BODY POLITIC

'A hugely entertaining fantasy . . . engagingly imagined'

The Times

'An intricate web . . . Johnston is a Fawkes among plotters . . . Quint's career looks set to blossom'

Observer

'A fascinating and thought-provoking debut that delivers much and promises more'

Val McDermid, *Manchester Evening News*

'A thrilling hunt-the-psycho novel with countless twists . . . accomplished . . . offers real proof of the vigour and class of current Scottish crimewriting'

Ian Rankin, *Scotland on Sunday*

'Imaginative . . . remarkable . . . shows that crime fiction can be not only thrilling but intellectually exciting as well'

The Economist

THE BONE YARD

WATER OF DEATH

'An acclaimed crime series . . . Johnston brings an intelligent perspective to the dark excitement of the thriller'

Nicholas Blincoe, *Observer*

'Both prescient and illuminating'

Ian Rankin, *Daily Telegraph*

THE BLOOD TREE

'Refreshingly original and entertaining'

Sunday Telegraph

'The platonic dystopia of Enlightenment Edinburgh is perfect for blending crime stories and satire . . . a pacy read'

Scotsman

THE HOUSE OF DUST

'Johnston's plotting is consummate and his character-isation deft. He is also a very funny political satirist so that although *The House of Dust* is set in the future he is, of course, commenting on Scotland and England today. Very enjoyable'

Observer

A DEEPER SHADE OF BLUE

'A sensual portrait of modern Greece, as well as a great page-turner: taste the salt, feel the heat as you follow the dramatic story . . . offers much more than the crime fiction genre usually encompasses: a rich and intelligent story, with fascinating characters'

Scotland on Sunday

'A new departure for an immensely talented author, and the change of scene from the Scotland of the earlier books to the author's new home of Greece pays great dividends'

Barry Forshaw, *Publishing News*

'A perfect setting for a tense thriller . . . This is an intelligent and satisfying book, part contemporary thriller, part the dark sister of *Captain Corelli's Mandolin*'

Scotsman

'The very best crime novels are those in which location, character and story combine in a single, powerful whole. With *A Deeper Shade of Blue*, Paul Johnston stakes his persuasive claim for a place in that pantheon'

John Connolly

Also by Paul Johnston

Water of Death
The Blood Tree
The House of Dust
A Deeper Shade of Blue

About the author

Paul Johnston was born in 1957 in Edinburgh, where he lived before going to Oxford University to study Greek. He made his home on a small Greek island for several years. He now divides his time between the UK and Greece. He is the author of *Body Politic*, winner of the John Creasey Memorial Dagger for the best first crime novel, *The Bone Yard*, *Water of Death*, *The Blood Tree* and *The House of Dust* all featuring Quint Dalrymple. His recent novel *A Deeper Shade of Blue* is the first in a series of crime novels set in Greece and featuring Alex Mavros, a half-Greek, half-Scottish private investigator.

BODY POLITIC

and

THE BONE YARD

Paul Johnston

NEW ENGLISH LIBRARY
Hodder & Stoughton

The right of Paul Johnston to be identified as the
Author of the Work has been asserted by him in accordance
with the Copyright, Designs and Patents Act 1988.

Body Politic first published in Great Britain in 1997 by Hodder and
Stoughton
The Bone Yard first published in Great Britain in 1998 by Hodder and
Stoughton
A division of Hodder Headline

This edition first published in 2003

A NEL paperback

2 4 6 8 10 9 7 5 3 1

A CIP catalogue record for this title
is available from the British Library

ISBN 0 340 83085 9

Printed and bound in Great Britain by
Mackays of Chatham plc, Chatham, Kent

Hodder and Stoughton
A division of Hodder Headline
338 Euston Road
London NW1 3BH

BODY POLITIC

In the last decade of the twentieth century people bought crime fiction like there was no tomorrow – which soon turned out to be the case for many of them. It isn't hard to see why detective stories were addictive. The indomitable heroes and heroines with their reassuring solutions prolonged the illusion that a stable society existed outside the readers' security windows and armoured doors.

Since the Enlightenment won power in Edinburgh, the popularity of crime novels has gradually declined, though not as much as the guardians think. They would prefer citizens to read philosophical investigations rather than those of Holmes and Poirot, Morse and Dalgliesh, but even in the "perfect city" people hanker for the old certainties.

I often have trouble deciding what to believe. All the same, the message that the Council sent on my birthday gave me even more of a shock than the first time I heard James Marshall Hendrix playing the "Catfish Blues".

I shouldn't have been so surprised. Sceptics and detectives have the same general principle: the only thing you can be sure of is that you can't be sure of anything at all.

Chapter One

Ghost-grey day in the city and seagulls screaming through the fog that had been smothering us for a week. Tourists started to head up George IVth Bridge for the Friday execution. I was the only local paying attention. If you want to survive in Edinburgh, you've got to keep reminding yourself this place is weirder than sweet-smelling sewage.

My shift with the squad of Parks Department labourers was due to finish at four but I'd made up my mind long before that. I had an hour before my meeting with the woman who signed herself Katharine K. It was 20 March 2020, I was thirty-six years old and I was going to break the rules.

"Are you coming for a pint, Quint?" one of the boys asked.

It was tempting, but I managed to shake my head. There would have been no escape if they had known what day it was. The Council describes birthday celebrations as "excessively self-indulgent" in the City Regulations, but the tradition of getting paralytic remains. It's one of the few that does. Anyway, I had a sex session later on and if you're pissed at one of those, you're in deep shit.

"Course he isn't." Roddy the Ox wiped sweat and snot

away with the back of his arm. "He'll be away to the library like a model arse-licking citizen." Every squad's got a self-appointed spokesman and I never get on with any of them. So I go to the library a lot. Not just to broaden my mind. I spend most of my time in the archives checking up on the people my clients report missing.

"Actually," I said, looking the big man in the eye, "I'm going to watch the execution." Jaws dropped so quickly that I checked my flies. "Anybody else coming?"

They stood motionless in their fatigues, turned to stone. Not even the Ox seemed to fancy gate-crashing a party that's strictly tourists only.

The way things are, I usually try to stick out from the crowd. Not this time. As I was the only ordinary citizen pushing a bicycle towards the Royal Mile, I tried to make myself inconspicuous. The buses carrying groups to the gallows gave me a bit of cover. So did the clouds of diesel fumes, at the same time as choking me. Fifteen years since private cars were banned and still the place reeks.

The mass of humanity slowed as it approached the checkpoint above the library's grimy façade. Rousing folksongs came from loudspeakers, the notes echoing through the mist like the cries of sinners in the pit. Some of the tourists were glancing at adverts for events in the year-round Festival which is the Council's main source of income. Among them were posters of the front page of *Time*'s New Year edition proclaiming Edinburgh "Worldwide City of the Year". The words "Garden of Edin" were printed in maroon under a photo of the floodlit castle. I've worked in most of the city's gardens but I've yet to see a naked woman – or a snake.

I kept my head down and tried not to bump into too many people with my front wheel. The guards had raised the barrier as the time of the execution drew near. Fortunately they weren't bothering to examine the herd of people. I felt a stickiness in my armpits that would stay with me till my session next week at the communal baths. Why was I taking the chance? The fire in my veins a few seconds later answered the question – I'd managed to get into a forbidden part of the city. I felt like a real anarchist. Till I started calculating my chances of getting out so easily.

I let myself be swallowed up by the crowd that had gathered round the gallows in the Lawnmarket. Guides were struggling to make themselves heard, speaking Arabic, Chinese, Greek, Korean. There was a small group of elderly Americans in transparent rain-capes. They were among the first from across the Atlantic; until recently the Council refused entry to nationals of what it called in its diplomatic way "culturally bankrupt states". A bearded courier in a kilt was giving them the sales pitch.

"The Royal Mile runs from the castle to what remains of Holyrood Palace," he bellowed, pointing towards the mist-covered lower reaches. "The palace was reduced to ruins in the rioting that followed the last coronation in 2002. The crown prince's divorce and remarriage to a Colombian drugs heiress signed the old order's death warrant." He paused to catch his breath and gave me a suspicious look. "The already fragile United Kingdom quickly broke up into dozens of warring city-states. Thanks to the Council of City

Guardians, Edinburgh has been the only one to achieve stability . . ."

The propaganda washed over me. I knew most of it by heart. I wondered again about the note I'd found under my door yesterday. "Can't wait any longer," it read. "Meet me at 3 Lennox Street Lane five p.m. tomorrow if you want work. Katharine K." The handwriting was spidery, very different from the copperplate required in the city's schools and colleges. The writer must have been hanging about on the landing outside my flat for quite a time. Despite the fumes from the nearby brewery, the place was filled with her scent. I knew exactly what it was: Moonflower, classified Grade 3 by the Supply Directorate and issued to lower level hotel and restaurant workers. Beneath the perfume lay the even stronger smell of a client desperate for my services.

It was coming up to four thirty and the guides took a break from their shouting competition. Looking around the crowd, I was struck by how many of the tourists were disabled in one way or another: some were in wheelchairs, some were clutching their companions' arms, a few even looked to be blind. The Council had probably been working on a braille version of the hanging.

Then there was a hush as the condemned man was led up to the scaffold by guards in period costume. The prisoner's hands were bound and a black velvet bag placed over his head.

The guides started speaking again. The bearded man was explaining to the Americans that this was Deacon William Brodie, the city's most notorious villain.

"Here, in the heart of the city where crime no longer

exists" – at least according to the Public Order Directorate – "Brodie committed his outrages. He was a cabinet-maker by trade, rising to become Deacon of Wrights and Masons. But by night he was a master-burglar, robbing dozens of wealthy householders."

Encouraged by their guides' gestures, the tourists began to boo. The English-speaking guide moved nearer the gallows.

"Brodie was eventually caught, but not before his reputation had gained a permanent place in the minds of his fellow citizens. A century later the Edinburgh writer Robert Louis Stevenson used him as the model for his famous study of evil in *Dr Jekyll and Mr Hyde*. The man in the kilt gave a fawning grin. "Don't forget to pick up a souvenir edition of the book in your hotel giftshop."

Under the gibbet final preparations were being made. I followed them closely, trying to work out how they faked it. There was no sign of a protective collar. It even looked like the victim was trembling involuntarily. I remembered summary executions I had seen, members of the drugs gangs that terrorised the city in the years after independence being put up against a wall. They had shaken in the same way, sworn at the guardsmen to get it over with. To my disgust I found that my heart was racing as it had done then.

The presiding officer, dressed in black tunic and lace collar, shouted across the crowd from the scaffold. "On 1 October 1788 Brodie mounted the set of gallows which he himself had designed – to be hanged by the neck until he was dead."

There were a few seconds of silence to let everyone's flesh creep, then a loud wooden thump as the trap jerked open and the body dropped behind a screen, leaving the rope twisting one way then the other from the tarred beam. The spectators went wild.

I pushed my way to the side, wheeling my bicycle past the tartan and whisky shops towards Bank Street. I felt a bit shaky. It had struck me that maybe the execution wasn't just a piece of theatre for the tourists. I mean, staging mock hangings in a city where capital punishment has been abolished and violence of any kind supposedly eradicated is cynical enough. Actually getting rid of the small number of murderers serving life with hard labour in the city's one remaining prison would be seriously hypocritical. But with the Council you never know. It's always boasting about the unique benefits it's given us: stability, work and housing for everyone, as much self-improvement as you can stomach. But what about freedom? Even suicide has been outlawed.

I turned the corner. By the Finance Directorate, a great, dilapidated palace that had once housed the Bank of Scotland, the barrier was down and the city guardswoman standing in front of it was definitely not friendly. She stuck her hand out for my ID.

"What are you doing up here, citizen?" She was in her mid-twenties, tall and fit-looking. Her red hair was in a neat ponytail beneath her beret and the maroon heart – emblem of the city – was prominent on the left breast pocket of her grey tunic. On the right was her barracks name and number. The heavy belt around her waist provided straps for her sheath knife and truncheon; since the gangs were dealt with, the City Guard no longer carry firearms. "Well?" she demanded. "I'm waiting."

I tried to look innocent. "I was working at the museum, Wilkie 418 . . ."

She didn't buy it. "Your flat's in the opposite direction." She had the neutral voice that all auxiliaries acquire during training. The Council has been trying to get rid of class distinctions by banning local accents. It's a nice theory. "You've no business to come this way."

She ran her eyes over my labourers' fatigues and checked the data on my ID card – height five feet ten inches, weight eleven stone in the imperial system: bringing that back was one of the Council's stranger decisions. Hair black, a bit over the one-inch maximum stipulated for male citizens. Eyes brown. Nose aquiline. Teeth complete and in good condition. Then she glanced at my right hand to check the distinguishing mark, showing no sign of emotion. Finally she gave me a stare that would have brought a tear to the eye of the Sphinx. She had registered the letters "DM" that told her I'd been demoted from the rank of auxiliary.

"I hope you don't think I'm going to do you any favours." The sudden hard edge to her voice rasped like a meat-saw biting bone. "You've no business in a tourist area. Report to your local barracks tomorrow morning, citizen." She handed me an offence notification. "You'll be assigned two Sundays' community service and your record will be endorsed accordingly." She glanced at my face. "You could do with a shave as well."

I stood at the checkpoint with the neatly written sheet in my hand for a few moments. Cheering from the racetrack that had been laid over the disused railway lines in Princes Street Gardens came up through the fog. The seagulls had given up auditioning for the City Choir and now I could hear bagpipe music from the speakers beneath the streetlamps. It sounded more mournful than any blues song I ever played. My appetite for meeting the fragrant Katharine K. had gone completely.

"Oh, and citizen," the guardswoman called humourlessly from the sentry box. "Happy Birthday."

I was late of course. As I was cycling like a lunatic through the swirls of mist on the Dean Bridge, I almost went into the back of one of the city's battered delivery vans. Their drivers have a reputation for using the vehicles to shift contraband but this one was going so slowly he had to be on city business.

"At last." The woman came towards me from the door of the house in Lennox Street Lane, then stopped abruptly. She examined me as critically as the guardswoman had, staring at my mud-encrusted trousers like she'd never seen filth before. She had a face to write poems about: high cheekbones, lips as promising as a lovers' assignation and green eyes that flashed in the dim light and told me stories I hadn't heard for a long time. Then her nose twitched and the spell was broken. "You are citizen Dalrymple, aren't you?" she asked in a hoarse voice that I felt run up my spine like a caress.

She wasn't the first of my clients to be dubious about the way I look. I nodded and fumbled with the padlock on my bike; only an idiot relies on the City Guard to look after his property outside the tourist areas. At the same time I ran my eye over her. She was about my height, but her build had more going for it. The short brown hair that stood up on the top of her head would have made her look permanently surprised if she hadn't been as languid as a well-fed lioness. I wondered who she'd eaten recently.

"Katharine Kirkwood," she said. "I wasn't expecting a labourer."

I took her hand and felt long, elegant fingers. Her scent washed over me like the tide of a lunar sea. "Quintilian Dalrymple," I said. "Investigator as well as labourer."

Her eyes blinked only once when she felt the stump of my right forefinger. "You give everyone that little test, don't you?" A smile nagged at the corners of her mouth. "How did I do?"

"Pretty well," I said generously.

"How did you lose it?"

"You don't want to know."

She looked at me curiously, then shrugged. "Come this way." She opened the street door and led me up dingy stairs to the first floor. That gave me an opportunity to examine her legs, black stockings beneath her issue coat. She passed that test too.

"You've got a key," I said. "Why were you waiting outside?"

Katharine Kirkwood faced a door which needed several coats of paint. She turned slowly and handed me the keys, her face taut. "I'm . . . I'm frightened." I hadn't put her down as the type who scares easily. "This is my brother's place." All of a sudden her voice was soft. "It's ten days since I last saw him."

"That's not long. You know what it's like in this city. People are always being picked up for extra duties or . . ."

"No," she said with quiet insistence. "Adam and I, we're

. . ." She left the sentence unfinished. "He'd have found a way to let me know."

I watched her as she leaned against the doorframe and tried to look optimistic. It wouldn't be the first time I found a body behind a locked door. If this one had been there for over a week, not even a jerrycan of her perfume would be much help.

"Haven't you been to the City Guard?"

"Those bastards?" Her tone was razor sharp. "I told them days ago but they still haven't found the time to take a look. Too busy licking the tourists' arses."

I nodded and knocked on the door less violently than the guard would have done. No answer. That would have been too easy. So I slipped the key into the lock and took a deep breath. Then pushed the door open and went inside.

Adam Kirkwood's flat conformed to the Housing Directorate's standard plan. In other words, it was a soulless dump. There was a square living room with the minuscule kitchen in a partitioned alcove, a bedroom off to the left and a toilet without shower or bath in the far corner. It contained the usual furniture; table, two stick-legged chairs, a sofa that looked like an elephant had been trampolining on it, a desk, uneven bookshelves and, to my relief, no body.

Katharine K. remained in the doorway till I beckoned, then came forward into the main room. "He's not here."

She breathed out slowly and turned to me. "Your turn for a test." She gave me a smile that was about as encouraging as the thumbs-down to a stricken gladiator. "I heard from one of the girls at work that you find missing people. Convince me you've got what it takes, citizen."

"Call me Quint." I've had to get used to clients who think investigators are magicians. Sometimes I refuse to perform, but not when they're female and have her looks. "You want a demonstration?" I scrutinised her, taking my time. I enjoyed it more than she did. "So, you work as a chambermaid at the Independence Hotel, you live in William Street, you're left-handed, you burned yourself with an iron five, maybe six days ago and you spend a lot of your free time in the staff gym."

She wasn't impressed. "Come on, all that's obvious from my appearance. And everyone knows where Indie staff live."

I shrugged. "I haven't finished. You have an unusually close relationship with your brother, your parents are dead, you used to be an auxiliary and you have a dissidence conviction." I gave her my best smile. "Also, you like Chinese poetry."

She glanced at the tattered book that was protruding from her bag. "Very observant. But most of that is just guesswork." She didn't sound quite as sceptical.

"You reckon?" I don't usually reveal how my mind works and a lot of what I'd said was just supposition, but I wanted her to think I was as sharp as they come. Maybe I was trying to convince myself too. "I saw your handwriting, remember? Only someone who doesn't care what people think would write a note to a stranger without using copperplate. And you aren't in a hurry to get off to evening classes either. Demoted auxiliaries like us aren't allowed to attend classes in case we have a bad influence on the others."

Katharine K. nodded. "You were one too. I was beginning to wonder. Don't tell me – Public Order Directorate?"

I raised my hands in surrender. The way she had shifted the discussion from her past to mine was impressive.

"Guardsman?" she asked acidly.

"Not exactly." I went over to the kitchen. It was tidy, a cup and plate on the draining-board. "Do I get the job, then?"

"I suppose so." She was right behind me, looking at the crockery, then touching the cup carefully as if she were trying to re-establish contact with her brother. "How do I pay you?"

"No cure, no pay. If I find your brother, it's up to you what you give me. None of my clients has much to spare after buying the week's food and electricity vouchers. I often get whatever they can lay their hands on at work. I had half a pound of coffee last month."

"Riches indeed." She finally took her fingers away from the cup. "Why do you do it?"

I've never been too sure of the answer to that question myself. "It's a way of staying alive." I moved over to the sofa. "You'd better tell me something about your brother."

Katharine K. sat down beside me and took a piece of hotel notepaper from her book of poetry.

"Adam Peter Kirkwood," I read. "Status – citizen. Born 3.12.1995, height six feet two inches, weight thirteen stone twelve pounds, hair dark brown, nose snub, teeth complete, distinguishing mark none, employment Roads Department, Transport Directorate, address 3 Lennox Street Lane, next of kin Katharine Kirkwood (sister)." I nodded. "That'll do for a start. I don't suppose you've got a photo?" The Council has strictly controlled the taking of photographs, seeing them as a major element in the cult of the individual that had helped to destroy the United Kingdom.

She showed me a small, blurred copy of a handsome young man who was looking straight into the camera with the hint of a mocking smile on his lips. "Just this, I'm afraid." The only way people can get pictures of their loved ones is by sneaking photocopies of ID cards.

"I'll track down his file and see what it says. If it's been brought up to date."

"Can you do that?" She was staring at me. "I thought citizens' files were classified."

"Depends who you know." That line usually provokes admiration, but Katharine Kirkwood just looked puzzled. "He's twenty-four, so obviously he's done his year on the border."

"Finished it three years ago."

"And you last saw him when exactly?"

"Tuesday before last, 10 March. I came round here. I often do."

I looked around the small room, keeping to myself the fact that over the last three months I'd had half a dozen cases of missing young people. I hadn't found any of them. "Anything different? Anything been taken?"

She got up and walked about, picking up and laying down objects that were clearly familiar to her. She went into the bedroom and re-emerged after a couple of minutes. "Everything's as it always is. Adam's very neat."

"Is there anything you haven't told me, Katharine?"

She looked like she was going to object to my use of her first name, but nothing came of it.

"I need to know. If it turns out he's part of some dissident cell, I'd prefer to be told before they start using me as a punchbag."

She shook her head. "No, he's not a rebel. You can be sure of that." She raised her hand to her forehead. "What worries me most is how he was the last time I saw him. Kind of nervous – not frightened exactly, but excited, as if something important was about to happen. I've never seen him like that before. He wouldn't tell me about it. Said it was secret."

I didn't like the sound of that and went into the bedroom to conceal my expression. If Adam Kirkwood was into something classified, I'd be giving myself a headache for nothing. Still, maybe she was worth it.

Where he slept was unusually tidy, more like a barracks than a private room. The deal wardrobe contained labourer's fatigues like mine and the few casual shirts and trousers that the average citizen possesses. A pair of size twelve running shoes took up one corner. When you look round a place you normally form an impression of the person who lives there. Not in Adam Kirkwood's case. I felt like an archaeologist breathlessly opening a golden sarcophagus to find nothing but dust and moth-eaten shrouds.

Back in the main room I continued snooping around, aware of Katharine's eyes on me.

"How are you going to track him down?" she asked.

I sat down on the sofa beside her. "I'll check the archives first. I know my way around there. I've got contacts in other places too – the Misdemeanours Department, the Labour Directorate – to see if he's been drafted into the mines or on to one of the city farms" – I skipped the hospitals, where unidentified bodies turn up more often than you might expect in a city whose population is carefully monitored – "the Deserters' Register. Did your brother ever talk about crossing the border illegally?"

Her eyes narrowed. "That's what the guard asked too. Adam isn't a deserter any more than I am. I don't like the Council but Edinburgh's safer than all the other cities. Neither of us wants to leave." She moved her hand to her eyes quickly. "It's my fault. I influenced him. He could easily have become an auxiliary. It was because of me that he didn't. He let his work at college go, failed all his exams and ended up as a labourer." She looked over at me. "Sorry . . ."

"Don't worry, I'm not proud. You haven't told me why you were demoted."

Her eyes opened wide and glinted shafts of ice. "That's got nothing to do with this. What about you? Why did they kick you out?" She looked down.

"Why do I have the feeling that I've suddenly grown jackass's ears?" I waited for her to raise her eyes again but she didn't oblige. "Forget it. I'll have to trust you."

"How kind." She smiled bitterly then stood up. "I've got the night shift. When will you know something?"

I moved over to the bookshelves. "In a couple of days. I live in Gilmore Place, number 13. Come round about eight in the evening." I pulled out the book that had attracted my attention. It was the same edition of Chinese poetry translations Katharine had in her bag. Between pages twenty and twenty-one I came across a single foreign banknote. I kept my back to her. "Any idea why your brother would have secreted fifty thousand drachmae in his copy of this?"

She was at my side instantly, staring at the garish pink bill. "I haven't the faintest idea," she said, her voice fainter than it was hoarse. "What's it worth?"

"More than you or I will earn this month. But where did he get it? You know it's illegal for Edinburgh citizens to have foreign currency."

Katharine shook her head in what looked like bewilderment. I was almost sure she knew nothing about this part of her brother's life but you never know – she could have been the most accomplished actress in the city. Glancing at her profile, I made another discovery. The line of her nose was exactly the same as Caro's. I thought I'd got over seeing aspects of her in other women. This case was already full of surprises.

I wheeled my bicycle back to Gilmore Place. It was dark now and the fog was even thicker than before, but City Guard vehicles were still careering about like decrepit maroon dodgems. My watch had finally succumbed to the soakings it got every day in the city's parks so I didn't have much idea of the time. Fortunately curfew wasn't imminent. Then I remembered the sex session. All citizens have to attend a weekly session with a partner allocated to them by the Recreation Directorate. The Council claims we get a more stimulating sex life, but everyone knows it's just another way of keeping an eye on us. At least it was a home fixture this time. A month ago I ended up stranded for the night at a crazy woman's flat in Morningside. She got her money's worth. Thank Christ the regulations forbid further encounters between partners of my status.

Back in my place I sank into the sofa, which was even more hamstrung than the one at Adam Kirkwood's. My room, a testament to Housing Directorate grot, was so similar I almost thought I was back at his. The only difference was that I had a lot more books. One of the few Council decisions I completely go along with is the banning of television. As a result Edinburgh citizens are seriously well read and cheap copies of most kinds of books are available. Nothing too subversive, of course, and writing in any Scots dialect is right out. I've forgotten all the dirty bits from Irvine Welsh books I memorised when I was a kid. But the worst thing the idiots in power have done is to ban the blues, though they had their reasons. My collection of recordings is hidden under a tartan rug with my guitar case on top. I listen to them with my head against my moth-eaten speaker, straining to hear and hoping the neighbours won't report me. What a thrill.

The street door three floors below banged open and heavy, ringing steps sounded on the stairs. Only the City Guard and citizens working in the mines are issued with nailed boots. Either I was about to have sex with a large female miner or someone in number 13 was in trouble.

I should have known that someone was me. My door took a pounding before I could get to it.

"Citizen Dalrymple?" The auxiliary was tall and barrel-chested, the kind of guy who gets picked first in playground team games. His black hair was longer than mine and the regulation beard thick on his face. "I'm Hume 253." He handed me an envelope bearing the seal of the Council. "This is for you."

I opened it, expecting one of the public order guardian's regular warnings to keep my nose out of his directorate's business. Instead I read: "CONFIDENTIAL: Murderer codenamed Ear, Nose and Throat Man appears to have resumed his activities. Accompany Hume 253 to Council meeting."

I was having trouble standing up, let alone concealing my shock from the guardsman.

"Are you coming, citizen?" the guardsman asked with an unusually patient smile.

I followed him out. Halfway down the stairs we passed a middle-aged female citizen with tired eyes and a soft, sad face. I wished I could have spent some time with her, but she was better off without me.

"I hear there's been a murder," Hume 253 said in a low voice. He must have been in his late twenties and on the surface he looked like a typical muscle-bound guardsman, but his enthusiasm was surprising. The average auxiliary these days displays about as much emotion as the tarts who service the tourists in the city's hotels. "What do you know, citizen?" he asked.

"Nothing," I lied as I climbed into the battered Land-Rover.

"The first killing in the city for five years," the guardsman said. It sounded like he approved. He let in the clutch and set off round the corner even faster than his kind normally drive.

I hung on to the worn edges of the seat and wondered exactly what kind of birthday present I was about to be given.

Chapter Two

"I don't want to die."

The fog had now reduced visibility to a couple of vehicle lengths. Only the knowledge that the disciplined citizens of Edinburgh wouldn't be jaywalking enabled Hume 253 to head towards the Royal Mile at high speed. Fortunately there weren't any tourists around Tollcross.

"Don't worry," the guardsman said cheerfully. "I passed out top of my driving course."

"Great." I blinked in the chill air that was whistling in through numerous holes in the bodywork. The best of the Land-Rovers were reserved for border patrols and farm protection. "What time is it?"

"Coming up to seven," Hume 253 said without taking his eyes off the road for more than a second. "The Council's daily meeting has been brought forward an hour because of the killing. That shows you how seriously they're taking it, doesn't it, citizen?"

"Call me Quint, will you?"

He knew I was trying him out. "Use of first names is prohibited between auxiliaries and ordinary citizens. So is inducing a guardsman to break regulations." He glanced at me, then laughed. "I seem to remember that my name's Davie, Quint."

So I'd found a guardsman who wasn't completely robotic. The more dedicated of them even address their barracks colleagues by number. "How long have you been in the Public Order Directorate, Davie?"

"Seven years, ever since I finished auxiliary training. I like it. I'm going to stay in the guard. Not even six consecutive tours on the border put me off."

That sounded more like your typical guardsman. I was interested in his background, though. "Did you have anything to do with the last operations against the drug gangs?"

He looked at me suspiciously. "How do you know about those?" Five years ago the Council sealed the border around what used to be Midlothian and laid into the remaining heavily armed criminals who had plagued the city since independence. Those guys were led by a ruthless bastard who called himself Howlin' Wolf, after the blues singer. There was some evidence that the Ear, Nose and Throat Man was one of the gang. The high casualty rate among guard personnel had led the Information Directorate to suppress all the facts, despite the success of the mission.

"You were involved, weren't you?" I said, waiting for him to nod. "How do I know about the operations?" I wondered if I would manage to shock an auxiliary. "I ran them."

"Shit!" he gasped, taking his eyes off the road long enough to make me nervous. "You're Bell 03."

The sound of my old barracks number was definitely not sweet music to my ears. "Used to be Bell 03," I corrected.

"They still talk about you in the directorate," Davie said. He was more excited than any auxiliary I'd ever seen. "If it hadn't been for you . . ."

"Fewer people would have died," I said, looking away. "That's all in the past. I don't want to talk about it." I wished I hadn't encouraged him. The stump of my forefinger was tingling and my gut felt like something with a sharp beak had just hatched in it.

The Land-Rover turned sharply into Mound Place and I caught a glimpse of the city from the high point; the blaze of illumination through the fog in the tourist area at the centre was like a weird version of the northern lights, but the suburbs where the ordinary people live had been cast into the outer darkness.

Davie pulled up outside the mock-Gothic façade of the Assembly Hall. The Church of Scotland used to hold its annual gathering here. It was typical of the Council's desire to replace religion with its own philosophy that it chose this location rather than the former City Chambers or Parliament House. They probably had too many associations with democracy. Banners were draped around the blackened walls proclaiming the Council's ideals; "Education, Employment and Health", "Edinburgh – Independent and Proud" and "The City Provides". Deep down I still felt some admiration for them. Then, beyond the flagpoles, I saw the memorial stones inscribed with the barracks numbers of auxiliaries who had died for the cause. Caro's name survived only in my mind.

"You all right?" The guardsman sounded strangely concerned. "Know your way?"

"I've been before the Council often enough, my friend. Thanks for the lift."

"Don't mention it. I'll be waiting to take you back." A grin split his face. "If they leave you in one piece."

I nodded wearily, remembering that Council meetings were more rigorous than City Guard physical training sessions, though at least they didn't take place at half past five in the morning. Then I felt the envelope in my pocket. What the hell was it all about? I raced up the steps three at a time.

Council members sat round a great horseshoe table in the main hall. I always used to find the setting a bit theatrical, but I could just remember the building's use as a venue in the Festival before independence. I sat down between the ends of the horseshoe, suddenly very aware of my dirty fatigues in the bright lights that were directed at me. I screwed up my eyes and saw the guardians. Behind them was the large bust of Plato that was the only concession to art in the austere chamber.

"Citizen Dalrymple." The deputy senior guardian's voice hadn't changed in the five years since I last heard it. She must have been over seventy by now. When I was a kid, she was a frequent visitor to my parents' house. She was the only university professor I ever met who found children more interesting than her subject – well, she was a sociologist. She also had a liking for vintage champagne. I wondered when she'd last sampled that. "It is some time since we last had the pleasure of seeing you," she said drily.

"I haven't been counting the days, guardian." Like all

those who pass through the rank of auxiliary, the city guardians don't use names. The roof would have come down if I'd addressed her as Edith.

"I'm sure you haven't. I think you know most of the Council members. Only my colleagues in the Medical and the Information Directorates are relatively new appointees."

I looked at the red-haired woman to her left, then at the improbably handsome man with the mane of silver-blond hair. His thin fingers formed an arch beneath his nose, giving him the appearance of a monk at prayer. The speaker was wrong. I knew Robert Yellowlees well enough. Before the Enlightenment he had played rugby for Scotland. After the party won the last election and took the city into independence, he worked as a surgeon. Later his research into neurology and endocrinology became known around the world, as journals I saw in the library confirmed. He could have jumped ship and worked anywhere, but he preferred to stay and move slowly up his directorate. He'd been in the pathology department when I was in the Public Order Directorate.

I couldn't avoid the unwavering glare of the figure sitting next to Yellowlees. While the other Council members had studied expressions of gravity on their faces, the public order guardian at least showed what he really felt – which was hatred of my guts.

The deputy senior guardian glanced at the unoccupied chair in the centre of the horseshoe. "I'm afraid the senior guardian is again unable to attend the meeting due to illness."

First I felt relieved, then uneasy. I made myself ignore both emotions.

"To the business in hand. Today's meeting has been brought forward because of the murder that has been reported." The speaker took a deep breath. "The murder of a female auxiliary right in the heart of the city." She was unable to restrain a shiver. "This was an act of unspeakable barbarity."

"Can it really be the otolaryngologist after all this time?" Yellowlees, the medical guardian, looked at me quizzically. I remembered he used to refer to the Ear, Nose and Throat Man by the technical term.

"It's incredible. After all the work that's been done to divert the urge to criminality . . ." The high-pitched voice trailed away. I looked at the bald head of the finance guardian which was glinting under the lights as he moved back and forwards animatedly. You'd have thought he'd be more concerned about the city's tourist income, but deviant behaviour had always been one of his specialities. Though he'd been a well-known economics professor before the Enlightenment, in certain Edinburgh bars he was more famous for his pursuit of male undergraduates. Under the strict celibacy rules that guardians submit themselves to, the only person he'd have laid hands on recently would have been himself.

"Quite so," the deputy senior guardian acknowledged, sympathetic but eager to continue. "I will not go into the details of this atrocity as I do not wish to prejudice the opinion of citizen Dalrymple. He is to investigate and find the murderer."

So that was it. For a nasty moment I thought the Council was finally on to me, even though I'd disposed of the ENT Man's body in a site I knew had never been disturbed. No matter how many times I told myself it was an accident, that he'd skewered himself on his own knife, I was responsible. I tried to strangle him like he strangled Caro. I wanted to kill the animal and that's what counts.

Hamilton, the public order guardian, shot to his feet, the iron line of his jaw visible even under his beard's thick grey curls. "I object."

I can't say I was surprised.

"This matter comes under the jurisdiction of my directorate. Citizen Dalrymple . . ." He paused, then repeated my name like it tasted putrid. "Citizen Dalrymple chose to withdraw his services from the Council at a critical time – while, I might add, the Ear, Nose and Throat Man was still at large. If it is indeed the case that the killer has struck again, this citizen can be seen as responsible. He never completed his investigation." The city's chief policeman looked round his colleagues. "Besides, he has been working as a labourer in the city's parks since then. What possible use can he—"

"One moment, guardian." The speaker interrupted him without raising her eyes from her papers. "There is to be no discussion about this. The senior guardian has sent a written directive." She turned to him. "You will provide citizen Dalrymple with everything he needs to track down the murderer." She looked around. "That applies to all directorates." Her eyes rested on me. "I'm afraid you may find the city's resources in the fields of forensics and criminology rather meagre. There has been little call for such expertise recently."

The public order guardian sat down noisily.

"We are dealing," continued the speaker, "with the killing

of a city auxiliary. This raises several concerns. The most significant of these would appear to be public awareness and the potential effect on the tourist industry. Your thoughts, please."

The information guardian got up, her flaming hair standing out above the sombre grey of her tweed jacket. She proposed keeping all news of the murder out of the *Edinburgh Guardian* and of Radio Free City. She was worried that such a major crime could lead to a loss of confidence in the Council. The public order guardian nodded vigorously in agreement. I might have been more convinced by the argument if the information guardian hadn't once been an award-winning investigative journalist on the *Scotsman*. People who change that much always make me suspicious. Anyway, I'd heard all this in the past. One of the most disturbing things about the Council is its obsession with secrecy. If the aim is to educate citizens to think for themselves, it seems to me that they should be trusted not to revolt as soon as things go wrong. Then again, who am I to talk? I've kept my mouth shut about what happened to the ENT Man and that makes me as egocentric as a pre-Enlightenment politician. Christ, how low have I sunk?

Whenever I give myself a bad time, it isn't long before I start looking for an alternative target. There was a whole shooting gallery of them in front of me.

"Excuse me," I said politely. Hamilton was the only one who smelled a rat; his glare was steelier than the toecaps of a guardsman's boots. "I suppose it's theoretically possible that my fellow citizens won't find out about the murder, but in my experience word always gets out, especially when measures are taken to keep things secret." I gave the public order guardian a cheerful smile, which deflected his hard man's stare for a second. "I mean, I heard about this supposedly confidential crime not long after I got your message."

That provoked more gasps than I'd expected, but Hamilton's reaction was about what I guessed it would be.

"I want the name of the citizen who informed you immediately," he demanded, his fists clenched.

I shook my head slowly. "No chance." I might have known my former chief would assume it was an ordinary citizen who had told me rather than one of his own auxiliaries.

"That will do," said the speaker sternly. "There is no need for names. Citizen Dalrymple's point is taken."

I sat back as the discussion turned to the danger of tourist volumes being affected if the murder was publicised. I couldn't see the Chinese being too bothered. Beijing became a Dantean pit of underworld activity in the years following the country's economic expansion. The Greeks weren't likely to object either. Since the discovery of oil in the Aegean twenty years ago, they've acquired a crime rate worse than those of Chicago and New York put together.

I found myself remembering the metaphor of the body politic, which had been a favourite propaganda device in the early years of the Council. It was probably one of my father's ideas. The ordinary citizens were the body of the city-state, while the guardians were its heart and brain and the auxiliaries its eyes and ears. But what if the heart was growing weary and the mind was no longer reliable? What if the eyes no longer provided 20-20 vision and the ears heard only what they wanted to hear?

The debate finally drew to a close and the deputy senior guardian looked at me. "So, citizen, we will expect a report from you every evening in person."

I didn't want them to think I was too much of a pushover. "And if I choose to remain with the Parks Department? No doubt the public order guardian would prefer that."

The speaker's expression froze. "I would remind you that this is a matter of the utmost importance, not just for the Council but for the whole city. You are not being given a choice, citizen. Failure to obey this instruction would have a very detrimental effect on the private investigation activities you pursue in your free time." The threatening tone was at odds with the guardian's white hair and wrinkled face, but I knew it was real enough. They let me trace missing people because auxiliaries have plenty of other work to do. I've even done the guard a good turn occasionally by letting them know about minor illegalities I turned up. But if I got on the wrong side of the Council, that would count for about as much as kids in one of the city's schools saying they hadn't done their homework because they reckoned Plato was irrelevant to the modern world.

So I shrugged and accepted the job without showing how interested I was. Rule one: never show your clients that you're fascinated by their case.

"Very well. The public order guardian will take you to the scene of the crime."

"One small point," I said. "I've got an offence notification for tomorrow morning." I heard Hamilton snort derisively and wished I'd picked up a few more public order violations. He might have ruptured himself.

"That is waived," the speaker said, without hesitation. "Citizen, I notice your watch has stopped. Never mind that you're breaking regulations, how do you expect to conduct a murder enquiry without a serviceable time-piece?"

I liked her turn of phrase. If I'd closed my eyes, I could almost have believed I was in a Sherlock Holmes story. "I'll get one, guardian," I said and turned to leave. "Without a moment's delay."

The public order guardian overtook me on the stairs and went over to a pair of auxiliaries in civilian clothes. He looked almost as imposing as he imagined he did in the tweed jacket and corduroy trousers worn exclusively by members of his rank, the brogues on his feet shining like a schoolboy's prize chestnuts.

"Hurry up, Dalrymple," he said over his shoulder. "This isn't a Sunday outing."

"Where's the body?" I asked in an even voice.

"The body?" he repeated, his eyes fixed on a point several inches to the right of my face. "We aren't going to see the body. Weren't you listening to the speaker? I'm taking you to the scene of the crime." He glanced at his watch. "There isn't much time."

I turned to the keen-looking young men who were standing behind their chief like a pair of little girls holding a bride's train. "Run away and play. This is grown-ups' business."

The guardian hesitated, then waved them back. "You can't talk to auxiliaries like that, Dalrymple," he hissed.

It was about time I got my relationship with my former boss sorted out. "Hamilton, you're still as much of a jackass as you used to be." I wasn't sure whether my use of his name had shocked him more than the animal imagery. "We both heard exactly what was said in there. I'm reporting to the Council, not to you. You're supposed to give me whatever I want." So far the show was going well. He looked like he'd swallowed a six-inch fishing hook. Time to reel it in. "So where's the fucking body?"

Hamilton went on the retreat. "It was a collective decision of the Council."

I looked at him in disbelief. "Don't tell me. You've moved the body, haven't you? I bet that's not all. I bet you've cleaned up after it too."

"Calm down, man," said Hamilton, signs of guilt I'd normally have enjoyed disturbing his features. "We couldn't wait any longer."

Outside I could see Davie standing by the Land-Rover. "Where's the scene of the crime?" I asked as I moved off.

"Stevenson Hall, the men's toilets on the ground floor." The guardian tried to keep up. "Aren't you coming in my vehicle?"

I didn't bother answering.

Davie looked impressed as he started the Land-Rover. "You've got guts, having a go at the chief."

"Maybe." I looked across at him. "But there's something I haven't got and you can supply it."

He turned on to Castlehill and headed for the corner at what used to be the Tolbooth church. It's the most soot-blackened building in central Edinburgh. Maybe that's why they've turned it into a strip joint. A group of enthusiastic Thai tourists had gathered outside.

"What do you need?" asked Davie.

"Your watch," I replied, putting out my hand like the beggars used to on Princes Street before the Council turned them into more productive citizens.

Through the fog the bagpipes were still wailing. I could just make them out above the roar from the Land-Rover's defective silencer.

"It's all yours." Davie handed a watch over that was a lot better quality than mine. "Anything else I can do? I'd give a lot to be in on this." His willingness to help was like a small child's and about as suspicious. What was he after?

I thought about it. I'd be needing an assistant, I was sure of that. On the other hand, he was a sworn servant of the Council.

Beware guardsmen bearing gifts.

Chapter Three

A large crowd was milling around outside Stevenson Hall; it used to be the Usher Hall, but the Council preferred the name of one of the city's most illustrious writers to that of the brewer who paid for the building. Its great dome was lost in the mist.

I had half an hour before the musical version of *Kidnapped* was due to begin. Shoving through the mass of people, I could see what had inspired the guardians' decision to remove the body. Cancelling the event would have caused a riot.

"Citizen, where do you think you're going?" A pale guardswoman stepped forward from one of the entrances, a hand on the grip of her truncheon. Ordinary citizens aren't allowed near Festival performances without special permission.

"It's all right, guardswoman," the public order guardian called from behind. "He's with me." It sounded like the admission caused him more angst than your average existentialist could handle.

"Sorry, guardian. He didn't look . . ."

"Never mind how I look," I said, suddenly feeling sensitive about my appearance. "Open the door, will you?"

Hamilton nodded and the guardswoman obliged. I found the men's toilet and was confronted by a sentry who looked like he wrestled elephants in his spare time and wasn't in the habit of losing.

"Let him pass," the guardian shouted from down the hall.

Before I went in, I rested my hands on the door for a few seconds and breathed in deeply. First impressions are important, especially when, thanks to the Council, there wouldn't be much to go on. Then I pushed the swing door open and ran my eyes around glistening marble and porcelain, seeing myself reflected in the row of mirrors. The smell of disinfectant was overpowering.

I almost hit the ceiling when one of the cubicle doors banged open. An arse in yellow overalls backed out.

"Right then, that's them all done." The old man straightened up slowly and gave me a leer. "Come to see the mess? Well, you're too late, son."

"Out, auxiliary," Hamilton ordered. "Now!"

The cleaner grabbed the bucket he'd put down at my feet and scuttled out past the guardian with his eyes lowered.

"Too late all right," I said, dropping to the floor. "Where was the body?"

"She was lying on her left side, head in that corner and back facing outwards." Hamilton pointed to the far right. "The bin for paper towels, which was empty, had been moved down this end."

I crawled forward with my magnifying glass. The tiles were almost dry. Pretty soon I gave up the search.

"Not a trace. You'll have to give that cleaner a commendation."

"Calm down, Dalrymple. I issued a permit and plenty of photographs were taken." Even in a major crime inquiry, the use of cameras has to be authorised. "They're being developed now."

"Wonderful. And what about all the other scene of crime activities? Sketches, collection of physical evidence, pathologist's report?"

"We followed procedure by the letter," Hamilton replied testily. "You're not the only investigator in the city. We also dusted for fingerprints all over the room and in the hallways – my people are checking records now. And don't forget, we've still got the post-mortem to come. We're sure to find traces of the killer on the body."

"Are we?" I found it hard to share his optimism. "Who's the pathologist?"

"The medical guardian."

I didn't make it obvious to Hamilton, but I found that interesting. You'd think Yellowlees would have more pressing duties. Still, he did carry out the post-mortems on the ENT Man's victims, so it made some sense.

"Who found the body and when?"

"A guardswoman: the one who tried to stop you outside. She came to relieve the victim at 0600."

"Jesus. She came on duty fourteen hours ago, found a colleague murdered and is now on crowd control? You're still treating your people like shit, Hamilton."

"Spare me the lecture," he said, avoiding my eyes. "For your information, she was taken back to barracks in the morning and allowed to rest after she'd given her statement. I told her commander to send her back after you were assigned the case. I presumed you'd want to talk to her."

"That's about the first thing you've got right so far." I'd forgotten how easy it was to bait my former boss. This time I got a reaction that was almost human.

"Look, you insubordinate little turd," he said, the veins around his eyes swelling like a nest of purple snakes, "you may think you're something now you've been let back into the fold, but to me you'll always be a prima donna who ran away when things got tough. If you don't want me to stamp all over you when this investigation's finished, you'd better observe the rules. For a start, don't call me by my name."

"Yes, guardian." Being told what to do always brings out the worst in me. "Sorry, guardian. Can I go now, sir?"

Hamilton kicked the door open, his face red.

"Where's the guardswoman now?" I asked over my shoulder.

"In the manager's office."

"I'm going to talk to her. Alone."

The guardian's reply was lost as the doors were opened and a horde of tourists stampeded in.

Napier 498 was standing by the barred window with her hands behind her back. She looked exhausted, her shoulders drooping and her forehead resting on the glass. I saw she was very young.

"I'm Dalrymple." I put my hand on her shoulder and felt the muscles tense. She turned, eyelashes quivering, then pulled herself together in proper auxiliary fashion and moved away from my touch. "You can call me Quint. What shall I call you?"

She pointed to the barracks number on her tunic, but let her hand drop almost immediately. Then, in little more than a whisper, she said, "Linda."

I led her to the swivel chair and sat on the desk next to it. "I know exactly how you feel, Linda, believe me. But I have to hear what you saw."

She kept her eyes down. "I made a statement. There's nothing more."

I've never read a statement that tells the whole story, no matter how careful people think they're being. I leaned closer. "You know who I am, don't you?"

"The guardian told me you have Council authority."

"That's not what I mean."

She looked up at me, her eyes less like an exhausted doe's. As I expected, the jungle drums hadn't taken long to beat.

"You were Bell 03. You wrote the *Public Order in Practice* manual we studied during the auxiliary training programme."

I nodded. "Some of your teachers probably told you that a lot of the material is irrelevant now that crime in the city has been controlled. But you saw what was done to one of your colleagues. Do you think any of your teachers can catch the killer?"

Napier 498 shook her head. "Catching the bus back to barracks is about the best they can do."

I smiled at her, overjoyed that cynicism was alive in the City Guard. "On the other hand, my record is a bit better."

"Legendary, more like," she said, colouring slightly.

"Thank you." Looking at the young woman, I suddenly felt a stab of guilt. I had turned tail and left the next generation in the shit. Then I thought of Caro and managed to justify what I'd done. "So trust me, Linda. Tell me what you found." I waited, but the gentle approach wasn't enough – I could tell by the way she was leaning away from me. I would have to shock her out of the reluctance to talk that's drummed into auxiliaries. "Your written statement is only a skeleton." Feeling like a worm, I hit her with my carefully chosen metaphor. "Flesh it out."

It never fails. The guardswoman's eyes narrowed and she sat up straight. "All right, citizen Dalrymple," she said, avoiding my first name like it might put running sores on her tongue. "I've been on the morning shift at Stevenson Hall all week. The guard vehicle dropped me off just after 0600 this morning – we were late because of the fog. We could hardly see a thing on the way down from the castle."

I was feeling bad about what I said to her and had an uncontrollable urge to make friends. "You're in the barracks up there?"

She nodded, giving me a suspicious glance.

"How much more of your tour of duty have you got left?"

"Four months." There was a slight loosening in the muscles round her mouth.

"Going to apply for another one?" I could see she was puzzled by these personal questions. They might have been a waste of time, but I reckoned I'd get more out of her if she didn't think I was a plague-carrier.

"I'm not sure." She gave a tremor. "I doubt it, after today."

I nodded. "Go on."

"The fog was even thicker around the hall. Because I was late, I ran to the door . . ."

"Did you see or hear anything unusual?"

"No. As I said, the fog was really dense. I could hardly even see the lights in the building." She paused. "And there was no sound. I didn't hear the Land-Rover driving off. It was like I had cotton wool in my ears."

"So you wouldn't have heard anyone walking or running away?"

She shrugged. "I don't think so."

I kept on at her. "Are you positive you were alone in the street? You didn't have any intuition that someone else was there?"

"Yes. No." She looked at me helplessly. "You're deliberately confusing me."

"No, I'm not. It's important."

"Yes, I did feel alone. I told you. I . . . I remember I shivered. I suddenly felt afraid. I ran to the door to find Sarah." The name made her choke and she bent forward, her hands over her eyes.

I let her have a few moments, then asked, "Her name was Sarah?"

Linda wiped her face quickly. "Sarah Spence. Knox 96. I knew her from the first day of my auxiliary training. She's . . . she was older than me – in her mid-thirties. She ran physical training classes on top of her normal guard duties."

"Describe her to me."

"Short and stocky, brown hair and eyes, a lot of freckles. The kind who would have turned to fat if she hadn't done so much exercise." A strangled sob escaped before she could get in its way. "Oh God, she was always so full of energy, laughing . . ."

"Obviously she could defend herself."

"Of course. She trained me in unarmed combat. That made it even more of a shock." She straightened herself up again. "Of a shock," she repeated, her voice falling away.

I gave her time to compose herself.

"So I knocked at the door and waited to be let in. She didn't come. I knocked again, then pushed the door. It was unlocked – against regulations. I was surprised, but I was still keen to see her before she was picked up. Her Land-Rover had been delayed too. So I walked in and called her name a few times. No reply."

"Did you notice anything in the hallway? Anything strange?"

"No, they didn't find anything."

"I'm not asking about what anybody else found, Linda. I'm asking if you saw anything."

She frowned then shook her head. "No, there was nothing."

"All right. Go on."

"She wasn't there – at the guardpost by the ticket office, I mean. The mobile phone was there, on standby, but there was no sign of Sarah. I walked down the corridor calling her name. Then I got to the men's toilets and, I don't know why, I pushed open the door. I hardly broke my stride, so I only caught a glimpse of it out of the corner of my eye . . ."

"It?"

She looked at me like I was a schoolboy who had just wandered into a research seminar on advanced cybernetics. "The blood, of course." She began to shake. "It was, oh

God, it was as if someone had thrown a bucketful over her."

I slipped off the desk and held her jerking shoulders. This time she didn't shy away. "Was there any on the floor near the door: footprints, stains, anything?"

"No!" she screamed. "No!" Then her struggling subsided. "No, there wasn't." Suddenly her voice was normal again. She stared at me in bewilderment. "But how could that be? She'd been . . . torn apart, but the blood was only in the corner where she was lying."

"Yes, how could that be?" I tightened my grip on her bony shoulders. "Tell me exactly what you saw as you approached her."

"The gaping hole," Linda replied without hesitation, her voice as bereft of emotion as a hanging judge's. "The great hole in her abdomen. Like an animal had taken a bite out of her." This time she didn't sob, but she seemed unaware that the door had opened quietly. The public order guardian came in.

"What about her face?" I asked quickly. "Did you see it?"

"No, thank God. Her tunic was wrapped around her head. It was soaked in blood." She was looking at the floor. "Is it true what I heard, that her liver was cut out?"

"You shouldn't pay attention to gossip, guardswoman," said Hamilton firmly. "Have you finished, Dalrymple?"

"Scarcely even begun, guardian," I replied. "Scarcely even begun."

"Where to now?" Davie asked. "The infirmary?"

I was looking at the mobile phone that was fitted beneath

the Land-Rover's rusty vent. "Yes, the infirmary. Remind me about reporting procedures in guarded premises, will you?"

"Every hour, on the hour. New code word each time."

Which is a pretty good example of the Council's mania for security. No wonder they need so many auxiliaries. I didn't share my thoughts with Davie, though I had a feeling he might have agreed.

"So what happened at Stevenson Hall last night? Did the killer time his arrival and departure to avoid the calls, or was he just lucky? Or . . . I wonder." I glanced at the bearded figure beside me in the dim light from the dashboard. This was a chance to find out how enthusiastic he really was. "Davie, while I'm at the post-mortem can you talk to the guard commander who was on duty this morning? Tell him you're working with me; he'll know that I have Council authority by now. Find out whether Sarah – I mean the dead guardswoman Knox 96 – gave all the correct responses."

"No problem."

Most auxiliaries would have had a hard time taking orders from an ordinary citizen, but Davie didn't seem to care. Maybe I would be able to make use of him. If he managed to squeeze an answer out of the commander.

The Land-Rover swung into Lauriston Place, just missing a horse-drawn carriage containing four tourists. We came to the gateway of the city's largest hospital. It bore the ubiquitous maroon heart emblem and the legend "The City Provides". Is that right? I thought. Provides what? Mutilation for female auxiliaries?

Before I was five yards away from the vehicle, I heard Davie speaking on the mobile.

* * *

I walked into the mortuary and my nostrils were instantly flushed out by the sweet and sour reek of formaldehyde.

"Ah, there you are, citizen," said Yellowlees, the medical guardian, with a warm smile. He looked so welcoming that I clenched my buttocks. Then I remembered the reputation he had for womanising years ago. "We're ready to begin." He was standing next to the slab where the cadaver had been laid out.

Hamilton came in, his face turning greyer than his beard when he saw the dead guardswoman. He'd always been squeamish at post-mortems. I'm not particularly proud that I can turn my feelings off temporarily. A nursing auxiliary with a bust like the figurehead on a tea clipper handed us masks and gowns.

Yellowlees nodded to her. "Very well, Simpson 134, start taking notes on –" he glanced at the tag on the subject's ankle – "Knox 96."

"She had a name, you know."

They all stared at me.

"Sarah Spence. In case you're interested."

Simpson 134 was the first to look away.

"Really?" Yellowlees turned briefly to the nurse, his eyes meeting hers above their masks, then stepped closer to the body. "It hardly matters now, does it?" He started the preliminary examination.

I soon realised that the medical guardian hadn't forgotten any of his pathologist's skills. The mortuary assistant scarcely got a look in as Yellowlees involved himself in everything, removing the plastic bags from head and hands, taking samples of dried blood from around the wound in the abdomen, scraping underneath the fingernails, telling the photographer exactly what angles he wanted. Then he lifted the tunic from around the head. I leaned forward. This was the interesting bit. As Sarah Spence had been lying on her left side, that part of her face and limbs was dark blue in post-mortem lividity. I saw immediately that her ears were intact and her nose unblocked. The guardians and I exchanged glances.

Yellowlees bent over her neck, then motioned to his assistant to turn the body over. "No doubt about the cause of death. Strangulation by ligature."

"The Ear, Nose and Throat Man's modus operandi," said Hamilton, nudging me.

"What?" I had suddenly been back in Princes Street Gardens, pulling a ligature of my own round a much thicker neck.

"All twelve of his victims were despatched that way."

Caro's face flashed before me, then was gone.

"Quite so," said Yellowlees. He pointed to the deeply scored line in the victim's flesh. "You can see the contusion where the ligature was twisted with considerable force. Unfortunately the killer took it away with him. We'll check for fibres, but it's possible he used strong wire."

Like I did.

"Turn her to the front," Yellowlees ordered, bending to lift the eyelids. "Note the haemorrhaging to the conjunctivae." He took a syringe and plunged the needle into the right eye. Hamilton stepped back quickly. "The vitreous humour. I should be able to give you a fairly accurate time of death after I've tested for potassium."

"What's your estimate from the body temperature?" I asked.

"I don't much like estimates," the guardian said, his eyes narrowing. "Still, you need all the help you can get. I'd say between four and six a.m.; as the body was found just after six, we're already in the frame."

I nodded and watched as he started examining further down the cadaver, cutting and plucking hairs then applying swabs to the vagina and rectum.

"There's extensive damage to the anus consistent with violent buggery."

"As with almost all the ENT Man's victims, male and female," said Hamilton.

"Correct." Yellowlees lifted his mask and lowered his face to the dead woman's buttocks, then sniffed.

"Jesus Christ." The public order guardian gagged and turned away.

"Curious." Yellowlees stood up straight and glanced at me. "A hint of spermicide. Tests will confirm that."

"A condom?" I said. "The Ear, Nose and Throat Man never used them."

"And we still never managed to track him down from his DNA profile." The medical guardian shook his head impatiently.

"He managed to keep himself out of all the Council's numerous files," I said, looking at the pair of guardians. "Pretty good going." He was a cunning bastard. Even though I buried him, I never knew his name. Members of the drug gangs always used aliases. I don't think the other Howlin' Wolf headcases knew his identity either.

After I got rid of him, I didn't try to find it out. Maybe I should have.

Yellowlees had replaced his mask and was peering at the arms and chest. "No evidence of a struggle. She must have blacked out immediately. It happens." Now he was over by the abdomen, reading off measurements. "Wound made by three incisions, forming a flap of skin six and a quarter inches by eleven inches by five and a half inches; said flap was pulled down to allow access to the liver, which was then removed."

"What kind of blade?" I asked.

"Non-serrated, single-edged, extremely sharp." The medical guardian shrugged. "As to length and thickness, I can't be sure."

I looked into the blood-encrusted hole. "Any evidence of medical knowledge?"

"Not a great deal. The killer knew where to locate the liver, but he could have found that out in any encyclopaedia."

"What about bloodstains? Surely he would have been soaked."

Yellowlees nodded. "I would have thought so, though bear in mind that the victim was already dead when mutilation took place. There wouldn't have been any spurting."

Hamilton came closer. It looked like he was only just winning the battle against vomiting. "We found all her clothing apart from the tunic in a neat pile under the washbasin nearest the door. Her equipment was laid on top. There were no stains on any of it."

I looked at him. "And there were no traces of blood anywhere except in the immediate vicinity of the body."

"That's right," said Yellowlees. "What are you getting at?"

"I'll tell you what I'm getting at. I think the killer took off his own clothes as well as the victim's. I think he cut her open when he was stark naked, then washed the blood off in one of the basins. He's some sort of cleanliness freak."

Simpson 134, the nurse, was staring at me, her eyelids so wide apart that I felt my own straining in sympathy. After a few seconds the medical guardian moved to her and put his hand on her arm briefly.

"I'd expect there to be traces of blood on the basin he used," he said.

"Not after the Council's decision to send in the city's number one cleaner."

Yellowlees ignored the sarcasm. "As I remember, the otolaryngologist didn't use to mind if he left bloodstains." That was a typical guardian understatement. The ENT Man treated his victims' blood like it was paint and he was Jackson Pollock.

"What are you saying?" demanded Hamilton. "That this isn't the same killer? The victim was strangled by ligature, sodomised and had an organ removed. That was the pattern in the past. What more do you want?"

I wanted an explanation of a lot more: like why the ears weren't cut off, why the nose wasn't blocked with earth, why the face hadn't been beaten till it was more black than blue, why a condom had been used and why the scene of the crime hadn't been left like a room in some late twentieth-century slasher film. And that was just for starters.

Yellowlees looked like he was thinking along the same

lines. He glanced at Hamilton doubtfully, then turned back to the body. His assistant had finished shaving the head and groin.

"Let's get on," said the medical guardian. He picked up a dissecting knife and made a large Y-shaped incision from neck to pubis, leaving the larynx intact for further examination. The sternum was then split and the dead woman's chest prised apart. That was when the public order guardian left.

"There's more to this than meets the eye," Yellowlees said. Even guardians sometimes speak in clichés.

"I'd go along with that," I said, suddenly noticing that the statuesque nurse was following the surgeon's every movement like she had been hypnotised. Not even auxiliaries are that brainwashed usually.

I left them to it. I'd attended too many post-mortems in the past. Perhaps a five-year lay-off had turned me into a sensitive soul; perhaps there's just a limit to how much of the human body's interior you can take. Unless you're a medic. Or a serial killer. I had a nasty feeling that was what I was up against, even though there was only one body in the morgue. At least I knew it wasn't the ENT Man. I'd have gone through the whole of his autopsy, but I couldn't allow there to be one. What happened was between me and him alone. I owed Caro that much.

Hamilton ambushed me in the foyer. Even though it was late in the evening, there were still patients waiting to be seen. Some of them were speaking a language I didn't recognise.

"Here. I've got these for you." The public order guardian looked like he desperately needed a cigarette, but the Council banned them years ago. He handed me a mobile phone and an embossed card bearing the Council seal. It authorised me to demand full co-operation from any guardian, auxiliary or citizen. "Anything else you need?" he asked mordantly. "Apart from a shave and a change of clothes." I could see he hadn't forgotten my jibe about the cleaner. It was hard to resist another one.

"I saw the hanging today. Do you ever use it to get rid of undesirables?"

Hamilton's eyes sprang open like a pair of Venus flytraps that hadn't seen a bluebottle for weeks. He stepped towards me as I jumped into the Land-Rover.

"Looks like you did it again," Davie said as he accelerated away. "What is it between you and the guardian?"

"You're better off not knowing. Take me back to my place, will you?"

"Right. I spoke to the guard commander who was on duty last night. Every call to Stevenson Hall got the correct response except the one at 0600. Napier 498, the guardswoman who was relieving the victim, made an emergency call at 0609. By that time a vehicle was already on its way to check out the place."

"Thanks, Davie." I made the decision. "What do you say to a temporary transfer? I need someone to work with me on this case."

"Bloody brilliant." He gave a great laugh that echoed round the Land-Rover's rattling shell like a crazed rodent trying to get out of a bass drum. "I wouldn't miss this for anything."

Either he was one of Hamilton's best undercover men

selling me a double dummy or he really was excited. I was too tired to work out which. The streetlights flashed three times in quick succession, making me blink.

"Curfew coming up. You better get a move on or you'll have to arrest me for being out after my bedtime."

"Don't worry, I'll vouch for you," he said with a grin. "Even if the chief won't."

The fog closed in around us as the lights were extinguished outside the tourist area to conserve electricity. In the early days, when the Council still called itself the Enlightenment and the nuclear power station at Torness was operational, citizens had to be off the streets by midnight. More recently, curfew time has been brought forward to ten o'clock. Whatever that points to doesn't come under the definition of enlightenment in any dictionary that I know.

Chapter Four

I was playing rhythm guitar in the band, cutting some riffs Muddy Waters could have related to, when the ENT Man appeared. Then I was on him, my blood on his filthy jacket. His head turned towards me as I garrotted him. In the light above the path I saw his teeth. They were as blue as a cheese that had been forgotten for decades in the deepest recesses of an underground storeroom in Copenhagen. The bastard was grinning, taunting me because he knew he could break my grip. When he got bored, that's what he did. Threw me sprawling to the ground, then came for me. I didn't think I had a chance of tripping him, but he went down like a hamstrung bull. On to his own knife. The beat drove on. Eventually I realised someone was hammering on my door. I staggered towards it.

"Morning." Davie examined me. "I won't ask if you slept well. You look like . . ."

"What's in the bag?"

"Barracks bread." He thrust it into my hands. "A sight better than anything you'll get in your local bakery."

"The coffee's over there." I went to dress.

"Coffee?" he called after me. "Where did you get that, citizen?"

I was groggier than a sailor's oesophagus, but it almost sounded like he was doing an imitation of your average hyper-inquisitive auxiliary. That wasn't enough to get him out of jail. As far as I'm concerned, people who thrive on getting up early belong to an alien race which has managed to infiltrate us without anyone noticing. Not a bad description of the Enlightenment.

Daylight was no more than a faint grey line under my tattered curtains. "What the hell's the time?" I shouted.

"You tell me. You've got my watch."

I found it in the carpet of dust under my bedside table. Ten past six. "Jesus, Davie, when I asked you to call me, I didn't mean at the start of your shift." The guard start two hours earlier than everyone else to police the rush hour.

He came in with a mug for me. "What shift? I thought murder investigations went on twenty-four hours a day."

"Up yours, guardsman."

He smiled and went back into the living room. While I was tying the laces of my boots, I heard him strum my guitar and have a go at "Such a Parcel of Rogues in a Nation". It was an Enlightenment favourite before independence but he couldn't do it much justice because of the state of my strings.

When I came out he greeted the clean black sweatshirt and trousers I'd found at the back of the wardrobe with a whistle.

"Citizen Dalrymple, you look almost respectable."

"Call me Quint if you want to stay on the case."

"You'll do anything to be different, won't you? A spell down the mines is what you need."

"They tried that once." I gulped coffee. "They didn't invite me back. Apparently I was a disruptive element."

Davie nodded slowly. "I can see that." He put my guitar back in its case. "You any good with this?"

"I haven't played for a long time."

"I noticed. What happened to your E-string?"

I had a flash of the ENT Man falling into the pit with my guitar string still round his neck. Then I thought of the dead guardswoman. Maybe she'd been strangled with a guitar string too. The idea disturbed me – too close for comfort.

I frowned at him when I realised he was still waiting for an answer. "I lost it, years ago. You know how difficult it is to get things like that replaced in Edinburgh."

He looked at me dubiously then followed me to the door.

The victim had been stationed at Knox Barracks on the west side of Charlotte Square. The building was formerly one of the city's record offices. After independence its façade had been ruined by the addition of rows of dormitory windows. The Council chose it as a guard depot because it's close to the tourist hotels and shops at the West End of Princes Street, and because it's within sprinting distance of the guardians' quarters in Moray Place. The dark, mist-sodden stonework looked like the hull of a long-lost battleship sunk beyond the range of the most sophisticated depthfinder.

Davie stopped the Land-Rover outside. I was remembering when there were parking meters on both sides of the road. I gazed into the fog that was still a thick carpet over the city. In the grass-covered centre of the square there used to be bookstalls and tents where writers made speeches at the time when the Festival only lasted three weeks every summer. Now there are booths containing slot machines and roulette wheels – for tourists only. Guard personnel stood at the gates even at this early hour.

"Try not to draw attention to me, Davie," I said before I got out.

"And how am I supposed to do that?" he said with a laugh. "Unless you grow a beard in the next two minutes, every auxiliary in the barracks is going to notice you."

"Well, anyway, let me go ahead, then see if you can find anyone in the recreation area. Tell them you were a friend of Knox 96 and see what kind of reaction you get." I shoved the rusty door open. "You can draw a replacement watch from the stores as well."

"You think of everything, bossman."

Which unfortunately was not the case. At that moment I had no idea how I was going to get anything but the most grudging of answers from the occupants of Knox.

At the entrance my way was barred by a grey-bearded guardsman. Most auxiliaries these days look like they're just out of primary school, but a few have survived from the early days. My ID and authorisation were scrutinised and the details entered in a logbook.

"I thought it was you, sir." The guardsman's eyes were suddenly more welcoming, though he didn't risk a smile.

Not that I had a clue who he was. His use of a proscribed form of address and the low number on his chest – Knox 31

– showed the length of his service. The twenty city barracks were originally set up in 2005 with fifty members each. Now they all have five hundred serving auxiliaries.

The guardsman waited while a group of his colleagues in running kit passed on their way to the all-weather track in Queen Street Gardens. I tried to place him but failed.

"Taggart, sir. I was with you in the Tactical Operations Squad."

Now I remembered. Even when I was in the directorate, I used names rather than barrack numbers – Hamilton used to love me for that. "God, Jimmy Taggart." I sneaked a quick handshake. "I didn't recognise you. All that grey hair."

This time he smiled. "Pressure of being an auxiliary, you know." The smile faded. "I'm not joking. You're well out of it." He looked away from my face. "I was in the back-up group the night we took out the Howlin' Wolf gang up on Soutra. If only those fuckin' phones hadn't gone down . . ."

It was impossible to shut out the flashing lights from the flares, the brittle sound of gunfire, then the screams of a woman I only identified when it was too late. I clenched my fists hard and managed to bring myself back to the present.

"Sorry, sir, shouldn't have mentioned it." Taggart stepped back as more auxiliaries came by. They glanced at me curiously. "Well, you'd better get up to the commander's office. You're here about the killing, aren't you?" He came closer again. "I knew Sarah Spence."

I looked around the hallway. "Can we talk later?"

He nodded. "I've got a break in a couple of hours. The refectory's usually quiet then." He acknowledged another colleague. "Don't believe everything they tell you."

"I'm not expecting them to tell me anything at all."
I walked down the corridor and breathed in the familiar
barracks smell: bleach mixed with sweat and the reek of
overcooked vegetables. The only light came from the high,
dirty windows.

The commander was waiting for me outside her office.
She was younger than me, her dark hair in the regulation
ponytail and her mouth set in a straight horizontal line
beneath pale cheeks and cautious eyes. There's nothing like
a senior auxiliary's welcome to make you feel optimistic about
the future of the human race.

"Citizen Dalrymple," she said. "Your reputation precedes
you."

"Meaning that the public order guardian told you to
expect me."

Straight-mouth nodded and led me into her office. It was
furnished in the usual austere fashion; it wouldn't do for
ordinary citizens to think that auxiliaries lived comfortable
lives. Not that any ordinary citizens would have got as far
as her office recently. The large windows looking out over
the square were all the room had in its favour. The carpets
and curtains were worn and the antique desk could have
done with the services of a restorer. Over the fireplace was
the city's maroon heart flanked by the words of the slogan,
"The City Provides". It was faced on the opposite wall by the
motto of the rank of auxiliaries: "To Serve the City". This is
one of the Council's better jokes – well, one of its only jokes,
and unintentional at that. The fact is, the Council deliberately
inspires competition between the barracks, which means that
they serve themselves first. "Loyalty to your barracks" is

the auxiliaries' real watchword. This leads to a pathological reluctance to disclose anything to outsiders, and you don't get much more of an outsider than me.

I decided to go in feet first. "So, what can you tell me about Sarah Spence?" I smiled as Knox 01's eyebrows shot up. "I mean, Knox 96."

"Knox 96," she repeated emphatically, opening a file. "Born 7.10.1986, height five feet two inches, weight nine stone two pounds, hair brown, eyes brown, distinguishing marks heavily freckled face and arms, completed studies at City College of Physical Education July 2007, started auxiliary training programme 1.9.2007, entered Knox Barracks on completion, 31.8.2009, served as physical education instructor—"

"I'm a big boy, commander," I interrupted. "I can read files for myself. Tell me things that aren't in there. Like did she have a lot of friends in the barracks? Did she have any contacts outside Knox? Did she prefer men or women at sex sessions?"

Her mouth looked even straighter than it had been. "Most of that is in the file, citizen," she said coolly. "For your information, she took male and female sexual partners."

"You're not answering my question. Which did she prefer?"

"What bearing can that possibly have on her murder?" The commander actually looked irritated. That was a good sign. Maybe I would find something out. "Oh, very well. Judging from personal experience I would say she preferred women."

She seemed to be expecting me to comment, so I didn't.

"As regards friends, yes, she was popular. She was the kind of person who organises, who's at the centre of things. She had no enemies I ever heard of." The commander was avoiding my eyes. "I don't think she had many contacts outside either. She was very much a Knox person." She stood up and handed me a list of barracks numbers. "These are the people she's . . . she was closest to." Suddenly her mouth wasn't straight any more. "Find him, citizen," she said, her voice taut. "Find the animal who did that to her." Then she twitched her head and became the senior auxiliary again.

"I'm working on it, commander," I said and left her to her files.

On my way to the refectory I passed the barracks gym. There were several pairs practising unarmed combat. I watched the auxiliaries in maroon judo suits going after each other with carefully controlled violence. The fact that the city was served by ten thousand trained killers didn't make me feel that great.

I saw Davie in the far corner of the eating room and ignored him. Taggart got up and led me to the self-service counter. I took a pint of milk and a plate of haggis and mixed vegetables. They serve that kind of food on a twenty-four-hour basis in barracks because of the shifts auxiliaries work. The food's better than what ordinary citizens can find in the subsidised supermarkets too. Since I'd missed dinner the previous evening, I decided against making a complaint at the next Council meeting.

"How did you get on, sir?"

"Stop calling me that, Taggart. I'm just an ordinary citizen now. Call me Quint."

"Sorry." He scratched his beard. "I was a constable before the Enlightenment. Things like that stick in the mind." He sat watching me eat and I knew he was wondering whether he could get away with bringing up the past again. I didn't give him any encouragement. "Did you find out anything useful?" he asked eventually.

"Not much. You know what it's like in barracks. They'd rather have their fingernails pulled out than talk about a colleague."

Taggart nodded. "I'm usually like that myself, but this is different. A murder, for fuck's sake. After all this time."

I studied the burly face opposite me. He had a two-inch scar above his right eye that had been sewn up by someone a lot less proficient than Yellowlees. "What do you think about it then?" I had a feeling he wanted to tell me something.

He leaned closer. "I'm a bit bothered by a couple of things. I'm sure you'll have heard that Sarah was all sweetness and light, a cheery soul and all that. It's true enough – as far as it goes. She wasn't always like that. There was a hard side to her as well. She was really sharp with people who went against her. I heard stories about her taking it out on girls who . . . you know . . . said no to her."

A pair of eager-looking guardswomen approached, making Taggart sit back rapidly.

I waited till they had gone. Even if he was right, I'd have a job getting any of his female colleagues to admit it. "What was the other thing?"

He leaned forward again. "I often do the night shift on Saturdays. I saw Sarah go out after midnight more than once. She always had an authorisation."

I lost interest in my food faster than a croupier in one of the city's casinos sizes up a tourist's wallet. "When was the last time?"

"Two weeks ago."

"But I checked the duty rosters." I looked through my notes. "Two weeks ago she had morning fitness classes and the afternoon shift at Stevenson Hall."

Taggart bit his lower lip and nodded slowly. "Like I say, it's a bit strange, isn't it?"

"Auxiliaries' movements in the central area aren't logged, of course."

"No, but since she had an authorisation, there should be a reference in the rosters."

"I don't suppose you can remember which directorate stamped her authorisation?" I knew before I'd finished the question that a positive answer was about as likely as the Supply Directorate doubling the sugar ration.

"I'm back on watch in a few minutes," Taggart said, collecting the crockery like a good auxiliary.

I needed to squeeze him a bit more. Whatever the Council thought about the ENT Man, I knew for a fact he wasn't at work again. But there were similarities in the modus operandi, Hamilton was right about that. I was going to have to carry out my own private investigation into the bastard's background. That meant doing what Taggart wanted and talking about the old days. I felt sick.

"What were you saying before about the Howlin' Wolf gang?" I asked as nonchalantly as I could. "Did you ever hear what happened to the survivors?"

Taggart didn't show any surprise at the question. I saw he

was the kind of veteran auxiliary who spent most of his free time boring the arses off his younger colleagues with tales of his heroic past. "I saw one of them the other day," he said, screwing his eyes up as if the coincidence stung him like an onion. I knew the feeling. "A pal of mine was in charge of a squad of prisoners clearing rubble at Fettes. I recognised him from the tattoo on his arm. They all had them, remember? This one's said 'Leadbelly'. Christ knows why."

Christ and me. They were all blues freaks. The Ear, Nose and Throat Man had "Little Walter" on his arm. I suppose they thought that was really funny.

Taggart would have gone on for hours, but he had his shift and I had my lead.

It was obvious from Davie's face when I got back to the Land-Rover that he hadn't got much out of his fellow auxiliaries. At least he was wearing a new watch.

The sheer walls of the Assembly Hall loomed out of the mist like a smoke-blackened Aztec sacrifice pyramid. I jumped out as soon as Davie stopped and sprinted into the building. Arriving late for a Council meeting was a good way to commit suicide. I'd been working in the archives and had lost track of time.

The medical guardian was on his feet when I got into the chamber.

"Never mind explaining, citizen," said the deputy senior guardian, raising her hand. "Our colleague has been giving us the results of the tests he ran on the victim. Unfortunately, they don't seem to be much help."

That didn't come as much of a surprise. I was too busy being relieved that the senior guardian was absent again.

Yellowlees looked at me without blinking, then acknowledged the speaker's remarks. "I'm afraid that's the substance of it. From the tests I can at least say that Knox 96 was in good physical condition and was not under the influence of drugs or alcohol of any kind. Nor did I find any trace whatsoever of the murderer – no hairs, blood, skin, semen. And no traces from the ligature. I can place the time of death between five and six a.m. from the potassium level in the vitreous humour." He looked around at Hamilton. "I can also confirm that there were traces of spermicide from a standard-issue condom in the guardswoman's rectum."

Hamilton was gazing unperturbed into the middle distance. Behind him was a board with photographs of the ENT Man's victims. That didn't exactly raise my spirits.

The speaker was trying to attract my attention. "Have you made any progress, citizen Dalrymple?"

"Not much. The medical guardian was lucky. At least he had a body to work on." I looked round the horseshoe table. The guardians suddenly found their papers more interesting than me. Which wound me up even more. "All I got was the best-cleaned shithouse in the city."

That got their attention. They probably hadn't heard one of those words for a long time. "I'll tell you this. I reckon there are going to be more killings. The bodies must be left where they're found. I haven't got a chance otherwise."

Some of them looked like they weren't too surprised to hear that.

"All right, citizen, you've made your point," said the deputy senior guardian drily. "Your report, please."

"I've been working on the victim's background." I saw Hamilton move his eyes upward dismissively. That was all the confirmation I needed to keep some of what I'd discovered to myself. "There's nothing irregular. I also spent some time with the auxiliaries from the public order directorate who handled the case before I was brought in. Again, there's nothing significant to report. Fingerprints found in the lavatory and corridor are either those of cleaners, who all have sound alibis, or are not registered in the archives, indicating they belong to tourists. There's no shortage of those in Stevenson Hall every night. The hotels have been checked and they all report that their residents were in by the tourist curfew of 0300."

"What's the point of all this?" Hamilton demanded, jerking his thumb at the board behind him. "We know who the killer is."

"Hardly," said Yellowlees. "Even if the ENT Man has started killing again, we don't have any idea of his identity."

The speaker raised her hand. "One moment. Are we to understand there is some doubt that the Ear, Nose and Throat Man is involved?"

"Absolutely none," said Hamilton, as firmly as a member of the Inquisition who'd just been asked if there was any possibility Galileo could be right about the solar system.

The deputy senior guardian didn't buy it. She turned to me. "Citizen?"

It was a tricky one. Life would have been a sight easier if I'd told them what happened to the ENT Man. They probably wouldn't even have thrown me into the cells for keeping quiet about it for five years. At least until I caught this killer. But it wasn't just my secret. It was all I still shared with Caro, lost beautiful Caro, whose photo, thank Christ, was obscured by Hamilton's head.

"We're waiting," prompted the speaker, her voice sharper.

I let Caro fade away. And decided to keep our secret. "Well, there are a lot of inconsistencies in the modus operandi. The ENT Man removed organs from his victims, but he also took their ears and blocked their noses, sometimes with earth, other times with pieces of cloth."

"He may have run out of time in Stevenson Hall," said Hamilton.

"You think so? This murder looks to me like a carefully calculated killing. The person who did this knew how to avoid the patrols and gain entry to a protected building."

"Whereas the otolaryngologist," said the medical guardian, his fingers forming a pyramid under his chin as he repeated the term, "the otolaryngologist tended to keep out of the way of guard personnel."

Except in two cases, I thought.

"As I remember," the shrivelled finance guardian said, "he didn't clean up after himself either." The old man glanced at the photos and twitched his lips.

Hamilton was shaking his head. "The woman was strangled, mutilated and sodomised. What more evidence is necessary?"

"Evidence that will enable citizen Dalrymple to catch him," said the deputy senior guardian. "There seems to be precious little of that." She looked at me again. "If you are dubious that it is the same killer, what grounds do you have for expecting more murders?"

It was a good question. They might give the impression of inhabiting a world light years away from the rest of us, but there's nothing wrong with the guardians' intellects. Except perhaps the public order guardian's.

"There was an outburst of serial killing in the years before the UK broke up. I read all the reports. The likelihood of a murderer who gets away with a killing of this kind doing it again is overwhelming." I was trusting a hunch as well, but I didn't think that would impress them.

"You'd better make sure you catch him then," said Hamilton grimly. "I propose that we increase the number of patrols in the tourist area at night. And that we continue to suppress all news of the guardswoman's death."

"You realise that every auxiliary in the city knows about it by now," I observed, giving him a grim look of my own.

"Auxiliaries are sworn servants of the city," said the speaker loftily. "They will not divulge the news to ordinary citizens."

And a formation of pigs had just been spotted over Arthur's Seat. "Even if they don't," I said, "it's possible that the killer needs publicity. By denying him that we may increase the chances of him doing it again." They all looked at me sternly. "Let's face it, censoring the news of the ENT Man's activities didn't exactly help us catch him."

I caught a glimpse of the bust of Plato at the rear of the chamber. The Enlightenment used his ideas as the basis of the new constitution and they're still debated every week in all the barracks. "You're the students of human nature," I said, trying to provoke a response. None of them reacted. It looked like I had them where I wanted. "By the way, I've taken on a guardsman as my assistant."

Hamilton was as reliable as one of Pavlov's dogs. His eyes sprang wide open and his fists clenched.

"Hume 253 is his barracks number," I continued. "He'll report to me alone during the investigation. No objections, I hope."

If the deputy senior guardian disapproved of my tone, she concealed it. Which is more than can be said for the public order guardian. Now he looked like a dog that had just been fed something worse than standard-issue haggis.

I hadn't finished with them. "It seems to me that we're failing to address the most important question raised by this case."

"No doubt you're about to tell us what that is," said Hamilton in a strangulated whisper.

I closed my notebook and stood up. "You're right, guardian – I am. What's behind the timing? It's five years since the ENT Man last killed. Suddenly his modus operandi is repeated in part and a guardswoman is murdered in Stevenson Hall in the early morning of 20 March 2020. Why?"

Back at my flat I cleared everything off the table and sat down to turn dross into gold. As I told the Council, the archives had yielded nothing worth reporting. I'd a faint hope that I would find some detail that had been omitted from the barracks documentation concerning the dead woman. Even a juicy big Public Order Directorate stamp showing that something had been censored would have done – then I could have squeezed

Hamilton about it. But there was nothing. It didn't take me long to come to the conclusion that I was as much at sea as the owl and the pussycat. At least they had a pea green boat.

The knock on the door came as a relief. I assumed it would be Davie, then with a shock I remembered Katharine Kirkwood. Maybe she couldn't wait until tomorrow. Her brother had been missing from my thoughts as well as from his flat. Still, the idea of laying eyes on her again was not unpleasant. I was disappointed.

"Billy?" I tried and failed to sound unsurprised.

"Quint, how the hell are you?" The short figure in a beautifully cut grey suit and pink silk shirt pushed past me. On his way he rammed a brand of malt whisky I hadn't seen for a decade into my hands.

"Christ, Billy, how did you find me?" I closed the door. "More to the point, after all this time, why did you find me?"

"I'm pleased to see you too. What kind of a welcome is that, for fuck's sake? I'm your oldest friend." William Ewart Geddes, Heriot 07, one hundred and ten pounds of financial genius and calculating bastard, walked into the centre of the room and looked around under the naked light bulb. "Nice place you've got here, Quint," he said with a sardonic grin. "I see you've still got your guitar. Not being a naughty boy and playing the blues, I hope."

There was a time when Billy was as fanatical about B.B. King and Elmore James as I am, but that was before the Council banned the blues on the grounds that music has to be uplifting or some such bollocks. The fact that most of the drugs gangs idolised bluesmen had nothing to do with the decision, of course.

"No, I haven't played for years," I said. "Not since I was demoted." I opened the whisky and inhaled its peaty breath. "That's the last time I saw you as well. Why the sudden interest?"

Billy accepted a chipped glass reluctantly and sipped the spirit neat, his small grey eyes blinking. The sparse beard that covered his thin face showed definite signs of officially disapproved clipping.

"You know how it is," he said. "No fraternisation between auxiliaries and ordinary citizens." He grinned again, showing suspiciously even teeth. "Still, you've had time to cool off. And now I hear you're back in favour—" He broke off to examine the small, blurred photo of Caro on the wall, the sharpness in his expression dissipating. The three of us had been at the university together. He looked like he was going to say something about her, but the glare I gave him made him change his mind.

"As for finding you, that was easy. I'm deputy finance guardian, remember. All I had to do was pull your rates sheet." He sat down gingerly on the sofa after inspecting it for anything that might damage his suit. Personally I'd have stayed upright if I'd been him.

"Deputy finance guardian? You look more like a stockbroker. Remember them?"

Billy laughed. "The clothes are nothing. You should see my flat."

"No, thanks. I'm only a citizen. Luxury's bad for my character." So's jealousy. I couldn't resist having a go at him. "Or so they used to say in the Enlightenment, didn't they?"

"Something like that," Billy mumbled, his cheeks reddening. The party had alway taken second place to his personal ambitions. Obviously they were now in the process of being achieved. "Listen, Quint, how about a night on the town? I've got a car."

"You're full of surprises."

"There's a new nightclub in Rose Street."

"Nightclub? You mean a place where semi-naked women prance around and tourists pay inflated prices for shitty whisky?"

"So you're interested." Billy raised an eyebrow. "You'll need a change of clothes."

I drained my glass. "I'll wear a tutu if I have to."

As I dragged my only suit out of the wardrobe, I almost managed to convince myself that I was only going because I wanted to find out why Billy had turned up after five years. But as I always turned the light out during sex sessions, it was also a long time since I'd seen a woman in anything less than a layer of off-white Supply Directorate underwear. Men are animals.

The Toyota that Billy drove might well have been the newest vehicle in the city. I decided against asking him where he found the petrol to run it. He'd either have ignored the question or revealed some deal I didn't want to know about. The Council banned the private ownership of cars because it was unable to negotiate a favourable price with the oil companies for anything except poor quality diesel. I wondered what its members thought about the deputy finance guardian's wheels. I had a flash of the clapped-out

2CV he used to have when we were students. The problem then wasn't obtaining fuel, it was finding somewhere to park. Now Lothian Road stretched ahead of us like a long deserted runway whose controller had turned the landing lights on in the forlorn hope of attracting some passing trade. Looking around, I realised that the fog was less thick.

Billy accelerated hard down the hill past Stevenson Hall and jerked a thumb. "It happened in there, didn't it?"

I might have known. He wanted me to fill him in about the murder. I fed him some scraps which he accepted impassively but which, I was sure, he was storing away in his memory. At school Billy was famous for his ability to memorise pages of material in seconds. Coupled with his business acumen, that had sent him straight into the Finance Directorate in the early years of the Council.

"Your parents all right?" he asked as he swung the car into the pedestrian precinct of Rose Street and acknowledged the guardsman who waved him through. When we were boys, Billy was a constant presence in our house in Newington. His own parents were divorced.

"Growing old with about as much grace as those archbishops the mob walled up in St Paul's years ago – the old man especially." Then I remembered that the next day was Sunday. Despite the investigation, I'd have to find time for the weekly visit.

"Don't suppose you see much of your mother," Billy said as he pulled up. "Right, let's get in amongst them."

The Bearskin was brightly lit. A pair of hypothermic girls wearing tartan shorts and crowned by headgear consistent with the club's name flanked the entrance. Placards in a variety of languages laid out the treats in store for prospective customers: live music ("the hottest in the city"), top quality food and the widest selection of beer and whisky in Edinburgh, as well as a floorshow Bangkok would supposedly have envied in the years before its decline.

Billy pushed through the mass of Chinese and Middle Eastern men – I couldn't see any female customers – and led me in without any money or ID appearing. The manager, despite his dinner jacket, smoothly shaved face and slicked-back hair, was an auxiliary, like most of the staff in clubs and casinos.

"Come on, Quint, I've got a table at the front." Billy went down a short flight of steps towards a thick curtain. It was opened by a beaming girl with dead eyes. Her skirt would only cover her knickers if she stood very still. A wave of sound broke over us.

The activities on stage were hard to avoid. Billy was already at a table, eagerly following the spectacle. I tried to play it cool, but my eyes were drawn all the same. The place was packed, the audience making almost as much noise as the band, whose members all wore kilts. A banner above proclaimed they were the only jazz band in the world with a bagpiper. Fortunately he seemed to have the night off.

We were very close to the tangle of limbs on the stage. The costumes suggested that the scene was set in the sixteenth century. Most of them were strewn across the floor. Mary, Queen of Scots, her petticoats lifted over her back, was being penetrated from the rear by a wiry young man presumably meant to be her secretary Rizzio. As the music rose to a crescendo, he withdrew, flipped his royal partner on to her back and started to tear off her remaining clothes to the raucous accompaniment of the crowd.

Billy turned to me with a desperate smile on his face, then glanced over my shoulder and nodded. I followed the direction of his eyes and saw an old friend, though she didn't seem to be very happy to see me. Patsy Cameron must have been in her fifties but she still looked the part, dressed up in a black velvet evening gown that showed the amount of bosom you'd expect from the madam of a cathouse in a Western. Which is more or less what she'd been before the Council decided to make use of her in the Prostitution Services Department. Patsy and I had got on pretty well when I was still in the directorate. Now she was avoiding my eyes like they'd give her an X-ray from twenty feet away.

Looking back at the stage, I saw that the queen was now completely naked. She sat up and gazed out at the audience. My heart missed so many beats that it hurt. She was without doubt the most stunningly beautiful woman I'd ever seen in my life. Although the tresses of her red wig partially obscured her face, the perfectly proportioned features were still visible. As were her full, hard-tipped breasts and limbs that looked like the pure white marble of an ancient statue. She moved her eyes slowly around the room, giving certain individuals the benefit of her erotically charged but totally inscrutable stare. The girl at the curtain's eyes had been dead, but this one's were on a different plane altogether – both superior and all-knowing, detached but at the same time infinitely provocative. I felt seriously out of my depth.

Then Rizzio, another member of the zombie eyes club, pushed her down, squatted on her chest and offered her his long, thin penis. She took it in her mouth and clutched his bony buttocks with her hands. The music started to build to a climax again as Mary, Queen of Scots inflated her cheeks in exaggerated movements. Eventually Rizzio pulled out and fountained over her breasts.

That was when I had another shock. Rubbing my eyes in the smoke from the tourists' cigarettes, I looked again. There was no doubt about it. The queen's left hand was normal, but the right one was a textbook example of polydactyly. Like everyone else, she had one thumb – but she also had no fewer than five fingers.

Chapter Five

Davie arrived at eight o'clock on the dot and almost fell over laughing when he saw the state I was in. I turned my nose up at his offering of barracks bread.

I only managed to formulate a coherent sentence after dosing myself with black coffee. "What do you know about Heriot 07, Davie?"

"The flash bastard in the Finance Directorate? He's got a reputation for looking after himself."

"How come he hasn't been nailed then?" I wasn't too happy about the way Billy had thrown his weight around at the nightclub. After the show had finished he got a hold of Rizzio and one of the waitresses and tried to interest me in a foursome. I prefer sex with women whose eyes have a bit more life in them. Besides, I was too pissed to do anything.

"Things have changed since you were an auxiliary," Davie said, shaking his head. "I'm beginning to see why you got out. You were one of those who thought the city should stay like it was in the early days, weren't you?"

"I was an idealist. Most people were then."

"Not any more, pal." His voice was harder. "While you've been doing your Philip Marlowe impersonation, a fair number of senior auxiliaries have been acting less altruistically. There's no shortage of smart operators like Heriot 07 who get what they can from the city. They cover their arses. If they're spotted, they pay people off. Or arrange a good kicking."

"Sounds like Chicago under Al Capone."

"Or London before the UK fell apart."

"Don't the guardians have any idea of what's going on?"

"That's the big question, isn't it?" Davie was looking twitchy. "Don't ask me, I'm only a guardsman." He turned away. "What are we doing today?"

I gulped down the last of my coffee. "It's Sunday. I have to call in on my father." Even when I was in the directorate, the visit had been a fixture. Hamilton, always the understanding boss, used to complain about me taking a couple of hours off on the city's single weekly rest-day. "But before that, we're going to look for a convict."

The fog had lifted completely and we drove along Comely Bank in bright sunshine. After the checkpoint between the tourist area and the suburbs, the surroundings took a rapid change for the worse. Although the streets were cleaned and rubbish collected regularly everywhere, the road surface, pavements and buildings were crumbling. In the centre, squads of cleaners, painters, masons and gardeners worked round the clock. Not in the parts where tourists never set foot. A flash in the sky caught my eye. A large silver and blue plane droned overhead on its descent to the airport – probably the daily flight from Athens with another load of tourists for the city's museums and fleshpots.

I looked at a small group of citizens gathered outside a church. Although the city is officially a secular republic, religion is tolerated as long as it conforms to the Council's standards of loyalty and civic responsibility. The thin but enthusiastic figures in their Sunday-best suits and dresses – smart enough despite the limitations of clothing vouchers – showed no dissatisfaction with the regime. People generally don't. In the sixteen years since the Enlightenment came to power, the Council has managed to retain the trust of the overwhelming majority of citizens. Probably because most of them haven't forgotten the economic chaos and the violence on the streets in the years before the last democratic election.

"You stay in the Land-Rover," I said as Davie pulled up at the East Gate of what had been the most striking building in north Edinburgh. Fettes College, once one of Scotland's foremost public schools, production line for generations of the politicians who had eventually brought the UK to ruin, was blown to pieces in 2009. I remembered playing rugby under the great grey-blue fairy castle walls when I was a kid. After independence and the abolition of private education, the school's proximity to the gangland area of Pilton had made it an attractive base for the drug traders. The Council concentrated on establishing order in the city centre first, then moved to retake Fettes. Bad idea. The gangs were better armed than the Parachute Regiment. Although the Council eventually drove them out, the buildings were blown up to show the guardians what the gangs thought of them. The top of the college's spire now lay hundreds of feet from its foundations. A small group of shaven-headed prisoners were loading stones on to a decrepit lorry.

"What do you think you're . . ." The guardsman shut up when he saw my authorisation.

I studied the labourers. They were sweating in the sunlight and had their shirt sleeves rolled up. That made it easy to spot Leadbelly.

"Bring that one to the Land-Rover," I said to the auxiliary. "Gently."

"Number thirty-five," he barked. "Get your arse over here."

I followed, shaking my head. You can always trust the guard to put people in the mood to co-operate.

"Wait outside, will you, Davie?" At least he did what I asked. I got into the driver's seat and beckoned to the prisoner to get in the other side. He was tall and I could see he had once been a hard man. Five years of the Cramond Island diet had turned him into a passable replica of a mummified corpse. He kept his eyes off me.

"So, Leadbelly, been digging any potatoes recently?" The reference to one of his namesake's best-known songs made him look at me quickly enough. A grin spread across his cracked lips and I saw that he had a serious shortage of teeth.

"'Digging My Potatoes' – shit, it's fucking years since I heard that. You know the blues?"

I nodded.

He gazed at me incredulously. "You know Huddie Ledbetter?"

"'Lining the Track', 'Matchbox Blues' – I've got some recordings from 1942."

He smacked his bony thigh. "You have? Christ, I'd bend over in front of a guardsman to have a listen to them."

"You may not have to go that far." I gave him my most encouraging smile.

His grin faded. "What do you want from me, man?" He peered at my clothes, noticing the lack of barracks number. "Who the fuck are you anyway?"

"Call me Quint."

"Quint? What kind of name is that?"

"There was a time when I was known as Bell 03."

"Is that right?" He leaned towards me. "You and me have had dealings."

You never know when it's going to happen, but sometimes you get lucky. I had been trying not to get excited by the slight chance that Leadbelly would turn out to be the gang member who put me on to the ENT Man. And it turned out he was. If I believed in a god, I'd have said thank you.

"You wrote me the note saying that the killer we were looking for would be in Princes Street Gardens the next Saturday night. You said he was going to get himself a tourist and really put the shits up us."

Leadbelly held his bloodshot eyes on me like he still needed final confirmation.

"At the end you wrote 'Axe the fucking . . .'"

"Psycho," he completed. "Okay, man, you're the genuine item." He grabbed my knee with a clawlike hand and brought his mouth close to my ear. "So did you?"

I didn't answer. He got the message though.

"What do you want now then?" he asked eventually.

"Tell me everything you know about him."

"After all this time?" He ran fingers with black nails over his scalp. "What's the point?"

"I've got Robert Johnson on tape too," I said.

"Never." He watched me nod in confirmation. "You're really something, man, you know that? Better get your notebook out then." He blinked and held his eyes shut for a long time, as if he were steeling himself to dive off a cliff. "Right, here it is. We called him Little Walter. Fuck, that was a good one. He must have been six foot two and sixteen stone."

At least. I felt his weight on me again, falling back as I tightened the ligature.

"And he was a shite. Fuck knows where the Wolf found him. He wasn't one of us, he didn't come from Pilton. He was good in a fight, mind, a handy man to have around. But he was weird, man. Christ, he was fucking insane. He had scars all over him; I'm sure he'd done most of them himself. And his breath reeked too. His teeth were even more rotten than mine."

I remembered. The bastard cocked his head, seemed to listen out. Then came the blue flash of his teeth in the light and the pitted skin of his face as he turned.

"And he was so fucking out of control. He once told me that he used to come when he throttled people. After I saw how he left that auxiliary woman in the farmhouse up on Soutra, I thought enough is a fucking nough."

I saw Caro lying on the stone floor, her left foot jerking like she was stretching it to get rid of cramp.

"I mean, he lived in a world of his own, man. He never paid any attention to our music, I don't think he even liked the blues. I'm sure he only let us tattoo him because he got a thrill from the needle." Leadbelly stopped and licked his lips as if he'd bitten into a putrid tomato. "Why are you making me talk about the sick fuck, for Christ's sake?"

"You ever hear his real name?"

"What do you think? We only used our gang names." He laughed harshly. "Like you assholes only use your barracks numbers."

"Not me, pal. How about family? Ever hear him talk about anyone he was close to?"

He choked on another laugh. "Close to? That shite only ever got close to the people he butchered. How come you never caught him? He left enough evidence, didn't he?"

"I nearly caught him once in Leith. He went back to the same place . . ."

"Yeah, he told us all about that. He reckoned he was something really special after he got away." He raised a finger. "Wait a minute, I do remember something about a relative. A brother. Walter said he was a right wee wanker and he'd shown him a thing or two when they were boys." He shook his head. "Didn't mention a name, though."

"Or anything about where he'd grown up, where he went to school, anything like that?"

"He was as silent as the grave I hope you put him in about all that."

I bet he was, the cunning bastard. "Anything else that could help me identify him?" I asked in desperation.

Leadbelly shrugged. "Here, can I get back now? The others'll be thinking you're getting me to rat on them."

"Wouldn't be the first time."

"Not fair, man. I did you a good turn. Walter was an animal."

I closed my notebook. End of the road. What the hell had I been doing? I knew where the butcher was; why was I raking around in dead man's dust? The chances of someone copying his modus operandi imperfectly were about as small as my chances of finding out the ENT Man's identity. I had to forget the old obsession once and for all.

The prisoner climbed out. Before closing the door, he leaned back in. "What about those recordings of Huddie?"

"Don't worry, I'll get them to you."

It was obvious he didn't believe me.

"Give me half an hour." I left my mobile phone with Davie and ran into the house in Trinity.

As a former guardian, my father had been given the large room that took up the whole third floor of the Victorian merchant's house. When he resigned in 2013, the Council's plans for the provision of homes for all the city's old people were well advanced, driven by the need for every able-bodied citizen to be available for full-time work. The old man was in his late sixties then and had no problem with the fifty-five steps to his room. He liked being alone, away from the resident nurse's prying eyes. But recently he'd begun to wheeze and he lived in fear of being moved downstairs. I knew that was about as likely as the roulette tables being opened to ordinary citizens – he had a tendency to wander off and the nurse wanted him as far from the front door as possible.

I opened his door without knocking. "Hello, old man."

"Hello, failure." My father didn't look up from his desk in the window but continued to run his finger along the page of the book he was studying. Finally he stopped and marked his place carefully.

"At least the fog's lifted." I was looking out over the Firth of Forth from the high window. I could make out the island of Inchkeith, which the Council once used as a penal colony. Further west I could just see the top of what remained of the Forth railway bridge – both it and the road bridge had been severed during the fighting that followed the city's declaration of independence. It suited the Council's policy of isolation from the rest of the country to leave the bridges unusable.

My father rose to his full height of six feet four inches and looked down at me, his breath catching in his throat. He never opened his eyes fully, which gave the impression of someone who was only half awake – that's my earliest memory of him. Like most things to do with him, it was deceptive. He was one of the quickest-thinking people I've ever met.

"What's happened to you, lad? You look almost respectable."

"I know. It's something I need to talk to you about."

The old man's eyes flashed and a sardonic smile grew across his mouth. "You surprise me. Don't tell me you want advice from a senile has-been, Quintilian."

He was the only person who liked calling me by my full name. He did choose it, much to his wife's disgust. Classical names were a tradition in the Dalrymple family and since the old man's academic field of expertise was rhetoric, the Roman orator Quintilian's name had been doubly appropriate. I'm not complaining. At least he didn't call me Demosthenes.

"This is serious, Hector." Even when I was at primary school, he'd insisted I address him that way. I don't know whether he subscribed to some late-eighties belief in equality between parents and children or whether he just liked the sound of his own name.

He sat down on the sofa beside me and stretched out his legs. Even indoors he always wore the guardians' tweed jacket and heavy brogues though he was no longer entitled to them. The polish from the old brown shoes made my nostrils twitch.

"Fire away, then," he said encouragingly. He was more sympathetic to his fellow men's weaknesses than some of his activities as one of the original guardians suggested.

"I've been taken on by the Council. To investigate a murder."

His eyebrows rose and he began to question me in detail. I didn't mention the ENT Man. He'd never heard about him.

"So what do you think?" I asked when he'd finished interrogating me. "You were information guardian. Should the Council be suppressing all news of the killing?"

He got up slowly then glared down at me. "Certainly not. You're as much to blame as they are. You should have seen where this would lead."

I didn't have a clue what he meant, but it was usually worth giving him some slack. "Which is where?"

"It's obvious, isn't it?" he shouted. "Why did I resign from the Council?"

I'd had enough of riddles. "What's that got to with it?" I shouted back.

"Answer the question, boy!"

The only way was to humour him. I bit my tongue. "All right. You left because you thought the guardians were going beyond the principles of the Enlightenment and taking too much power for themselves."

"Exactly." He was nodding his head like a teacher whose thickest pupil had just grasped that two and two don't make five. "Which, for all the high-mindedness of the first Council members, would inevitably lead to corruption."

"And murder?"

"Why not? I'd say that this killing is a direct result of the Council's concentration of power in directorates personally controlled by its members."

Now he'd lost me. "Hang on a second. Lewis Hamilton's got about as much idea of how to handle a murder case as I have of respecting my elders and betters, but you can't deny his directorate's cut down crime in general. What's corrupt about that?"

Hector shook his head. "You're taking what I said too narrowly. I'm talking about the regime as a whole. If there's no debate, no opposition, as has happened now that absolute power rests with the Council, there's bound to be a lowering of standards, just like there was in the House of Commons before it self-destructed."

He may not have been a guardian any more but he still spoke in the long sentences favoured by that rank. Still, what he'd said about corruption had made me prick up my ears. "How come you've never spoken about this before?" I asked. "Have you given up on the Enlightenment completely now?"

"Of course not." The old man went over to his desk. "When we founded the Edinburgh Enlightenment at the turn of the century, we were convinced that the only way out of the political and economic nightmare in the United Kingdom was by decentralising power. Not the feeble assemblies that some of the old parties had set up, but the real thing – regional government by bodies of experts, some of them even philosophers like Plato's guardians. Here, I want to show you something." He started rummaging around in his papers.

I thought about the early years. I was still at school when the party was formed – sixteen, and almost as fascinated by Edinburgh's new politics as I was by the blues. The world was changing day by day. Oil in the Aegean had lead to the end of American investment in the North Sea and a slump in the UK's already weakened economy. At the same time China, bolstered by the return of Hong Kong, had become the dominant economic power and the USA had reverted to the self-obsession that's a hallmark of their history.

It wasn't long before crime reduced the majority of British cities to battlefields. Drugs were the country's only significant industry. The government reintroduced the death penalty in 1999 and became increasingly assertive in its handling of foreign policy, egged on by the tabloid press. Following a European Union directive to withdraw British forces from Gibraltar, Downing Street threatened the use of nuclear warheads against Spanish ships. This resulted in international sanctions and the sealing of the Channel Tunnel. The catastrophic accident at the Thorp installation at Sellafield in 2003 was the final straw. The country fell into total disorder and the Enlightenment got the opportunity it needed. Edinburgh citizens voted the party in with a huge majority after a London mob barricaded MPs in the chamber during their last emergency debate and burned the place to the ground. I can't say I was too upset.

"Got it." Hector held up a piece of paper triumphantly. "Read that."

I looked at the typed sheet. It was a page from the minutes of a Council meeting six months after the election victory. I studied it with mounting amazement. "'As a result of negative votes by the education and public order guardians, we do not approve the information guardian's proposal that the Council commit itself to resign en masse if evidence of corruption in any directorate is brought to light.'" I glanced at my father and whistled. "Jesus. You tried to get them to agree to that and they refused?"

His eyes were unusually wide open. "You see what I mean? That proposal was an integral part of the Enlightenment's planning from the beginning – it was the ultimate safeguard. But once we were in power, people's priorities changed."

"I'm not surprised Hamilton voted against it, but the education guardian . . ."

"Who is now the senior guardian." The old man sat down, his limbs suddenly loose and his jaw slack. "From that day on I never felt the same about the Council. I stuck it out for another nine years, but organising propaganda is hard when your heart isn't in it."

It was one of the few times I'd seen my father looking like he needed support. I wish I'd shown him that I felt for him, but neither of us was ever much good at displays of emotion. The Enlightenment deadened us completely.

Pretty soon afterwards Hector sat up straight. His periods of introspection were always short. "Look on the bright side, Quintilian," he said. "People are better off than they were and they know it. Electricity and water may be in short supply, but there's enough. There are no cars or private telephones or personal computers. There's no television, though only a cretin would choose to sit in front of what used to be served up every evening. But think of all the benefits: jobs, a reliable health and welfare system, safety in the streets, education throughout their lives for all." He glanced at me and smiled ironically. "Except for people who've been demoted, of course." He looked away, shaking his head. "Those were our ideals and they've actually been achieved. Sometimes I still find it hard to believe."

I admired his ability to criticise the regime and then salute its achievements, but I wondered how close he was to the reality of life in the city now. "I saw Billy Geddes last night," I said, then told him about the Bearskin.

"Sounds like he's turned out to be one of the backsliders I was talking about," Hector said scathingly. He was never keen on what he referred to as "affairs of the cock".

"Maybe he isn't that bad," I said, scrabbling around for something to put up in mitigation. "Maybe he's just keen on cars and flash clothes."

"I'd have him down the mines before he could zip himself up."

He had a point. I was having a hard time with Billy myself.

"I never agreed with all that entertainment for the tourists," the old man added. "At least the gambling and whoring. I'm no Calvinist, but to me that's just dirty money."

I had a sudden vision of the perfect woman on the stage and wondered how she'd got involved in that kind of work. "The Medical Directorate checks all the women regularly," I said. "There hasn't been a case of AIDS for years."

"Not that we've been told about," Hector said. "There hadn't been a murder . . ."

Boots were pounding up the stairs. The noise grew louder, then Davie burst in, my mobile phone in his hand.

"Quint, you're wanted. Come on."

"What is it?"

Davie struggled to catch his breath. "They've found another body . . . in Dean Gardens." He looked at my father, then back to me. "Male this time . . . same modus operandi, it seems."

Hector was looking worried. I didn't feel too good myself.

"Sounds like you've got a psychopath on your hands, Quintilian. Be careful."

Davie set off out the door and I followed. "I'll try to come again next Sunday. Keep well, old man."

Halfway down the stairs I heard him calling out. Something about me not telling him if I'd seen my mother. At that moment, she was the last thing on my mind.

Chapter Six

"Shit, Davie." I clutched the seat. "I told you, I don't want to die."

"Don't worry. There hasn't been a fatality on the roads for years." He kept his foot on the floor and called ahead to the next checkpoint. We raced through and were soon crossing the Dean Bridge. The parkland dropping steeply down to the Water of Leith was bright green in the sunlight, the only trace of the days of fog a silver sheen on the leaves and grass that had almost evaporated. Along with the last slim chance of this being a one-off killing.

Then the Land-Rover swung round hard into Academy Place and I remembered two things. The first was irrelevant, a desperate attempt by my mind to distract itself from what lay in the park; it had come to me that the street used to be called Eton Terrace before the Council took steps to change all names with suspect cultural connotations. The second thing gave me a jolt of electric-chair proportions. Adam Kirkwood's flat, where I'd been with Katharine two days earlier, was a couple of hundred yards further on. I hoped to hell he wasn't the latest corpse.

I counted six guard vehicles, including the public order

guardian's with its maroon pennant. The windows of the houses lining the street were filled with spectators. No chance of the Council keeping this killing quiet.

Lewis Hamilton emerged from the gap in the railings where the gate to these formerly private gardens had been. "Dalrymple, it's about time you turned up." His cheeks had an unhealthy tinge and I reckoned he'd been closer to the dead man than he would have liked.

"Who found the body?" I headed down the slope to the bushes where a group of guardsmen and women stood.

"We did," said the guardian. "A woman who refused to identify herself telephoned from the callbox at the end of the bridge. Probably one of the local residents who didn't want to get involved."

"Very public-spirited of her."

"There are rotten apples in every barrel, citizen."

That was too inviting to ignore. "I thought your directorate had got rid of all of them."

He gave me a glare that made me feel a lot better. "Clear the way," he ordered curtly. It wasn't the first time I'd seen him taking things out on his auxiliaries.

I pulled on rubber gloves and dropped to my knees. There were a lot of footprints on the grass at the edge of the bushes but it was clear they were all recent – from the guard and the woman who'd raised the alarm. It was also obvious what had drawn her to the spot. The stench of decomposing flesh was like a curtain I'd just poked my head through. Beyond the branches a discoloured mass was visible. Even at ten yards' range I could see that the body was completely naked.

There was a small clearing beyond the outer foliage. I

approached from an oblique angle to avoid touching any footprints. As I got nearer the corpse their number increased and I marked the deepest indentations so that casts could be taken. I already knew what kind of footwear had made them – non-nailed citizen-issue boots, size twelve. That was all I needed. The Ear, Nose and Throat Man took size twelves. That's how I was sure the man in Princes Street Gardens that night was him, even before I got close. He was wearing a pair of ancient cowboy boots with square toes – I'd found prints from them at several of the murder sites. Jesus. He couldn't still be alive. I clung to that certainty. After he skewered himself, I pushed him into the foundations of the stand they were building beside the new racetrack. Then I heaped a great load of earth over him till I passed out because of the loss of blood from my finger. But I came to before the workmen arrived the next morning and I saw them pour the concrete over him. It was a coincidence, the shoe size, but it shook me for longer than it should have.

I crawled around with my magnifying glass but found nothing else in the way of traces. No fibres from clothing, no buttons torn off in the struggle, no strands of hair.

Davie came in on his hands and knees, carefully avoiding the marks I'd drawn around the footprints. He looked across at the body and grimaced. "How long do you think he's been here?"

I couldn't put it off any longer. "I was just getting round to having a look."

Davie was holding a handkerchief to his face. "After you."

"Thanks a lot." I moved forward. The man was lying on his left side, his limbs swollen under greenish purple skin.

The abdomen was grotesquely distended. A couple of yards behind his head was a neat pile of clothes, boots placed on top. He was short, no more than five feet five inches, and heavily built. At least I could be sure he wasn't Adam Kirkwood. I could also be sure that something violent had been done to the lower part of his back.

Taking a deep breath, I bent over the blackened hole. And almost threw up. It was seething. I had an idea there would be insect infestation, but not this much. The temperature under the fog carpet hadn't been too low so the maggots were fat, clustered over what was left of the flesh around the ribs. I reckoned they were in the third instar of growth. The flies had laid their eggs in the cavity which had once been occupied by the dead man's right kidney. I turned towards the upper part of the body and froze solider than the permafrost on a Siberian steppe. Something had moved.

"What is it?" Davie asked immediately.

I shook my head to shut him up. Again there was a quick, confined flurry. It came from the right armpit. I leaned forward slowly, drawn on despite the urge to escape my stomach manifested by the mug of coffee I'd drunk earlier. Then I saw it.

The rat was so bloated that it could hardly pull itself out of the corpse. It looked at me with glassy eyes then opened its mouth to pant. Its head twitched from side to side as it calculated angles and distances for its escape. I wasn't planning on getting in its way.

It made its move with surprising speed. The long hairless tail was past me even before I could sit back. But it hadn't taken account of Davie. He grabbed the tail and held the animal at arm's length. I hadn't put him down as a pet lover. The rat wriggled frantically and tried without success to bite him. It was too fat to double up.

"Don't we want to examine it?" Davie asked. "The stomach contents might . . ."

"Jesus Christ, let the bloody thing go. We've got a whole, well, almost a whole body to dissect. Not to mention about a million bluebottles."

There was a rustling noise behind me.

"What have you got there, guardsman?" asked Robert Yellowlees. "We can always use those in the labs. Give it to my assistant."

Davie grinned at me and departed.

The medical guardian inspected the body, running his rubber-sheathed hands over the limbs and sniffing like a discerning wine drinker.

"You were right, citizen," he said. "We're dealing with a multiple murderer. Whether it's the otolaryngologist or not." He pointed to the victim's neck. "Strangled by ligature like the guardswoman. And an organ removed. There isn't much doubt that it's the same killer."

I looked at the dead man's swollen face. He had a misshapen nose that had been broken at some stage. There was no evidence of it having been blocked. The ears were intact too. His close-cropped hair was grey and I put his age at around forty-five. The mouth, caught open in a rictus that looked like he was trying to call for help and yawn at the same time, revealed discoloured teeth and gaps where several had fallen out. Another one who hadn't taken advantage of the city's dental services.

Yellowlees was writing notes. I went over to the pile of clothes. In the breast pocket of a donkey jacket I found a wallet containing only an ID card. There were none of the booklets of food, clothing and electricity vouchers that citizens usually have on them. Still, it seemed hard to believe robbery was the motive. Any self-respecting thief would have taken the ID to sell to the dissidents. No self-respecting thief would have had a man's kidney out.

I read that the victim's name was Rory Talbot Baillie, aged forty-eight, driver in the central vehicle pool.

"Around ten days since he was killed," Yellowlees said, a thin smile flashing on his lips. "Before you ask. The entomologists will be able to confirm that from the maggots. I'll run my own tests as well, of course. I'd say that the kidney was removed with a blade very similar to the one used in the other murder." He turned to go then stopped. "Oh, and the anus was penetrated. Will that do you for the time being?"

I spent three hours supervising the scene-of-crime auxiliaries. They seemed to have a reasonable idea of what they were doing. Perhaps they'd read my manual. Davie certainly had. He took charge of the photographer and made sure all the angles were covered. We had some trouble taking plastercasts of the footprints as the ground was still soft, but eventually we got some good ones. An auxiliary got on to the Supply Directorate and was told that two thousand three hundred and six pairs of size twelve citizens' boots had been issued in the previous year. That was a great help.

Hamilton came over when things were winding down and the body was long gone. "What do you make of it,

Dalrymple? It's our man, isn't it?" His cheeks were glowing like those of a believer who's just had his faith confirmed by a thumbs-up from an effigy of his god.

"Bit early to say," I said, keeping encouragement to a minimum.

"Come on, man. Size twelve footprints. What more do you want?"

"There's no shortage of large men in Edinburgh," I observed. "Thanks to the Medical Directorate's dietary guidelines."

The guardian was impervious to irony. I've often noticed that with members of his rank.

"Damn the fog." That made me bite my lip. Now he sounded like an eminent Victorian. "The body would have been found much more quickly under normal weather conditions."

"I checked with the meteorology centre. The fog came down on the afternoon of Friday the 13th. We're waiting for an accurate time of death, but it looks like the murder happened when the atmosphere was still clear." A thought struck me. "Of course. It must have been at night. And this area's outside the central lighting zone."

The guardian looked at me dubiously. "So?"

"So no witnesses. Your people are taking statements from residents but I'm not holding my breath."

"No. There would have been a call by now."

"But if it was night, how did the killer see what he was doing?"

Hamilton stared at me. "What are you getting at?"

I stared back. "He must have had a torch. Tell me,

guardian, who are the only people in Edinburgh issued with torches and the batteries for them?"

"Auxiliaries," he mumbled.

"Sorry? I didn't catch that."

"Auxiliaries," he repeated, his eyes steely. "Guardsmen and women, as you full bloody well know." He turned away, wiping his mouth. This time he resembled one of the faithful who's just been tempted into heresy by a hirsute gentleman with a full set of horns and hooves.

"Who won that round?" asked Davie. "Don't tell me. The chief looks like he's going to throttle someone."

"Very apt. Let's leave him to it."

"Where to? The infirmary?"

"Yellowlees will be desperate to start the post-mortem, but there's somewhere else I need to go first." I gave him directions to Adam Kirkwood's flat.

The lane was quiet. I got Davie to park round the corner so we'd be less conspicuous. That was a waste of time. The sound of his boots on the pavement told the locals that the guard was on its way.

The street door was open. I led him up the stairs to the flat. The door was closed. I got out the strip of plastic I always carry.

"How about knocking?" Davie suggested.

"I thought your lot preferred to break doors down."

The lock clicked and I pushed the door open slowly. A familiar scent filled my nostrils.

"What the fuck are you doing?" Katharine Kirkwood

appeared from behind the kitchen curtain with a carving knife in her hand. "Quint. God, you nearly gave me a heart attack."

"Put the knife down, citizen." Davie had his hand on the butt of his truncheon. "Slowly."

"It's all right," I said. "This is one of my clients. Katharine Kirkwood, Hume 253. Also known as Davie."

They looked at each other suspiciously.

"Quint, what's going on?" Katharine asked after she'd put the knife back in the drawer. "You break in here with a guardsman in tow. I thought you were an independent investigator." She gave me a questioning look. "At least that's what you led me to believe."

"I am." I opened my arms in a feeble display of innocence that I could see she didn't buy. "I've been taken on by the Council for one particular job."

She walked over to the sofa and picked up her bag. Despite the limited choice of clothing in the city, she had managed to dress in an idiosyncratic way. The tight black trousers made her legs look even longer than they were and the long chiffon scarves, magenta and brown, gave her an exotic air.

"And this job includes sniffing around my brother's flat, does it?"

"Not exactly. Look, I can't tell you what's going on . . ."

"Of course you can't." Katharine gave Davie a glare that Lewis Hamilton would have been proud of. He put back a book he'd taken from the shelves. "It's classified, like everything else official in this place."

"Right. I needed to check if your brother was here, that's all."

"Well, as you can see, he's not." She moved towards the door.

"And you haven't seen him since we last spoke?"

"No, I haven't." Her voice had softened. "Have you found anything out?"

I didn't fancy telling her I'd done nothing about her brother at that point. "Look, come round to my flat tonight as we arranged. I can't talk now."

She nodded without looking at me and headed out. "Since you managed to get in on your own, I suppose you can close up again when you've finished."

I checked the place out. Everything was the same. There were no more foreign banknotes in the book of Chinese poetry and the size twelve running shoes didn't look like they'd been moved. Davie watched me with undisguised curiosity.

"Who was that female?"

"I'll tell you later. We'd better get up to the infirmary."

"You're forgetting this." He held up a clear plastic bag in which he'd put the long-bladed knife Katharine had brandished.

"Well done, guardsman. You beat me to it."

The post-mortem went on for hours. A team from the university zoology department spent an hour removing the insect life from Rory Talbot Baillie. Then Yellowlees confirmed what we already knew concerning the cause of death and the wound in the back. I could have spent the afternoon in the archives looking into the dead man's background, but that could wait till the morning. One reason for staying in the mortuary was to watch Hamilton's face change colour more often than a chameleon in a disco. As long as I was there, he felt he had to be too. Simpson 134, the nurse with the prominent chest, took notes – when she wasn't following the medical guardian's every move.

As I was leaving, Hamilton came up. "You know, Dalrymple," he said in a low voice, "your idea about the torch and batteries doesn't mean a thing. The Ear, Nose and Throat Man could easily have got hold of them on the black market. And remember, the boots were citizen issue, not auxiliaries'." He stepped back, looking pleased with himself.

There was something in what he said, but I didn't feel like letting him off the hook. "I'm glad you admit that there is a black market in the perfect city, guardian." His scowl encouraged me to go on. "And as for the boots, correct me if I'm wrong, but aren't auxiliaries issued with standard boots for fatigues?"

He didn't correct me. There was something else I was tempted to bring up but I decided to keep it for the Council meeting. The guardian looked like he had enough to wrestle with for the time being.

Before the meeting I stood by the railings and looked down over Princes Street Gardens. The last race had just finished and the tourists were going back to their hotels to get ready for a night on the town. There was no way the butcher could have been alive when I buried him, no way he crawled out before the concrete was poured – I would have seen a trail. I remembered the sick grin on his face as he slashed my finger off with one of his knives and felt myself shiver. No, he was dead all right. The alternative was too horrific to consider.

I passed by the Land-Rover on my way into the Assembly Hall. If Davie was surprised by the request I made, he didn't show it. I pocketed what he gave me and went inside.

The guardians were less disturbed than they'd been after the first murder. You can get used to anything. A cynic would say that the death of an ordinary citizen was less important to them than an auxiliary's, but even I wouldn't go along with that. They were concerned enough, but they showed their usual tendency to get bogged down in philosophical debate. This time the subject was cannibalism. We never determined what the ENT Man did with the organs he removed. The possibility that he ate them had been difficult to overlook. The same applied now.

The deputy senior guardian caught me looking at my watch. "You don't seem to have much to contribute on the subject, citizen."

"It's all a question of evidence, guardian. We don't know why the killer's removing the organs. Since there's nothing to back up any conjecture, why waste time talking about cannibalism?"

"Very practical," she said drily. "How do you think we should be proceeding?"

"First, we should publish full details of this murder in the *Guardian* tomorrow. You'll find that half the city knows already, so you may as well give the killer some publicity. That may prompt him to do something careless."

The red-headed information guardian nodded in agreement. Even ex-journalists love a murder.

"Very well," said the speaker. "Subject to the senior guardian's approval. What else?"

"I have a question," I said, feeling around carefully in my pocket. "For the medical guardian."

Robert Yellowlees was watching me, his fingers in the usual pyramid under his nose. "Go ahead, citizen," he said.

I took Davic's auxiliary knife out. The naked blade flashed in the light from the spots above the horseshoe table. "Could the weapon used to remove the organs have looked anything like this?"

The guardians looked like a flock of pigeons that had been infiltrated by a ravenous cat.

Except Yellowlees. He smiled broadly. "Long, well-honed blade, single edge, non-serrated, sharp point – yes, it fits the bill. Not exclusively, of course."

From then on the atmosphere was distinctly frosty. If there was one thing that had never been obtainable on the black market, it was auxiliary knives. I think they got my drift. The trouble was, I was no nearer to catching the lunatic who'd done the cutting.

"You look pissed off," Davie said as I climbed into the Land-Rover.

"Pissed on, more like. I'm having difficulty convincing our beloved guardians about something."

"Want to talk about it?"

I thought about that. Over the past five years I'd got used to working things out on my own, with a bit of help from the old man occasionally. But the fact that Davie didn't know about the ENT Man might be an advantage. "All right.

Drive up to the Lawnmarket. We don't want Hamilton to see us having a heart-to-heart, do we?"

On the Royal Mile the souvenir shops were still open, tourists wandering around with their purchases in lurid tartan plastic bags that invariably clashed with their clothes.

"Pull up over there." I pointed to the gallows where I'd seen the hanging two days before. "Have you ever heard any rumours about the mock executions they stage here?"

"Rumours?" He looked puzzled. "The only story I heard was the executions were the chief's very own idea. He persuaded the tourism guardian to go ahead with them."

"Is that right?" I wondered if Hamilton was clutching at any way, even as theatre, to keep the ultimate deterrent alive. Or had he taken it upon himself to dispense summary justice? "Forget it," I said to Davie. It seemed to have nothing to do with the case and I didn't want to test his loyalty too hard.

I needn't have worried. He'd already forgotten the subject and was busy exchanging smiles with a guardswoman who'd walked up.

"Friend of yours?" I asked as she moved away.

"Auxiliaries don't have friends, citizen. You know that." Then he grinned. "I have spent the occasional sex session with her though."

"Oh aye. Don't you think those sessions are a bit soulless?"

"Why? There's nothing wrong with safe sex." He was avoiding my eyes.

"What about emotional involvement?"

He shrugged. "What about it? It just gets in the way."

"Come on, Davie. Haven't you ever fallen for a woman?"

"I thought we were going to talk about the investigation."

"We are. Just answer that simple question first."

He let out a long breath. "All right. Yes, I've been in love, whatever that means. Satisfied?"

I gave him a smile. "For the time being. Right, let's look at the second murder. Yellowlees and the forensics people will confirm the time of death tomorrow. I'm not expecting any surprises, so what are we going to do?"

"Check family, friends, workplace of the victim."

"Yes, there's going to be plenty of legwork over the next few days. But there are other angles too. Put yourself in the murderer's shoes. Or boots."

"Killing someone in a public park isn't a job you'd do in daylight."

"Good one, Davie. That's just what I said to your boss."

He scratched his beard. "So the murder happened at night . . . Christ, he must have had a torch." He turned to me. "Now I understand why the guardians were down on you. You think it was an auxiliary. Bloody hell, Quint."

"Hang on a minute. There isn't much to go on. The boots weren't auxiliary issue. All I'm saying is that we should open our minds to the possibility."

He didn't go for it. "There's no way one of us would go around throttling people and removing their organs, no way."

I hadn't expected him to be convinced easily. In fact I'd have been suspicious if he hadn't objected. The auxiliary training programme is so intense that self-doubt is an early casualty. I put my hand in my pocket. "Here's your knife, by the way."

He looked at it for a moment. "You told them one of these could have been used on the victims, didn't you?"

"Actually, it was the medical guardian who said so."

"But you asked the question."

"I asked the question."

He shook his head slowly. "Have you got a burning desire to spend the rest of your life down the mines?"

I laughed. "I told you. They won't have me back there. Any other thoughts?"

"The killer's clothes. They must have been heavily blood-stained. It's too bloody cold at this time of year to go prancing around in the nude like he did in Stevenson Hall."

"I agree. I got Hamilton to organise search parties in a mile radius from Dean Gardens. There's a good chance he'll have dumped his clothes."

"Meaning he had others with him to change into."

"Meaning, as if we didn't know it, that the murder was carefully planned."

Twilight was well advanced though the bright lights on the Royal Mile made it hard to tell.

"Come on," I said. "We'd better get going. I've got a meeting with Katharine Kirkwood."

Davie started the engine. "You haven't told me who she is."

I looked down the street to the ruined palace. "I haven't found that out myself yet, my friend."

Chapter Seven

Davie parked outside my flat and joined me on the pavement.

"What are you doing?" I asked.

"I'm coming with you."

"No, you're not. This has nothing to do with the murders."

He looked dubious. "Why did we give that knife to forensics then?"

"Just covering every angle. See you in the morning."

He laughed. "If you're sure you can manage on your own."

"Goodnight, guardsman." I pushed open the street door. Traces of her perfume confirmed that she was in the vicinity. I ran up the stairs.

Katharine Kirkwood was sitting against my door, knees apart. "Here you are at last." She examined her watch in the dim light of the stairwell. "I've got to get home by curfew time."

I led her into my rooms. "You don't have to worry about that." I showed her my Council authorisation.

She glanced at it. "I suppose this means you're going to

stop looking for Adam." She fixed me with an acid look. "If you ever started."

I went over to the table and picked up the whisky bottle. "Drink?"

She shook her head dismissively.

I didn't fancy drinking on my own. "Sit down. I need to ask you some questions."

"About Adam?"

I nodded slowly. "What were you doing in his flat this morning, Katharine?"

"What do you think? I'm worried about him." She looked away. "I miss him."

"Look, I'll be straight with you. I was called to a Council meeting straight after I met you on Friday evening. I haven't had time to check anything about your brother."

"Great." She stood up and walked to the door.

"I haven't finished."

Katharine opened the door. "But I have," she said over her shoulder.

I had to tell her. "There's been a murder."

She stopped dead in the doorway.

"Don't worry," I added quickly. "Adam wasn't the victim."

She came back in. "So that's what all those guard vehicles were doing at Dean Gardens." She sat down opposite me. "You're investigating that?"

"Among other things."

Katharine took her bag from her knees and loosened her coat. "You must be a real detective."

"I have some relevant experience."

"What's this murder got to do with me? Or with Adam?"

I decided to try the victim's name out on her. "Do you know a citizen called Rory Baillie?"

She shook her head after a few moments' thought.

"Did you ever hear your brother mention that name?"

The same reponse. It seemed genuine. "Rory Baillie was killed by someone wearing size twelve citizen-issue boots."

Katharine was looking straight at me, her elbows resting on her knees. She wasn't going to give me any help.

I shrugged. "Your brother takes that shoe size, he lives down the road from the murder site and he hasn't been seen for over ten days."

Her eyes opened wide. "You think Adam killed someone?"

"No. But I need to find him so I can rule him out as a potential suspect."

She stood up and stared down at me. "You've got it all wrong. Adam couldn't kill anyone. He may be tall and strong but he's never been aggressive."

"I need to know more, Katharine."

She raised her left hand to her forehead and drew long fingers across it. "All right." She sat down again, her hotel-issue skirt riding up over black-stockinged thighs. She didn't pull the skirt back down. "It was true what you said, even if you were only guessing. I'm very close to Adam. Our parents were doctors, Enlightenment supporters. Not that they had time to get very involved with the party, they were so busy. Adam and I were often on our own at home. He's so much younger than I am. I was always looking after him." She gave a curious, winsome smile that changed the appearance of her face completely. "I still think of him as a little boy." Then her expression hardened again. "Our parents died in the flu epidemic of 2010. Adam was fifteen. I was in the City Guard at the time. They gave me the afternoon off to get him settled into the orphans' barracks."

"They're a caring crowd in the Public Order Directorate."

She nodded without smiling. "That was when I first had doubts about the system."

"And doubts are something auxiliaries aren't allowed to entertain."

"You've been through the same process, haven't you, Quint?" She was doing it again – turning the discussion away from her to me.

This time I wasn't going to let her get away with it. "So why exactly were you demoted?"

Katharine finally became aware of the state of her thighs and covered them in a rapid movement. She held her lower lip between her teeth for a few moments. "A couple of months later I finished my tour of duty in the guard. I was transferred to the Prostitution Services Department."

I had a flash of Patsy Cameron, that department's head, in the Bearskin and wondered if Katharine knew her. "In what capacity?"

She laughed harshly. "It said 'General Duties' on my transfer papers. You can imagine what that meant."

I looked at her and tried to work out how much of what she'd said was true. Then I heard the sound of a Land-Rover pulling up in the street below and thought of Davie. I was guilty about excluding him, but I reckoned Katharine wouldn't have said anything with a guardsman present.

There were footsteps on the staircase. I opened the door just before the knocking started.

A slim female form in a guard uniform fell against me. "Sorry, citizen," she said with unusual civility. She handed me an envelope.

I recognised the seal immediately. "That's all I need." It was a summons to the senior guardian. "We haven't finished," I said to Katharine. "Can you wait here? I'll be back as soon as I can."

She looked at me then nodded. "Why not? My place isn't any better."

I expected to find her there when I returned about as much as I expected the murderer to give himself up without a fight.

The guardians pride themselves on their rejection of private property and the trappings traditionally enjoyed by those in power. Their ascetic lifestyle and separation from members of their families are an example to auxiliaries, as well as a guarantee of their probity to ordinary citizens. But like all fanatics, they ruin their case by overstatement. The senior guardian's Land-Rover must have been the oldest in the fleet, the maroon pennant fluttering over bodywork that wouldn't even have had scrap value in the days when there was such a thing as a used car market.

The guardswoman was used to the ancient vehicle's ways, dextrously slipping from gear to gear without too much stirring of the slack lever. If she had any idea of who I was, she wasn't showing it. She stopped at the Great Stuart Street barrier and pointed the direction.

"It's number . . ."

"Don't worry, I know which one it is. Thanks for the ride."

The auxiliary's face remained impassive. "I'll be waiting for you here."

I couldn't resist the temptation to slam the door. The guardsman who checked my ID wasn't impressed.

"You are aware of the regulation about silence in the proximity of Moray Place, aren't you, citizen?"

"Must have slipped my mind."

He let me into the circular street which contains the guardians' residences. Their demand for silence was a typical example of their tendency to overlegislate. It's one thing to exclude all vehicles from the street, but telling citizens to keep quiet as they pass is comical. Not that any action is taken over the racket from the gambling tents in Charlotte Square; tourists can make as much noise as they like as long as they keep spending money.

The senior guardian had retained control of the Education Directorate and lived where the Educational Institute of Scotland had been located before independence. The black door opened a second after I put my finger to the bell and a female auxiliary in a grey suit admitted me.

"Go up to the second floor, citizen."

I climbed the elegant staircase slowly, trying to put off what was about to happen. It was over a year since I'd been in the building and then I'd been torn to shreds. I ran through the report I was going to make and tried unsuccessfully to decide which of my ideas I should come clean about.

Another administrative auxiliary opened the high door to

the guardian's study. I walked in reluctantly, rubbing at a dusty mark I'd just noticed on my trousers. The room was lit by a single lamp which cast a glow around the desk and left the walls and peripheral furniture in gloom. The city's senior executive was standing, back to me, beside the thick curtains.

"Good evening, citizen." The voice was lower than it had been, but its edge was still perceptible.

I walked up to the desk. "Hello, Mother." I waited for her to turn, knowing that my use of that form of address would have annoyed her. "You sound tired."

The laugh that prompted was humourless, almost bitter. I was surprised. Whatever else I could accuse my mother of, she'd never let self-pity get the better of her.

"If only being tired was all I had to put up with." Then her voice softened. "Do not look away, Quintilian, I beg you."

This was very strange. Not only had she used my full name, which she'd always disliked, but she almost sounded like she was getting emotional. Then I got a real shock. As she'd guessed, my first reaction was to take my eyes off her. After a struggle, I managed to hold my gaze steady.

"My God, Mother, what's happened to you?"

She was still unbent despite her seventy-four years, but there the resemblance to the woman I'd known ended. She had put on a lot of weight. What remained of her hair, which had once been a mass of thick curls, was sparse, giving the impression that handfuls of it had been pulled out. There were purple lesions on her arthritic hands and a pinkish rash on her face. But it was the shape of her face that had changed most. Even the year before it had still been finely drawn, the cheekbones prominent and the skin delicate. Now it was round and swollen, the eyes sunken. Moon face, I thought. She looked like the man in the moon.

She sat down slowly, laying her arms out on the surface of the desk. "It's the lupus."

"But it was never like this before." I wanted to sit down badly but I wasn't going to without an invitation. "You just had occasional fevers and pain in your joints, didn't you?"

"Sit down, for goodness sake," my mother said irritably. Hector and I had always been wary of rousing her temper. "Don't worry, I still have fevers and joint pain. Apparently I've been lucky to escape these recent symptoms for so long."

The Georgian chair I was sitting on was seriously uncomfortable. "And there's still no cure?" I asked, moving my legs.

"Sit still!" She shook her head. "Not yet. The medical guardian's treating me with something he's optimistic about. Up until last month all he could prescribe were painkillers and drugs for the lesions. The problem is to stop the disease advancing. It seems systemic lupus erythematosus can attack any organ – kidneys, heart, even the brain." She smiled for the first time since I'd arrived. "Maybe your old mother's finally going to be certifiable."

I looked away, catching a glimpse through the gloom of the single work of art the guardians allow themselves to choose from the city's collections. For some reason my mother had taken a Renoir of a buxom woman suckling a child.

"I have approved the Council's recommendation to publicise the second murder," she said, opening the thick file in front of her. Clearly she was still able to work even though she wasn't showing up to meetings. "I gather you are doubtful that these latest killings are the work of the Ear, Nose and Throat Man."

"Because of the differences in the modus operandi."

She looked at me sternly. "Is that the only reason?" She waited to see if I had the nerve to answer. I didn't. "I'm not going to press you about what happened five years ago. I wasn't senior guardian at the time, so it doesn't directly concern me."

She was my mother at the time, but given the guardians' renunciation of family life, I suppose that didn't concern her either.

"I know that you were under a lot of pressure, running the operations against the drugs gangs as well as the investigation into the murders."

This was her attempt at compassion. No mention of Caro, of course. She knew about our ties, but it suited her to see us as nothing more than a pair of auxiliaries who spent time together only on duty and at sex sessions.

"I also know that you were never one to shirk your duty, Quintilian. For all your childish egocentricity. Do we understand each other?"

I don't know how much she understood me, but I knew what she meant all right. She was twisting my arm. Any displays of petulance during this investigation and she'd start asking awkward questions about that night in the gardens.

She turned a page. "I also gather you think an auxiliary might be involved."

"There's a chance of that."

"A lot of circumstantial evidence, if you ask me. Anyway, you're forgetting one essential point."

"What?" I demanded. I was pretty sure I hadn't overlooked anything significant.

"The inherent illogicality."

I nodded slowly and tried to restrain myself. I might have known she would bring philosophy into it. She was a professor in that department at the university before the Enlightenment came to power. "You mean auxiliaries are trained to serve the Council so blindly that they can never break the law?"

She refused to be drawn. "Auxiliaries, like all citizens, are encouraged to think for themselves. There's no question of them following instructions blindly. The whole thrust of our educational system is towards the fostering of independent but discriminating thought."

"Spare me the lecture, Mother."

"It is not a lecture. There are certain basic precepts that the people accept, one of which is the inviolability of the body." She smiled briefly. "Despite what's happened to my own body, even I can uphold that. We abolished capital punishment for that reason, we eradicated physical violence in all its forms from the streets."

"Someone slipped through the net. In fact, a lot of people did. There's no shortage of rejects. Look at me. The system didn't want me."

She raised a finger. "You, Quintilian, were always wilful. But even you would accept that the city is a better place now."

"Maybe," I conceded. "But at what cost?"

"Cost? There is always some cost. In the past the poor and the unemployed bore it. Now everyone makes sacrifices. Surely you don't disagree with that principle?"

"Not as far as it goes. But what about the effect on people's hearts and minds?"

"Since when have you been an expert in those fields?" she asked caustically.

I stood up and leaned over her desk. "I don't have to be an expert to see that someone out there has been so messed up by your system that he's going around cutting people up."

She nodded reluctantly. "I'll grant you there's at least one madman in the city. Who knows? Maybe there's a cell of dissidents at work. The point is, how do we put a stop to the killings?" Apparently it was a rhetorical question, as she raised her hand shakily to shut me up. "Listen carefully. No doubt you think we guardians are out of touch with the realities of life in Edinburgh. All right. I'm prepared to concede that some of my colleagues would be better off in retirement homes like your father."

I'd have been surprised if there was any display of emotion to go with this mention of Hector.

"But I'll say this too," my mother continued. "If – and I see it as only the remotest possibility – if an auxiliary is involved, there will be some entirely logical reason. So concentrate on the question of motive. An auxiliary is incapable of acting irrationally, I assure you."

I was an auxiliary when I went after the ENT Man, but she didn't know that, of course. Maybe that was a rational act. I looked at the moon-shaped face and devastated hair. I couldn't help myself admiring her. But I knew without recourse to philosophical definitions that admiration is not the same as love.

"I'll bear that in mind, Mother," I said as I turned towards the door. "Unfortunately I've got even less of an idea about the killer's motive than I have of his identity."

In the Land-Rover on the way home I looked out at the city. The streets shone in bright moonlight and the floodlit mass of the castle rock reared up to my left – the illuminated heart of the Council's regime. At least that's how it's presented to the tourists. Citizens are more inclined to remember it's the headquarters of the City Guard.

I made myself go over the points I'd chickened out of bringing up with my mother. She always did have an imperious air that made contradicting her difficult, but this time I'd done even worse than usual. I wanted to ask her why she'd voted against the anti-corruption safeguard my father showed me. She'd probably just have wheeled out the standard line about how the citizen body now trusted the Council implicitly, while in the past they'd justifiably no faith in either their elected or hereditary rulers. Given the chaos inspired by the last UK government and the discredited monarchy, I couldn't have argued with that. But were the Council and its servants still worthy of that trust?

I also wished I'd had the nerve to ask her how much she knew about the activities of senior auxiliaries like Billy Geddes. I'd have liked to know what she thought she was doing drafting me on to the investigation without so much as a personal note too. She wouldn't even have bothered replying to that question.

It was only when I found myself on the pavement in Gilmore Place breathing in lungfuls of exhaust fumes that I remembered Katharine. No doubt the guardswoman would have reported the presence of a female citizen in my flat to my mother's office. Much joy might she have of that piece of information. The smile froze on my lips when it occurred to me that Katharine had probably been back in her own flat for a long time.

I opened the door and fumbled for the box of matches by the candle.

"Is that you, Quint?"

I jumped like a ewe surprised by a sex-starved shepherd. As the flame flared, I saw that she was sitting in the same place on the sofa. "Shit! Why didn't you light the candle?"

"Candle?" She shrugged. "I'm not afraid of the dark."

"Well I am," I shouted. "I assumed you'd gone."

"Why?" She sounded puzzled. "I said I'd wait for you."

I nodded. "Sorry. I just had a testing time with the senior guardian."

"Yes, you look like you've been in a fight. Have a drink." She pushed the bottle towards me. "Do you often visit the senior guardian?"

I shook my head and poured some whisky. I had a feeling she was about to start picking my brains.

"Want to talk about it?"

I did, but how could I trust her? Anyway, I was suddenly feeling completely exhausted. "It's classified," I said, resorting to the coward's defence. "Look, I'm going to have to crash. We can talk in the morning. You take the bed. It won't be the first time I've passed out on the sofa."

"Quint?" Katharine said quietly, lifting the candle and pointing to Caro's photograph. "Who is she?"

My stomach knotted. I took a couple of deep breaths. "Someone I lost," I said in an even quieter voice than hers.

She looked at me but didn't say anything else.

"Goodnight," I said abruptly. I wanted to be alone.

She got up. "I want to help, Quint. To find Adam, I mean. And . . ." She didn't finish the sentence.

"There are some clean sheets in the bottom drawer."

"I'm the last person who needs clean sheets," she said over her shoulder. "Goodnight, sweet prince."

I was ready to drop but sleep didn't come immediately. I was thinking about what had led to Katharine's demotion. I'd sometimes heard rumours that the Prostitution Services Department used auxiliaries as undercover tarts to gather information on tourists in the city's hotels. Like most men who never go with whores, I always found them desperately alluring. A vision of Mary, Queen of Scots in the nightclub came to me; the way she'd gazed out over the crowd made it seem like every man there was naked and under her power. Then I thought of Katharine in my bed next door. Caro was absent from my dreams that night.

I often hear music in my sleep. This time it was Bessie Smith. She was singing "Mama's Got the Blues".

Chapter Eight

I was following Caro up a hillside. No matter how hard I tried, I couldn't get any closer to her. The Ear, Nose and Throat Man was coming up on me though. I could smell the stink from his rotting teeth. Eventually Davie's pounding woke me.

"You should give me a key, Quint," he said. "Then I could bring you breakfast in bed." He took in the clothes scattered around the sofa. "Or not, as the case may be." He went over to the electric ring. "Did you forget where the bedroom is?"

"Shut it, guardsman." I struggled into my trousers. Then I noticed that the bedroom door was open. On the neatly made bed I found a note. "Morning shift. Thanks for the bed. *I want to help*. K." I still wasn't sure how to take the offer.

The mobile phone rang as I was finishing the coffee Davie'd made. He answered it, his back straightening, then handed it to me. "The chief."

"Dalrymple? Get yourself down to Dean Terrace." Hamilton sounded like a teenage boy who's stumbled on his father's store of dirty magazines. "We've found a plastic bag full of clothing."

123

"I'm on my way. For Christ's sake, don't touch anything."

By the time I'd got my jacket on, Davie was already halfway down the stairs.

"That's it down there." Hamilton pointed at a shiny maroon object that was lodged between two rocks under the bridge.

I put on a pair of rubber gloves and clambered down. The Water of Leith sucked and pulled at the piles as it flowed past. It was only a couple of feet deep and choked with vegetation. Looking back to the slopes of the park four hundred yards upstream where the body had been found, I wondered if the river could have carried the bag this far. I leaned forward and lifted it up. I had to pull hard to dislodge it. A sodden sleeve flapped about like the neck of a dead swan.

One of the forensics team stood waiting with a photographer. I handed him the bundle and watched as he removed a labourer's tunic and trousers, both size extra-large, then a pair of thick socks. There were bloodstains on everything.

"Apart from the sleeve, everything is dry," the scientist said.

"Meaning the bag was carefully placed there, not swept down by the water," I added.

Hamilton looked at me uncomprehendingly. "Have your report ready as soon as possible," he said to the forensics man, who was packing the clothes carefully in separate bags. Then he led me away. "What do you mean the bag was placed there?"

"If the bag had just been dumped in the water, how likely is it that the contents would have been dry?"

He nodded slowly. "But couldn't the murderer just have dropped the bag off the bridge as he was sneaking off? Maybe a guard vehicle made him panic."

"I don't think so. It was wedged solid between the rocks."

Hamilton gave me a confused look. "Explain."

"It's simple enough. The killer wanted us to find his clothes."

The guardian laughed. "Don't be ridiculous, man. How often do murderers deliberately plant evidence?"

I could think of several cases but there was no point in quoting them to him. I knew what he was going to say next as well.

"Anyway, however the clothes got here, they rather put paid to your theory about the killer being an auxiliary, don't they?" He smiled with more satisfaction than guardians usually allow themselves. That was a mistake.

"I had the impression that all barracks keep a stock of labourers' clothes for auxiliaries engaged in maintenance work."

The smile disappeared quicker than the sun on an August morning in the city. "You don't give up, do you, Dalrymple? Until the going gets tough." He turned on his heel and headed for his Land-Rover.

"Not again," groaned Davie as he came up. "The guardian's going to have your head if you're not careful."

"I'm sure he'd love to have it over his fireplace in the castle. Find anything out from forensics while I was distracting your boss?"

He grinned. "Is that what you were doing? As a matter of fact, I did. That carving knife we gave them. No traces of anything human."

I walked away from the river.

"Let's go and see the widow."

Davie drove down the broad avenue where the regional police headquarters used to be located. The buildings, surrounded by a high barbed-wire fence, are now Raeburn Barracks, responsible for Pilton to the north where the drugs gangs used to hang out. Ahead of us lay the ruins of Fettes where I met Leadbelly. I remembered that I hadn't sent him the recordings I'd promised. He wouldn't be surprised.

I slumped down in the seat. "Christ, Davie, if evidence was oxygen, we'd have suffocated days ago."

"Aye, there are a good few dead ends. The guard didn't turn up any witnesses at Dean Gardens, I heard. Surprise, surprise." He glanced at me. "Still, maybe we'll find out something from Baillie's wife."

I wasn't sure whether that qualified optimism was his own or a result of auxiliary-style positive thinking. Looking at the forbidding estate ahead – growths of grey concrete against the steely estuary – I wished I could share it.

Before the Council took charge I'd never been to Pilton. Although the area isn't much more than a mile from the northern extent of the city centre, it belongs to a different world. The drug traders recruited their hard men from the gangs that had always operated there. It was the city's open sore until the Public Order Directorate went in and the real fighting started. Since then the Housing Directorate has done what it can to rebuild and the streets are patrolled by the City Guard, but the place still looks like a war zone. Every window is fitted with solid shutters that are closed as soon as night approaches. I wondered when Hamilton had last been down here. Let alone the senior guardian.

A group of adolescents of both sexes was gathered round a lamppost that stood at a crazy angle. They watched us pass sullenly.

"Shouldn't they be at school?" My mother's educational planning set great store on the removal of truancy from the list of the city's social problems. There were squads of auxiliaries who went around counselling parents and pupils about the value of attending school.

Davie laughed grimly. "You want to make them go?"

"No." I didn't fancy the tough faces and empty eyes much. "What is the city coming to?"

"Don't ask me. I haven't finished the political philosophy course yet." He pointed ahead. "It's that block there."

We had reached the centre of a web of streets uncluttered by any vehicles. There were no people around here; all were busy at whatever work the Labour Directorate had assigned them. The dead driver's wife was to have been picked up by a guardswoman from the bakery where she worked as a counter assistant and brought home.

Inside the street door the sharp smell of disinfectant didn't disguise the inadequate sewerage. Working for the Parks Department meant that I was allowed to live just outside the tourist area. If I'd lived in Pilton, I wouldn't have been a drop-out from the system for long.

The information board in the lobby told us that Baillie R. and J. were in flat C on the third floor. I ran up concrete stairs that had been chipped away by the residents' heavy boots. The door of the flat had once been dark blue. I paused to draw breath then knocked softly. A heavily built guardswoman opened up immediately.

"Where is she?" I asked, looking round the room. Its standard-issue sofa and armchair, dining table and chairs all showed signs of wear, but the place was spotlessly clean.

"She went to the toilet," said the guardswoman, Raeburn 244.

I went over to the table where a large Bible lay open. It was over a hundred years old, the heavy type as stern as the Church which had authorised it.

"How long has she been in there?"

Raeburn 244 looked at her watch then met my stare with wide eyes.

"Shit!" I ran down the narrow hallway that led to the other rooms. "Mrs Baillie? Are you in there?" I shoved hard with my shoulder without waiting for an answer. The poor quality wood and hinges gave way as fast as an old-style princess before an offer from a tabloid newspaper.

A thin woman was crouching over the toilet bowl. At first I though she was throwing up. Her head, brown hair flecked with flour from the bakery, was moving backwards and forwards. Then her hand shot up and pulled the chain with surprising speed. I saw a mass of colour in the foaming water which didn't look like vomit. Pushing her out of the way, I rammed my hand down as the last of it was disappearing. A soggy lump caught in my extended fingers. I heard the woman sobbing.

"I hope you haven't been eating this, Mrs Baillie," I said, shaking my head. "It isn't good for you."

The pinkish mess had unravelled into what was clearly a banknote. Although the writing was in a foreign alphabet I had no trouble identifying it. I'd seen one in pristine condition a few days earlier. It was a fifty thousand drachmae note, all the way from Greece's sun-kissed shores and oil-rich waters.

"How many of these did you manage to flush away, Jean?"

The woman's eyes followed Davie and the guardswoman, who were taking the flat apart. "I'm no' sure. Maybe ten."

Half a million drachmae. In a city where foreign currency is restricted to tourists and the needs of citizens are covered by vouchers, that's big money, especially for a driver to have.

"Where did your husband – I presume it was your husband, not you?" I watched her carefully as she nodded. "Where did he get this money?"

"Ah dinnae ken, citizen, honest ah dinnae."

"Watch your language," said the guardswoman.

I raised my hand to silence her. The last thing I needed now was for Jean Baillie to be reminded of Council language policy. I didn't give a bugger if she said "ah dinnae ken".

The woman had lowered her head after the rebuke and her veined hands shook against the maroon of her overall. She eventually looked up when I didn't speak, eyes pleading for another question to make things easier. I kept quiet.

"He . . . Rory . . . he worked extra shifts. At night, a lot of the time. I only found that money this morning . . . I was tidying up his clothes in the wardrobe." Her voice almost broke, but she held on.

I believed her. "You don't have any children, Jean?"

She shook her head slowly. "I couldn't. Or he couldn't." She dropped her head again. "He tried hard enough."

That sounded promising. I changed the subject temporarily. "You read the Bible a lot?"

"Aye." She was suddenly more in control of herself. "I go to St Margaret's every Sunday." Like most of the believers who remain in the secular city, she was ardent about her faith.

"And your husband? Did he go with you to church?"

Jean Baillie laughed, a harsh scrape from a throat dried in the bakery for years. "Rory? He wouldnae go near a church. He spent all his time chasing fancy women and . . ." Her voice tailed off.

"And what, Jean?" I asked softly.

She stared up at me fiercely. "And nothing. I don't know what else he was doing."

"Why did you try to get rid of the money?"

She shook her head but didn't answer. The guardswoman came over but I waved her away. I was sure Jean Baillie hadn't done anything criminal. The same couldn't be said for her husband.

The widow wasn't able to answer my other questions either. She didn't know any of her husband's workmates; she didn't know where he'd been on the night of his death. I tried a long shot.

"Did Rory ever mention an Adam Kirkwood?"

I saw Davie look over and stare at me. We waited for the woman to reply. In vain. Eventually she shook her head slowly, hopelessly.

Down in the street the same group of teenagers had gathered near the Land-Rover. They hadn't touched it yet, but I reckoned it wouldn't be long before they had a go. When we came out of the block, they shambled away with calculated nonchalance.

"Get on the mobile and tell the directorate to send a squad down to search the sewers," I said to Davie as we climbed in. I caught a glimpse of Mrs Baillie at her window. She was gazing out to the north where the hills of Fife were visible beyond the Firth of Forth. I was pretty sure that for all its marauding gangs and violence, she was praying to her god to pluck her up in a pillar of fire and lift her over there.

Another one who the system failed.

As we were passing Raeburn Barracks, Davie turned to me. "Why did you ask her about that Adam Kirkwood guy?"

I came clean and told him about Katharine and her brother. He didn't seem too pissed off at being excluded.

"You think he and Baillie might have met in the vicinity of Dean Gardens on the night of the murder?"

"It's possible." I took the banknote I'd found in Adam Kirkwood's flat from my wallet. "There's also the small matter of this."

Davie whistled. "Christ, the same currency and denomination. I told you we'd get lucky."

"Yes, but keep it to yourself for the time being." I gave

him a Hamiltonesque glare. "And wipe that bloody grin off your face, guardsman. All this does is make things even more complicated."

He nodded, the smile still on his lips. "I'm assuming we're heading for the drivers' mess in Melville Street."

"You know, you're too bright to be in the guard, Davie. Ever thought of a transfer to the Parks Department?"

He shook his head violently. "No way. I couldn't face clearing up all that horse shit after the races."

"We're going to be clearing up a lot worse than that in the near future, my friend."

Yellowlees came on the mobile as we were driving over the Dean Bridge. "I've just finished comparing notes with the entomologists, Dalrymple. We've concluded that the time of death was between four and six a.m. on Friday 13 March."

"It certainly wasn't a lucky day for Rory Baillie."

"What? Oh, I see what you mean. You might like to know that the killer used a condom in this case too." The guardian paused as if he were waiting for me to volunteer information. "Making any progress?" he asked when I didn't.

"Slowly but surely," I lied, then signed off.

We left the guard vehicle on Queensferry Street and walked round the corner to Melville Street. Davie stopped at a kiosk and took a copy of the *Edinburgh Guardian*.

"Look, Quint, you've made the front page."

"That's all I need." They'd dug out a photograph of me so that the killer would know who he was up against. Above it was the headline "Dalrymple Investigates". I read the beginning of the lead article out. "'Quintilian Dalrymple, former senior detective at the Public Order Directorate, has been appointed to head the investigation into the murder of a citizen in Dean Gardens.'" I looked further down. "Jesus, listen to this. 'Citizen Dalrymple, who was forced to retire from active service because of ill health, has the full confidence of the public order guardian.' Two heaps of your favourite substance in one sentence, Davie. They've printed the number of my mobile, too. Wonderful."

Davie didn't seem too keen to hear any more of that in public. He grabbed my arm and led me down the street, taking back his paper. "Come on, citizen. Time to play detective. Here's the drivers' mess."

An open door led into a broad hallway. The building had once been a school, then offices, before it became the centre for all drivers of city vehicles apart from the guard's. The Transportation Directorate has overall control of the facility, but the drivers have always had a reputation for being individualists – as far as such creatures survive in Edinburgh.

The auxiliary in charge was middle-aged and overweight. I decided to play things low-key and kept my authorisation in my pocket. He didn't show any interest in my request for information about Rory Baillie. The magazine he was looking at did pertain to vehicles, but only in as much as they offered partially clothed women the means of sexual gratification.

"I hardly knew the man," he said. "Go and see Anderson, the drivers' co-ordinator."

Davie leaned across the desk, grabbed the magazine and jammed it up against the auxiliary's neck. "I don't like what I'm seeing here, Ferguson 73." He glanced at me. "Show him your authorisation. Obviously he's been too busy to read the *Guardian* today."

The auxiliary slumped forward as Davie pulled the magazine away. He rubbed his throat and gulped, his jowls vibrating like a petrified chipmunk's. Within seconds he'd called Anderson on the internal phone and told him to bring the relevant files.

I smiled at him while we were waiting. The fat man's skin had acquired a sheen of sweat. Auxiliaries have been demoted for obstructing the bearer of a Council authorisation, but I had a feeling he was more worried about his magazine. He would have paid a Scandinavian tourist plenty for it.

The co-ordinator bustled in with an armful of folders. He was balding, with the professional driver's paunch and fondness for black leather. If leather trousers had been available from the city's clothing stores, Anderson would have had a wardrobe full of them. As it was, his jacket was scuffed and his belt looked like it was about to give way. He must have had both items since before the time of the Enlightenment. Only his standard-issue boots looked new. The shine on them suggested he'd once been in the army.

"Hello there, gents," he said cheerily. "Here's all the stuff I've got on Rory: personal file, time sheets, medical record, the lot." He dumped the papers on his boss's desk and shook his head. "Poor sod. We thought he'd been drafted to the farms or down the mines." He turned to me. "Is it true what they're saying, that one of his kidneys was cut out?"

"It is." I motioned to him to sit down. "We'll go through the records later. In the meantime, I'd like you to fill me in about Baillie. How well did you know him?"

"Hardly at all," he said with a shrug. "Even though we were in the army together." He ran his hands down his jacket. "Rory was a secretive bugger."

"Tell me everything you can about him," I said.

The sun appeared suddenly above the buildings and light flooded into the room, making everyone screw their eyes up. The fat auxiliary mopped his face with a filthy handkerchief.

"Good driver," the co-ordinator said. "Plenty of experience in all kinds of vehicles – cars, Land-Rovers, trucks, ambulances, oil tankers." He looked at Davie and me. "There hasn't been much call for armoured cars since you lot dealt with the gangs," he added ironically.

"Watch it," growled Davie.

"Did he have any particular speciality?"

"Not really. As Ferguson 73 will confirm, we run a fair system here." His emphasis on the word "we" made it clear who was really in charge. "Everyone changes round regularly to maintain efficiency."

"Very commendable," I said, not buying that explanation for a second. "Why do I get the impression you're stonewalling, citizen? Would you like Hume 253 here to take you up to the castle and interrogate you with his friends?"

Anderson's shoulders dropped and his cocksure attitude vanished in the sunlight. Ferguson 73 started waving his hands about in a belated and wholly unnecessary attempt to make his subordinate see reason.

"Look, citizen," the driver said desperately, "I don't know anything about what Rory was up to."

"But you suspected something."

Anderson nodded. "Aye. I mean, we've always had a

reputation for being on the make, we drivers, especially when we're on the tourist buses and horse-drawn carriages. Christ, they offer us tips. We can't offend them by saying no."

Davie and I didn't say anything. The commander put his head in his hands. It was obvious he was on a percentage.

"But Rory," Anderson continued, "Rory was something else."

"What do you mean?"

"He always had a lot more in his wallet than the rest of us, even though his roster was the same as everyone else's." The co-ordinator shrugged. "I've often wondered where he got it."

"Those tips you mentioned – how much do you make from them?"

"Say five US dollars, maybe ten of those Chinese things . . ."

"Renminbis," said the fat commander hoarsely.

"Ever get anything from the Greeks?"

Anderson smiled. "Oh aye, they're very generous. They'll give you five thousand of their currency on a good day."

I wrote the numbers down in my notebook. "What could a driver expect to make from tips every year?" I glanced at the man behind the desk. "Net of what he pays your boss here."

The driver grinned. "No one works the tourist routes more than two months a year and often the guard stop us accepting tips." He scratched his chin. "Say three hundred dollars US."

Or around three hundred thousand drachmae, I calculated. Still a lot less than Baillie's wife had flushed away. I turned to Ferguson 73. "Right, here's how we're going to do this. Personally I don't give a shit that you've been taking a cut. As long as you tell me everything that's been happening in this facility and go through the files with us, I'm prepared to forget about your financial arrangements. If you're good, you might even get your magazine back."

The commander's face lit up and he started simpering like a trainee auxiliary at his first sex session.

I raised my hand. "But remember, my colleague here is in the Public Order Directorate. If he thinks either of you is holding out on us, expect tackety boots and thumbscrews."

The threat seemed to work. We spent hours in the mess but there was nothing that cast any light on the source of Rory Baillie's wealth. The only interesting thing we discovered was about the night shifts Jean Baillie said her husband often worked. There was no reference in the duty rosters to him having driven any vehicle after eight p.m. for over six months. So what was he doing at nights?

Back on Melville Street it occurred to me that Katharine Kirkwood lived less than five minutes' walk away. Like her brother lived a few minutes walk from where Rory Baillie was murdered. Coincidence?

As I was closing the Land-Rover door, Anderson appeared round the corner. He was panting from the short run.

"Just a minute, gents." He looked over his shoulder. "Something I didn't want to say in front of the fat shite. Rory, he caught me eyeballing the wad he was carrying . . . must have been a month or so ago. He told me he had a friend he helped sometimes." The driver leaned further into the cab. "He said the friend was in the Finance Directorate."

I didn't have to rack my brains for long to come up with an idea of who that could be.

Chapter Nine

Thursday evening. After a few sunny days, the fog had returned and was settling over the city as thickly as the mustard gas in a Wilfred Owen poem. I trudged up the Mound, the prospect of another Council meeting with nothing much to report weighing on me more heavily than the concrete overcoat worn by the ENT Man. B.B. King once sang about outside help – he didn't want any, but I could have done with some. I'd just spent the afternoon in the archives and I kept losing track of the time. That's always a bad sign during an investigation. If my mind starts wandering, I know the trail's going cold.

Then, out of my favourite colour, the idea came to me. I ran up Mound Place and sat down in the vestibule of the Assembly Hall to scribble some notes. Shortly afterwards a pair of gleaming brogues appeared in front of me.

"Come on, Dalrymple, you'll be late. Again."

At the sound of Hamilton's voice I closed my notebook hurriedly.

"Working on anything interesting?"

"Are you?"

The guardian shook his head. "But I don't have to, do I? You're the special investigator."

I followed him up the stairs and wondered about the old sod. Hamilton's involvement with the hangings still nagged me, but it had nothing to do with the murders. I'd like to have nailed my former boss, but that was another obsession from the past I had to forget.

"Your report, citizen," said the deputy senior guardian brusquely as the meeting came to order. As the days went by, she, along with most of her colleagues, had become noticeably sharper under the strain. The city's intellectuals, who prided themselves on their deep knowledge of the human condition, were finding the killings harder to live with than ordinary citizens. Most of the latter found Baillie's murder fascinating, a source of endless speculation and gossip.

"Perhaps you could give us a recapitulation of all the evidence you have collated to enable us to gather our thoughts," the speaker added wearily, her command of the guardians' tortuous syntax apparently unaffected.

I started off slowly, trying to spin out the little I had to report. "Well, guardians, extensive research has revealed little of significance. Sarah Spence had an exemplary service record and the only unresolved matter is where she was on the Saturday night twelve days before her death. The rosters of all directorates have been examined and no reference to her has been found."

"But you reported yesterday that the guardsman at her barracks remembered seeing an official authorisation," said Hamilton.

I'd told them about that to pad out an even more vacuous report. "True enough. So we're left with two possibilities.

Either Taggart" – I heard the public order guardian's intake of breath – "I mean Knox 31 was mistaken, or somebody removed all traces of that authorisation from the records."

"No doubt you favour the latter," Hamilton said ironically. "You were always keen on conspiracies. I'd be more inclined to think the guardsman confused the dead woman with someone else."

"What, one of your men made a mistake?"

The speaker looked at me sternly. "Continue, citizen."

"Right. Rory Baillie. Twelve fifty thousand drachmae notes and thirteen US hundred dollar bills were recovered from the sewers outside his flat." I glanced along the row of stony faces. "This raises more questions than it answers. For a start, none of the serial numbers on the banknotes tallied with the currency records at the airport and Leith docks."

"Meaning that some of our visitors bring in more than they declare. That's quite normal, citizen." The scratchy voice was that of the finance guardian, Billy Geddes's boss.

"The problem isn't only the existence of undeclared foreign currency in the city," I said to the wizened old economist. "Though if you ask me, it doesn't seem to be in line with Enlightenment principles. The significant point is the amounts. Even the most generous tourist is hardly likely to tip a driver fifty thousand drachmae. So what was Rory Baillie doing to earn that sort of money?"

No one came up with an answer. I could have asked the same question about Adam Kirkwood, but I'd kept him out of my reports; I didn't think Katharine's case had anything to do with the Council. But I'd checked Adam's banknote. It hadn't been declared either.

"Is that all, citizen?" the speaker asked.

I shook my head. "We've been trying to track down some of the women Baillie spent his time with, but no one was willing to talk." I gave them a bitter smile. "It isn't only in the barracks that speaking to strangers is discouraged."

"Thank you for that observation. Kindly confine yourself to reporting the facts." The deputy senior guardian looked at me like a hassled schoolmistress who's just been pushed over the edge by the class smartass.

I felt a bit sorry for her. "All right. A final point about Baillie. I've double-checked all the records and there's no reference anywhere to him working nights. That contradicts what his wife told us."

"Maybe he was lying to her to cover up his extramarital activities." Robert Yellowlees gave a brief but unusually sympathetic smile for a guardian. His colleagues didn't look too impressed.

"Maybe. But we're assuming he was murdered after curfew, when the lights were out. If he was with a girlfriend, wouldn't he make sure he was at her place by then?"

"He would," put in Hamilton. "The chances of him avoiding all the patrols are minimal."

I was less sure about that than he was – after all, the murderer had managed to get away twice – but I didn't argue. The likelihood was that Baillie had an authorisation and everyone in the chamber knew it. I gave them a couple of minutes to think about the fact that someone was manipulating the city's precious bureaucracy.

Then I hit them again. "There's more bad news. There was no forensic evidence pointing to the killer on the clothing found in the Water of Leith – only blood and other matter from the victim. Either the murderer was very lucky not to leave traces or he was very careful."

"We're assuming the latter, of course," said Yellowlees with a humourless smile.

"Of course." I looked around the guardians. They looked about as bereft of ideas as a 1990s cabinet. Time to give them a nudge with the cattle-prod. "I had a thought on the way up here. Both the victims were killed in the early hours of a Friday morning."

"So?" said Hamilton.

"So maybe there's a pattern. This is Thursday evening." The guardians' eyes were all wide open now.

"What odds will you give me on another killing in the next twelve hours?"

Davie drove up Ramsay Lane towards the castle. The fog was very thick now. Just what we wanted, especially tonight. Burke and Hare conditions.

"What are we doing up here?" Davie asked.

"I need something from Hamilton."

"Round six of fifteen."

"Have you been counting?"

"Got to do something while I'm hanging around." He accelerated through the checkpoint and on to the esplanade.

"Tell me, Davie," I said, watching him closely. "What do you know about the directorate's undercover operations?"

He looked like I'd just punched him in the balls.

"Not much," he said quietly. "Why do you ask?"

He was a lot paler than he had been when we were

next to Baillie's body. "What is it, Davie? What's the matter?"

He looked away to the damp tarmac, then turned back to me. "You remember I told you I had a girl. She . . ." He didn't finish the sentence.

"She was selected to go undercover?"

He nodded slowly. "Two years ago. I haven't seen her since."

"Christ."

His chin jutted forward. "You know what's the worst thing about it?"

I did, but I let him tell me.

"It's the uncertainty. She could be dead, could have been dead for a long time and I just don't know." His hands were clamped to the steering wheel.

I wasn't proud of the pain that my question had etched into his face, but at least I'd found an auxiliary who could pass for a normal human being.

Hamilton hadn't got back to his office yet. I flashed my authorisation at his secretary, a thin young man with grey lips, and went into the guardian's private bathroom. I hadn't had a chance to visit the public baths for a week. The water temperature would have struck even a Spartan as low and the soap was as carbolic as Hamilton's temper, but I felt better afterwards.

Hamilton ambushed me in his outer office. "Dalrymple, what the—" He broke off and led me into his sanctum. "You're pushing your luck, laddie. What do you want?"

"I've got a problem."

The guardian sat down behind his broad Georgian desk and started looking through the files in his in-tray. "Really? Don't tell me you need my help? I thought you preferred to work independently." He raised his eyes. "Not that it's got you very far."

As Davie said, time for the next round. I tossed my authorisation on to his pile of papers. "You remember what that says about co-operation, don't you, guardian?" I tried hard to make his title sound like an insult. "You choose. Either comply with the request I'm about to make or explain your refusal at the next Council meeting."

Hamilton's eyes were colder than the water in his shower. "That rather depends on the request," he said, his voice taut.

"One of the people I'm checking has a file that's classified Restricted. You keep those in the directorate archive here, don't you?"

"You want to see a Restricted file," he said slowly. "Why?"

"That's not a question I have to answer."

He picked up a pen. "Name of the subject?"

"Katharine Kirkwood." I watched his reaction, but I couldn't tell if the name meant anything to him.

"Very well. Wait here."

I raised my hand. "I want the complete file. Don't forget, I spend half my life in the archives. There's no way you'll be able to pull any pages without me noticing."

Hamilton shot a ferocious look at me and walked out. I was surprised how quickly he came back with the maroon cardboard folder.

"There you are." He seemed to have calmed himself down.

"So, do you think the precautions we've taken for tonight are adequate?" After my idea about the killer working to a pattern, measures had been approved to monitor movement around the city centre even more than normal.

"Look at the fog," I said, pointing outside the leaded windows. "There could be a massacre without anyone noticing."

"Don't be ridiculous. We'll catch the bugger." He looked at me. "Remember, the contents of that file are confidential."

Large black letters to that effect were stencilled on the cover. "I can read, you know."

"Which means that the subject is not to be given any hint of what we have collated."

"Why?" I headed for the door. "Do you know something she doesn't?"

William Street, once the location of fashionable bistros and sandwich shops patronised by lawyers and their weak-kneed secretaries, is now occupied solely by female citizens who work in the nearby West End hotels and shops. There was less than half an hour till curfew. I sat in the Land-Rover under the streetlight and read the file.

"That's hers, isn't it?" Davie said, keeping his eyes off the typed pages. "What's she got to do with the murders, Quint?"

"God knows. Have you got that carving knife? I'll give it back to her."

"Mind she doesn't use it on you."

"I'm planning on keeping my hands to myself, don't worry."

Davie grinned. "I wasn't thinking of your hands. You know what they call this street?"

"I do, guardsman." The large number of women residents have led to it being referred to as "the Willie" in common parlance. "I thought auxiliaries kept themselves above that kind of thing."

"Did you now?"

I left the maroon folder on the seat. As I went over to number 13, I wondered if Davie would resist the temptation to have a look. That would be a test for him.

"Quint." Katharine stood in the doorway wearing a dressing-gown. "Have you found Adam?"

I shook my head. "I've made some other discoveries though."

She looked at me then turned quickly. I followed her in, my eyes drawn to her bare feet. They were unusually long and thin and I could see the networks of tiny veins around her ankles. I wasn't aware that hotel maids were required to paint their toenails.

Katharine sat down on a pile of cushions on the floor and motioned me to the sofa.

"We didn't finish our conversation the other night." I glanced around the small flat. It was no more than a bedsit with a door off to the toilet in the corner. The sofa I was sitting on converted into a bed and the only other furniture was a small table with a couple of rickety chairs, a kitchen cabinet and a chest of drawers. The Supply Directorate wasn't particularly generous to single female citizens, especially those with the kind of record I'd just been reading. Katharine had tried to put her own stamp on the place: she'd hung rugs made from scraps of different coloured material on the walls and stuck up pages copied from the large number of books that lay around the room. The extract nearest me was from one of Eliot's Sweeney poems.

I took the carving knife out of my jacket pocket, watching her face. It remained impassive. "This is from your brother's flat. Can you take it back?"

She knew I was putting her on the spot and she didn't like it. Her lips were set in a tight line. But she was curious too. "What were you doing with it?" She sat up straight. "You were running tests, weren't you? Why didn't you listen to me? Adam couldn't have killed that man in the gardens."

"I can't take your word for that, Katharine."

She nodded slowly. "No proof."

"Not only that." I pulled out my notebook. "You've been behaving like a civil servant before the Enlightenment."

"What do you mean?"

"You've been economical with the truth."

She stiffened even more. "Like you said, we didn't finish our conversation. You were called away."

"I was. I seem to remember that you offered your help. You can do that by telling me more about yourself and your brother." I handed her the knife, pushing Davie's comments to the back of my mind. Katharine took it nonchalantly and laid it on the floor.

"Haven't you checked us out by now?"

"The archives don't contain everything." I'd been through Adam Kirkwood's file, which wasn't restricted. Davie and I had also questioned his workmates, who'd assumed he was in the mines. He seemed to be an adequate worker who kept himself to himself. None of them saw him out of work hours. There remained the question of the foreign banknote. Katharine was another puzzle. I'd been to the hotel and checked the duty roster. She was off duty on the nights of both murders. I was wondering how much of her past she would reveal voluntarily.

"What happened when they transferred you to the Prostitution Services Department?"

She looked at me curiously. "I still don't understand what that's got to do with Adam or with the killing."

"Any chance of you letting me be the judge of that?"

She laughed. "All right. I refused the transfer, of course. They kept on at me for days. If they'd offered me something else I might have agreed, but they have that rule about auxiliaries never refusing duty. You know all about that. So I was demoted."

So far, as per her file. "What next?"

"I was assigned work as a cleaner in one of the hotels down in Leith. That was someone's idea of a joke, I suppose. I spent more time fighting off drunken Scandinavian tourists than mopping floors." She smiled bitterly. "If it was a joke, it backfired. It was in the hotel that I met the contact from the dissident group."

I knew from the file that his name was Alex Irvine. She had what was referred to as "sexual involvement" with him.

"They had links with the democrats in Glasgow, who used them pretty cynically. We blew up a few buildings."

"And got caught."

"Naturally. Even at that time the Public Order Directorate

was good at planting informers." She looked at me coolly. "As you know very well."

I lowered my eyes. "I wasn't involved with that kind of operation." Hamilton became a great advocate of undercover work during the drug wars. I always preferred the investigative approach. "What was your sentence?"

"Three years on Cramond Island." Her voice was flat. "I was lucky. They put the cell leaders up against a wall."

She hadn't concealed anything. I should have been pleased, but her apparent frankness disturbed me. Maybe three years on the prison island, connected to the mainland by a causeway submerged at high tide, was enough to make anyone talkative. One of the few outbursts of resentment against the Council led to the facility being renovated two years ago. Conditions had been even worse than those in UK prisons before the breakdown of central government.

"Must have been tough."

"I read a lot of books," Katharine said impassively. "The Council chose them, of course."

"And when you were released, they gave you no choice of work?"

"I would have done anything." She shivered violently. "It was so fucking cold on that island. I still have it in me." She curled herself up into a tight ball. "I don't think I'll ever feel warm again."

"How was Adam affected by what you went through?"

"It didn't turn him into a murderer, if that's what you're thinking. It just made him give up the idea of becoming an auxiliary."

I had to be sure about one thing. My mother's words about

motive were ringing in my head. "How do you feel about what they did to Alex Irvine?"

I realised as soon as I said it that I'd cocked up badly. She hadn't mentioned the dissident's name.

Katharine's whole body went rigid. "You bastard." She stood up and looked down at me like I was something that had crawled out from between the floorboards. "You knew all this already, didn't you? You've been giving yourself a hard-on listening to me cough it all up."

Fortunately she'd forgotten about the knife. There was no need for her to answer my question. It was obvious what she felt about the people who'd killed her lover. But that didn't mean she was capable of murder, and there wasn't much point in asking her that. I felt my fingers trembling. From self-disgust more than anything else.

"Get out!" she shouted, striding towards the toilet.

I wasn't too shaken to miss the sight of her body, naked from ankle to throat, as her dressing-gown parted. Her pubic hair was a thick brown mass and her breasts firm and hard-nippled.

"Out!" she repeated, catching the direction of my gaze but too incensed to bother covering herself.

I left red-faced, like a schoolboy caught spying on matron. As I was halfway down the stairs, the lights went out.

Davie was talking to a guardswoman in the Land-Rover. He had moved the file so she could sit on the passenger seat. There was no way of telling if he'd read about Katharine. For some reason that disturbed me.

Chapter Ten

I was in the Bearskin, strange wailing music from the jazz band rising and falling like someone was playing with the volume control. The bagpiper was on duty this time. While the crowd was cheering, I looked at Billy Geddes and then at the woman he acknowledged: Patsy Cameron from Prostitution Services. She didn't flinch as she stared back at me. Her eyes were the cold fire of a star that burned up a long time ago.

The slam of a Land-Rover door in the street below woke me up. Boots that sounded like auxiliary issue number tens came up the stair. I parted the curtains and was greeted by the first grey tinges of an Edinburgh dawn. The fog had lifted.

I opened the door. "Jesus, what happened to you?"

Davie's face and uniform were blackened, his beret shoved back on his head.

"Fire!" he gasped hoarsely. "Fire in the Independence. Didn't you hear the sirens?" He grabbed the jug of drinking water and gulped down its contents. "Every fire engine in the city was called out."

"In the Independence Hotel?" I thought of Katharine and wondered if she'd been working overnight. "What about casualties?"

"Amazingly few. Every auxiliary in the central barracks was mobilised." He grinned ruefully. "Including me. We got the guests out pretty quickly."

"What about the staff?"

He looked puzzled for a moment. "Most of them got out themselves. Oh, you mean the Kirkwood woman." He gave a shrug. "I didn't see her."

I stood in the middle of the room, my legs tingling in the chill. Had the murderer suddenly turned arsonist?

"The blaze started somewhere near the kitchens," Davie said, raising his head from the kitchen sink where he was dousing himself. "I heard the hotel manager telling the fire chief that there have been some problems with the electrics recently. By the time I got there – about half four – it had spread all over the building. It's still burning at the south end but they've got it under control in the other parts. Christ, you should see the place. It looks like the photographs of Sarajevo they showed us in modern history classes."

I went to dress. "You'll need to get me down there."

"Why?" Davie followed me into the bedroom. "I thought you were expecting someone to be murdered last night."

I sat down and pulled on my boots. "You should have called me, Davie. A major fire on the night we were expecting our friend to strike again doesn't sound like a coincidence to me."

"Bloody hell."

"Find out where the public order guardian is, will you?"

Davie picked up my mobile and asked the castle for Hamilton's location. "He's at the hotel."

"Amazing." I picked up my jacket and went towards the

door. "Don't tell me he's had the same thought as me. The case isn't that weird. Yet."

The great mass of the Independence stretches a hundred and fifty yards up Lothian Road at right angles to Princes Street. Before the Enlightenment, when it was called the Caledonian, its façade was brownish red. Since we started using coal again in the city, it's gone sooty grey. Now it was marked by great smudges of black around windows shattered by the heat. Glass covered the road in a glittering carpet and smoke was billowing from the hotel's southern end. The guard had erected roadblocks. Beyond them fire engines, dwarfed by the giant building, were spraying thousands of gallons of Edinburgh's precious water on the flames that flickered round the window-frames.

"I see what you mean," I said as Davie pulled up at the barricade below Stevenson Hall. "This is a disaster area."

We walked down on the opposite side of the road from the blaze. Bad move. Even there the heat was enough to make the air blister your throat. We had to push our way through a crowd of exhausted firemen and women.

As we got nearer to Princes Street the temperature began to come down. That end of the hotel was less damaged. A group of auxiliaries had gathered around Hamilton and Yellowlees. They stood on the horse-drawn carriage rank outside the main entrance like a gaggle of schoolkids on an excursion, scribbling notes on their clipboards.

"Bureaucracy even when Rome burns," I said.

Davie smiled. "Especially when Rome burns, we were taught."

Hamilton caught sight of me and exchanged glances with the medical guardian. Then he strode over. "What are you doing here, Dalrymple?"

"What a relief. I was wrong about his mind working like mine," I said under my breath. "Morning, guardian. What's the story?"

"The story," he said, eyes boring into mine, "is that this has nothing to do with you. Why don't you go back to ferreting around in the archives? This is a job for professionals."

Yellowlees walked up. He looked less hostile.

"Let's be civilised about this, gentlemen." I moved them further away from their subordinates. "I don't want to have to start flashing my authorisation around, but if that's the way you want it . . ."

"What's your interest here, exactly?" the medical guardian asked.

"Hasn't it occurred to either of you that there may be a connection between this fire and the killer we're looking for?"

"Come on," Hamilton scoffed. "This was an accident – a pretty horrendous one, I grant you, but these things happen."

"Hold on," Yellowlees said, putting his hand on his colleague's arm to shut him up. He suddenly looked seriously worried. "You think the fire might have been started deliberately?"

"Given what the murderer's done so far, you have to admit the possibility."

"Rubbish." Hamilton made to turn away. "I've got more important things to do than listen to conspiracy theories."

"Wait," Yellowlees said imperiously. "This could be important." He looked at me. "What do you want from my directorate?"

"Full casualty lists, current locations of all the injured, plus a list of any injuries which might not be a result of the fire." I turned to Hamilton. "Are you in on this?"

He bit his lip, then nodded.

"Thank you. I need to know how and why the fire started, whether any suspicious activities were witnessed. I also want full lists of all residents and staff, as well as where they are now."

"Is that all?" the public order guardian demanded sarcastically.

"No. I need the barracks numbers of all auxiliaries involved in fighting the fire and in the rescue operation."

"There are hundreds of them, man." Hamilton's eyes opened wide as the coin dropped. "Why do you want this information? Are you still obsessed by the idea that the killer's an auxiliary?" He jabbed his finger into my chest. "If you're wrong, I'll have your hide."

I faced him, then glanced at Yellowlees. "And if I'm right?" I asked quietly.

"I've found her," said Davie, lowering the mobile from his mouth. "She's in the infirmary."

I'd asked him to locate Katharine while I went through the papers that auxiliaries were bringing in continuously. "What happened to her?"

"They said a piece of burning wood fell on her arm. It's not serious. She's been given a sedative."

So she had been on the night shift. "Thanks, Davie. Come and give me a hand here."

We were in the Public Order Directorate's mobile operations unit, a broken-down caravan which had been parked outside the hotel entrance. Beyond the guard cordon, crowds of tourists stood watching what was going on, gazing up at the clouds of smoke that were gradually being reduced. I was surprised the Tourism Directorate hadn't started selling tickets.

"What are we doing exactly?" Davie asked, peering at the piles of paper I'd made on a fold-down table.

"Looking for a needle in a very large haystack."

"But we've got nothing to go on," he said with a groan. "And not to put too fine a point on it, I'm fucking knackered."

I was at the window, straining forward. "Don't worry. I think my hunch just paid off."

We watched as a firewoman staggered out of the hotel and fell to her knees in front of the caravan. She leaned forward on to her hands, the breathing apparatus dangling from her abdomen like exoskeletal entrails. Even under the layer of grime, her face had the pallor of a corpse. Before anyone could reach her, she vomited copiously on the tarmac.

"What the . . . ." Davie yelled as I pushed past him and jumped out.

"Let me through!" I shouted as auxiliaries crowded round. I reached the firewoman and knelt down beside her. "What is it? Take a deep breath and tell me." I rubbed the muck from her barracks number, aware for a second of a soft breast. "Come on, Cullen 212, it's a matter of life and death."

She managed to control her breathing. "Death, citizen," she said with a gasp. "Definitely a matter of death." She started to laugh, then sobbed. "Man in a linen store on the third floor at this end of the hotel. The fire had nothing to do with what happened to him."

"Can you show me?" I took her arm and pulled her up.

Cullen 212 nodded slowly. "I'll take you to the corridor, but I'm not going in that cupboard again." She was staring at me, her face taut with horror.

"Jesus, Quint," said Davie as we followed her inside. "Some bloody hunch."

A guardswoman passed us in the hall. Her face was blackened and her tunic torn, but I recognised her immediately. It was Mary, Queen of Scots.

There was a strong smell of smoke in the passage on the third floor but we didn't need the breathing gear we'd been handed on the way up. Open doors to guests' rooms revealed the panic caused by the fire – covers thrown back from beds, drawers and wardrobes with clothes hanging from them. A trail of paper led from one room into the corridor, typed pages that some desperate resident had tried to save. Another room had heaps of expensive clothing on the floor, as if the owner had tried to decide what to take with her. What struck me most of all was the eerie silence in this part of the building. The sounds of the firefighting at the other end were muted, almost inaudible, like the creaking from the hullplates of a stricken ship that scarcely got through to the first-class smoking room. Our heavy boots sank into the thick pile of the carpet.

Cullen 212 stopped abruptly at a corner. "It's down there, at the far end on the left." She pointed ahead, her arm shaking.

"Right." I felt a dull ache in my stomach. "Let's go, Davie."

The two of us went on, sticking close together. My breathing was rapid and it rasped in my throat. Davie seemed unperturbed though a nerve twitched on his cheek.

"Okay, let's take this slowly," I said as we reached the door. "We've both seen worse."

"Speak for yourself. The worst I normally see is drunken tourists in Rose Street."

"That bad?" I put my fingers on the handle of the store-room door. It was the only one closed in the whole corridor. I took a deep breath and opened it, then reached for the light switch. Nothing. We both shone our torches in.

In the flashes reflected from the piles of sheets and pillow-cases, the small room took on the appearance of the sacred inner chamber of an ancient temple – one belonging to a civilisation that performed human sacrifice. The naked victim was in a seated position, his legs and arms wide and his head flung back on a stack of linen. There was a lot of blood on the right side of his face and, as I looked more closely, I made out the scored line left by a ligature on his neck.

I fumbled in my pockets for rubber gloves, pulled them on and examined the man's face.

"The right eye's been removed," I said. "There's extensive laceration. Christ, I think the bastard used his fingers." I lowered the torch and studied the throat, straddling the body. "Strangulation by ligature." I looked over my shoulder at Davie. He was leaning against the doorframe, his eyes bulging. Then I heard the faintest of croaking sounds and pressed my ear against the man's bare chest.

"Jesus, I don't believe it. He's still alive. Get on the mobile, Davie." I felt for a pulse. It was feeble and irregular, but it was definitely there. I piled blankets over the man and stepped back, running the torch around the closet. Apart from a pair of silk pyjamas and the slippers near the victim's feet, there was nothing.

I heard a stampede in the corridor. A team of medics barged in and took charge. I ran into Hamilton as I came out.

"Why wasn't I informed of this?" he demanded, peering into the storeroom. "Oh my God."

"It's our man all right," I said. "Same strangulation method, an organ removed. I think he ran out of time."

The victim was brought out and laid on a stretcher. Before they strapped him down, I took hold of his left wrist.

"Take a look at this."

The public order guardian bent over, then quickly looked up, his face ashen. "He's a foreigner."

"Exactly." The mutilated man was wearing a Swiss watch that not even Billy Geddes would risk being seen with. He had also cultivated a long nail on his little finger.

The public order guardian looked like a condemned man who'd just seen the scaffold come into view. "A tourist," he mumbled. "This is getting beyond a joke."

His understatement might have made me laugh if the implication hadn't grated – the situation only became critical when foreigners were killed. I could see how his mind was working. In the years since independence, the security of tourists has become one of the Council's priorities. There had never been any incident affecting the volume of visitors to Edinburgh. As the guardian responsible for crime prevention, Hamilton was in an ocean of shit.

"We need to identify him as soon as possible," he said, still in a partial trance.

I nodded. "Shouldn't be difficult. Obviously there's no ID on him, but the staff will recognise him." I saw the guardian's mouth open. "Don't worry. I know the Council will have to decide on whether to go public on this. I'll make sure I only talk to auxiliaries at this stage. They'll keep their mouths shut, won't they?"

Hamilton walked off without replying.

Davie shook his head. "You never give up, do you, Quint?"

I caught his eye for a second. "No, my friend, I don't."

As it turned out, there was no need to involve anyone else in the identification. After I left Davie in charge of the forensics team in the linen store, I found the intended victim's passport in the third room I checked down the passage. It was tricky recognising a face with one eye missing and blood over half of it, but the thick, curly black hair and dimpled chin helped.

"In here, Davie," I shouted. I took the passport out of the drawer of the dressing table. "Andreas Roussos," I read. "Born 11.12.80, Athens." I'd seen Greek tourists with long nails on their little fingers before. You don't have to be a detective to know why they grow them.

"How long's he been in the city?" Davie asked.

The maroon stamp with the heart motif showed 4.1.2020.

"He can't have been an ordinary tourist," I said. "See if you can find out whether he was a guide. There'll be a file in reception if the fire didn't get to it."

Davie nodded and left the room. I closed and locked the door after him. Searching rooms is hard enough without interruptions.

Andreas Roussos had a dressing-gown that a Byzantine emperor would have been proud of – purple and gold with a double-headed eagle motif. There was a diamond-studded bracelet on the bedside table too. It looked like he was a major player in some very lucrative business. I smelled something rotten under the eau-de-cologne.

The wardrobe was full of Parisian suits and shirts, as well as Italian shoes. What have you been up to in our fair city, Mr Roussos? I wondered as I lifted up the mattress. Nothing. The chest of drawers was equally devoid of interest, unless you happened to be a connoisseur of G-strings and thongs. I crawled around the edges of the thick carpet – no expense being spared by the Supply Directorate when it comes to the city's hotels – but I found no gap between the closely positioned tacks. Then I squatted down in the middle of the room and let my mind go blank. I often get inspiration doing that. Andreas Roussos appeared before me in one of his well-cut suits, admiring himself as he knotted one of the garish ties from the wardrobe.

Got you. I jumped up. It had to be the mirror. I lifted the gilt-framed glass down from the wall. The back was plastered with tape. I ripped it off and discovered four brown envelopes. From three of them came wads of brightly coloured banknotes. They were US dollars and Greek drachmae, all of high denominations, including plenty of fifty thousands. That left one envelope. It was larger and had a stiff insert. Photographs. I pulled them out. And found masturbators' paradise. Dozens of pictures of naked bodies, male and female, from all angles. I spread them around me on the floor and sat in the middle of an island of black and white flesh.

There were two unusual things about the photos, both contesting the idea that Roussos was a purveyor of dirty postcards. They all had what looked like serial numbers stencilled on them – AT231, HF76 and the like. And although the major features of every torso appeared in close detail, not a single one of the photos showed a face or head. The people these were intended for were obviously only interested in serious sexual activity, without the distraction of a pretty face.

"What can you tell us then?" Hamilton's voice was almost back to normal. Maybe he was relieved he'd escaped another post-mortem.

The medical guardian finished rinsing his hands at the sink recessed into his office wall and turned to us. His face was sallow and he looked unusually nervous.

"The man was lucky. His assailant thought he'd held the ligature tight long enough to strangle him. Not only did the Greek survive, but it looks like he's escaped brain damage too." Yellowlees shook his head. "His right eye socket's a hell of a mess though. The butcher dug his fingers in and pulled the eye out with his fingers, would you believe? Then he slashed around to sever the ocular muscles." He glanced at me. "With a suitably sharp blade. I can't tell you anything more about it this time."

"When will I be able to question him?" I asked.

"Not till tomorrow at the earliest. He's heavily sedated."

"Was there any penetration of the anus?"

Yellowlees shook his head.

I turned to Hamilton. "You'll remember the ENT Man never showed any interest in eyes."

"Doesn't prove anything. He's our man. And don't tell me the fact that there was no sodomy here is significant. He was interrupted by the fire alarm."

I let him stay in his own little world.

Hamilton glanced at his colleague, then at me. He looked like a little boy about to try and talk his parents into letting him stay in their bedroom on a Saturday night so he can improve his education. "Em, how exactly are we going to frame our reports to the Council?"

I wasn't going to play this game. "How about telling them what we know?"

The two guardians stared at me like I was an impossibly naive trainee auxiliary.

"It may not be quite as simple as that," Yellowlees said. "This thing is getting out of control, citizen." He smoothed back his silver hair. "We need to – how shall I put it? – protect our interests."

"You mean cover your arses?" I said. Even as much of a drop-out from the system as me knows that there are internal politics under the calm surface of the Council. But I couldn't see why Yellowlees was worried. Hamilton was another story, but I wasn't going to lose any sleep over him.

"Don't push your luck, Dalrymple," said my ex-chief.

"You haven't exactly covered yourself in glory either. What pearls of wisdom are you going to give them?"

I shrugged. "The Greek's been in residence at the Indie for eleven weeks. According to the business card I found in his wallet, he's an insurance consultant."

"He's been earning some hefty commissions," grunted Hamilton.

"In cash, too," I said. "We've started checking on who he's been meeting and what he's been doing. I'm also looking to see if the serial numbers on any of the banknotes are close to those we found in the sewer outside Baillie's place." I didn't say anything about the photos. It wasn't just that I was worried about the guardians suffering a collective heart attack at the sight of so much naked flesh. I wanted to do some research of my own first.

Yellowlees came up to me. "My God, Dalrymple, you've got to do something about this lunatic. Who knows who his next victim will be?"

I'd never seen the medical guardian so emotional.

He realised we were staring at him. "Sorry. Not enough sleep recently."

"Come on." Hamilton moved towards the door. "We'll be late."

"You haven't told us what you're going to report." I said. "Are you going to ask for another news blackout?"

He looked at me icily. "I'm going to tell the Council that the city is in grave danger and that we need to declare a state of emergency."

"You're joking." I groaned, knowing the likelihood of the old jackass being deliberately humorous. "How can we investigate with citizens confined to their homes except for the hours of work? The City Guard marching around carrying firearms is hardly going to make people co-operate, is it?"

Hamilton had already left the room. As I followed him, I almost collided with the nurse who'd attended the post-mortems, Simpson 134 of the staggering chest. She didn't even notice me. Her expression softened when she saw Yellowlees, but she still looked like a woman who's just spent Hallowe'en in a particularly lively cemetery.

The Council meeting went on for hours. The Greek consulate had been informed about the attack on Andreas Roussos and had insisted that it be kept confidential. That made Hamilton very happy. Edinburgh locals probably wouldn't have been interested; they were engrossed by the fire and the death toll from it, which rose to eight during the evening. There were over a hundred detained in the infirmary.

I got off lightly since my prediction about the killer working to a pattern had been right. Hamilton was given a hard time by the speaker because of his failure to advise me about the fire. He was then told to report to the senior guardian later on. I tried not to laugh. That wasn't the end of his troubles. The Council threw out his demand for a state of emergency because of its potentially catastrophic effect on the city's finances from cancelled bookings. Holidaymakers like armed auxiliaries in the military tattoo, not on every street corner.

After the meeting Davie drove me to the infirmary. He looked so worn out that I sent him back to his barracks, telling him I'd walk home.

I found Katharine in a ward full of casualties from the fire. She was asleep. For a few moments I studied her features in the glow from the bedside lamp. The deep auburn of her hair contrasted starkly with the pallor of her face, which had a softness that I hadn't been aware of when she was awake. Suddenly she seemed to sense my presence and her eyes opened. They weren't as hostile as I'd expected.

"I wanted to see you," she murmured.

I smiled. "Good." I sat down carefully on the bed. "I wanted to see you too."

She looked at me then shook her head. "That's not what I meant." She lifted her unbandaged arm and motioned to the jug on the bedside table. "Thirsty."

I filled a glass and held it to her lips, feeling the warmth of the skin around her mouth.

"Thank you," she said. "What happened at the Indie?" She spoke so softly that I had to lean close to hear.

"There was a fire. Don't you remember?"

She shook her head violently and winced. "Of course I remember the fire. I mean, what happened on the third floor? I was on duty there."

"What?" I slid my arm behind her back and helped her into a sitting position. "Did you see something?"

"Not enough to help you very much." She looked into my eyes. "There was another murder, wasn't there?"

I shook my head. "Not quite. The bastard tried his best."

She shivered and twitched her hands. "No, it wasn't a—" She broke off and turned away, stifling a sob.

I put my hand on hers. "Calm down, Katharine. Just tell me what you saw."

She took a deep breath and started to speak slowly. "It was a few minutes before the alarm went off. I was at the end of the corridor near the stairs. Down the other end I saw a dark-haired guest in his pyjamas. He went into the linen store." She shook again briefly. "With a woman."

"With a woman?" I had difficulty getting the words out. "What did she look like? Come on, think."

Katharine pulled her hand away, blinking in pain with the movement of her injured arm. "I only got a glimpse. Then the bell rang and people started coming out of their rooms. I got caught up in them." She paused. "There was an old man in the middle of the crowd, you know. They almost pushed him down the stairs . . ." She began to sob, then gradually controlled her breathing.

"The woman, Katharine," I said, squeezing her hand again. "What did the woman look like?"

She sat motionless, her eyes fixed on the wall opposite. "She was tall, wearing high heels, quite well built. Her hair was very blonde. I didn't see her face." She stopped abruptly, her mouth staying open. "My God, Quint. I don't think it was a woman. It looked more like a transvestite. There are always some on duty in the hotel."

I sat back, my head spinning. Hamilton and Yellowlees reckoned things were getting out of control but they didn't know the half of it. I needed to get my mojo working. Fast.

Chapter Eleven

I walked away from the infirmary into the night. The breeze still carried the smell of smoke, though the fire at the hotel had been out for hours. I tried to make sense of what was going on. In the afternoon I had checked Adam Kirkwood's flat and found it exactly as it had been. Was he the transvestite his sister had seen? I had no evidence, but I had bugger all evidence for anything. That's why I was reduced to following up marginal leads.

A car braked and stopped just in front of me on Lauriston Place. It was Billy Geddes's Toyota.

"Get in, Quint."

"What are you doing around here?" I got in without any show of enthusiasm. "No sex clubs in this part of the city."

Billy accelerated away. "Looking for you." His hands gripped the steering wheel hard.

"Oh aye." I was instantly curious. "Need to get something off your chest, maybe?"

"You don't make things easy, do you?" He shook his head. "Fucking smartass. As it happens, I have got something to tell you."

"Come home for a nightcap. I've got some unusually good whisky."

"Wonder where you came by that. Spare me your pit. I'll take you to my place."

"Great, Billy." At least it would be interesting to find out if his years in the Finance Directorate had left him with any understanding of what telling the truth entails.

I wasn't much the wiser after my first hour in Heriot Row. Billy had led me up the ornate Georgian staircase to his apartment on the first floor. From the high windows I looked out over the lights in the street below. The voices of a group of auxiliaries jogging on the all-weather track in the gardens beyond floated up in the still night air. Well, it wasn't that still. From the gaming tents in Charlotte Square came the pounding of music, interspersed by the raucous yells of the winners.

Although even senior auxiliaries are supposedly issued with the same furniture as us ordinary citizens, their residences in the streets near Council members' accommodation aren't checked by Supply Directorate inspectors. I recalled the Latin question my father came up with all the time in the early years of the Enlightenment: "Quis custodiet ipsos custodes?" It didn't look like anyone was keeping an eye on the next generation of guardians.

"Look at this." Billy nudged me and took me over to the polished Regency table that stood in the centre of his large sitting room. "It's a first edition of Hume's *Treatise*."

"Bloody hell." I ran my hands over the stiff pages of the old book carefully. "Where did you get it?"

Billy raised a finger to his nose. "Contacts, Quint. That's what it's all about." He went over to the drinks cabinet by the Adam fireplace and raised a decanter. "This is from Jura."

I was seriously tempted to taste the whisky. Brands like it had disappeared from the city when relations with the unstable states in the north and west were cut after independence. The whisky available to ordinary citizens was a low-quality blend from the few distilleries around Edinburgh. Only the tourist shops stocked the few expensive brands that remained in the bonded warehouses.

"No, thanks." I didn't fancy being bribed. "I suppose you got that from one of your contacts."

Billy smiled and shrugged. "That's the way things work."

"Is it fuck." I poked him in the chest with my left fore-finger. "That's exactly the kind of thieving the Enlighten-ment was formed to fight. Remember all those corrupt bastards in London?"

"Grow up, Quint. Things are different now."

"Bollocks. You're the one who's different. You used to go on about how people in power had to be above suspicion."

Billy drew back his thin lips. "I *am* above suspicion," he said quietly. "Let me teach you about the reality of life in Edinburgh." He gave me a bitter smile. "Unlike you, I've actually applied myself to working for the city ever since the Council was set up."

That's the problem with old friends – they know how to get to you. What Billy said was true enough. I'd dropped out, failed to honour the commitment I made to the Enlighten-ment when I was eighteen. Maybe I didn't have a right to criticise those who'd remained in harness.

Billy was standing in front of the carved fireplace. His voice was calm and self-assured, which pissed me off even more.

"Even if I were to come under suspicion, no one would investigate me very carefully." He glanced over to me. I'd taken refuge in a Charles Rennie Mackintosh chair that was even more uncomfortable than it looked. "I'm worth more to the city than just about anyone else in it. Without me, Edinburgh would be full of citizens rioting for bread, and the Council knows it."

"Come off it, Billy," I said wearily. "Nobody's that important. The structure of guardians and auxiliaries is supposed to ensure that individuals can't become indispensable."

He choked on his whisky and almost spilled the contents of his glass over his immaculate grey suit. "Fucking hell, Quint," he gasped. "You of all people should know what a pile of crap that is. Why did you become an outsider? Because you rate your precious ego higher than anything else."

I glared at him. "We're talking about you, not me. What makes you so important?"

Billy opened his hands like a magician producing doves from a handkerchief. "I make the deals that keep this city solvent. Like I said, it's all a question of contacts. Personal contacts. I've got them in the countries we trade with, in the companies we buy from, in the embassies we work with, in the foreign police forces we send auxiliaries to train, even in the neighbouring states we technically don't recognise." He grinned. "The finance guardian signs the contracts, but I negotiate them. I make the decisions."

I believed him. So far. Although Billy had always been a smooth operator, he never bothered boasting about it. I only had to look at the opulent room to be convinced. That's why he'd brought me here.

"What exactly was the nature of your relations with Andreas Roussos, Billy?" I asked quietly.

He looked up from his glass and smiled. "Sharp, Quint, very sharp. Not much gets past you."

Flattery from Billy was the last thing I'd set my heart on. "Just about everything this psycho's done has got past me so far. Answer the question."

"I'm going to. That's why I had the infirmary advise me as soon as you left." He pulled open a drawer. "Want a cigar? I've got some Havanas here . . ."

"Answer the fucking question."

He stopped fumbling with the illegal box. "All right. You would have found witnesses in the hotel who saw me with the Greek, so I thought I'd get in first. There's nothing much to it. He represents an insurance company which looks after its clients' welfare while they're on holiday in the city." He ran the tips of his fingers across his forehead. "Your murderer – I assume it's the same guy?"

"Looks like it."

"Your murderer picked a good one to attack. We'll probably lose a lot of customers."

I stood up and walked over to him. "Is that it?"

Billy shrugged. "What more do you want?"

It was time for the third degree. "I'll tell you what more I want," I yelled, holding up the fingers of my left hand and counting them off. "One, why did Roussos have a stash of what I'm sure will turn out to be undeclared foreign currency hidden in his room?" I didn't mention the photos. I had a feeling Billy knew something about them, but I didn't want to show my hand. "Two, why did my murderer, as you call him, try to kill this particular foreigner? Three, why have you been chasing after me ever since the first killing? That'll do for a start."

"You mean there's more?" he asked with a wan smile.

"Bloody right there is." I moved right up to him. "What kind of an investment have you got in the Bearskin?"

It didn't work. He wasn't scared of me. Even if I'd thrown him around the room a bit, he'd still have kept quiet. After all, he reckoned he was the Council's favourite son. At least I'd let him know I was on his trail. Wherever that might lead.

"What kind of a friend are you?" Billy said as I headed for the door. "I offer you help and all you do is shout at me."

I followed his example and declined to answer, giving the front door a good slam on the way out. The worst thing about growing older is seeing how your friends turn out. All is flux, an ancient philosopher said. I don't suppose I bear much resemblance to my former self either.

As I approached Darnaway Street a thought struck me. Who informed Billy Geddes that I'd left the infirmary? I couldn't think of any reason why he should have a contact in the city's main medical facility.

A wave of exhaustion swamped me as I was passing the charred walls of the Independence. It was easy to flash my authorisation and get a guardswoman to drive me home. Billy would have found that minor abuse of power highly amusing.

* * *

Saturday morning was warm and sunny. That was about all that could be said in its favour. I went round to the infirmary to question Roussos and found Hamilton deep in conversation outside the Greek's room with a distinguished-looking guy in a herringbone tweed coat. He had a moustache thick enough for a barn owl to roost in.

"Ah, Dalrymple," the public order guardian said in a nervous voice that made me immediately suspicious. "This is Mr Palamas from the Greek consulate."

The diplomat eyed my unofficial clothing and decided against shaking hands.

"Mr Palamas has been visiting his compatriot to check on his progress."

"Fortunately for you, guardian, he is making a good recovery." The Greek shook his head theatrically. "That such a thing should happen in your city . . ."

"When can I interview Mr Roussos?" I asked.

Hamilton started shaking his head before I finished my question.

Palamas looked down his long, fleshy nose at me. "As I have just explained to your superior, Mr Roussos is not to be interviewed by any city official."

I looked at Hamilton. He opened his hands helplessly.

"Mr Roussos has told me he saw nothing of his assailant. There is therefore no point in interviewing him. The guardian has agreed to this. Good morning." Palamas walked away with his nose in the air.

"Are you out of your fucking . . ."

"Quiet, man. This is nothing to do with you. The senior guardian is aware of my decision." He paused to let that sink in.

"Since when do attempted murder victims get let off making statements? How the fuck am I supposed to catch this maniac?"

"It's out of my hands, citizen." Hamilton twitched his head like a fly was annoying him. A fly named guilt. He knew he should never have agreed to exempting a witness from questioning. If what Katharine had told me was right and the attacker was dressed up as a transvestite, Roussos must have hired him and obviously must have seen him close up.

"It's because of commercial considerations," Hamilton said in a low voice. "The Greeks are worth a fortune to us. If they don't want one of their people to be bothered, what can we do?"

I knew exactly what he could do and I told him. He didn't look too impressed.

So then I went to see the city's chief prostitute. I got a surprise on the way into the Tourism Directorate building on George IVth Bridge. Simpson 134, the buxom nurse who spent her time making eyes at Yellowlees, came out, a well-stuffed briefcase in her hand. She pretended she didn't see me but I was sure she did. What the hell was she doing there? A bit of moonlighting in her off-duty hours?

The Prostitution Services Department is on the second-top floor of the building. That shows how important it is to the Tourism Directorate. Men come all the way from the Far East to have a good time with Edinburgh's finest. No doubt they find the experience very enlightening.

The sun was streaming in the large windows. I sat in the office of the controller and waited for her to come out of a budget meeting. Her desk was clear and all her filing cabinets locked. I began to get bored.

"Hello there, Quint," Patsy Cameron said, bustling in eventually and taking off the jacket of her pinstriped suit. She looked a lot more pleased to see me than she had in the Bearskin the other night. "Sorry I'm late. Financial planning seems to be how I spend all my time these days."

"Beats lying on your back with your legs open though."

She looked across at me, eyes cold, then laughed. "Really, citizen, what kind of way is that to speak to a senior auxiliary?"

"Sorry, Patsy." I looked across to the barracks number on her ample bosom. "I mean Wilkie 164."

"Never mind that nonsense. I was Patsy Cameron when you took me in during the anti-whoring campaign fifteen years ago and I'm the same person now." Although she was over fifty, the controller's hair was blonde and her face surprisingly free of wrinkles. Only the remains of a heavy accent hinted at a less than typical background for a person in her position.

I used to like Patsy, but I hadn't seen her since I dropped out. She was one of the Enlightenment's success stories, an ex-prostitute who'd gone through the adult education system and done well for herself. I often worked with her during the Public Order Directorate's campaigns to keep women off the street. I hadn't realised then that most of them would end up doing the same job in the service of the city. Now that the Council was in open competition with Amsterdam and anywhere else you can think of, Patsy must have got a job for life.

"I'm told you're back doing what you're best at, Quint," she said, opening one of the files she'd brought in.

"I'm not doing it too well now. That's why I need your help." I also needed to con her and I wasn't too sure if I was up to that.

The controller put on a pair of standard-issue glasses, the plain plastic frames clashing with her luxuriant coiffure. "Fire away," she said with more enthusiasm than I'd expected. Maybe she wanted something from me in exchange.

"First, I need to check out the transvestites who work the Indie." I told her a witness had spotted one, without mentioning Katharine.

"I'll give you everything I've got on the boys who were on the roster on Thursday night." She pursed her lips. "Won't necessarily prove a lot – most of them freelance in their spare time."

"Freelance?"

Patsy laughed. "So to speak. I'll give you the full register of t-vs." She looked across at me. "What else?"

Now came the tricky bit. I needed a way into the department's main archive to see if I could find any other photos like the ones I'd found behind Roussos's mirror. I could only think of one name to use.

"Katharine Kirkwood. I need to go through her file."

Patsy eyed me cautiously. "Let's have a look at that authorisation of yours."

I handed it over and watched her scrutinise it.

"Aye, well, it looks like I can't refuse you anything." She

gave me a practised tart's leer, her lips parting to show gleaming and even teeth – dental work obviously done before private practices were abolished. "You know she has a security file?"

"I've seen it."

"Have you now? Well, the files we keep aren't always the same as the ones those idiots in the Public Order Directorate have." She shook her head and quickly regained her senior auxiliary's air. "Sorry. The old prejudices die hard. What's your interest in our fair Katharine?"

I had the sudden feeling I'd bitten off more than I could comfortably get through in a single dinner sitting. When I'd used Katharine's name I hadn't expected Patsy to know her. I mumbled some garbage about how I was checking everyone who'd been injured in the fire.

Patsy caught my eye. "You know, we play hard in this department. You might not like everything you read in our files."

"I can take it."

She raised her eyebrows sceptically then pressed the button for her secretary. "You'll be locked in the archive. And Quint, nothing leaves the building, all right?"

"I'll mention your co-operation in my report, Patsy."

The controller was already engrossed in her papers. It seemed she didn't want anything from me in return. "Screw you, citizen," she said, without much sign of humour.

I suppose I was just another man to be satisfied and shown the door.

Things got worse as the day went by. The transvestite lead

didn't get us very far. I went through the roster and had Davie check the boys out. There had been three on duty in the hotel when the fire started. The logsheets showed that two of them had been in rooms a long way from the scene of the crime when the alarm went off, and the other had been in the staff messroom with several female prostitutes. The clients, a Norwegian and a Chinese, weren't too keen on providing alibis, but Hamilton twisted their arms. There were seventeen other t-vs on the department's register and they were being traced, but I had a feeling the trail was cold.

The photos were a waste of time too. I didn't find any similar ones in the random sample of files I pulled in the archive and none of the serial numbers matched. Either these particular naked bodies had nothing to do with Patsy's department or efforts had been made to keep them secret. Of course, I could have asked her about them but where would that have got me? If she was involved, she'd make sure I didn't get a sniff – she knew everything there is to know about tricks.

Katharine's file was the perfect end to a shitty spring day. I decided she *was* worth talking to Patsy about. On several counts.

"Do all your operatives fuck as much as she does?" I asked, holding the maroon file up as I walked into the controller's office in the late afternoon.

Patsy shrugged. "I suppose she does have a bit of a talent for it."

"I like the auxiliary-style understatement, Patsy. This woman makes Catherine the Great look like an under-achiever. What do you do with all this information she gathers about her clients?"

The controller went coy on me. It didn't suit her. "Oh, you know, it pays to know about clients' needs – in case they come back."

"It would never occur to the Tourism Directorate to blackmail the ones who get out of hand, would it?"

"Is that an accusation, citizen?" she asked. An Arctic fox's eyes would have been warmer.

"Just an observation. I get the impression you know her pretty well. Fill me in."

"I hope this is relevant to your investigation."

"Trust me."

"Ha." Patsy loosened up a bit. "Actually, I do know her quite well." She shook her blonde mane a couple of times. "If you can really know someone as cold-blooded as her. She's one of our stars. A year ago I even asked her to give up the hotel and come to work with me here." She laughed. "She told me right where I could go. Our Katharine doesn't think much of the Council and its works."

"I noticed." I was trying to come to terms with my client's activities and failing abysmally. What difference did it make to me if she serviced every tourist in the city? I wondered if her brother had any idea of all this.

Patsy gave me a knowing look. "I told you we played hard."

I didn't want to be left on the touchline. "I saw you enjoying the show in the Bearskin the other night. Does your department supply it with boys and girls?"

For a split second the controller looked nervous. "No. The word is that Heriot 07 and his pals are running that place themselves."

"Any idea who his pals are?"

"He's a friend of yours, Quint. Ask him." She went back to her files.

Patsy was good, very good. If I hadn't known her in the past, I'd probably have believed her. But what I was certain wouldn't happen just had – she'd let her guard drop. That was all it took to make me very sure that the key to the investigation wasn't the t-v Katharine said she'd seen, nor was it Katharine herself, despite the doubts her file had raised. It was the city's deputy finance guardian, William Ewart Geddes.

"We can't do it, for fuck's sake." Davie sat in the stationary Land-Rover outside my flat with his head bowed. "He's a deputy guardian, not some poxy dissident."

I watched him as the last of the twilight drained away and scrabbled around for another way to convince him. "He's involved with the Greek who was attacked a sight more than he's admitting. That means he's also linked to the killings."

"You're guessing, Quint." He turned to me, the cheeks above his beard pale. "I'll get demoted. Unauthorised action against an ordinary citizen is bad enough, but against a senior auxiliary . . ."

I let his words trail away unanswered. I'd decided to go ahead with surveillance on my own if I had to. I'd have liked to follow Katharine when she came out of the infirmary too, but Billy had priority.

Davie realised I was set on it. "You're all right. When you get caught they'll just send you back to the Parks Department."

I reckoned I might as well have a go at steamrolling him. "You've forgotten that my Council authorisation gives me the power to demand anything of you."

He didn't buy it. "They didn't mean you to use it like that. I want confirmation from the Council."

"Which they won't give. Billy Geddes is their favourite human being." I glanced at him. "Anyway, what do you mean *when* I get caught? *If* I get caught."

"Don't kid yourself. Hamilton will be on to you soon enough. He's watching us like a hawk." Davie's voice had lost its usual confidence.

"Has he said something to you?"

"Nothing specific. Dropped a hint or two about my future career."

"Bastard." I grabbed his arm. "Look, if these murders go on, you won't have a career. The city's getting restless. What'll happen if there are more killings?" I went for the jugular. "Don't tell me you're frightened of that stiff-necked old cocksucker?" I sat back and waited for the explosion.

Nothing happened. I might have known. Davie let his muscles go slack and breathed in deeply. Auxiliaries are trained to withstand every kind of mental and physical pressure – at least that's what it says in the survival manual.

"I could take you in, you know, Quint," he said calmly. "Abusing a guardian is a serious offence. Your authorisation doesn't give you immunity."

"I don't think your boss would win a slander case. If such a thing could be brought in the city nowadays."

Davie laughed. "Maybe not. I've heard worse said about

him." He scratched his beard thoughtfully. "I doubt he's into fellatio though."

"I didn't mean it literally." It looked like he'd capitulated. Badmouthing Hamilton was obviously a good tactic. "Are you looking forward to dressing up as a tourist?"

"You don't really think Heriot 07's the killer, do you?"

I shrugged. "Anyone can wear size twelve boots. Billy's cunning enough to dress himself up as a t-v and then feed me a load of horseshit to distract me." I remembered how feeble he'd been in PE classes at school. Maybe he'd started weight-training. It wouldn't be the only thing he'd changed in his life. "No, I can't see any motive. I reckon he's involved in something the killer's targeting."

Davie looked across in the near darkness. "All right, I'll do it." He raised a hand. "On one condition."

I owed him at least one. "Whatever you like."

"Under no circumstances am I dressing in drag."

I put a brave face on it. "Okay. See you tomorrow." I jumped down from the guard vehicle and went up to my flat.

The absence of Katharine's perfume was almost as over-powering as its presence had been before.

Chapter Twelve

I slept badly and the tramp of workers heading for the assembly points woke me. I stood wrapped in a blanket at the window, watching the first light of dawn filter into the street below. The last Sunday of the month is when the shifts are changed in the mines and on the farms. The lucky ones coming off duty would be on their way to the pubs that open early for them, while their replacements, grim-faced and shivering, boarded the buses in silence. I remembered the times I stood in line and was surprised to find that I felt nostalgic about them. At least then I hadn't always been dreaming of mutilated corpses and a killer who vanished into the mist. I had a bad case of the ghost blues.

Davie arrived carrying a hold-all. "I scoured the barracks and managed to find some casual clothes that look a bit like a tourist's." He held the bag open.

"A pretty poor tourist," I said. "They'll do." I went over to the kitchen area and rooted around for my scissors. "But first we'll have to sort out your facial hair."

His jaw dropped. "Wait a minute. You didn't say anything about that yesterday. I'll get thrown out of the guard."

"Don't worry. I'm not going to cut it all off. Just a trim.

You look like bloody John Knox." I pushed him down on to the sofa and set to work.

"Mind you don't cut anything vital." Davie was sitting very still.

"Relax. It took me a few years, but my left hand can do everything my right hand used to do before I lost my finger."

"Everything?" Davie asked with a grin.

"Everything, guardsman. There you are. Women will be queuing up."

"That'll make a change." He got up and brushed away the thick curls.

"Hang on," I said. "Does Heriot 07 know you?"

"Not unless he's seen me with you." He peered at himself in my small standard-issue mirror. "He won't recognise me even if he has. I look like a chicken that's in the middle of moulting."

"Drop your shoulders a bit, for Christ's sake. You've got to lose that guardsman's purposeful walk." I went to dress. "First stop Hamilton's office to fix up the paperwork. We won't get far without that."

Davie followed me, a thoughtful expression on his face. "We're going to the castle?"

"Yes, why? Got a girlfriend there?"

He nodded slowly, but it didn't look like he had a furtive grope on his mind.

The public order guardian leaned back in his chair and drummed his fingers on the desktop. "Why exactly do you need these undercover clearances, Dalrymple? What are you up to?" He turned to Davie and looked with distaste at his trimmed beard.

"It's a long shot," I said nonchalantly. "I'd rather keep it under wraps at this stage. It probably won't come to anything." If Hamilton discovered I was trailing a senior auxiliary, the blades of the fan would be permanently clogged with excreta. But I had to have the undercover passes – "ask no questions", as they're known in the directorate. Without them our surveillance activities would be interrupted all the time by curious auxiliaries.

The guardian's expression softened. "Oh, all right." He scribbled a note. "Give this to my assistant, guardsman." He fixed Davie with his eyes again. "I hope you're not getting yourself into anything which demeans your rank."

"I'll make sure regulations are observed, guardian," Davie said compliantly, avoiding my eyes.

"Sit down, man," Hamilton said to me wearily. He shuffled the papers on his desk with the look of a man who can't decipher the clues of the crossword, let alone have a go at the answers. "How on earth are we going to find this" – he pushed the papers away – "this savage?"

I was surprised at the change in his bearing. Maybe the Council's rejection of his demand for a state of emergency had knocked the certainty out of him. It struck me that the guardian actually had little experience of this kind of crime. He was an organisation man, an administrator at heart. And like all administrators, a plotter. The question was, how far did his plotting go? Was he just protecting the interests of his directorate or had he got involved in something a lot dirtier? Now I was the one who didn't have a clue.

* * *

Davie was waiting for me in the outer office. An attractive red-haired guardswoman lowered her head as I came out, but I saw the smile on her lips.

"Let's go," I said to Davie. "Got the 'ask no questions'?"

He nodded, looking extremely pleased with himself.

Although it was a Sunday morning, senior auxiliaries like Billy Geddes are expected to make an appearance at the office. Davie changed into his tourist clothes and went off to keep an eye on the Finance Directorate in Bank Street. I didn't expect Billy to go anywhere revealing during daylight, but there was a chance he might meet someone during his lunchbreak.

I walked across the esplanade and down to the infirmary. There was a lot of noise in the ward containing the fire victims, patients garrulously comparing experiences and nurses clattering around with trolleys. But the figure in Katharine's bed was inert. I was a few yards from it before I realised that the occupant had grey hair and fleshy shoulders.

"She discharged herself an hour ago, citizen," said a familiar voice. "She shouldn't have. The doctor didn't have a chance to examine her arm again. But I couldn't stop her."

Simpson 134, the senior nurse I'd seen the day before on my way to the Prostitution Control Department, was standing in the centre of the ward. Her subordinates moved around her like drones in the service of a queen bee. I paid less attention than I might have to her chest because I was cursing myself for not putting a guard on the door. She heard some of the words I came out with and looked about as impressed as the former king did when the mob told him where he could put his crown.

"Any idea where she went?" I asked.

"She said she was going home."

The nurse's mordant tone puzzled me. "Is something troubling you, Simpson 134?"

She eyed me coldly. "The city is being terrorised by a lunatic and you ask if something's troubling me? Why aren't you chasing the killer instead of that female citizen?" She turned away abruptly and walked out.

There was a guard vehicle by the gate. I flashed my authorisation and got the guardsman to take me to Katharine's flat. I felt uneasy. It seemed unlikely that she could have met anyone or that anything could have happened to her in the short time since she left the infirmary. A worrying thought came to me. If she had seen the killer from the far end of the corridor, then it was very possible that he had seen her too.

"You look like you've seen a ghost." She stood at the door, her hair wet and a towel round her shoulders.

I felt a wave of relief dash over me, then recovered the power of speech. "Are you all right? They said you shouldn't have left the infirmary."

"Checking up on me?" Katharine asked, her eyes wide open and ice-water cold.

"You're a witness, for God's sake."

Her expression slackened. "I suppose I am. Sorry." She let me into the flat.

"Is your arm okay?"

She flexed it slowly. "A bit sore but I'll manage." As she

sat down on the sofa, her dressing-gown parted to reveal a length of thigh.

I gulped and tried to look elsewhere. "Why did you discharge yourself?"

"It's a madhouse there," she said, shaking her head. "Even in the middle of the night there are porters running up and down the corridors with patients on trolleys."

I pulled out my notebook and flicked through the pages. There was no need to remind myself of what I was going to ask her, but I was looking for a way to put it off.

"What is it?" Katharine asked with a smile that made my heart beat faster. "You've got that faraway look again."

No point in delaying any longer. "Andreas Roussos in room 346: did you provide sexual services to him?"

She didn't turn away. Only the disappearance of her smile suggested that the question might have had some effect. "You've been checking up on me, haven't you?" she said quietly. "I was hoping you wouldn't get around to the department's files."

"Answer the question, Katharine."

"All right. Why do you think I was so sure it was a t-v I saw with him? He wasn't interested in women, Quint."

I thought about the fact that the murder victims had been sodomised. Maybe there was a link there with the Greek's sexuality. I didn't fancy it much. I had a feeling we were supposed to think the killer was a sex freak like the ENT Man.

Katharine sat up and leaned over to me. "I want to help, Quint. Why won't you let me? You've forgotten all about Adam."

I hadn't. It was just that he was missing while she was right in front of me. He didn't have her track record either. "Why do you do it? No one's forcing you to fuck all those men."

She looked down at me without flinching. "What's that got to do with your investigation?"

"I'll tell you. From the start you've held things back from me. I had to ferret out your dissidence conviction and the fact that you whore for the Tourism Directorate. How do I know you haven't got more secrets?" I piled on as much indignation as I could. "On top of that, you expect me to accept your help? Christ, Katharine, you're not living in the real world."

"And everyone else in Edinburgh is?" she asked ironically. "Anyway, I thought you knew everything about me from the moment we met. Remember that little demonstration you gave?" The smile disappeared from her lips. "I told you, Quint. After my time on Cramond Island I do what I'm told."

That was bullshit. It was clear from Patsy's file that Katharine wasn't being coerced. I kept on at her. "Does that include throttling the guy in the linen store?"

Her mouth opened slightly and I heard her breathing quicken. "What do you mean?" she asked in a whisper.

I stood up and faced her. "Why should I believe your story about the transvestite? Maybe you ripped the Greek's eye out with those long fingers of yours."

The next few seconds would be crucial. She was about the most enigmatic person I'd ever come across, but I was still confident I'd be able to tell if she was lying.

"You've made your mind up already, haven't you?" she

said, holding my gaze. "There's no point in me saying anything."

I waited for a bit, then snapped my notebook shut. If she'd started to weep or plead, if she'd opened her legs and offered me sex, I'd have been seriously suspicious. As it was, she convinced me that she hadn't been involved in the attacks on Roussos and the others simply because she didn't care about them. Or about anyone else except her brother, it seemed.

"I want to assign a guardswoman to you," I said on my way out. "The assailant might have seen you."

"Forget it," she said, her voice harsher. "I can look after myself."

I didn't press the point. Suddenly the idea of arguing with her took on the aspect of Everest's south-west face from below. I went downstairs to the safety of the street.

"Dead ends," said Hamilton laconically.

I looked out from the window of his office in the castle. The city looked unreal in the late afternoon sun, a thin layer of mist hanging over the buildings like the last exhalations of an intelligent but slow-moving species of dinosaur. "Looks that way," I said.

"Do you think we can rely on the official t-vs' alibis?" The guardian pronounced the initial letters with distaste.

"Yes. We'll have to look elsewhere for the butcher."

"But where, for God's sake? My people have checked all the gaming tents and nightclubs. Some of the staff remembered Roussos, but no one could say if he'd been with anyone else. The same in the hotel."

"Did the consulate confirm his job?"

"He's an insurance consultant all right. Unless the contract they showed me was a fake."

That wouldn't have surprised me, but there was no way of proving it. I walked towards the door. "Keep up the good work, guardian."

"Where are you going?" he demanded.

"To follow up my long shot. Looks like it's our only chance."

I leaned my bicycle against the front of the tourist shop opposite the Finance Directorate and went in.

Davie was behind a curtain. "She's seen my 'ask no questions'," he said, glancing at a middle-aged auxiliary in a tartan plaid behind the counter who was studiously ignoring us. "And I showed it to the guardsman in the checkpoint." He shrugged apologetically. "Had to – I did my auxiliary training with him. Don't worry, he'll keep quiet."

I looked over at the imposing building, formerly the headquarters of a bank. It stands on a prominence overlooking the gardens and is about as close as you get to architectural opulence in the city nowadays. The Council would claim that they've just left it as it was, but I wouldn't buy that. Money still talks, whatever they say.

"Is he still in there?"

Davie nodded. "Been there all day, apart from when he went for a wander on the Royal Mile at lunchtime. He didn't meet anyone."

"Or hand over anything?"

"I don't think so. It was pretty crowded. I suppose he

could have slipped a note to someone. There were a lot of foreigners around."

"How many of them were Greeks, I wonder?" I frowned at him. "Next time stay as close as you can to him."

"Easier said than done. The High Street's like a wheelchair track. Have you noticed how many of them there are these days?"

"Yeah, it's . . . hang on . . . here we go."

Billy Geddes had appeared outside the Finance Directorate. He stopped and exchanged a few words with the guardsman at the entrance.

"I'll take him now," I said, jamming my woollen hat over my ears and wrapping a scarf round the lower part of my face.

"I thought you might have dressed in drag," Davie said with a grin.

"Not on my bike. That would be a bit of a giveaway."

Billy's Toyota was driven up by a porter. He got in and moved off down the Mound, followed by a Supply Directorate lorry that was pumping out clouds of fumes. I took a deep breath and dived into the smog. There was no getting away from it. Billy Geddes was a lucky bastard to have his own car and I was jealous as hell. Not that I was going to let that prejudice my handling of the investigation.

Either Billy wasn't really a bad boy or he was being very careful. He went straight back to his flat and stayed there. I took cover in the bushes lining the lower edge of Queen Street Gardens. Twice I was approached by track-suited auxiliaries. They backed off when they saw my "ask no questions". Twilight deepened and the lights from Billy's high windows shone out over the street. I caught a glimpse of him moving past, a mobile phone to his ear. There was no way of finding out who he was talking to.

Later the lights were dimmed, though not extinguished completely. I was shivering in the gloom, trying to convince myself that I wasn't wasting my time. Even the unchanged sheets and coarse blankets on my bed began to tempt me. I forced myself to concentrate on the elegant Georgian façade across the road. Nearby was number 17, where Robert Louis Stevenson lived as a boy. Perhaps he had the first intimations of Dr Jekyll here when the mist was swirling around, swallowing the drumming of horses' hooves from passing carriages. The doctor and his sinister doppelganger seemed very close. Then I thought of the Ear, Nose and Throat Man's hulking figure, a knife glinting in each hand, and felt a tingling in the stump of my finger.

I was so caught up that I hardly heard the dull click of the door closing behind Billy. I looked over in time to see his small figure move quickly down the steps and along the street. There was no sound from his feet – he must have put on a pair of well-worn shoes – and that made me wonder what he was up to. I stepped away from the bushes and ran along the grass by the all-weather track, hoping he'd think I was a jogger. It was too late to vault the fence. I'd have to wait till Billy was off Heriot Row and use the nearest gate. The question was, where was he heading?

When he got to India Street, he turned and walked down-hill rapidly. I sprinted to the gate then froze as I saw Billy stop and look round. Fortunately I was obscured. He carried on. Then disappeared.

My heart skipped a couple of beats. I went down India Street cautiously, looking at all the basement flats and the steps down to them. Nothing. Then it came to me. I'd forgotten about the narrow entrance to Jamaica Street. There was a bar patronised by senior auxiliaries further down. The lights were low, curtains covering most of the window space. A buzz of voices was audible despite the heavy door. Billy must have gone for a pint. I got my breathing back to normal and wedged myself behind a large rubbish container to see if he came out with anyone interesting. If I'd been spotted by a resident, the guard would be along any minute. They weren't.

Half an hour later I heard high-heeled footsteps coming from the darkness beyond the bar and swore under my breath. My geography was all screwed up. Jamaica Street looked like a cul-de-sac, but there were actually a couple of lanes leading on from it. They were unlit by streetlamps. Billy could have met someone there or kept going and shaken off a tail as incompetent as me. The footsteps came closer. I crouched motionless, wondering if they were a woman's or a transvestite's. As they passed, I looked out and got a clear view of the straight body and unmistakable chest of Simpson 134 from the infirmary. Except instead of a nurse's uniform, she was dressed up in a flashy wool coat, black stockings and shoes that didn't come from the Supply Directorate. She was also carrying the briefcase I'd seen her with outside Patsy's office. She turned the corner and vanished.

Jigsaw pieces began to come together in my mind. She

must have been Billy's contact, the one who told him when I left the infirmary. But what was she doing meeting him in a pitch-black backstreet?

A faint noise came from the lane. Billy turned the corner and pulled open the bar door, to be greeted by raised voices.

After a few minutes, I decided to leave him to it and set off home. My long shot had hit an interesting target but I couldn't say I was much further on. None of what I'd seen was worth reporting to the Council. To confront them I needed evidence and that was in shorter supply than Danish bacon in the city's foodstores.

As I crossed Heriot Row I had another thought. I'd completely forgotten to make the Sunday visit to my father. There was definitely something wrong with my memory.

Chapter Thirteen

When Davie arrived at six the next morning I was already working on the lists Hamilton had sent over.

"What's all that?" he asked.

"Auxiliaries who were involved in the fire and the rescue."

"Have you found me there?"

"Don't worry, you're not a suspect." I glanced at the faded labourers' fatigues he'd dressed himself up in. "Your feet aren't the right size."

"What a relief."

I threw down my pencil. "This is a waste of time. There were hundreds of your lot at the Indie. Even if the killer is an auxiliary, he could have been off duty on Thursday evening and gone to the hotel earlier."

"To start the fire, you mean? What did the fire chief's report say about arson?"

"He's still investigating, but there's a good chance it was started deliberately. The heat around the kitchens was so intense that there's not much evidence."

Davie scratched what remained of his beard. "You know what I think? If he was dressed as a t-v, he already had the freedom of the hotel. So he didn't need a distraction."

I looked up at him. "What are you getting at?"

He shrugged. "Maybe he set the fire just to show us what he can do."

I shivered and pulled the blanket tighter around my shoulders. "Bloody hell, Davie, that's an idea which makes me look forward to the rest of my life." It was also one with a definite ring of truth. I told him about Billy Geddes and the nursing auxiliary.

"Why don't you take her in and interrogate her?" he asked.

I shook my head. "That would make Billy run for cover. Anyway, he'd just say he was giving her a knee-trembler against the wall."

"Very likely. That woman would crush all his ribs."

I laughed. "I'm going to ask Hamilton to put a guard on her. We can say it's for her safety. Then at least we'll know where she is all the time."

"You want me to stay on Heriot 07?"

"Yes. Hide yourself in the bushes opposite his flat till he comes out then tail him."

He looked unusually anxious.

"What's the problem? You've got your 'ask no questions'."

"It's not that." His cheeks reddened. "I've got something I have to do in the castle."

"Something to do with that redhead in the guardian's office, guardsman?"

"You could say that."

"I'll try to spare you later on." I looked at my watch. "Let's get going. I want to see my father before the fun starts."

I knew Hector would be unimpressed that a mere double murder investigation had stopped me visiting. Besides, I had something to tell him.

The door on the top floor was half open. I looked in and saw the old man bent over his desk. I could hear the rasp of the fountain pen he always used. It was a mystery where he found the ink for it – the city's stationery shops provide only pencils and cheap ballpoints. He didn't look up when I went in. I took in his worn cardigan and the loose skin on his neck. His characteristic wheeze came regularly, like the revolutions of a decrepit but still serviceable pump.

"Hello, old man."

Hector sat up and swung round with surprising speed. "Ah, there you are, failure." He gave me a smile that was both ironic and welcoming. "Let me finish this page."

I went over to the window and looked out over the waves that were dancing away in the sunlight. My father had started writing again.

"I saw her last week," I said when I heard his pen stop.

He put the cap on the pen and laid it carefully on the desk. "The standard view of Juvenal is that he hated women." He put his hand on a pile of books, all containing slips of paper covered with minuscule notes. "That's what the experts say." He got to his feet, hands spread on the desk for support. "What I say is bollocks to that. The old bugger was so obsessed with women that he spent all his time abusing them and . . ."

"I said, I saw Mother."

Hector turned to me, his eyes wide. "I'm not deaf,"

he shouted. Then he asked more quietly, "Why do you think I'm spending my dotage trying to make sense of this Roman misogynist? There must be more to life than despising women." He lowered his head. "Or in my case, one particular woman."

I moved closer. "She looks terrible. The lupus is much worse."

"And what the hell can I do about that?" he demanded, clutching at my arm as I went to close the door. "Did you come down here just to tell me her condition's worse? Surely she's not asking for my sympathy?" He suddenly looked his age.

I led him to the sofa. "You know Mother. Sympathy's not something she's ever needed." I kept my hand on his forearm.

"Are they looking after her properly?"

"I think so. Apparently the medical guardian's treating her himself."

"Is he?" My father looked at me curiously. "But even the great Robert Yellowlees hasn't found a cure yet?"

I shook my head, remembering that the old man was one of the few people in the city with a poor opinion of the medical guardian. He thought his loyalty to the Enlightenment took second place to his research interests.

"He's working on a new approach, Mother said."

Hector twitched his head impatiently. "And what about your investigation? Did your killer have something to do with the fire at the hotel?"

"I think so." I gave him a downbeat report, keeping Billy Geddes out of it. That didn't escape him.

"What about your friend in the Finance Directorate? Did you find anything more out about his activities?"

"Sort of," I answered, remembering too late how much he loathed vagueness.

"What the hell does that mean?" he raged. "You went to university, didn't you? Express yourself properly."

"Sorry," I replied lamely. At least Hector was back to his normal self. "What I meant was that I've discovered things, but I can't link any of them to the murders." I glanced at my father, who was studying me through his battered spectacles. "I'm sure there is a connection though."

He smiled broadly. "At least there's one thing you're sure of." He got up and moved purposefully towards his desk. "You'll work it out," he said, picking up his pen. "You always did." His face clouded. "Until Caro was . . ."

"I thought we agreed we wouldn't talk about her again."

He raised his hands placatingly. "Mea culpa, Quintilian." He frowned. "It's just that the city has needed you these past five years. You might have stopped things going the way they have."

I walked to the door. "I'm an investigator, not a political philosopher."

"What's the difference?"

"I'll see you next Sunday."

"She's much worse, you say?" Hector's voice was almost inaudible.

I nodded then turned away. Before I reached the stair, I heard the scratch of his pen start up again.

"Hume 253, advise your location," I said into the mouthpiece of my mobile, using Davie's barracks number because of the severe guardsman in the driver's seat.

"My location?" Davie demanded. "Up to my knees in the hole you told me to dig."

"Subject's still in his hutch then?"

"Correct. Maybe he thinks he can have the day off after working on Sunday. When are you coming to relieve me?"

"As soon as I pick up the relevant vehicle."

Davie grunted. "Try and get here before I strike oil."

"A piece of advice. If you want to avoid blisters, keep spitting on your hands."

The driver gave me a sidelong glance.

"Now you tell me," moaned Davie despairingly.

The fat commander of the drivers' mess peered at the ancient Ford Transit like an ornithologist who's just spotted a dodo in his back garden. "We can't give him that," he said.

All around us mechanics in heavily stained overalls were tinkering with vehicles ranging from ten-year-old taxis bought on the cheap from Slovakia to minibuses with more rust on them than the German High Seas Fleet in Scapa Flow.

Anderson touched the crack that ran down the centre of the windscreen and laughed. "It'll be fine." Although it was hot in the garage behind the drivers' mess, he was still wearing his leather jacket. "It hasn't been used for a few years, mind." He leaned into the cab. "Only 148,000 on the clock. You'll not be planning on doing too many more, will you?"

"I shouldn't think so." I looked at the Parks Department stickers that had been fixed to the doors. "Where is there to go?" I sat behind the wheel.

"Citizen Dalrymple," the auxiliary said, "you do have a driving licence, don't you?"

"Of course," I replied, trying to remember how the controls worked. "I took my test when I was seventeen."

"Could I see it?" the fat man asked officiously.

I turned the key. To my surprise the engine fired immediately. I closed the door. "You'll just have to take my word for it." I stirred the gear lever and produced a grating cacophony.

Anderson jumped in from the other side and found first for me. "Just out of interest, when was the last time you drove?"

I lifted my foot cautiously from the clutch pedal. "Six or seven years ago, I suppose." I saw the leather jacket exit rapidly. "It's like riding a bike, isn't it?" I shouted after him. "You never forget."

The van juddered its way out of the garage. I wasn't sure if Anderson had wished me good luck or something else that rhymes with it.

I parked fifty yards from Billy Geddes's flat and walked through the gardens towards the pile of earth that was being heaped up by a broad-backed labourer.

"Hit bedrock yet?"

"Hours ago." Davie wiped his forehead with his sleeve.

"Any sign of our man?"

"He's still inside. I saw him through the window a few minutes ago."

"And there's no rear exit, unless he's prepared to shin down a rope." I looked at Davie. Without the heavy beard and guard uniform he was very different. "Christ, you look almost human now."

"Thanks a lot." He tensed. "There he is."

Through the bushes we watched Billy Geddes come down the steps, resplendent in a light blue suit and pink tie. He obviously wasn't bothered about sticking out from the crowd. He glanced up and down Heriot Row, paying no attention to the Transit, then got into his Toyota.

"Time to knock off here," I said.

We ran to the van. I jumped into the driver's seat and started the engine.

"When did you learn to drive?" Davie asked suspiciously.

"Not another one." I accelerated away, narrowly missing a couple of track-suited guardswomen. "I learned before the Enlightenment, if you must know." The lights changed and I had to brake sharply. "Haven't had much practice recently."

"So I see." Davie's knuckles were white.

Fortunately the Toyota stayed in sight. It went round St Andrew Square, turned left on to Princes Street and headed up Waterloo Place, past the former main post office which is now a video game centre for the tourists. Then Billy drove up the road behind the old Royal High School and stopped.

"What's he up to?" I said. "Going for a walk during office hours? What kind of example is that to set?" I parked on the pavement and climbed over my seat into the back of the van. "Keep an eye on which way he's going."

Davie got out and watched the short figure start off up Calton Hill.

When I was ready, I opened the back door and walked over to Davie. "Hello, big boy."

"Christ, Quint, is that you?"

It looked like my disguise worked.

"Do you get a kick out of wearing women's clothing?"

"Not really. I'm just trying to get an insight into the transvestite mentality."

Davie didn't look convinced. I'd put on the uniform of a certain kind of female American tourist: mauve slacks tight over the arse and baggy everywhere else, crinkly showerproof jacket, sneakers, baseball cap pulled low, shoulder bag and camera. The yellow bouffant wig I'd ordered from the Theatrical Productions Department was set off by an excess of rouge and glistening purple lipstick.

"Do you think I'll get picked up?"

Davie stifled laughter. "No danger of that. Does the camera work?"

"You better believe it, lover boy. One of the directorate's finest." I set off up the hill. "I've taken my mobile, but don't call me in case he hears it."

Over my shoulder I heard Davie muttering, "Madam, there is no way I'll be calling you."

Billy was standing by one of the National Monument's ten columns. The tableau in front of me was loaded with symbolism. There was the city's financial genius dressed up in non-regulation clothes silhouetted against the tourist-ridden, soulless state he'd helped create. Not that Billy was the only long-standing member of the Enlightenment on the hill at that moment. Despite my demotion, I'd never actually handed in my party card.

A group of Filipinos came past, chattering and taking photographs of the sights their guide pointed out. The clicking of their cameras reminded me that I should be capturing Billy on film. I wondered what he was doing up here. One thing was certain – he wasn't simply taking the air. Even at school he never had any time for activities that didn't provide some tangible benefit.

Time dragged by and I began to feel conspicuous. Amateur theatricals are all very well in the local church hall, but you've got to be a hardened female impersonator to hang around on a windswept hilltop.

Then Billy moved away from the pseudo Parthenon towards the Nelson Monument. There was a rattle and a thud as the time ball dropped from the top of the inelegant Gothic tower, provoking a round of applause from the Filipinos. I took up position behind the column where Billy had been standing and checked my watch. By the time I looked up again, he'd met someone I knew.

It was Palamas, the Greek diplomat with the moustache Nietzsche in his moments of sanity would have been proud of. He was wearing the same herringbone coat and carrying a black leather briefcase. I raised the camera and shot the pair of them repeatedly before they went into the Nelson Monument and disappeared.

I called Davie. "He's made contact – with a guy from the Greek consulate."

"What are they doing?"

"They're up the tower. I'll wait for them here then tail the Greek. You take our man. Out."

I fancied trying to eavesdrop on their conversation, but I

wasn't confident enough of how I looked to risk meeting Billy in the narrow confines of the building. After half an hour he reappeared, carrying the briefcase, and headed down the hill towards his car. As he passed me, he didn't even turn his head.

Five minutes went by before the Greek came out. This time I had a narrow escape. He gave me a long glance and seemed to be weighing up making a move on me. He must have been short-sighted. Either that or his taste in sexual partners was a matter for serious concern. Then he saw the error of his ways and stalked off to the consulate.

I went back to my flat to change. That was enough of life from the other side of the great sexual divide.

Davie called not long after I got home.

"Subject returned to his place with the briefcase, then came out empty-handed and went to the Finance Directorate."

"Care to hazard a guess at the contents of the case?"

Davie grunted. "Why don't we search the flat and take him in?"

"And do him for accepting bribes?" I thought about it for a moment. As well as all this, I was pretty sure Billy was behind the authorisations Sarah Spence had to leave her barracks after midnight. But he'd have made sure all reference to them in Finance Directorate records had been expunged. I shook my head. "We've nothing that'll get us any nearer to catching the murderer yet."

"Listen, Quint, there's something I want to do. Can you take over in Bank Street for a bit?" His voice was suddenly breathless.

"The redhead?"

"Aye."

"All right. I'll give you an hour."

"As long as that?" He didn't sound too disappointed.

I hadn't been behind the curtain in the tourist shop opposite Billy's office for more than twenty minutes when Davie burst back in. He had a large brown envelope in his hands and the wide-eyed look of a man who's just struck very lucky in the draw for the weekly sex session.

"That good?" I asked.

He ran over to the counter and pulled the female auxiliary out. "Early closing," he said firmly.

She was out in a flash.

"What is it?" Now he was pulling me to the counter, having locked the shop door.

"Look what I've got hold of." He took a buff folder out of the envelope. On it was embossed the city's heart emblem. The words "Guardians' Eyes Only" were stamped in large black letters above and below it. Considering the fact that possession of this file constituted guaranteed grounds for demotion, Davie was looking very pleased with himself. I didn't think I'd had that much of an influence on him.

"You realise the risk you're . . ." I stopped when I saw the file's title. "'Citizens Reported Missing as of 1.1.2020'. Bloody hell. Let's have a look."

There was a thick wad of City Guard Missing Persons forms. What grabbed my attention was the cover sheet. Forty-eight people, twenty-eight female and twenty male citizens, had gone AWOL in the last three months. All of them were under twenty-six years old. Underneath the front page was a list of the names. I felt my heart race. One of them was Katharine Kirkwood's brother Adam. There were six others that clients had asked me to find.

"Do I get a coconut?" Davie asked with a grin.

"If Hamilton finds out you took this, you'll get a whole lorry-load of them dumped on you. The redhead?"

"She made sure she was out of the office long enough for me to have a look at the guardian's personal files. This one was on top. I saw Adam Kirkwood's name and thought you'd go for it."

"But why didn't you tell me what you were up to?"

He shrugged and looked awkward. "Well, you know, I wanted to show you I could do something on my own initiative."

I laughed. "Christ, Davie. Not even I would have gone through Hamilton's confidential files."

He chewed his lip, as if the significance had finally struck him. I had plenty more bad news for him.

"Well done, pal. But I haven't got a clue how this fits in to the rest of what we're investigating. If it fits in at all."

"All these people missing while there's a psycho on the loose? Course it fits in." He was looking pleased with himself again.

"Maybe. But there's another problem we have to solve first."

"Hit me. I can handle anything."

"Uh-huh. After you've copied the file, you'll have to figure out a way to get it back without anyone noticing."

He wasn't beaten. "Good enough. I thought you might

be going to walk into the chief's office with this in your hand."

I shook my head. "No chance. For the time being this is our little secret, guardsman."

The Council meeting that evening was a bit difficult. I got my head in my hands for not being available throughout the day. I got my own back by telling them exactly what I thought about the fact I hadn't been allowed to question Roussos in the infirmary. Hamilton looked embarrassed about that. So much so that he forgot to mention that I was working on a long shot. Just as well.

I went back to my place after the meeting, having arranged to relieve Davie outside Billy's at midnight. I sat outside in the Transit trying to work out what to do about the missing young people. I knew one thing for sure. There were far too many for them just to be deserters – and the fact that the Council had a file on them meant that they weren't in the mines or on the farms. Christ, I'd even noticed an increase in my own workload before the killings started, but I'd forgotten all about it till now. Davie had remedied that. But what about Adam Kirkwood? What was I going to tell Katharine?

Then I saw her come round the corner. She had on a skirt that stopped about six inches above the knee. I noticed that because she was wearing red stockings and high heels that made her legs as striking as a smiling face in a philosophy seminar. I watched as she drew nearer. In the gloom she didn't see me. She went in the street door.

I didn't get out straight away because I was still wondering whether to say anything about her brother. Then I chickened out, decided to keep my mouth shut and followed her in. Her scent lingered in the musty air. By the time I reached the third floor, she was on her way down. Her legs looked even more stunning from that angle. There was the hint of a smile at the corners of her mouth. We stood looking at each other.

"I thought I'd missed you."

"You were lucky."

"I should say so." She gave a light, mocking laugh then turned back up again.

"What a surprise," I said, my eyes fixed on the back of her thighs.

She didn't answer, waiting for me to open the door. Then she walked in and dropped her jacket on the end of the sofa. The white blouse she was wearing was almost transparent. I could see the points of her breasts. She caught me staring.

"I'll have a drink," she said coolly. "Before we get down to business."

I poured whisky into a glass, wondering what she was after. I knew very well what I was after.

"Thanks." She raised the glass. "Are you not having one?"

I sat down in the armchair opposite her and shook my head. "I've got to work later on."

"He works nights too," she said with a smile. "The dedication." She put the glass to her lips and touched the rim with her tongue, unwavering eyes locked on me.

I suddenly felt breathless, like an astronaut, in the old days before space travel became too expensive, whose safety line has broken. "What is it you want, Katharine?" I asked weakly.

"What is it I want?" she asked, taking a sip of whisky. "I'd have thought that was obvious." She opened her mouth, the tip of her tongue glistening as it protruded for a second. "I want you." Then she moved over, stood in front of me and lifted her skirt up. She was wearing the full tart's get-up, suspender belt and knickers matching her stockings. I hadn't forgotten what I'd read about her in Patsy's file. I just didn't give a damn.

"Kath . . ." I began, then lost the power of speech as she straddled me, knees against my abdomen.

She knew exactly what she was doing. Lowered a hand to the bulge in my groin and squeezed, leaning back as I ran my hands down her buttocks. I slid my fingers under the elastic of her knickers and pressed them forward. To my surprise I found she was wet.

"Come on," she whispered, "I want you now." She unfastened my belt, unzipped me and touched my cock. Before I could move she rolled a condom over me with practised skill. And pushed down, directing me into her. My hands were on her breasts, which became taut as she leaned back again. I felt the dark brown nipples harden even more. Looking at her face, I saw that she had her eyes closed. I kept mine open.

As in all the best erotica, we came together. At least it seemed that way to me. When I spurted, she shuddered then slumped over me, her breath warm in my ear and the scent of her in my nostrils. I floated off into deepest space.

But she wouldn't let me go. Clenched well-exercised muscles and held me inside her.

"Actually," she murmured, "there is one other thing I want."

"To help find Adam?" I gasped, my breathing still all over the place.

"You're way ahead of me," she said, sitting up straight and looking down at me. "Well?"

If she's working with me I'll be able to keep an eye on her, I told myself. It wasn't a difficult decision.

"All right," I said, pushing her off gently. As she stepped back I caught sight of Caro's photograph.

There was the sound of water being splashed around in the toilet. Eventually Katharine emerged, shaking her head.

"You can tell the city's washing facilities were organised by men. Have you any idea how difficult it is for a woman to wash herself in a basin?"

"I suppose you've got used to the bidets in the Indie."

She sat down and looked at me curiously. "What's the matter?"

I turned away, but not before Katharine saw the photo.

"Who is she, Quint?" she asked softly.

It was the tone of her voice that did it. Hoarser than usual, somehow suggesting a capacity to understand that I suddenly needed badly.

So I told her about Caro – about the law lectures we attended together at the university, about her belief in the Enlightenment and about our time in the Public Order Directorate. She didn't interrupt or comment, didn't show how she felt at all. Until I got to the last operations against the drug gangs and stopped. I couldn't go on.

"You have to share it with someone, Quint." Katharine was looking across at me with eyes that had none of their usual steeliness. "You've kept this bottled up for years, haven't you?"

I nodded slowly. "You're the first person I've ever spoken to about Caro's . . . about what happened."

"I've had a lot of experience of confessions."

"Is that what this is?"

"Of course." She smiled to encourage me.

It worked. I found that I could go on. "It was five years back. The leader of the worst gang was holed up with about twenty of his men in a farmhouse on the northern slopes of Soutra."

"Just beyond the city's borders."

"Yes. We bent the rules – it was my decision. Caro was in charge of the scouting group and I was with two other squads to the rear, waiting for her signal." I stopped to get my breath. Usually my heart pounded like a piston engine when I woke up after dreaming about that night, but it was beating normally now. "Then everything went wrong. Their sentries must have spotted Caro's group. They grabbed them before we realised what had happened. We'd had problems with the mobile phones earlier. We didn't react quickly enough."

"These things happen," Katharine said. "It wasn't your fault."

"Then we heard screaming, men's voices, and afterwards a high-pitched shriek that seemed like it would never stop. I didn't recognise it. We went in then. They were waiting for us, they knew exactly how many of us there were. A lot of my people were taken out. Not me, though. I had a charmed life.

Ran right through the centre of their line and reached the barn. By the time I got there the screaming had stopped."
I had to stop, swallow saliva. The same thing had happened that night too.

"I was on my own. The guard were still fighting their way through the outer defences. The bastards had fortified the place. And all I had was my service knife. My pistol had jammed on the way in."

Katharine moved round the table and sat on the arm of my chair. She didn't touch me.

"There was nothing else for it. I burst in the door and headed for the light in the centre of the barn. I had to jump over the bodies of a couple of guardsmen from Caro's group. There were four men in a huddle round the hurricane lamp. When they heard me, they broke up and . . . and I saw her."
I looked round at Katharine. "I thought she was all right at first. Except . . . except her foot was jerking crazily. Then I saw the blood round her mouth."

Now Katharine put her hand on mine for a few seconds. It was cool, absorbed some of the heat.

"I put my arm under her shoulders and tried to find a pulse. I was too late. She'd been strangled. I put my fingers into her mouth to try to clear her throat. She'd . . ." I turned to Katharine again, suddenly not wanting to spare her anything. "She'd bitten through her tongue. It came out on my fingers. Like a little fish."

Katharine gripped my hand hard. "Oh my God."

"Then I was hit over the back of the head. I came round in the infirmary." I pulled my hand away and slumped back in the chair. I was totally drained.

She was silent for a time, then nodded at my right hand. "You got that injury then?"

"Soon afterwards." I wasn't going to tell her about the Ear, Nose and Throat Man, about how I'd seen him break away from the group first, a length of rope dangling from one hand. I had to keep something secret. For Caro.

Katharine got up and moved over to the sofa. "You've never forgotten her, have you, Quint? But you have to. It's finished."

"You want me to let myself become a soulless robot like everyone else in Edinburgh?"

She shook her head slowly. "No. You just have to stop caring so much."

"Like you stopped caring for that dissident – what was his name?" I remembered it perfectly well, but I wanted to shake her.

"Alex." She looked at me without animosity. "I think I've got over him. He's out of the Council's reach now."

I envied him. For all my pathetic attempts at independence, the Council still had its claws deep into me.

Chapter Fourteen

The buzz of the mobile phone woke me. I fell out of the chair and crawled over to my jacket.

"What the hell's happened to you?" asked Davie in a caustic whisper.

"Good question," I replied. "What time is it?" I fumbled for matches and lit a candle. Katharine was asleep on the sofa.

"You took my watch, didn't you?"

"Christ, half one. Sorry, Davie. I'll be down right away. Out."

Katharine stirred, then sat up and stretched her arms. "Going to work? I'll come with you?" There was no trace of sleep in her voice.

I nodded. An extra pair of eyes would be useful during the surveillance. She was pulling on her short skirt.

"You're not exactly dressed for what we're going to do. I'll see if I can find you something warmer." The first clothes I came across in my bedroom were the American tourist outfit. I didn't bother giving her the wig.

On the way downstairs I made the decision. "There's something I have to tell you about Adam."

She pushed me up against the wall, almost knocking the

candle from my hand. "You bastard," she hissed. "You've waited all this time?"

I put my hand between her breasts and shoved her backwards. "Calm down, Katharine. It isn't bad news." I shrugged. "It isn't really any kind of news."

"What the fuck are you trying to say?"

"Look, this is seriously classified. If the Council finds out we know this, we'll both be in Cramond Island before you can blink."

"If you don't tell me right now, you'll be in intensive care before you can blink."

"All right." I led her down the stairs and out into the street. There was a moon so we managed to get to the Transit even though the candle was immediately blown out. "The guard did register Adam as missing."

"I know that, for Christ's sake. I more or less filled the form in for them. The problem is they haven't done anything about finding him."

"I think they tried." I opened the door and let her in. "He's not the only one though. Forty-seven other people have gone missing in the last three months. The weird thing is, they're all under twenty-six."

Her face was yellow in the dull light from the dashboard. "What does it mean?" she asked slowly. "I don't understand."

"Me neither. But it makes you wonder. Forty-eight citizens missing and a killer on the loose." I heard her sharp intake of breath. "Shit, sorry. I didn't mean . . ." I glanced at her. Even in the unflattering clothes she looked striking, her high cheekbones prominent in the glow.

"Where are we going?"

"Heriot Row." I started the engine and drove down to Tollcross. "We're tailing someone." It suddenly occurred to me that Katharine might have seen Billy in the hotel with the Greek. "An auxiliary." I watched her out of the corner of my eye. She didn't react. "Heriot 07. Know him?"

"I know him." She sighed. "He's around the hotel all the time, playing God. He must be on the take." She turned to me, a faint smile on her lips. "I think I'm going to enjoy this."

I knew the feeling. No one likes catching auxiliaries out more than demoted auxiliaries.

When I parked the van at the end of Heriot Row, she was out like a shot. I took the opportunity to make a quick call on the mobile.

The moon was casting long shadows from the bushes in the gardens. We kept to them as we approached Davie's position.

"I've brought reinforcements," I whispered. "Well, one reinforcement."

Davie looked up from his hide and examined Katharine. He didn't make any comment.

"What happened to your beard?" she asked quietly. "I can hardly tell you're an auxiliary."

He shook his head with what looked like disbelief and turned to the front again. "He's inside – fast asleep if he's got any sense. I saw him against the bedroom light not long before he switched it off." He looked down at his notebook. "At twelve eleven." He stood up and stretched his legs. "I'll be back at 0800. Good hunting."

Katharine watched him move away stealthily. "I'll take the first watch, if you like." She patted her thigh. "You can put your head here."

I tried not to accept the offer with too much alacrity. "Wake me if you see anyone go in or come out."

"Yes, citizen."

I was only going to doze but I'd forgotten what the road to hell is paved with. Besides, my pillow was unusually soft.

Birdsong started up like a battery of tuneful road-drills. The virtual disappearance of vehicles from Edinburgh's streets has led to a massive increase in the number of birds and that morning it seemed like they were all gathered on the branches directly above me. For a moment I thought the ceiling had been removed from my bedroom. Then I remembered where I was.

My head was resting on a shoulder bag. Sitting up quickly, I caught sight of Katharine. She was watching the windows of Billy's flat, her back against the trunk of a rhododendron.

I looked at my watch. "Bloody hell, six thirty. You should have woken me hours ago."

She turned and smiled. "Good morning to you too." She stretched her arms, wincing as the bandage on her burn moved. "You were sleeping so sweetly that I decided to leave you to it."

"Well, I did have a tiring evening."

"As I remember, you never got off your backside."

I had a look through the binoculars. The curtains were still drawn across Billy's bedroom window. The Toyota was exactly where it had been. "I take it you saw nothing?"

"No one went in or came out."

"Good." I touched her knee. "You should get some rest."

"I'm all right. There'll be plenty of time for rest when this is all finished."

"Don't hold your breath. It might take weeks."

The pounding feet of an early morning jogger came towards us. We both froze and waited for them to pass, but they slowed down. Looking through the foliage, I saw legs in a maroon track suit and auxiliary-issue running shoes. I reached into my pocket for my "ask no questions".

"Raise your hands and come out slowly. You have five seconds to comply."

Katharine licked her lips but remained where she was. The auxiliary came nearer.

"Fuck you, Davie," I said in disgust. "Get down before you're spotted."

He joined us in the small clearing, removing the scarf he'd wrapped round his face. He had a Thermos of coffee and a loaf of barracks bread.

"What are you doing here so early?" I demanded.

"Just out on my morning run." Davie grinned. "I reckoned you'd been in the bushes long enough with this female citizen."

Katharine looked at him sharply. "I thought guardsmen were supposed to be above that kind of innuendo."

"Pardon me," Davie said ironically. "I forgot you were a lady of high moral standing."

"Shut up, you two," I said. "We're supposed to be a team."

"Is that right?" asked Davie. "I'm glad someone told me."

Katharine stood up and glanced around. "I'm going for a pee. Keep some coffee for me."

"What's the matter with you, Davie?" I pulled out my mobile. "I want to keep an eye on her. The killer might have seen her." A thought struck me. "You looked at her file that time I left it in the Land-Rover, didn't you? That's why you're down on her."

"She was a dissident, for Christ's sake." He looked guiltier than a kid who's been caught with his telescope trained on the neighbour's bedroom. "Sorry."

"Forget it." I made a couple of calls.

"What was all that about?" Davie asked when I finished.

"Katharine's in the clear. I put a sentry at each end of the street overnight – just in case she tried to wander off." I kept my eyes lowered.

"What a way to treat a member of the team."

"Thank you, guardsman. Now piss off back to Hume and get changed. There's something else I have to check up on."

When Davie came back, Katharine and I left in a guard vehicle. She didn't seem too bothered when I told the driver to take us to the castle. When we got there, I asked her to wait in Hamilton's outer office. I didn't want her to see the file I needed yet.

The public order guardian's reaction when he saw me was strangely muted. He listened to what I had to say about Katharine with about as much interest as an atheist forced to have dinner with the Pope.

"I suppose you know what you're doing, using a convicted dissident," he said dully. He looked anaemic, his movements sluggish. Remembering the suspicions I had about him, I suddenly felt like an idiot. On the other hand, maybe he was guilty about something. He didn't object when I asked to see Alex Irvine's file.

The first page got me going. He was a big man, six feet two in height, and he took a size eleven boot. That was near enough the murderer's. I ran through the record of his interrogation. Under the strongarm methods of one of Hamilton's expert headbangers, Irvine had admitted killing three auxiliaries, one with a knife and two with a length of rope. Better and better. My suspicion that he'd somehow escaped the execution squad and come back to take his revenge against the city was getting out of hand. Then I came to the death certificate. There was a close-up photograph of a face with the entry wounds from three bullets. But I had to be sure.

I went to the outer office. "Katharine, come in for a minute, will you?" I tried to keep my voice level. I was not having a good time.

She looked briefly at the guardian, her face impassive. Then looked even more briefly at the photo I showed her. And closed her eyes once, long enough for me to make out moistness at the corners.

"It is Alex Irvine, isn't it?" I prompted, touching her arm.

She pulled away like I was a leper. "I suppose you're going to tell me you had to be sure he was dead." She didn't wait for me to confirm that. "It's Alex," she said as she headed for the door. "The first photo I've ever seen of him."

The phone on Hamilton's desk rang. His expression livened up after a few seconds. "Something strange, Dalrymple," he said, his hand over the receiver. I saw Katharine stop in the doorway. "It's your father. Apparently he's disappeared."

We followed the guardian's Land-Rover down to Trinity. Katharine sat beside me, her face blank. It was almost as if she'd forgotten what I'd done to her in the castle. Or perhaps finding her brother was all that mattered and I was her best option on that score.

The resident nurse in the retirement home was convinced that Hector had wandered off with a book to enjoy the spring morning. It wouldn't have been the first time. But regulations required her to report any absentee immediately and as my father was a former guardian, the local barracks commander had informed Hamilton. I was surprised the guardian had come down himself – he never got on with the old man. Then I thought of the top-secret missing persons file. Surely he didn't think Hector had any connection with the forty-eight young people? I suddenly felt uneasy.

I went up to the third floor. Hector's room looked the same as it had the day before, apart from his desk. The books on Juvenal that he was working on had all been tidied away. The bed was as neatly made as ever. My father insisted on making it himself. He'd always been an early riser and he might have let himself out before the main door was unbolted. But someone would have seen him.

The nurse, Simpson 172, shook her head impatiently when I asked her. "No, I've already checked with all the residents. And the door was bolted too."

"How about the back door?"

"That too."

"And all the windows were locked?"

"Of course."

I lost my patience with the woman. She was the kind of lazy and unimaginative auxiliary that somehow slips through the selection net. "That only leaves one possibility, then," I said, giving her a rancid smile. "Unless you do conjuring tricks in your spare time."

"That'll do, Dalrymple," Hamilton said from behind me. "What is this possibility you're talking about?"

"It's obvious. Somebody let my father out, then bolted the door after him."

It didn't take me long to find the guilty party. The only resident Hector spent any time with was an old guy called Joe Bell. He was in the lounge, playing dominoes. He got up when he saw me and came over, his back bent from years working on the roads.

"Hello, son. I was wondering when you'd turn up." His rheumy eyes opened wide as Hamilton came over.

"It's all right," I said. "Come into the office."

The nurse was sitting stiff-necked at her desk. She stood up when she saw the guardian, then cast a disapproving eye over Joe Bell and Katharine.

"Joe, you can tell us what you know," I said, nodding at him. "We have to be sure that Hector's disappearing hasn't got anything to do with the killer we're looking for."

"Jesus Christ," the old man said.

"What kind of language is that, citizen?"

"Do you mind?" I asked acidly. I remembered my father

saying that Simpson 172 was called Florence Nightingale behind her back.

Joe Bell smiled at the nurse's affronted look. "Well, I suppose it's all right. Hector wouldnae mind me telling you, son . . ." He paused, licking his chapped lips.

"Well, go on then, man," said the guardian impatiently.

Joe Bell looked at me and raised an eyebrow.

I got the message. "Is there anything you'd like in return for this information?" I asked with a grin.

Hamilton looked like he was about to do an impression of Mussolini with a hangover. I waved a finger at him.

"Well . . ." Joe pointed shakily at the nurse. "She doesn't give us our whisky ration. Says it's bad for us . . ."

"Which it is," the auxiliary said primly. "I always have to clean up afterwards."

"Perhaps you could make an exception today," I said. It wasn't a request.

Simpson 172 pursed her lips then nodded.

"Thanks very much, son," said citizen Bell, his face a picture of bliss an icon painter would have been canonised for.

"So you let Hector out and closed up after him this morning?"

"Aye."

"He didn't say where he was going?"

Joe shook his head, then glanced at the guardian. "Just before I shut the door I looked out. I saw a vehicle at the end of the road. Hector seemed to be going to it."

"What kind of vehicle?" Hamilton asked.

Joe found the question very amusing. He laughed until he

began to choke. "What kind?" he repeated. "It was one of your lot's. It was a bloody guard Land-Rover."

Considering Hector's feeling about the guard, I couldn't see him asking for a lift.

"Did you see him get in?" the guardian demanded.

Joe shook his head. "Florence here finally woke up and started down the stairs. I had to close the door sharpish."

"It's a pity you didn't come on duty when you should have," Hamilton said scathingly to the nurse.

"Will you check if there were any patrols around here at that time?" I asked him.

He nodded. "I've already circulated an instruction to all barracks to look out for your father."

My mobile buzzed. I turned away.

"There's movement here," Davie said. "Subject's coming out. I'm off to the van. Out."

Hamilton was curious. "What's going on?"

"I'll keep you posted." I beckoned to Katharine and we moved off.

"Dalrymple," the guardian called. "I'm sorry about all this. We'll find Hector."

I was surprised by how sincere he sounded.

A middle-aged female auxiliary with sad eyes drove us down Inverleith Row.

"So, another one goes missing," Katharine said. "I can't see what your father's got to do with the murders. Or with Adam."

"Join the club." I shook my head, unwilling to talk in front of the driver. Then my mobile rang again. It was one

231

of my mother's assistants requiring my presence immediately at Moray Place.

"Shit," I said under my breath, then redirected the driver. "You'll have to contact Davie and find out where he's heading," I said to Katharine. "I can't get out of this."

She nodded and reached for the Land-Rover's mobile.

"Aren't you exhausted?" I asked. "You hardly slept."

"I'm fine." She smiled bitterly. "I'm used to all-night performances."

I couldn't think of an answer to that. At the Darnaway Street barrier I jumped down.

"I'll catch up with you as soon as I can." In the second it took the auxiliary to engage first gear, I looked at Katharine. I was letting her loose on the investigation without any supervision. When she'd gone, I put in a call to make sure Davie kept an eye on her, but his mobile was engaged.

They were on their own.

"Mother, what's happened to you?" I stood on the landing outside her study and stared.

She walked towards me with no awkwardness, the pain apparently gone from her joints. "I feel twenty years younger," she said, her voice strong and unwavering.

I walked around her. She allowed me to examine her, an almost coquettish smile on her lips. Although her hair was still devastated, her face was no longer so moon-shaped and her skin had fewer blemishes. She led me into the room, stepping out like a model on a catwalk. The sudden change in her character was about as likely as the existence of teetotallers in the House of Commons before independence.

"You remember I told you that the medical guardian was working on a new approach?" my mother said. "This is the result."

"He's actually found a cure for the lupus?"

She raised her hand, more to restrain her own excitement rather than mine. "Not yet. But this treatment substantially neutralises the effects of the disease." Her face was glowing. "I'll be able to go on working for years."

I frowned at her. "You know Hector's disappeared, don't you?"

She nodded, avoiding my eyes. "The public order guardian has informed me. It's hardly the first time."

I considered bringing up the forty-eight missing young people but decided against it. She would insist on knowing how I'd found out. "It's the first time when there's a murderer at large."

"Do you really imagine the killer has any interest in your father, Quintilian?" She ran her fingers slowly down her cheeks as if to ensure the smoother surface really belonged to her.

"You don't care, do you?" I leaned over her desk. "Why should you? After all, it's years since you've seen him."

Her eyes flared and she opened her mouth like she was going to argue about that. Then she looked away. "Stop it," she said softly. "This is of no benefit to either of us."

"No benefit!" I shouted. "You always think about who benefits, Mother. Christ, this isn't a philosophy tutorial. Aren't you even slightly concerned?"

She moved over to the fireplace, her eyes fixed on the marble fluting. "What I feel, Quintilian, is no business of yours." She gazed at me sternly. "What's important is that you find the murderer. You are not to allow your father's disappearance to distract you."

As usual when I'm told to do something, my inclination was to do the opposite. But in this case I couldn't fault my mother's reasoning. Her lack of feeling for Hector was nothing new. I turned to go.

"One other matter," she said. "Heriot 07."

I stopped in my tracks. Surely she couldn't have discovered we were tailing Billy Geddes.

"Have you seen him recently?" Her tone was neutral.

"Yes, I have." I watched her carefully. "Why the interest?"

Her expression gave nothing away. "As I'm sure you know, he has been allowed to handle certain activities with a free hand."

I wasn't sure if I was really hearing this. My mother in league with the city's chief fixer? "I know he parades around like a semi-reformed drug gang boss."

"Don't be ridiculous," she said sharply. "He has been permitted certain privileges, but he's worth them. Without the income he provides, the city would be insolvent."

"He's on the take, Mother."

"Rubbish. We tolerate his car and his clothes, that's all."

I looked at the Renoir and shook my head. "I don't think it stops there."

She looked at me without twitching a muscle. "Then find out and report. To me, though – not the Council."

I headed for the door.

"And Quintilian?" She waited for me to look back. "Be

careful. Heriot 07 has some powerful friends." She turned to gaze into the mirror above the fire.

I went down the stairs slowly, trying to work out exactly why the senior guardian had called me to Moray Place.

I called Davie on the mobile as soon as I got outside. It seemed Billy Geddes had just walked into the former Royal Scottish Museum in Chambers Street. Whatever he was after, I was bloody sure it wasn't culture.

Chapter Fifteen

I got the guardsman who answered my call to drop me where the Transit was parked at the corner of George IVth Bridge and Chambers Street. Through the window I saw Davie slumped forward over the steering wheel. He was so still that for a few panic-stricken seconds I thought something had happened to him. When I pulled the door open, he stirred.

"Wakey fucking wakey, Davie. God, you gave me a shock. It looked like you were murder victim number three."

"Sorry." He rubbed his eyes. "Not enough sleep recently."

"I know the feeling. Where's Billy?"

"Still in the museum. Katharine's on him." He punched me lightly on the chest. "Hey, she told me about your father. Don't worry, he'll turn up."

"That's what everyone's saying." I nodded at him. "Thanks, Davie." I was touched by his concern. "I hope Katharine's keeping her distance."

"She seems to know what she's doing. She made me requisition a scarf and a horrendous tartan jacket from one of the tourist shops. She looks like a mobile carpet."

"Is that right? I'm obviously out of my depth. I'll just go as I am." I pulled my scarf up over my mouth.

"She's got a mobile, by the way. I had one sent down from the castle. Shouldn't she have an 'ask no questions' as well?"

"I wouldn't worry," I said as I got out. "She seems to be getting on fine. Wait for me here. Awake if you can manage it."

"Yes, sir."

I turned into Chambers Street. There were signs on every available wall advertising the exhibits in what's now called the Museum of Edinburgh. As I ran up the broad steps below the main entrance, I remembered going up them countless times with my grandfather – he loved the place.

The buzz of my mobile made me stop.

"Quint, where are you?" Katharine's voice was low.

I told her.

"You'd better get inside. Subject's been giving a man with a dark complexion the eye and I don't think it's because he fancies him. I'm in the natural history hall, under the whale's tail."

I flashed my "ask no questions" at the ticket clerk. The museum was free when my grandfather used to take me but the Council changed that years ago. I went into the east hall where the blue whale's skeleton hangs from the roof arches. Looking around cautiously from behind a pillar, I saw Billy Geddes at the far end. A stocky female in a virulent red and yellow jacket was examining a display case full of monkeys. I strolled over to her.

"Heriot 07 just nodded to the other guy," Katharine whispered. "They're getting closer."

"Stay down here. Billy might recognise me. When they

split up, I'll follow the other guy. You stick with Billy." I glanced at the jacket. "Couldn't you find anything a bit less conspicuous?" She must have padded it out with a lorryload of pullovers.

"I like to be centre-stage." She pouted like a vamp who'd turned to fat and moved away, showing interest in a gruesome exhibit about the craft of taxidermy.

I went back into the main hall and ran up the curved staircase to the first floor. From the balcony I could see Billy and his contact clearly. I had the camera in my pocket but I didn't want to risk attracting their attention with the flash. The other man had greasy black hair and was wearing a tan leather jacket that Anderson in the drivers' mess would have killed for. He was younger than both Andreas Roussos and Palamas, the diplomat Billy had met on Calton Hill, but I was pretty sure he was the same nationality. Unfortunately, I couldn't make out his fingernails.

The two of them were carrying on an animated conversation, oblivious to Katharine who was about twenty yards away. Then Billy looked around. I felt my stomach turn over and tried to disappear behind a supporting column. Billy caught sight of the skinned otter in the taxidermy display and wrinkled his nose in disgust. His contact tapped him on the chest impatiently and Billy produced an envelope from his pocket. It was secreted in the man's jacket before I could blink.

The olive-skinned man turned and walked quickly away. I went down the stairs three at a time, assuming that Billy would be hanging back to let him get clear. By the time I got out of the museum, my man was heading right towards the South Bridge. He seemed to be on the lookout for a cab. I called Davie and told him to pick me up. By the time the Transit arrived, the man had stopped a taxi.

"Follow that cab," I shouted as I jumped in.

"Very funny," Davie growled, accelerating away.

"I've always wanted to say that."

"How sad."

The taxi driver ahead went through the checkpoint at the top of the North Bridge, drove down to Princes Street then turned left.

"Which hotel do you reckon?"

Davie's chin jutted forward. "He looked foreign, right enough. Maybe he's heading for one of the consulates."

"Doubt it. He's hardly dressed like a diplomat."

"True enough. How about the Boswell?"

"Too full of geriatrics for this specimen. I go for the Waverley. Bottle of malt on it?"

"How am I supposed to talk the barracks steward into giving me one of those?"

I grinned. "That's part of the fun."

The taxi slowed down then drew up outside the Waverley. It was built on top of what used to be the railway station.

"Shit," said Davie with a groan. "How long have I got to come up with the whisky?"

"I'm a generous soul." This time I had no problem with using the camera. I fired off several shots of the man as he got out of the cab. Now I'd be able to identify him in the archive. "I'll give you twenty-four hours."

My mobile buzzed before he could express his gratitude.

"Subject just went into the Finance Directorate," Katharine reported.

"Right. I'll pick you up at the gallows. Out."

"What's the plan?" Davie asked.

"Katharine's an expert at getting into hotel rooms. I want to have a look at the contents of the envelope Billy passed to our friend here."

"Oh aye?"

"I'm prepared to make another bet. He knows Andreas Roussos. In fact, it wouldn't surprise me to find out that he was staying at the Indie before it went up in smoke." I looked at Davie. "Any takers?"

There was no reply.

I called for a guard vehicle and left Davie watching the door of the hotel. Katharine didn't seem too concerned when I asked her to go home and change into something a bit more seductive than her carpet. I sent her off in the Land-Rover and went into the castle to get the film developed.

While I was waiting, I went to see Lewis Hamilton. He was sitting at the conference table in his office with several mountain ranges of files in front of him.

"Ah, Dalrymple," the guardian said, looking up blearily. "Any news?"

"Nothing concrete yet. Have you picked up any trace of my father?"

He shook his head, avoiding my eyes. "I put my best auxiliaries in charge of collating the reports from the barracks." He stood up and ran a hand through his hair. "None of them had a patrol vehicle near the retirement home this morning."

"Really?" I frowned at him. "Have they all been checked?"

He nodded. "And all the directorates."

"So where the hell did that Land-Rover come from?"

"Maybe the old citizen was mistaken."

I looked out over the city, wondering where Hector was. If he'd just wandered off, the likelihood was that he'd have been picked up by now.

"You're not thinking the killer's involved, surely?" said Hamilton. "His modus operandi hasn't included kidnapping."

But someone's has, I thought. I considered telling him that I knew about the young men and women who were missing, then rejected the idea. Obviously the Council was suppressing any mention of them. Christ, maybe the guardians themselves were all involved in some massive scam. Letting Hamilton know that I'd seen the file might be a good way to end up dressed in eighteenth-century costume on the gallows.

"Look, I'm not going to be at the Council meeting this evening," I said. I saw his eyebrows shoot up. "You can handle the daily report, can't you? After all, there isn't exactly a lot to tell your colleagues." I picked up a file from the table. "What are you doing?"

He shrugged, looking sheepish. "Trying to compile a list of auxiliaries who had Thursday nights off duty and also attended the fire."

I'm sure he was expecting me to comment on the fact that he was even considering the possibility of an auxiliary being linked with the killings, but I couldn't be bothered. Besides, he was carrying out a piece of drudgery that I'd started doing myself but had given up on the grounds that anyone clever enough to commit the murders was capable of covering his tracks by swapping shifts.

"Keep up the good work," I said, unable to resist a dig.

He didn't pick it up. "Dalrymple," he said as I reached the door, "I never wanted Hector to leave the Council, you know. Only . . . priorities changed. The real world was harder than we'd imagined."

The tyrant's excuse through history. I remembered that he and my mother had vetoed the anti-corruption safeguard. You could say they were responsible for all that had happened recently. The question was, how directly?

Katharine looked at me unflinchingly after I sent Davie off to keep an eye on Billy Geddes. We were in the back of the Transit, lit by the streetlamps on Princes Street.

"Let me get this straight," she said. "You want me to pick up Heriot 07's contact and locate the envelope?" Her eyes glinted and stayed on me.

"You can handle that, can't you?"

"And exactly how far do you want me to go?"

I looked out at the hotel, then at my knees. "As far as you have to. This is our best lead."

"All right."

I felt her gaze suddenly move off me. She stood up and undid the buttons of her coat, then lifted her short skirt and smoothed the top of her black stockings. I knew very well that the show was for my benefit. She wanted me to be aware of the potential consequences. Given the thin white blouse and almost transparent bra she was wearing,

I had no doubt what they'd be. Unless our man had other inclinations.

I picked up the file I'd pulled on him. "Nikos Papazoglou," I read. "Born 1997, Thessaloniki. Accredited as a resident tour group leader four months ago. Until last week, he had a room on the second floor of the Independence. Staff report seeing him often with Andreas Roussos in the bar and restaurant. Did you ever see him in the hotel?"

Katharine put her compact back in her bag and reached for one of the photographs. "No. How much do you think he earns? That jacket he was wearing's a bit special."

"Maybe he wins a lot on the gambling tables."

"And maybe I'm the Virgin Mary." She slipped on a pair of high-heeled shoes and went to the rear door of the van. "See you later, citizen."

I watched her go, not too happy about what I'd given her to do. Or about her acceptance of the job without complaint. Then there was the danger of the situation she was going into. I wanted to go after her; Christ, I wanted to protect her. It was a long time since I'd felt that way about anyone.

I called Davie. He told me that Billy had returned to his flat and was still there. Then I called the guardswoman who'd been assigned to watch Simpson 134. She said that the nursing auxiliary was on duty in the infirmary. There was nothing to do except wait for Katharine.

I sat watching the tourists on their way to the pubs and clubs in Rose Street, then lost myself in a maze of unanswered questions. Where had the guardswoman whose body we found first been going on Saturday nights with the official authorisation I'd never managed to trace? Could there really be a connection between her, the driver Rory Baillie and the Greek who'd lost an eye? What was the significance of the different mutilations? And what about Billy? What kind of scam was he running with the Greeks?

A noise at the rear door roused me. It opened and Katharine climbed in, a broad smile across her face.

"God, that was quick."

She waved two sheets of paper at me. "Look what I've got."

I scrambled over from the front seat and grabbed them. "You took them? Now he knows someone's on to him."

"Take a closer look, Quint."

"Photocopies. You have done well. But how did you get them?"

She had pulled off her shoes and was sitting with her knees apart, completely unconcerned by the direction of my gaze. "Simple. When I didn't find him in the bar or restaurant, I went up to his room. I was going to pretend that Heriot 07 had sent me, but he didn't answer my knock. I could hear a terrible racket coming from the bathroom – he could do with some singing lessons – so I tried the door. The stupid bugger had left it open. I found the envelope in the drawer of the bedside table, ran down the corridor to the photocopier they have for businessmen on that floor, copied the pages and put them back. All before he'd finished treating his dandruff." She shot a glance at me. "No exchange of body fluids required."

I was relieved about that, though I tried not to show it. I examined the photocopies. They looked like balance sheets – there were a lot of numbers, most of them strings of zeroes.

But there were also combinations of letters and numbers which I recognised. I pulled out my notebook and found the references I'd copied from the headless photographs in Roussos's room: LR462, AT231, PH167 and so on. All thirty of them were on the pages. Some of them had numbers without many zeroes against them, others had plenty. A column on the right wasn't too hard to decipher. It showed dates. Some were in February, some in March and the last six were in the middle of April.

"Some sort of code," Katharine said.

"Brilliant."

"What does it all mean?" she asked, watching me carefully. "Do you think the letters could be initials?"

I told her about the photographs. Katharine grabbed my leg hard. "You bastard. You should have shown them to me. I could identify Adam. These are the missing people, aren't they?"

"Calm down," I said, prising her fingers from my thigh. "The photographs don't show anything except torsos and limbs. There are no scars or marks on any of them." I squeezed her hand gently. "You're right, these letters probably refer to people. But I already checked the initials of the ones who've gone missing against the references on the photos. They don't match."

"So it's a code, like I said." She was looking at me like I was shit on her stilettos.

I felt my face go scarlet. "Look, I'm sorry I didn't show you the photos. They're a bit gross and . . ."

"Fuck you, Quint," she shouted. "You're happy enough to send me off to lick the guy in the hotel's balls but you get all coy when it comes to giving me a chance to find Adam."

"All right, I'll let you see . . ."

My mobile buzzed.

It was the guardswoman in the infirmary. She was scarcely able to identify herself. "Citizen . . . it's Simpson 134 . . . I went . . . to the toilet . . . she . . ."

"Take a deep breath," I said, trying not to scream as I climbed into the front of the Transit. "Tell me what happened."

"She was attacked. I don't know if she's alive or . . ."

"Call the public order guardian. And make sure there's a guard on every exit. I'm on my way."

"What's going on?" Katharine joined me in the front.

"Either the killer's changed his timetable or we've got another one on the loose."

"I'm coming with you."

"No, you're not. I need you to stay here and watch Papazoglou, Katharine."

Again, she didn't demur. "Keep in touch."

"I will, pretty lady."

She raised an eyebrow and got out of the van.

Hamilton was getting out of his Land-Rover when I arrived at the infirmary.

"It doesn't stop," he said despondently.

"It might if your directorate did its job."

He looked ahead. "Don't worry. I'll have the guards-woman's head."

"That'll be a great help." I pushed through the knot of

auxiliaries at the main entrance and found a tear-stained girl whom the others were ignoring.

"How long were you away from her?" I asked, giving her an encouraging smile. She couldn't have been long in the guard.

"No more than five minutes, citizen. She was working in her office and I thought I could . . ."

I raised my hand. "Where is Simpson 134 now?"

The guardswoman pointed. "In intensive care. The medical guardian got her there straight away."

I wondered how Yellowlees was taking it. "Show me the scene of the crime."

She walked away quickly, avoiding the public order guardian's glare. I motioned to him to keep his distance and caught her up.

"Simpson 134 went down to one of the storerooms. That's where she was attacked." The guardswoman glanced at me, her face white. "One of the porters heard something but the attacker got out of the window before he saw him."

She led me into a gloomy corridor. At the far end I could make out a guardsman and a short figure in grey overalls.

"I'll be all right from here," I said.

The guardswoman stopped, clearly reluctant to face the guardian. There was nothing I could do for her.

"What's your name, citizen?" I said to the balding, middle-aged hospital porter.

"Gregson," he said, keeping his eyes lowered.

"Your first name."

Now he looked up, puzzled by my last question. When he saw I wasn't in uniform, he replied, "Andrew."

"Mine's Quint."

"Citizen Dalrymple," supplied Hamilton from behind me. "He's in charge of this investigation."

The porter nodded, then began to speak rapidly as if he wanted to get his story out as soon as possible. "It was like this. I'd just wheeled an old fellow into geriatrics and I was on my way back to reception. Then I met my supervisor and she says to me, 'Go down to the stores and get me a socket set so I can fix the wheel on that trolley.' When I was halfway down the corridor, I heard this noise. I couldn't place it at first. It was a bit like one of they big clocks that tick really slowly. A kind of croaking, then a long-drawn-out gasping that fair made me shiver."

"What did you do?"

Andrew Gregson wiped beads of sweat from his forehead. "I started to run." He looked down ruefully at his heavy boots. "That's what let the bastard know somebody was coming. By the time I got to the door the choking noise had stopped. Then I heard the pounding on the window. I tried the door but he'd taken the key and locked it from the inside." He shrugged. "It took me a good few shoves with my shoulder to break it down. By then he was out of the window and away."

"You nearly got him, Andrew."

"Judging by the state of her, I'm bloody glad I didn't." He took me by the arm and led me through the broken door.

The room was lit by fluorescent strips. It was full of floor-polishers and vacuum cleaners, buckets, half-dismantled trolleys and general maintenance stores. In the centre was a space between two piles of mattresses.

"She was leaning against them," the porter said hoarsely. "Her head was at a funny angle and she was still making a noise, but it was very faint." He gulped. "Her skirt was up . . . over her thighs and her . . . her stockings were ripped." He stopped and stared down at the place where Simpson 134 had been. "She was almost gone but she must have realised I was there."

"How do you know?"

Andrew Gregson's eyes met mine. "Because she spoke to me."

I felt my heart jump. "She said something to you?"

"Well, she tried. Poor woman. I couldn't stand her but no one deserves to be throttled like that."

"Andrew," I said insistently, "what did she say?"

He bit his lip then shook his head. "I couldn't really understand it. It sounded like she was saying 'sick'. Three or four times she said it, then she slumped over. And the medical guardian came rushing in and pushed me out of the way."

"Sick"? It meant as little to me as it did to him. But in terms of the body politic, it was certainly appropriate.

The fingerprint squad dusted all over the storeroom, but I wasn't surprised when they found nothing on the window and door except smudges. Obviously the nurse's assailant had worn gloves. Outside, all I found were scuff marks on the grass, suggesting socks had been worn until he got to the tarmac road. Those indications, along with the fact that a ligature had been put round Simpson 134's throat, made me quite sure it was the killer – even though it was

Tuesday, rather than the Thursday evening he'd preferred until now.

Yellowlees appeared in the shattered doorway as I was getting ready to leave. He looked around with wild eyes for a few seconds, then stared at me dully.

"She died five minutes ago," he said.

I felt as hopeless as the medical guardian sounded.

Chapter Sixteen

Yellowlees led Hamilton and me back up the corridor, the limbs hanging from his tall frame like an unstrung marionette's. "You'll want to see her, I suppose," he said in a faint voice.

Simpson 134 lay on her own in a small room. The medical guardian pulled the sheet down carefully, holding his eyes on the body. Her face was bloodless, white as chalk, in contrast to the livid line around her neck. The ligature had been twisted with enough force to break the skin. It was surprising she'd lasted long enough to say anything.

"Any idea what she was trying to say?" I asked.

Yellowlees shook his head then replaced the sheet. He stood there like a statue. If I hadn't taken his arm and led him out, I think he'd have been there for hours.

In his office he sat down heavily at his desk and watched Hamilton close the door with staring eyes.

"There are some things I have to know, guardian."

"Is this really necessary, Dalrymple?" The public order guardian seemed strangely protective of his colleague.

"It is." I gave Hamilton a glare that would have warmed Katharine's heart and turned to Yellowlees. "What exactly were Simpson 134's duties?"

"Margaret . . ." The medical guardian shivered as if saying her name was an act of betrayal. "She was one of the infirmary's most senior nurses. She assisted me in the labs, in theatre, with administration . . ." His head sank down.

"You realise it's the same killer?" I said.

Yellowlees nodded slowly. "At least he didn't have time to—" He stopped abruptly and took a few deep breaths.

"Why do you think he came after her?"

He raised his hands from the desk and watched the fingers twitch before rubbing them together. "I don't know." He didn't look at me. "Maybe she saw him and asked him what he was doing. She was fearless."

I remembered Simpson 134's angry question about the investigation when I'd been looking for Katharine; she seemed to have a personal interest in the killer's capture. Had she known something that Yellowlees didn't? Did he know that she'd met Billy Geddes that night I'd seen them in Jamaica Street Lane? I was pretty sure that she and the guardian had no secrets from each other.

"Do you know if she had any connection with the murdered guardswoman Sarah Spence? Or the driver Rory Baillie?"

He was shaking his head, eyes still lowered.

"How about the Greek Roussos who lost his eye?"

He glanced up. "Don't be ridiculous. What could she possibly have had to do with him?" His lips twisted in an odd smile.

Guardians, like all auxiliaries, are supposed to respect the truth. In my experience that doesn't stop most of them becoming accomplished liars. Normally Yellowlees was very smooth. Not now though. He'd tried to brazen things out and I wasn't buying it. I played what I thought was my ace.

"Tell me, what do the organs that have been taken from the victims have in common?" I saw Hamilton's eyes open wide.

Yellowlees suddenly seemed more in control. "That's obvious, citizen. Liver, kidney, eye. They can all be used, in part if not in whole, for transplantation."

"Which, of course, isn't practised in Enlightenment Edinburgh."

The medical guardian nodded. "It goes against the constitution's directive about the inviolability of the body." He gave a bitter smile. "Besides, the abolition of private car ownership has reduced traffic accidents to a minimal level and the supply of organ donors has dried up." He walked towards the door. "Excuse me. I have to see to Margaret."

Hamilton and I were left alone.

"You knew they were lovers," I said.

Points of red appeared on the public order guardian's cheeks. "It was something the Council was aware of, yes. I can't say I approved, but others regarded it as nothing more than a minor foible."

Others obviously included my mother. As senior guardian, she must have known what Yellowlees was up to. I wasn't sure what to make of that. I wasn't sure what to make of anything. I resorted to my usual fallback position. When in doubt, hit the archive.

It didn't get me very far. I got the supervisor to open the building for me despite the late hour and sat at a huge table with the photos from the Greek's room on my left and the files of the forty-eight missing young people on my right. I was trying to link their ID card mugshots with the headless torsos. It was a waste of time.

Well, not completely. All that naked flesh made me think of Patsy and the Prostitution Services Department. And then I remembered something. I'd seen Simpson 134 coming out of the building as I was on my way in to see Patsy. With a large briefcase. What the hell was she doing there? What was in the briefcase?

I wondered about Patsy. Could she be the connection? I'd got the impression that she was nervous about Billy's involvement in the Bearskin. But maybe she'd actually been nervous about my interest. Maybe she was in business with Billy.

And that was where I got stuck. I already had the Council's golden boy under surveillance. It would be a struggle for Davie, Katharine and me to keep a trace on Patsy too. Unless I went to the Council and told them about my suspicions. Which I didn't want to do. Some individual or individuals on the Council were in this up to their necks. I needed conclusive evidence if I wasn't to become the forty-ninth missing person. Or fiftieth including my father.

So I went back to thinking about the killer's modus operandi – it was *like* the ENT Man's, but not exactly the same. That was significant, I knew it was. Everything came back to the ENT Man, but I just couldn't work out how. This time even the archive failed me.

It was after one when I got to the Transit. Katharine told

me the Greek had stayed put all evening so I spoke to the hotel's senior auxiliary and asked him to call me if Billy's contact moved that night. Then Katharine and I went back to my place.

I should have got as much sleep as possible before relieving Davie outside Billy's flat, but things didn't work out that way. Afterwards we lay sprawled on my bed and Katharine dropped off. Sleep wouldn't come to me though. I was thinking about my father, still unaccounted for. Surely there wasn't any link between his disappearance and the killer's latest strike? I was getting nowhere. I got up and tiptoed out of the bedroom, overcome by an irresistible urge to listen to the blues. But even looking through my tapes didn't provide any escape. I came across my Leadbelly recordings and thought of the convict I'd promised them to. There I was, back at the ENT Man.

And suddenly my heart took off like one of the intercontinental ballistic missiles the last UK government had threatened to launch at its fellow European Union states. The Ear, Nose and Throat Man. Two things that Leadbelly said about him came back to me: that the butcher had mentioned a younger brother and that he had never showed much interest in the gang's music. It was the second that struck me most. I remembered how the ENT Man looked as I came up behind him in the gardens, the way he held his head. Cocked to one side, like he was straining to hear. Christ, he cut his victims' ears off; maybe the bastard had something wrong with his hearing. In which case there would be records. I knew exactly where to look.

Katharine woke as I was pulling my clothes on.

"Stay here and keep your mobile on," I said. "It's going to be a busy day."

The Council had concentrated all the city's facilities for the treatment of the deaf in what had once been a school for children with hearing problems. I drove past the Haymarket and into the total darkness outside the central area. The great grey turreted building lay beyond an expanse of lawn but I had to use my memory to find it. The place was as lost in the mist as a fairy castle. Or a vampire's. I stopped the Transit in a shower of gravel outside the main entrance.

A startled guardsman appeared at the door. "It's three in the morning, citizen. What the . . . ?"

I stuck my authorisation into his face. "The records room. Take me there."

He hesitated, glancing at the mobile phone on the table beside him.

"Now, guardsman!" I shouted. "Call your commander afterwards."

"Yes, citizen." He set off down the corridor at speed, his nailed boots echoing around like the dying fall of shotgun pellets fired out of range. At last, deep in the guts of the building, he skidded to a stop outside a heavy door.

"Let me in and lock the door after me," I ordered. I didn't fancy being disturbed by anyone the guard commander might advise of my presence.

Inside there was the familiar archive smell: dry paper and cardboard, dust in places where the cleaner's broom never reaches and the still-acrid tang of sweat from the poor sods who spend their lives shuffling files. I'd already decided where I was going to start. I estimated that the ENT Man was in his mid-thirties when he died. So he could have been treated from the early 1980s, but there wasn't time to trawl through that many files. There was a fair chance that when he was an adult he deliberately kept himself out of the Enlightenment's bureaucracy so I went for the 1990s. It took me fifty-eight minutes to nail him. The photograph was of a fourteen-year-old boy but I recognised the misshapen features and empty eyes immediately.

His name was Stewart Duncan Dunbar. Knowing it suddenly made him seem even more real than when I saw him in the flesh – like a vengeful ghost made corporeal, an evil spirit made human. I skimmed through the details, my fingers catching on the edges of the documents. Born 6.7.80, admitted to the school for the deaf 7.1.94, expelled 24.6.95. Surprise, surprise – he'd been a seriously disruptive pupil and was eventually kicked out for trying to rape a girl in the toilets. What was interesting in a worrying way was the nature of his deafness. Severe damage to the tympanic membrane caused by the insertion of pointed objects. I hazarded a guess that he'd injured himself in pursuit of some desperate sexual thrill. The last tests performed on him showed that he retained some vestigial hearing and that he'd made progress with lip-reading. Good enough progress to conceal his condition from the others in the Howlin' Wolf gang. And from me. Not that I had much of a conversation with the animal.

Then I found a couple of other things, one I'd been hoping for and another which made me shiver. The first was that he had a brother, one Gordon Oliver Dunbar – Leadbelly was right about that. The second was that their family address had been 18 Russell Place. That was less than a hundred yards away from my father's retirement home.

In the castle, the guardsman on watch leaped to his feet as I pushed open the door to Hamilton's outer office.

"You can't go in there, citizen. The guardian's . . ."

I pushed past him and turned the lights on.

Hamilton sat up on the couch, a blanket slipping down to reveal pale skin and a surprisingly grubby standard-issue singlet. "What the hell . . ."

"Sorry to disturb your slumbers. I need to use your computer."

"Why?" He started buttoning his shirt quickly.

"I've found out the ENT Man's identity." I went round to the screen and keyboard behind his desk.

"You've what?" His mouth gaped like an idiot's.

"Don't get too excited. That doesn't mean he's the killer."

Hamilton sat down and reached for his brogues. "Well, don't ask me how the bloody thing works. I always get my assistants to handle it."

I started to tap away. "Don't worry. I think I can manage." Only guardians and senior auxiliaries are provided with computers; the Council limits the number of machines ostensibly because of the shortage of electricity but in reality to control the flow of information. "I need your entry code."

"Oh." The guardian looked sheepish. "It's 'Colonel'."

"Uh-huh." I entered it. "Right, we're into the main archive. Let's go to the index of citizens' names."

"What are you after?" Hamilton was leaning over my shoulder.

"The ENT Man's brother. How much do you want to bet that he's an auxiliary?"

"Are you still obsessed by that idea? Anyway, what makes you so sure the ENT Man himself's not the killer?"

I was tempted to come clean but a picture of Leadbelly came to me, not for the first time that night. I didn't want to join him carting stones on bomb sites and sleeping in a cell on Cramond Island. Hamilton would have done me, accident or not; after all, I'd kept quiet about it for five years.

"Here we are. Gordon Oliver Dunbar. Barracks number Scott 391." I looked round at the guardian. "Just as well you didn't put your shirt on it. Or your singlet."

"I don't understand the point of all this. What's this auxiliary supposed to have done?"

"He might well be the butcher we're looking for." I went back into the main archive and called up details on Scott 391.

Hamilton was slow but he got there in the end. "How did you find this name?"

I felt his breath on the back of my neck. "That doesn't matter just now. It—" I broke off as words came up on the screen.

"'No reference found'," Hamilton read. He gave a dry laugh.

"Shit! That can't be right." I tried again, hoping I'd made an input error. Same response. I stood up in frustration, jamming the back of the chair into the guardian's midriff. I went over to the window without apologising. A few pinpoints of light were dotted about the city centre. Dawn was still an hour away and the outer reaches were plunged into a darkness denser than in any Edgar Allan Poe tomb. That was it. I rushed back to the keyboard.

"The main archive only has files on the living." I called up the "Auxiliaries – Deceased" archive and typed in the barracks number. "This has got to be it." The cursor stayed where it was as the computer searched. "Come on, you bastard, come on." I smelled Hamilton's sour breath. Even if Scott 391 was dead, he might still be the connection I needed.

Then the cursor jumped and the file came up.

"Scott 391," I read. "Date of birth 28.5.85, registered date of death 5.3.2020."

"He died over three weeks ago," said the guardian.

"Before the first murder," I added, not giving him the satisfaction of pointing that out.

"Exactly. Now will you tell me exactly what this is all about?"

"Cause of death," I continued. "Bullet wound to head during operations against scavengers near Soutra border post." Everything came back to Soutra, I thought, seeing Caro's body at the farm for a second.

"Oh yes, I remember the report about that," said Hamilton. "Bloody dissidents. They got away as well."

I motioned to him to be quiet. I needed to work out what to do. Scott Barracks where the dead auxiliary had been based is in Goldenacre and its territory includes both my father's and the ENT Man's family home. I remembered the guard vehicle Hector was seen walking towards. Was there a connection? Then there was Patsy. What was I going to do about her? What could she have to do with all of this?

"Where are you going, Dalrymple?" Hamilton asked uneasily as I headed for the door.

"I'll let you know as soon as I make my mind up."

It was six in the morning. I didn't think Billy Geddes was likely to make an early start, so I called Davie and told him to meet me at my flat.

He arrived looking like he'd been dragged through a bush backwards. "Where have you been all night?" he demanded. "I couldn't get through on your mobile."

"Shit." I pulled it out of my pocket. "I turned it off about three. I didn't want any interruptions." I turned it on again.

"Lucky for you that Heriot 07 didn't do anything naughty." Davie glanced at Katharine. She'd emerged from the bedroom with her hair sticking up like a bomb had gone off under it. "Oh aye." He looked at me knowingly.

"I've been out all night, guardsman."

"Oh aye." He rubbed his eyes with muddy fingers. "Any chance of me getting some sleep?"

"Of course." I gave him a tight smile. "When the investigation's over."

"She looks like she's been in bed all night," he complained.

Katharine was ignoring him. "Have you made some kind of breakthrough?" she said to me.

"Sort of." I wasn't going to tell them about the ENT Man, so I was vague about his brother and concentrated on the other angles. "There might be a connection between Billy Geddes, Patsy Cameron and the medical guardian."

"Patsy Cameron in Prostitution Services?" Katharine asked, her eyes locked on me.

I nodded. "I'm pretty sure the nursing auxiliary who died last night was involved." I filled Davie in about events in the infirmary.

"Simpson 134 and the medical guardian were more than just good friends," he said.

"You know about that?"

"Christ, everyone in the guard knows about that. So you reckon they were doing more than just screwing?"

I shrugged. "We need evidence. I'd like to keep an eye on Yellowlees, but right now I've got other priorities. Davie, you'll have to watch Geddes again. Katharine, can you . . ."

"Tail Patsy Cameron?" She didn't look like she was too bothered by the prospect.

"You'll need a less conspicuous disguise, I think. Make sure she doesn't spot you."

Katharine nodded impatiently. "I think I can manage that, Quint."

"What about you?" Davie put in. "What are these other priorities?"

"I'm going down to Scott Barracks to do some digging."

"In the gardens? Apparently if you spit on your hands . . ."

I didn't respond to that. It had just struck me that tomorrow was Thursday. The killer was probably getting ready for another attack. Then again, today was April Fools' Day. I wondered how much of a sense of humour the butcher had.

I stood on Goldenacre looking up at the façade of the stand. I had a dim memory of watching a rugby match with my father when I was a small boy: a freezing winter's afternoon high above the pitch, being buffeted by the wind. I couldn't remember anything of the match itself. It probably involved some of Hector's students. He used to follow the rugby before the Enlightenment gave him other things to think about.

Scott Barracks is a custom-built block beyond the rugby field. It stands between the once affluent area of Goldenacre and the outskirts of Leith, where civil unrest was endemic in the first ten years of the Enlightenment. The lack of large buildings in the vicinity forced the planners to erect a dreary three-storey block of mess rooms and sleeping quarters. Auxiliaries from the barracks always had a reputation for being headbangers. I wished Davie was with me.

I flashed my authorisation and went into the entrance hall. The place had the usual institutional smell, the drab paint and scuffed woodwork of all barracks – but there was something else to the atmosphere. The guardsmen and women on duty seemed strangely depressed. There was none of the enthusiastic officiousness encouraged by the Council. I was directed to the commander's office by a young woman who looked like she hadn't slept for a week. I knocked and went in without waiting for a reply.

Scott 01 raised his head slowly and looked at me without blinking. He was hollow-eyed and prematurely bald. He couldn't have been much over thirty and even before he said anything I could see that he was having a hard time holding the job down. His beard was flecked with grey and it was probably a long time since he last smiled.

"Dalrymple," I said, showing him my authorisation. If he knew about me, he wasn't showing it.

"What can I do for you, citizen?" His voice was unusually high-pitched, reedy as a shepherd's pipe on a distant hillside.

"I need immediate access to your records room."

That got a flicker from his eyelashes. "If you need a file, I can have it brought to you here, citizen."

And then you can see which one I want, I thought. "No, thanks. I want you to escort me to the archive personally and I want no one else to know I'm in there."

"Can I see your authorisation again?" he asked.

I'd run out of time. "No, Scott 01. If you've got a problem, call the public order guardian." I beat his fingers to the phone. "After you've taken me."

"Very well." The commander closed the file he'd been working on and stood up.

I wondered if he'd move any faster if I shouted "Fire". Probably not. Auxiliaries are trained to keep a hold of themselves. Or at least to look like they're keeping a hold of themselves.

A group of guardswomen passed us in the corridor. They lowered their voices and their faces when they saw the commander and me. The first two were nondescript but the third wasn't the kind you look away from. I recognised her immediately. It was Mary, Queen of Scots. She gave me a quick glance and was gone. I didn't catch her barracks number.

I waited impatiently as Scott 01 unlocked the records room. In accordance with security regulations its door was steel plated and equipped with three separate locks. In the early years of the Enlightenment there had been frequent break-ins by relatives trying to discover the whereabouts of auxiliaries after they'd been separated from their families. More recently the Education Directorate has been working hard to explain the need, as the Council sees it, for the city's servants to be anonymous and breaches in security have fallen away.

The commander stood back at last and let me into the windowless room. Then I waited till he'd locked me in. No doubt he'd be haring back to his office to call Hamilton.

Now for the ENT Man's brother. I pulled Scott 391's file, relieved to find that the thick maroon folder hadn't yet been sent to the central archive. The barracks are reluctant to hand over information on their people, even to other auxiliaries. So I sat down and learned all about the dead guardsman.

Or rather, tried to fill in the gaps. Auxiliaries have to write a Personal Evaluation at the start of the training programme. Scott 391's was remarkable because of the complete lack of reference to his older brother. He went on at some length about his parents, who were lawyers and strong supporters of the Enlightenment; he described his feelings about several schoolfriends and filled three pages about a girlfriend; he even wrote about the family house in Trinity and what he got up to as a kid in the area. But about his brother Stewart, not a word.

I went on through the file, tracing the guardsman's life through school, where he was particularly good at biology, to tours of duty on the border after he'd finished auxiliary training, to community service in Leith. He seemed like a conscientious enough guy, without much imagination. He fitted in well. It seemed pretty clear that he'd had no contact at all with his brother since the beginning of the Enlightenment, unless he'd been very clever about it. Auxiliaries get very little free time and they have to ask permission to move outside barracks areas – which, of course, would be recorded in the file. Gordon Oliver Dunbar spent most of his time off pumping iron in the barracks gym or writing seriously dull papers on Plato for the debating society. Then I got to the section about his sexual activities.

I felt a bit guilty. I always do when I go through other people's files. The problem is, I like it. I get a kind of vicarious pleasure from witnessing other lives, the successes and failures, the dreams and unachieved ambitions. No doubt voyeurs get the same rush.

My subject was definitely hetero. All his sessions were spent with female auxiliaries. I took a note of the numbers for the last couple of years, as well as those of his friends – not that they're described as such in Enlightenment-speak. His "close colleagues" amounted to eighteen barracks numbers. Either he was a liar or he was distinctly popular. It would take hours to go through all their files and, anyway, I wasn't sure what I was looking for. The poor sod had died before the first murder.

I went on to the end of Scott 391's file, turning the pages with rapidly decreasing interest. Then I got to the end and sat up like I'd been jabbed with a picador's lance. I tore out the memo that had been stapled in last and hammered on the door for it to be opened.

Scott Barracks is less than two hundred yards from the

crematorium that serves the northern half of the city. The night the coffin containing the ENT Man's brother was delivered, something very unusual had happened there.

Chapter Seventeen

I parked the Transit outside the low brick building. The sign said that services, secular of course, were held only in the afternoons. Judging by the state of the place, I reckoned that the mornings were devoted to maintenance and cleaning. The Council had obviously shied away from rebuilding the dilapidated facility.

A thin, balding man with yellowish skin appeared on the steps. He rubbed his hands nervously and came over to the van. "Are you wanting to work in the gardens?" he asked, peering at the Parks Department sticker. "Only, they usually come on a Monday."

I jumped down and showed him my "ask no questions". His lack of beard and uniform showed he wasn't an auxiliary so there was no need to let him know my identity.

"Em, I hope there's no dissatisfaction with my work," the official said warily. "I've always followed the Council's instructions to the letter."

I shook my head. "There have been no complaints. You are . . . ?"

"Douglas Haigh," he said, thumbs on the seams of his worn grey trousers and the upper part of his body bending forward like a heron following a fish. "Haigh with 'g-h'," he added. "I've been here for thirty years. How may I help you?"

"I need to see your records, citizen." I stepped away from him and into the building. I didn't fancy his cadaverous appearance much. It looked like devotion to his work had kept him in a job that would normally be an auxiliary's.

"My records? Certainly." Haigh overtook me and headed down the corridor with long strides. "What precisely do you want to know?" He had started rubbing his hands together again.

"You sent a memo to Scott Barracks on 8 March. It was a Sunday . . ."

"I work seven days a week," he put in.

"What a surprise," I said under my breath, pulling the sheet of paper from my pocket. " 'I wish to point out that Scott 477, the sentry on duty on the night of 7–8.3.2020, was guilty of several serious breaches of procedure. One, he . . .' "

"My word, yes. I remember that night very clearly." He led me into a small office set back from the passageway that was echoing from our footsteps.

"You were here during the night?" That sounded promising.

Haigh sat down in an ancient chair that he had bound together with plastic-covered wire and motioned me to the other even more rickety seat. "Indeed I was." He gave a brief, thin-lipped smile. "I don't like the flat I was assigned. Saturday nights are quiet here. There are usually no deliveries. But there was one that night." The joints of his fingers cracked. "And a very curious one it was too."

I leaned forward. "Why was that?"

"Well, first of all, the documentation was incomplete. If I hadn't happened to be here when the delivery was made, I would have had a terrible job chasing up the missing information."

"What exactly was missing, citizen?"

Haigh cleared his throat like a professor about to start a lecture. "The Consignment of Human Remains form must show the barracks numbers of the auxiliary who approves release from the hospital or wherever the death was registered. It must also show the number of the guardsman or woman who accompanies the coffin and the name of the civilian driver." He spread his arms dramatically. "In this case, none of them was filled in."

I suddenly realised that the old ghoul was about to give me something precious. That was what prevented me from grabbing the desiccated bureaucrat by the throat to speed things up.

Haigh turned quickly to the grey metal cabinets behind him and produced a folder. He must have seen the look on my face.

"I took down the guardswoman's and the driver's details," he said proudly. "And I even succeeded in obtaining the nursing auxiliary's number."

I snatched the file from him. The top page was a mass of boxes and numbers, some filled in, others ticked or crossed out. It was what I found at the bottom that made me whistle. The dead guardsman had been logged out of the infirmary by Yellowlees's girlfriend, Simpson 134. The guardswoman accompanying the coffin was Sarah Spence, the murder victim we found first. After that, I wasn't too surprised to see Rory Baillie's name in the box marked "Driver". But what the hell did it all mean?

"Anyway," Haigh continued, "after the coffin was brought in, I went off home, thinking that was enough disorder for one night."

The memo I'd taken from the barracks was making sense now. "And when you came back in the morning, you found all the screws on the coffin loose and the documents strewn across the floor."

"Quite so." He shook his head. "The sentry must have had a look at the body. After all, he was in the same barracks." Now he was rubbing his hands like Lady Macbeth on speed. "I wonder if that's what drove him to kill himself."

"What?" I looked up in astonishment. "The sentry committed suicide?"

Haigh's face turned even paler. "Oh, I . . . I assumed you knew about that. I . . . I didn't mean to . . ."

The constitution is firm about suicide. People who kill themselves become non-citizens without any memorial. No one, not even family and friends, is allowed to talk about them. The rules are even stricter when it comes to auxiliaries. No wonder Haigh was worried.

"I'm s . . . sorry," he stuttered. "I heard it from one of the sentries last week. I . . . promise I won't . . ."

I raised my hand. "It's all right, citizen. You've been a great help." As I left his office I saw a self-satisfied smile creep across the parchment of his face.

*   *   *

The commander of Scott Barracks looked up wearily when I burst back into his office.

"You had a suicide here recently," I said.

That seemed to bring him even nearer to the end of his tether. "Scott 477," he said in a faint voice. "It was a great shock. The barracks hasn't been the same since."

Now I understood the atmosphere of the place. "When did it happen?"

"A week ago today – 25 March."

I checked the barracks number in my notebook. "Scott 477 was a 'close colleague' of Scott 391, the guardsman who was killed on the border."

The commander nodded. "He was. And he was very down about his death. But . . . but he wasn't suicidal. I spoke to him at some length after I received the memo from the crematorium manager." He shook his head slowly. "There was something else. Something happened afterwards."

I thought about the date: 25 March. The news of Rory Baillie's murder had been made public by then. Could there be a connection? Something else struck me.

"How did Scott 477 commit suicide?"

There was a flash of hostility at my question in the commander's eyes. "He hanged himself, if you must know. In the storeroom."

I nodded. "I'll need to see his file. You can have it brought to me here."

Before it arrived, my mobile buzzed.

"It's Davie, Quint. Where are you? Billy Geddes has just left the Finance Directorate. He's heading down the Mound on foot."

"Keep on his tail. He can't be going far if he's walking."

"Quint, he looks pretty bloody keen. I smell big money. Are you coming?"

Did the former king have a predilection for feminine sanitary goods?

Davie, dressed as a labourer, was standing on the concrete path above the racetrack at the west end of Princes Street Gardens. Below, preparations were under way for the twelve o'clock race. Grooms were parading horses around the enclosure and large crowds of tourists were clustered around the Finance Directorate's betting booths.

"Where's our man?" I asked as I joined him.

Davie pointed to one of the refreshment stalls. There were fewer people there in the minutes leading up to the off. Billy was very conspicuous, the only man wearing a suit and an open camel-hair coat. He checked the time and looked around anxiously.

"He's waiting for someone," Davie said.

"You'll make an investigator yet."

"Here we go. Who's this then?"

I recognised the dark-haired figure in the tan leather jacket immediately. It was Papazoglou, looking even more shifty than he had in the museum. One hand was stuffed into his pocket and the other held a briefcase that he seemed to be very attached to – he kept it tight against his leg. The two of them met and exchanged a few words. Then the Greek handed over the briefcase.

"What now?" asked Davie.

They separated, Papazoglou heading towards the Mound

and Billy to the right. Suddenly Billy stopped, turned back as if he'd forgotten something – and saw me. He stood stock still for a few seconds, his face inscrutable, then kept going in his original direction.

"Fucking hell. Call the guard on the exit over there and get the gate locked. I think it's time to pull the plug on Heriot 07's deals."

Davie spoke rapidly into his mobile then signed off. "Done."

The voice of the race announcer boomed out from speakers hung on trees and lampposts. There was a rush of bodies towards the fence alongside the track. Billy was caught in the crowd.

"Christ, we'll lose him," said Davie.

"You cover the left." I ran down the slope.

"I can't stand horse-racing," he shouted as he followed me.

The six horses were in the stalls by the time I reached the concourse in front of the track. The spectators fell silent and the chimes of the clocks in the vicinity started to ring out.

Then I caught sight of Billy. He was pushing his way along the white rail, oblivious to the abuse from tourists he was banging into. The tolling of the bells seemed to rise to a crescendo and I realised what he was going to do.

"No, Billy, no!" Then I flinched as the gates of the stalls crashed open.

Billy had ducked under the fence and started to run across the track. He must have thought he could reach the upper exit. He didn't stand a chance. In an instant the horses were on him. Spectators screamed as his body was bundled up like a ball of rags and kicked around the turf by a blur of hooves.

"No, Billy, for fuck's sake, no," I heard myself repeating. People got out of the way as they turned away from the track. The announcer was keeping quiet and all that could be heard now was the pounding of hooves further down the gardens as the jockeys tried to rein in their mounts.

The first thing I came to on the closely cut grass was the briefcase Billy had received from the Greek. It had been knocked open but none of the banknotes from the large number of wads in it had slipped out. The crowd hadn't even noticed the money. I closed the case and left it where it was, then ran over to where Billy lay. He was still crumpled in a ball, only his left arm extended. The forearm was bent back from the elbow at an angle that was all wrong. His face was pressed into the ground, the single eye that was visible half open and glazed.

Kneeling down beside him, I felt for a pulse. "Why, Billy?" I mumbled. "Why? Couldn't you see it was hopeless?" I knew he couldn't hear me.

Davie ran up. "They've got his contact at the Mound gate." He bent down. "Is he dead?"

I looked up at him in amazement. "No, he isn't. There's a pulse, would you believe?" I pulled off my jacket and laid it over the battered body.

"There's an ambulance on its way."

I stood up slowly. "They'd better be quick."

"Why did he make a break? There wasn't anywhere for him to go."

"I don't know. Panic, the survival instinct." I went back

to the briefcase. "One thing's for sure. There's a hell of a lot of money involved."

The ambulance drew up, siren blaring. There was a guard vehicle behind it. Hamilton jumped down and ducked under the fence.

"What happened here?" he asked, peering at Heriot 07.

"The deputy finance guardian may well have made his last transaction," I said slowly.

The medics lifted Billy carefully on to a stretcher and moved him towards their vehicle.

Hamilton was glaring at me. "Have you had Heriot 07 under surveillance?"

I turned away. "He was the long shot," I said over my shoulder. "Pick up the money, guardian. It belongs to the city."

I watched the ambulance drive away.

"This is all foreign currency," Hamilton said. "Where did it come from?"

"Heriot 07's been selling the city's assets," I said. "Come on. Let's see what the medical guardian thinks. I'm sure he'll be keen to treat Billy personally."

Robert Yellowlees finished drying his hands at the basin in his office and turned to face us.

"I've never seen anything like it," he said, shaking his head. "Most of his ribs are broken, one lung is punctured, his left elbow is shattered, his skull's cracked in two places – and he's still alive."

I wondered how important that was to Yellowlees. "How long will he be unconscious?"

The medical guardian shrugged. "Who knows? The brain scan showed remarkably little damage. He may well regain consciousness soon." He didn't sound very optimistic. "You want to question him, I suppose."

Bloody right I do, I said to myself.

"He hasn't got some connection with the murderer, has he?" Yellowlees narrowed his eyes. "With the bastard who killed Margaret?"

I watched him as he walked round his desk. His normally steady surgeon's hands were trembling. Again I wondered what he knew about Billy's activities.

"We'll need to keep a close guard on Heriot 07," I said, turning to Hamilton. "Davie – I mean Hume 253 – will supervise. He'll need a couple of experienced squads."

"I'll see to it." Hamilton came up to me. "Still nothing on your father, I'm afraid." He went out.

Before I could say what I wanted to Yellowlees, my mobile went off. I moved away when I heard Katharine's voice. "I'm in conference," I said.

"Got you. I'll do the talking. I can't speak for long anyway. Patsy Cameron's on the move. On foot. I'll shadow her."

I looked round at the medical guardian. He was watching me, making no attempt to disguise his interest. "Are you sure you can handle it? The subject may have some unpleasant friends."

"I'll be all right. Don't call me in case I'm close to her."

"Don't take any independent action," I said, realising before I'd finished that she'd rung off.

"What was that all about?" Yellowlees asked.

I ignored the question. "I need your help, guardian," I said, walking up to the desk. "There's a medical file I want." His face remained impassive. "An auxiliary who was killed on the border a few weeks ago. Scott 391." Unless the file had been doctored, it might give me an idea of what the sentry saw when he opened the coffin in the crematorium.

Yellowlees was finding the papers on his desk a lot more interesting than my face. Finally he raised his eyes. "I remember the case," he said hoarsely. "Bullet wound to the head."

I heard the door open behind me. It was Hamilton.

Yellowlees looked both relieved and anxious. "Lewis was asking me about it this morning." His gaze dropped again. "Since Margaret . . . died, everything's fallen apart here." He shook his head at me helplessly. "I can't locate the file."

He was treating my mother so I gave him one last opportunity to come clean. It was obvious that the file contained something that he didn't want me to know. "Are you quite sure about that, guardian? There could be serious consequences."

No reaction. Well, I tried. The medical guardian would have to take his chances. I filled them in on what I found out at the crematorium. "It looks like the murderer is working his way through a list of victims. They all had some connection with the dead guardsman except the Greek in the Indie – and I suspect the killer must have seen him with one of the others."

"But what's the motive?" asked Hamilton. "If he's got a list, he must have a reason for attacking these people."

"I'm not clear about that yet." I glanced at Yellowlees. "But I can hazard a guess at who's next on the list."

I left them to think about that. If the medical guardian wouldn't talk, maybe Billy's Greek contact would.

Chapter Eighteen

Interrogating Nikos Papazoglou turned out to be as productive as asking an auxiliary to sing "God Save the King". The Greek stared sullenly at the wall in the cell, mumbling over and over again, "I want to call the consulate," in heavily accented English. Eventually I lost my cool.

"All right," I shouted. "I'll let you talk to your people." I slapped down in front of him the copies Katharine had taken of the pages Billy passed him in the museum. "After you tell me what this is all about and why you gave Heriot 07 that case with two hundred and seventy-five million drachmae."

When he saw the papers, the young man gave an involuntary start and his eyes opened wide. "How did you—?" He broke off and went back to stonewalling. "I don't know what you're talking about, mister."

I leaned over and glared at his sallow face. "You know what happened to Andreas Roussos, don't you?" I said, my voice not much more than a whisper. "You know that someone took his eye out? Without an anaesthetic. As I see it, you've got two choices. Either you tell me what these pages mean and I let you out of here in five minutes . . ." I paused and moved in closer to him. "Or I print in the newspaper that you had links with Roussos and the killer comes after you." I sat back and smiled. "I wonder which organ he'll go for this time."

Papazoglou's chin quivered and his tongue appeared between dry lips. Then he raised his hand so quickly that the guardsman at the door jumped forward with his truncheon raised.

"Okay, okay," the Greek jabbered, cowering. "You guarantee I face no charges?"

"Sure," I lied.

He raised his hand very slowly, eyes fixed on the auxiliary, and wiped the sweat from his forehead. "All right. These papers are—"

There was a clang as the bolt was drawn back and the door pulled open. Hamilton came in, followed by a man with a heavy moustache who I'd been hoping I wouldn't see that day.

"I'm sorry, Dalrymple. Mr Palamas from the Greek consulate insisted on being brought down."

The Greek I'd seen on the Calton Hill with Billy ignored me, standing behind Papazoglou and addressing his lecture to the public order guardian.

"Under Edinburgh law, the prisoner is entitled to have a representative of his country present at all interviews. I am concerned that we were not officially informed that this" – he looked at me like I was an Untouchable – "this interrogation was taking place."

Hamilton opened his arms in a gesture of hopelessness. "I apologise on behalf of the Council for this lapse."

I stared at him in disgust, my arms folded tightly to stop myself offering violence to a guardian.

Palamas nodded brusquely. "What are the charges, please?"

Hamilton glanced at me.

I shrugged; now that Palamas was pulling strings, Papazoglou would clam up. There was no point in holding him.

"Em, no charges will be pressed," the guardian said lamely. "Guardsman, escort these gentlemen to the esplanade."

I watched as Papazoglou left, relief etched into his face like acid. "Couldn't you have stalled him for a bit longer? I almost got what I wanted."

Hamilton was examining his feet. "He got on to the deputy senior guardian. What could we do? You know how important Greek business is to the city."

I wished I knew a lot more about that particular matter. I could either tell Hamilton that I'd found out about the missing young people and that I suspected Patsy Cameron of being involved in some horrendous scam with Billy, or I could hit Billy's flat. The latter would be much less hassle.

"How did Palamas know we had Papazoglou?" I asked on my way out.

"Every Greek at the race meeting saw him being arrested by the gate." Hamilton sighed. "At the rate you're going, there won't be any tourist trade left in the city."

I parked the Transit outside Billy's flat and got the guardswoman who'd been sent down after he was injured to let me in. The hallway was cool and the smell of floor polish filled my nostrils as I ran up the marble staircase.

Inside the flat there was dead silence. I stood motionless for a few moments, breathing in deeply and listening. I suddenly had a premonition that someone was about to appear, someone who didn't care too much about my health. I could have called the sentry up but instead I ran from room to room like a child certain that a monster was lurking. There was no one, of course. I'd been living on my nerves too much recently. Tearing the place apart would be good therapy.

For a senior auxiliary sworn to live according to the Council's ascetic standards, Billy had accumulated an amazing collection of luxury goods. The wardrobes in his bedroom were stuffed with Italian suits and shoes, silk shirts and ties, a couple of leather jackets – even a fur coat which the label showed to have originated from independent Siberia. Billy must have made a business trip there. It wasn't the greed that pissed me off, it was the waste. He could get away with dressing up in flash suits, but not even Billy would venture out wearing a fur coat in Edinburgh. Mind you, in winter most buildings are cold enough to warrant one.

The kitchen was insanely overstocked. There was a full range of French saucepans that would have been worth a small fortune in that country before the Moslem fundamentalists reduced it to a collection of bankrupt city-states. The cupboards were full of tinned foods that are never available in the city's shops: tomatoes, olives, kidney beans, stuffed vine leaves. I even found the components of a pasta machine. I can't remember the last time I ate spaghetti.

After an hour I began to run out of steam. The only documents I'd found were from standard Finance Directorate files and there was no sign of any foreign exchange. I began to suspect that Billy had organised a hiding-place. I squatted down on the carpet in the middle of the sitting room and looked dispiritedly at the heap of his personal possessions that I'd piled up.

"Shit, Billy," I muttered. "What the hell have you done with it all?" Pins and needles started to attack my feet. I got up and went over to the table where he kept the first edition of Hume's treatise. The first creak of the uneven floorboards made no impression on me. Then I shifted my weight to the other foot and the noise came again, this time louder. Eureka.

I ran to the wall. Although the carpet looked like it had been secured with tacks, it came up easily when I stuck my fingers between it and the skirting board. I quickly moved the furniture aside – a couple of armchairs, a coffee table, an escritoire and a Georgian display cabinet that almost broke my back – and rolled up the heavy floor covering. Where the small table stood, there was a two-foot square cut in the underlay. I lifted it and the boards beneath it, thinking how Billy must have been laughing to himself at the idea of me innocently standing there when he showed me the book. And struck gold. Literally.

The hole contained six bars of that metal, over twenty thousand US dollars and so many wads of Greek drachmae that I didn't waste time counting them. There was also a thick folder of statements from a bank in Berne, a file of papers similar to the one Billy had passed to Papazoglou and, right at the bottom, the confirmation I needed to connect the deputy finance guardian both to Yellowlees and to Patsy Cameron. What was Billy doing with a copy of a research report entitled "Towards the Effective Treatment of Systemic Lupus Erythematosus"? Was he bankrolling the medical guardian's research? Or blackmailing him, perhaps?

And what was he doing with Prostitution Service Department appraisals of ten male and female citizens? Their names had been blacked out and replaced with letter and number references which tallied with ten of those on the headless photographs in Roussos's hotel room. The appraisals included physical and mental profiles and aptitude ratings for specific sexual services. They were all initialled PC. Things were falling into place at last.

My mobile buzzed. I had a job finding it under the carpet at the edge of the room.

"Quint, Davie. Subject is leaving the infirmary. Do I follow?"

"Bloody right you do." I put Davie in charge of Billy's security so that he could also keep track of Yellowlees. "What about Heriot 07? Has he come round yet?"

"Negative. I've got three guards in his room and another half-dozen in the corridor outside. That do you?"

"Yes. Let me know where the subject's headed. And Davie?"

"Aye?"

"Don't lose him. The killer's probably after him."

"Christ."

"Exactly." I signed off and looked down at the money and documents around the hole in the floor. Suddenly I had a flash of the gaping wounds the murderer had cut in the bodies of his victims. How did what he was doing fit in with Yellowlees and the ENT Man's brother? How did it fit in with Billy and Patsy? There was something missing from the equation and I couldn't work out what it was.

I ran down the stairs, this time impervious to the smell of polish. Something much ranker had filled my nostrils in Billy's flat and I was sure it was about to get worse.

The cloud had thickened over the city and it began to drizzle as I drove towards the castle. I reckoned it was time to come clean with Hamilton. There was too much going on for me to handle without more back-up. Even if there were some Council members who were bent, it wasn't likely that Hamilton was one of them.

I didn't get the chance to find out. He came on the mobile when I was halfway up the Mound.

"Dalrymple, that female citizen you've got working for you . . ."

"Katharine Kirkwood?" I felt my stomach somersault. "What's happened to her?"

"A tourist found her lying unconscious in Reid's Close off the Canongate."

"Where is she now?"

"She's still there. An ambulance is on its way."

I accelerated out of the corner at the Finance Directorate and drove down towards the ruins of Holyrood Palace. I left the Transit on the pavement behind the ambulance. A guardsman stepped forward, then stopped when he saw my authorisation. A couple of his colleagues were talking to a male tourist who looked shocked. I ran into the narrow close. The high walls were dark grey, the flagstones wet from the drizzle. Round a corner I found the medics. They were bent over a figure in a light blue raincoat. A woollen hat lay on the ground between me and them.

I went closer. "How is she?"

The more senior of the two male medics turned to me. "Coming round. She took a heavy blow to the back of the head."

"Quint?" Katharine's voice was weak. "Is that you, Quint?"

"What happened?"

"She . . . someone was behind me suddenly . . . hit me . . . I didn't see . . ."

The medic stood up. "She should be X-rayed. She's probably concussed."

I knelt down and took her hand. Her eyes seemed unfocused. "Katharine, you'd better go to the infirmary. They think . . ."

"No!" she said, her voice suddenly back to normal. "I'm staying with you. I was on to something. She must have seen me . . ."

I looked round helplessly at the medics. "Keep an eye on her for a moment."

I went back down the close and found Hamilton questioning the tourist. "Did he see anything?" I asked.

The man had a Korean flag on his baseball cap, jacket and shoulder bag. His English appeared to be Korean too.

"From what we can understand," said the guardian, "he was trying to find his way back to his hotel from the palace."

"Bit of an indirect route," I said dubiously.

Hamilton shrugged. "He's got a copy of *Jekyll and Hyde* in his bag. Maybe he was in search of local colour."

"And he found Katharine in there?"

There was another burst of incomprehensible English from the tourist, accompanied by what seemed to be positive head movements.

"We'll take that as a yes, shall we?" I turned to the Korean. "Did you see anyone else? Was anyone coming out when you went in?"

More yabbering, but the gestures looked negative. I took Hamilton aside. "Get your people to find an interpreter before they take a statement from him. I don't think he's involved in this, but if we stall we can keep an eye on him."

Hamilton looked confused. "Not involved in what? What exactly was the woman—"

He broke off as Katharine came staggering from the close, her face white and her right arm against the wall.

"What are you doing?" I said. "You're not supposed to be walking about."

She pushed one of the medics away. "I told you, Quint. I'm staying with you till we catch her."

"Catch who?" the guardian demanded. "What's going on here, Dalrymple?"

I took a deep breath. Now was the time to tell him about Patsy. So I did. I was a bit vague about the connection with the missing young people, but that didn't seem to bother Hamilton. A tight smile began to show on his face as I spoke.

"So the controller of Prostitution Services has been up to no good," he said when I finished. "I can't say I'm surprised. I never approved of her promotion to senior auxiliary rank."

You sanctimonious old bastard, I thought. Where would the Council be without the income from Patsy's department?

"You didn't see her?" he asked Katharine.

She shook her head. "But obviously she saw me. I followed her from outside her office to a café on the Royal Mile. She sat there for over an hour, then went into some shops. I had that woollen hat pulled down low over my forehead, but she must still have recognised me. Led me down here and hid in one of the doorways and hit me from behind, the bitch."

"She may have had help," I said. "You're lucky you weren't injured more seriously."

Hamilton was desperate to get involved. "Shall I instruct all guard units and barracks to look out for the controller?"

I raised my hand. "Wait a minute. I need to think." I walked back into the dank close, stood in a granite corner and let the stream of images bombard me. The Bearskin, Patsy's office, the Greek's hotel room where I'd found the headless photographs, the hiding-place in Billy's flat with the Prostitution Department appraisals. All those places had links with Patsy. But there was something else, something relevant that I couldn't quite grasp. I put my hands against the damp stone and tried to hatch the idea that had begun to torment me. There wasn't much time. Even if Patsy hadn't recognised Katharine until she was knocked unconscious, she'd seen her close up here. She knew of my interest in Katharine and it would be clear that I was closing in on her. So where would she go? None of the obvious places, I was sure of that. Patsy had been a smart operator before she joined the Enlightenment and I knew she hadn't forgotten any of her old tricks. So where had she gone? I ran my mind back over the places: the Bearskin, her office – Christ, her office. Suddenly I saw Simpson 134, the dead nurse, the time she came out of the building where Patsy worked. Simpson 134. She was involved with Billy, she'd met him. That was it. I knew where Patsy was.

"Let's go," I said, running back out to the pavement. "To Jamaica Street Lane North."

Katharine came with me to the Transit. As I drove off, Hamilton's guard vehicle in my rearview mirror, I thought of the night I'd hidden behind the refuse bin and waited for Billy to reappear from the lane. He wasn't the kind of guy who would have a meeting out of doors in the dark. He had a hideaway down the lane and I was positive that's where Patsy had gone. I was also positive that we wouldn't find her there alone.

I stopped on India Street, near the bar I'd seen Billy go into that night after he met Simpson 134.

"What's the location?" Hamilton asked.

"I'm not sure," I said, watching his eyebrows jump. I wasn't sure how to go about identifying the building where Patsy was either. If the people I suspected were there too, using the City Guard's stormtrooper methods mightn't be a good idea.

"Quint?" Katharine said. "What if I walk down the street? That would probably bring Patsy out."

"More likely get you killed." I thought about it. "On the other hand . . ."

"Where are you going, Dalrymple?" Hamilton shouted as I reached the corner.

"To talk to Patsy." I smiled at Katharine. "Right idea, wrong person to carry it out. Patsy and I used to be friends." I turned to Hamilton. "Put a roadblock at the other end of the lane. If I don't contact you within five minutes, send in the cavalry."

"Quint . . ."

I faced the front. "Stay here, Katharine."

The buildings in the lane had originally been stables and servants' quarters, two-storey blocks that had been renovated by young professional people in the years before the Enlightenment. Now most of them are set aside for middle-ranking auxiliaries. Most of them. Billy must have managed to get his hands on one. What number was it? Only one way to find out. My palms were wet and I wasn't in complete control of my breathing.

"Patsy!" I yelled. "Patsy! We need to talk!"

I looked around the damp stone façades. Nothing. I walked on a bit further.

"Patsy! I'm on my own. I'm not armed."

No reply.

"Patsy! You're better off . . ."

A window to the left above me rattled open. I stopped and waited. There was no one visible.

"Patsy . . ."

"Will you stop shouting, Quint? I might need glasses, but I'm not deaf." Patsy's head appeared. "Here, you'll need these." She dropped a ring of keys.

Before I used them, I called Hamilton and told him to stay where he was.

I found Patsy on the first floor. It was a small flat but

through the rear window I could see a series of low buildings in what would originally have been a garden.

"I'm impressed, man," Patsy said with a slack smile. "How did you find out about this place?"

I tapped the side of my head with my forefinger. "Where are they, Patsy? In there?" I pointed to the outhouses.

"Has Billy talked?" Patsy said, her voice hardening.

I let her think he had.

"That little shite. He swore he'd look after things with the Council," Patsy said bitterly. Then she laughed. "I should have known. Never trust a man. Aye, they're down there. Asleep probably. We've been giving them tranquillisers to keep them quiet."

"How many are there?"

"Six boys and four girls. The rest are all away to Greece. These ones were to leave at the end of the week."

"Is there one called Adam Kirkwood?"

"I knew we shouldn't have taken Katharine's brother. He was too much of a good thing. Maybe it runs in the family." She nodded. "Aye, he's still here."

I took out my mobile and asked Hamilton to put Katharine on. Then we went to find Adam.

Patsy told the two hard men who were watching over the sex slaves to forget about putting up a fight. They hadn't looked exactly keen when they saw the double squad of guardsmen Hamilton sent in. Katharine ran over to the bed her brother was occupying in the makeshift dormitory and tried to bring him round with a tenderness I hadn't expected. It was difficult to rouse him and the others. Ambulances took them to the infirmary for check-ups. Katharine went with Adam after giving Patsy a look that would have made a statue's eyes water.

"I haven't much time, Patsy," I said, waving Hamilton back. "Tell me what's been going on here."

Patsy looked at me quizzically. "I thought you said Billy had talked?" Her lips creased. "Fuck you, Quint. You made me . . ."

"Forget it, Patsy. If you want me to keep the public order guardian off your back, you'd better co-operate. Whose idea was it to sell off citizens as sex slaves?"

She laughed scornfully. "Whose do you think?"

"But Billy couldn't have done it without you."

"I provided the technical know-how." She sat down on one of the beds and smoothed the cover. "He worked the deal with the Greek Roussos in the Indie and found this place." She looked around at the drab walls and shook her head. "The kids were better off on their backs in Athens than in this shite-hole. We told them they were in line to become cultural representatives and gave them some Greek money to impress them. And we told them not to tell anyone else till their jobs were confirmed."

That explained the banknote I found in Adam Kirkwood's flat. "And when you'd run preliminary checks on them, they were picked up. Did you give them any choice?"

She shrugged. "No. After they were picked up, we made sure they couldn't get away."

"Simpson 134 checked their medical records?"

"That's right. The Greeks only wanted young, fully fit specimens. And photographs they could drool over."

"What about Rory Baillie?"

"We used him to drive them around; I trained them with Sarah Spence in different places. Some of them were in the Bearskin that night you were there."

I walked over to her. "Billy's in intensive care."

Patsy looked like a snake had started to glide up her leg. "The killer?"

I shook my head. "He ran in front of the horses in Princes Street Gardens – trying to get away from me."

She stared at me. "Are you proud of yourself, Quint?"

"No." I bent over her. "Christ, Patsy, you knew a maniac was butchering the others in your scam. Why didn't you run earlier? Why didn't Billy?"

She looked up at me. "There was so much money coming to us. I could've got out of this bastard city and started somewhere else." She stood up slowly. "Besides, it didn't make any sense. We couldn't see what the murders had to do with this business. It isn't all just some crazy coincidence, is it?"

"What do you think? Patsy, what about the medical guardian? Did he have anything to do with this?"

I knew before she spoke that the answer was negative. I turned to go.

"Quint," Patsy called. "You'll do what you can for me?"

I passed Hamilton in the doorway. She was his now.

Davie called before I got to the Transit. "Subject went into his residence a minute ago. I'm trying not to look too suspicious in the gardens in Moray Place."

"Right. Keep on him."

So Yellowlees was out of the infirmary. But his files weren't.

Time to take a look. The fact that Katharine was there gave me an extra incentive. I was wondering what my payment for finding her brother would be.

Then, as I drove towards the centre through the drizzle, I remembered my father. Like the murderer, I'd lost track of him in this lunatic city. Maybe Patsy had the right idea. Maybe it was time to get out. But first I had a lot of unfinished business.

Chapter Nineteen

In the infirmary a ward had been set aside for the sex slaves. A senior nursing auxiliary told me she'd contacted the medical guardian and told him about the ten tranquillised patients. She was surprised that he hadn't arrived to take charge. I wasn't, but he might still turn up any minute.

Katharine was sitting by her brother's bed holding his hand. Her face was close to his and they were deep in conversation. Adam Kirkwood was pale, but he looked healthy enough. Patsy had been feeding the slaves up. I turned back before I reached them, but Katharine spotted me.

"What are you up to now, Quint?" she asked.

I shrugged. "I've still got a murderer to catch."

She stood up, pulling her brother into a seated position. "*We* have, you mean."

"Katharine, you've got your brother back. You've done your part."

She looked at me like a schoolmistress about to sort out the class villain. "There's a connection between the killings and what Adam's been through, isn't there?"

"It looks that way to me."

"So Adam and I have a right to be involved."

"What are you talking about? This is a murder investigation, not a human rights forum."

Her eyes flashed. "Oh, I see. When it suits you, you take my help. When it doesn't, you dump me."

"What's this all about, Katharine? Adam's back. What more do you want?"

She came up to me. The look on her face almost made me run away. "Look, Quint," she said in a harsh whisper, "I've been fucked by the Council and I don't care about myself any more. But Adam's still young. He didn't know much about what life's really like. Patsy Cameron and the rest of them have seen to that though. I'm going to stick with this to the end, then I'm going to make them pay."

"Personal vendettas don't help."

"Don't they?" she replied indifferently. "Come on, Adam. Citizen Dalrymple needs our help."

I watched as her brother got out of the bed unsteadily. I couldn't see him being much use but the mood Katharine was in, I didn't fancy objecting.

"Lock the door, Adam," I said.

We were standing in Yellowlees's outer office.

"What are we looking for?" Katharine asked.

I started to pull open filing-cabinet drawers. They were all unlocked, which was a bad sign. "The organs that the murderer cut out can all be transplanted."

"But transplantation's illegal, isn't it?" Adam Kirkwood said. For a big guy, he had an incongruously high voice.

"So's selling people as sex slaves," said Katharine.

"Quite." I went over to the door leading into the medical

guardian's inner sanctum. It was locked. I put my shoulder to it and the poor quality wood quickly gave way. "I'll look in here. You two see if you can find anything about transplantation out there. And tell me if you find any files about the auxiliary Scott 391. I'll explain later." I hadn't said anything about Yellowlees's lupus research and his treatment of my mother. If there were any papers about that in the infirmary, they would be in his private office.

But there was nothing. We found patients' reports, memoranda on infirmary administration, personnel files on medical staff and a heap of other documentation but not a hint about transplants or about the lupus. And nothing about the dead auxiliary.

Katharine squatted down by the mound of files. "I don't get this," she said, pulling Adam down beside her. "Obviously the organs the murderer removed couldn't have been used for transplantation."

"No, they were hacked out pretty crudely."

"So why do you think there might be transplants going on in the infirmary?"

I told them about Scott 391 – how the sight of his body in the crematorium had affected the sentry there and how Yellowlees had mislaid his file. "It could be that organs were removed from him."

Katharine's forehead was furrowed. "But what's that got to do with the killer mutilating corpses?"

"Search me," I replied. And what's it got to do with the ENT Man? I asked myself. "Whatever the reason, my hunch is that Yellowlees is the next victim on the killer's list. He got the guardian's girlfriend last time and . . ."

"Your hunch?" Katharine said scornfully. "You run investigations on hunches?"

"They've never failed me yet." I nodded at Adam. "My hunch about Jamaica Street Lane was right, wasn't it?"

Katharine stood up. "But you need evidence, even in this city. And you haven't got a thing, have you?"

"If I had, I'd have arrested the guardian."

Her eyes narrowed. "Quint, you're a bastard. You're using Yellowlees as bait, aren't you?"

I shrugged. "My father's still missing. I think there's some connection with all of this."

"I thought you disapproved of personal vendettas," she said with an ironic smile. "God, you're as much of a hypocrite as the rest of them." She took her brother's hand and pulled him to his feet. He was looking pretty queasy.

On the way to the exit I checked with the security squad commander. Billy Geddes was in a stable condition and no one had been near him except the nurses. A stable condition meant that he still hadn't come round. I wished I could have had five minutes with a conscious Billy: he would at least have explained why he had a copy of Yellowlees's lupus research in his flat. But that would have been too easy.

I headed for the Transit and the Assembly Hall. I couldn't shake Katharine and her brother off. It didn't look like I was going to get much of a reward for finding him after all.

I called Davie before the Council meeting started. "Where are you?"

"On the Mound. I saw the medical guardian go in to the Assembly Hall five minutes ago."

"Right. Trail him when he comes out and keep in touch. I'll be close. And Davie?"

"What, Quint?"

"Be careful, my friend. I've got a feeling we're near the end of this caper."

"Not before time. I want my bed. Out."

I laughed then ran over to the entrance as Hamilton's Land-Rover pulled up.

"We'll tell them about Billy and Patsy Cameron, but not about the dead guardsman and the fact that Yellowlees lost his file, okay?"

The public order guardian was looking pleased with himself. No doubt he'd spent a happy time ripping Patsy to pieces. "Very well, Dalrymple. By the way, I had the senior guardian on the line. She was shocked to hear about the sex slaves."

I bet she was. She'd be even more shocked if she knew that Billy had a copy of Yellowlees's research.

"She also offered both of us her congratulations on the outcome of the investigation," Hamilton added with a self-satisfied smile.

I was unimpressed that she hadn't bothered to call me personally. "In case you've forgotten, there's still a killer on the loose," I said. Hamilton was an easier target than my mother.

The Council meeting was a ludicrous performance, the guardians trying to outdo each other in expressions of disgust and horror at the news of the sex slave scam. The only one who kept a low profile was Yellowlees. He sat through it all without making any comment, his fingers in the usual pyramid beneath his nose and his mane of hair as tidy as ever. But he didn't look at me once.

I thought about my mother again. A few days ago she had been much better. I'd expected to see her resume her place at the centre of the horseshoe table by now, but the deputy senior guardian was still acting as speaker. Was the treatment losing its effect? Or did she have some other reason for keeping away?

At the end of the meeting, Yellowlees left the chamber without speaking to anyone.

"What now, Dalrymple?" asked the public order guardian. "Did you find out anything more about that dead guardsman?"

"I'm still working on it," I said vaguely. I'd been hoping he'd forgotten about the ENT Man's brother. I should have been down at Scott Barracks checking out his close colleagues and trying to find out why the sentry in the crematorium had committed suicide. But there wasn't time for that. I was sure the killer was about to strike again. I'd given Yellowlees a chance to come clean and he'd rejected it.

Hamilton walked on. "I'm going back to the castle to continue the interrogation." He seemed to be so keen on nailing Patsy that he'd lost interest in the murderer. Maybe he was hoping that we'd scared him off.

"What about my father?" I called after him.

He stopped and turned round. "We're still looking," he said feebly. "What else can we do?"

I didn't respond and went past him to the Transit, hoping

that might distract him from his assault on Patsy. That was all I could do for her.

Katharine was waiting for me. Her brother had crashed out in the back of the van. "Well, what next?"

"We wait." I looked at my watch. "It won't be long."

I got that right.

My mobile rang ten minutes later.

"I've lost him." Davie sounded desperate.

"Where are you?" I started the Transit and slammed it into gear.

"Corner of Frederick Street and Rose Street. A bloody great group of Japanese came out of a shop and . . ."

"Stay there," I shouted, slewing round the bend and on to the Mound. "Did you see anyone with him before you lost him?"

"No!" Davie shouted above a babble of foreign voices.

The mobile slipped from between my ear and neck. "Shit." I braked hard behind a horse-drawn carriage that was overloaded with women wearing chadors.

"Quint?"

I felt Katharine's eyes on me as I jumped the lights on Princes Street. "What?"

"If you put me through the windscreen of this wreck, there'll be big fucking trouble."

She wasn't just making polite conversation.

Davie was waving his arms frantically. "The guardsman at the far end of Rose Street saw the guardian a few minutes ago. He was getting into a taxi with a male tourist wearing a pinstripe suit and a baseball cap." He pushed in beside Katharine and peered at Adam Kirkwood in the back.

"Height?" I asked as I turned into the pedestrian precinct.

"Who's this?" Davie asked.

"What bloody height was the tourist?" I shouted.

Davie spoke on his mobile. "About five feet nine inches, he says."

"Five feet nine inches?" I repeated. "But the murderer takes size twelve boots."

"Watch out!" Katharine screamed.

I stood on the brakes as a pair of Arabs squared up to each other in the middle of the road, oblivious to the Transit. As I waited for their friends to separate them and while Katharine was introducing Davie to Adam, I glanced out of the side window. We'd stopped right outside the Bearskin. It was impossible to avoid the photographs of the show. And at that moment it came to me with the shriek of a Hendrix high note and the pounding certainty of a bass riff from Willie Dixon. I understood what Yellowlees's lover had been trying to say about her assailant. I knew who the killer was.

Then my mobile rang again.

I scrabbled around for it on the floor.

"Dalrymple? Is that you, Dalrymple?" The medical guardian sounded like he'd just completed a five-mile run. "I'm . . . I'm to tell you . . . to tell you to come . . . to Moray Place . . ."

The connection was broken before I could say anything; before I could tell him I knew who had captured him. Not that it would have done him any good. I put my hand on the horn and held it there.

*   *   *

"Why the guardians' residences?" Davie asked.

"It's the last act," I said. "All is about to be revealed." I turned on to Heriot Row.

"Shouldn't we tell the public order guardian?"

"He'll have been informed already, I'm sure of it, Davie. This is going to be a performance that all the guardians are expected to attend." I turned to Katharine. "I want you and Adam to wait in the van. Things might get nasty."

She was looking straight ahead. "I told you, Quint. I'm staying with you."

I couldn't be bothered to argue with her.

"Here," said Davie. "You'd better take this." He handed over his knife.

"No, thanks. There's been enough killing."

"You were right." Davie pointed ahead. "The word's out."

Guardsmen and women were swarming around like bees whose queen is under threat.

After we stopped I beckoned to Davie to lean across Katharine and put his ear to my mouth. The murderer wasn't the only one who had stage directions to give.

The commander at the barrier scrutinised my authorisation then looked dubiously at Katharine and Adam. She'd insisted on bringing him along too, God knows why.

"Oh, for fuck's sake, they're with me." I grabbed Katharine's arm and pushed past the auxiliary into Moray Place.

"Where are they?" she asked, wincing. I'd taken hold of the arm she burned in the blaze.

There was a clatter of boots from a squad running to take up position outside the senior guardian's residence. When they'd passed, I walked over to the edge of the gardens that form the centre of the circular street, and gazed into the darkness at the heart of the Enlightenment.

"They're on the grass," I said.

"I can't see any . . ."

The floodlights ignited with a crack and a hum. I was blinded by the white light for a few seconds. I'd rarely seen the gardens lit up. The guardians only use the illuminations when they want to impress foreign dignitaries.

Then I saw the two of them. They were standing close together in the middle of the well-manicured grass. The medical guardian's head was lowered and his shirt was out of his trousers but I didn't look at him for long. It was the figure next to him that I was drawn to, the figure in the pinstripe suit. That individual's head, under a wide-peaked baseball cap, was also lowered, obscuring the face. There was a glint from their wrists and I made out a pair of handcuffs.

"Stay here," I whispered to Katharine. "I've got to go out there."

"Why?" she demanded, her eyes flaring as she turned to me. "Have you got a death wish?"

"Don't tell me you care." I leaned forward and kissed her hard on the lips. I saw her brother grin. "Watch my back," I said, then pushed her gently away.

And stepped out from the line of bushes into the light.

I stopped when I was about ten yards away from them. With a sweeping movement, the figure on Yellowlees's right raised the hand untethered by the cuffs and grasped the peak of the cap. I could read the words around the heart emblem on it. They said "Edinburgh – International City of the Year". I was also able to count the number of fingers as the cap was pulled off.

Mary, Queen of Scots lifted her head and shook it a couple of times. Fair hair billowed out around her perfect features like the aura around a Pre-Raphaelite pin-up.

"So, here you are, citizen Dalrymple. I've been looking forward to meeting you." Her voice was warm and welcoming, very unlike the average auxiliary's. Then again, she wasn't by any standards an average auxiliary. "Stand still, guardian," she said, her voice still friendly. But her hand moved to her pocket quickly and re-emerged with her service knife, which she put to Yellowlees's throat.

"Are you all right?" I asked him.

He nodded, keeping his eyes lowered.

"We haven't been introduced," I said to the woman. "You're from Scott Barracks, aren't you? Close colleague of 391 and 477."

"Very good. I thought you might be getting close." She looked at me and I felt my spine freeze. "Scott 372 is how they refer to me in this festering city." She glanced behind me. "Who's this?"

I turned, my heart missing a beat as I saw Katharine coming towards us. In the background I suddenly caught a glimpse of my mother in the window of her study. Her face looked moon-shaped again. There was a tall figure I couldn't make out at the curtain beside her.

"Come and join us," Scott 372 said with mock civility. "The more, the merrier. Just tell all my fellow auxiliaries to keep back if they want the guardian to stay alive, citizen."

I made the call and saw Hamilton raise his hand in acknowledgement from the bushes.

"Now throw your mobile over here." There was an easy smile on Mary, Queen of Scots' face, the smile of someone who's in complete control. "Let's see what you've got in your pockets."

I tossed over my phone then dropped my notebook, keys and wallet.

"And you," she said to Katharine. "What brought you out here? Don't you trust your boyfriend?" She smiled, this time sardonically.

"Why don't you come over here and empty my pockets yourself?" Katharine asked.

"No, thanks." The auxiliary gave Katharine the imperious look I saw in the Bearskin. "Do it or the guardian dies."

I glared at her too and finally she produced a knife. She must have convinced Davie to give her his. She threw it away to the left.

"Sensible move." Scott 372 turned her gaze back on me. I tried to see beyond the mask of her beautiful, unperturbed face but didn't get very far. Her eyes were vacant, definitely not the windows of her soul. I wondered if I would be able to provoke her. It was worth a try.

"What's your name?"

She laughed. It wasn't a pleasant sound and I saw

Yellowlees glance at her nervously. "I don't have a name, citizen. You know that."

"I'm sure Gordon Dunbar didn't call you Scott 372 during sex sessions."

I saw her lips tremble momentarily. It looked like I'd got to her. Now what?

"All right," she said, her voice hardening. "My name's Amanda."

"Well, Amanda, release the guardian. I guarantee you'll be treated fairly. I know there's corruption in the city. You can help me root it out."

She laughed again, this time an even more metallic, pitiless noise that was about as far from humour as you can go.

"Spare me, citizen. I'm an expert at rooting out what's wrong in the city." She looked at me like I was a trainee footman in her court. "I don't need your help."

"What are you going to do now?"

"Extract a confession from this butcher here."

The medical guardian's head shot up as Amanda slammed the butt of her knife into his solar plexus, then he slumped down. She pulled him upright again.

"You can both witness what he says. Then you'll under-stand everything that I've done."

"Everything you've done?" Katharine said scathingly. "You're protecting someone. You can't be the murderer . . ."

I jammed my elbow into her ribs.

There was a hint of a smile on Amanda's mouth as she turned to Yellowlees.

"Stop her, Dalrymple," he said, his eyes wild. "This is all a terrible mistake."

Amanda shot a cold glance at Katharine. Then punctured the skin below the guardian's Adam's apple with a lightning-quick movement. A thin jet of blood spurted out. Yellowlees gave a loud gasp and raised his uncuffed hand to the wound.

"I don't understand what you want from me," he said desperately. "I don't know . . . I've . . . I've never even seen you before."

The hesitation was enough for her. "You may not have seen me, but you certainly saw Gordon, Scott 391." Her voice was rising in a crescendo. "Didn't you?" she screamed.

The guardian didn't answer. She stuck her knife into his thigh and pulled it out so quickly that I hardly saw her hand move.

His face twisted in agony. "Oh Christ . . . yes . . . I . . . I know who he was . . ."

"You cut Gordon to pieces," Amanda said, her lips close to his ear. "That nurse of yours wouldn't tell me, but I know you did. Who else but a guardian would dare to carry out transplants in Edinburgh?"

"No, you're wrong." Yellowlees was almost weeping now. Blood trickled between the fingers he had clamped to his thigh. "You're wrong! There were no transplants."

The way he was pleading convinced me. I heard plenty of confessions during my time in the directorate and I learned to tell when bullshit turns into the truth.

"You don't deny you extracted organs from Scott 391?" I said. That was what the sentry had discovered when he opened the coffin in the crematorium.

He shook his head dumbly, cowering from the blow he was expecting. This time it didn't come.

"That's better," said Amanda. "Now tell us how many transplants you've carried out."

She was obsessed by transplants. Suddenly I realised she'd misunderstood what the medical guardian had done with her friend's organs.

Yellowlees was staring at her, his mouth open. He'd realised that if he said the wrong thing now he was dead.

I tried to distract Amanda. "It was your research, wasn't it, guardian? That's what was behind all this."

Yellowlees grabbed the lifeline I'd thrown him gratefully. "Exactly. My research into lupus requires certain hormones and cells. I only extract them from . . . dead tissue." He was avoiding the auxiliary's eyes. "As in the case of your friend."

Amanda turned to me. Her lips parted and the tip of her tongue protruded. She was staring, as if what I'd said was inconceivable. Then she snapped to attention again. She'd dismissed the idea that she'd been mistaken.

"You're lying, guardian," she said sharply. "I know you've been doing transplants."

Yellowlees looked at me imploringly. "Help me, Dalrymple. Your mother's benefited from my work." He tried to step forward, then juddered to a halt like a dog on a lead as Amanda pulled him back. "I was only interested in my research. I had nothing to do with the illegal deals the others were running, you must believe that."

I did, but I wasn't calling the shots. I had a nasty feeling he'd overplayed his hand.

"Others?" said the auxiliary, her features alert. "Which others?"

The guardian swallowed, then dropped his head. "Heriot 07 . . ."

I had a feeling that if he ran through the names of the murder victims he would only convince Amanda he was involved. I tried to muddy the waters. "You realise that your research led indirectly to Margaret's death?"

"I know that," Yellowlees said weakly. "I can't stop thinking about Margaret . . ."

"Which others?" Amanda said inexorably. "Heriot 07 and who else?" She saw me move. "Stay where you are, citizen."

The guardian raised his head as warily as a cow in an abattoir. "The Greek Roussos, the driver Baillie, the guardswoman Sarah Spence . . ."

The auxiliary's chin went up like she'd been electrocuted. "That bitch?" she hissed, pulling Yellowlees closer. "Well, don't worry about your precious Margaret any longer. Soon you'll be . . ."

Before she finished the sentence I raised the stump of my forefinger to my chin, hoping that Davie had positioned spotters all round the gardens.

For a split second everything seemed to stand still – Amanda with her knife to the guardian's neck, Katharine by my side, the guardsmen lined up beyond the grass – we were all like players on a stage, motionless before the curtain falls.

Then the lights went out with a loud crack and I leaped forward into the blue-black night.

Chapter Twenty

I'd arranged with Davie for the lights to go off for ten seconds. They seemed longer than the slowest-moving episode in the French New Wave films my parents used to watch on their video in pre-Enlightenment times. I reached the spot where I thought the auxiliary and the guardian had been, but found no one. Then I heard a thud and a groan to my right. Before I could move I was hit in the chest by a blow which would have broken ribs if it hadn't struck my sternum. I went down in a heap, winded. At the same time the lights came back on. Someone ran past and dived on to the scrum of bodies in front of me.

By the time I crawled over there, only one of them was moving. It was Amanda. She stood up unsteadily. Beyond her I could see Katharine lying on her side unconscious, her mouth open. Her brother was crumpled on top of Yellowlees. I saw legs in dark blue pinstripe come close and tried to sit up. I still couldn't catch my breath. My heart was pounding. I saw the knife in the murderess's hand, the blood on it. She bent over me. I waited for the thrust of the blade.

"Come on, citizen. I didn't kick you that hard." She put

her arm under my back and sat me up. "I don't know about your girlfriend." She looked over at Adam. "Who was that madman? I think I may have killed him." She said the words as if they were a meaningless platitude.

"Yellowlees," I gasped, noticing that she no longer had the handcuff on her left wrist. "What happened?"

"I don't think he'll be doing any more surgery."

"Drop the knife." Davie had an automatic pistol in his hand. "Stand up slowly and put your hands on your head." He glanced down at me. "Are you all right, Quint?"

"I'll live. What about Katharine?"

An army of guard personnel surrounded us. I saw a couple of medics squat down beside her. I managed to stand up, in time to see Amanda's hands being cuffed behind her back. Hamilton was on his knees with more medics beside the medical guardian and Adam. I stumbled over and crouched down.

"They're both gone," the public order guardian said hopelessly. Yellowlees's throat had been cut from ear to ear. If he hadn't been lying face down, there would have been blood everywhere. As for Adam, there didn't seem to be a mark on him. Till I looked at his chest and saw the stain over his thorax. You didn't have to be a cardiologist to realise which organ had been perforated.

"We have failed to look after our young," said my mother from behind me. "The heart of the body politic no longer beats."

I looked up at her. She was leaning against my father, her face a blotched and flaking ruin.

*   *   *

"She's coming round," the medic said. "Heavy blow to the chin, but her jaw's still in one piece."

I kneeled down beside Katharine and helped her sit up. Her eyes rolled then focused on me.

"What happened? Where . . ." She was slurring her words. She started to look around. "Where's Adam?"

"Why did you follow me out here, Katharine? I told you to . . ."

She grabbed my arms hard. "What's happened to Adam?"

There was nowhere to hide. "When the lights went out, he ran out. To help you, I suppose . . ."

"She killed him," Katharine said dully. "The bitch killed him."

I nodded slowly. "She killed the guardian too."

Her eyes flared. "I don't give a fuck about the guardian. He deserved everything he got. But Adam . . ." She let out a single, devastated sob. "Adam . . . never laid a finger on anyone. That's why they all took advantage of him." She pushed me away and got to her feet. "I want to see him."

Hamilton stepped up. "Come with me. He's in that ambulance." I was surprised by the sympathetic look on his face.

"It's over now, Katharine," I called after her feebly.

She turned and skewered me with a glare. "It's not over for me, Quint."

"I'll catch up with you later."

"Where are you going?" she demanded suspiciously.

I squeezed her arm. "Things to clear up. Keep your mobile switched on."

"You're not going to interrogate her now, are you?" She brought her face up to mine. "I want to be there when you do."

I wasn't going to commit myself to that. I shook my head. "I've got some family business to sort out."

She kept her eyes on me. "So have I."

My mother looked like she'd collapsed into the armchair by the fireplace in her study. Otherwise I would have been harder on her.

"You had him here all the time, didn't you?" I glanced at my father. He was leaning against the marble mantelpiece and looking uncomfortable.

She nodded.

"Thanks for telling me. You realise I might have caught the murderess more quickly if you hadn't put that distraction in my way?" I bent over her. "Did you know that Billy was funding Yellowlees's research so he could sell the results?"

"No, Quintilian," she said weakly. "Anyway, you've no hard evidence of that."

I'd seen the look on the medical guardian's face when he mentioned Billy's barracks number. "You must have known that Yellowlees couldn't have made that kind of breakthrough without finance."

"He was . . . reticent about how he'd been able to make such progress," she said, looking away. "I know, I should have pressed him." Her eyes, almost invisible under swollen flesh, moved back to me slowly. "As you see, I've already stopped using the serum."

I didn't feel congratulations were in order. "You sent for Hector, didn't you? Why?"

Her distended cheeks took on an even redder tint. "Vanity. I . . . I wanted him to see how much younger I looked."

I glanced at my father again. He shrugged awkwardly.

"I got what I deserved," my mother said with a faint laugh. "He was horrified by what he called the unnatural reversal of my condition. He wanted to get you to investigate the medical guardian." She shaded her eyes with unsteady fingers. "I couldn't allow that so I kept him here."

I was amazed. I couldn't say I knew my mother well. Over the past fifteen years I'd rarely seen her. But the idea that she was concerned about how she looked seemed almost as much of a betrayal of Enlightenment principles as Billy's deals. Then again, I was an expert in betraying the Enlightenment. Maybe it ran in the family.

"I want all of this to be given full publicity," I said.

My mother raised her head, wincing with the effort. "That is a matter for the Council to decide." Her tone was more like it used to be.

"I want everyone to know that senior auxiliaries were stealing from the city, that they were selling the city's young people as whores. I want the medical guardian's use of illegally obtained organs for . . ."

My mother raised her hand. "All right, Quintilian. I'll put those points to the Council," she said wearily. "Where are you going?"

"I have some unanswered questions."

Hector caught up with me on the stairs. "You've done well, failure. I knew you'd get to the bottom of it."

I shook my head. "All I've done is react to events."

The old man smiled. "Very modest." He continued downwards.

"Where are you going?"

"Back to my books. I've been without them for days."

"More Juvenal?"

"I haven't seen anything here to put me off him."

I got him into a Land-Rover, then walked towards the Transit. Just before I turned out of Moray Place, the lights in the empty gardens went out.

Like the sun in a minor constellation imploding.

I called Hamilton and asked him where Katharine was. She'd stayed in the infirmary with Adam's body. I couldn't think of anything to say to her as I drove to the castle.

The cell where the murderess had been taken was in the depths of the barracks block, at the end of a long, dank passageway. Guard personnel stood at five-yard intervals, carrying rifles with fixed bayonets. I hadn't seen those for a long time.

"I've given instructions to shoot to kill if she makes a break," said Hamilton.

"Brilliant. Don't you realise that she's finished killing? She could have knifed me but she didn't."

The guard commander at the heavy steel door waited for the guardian's order, then unlocked it. The clang as it opened echoed down the corridor and came back at us like a vengeful spirit.

"Christ almighty," I groaned. They had stripped Scott 372 down to her auxiliary-issue khaki singlet and knickers. Her wrists and ankles had been cuffed to a solid wooden chair that was bolted to the stone-flagged floor. "How's she going to make a break?" I asked. "Unless she happens to be related to Houdini, of course."

"You can't be too careful," the guardian said impassively.

"Aren't you freezing?" I said to the prisoner.

Amanda lifted her head. "I'm a cold-blooded creature, citizen," she said, a smile flickering across her lips. "Haven't you noticed?"

I stood looking at her, struck again by how perfectly proportioned her features were. Let alone her body. But she was right. Her eyes were glazed like a reptile's.

"So," she said, giving Hamilton a glance that would have dissolved most men's bowels. "It's interrogation time."

I sat down opposite her and rested my elbows on the table. "I was rather hoping for a confession, Amanda."

My use of that name made her smile again. "You don't have to sweet-talk me, Quintilian." She pursed her lips curiously as she pronounced my name, like she was going to whistle. She repeated it and laughed as innocently as a child learning a new word. "I'll tell you everything, Quintilian. Only you though, no one else. Especially not anyone from the Council." Her tone remained even but I noticed that her fingers – all eleven of them – had tightened on the chair arms.

I turned to the guardian.

He bit his lip then shrugged. "Very well. But the tape recorder is to run continuously."

Amanda laughed, this time harshly. "Don't they trust you?" she asked me.

I waved Hamilton away. A technical auxiliary brought in the tape recorder and set it up. As soon as the door closed behind him, the murderess began to speak.

"You bastard, Quint. I should have been there." Katharine was standing at the window, her back to me. "You owed me that."

I looked at her from the sofa and wondered how much longer I could keep my eyes open. I'd got back from the castle in the early afternoon after listening to the confession for over twelve hours.

"What is this great debt I've suddenly acquired?" I demanded. "It seems to me you owe me an explanation of what you were doing following me out to the middle of the gardens." I closed my eyes when she didn't say anything. "Anyway, I told you. She wouldn't speak to anyone except me."

"Oh, the great Quintilian Dalrymple," she said scathingly. "What makes you so special?"

"She needed someone who could understand what she did." I opened my eyes when I heard Katharine coming over quickly.

"If you're so fucking clever, why can't you understand that I followed you out there because I was worried about you, because I . . ."

She buried her head in the cushion beside my leg, sobs jerking her shoulders.

I put my hand on her back. "Come on, you'd only have tried to hurt her."

"And what if I did?" she said, looking up at me with wet eyes. "Could you blame me?"

"No." I pulled her towards me. She didn't resist. "But this isn't only about Adam, Katharine."

"Tell me what she told you," she asked quietly. "At least I'm entitled to that."

I nodded, then made the mistake of closing my eyes for a few seconds before I started to speak. Faces flashed in front of me. I made out Caro's and Katharine's, then they were both replaced by the flawless mask of the murderess, her lips moving as she spoke. I opened my eyes with a start and she disappeared. But her voice still rang in my ears, sweeter and more deadly than any siren's song.

"You know, Quintilian, none of it would have happened if Fergus – Scott 477 – hadn't been on sentry duty at the crematorium the night Gordon . . . the night Gordon's body was taken there."

"Gordon and you were more than just close colleagues."

"Gordon and I . . . Gordon and I knew each other all our lives. Our parents were neighbours."

"In Trinity."

"You have been doing your homework. When Fergus saw from the documents who was in the coffin, he called me."

"Wait a minute. Gordon had a brother. Stewart Duncan Dunbar. Tell me about him."

"That animal? Until Gordon died, I hadn't thought about him for years. Why are you interested?"

"You remembered him after you saw Gordon's body, though, didn't you? That's why I'm interested."

"How . . . how do you know all this?"

"Never mind that just now. What did the older brother do to Gordon?"

"The same thing he did to me."

"When did it happen?"

"Before they packed the pig off to the school for the deaf."

"What age were you?"

"Eight. He . . . why are you making me go over this? I kept it locked away for years."

"You learned things from Stewart Dunbar, didn't you? Like how to use a ligature."

"How do you know that? There's something I don't understand here. Do you know the pig?"

"I met him. He had a connection with the directorate."

"Where is he?"

"In a safe place."

"They don't know, do they? Remember the tape."

"What did Gordon's brother do to the two of you?"

"No, I don't want to . . . oh, what does it matter now? It's relevant to your inquiry, I suppose. What you've got to understand is that their house was like Bluebeard's castle. The parents were never there. They were lawyers, fanatical supporters of the Enlightenment."

"Till they were found to have connections with the democrats in Glasgow and exiled."

"That was much later. Who's telling this story?"

"Sorry. So what about Stewart Duncan Dunbar?"

"We never called him by his first name. It didn't seem appropriate. To Gordon and me he was the Beast. His room was like a laboratory. One that belonged to a scientist who'd gone right off the rails. There were animals splayed out on boards, cut open. Rats and rabbits, mainly, but he took the neighbours' cats too. God, the smell."

"And the ligature?"

"When he reached his teens, he began to get even worse. He started doing things to his body – cutting himself, sticking pins into his thighs, putting pencils in his ears. That was how he damaged his hearing. His father found him thrashing around on the floor with the pencil points in his ears and an erection. Oh, and he was laughing."

"The ligature, Amanda."

"I'm coming to that. He got us into his room one day and locked the door before we could resist. Then he went for Gordon. Suddenly he had a leather bootlace round his neck. He passed out almost immediately. I tried to get the animal off him so he concentrated on me. I can still smell his breath. He never brushed his teeth. They were blue with decay. I had to turn away. Then he pulled my pants down and sodomised me. A few minutes later he did the same to Gordon."

"And you were eight years old?"

"That time the parents listened to us. But instead of having him put away, they got him into the deaf school."

"Did you see him again?"

"Only once. After he'd been thrown out. He was proud of it. He ran away not long afterwards. It took me a long time to blot him out. Gordon helped me, we helped each other. But I learned something from the Beast that was reinforced by the auxiliary training programme."

"What was that?"

"The poetry of violence."

*   *   *

I woke with a jerk, sweat all over my face. I was still on the sofa. Katharine's head was against my thigh, her breathing regular. I vaguely remembered sleep overwhelming me while I was telling her what Amanda had said. I lay still, feeling Katharine's warmth and aware of her scent. Outside it was still light though the sun was well down in the west. I would have got up to stretch my cramped legs but I didn't want to disturb Katharine.

So I sat and thought about the poetry of violence. I knew something about that too. I saw the Ear, Nose and Throat Man turning on me, the light falling on his scarred face and rotten teeth. But instead of seeing Caro's body, as I used to when I remembered the butcher, I pictured Amanda. The skin on her arms was smooth, sheathing well-toned muscles. When I'd stood up from the table in the cell, I glimpsed the curve of her breasts beneath the singlet and the lines of her bare, marble thighs.

And her voice went on, running through the catalogue of her crimes in an easy, even tone. Apart from when she was talking about Stewart Duncan Dunbar, she never hesitated. Like the radio announcer reading the inter-barracks rugby results on a Sunday evening.

I couldn't stop myself closing my eyes. I went straight back to Amanda in the cell.

"Fergus called me when he saw Gordon's barracks number on the documents at the crematorium. There was some bureaucratic problem and the delivery squad didn't notice how upset he was. It was the shock. I felt it too. There had been no news of Gordon's death. When he didn't come back to barracks, we assumed he'd been assigned an extra tour on the border. It wouldn't have been the first time."

"You opened the coffin."

"I had to see him one last time. And when I did . . . I knew without even thinking about it that I was going to track the bastards down."

"You thought auxiliaries were being killed for their organs."

"That's the way it looked. They'd taken his brain, eyes, liver, kidneys, pancreas, as well as other parts I couldn't identify. Since the documents were official, I knew auxiliaries must have been involved."

"Fergus committed suicide when he realised what you were doing, didn't he?"

"I'd been using his clothes and boots. He put two and two together when he heard about the murders."

"You used a bootlace like Stewart, didn't you? And you disguised yourself to get us off your trail. That way you gained time to find everyone who was involved."

"And to make them sweat. They deserved that."

"So it was all a question of personal revenge."

"No. I'm a good auxiliary. I wanted to purge the city of the disease that was afflicting it."

"You never thought of going to your superiors?"

"Is that supposed to be funny? Who could I trust? I was already performing at the Bearskin. I'd seen plenty of senior auxiliaries in the audience."

"How did you come to be working there?"

"It was that bitch Knox 96 – Sarah Spence – she recruited me last December. She'd been after me for weeks. I preferred performing to letting her go down on me. Killing her wasn't exactly a hardship."

"You didn't realise she was involved in a sex slavery deal Heriot 07 and the Prostitution Services controller were running?"

"Is that what the medical guardian meant? It makes sense. There were always these young, half-brainwashed citizens wandering around the club. I was too busy chasing the people who killed Gordon."

"It's not clear that he was killed deliberately. I think Yellowlees was telling the truth when he said he only took organs from bodies that were dead before they reached the infirmary."

"It's too late to ask him for confirmation now."

"Your system was to kill every Thursday night. Because . . ."

"Gordon died on a Thursday. I had to keep him alive somehow."

"And you were very careful to leave no prints, no traces to incriminate yourself. When you mutilated Sarah Spence in Stevenson Hall, you took off all your clothes, didn't you?"

"Yes. I dumped the rags I used to clean myself in the barracks furnace later."

"And the damage to her anus?"

"I used my truncheon. With a condom on it."

"To make sure we thought you were male."

"I had it all worked out. I had a good teacher."

"Who?"

"Bell 03. The guy who wrote the *Public Order in Practice* manual."

"You . . . you shouldn't believe everything you read in

books. As for the driver, Rory Baillie, you trailed him from the mess?"

"Believe it or not, I didn't intend to kill him. After all, he wasn't an auxiliary. I wanted information from him."

"But it was a Thursday night."

"My only night off."

"What made you change your mind about killing him?"

"I found foreign currency in his wallet. And an infirmary authorisation issued by Simpson 134."

"After you killed Baillie, you planted Fergus's clothes in the Water of Leith to make sure we didn't suspect a woman."

"You found them, did you? It never said in the *Guardian*."

"What about Roussos, the Greek in the Independence?"

"I was after Simpson 134, the nursing auxiliary. She was difficult to get close to. One day I saw her meet the foreigner and hand an envelope over. So I concentrated on him."

"You thought he had something to do with transplants?"

"There are enough tourists in wheelchairs to make you wonder."

"After you sold a double dummy by dressing as a male transvestite, how did you persuade Roussos to go into the linen store?"

"That was his idea. He said he liked doing it in unusual places."

"You know he was alive when you removed his eye?"

"Yes. The fire alarm went off earlier than I thought it would. My incendiary device did a good job."

"You killed innocent people."

"Who's really innocent, Quintilian? I know for certain you aren't. And you're the hero of the city now. I'd rather be dead than a hero in this cesspool."

I sat up with a start, this time waking Katharine.

"Are you all right?" She ran her palm over my forehead. "You're very hot."

"Bad dream," I said, struggling to get the words out. I looked around, suddenly sure that the murderess was in the room with us.

Katharine pulled me to my feet. "If we're going to sleep, we may as well use the bed."

I followed her, glancing back one last time to convince myself Amanda wasn't there. The muscles on my arms and the bruise on my chest were aching. Katharine pulled back the covers and started to take her clothes off. I saw the triangle of hair in her crotch and the dark rings of her nipples but felt no response.

"Can you understand why she killed?" I asked.

She looked across at me and nodded. "Revenge for someone she loved." She shuddered. "I can sympathise with that. From what you said about Caro, so can you."

I sat down slowly. She was right. We were all guilty of murder, in thought if not in deed.

"After the fire I went back to tracking Simpson 134. Eventually I took a chance and went to the infirmary. Someone came down the corridor before I could get her to tell me what had been done with Gordon's organs. I'd already decided that the medical guardian was responsible."

"The nurse almost identified you. She saw your fingers."

"I was lucky then. I thought you might be getting close. That's why I gave up the Thursday routine. Do you think the show I put on for the guardians was a success?"

"Brought the house down. You know, you could probably have got to the border with Yellowlees as a hostage. Some of his colleagues would have done anything to keep him alive."

"Maybe I should have given myself another chance. What will they do with me?"

"Solitary for life."

"Kill me."

"What?"

"Kill me before they come. I'm begging you, Quintilian."

"I can't. I'm not a killer."

"I don't believe you. Besides, this would be a mercy killing."

"What did you do with the organs you removed?"

"They're under a consignment of fish in the Scott Barracks cold store. I was going to send them to the Council when I had a complete collection."

"Jesus."

"Kill me. You can't let me rot on Cramond Island."

"It's too late, they're coming."

"You're no better than the rest of them. You dress up as an ordinary citizen but under the surface you're still an auxiliary. And a coward."

The word shot through me like the volley from a firing squad. I sat up, disentangling myself carefully from the sheets, and went into the living room. Outside it was dark but the curfew hadn't come into effect yet. I looked down at the road in the glow from the streetlights. Suddenly I was certain that I didn't want to sleep again for a long time. In my dreams I couldn't separate myself from Amanda. She'd used the manual I wrote to kill, in the mistaken belief that the city had been selling organs for profit. But even when I was awake, I couldn't condemn her. Gordon, Katharine, Adam, Billy, Amanda and I all had the same background. We were the children of families where love and affection had been replaced by devotion to the cause. The real criminals were in the Council.

The lights flashed three times then were extinguished. Ten o'clock. The realisation crept up on me like a footpad in the night. In the perfect city, the only way to express free will was to commit murder.

Chapter Twenty-one

I finished my report on the investigation as quickly as I could and spent the next week trying to forget the murderess. Without much success. After a couple of sleepless nights and days spent wandering aimlessly around the city, I even considered going back to the Parks Department – after all, I still had the Transit. Katharine talked me out of that. After Adam's cremation, she seemed to accept his death. In the castle they carried out psychological tests on Amanda, followed by what passes for a trial in Edinburgh. I kept away.

The next Thursday Katharine and I were called to the Council chamber. Two chairs had been placed in front of the horseshoe. The medical guardian's place was empty. It looked like a tooth had fallen from an old man's gum.

My mother kept her head lowered over a pile of papers while we were ushered in. Finally she raised it slowly and looked at me. Her face was even more swollen than before and her hair thinner.

"The meeting will come to order," she said, her voice unsteady. "The contents of the various reports on the activities of the self-confessed murderess Scott 372 are noted. Are there any further comments before we close the file on her?"

No one could find anything to say.

"Next business. Public order guardian?"

Hamilton got to his feet. "My interrogation of the Prostitution Services controller is now complete. Steps have been taken to locate the citizens who were sent to Greece. They will be repatriated as soon as possible."

My mother nodded and made a note.

"As regards Heriot 07," Hamilton continued, "he is making progress. The doctors expect him to be able to face questioning soon."

I'd visited Billy earlier in the week. He was just about coherent and had been told he'd be spending the rest of his life in a wheelchair. I couldn't find much to say to him.

"I trust that Heriot 07 will return to the Finance Directorate when he is fully recovered." Billy's chief looked expectantly at the senior guardian as if what he'd said was perfectly natural.

My mother gave me an uneasy glance. "That will need to be discussed at a later date. Heriot 07 is guilty of serious crimes."

"But where would we be without him?" said the finance guardian. "He made all the deals that . . ."

"That will do, Donald," my mother said firmly. "If you'd kept a tighter rein on your deputy, perhaps none of this would have happened."

The old man looked like he'd just stood on a six-inch nail. He waved his hands weakly and slumped down on to his chair. He wouldn't be in a job for long, I reckoned. Running my eyes along the guardians, I was struck by how wan and impotent they appeared – like the survivors of some natural catastrophe who had come so close to annihilation that they would never be able to return to the way they used to live. Even the younger ones sat slackly in their chairs. The only Council member with any life in him was Hamilton. I soon found out why.

"Senior guardian," he said, getting up again and glancing at me meaningfully. "I would draw your attention to the memorandum I drafted concerning citizen Dalrymple. The recordings of the prisoner's confession suggest that he is in possession of information which may relate to the murderer codenamed the Ear, Nose and Throat Man. My directorate's opinion is that there are grounds for his arrest."

I admired his spirit, going into battle with my mother over me. Perhaps he thought she was in a weak enough condition to accept his advice. When I saw her glacial expression, I realised he might well have a point.

Then she drew herself up and turned to him imperiously. "Guardian, without citizen Dalrymple's work this case would not have been brought to a satisfactory conclusion. You of all people must be aware of that." She gave the irony a few seconds to sink in. "I have considered your memorandum and have concluded that further investigation of a five-year-old case is not in the city's interest."

She got that right. Hamilton's face was bloodless. He sat down without looking in my direction.

I suppose I should have been grateful to my mother but I didn't want her to think she'd bought my silence. "What about the medical guardian's activities? Doesn't the city have a right to know what he was doing with the organs he obtained illegally?"

"You never give up, do you?" my mother said with an infinitely weary sigh. "The body competent to judge the rights of citizens is the Council of Guardians and it is perfectly capable of doing so without reminders from you."

"The body?" I said. The joke was lost on them.

"Come on," said Katharine, standing up. "There's nothing for us here."

"On the contrary," my mother said before we got far. "There is a great deal of work for you here."

I slowed down a little, not enough to suggest I was interested in what she was saying.

"I would be gratified if you were both to accept an invitation to join the Public Order Directorate."

I turned to see Hamilton close to cardiac arrest.

"In appropriately senior positions, of course."

I looked at Katharine. Her lips twitched into a bitter smile.

"I think we'll need some time to think about that," I said.

"Don't take too long." The senior guardian's expression slackened. "As my colleagues are aware, the Council will shortly be restructured. That's why we have delayed naming a new medical guardian." She lowered her head. "I shall be retiring."

I wasn't sure whether to congratulate her or ask her why she'd waited so long, so I did neither. "We'll let you know our decisions," I said. "In the meantime, Scott 372 is waiting to be escorted to Cramond Island."

"There's no shortage of guard personnel capable of that task," my mother observed drily.

"She's my prisoner."

"Very well." She was already poring over another file. "Don't lose her," she said without looking up.

I raised my eyes to the ceiling of the chamber and followed Katharine out.

Hamilton came down the stairs behind me. "Look, Dalrymple," he said, his voice unusually tentative. "It was my duty to write that memo, you do realise that, don't you?"

That wasn't worth an answer.

"What about the directorate? Do you think you'll come back?"

I knew the prospect was about as palatable to him as having Patsy Cameron installed as his personal assistant. No way was I going to put him out of his misery yet.

Evidently Katharine's mind was working the same way. "As far as I'm concerned, the invitation deserves serious consideration," she said sharply and walked out into the evening sun.

Hamilton stared after her. "Strange woman," he murmured.

"She thinks the guilty aren't being adequately punished. In some cases I think she's right."

"You mean the murderess?"

"No. Locking someone up in solitary for life is the worst punishment I can imagine."

"Who then?"

"Billy Geddes, for one. That talk about him staying in his job – are you people hypocrites or just cynical bastards?"

"His expertise would benefit the whole city. With the money . . ."

"Spare me the economics lecture. What about Patsy Cameron? I suppose she's back in Prostitution Services."

"No, she is not, citizen. I have my own ideas about what should happen to her."

I wondered if they involved an eighteenth-century costume and a length of rope.

"Guardian, do me a favour," I said, making the words sound more like an order than a request. "Stay away from the esplanade. I want to handle Scott 372's transfer without you getting in the way."

That shut him up.

Twilight had turned to darkness by the time the squad of guards appeared.

"Here she comes," Davie said, pointing to the castle gatehouse.

I looked over from where the Land-Rovers were parked on the esplanade and watched as Amanda walked slowly towards us, flanked by a heavily armed escort. I felt Katharine stiffen by my side. The prisoner had been given yellow and black striped overalls and labourer's boots, and her hair had been cut short. She still looked like the representative of a superior race. When she caught sight of me, she smiled. She ignored Katharine completely.

"Quintilian," she said. "I was hoping I'd see you again."

We were bathed in light as the vehicles' headlamps came on. The whiteness made Amanda's features even sharper in outline.

"No talking, prisoner!" the guard commander shouted.

"It's all right," I said. "I'm responsible."

Katharine looked at me tensely. "Gag the bitch," she said in a loud whisper. "Are you going to sit in the Land-Rover and have a conversation with her?"

"You don't have to come," I said. "It'd be better if you didn't." I'd tried to get her to go back to the flat but she insisted on seeing the murderess to her cell.

"Don't start that again," she said grimly. "I'm coming."

"Shall we get on then?" asked Amanda politely.

Davie opened the vehicle's rear door and watched as a guardsman secured the prisoner's hands, attaching her handcuffs to the stanchion behind the front seats.

"How many men do you want in there with her?" said the commander.

"One'll do," I replied. "The three of us will be in the front."

"And we'll be right behind you." The grizzled auxiliary strode away to his vehicle.

Doors slammed all around, then engines revved. Katharine and I climbed in. Davie drove off across the esplanade and down on to the Royal Mile.

"So what's next on the agenda, Quintilian?" asked Amanda. She was right behind me but she still needed to raise her voice above the engine noise. "Any more multiple murderers to be caught?"

"Shut her up, for God's sake," Katharine said, turning round to face the prisoner. "If you don't, I will, Quint."

"Calm down, will you?" I looked round as well, first at the guard then at Amanda's handcuffed wrists.

"Bloody right," said Davie. "How do you expect me to drive with all this racket?" He slowed down to take the left turn on to Bank Street by the gallows.

And suddenly I remembered Yellowlees when the lights went out in Moray Place. Amanda had been cuffed to him but when the lights came on again she was free. I jerked my head back round and saw the intent expression on her face. But before I could do anything, she struck, lashed out with her right foot and caught the guardsman sitting opposite on the chin. His head shot back with a sickening crack and he slid lifeless to the floor. At the same time Amanda slipped her right hand out of the handcuff and looped her arm round my neck. I felt the grip tighten.

"I can kill him in a split second," she shouted to the others. "You know I can!"

I sat motionless, my body taut. She only had to wrench her arm round and my neck would snap like a stalk of dried grass. I knew Katharine and Davie understood that – the hold was one that all auxiliaries are taught. The pressure of Amanda's six fingers at the top of my spine sent tingling shafts all over my body.

"What do you want us to do?" I heard Davie ask calmly.

"Call the escort commander and tell him to get his vehicles off our tail. Be very explicit about what I can do to citizen Dalrymple."

He spoke on the mobile. "Where do you want me to drive?" he asked when he'd finished. We were still on the Royal Mile; he'd aborted the turn into Bank Street.

"Go straight ahead," Amanda said. "We're going to take a trip to the border. Turn right on to the South Bridge and head south out of the city." I felt her lean over. "You. Katharine. Call ahead to each checkpoint and make sure they let us through."

"How did you get free?" Katharine asked hoarsely.

"These handcuffs aren't designed for women. I've got thin wrists." Amanda rested her head on the back of mine. "You were weak, Quintilian," she murmured. "You should have killed me when you had the chance."

I felt her warm breath against my skin. Her body was curiously odourless apart from the faint residue of carbolic soap and the musty prisoner's clothing. Members of the superior race probably don't sweat. Outside it was completely dark. We had passed the last of the suburbs. I closed my eyes and wondered if this was how it would end – a quiet interlude before sudden blinding pain and permanent night. With the murderess's lips against my neck I almost felt comfortable, despite her vice-like grip. I remembered how she looked in the interrogation cell. Firm breasts, the nipples visible under thin fabric, smooth thighs leading to her secret place. How did she feel when she killed? How did she feel with my life in her hands? I lost track of time and drifted away, unafraid, into a limbo. I thought I could hear a guitar playing. John Lee Hooker was crooning "Think Twice".

The next thing I knew was Katharine's voice on the mobile advising the border guards at Soutra not to approach the Land-Rover. I opened my eyes and saw the lights of the fortified post standing out against the dark mass of the hillside that marks the extent of the city's territory. The farmhouse where Caro died was only a few hundred yards away.

"You're going to cross the fence, aren't you?" My voice croaked from parched throat and lips.

"*We're* going to cross the fence, Quintilian." The pressure on my neck relaxed slightly. "You were the one who gave me the idea. I haven't got much else in my diary for the next few years." She leaned closer again. "Besides, I haven't finished purging the body politic."

I felt the blood surge through my veins. The idea of going away with her was strangely attractive, even though I knew she only wanted me to cover her escape.

"Call the post again," Amanda said to Katharine. "Don't worry," she breathed in my ear, "we'll soon be on our way."

It happened in an instant. Before I could speak, before I could tell her that I would go with her willingly, I felt a momentary tightening of her grip, then heard a gurgling noise. There was a viscous wetness on my neck.

"So go, bitch," Katharine said. "What are you waiting for?" She pulled away the arm that was suddenly heavy on my shoulders.

I turned round, the pain from trapped nerves lancing into my shoulders, and saw Amanda fall back slowly to settle on the legs of the guardsman she had killed. The haft of the knife Katharine had taken from Davie's belt protruded from her throat, blood welling up around it like a subterranean spring. By the time I clambered over the seat, the quivering in all her fingers had completely stopped.

"Come with me." Katharine took my arm and led me towards the border fence. "You were going to go with her." She looked at me accusingly for a second then glanced back at the guard vehicles that had pulled up around the Land-Rover. "What's there to keep you in this bastard city?"

"Nowhere else is any better," I said dully. In the dark I was scarcely conscious of Katharine but I could still feel the warmth of Amanda's breath on my neck, as well as her gradually congealing blood. I didn't want to wipe it away.

"Well, I'm not staying. They'll put me in the cell they had ready for her."

"Because you committed murder? I think we'll be able to argue sufficient cause."

She turned away. "I don't want strings pulled on my behalf. Christ, Quint." She shook the wire in frustration. "Why don't you come with me? Don't you want to be with me?"

I couldn't find an answer that would have satisfied her.

"It's torn your heart out, the perfect city." She looked back at me and shook her head. "And still you stay." She tried to pull herself up the high fence.

"Here." I cupped my hands for her foot.

Katharine grabbed my shoulders and kissed me once, hard, on the lips. "Don't turn into one of them."

"Katharine," I asked before I lifted her up, "did you kill her for Adam or for me?"

There was no reply. I helped her over and heard her tumble into the grass on the other side. There was a rustle, then she vanished like the last wind of winter.

As I turned to walk back to the lights I felt something against my foot. I knelt down and found a book. When I picked it up, I caught her scent. I knew without looking that it was the copy of Chinese poetry she always carried, the same one that her brother had in his flat. I don't know whether she dropped it deliberately or not. Maybe she meant it to be my reward for finding Adam.

The next day was warm. I opened all the windows of my flat and let the breeze raise the dust from my bookshelves. Katharine's poems were translated by Arthur Waley, so I slotted them in where they belonged alphabetically. They ended up between Barbara Vine's *No Night is Too Long* and Colin Wilson's *Casebook of Murder*. I thought I'd done it quickly, but her perfume came off the spine like a friendly bacillus and made me step back.

There was only one thing for it. I dug around in my tapes for the recordings I was going to send Leadbelly, then found what I was really after: the bootleg of the Millennium Blues concert that packed out the Albert Hall on Hogmanay, AD 1999. B.B. King, Clapton, Thorogood, Moore, Cray, Page, they were all there. This time I wasn't going to listen with the volume turned low and my ear pressed against the speaker. I gave Gilmore Place and the whole neighbourhood "The Lemon Song" and felt a hell of a lot better.

It wasn't long before I saw a guard vehicle pull up. A few moments later, my door burst open.

"Really, citizen, you should be more careful. This music could start a riot."

"Why do you think I'm playing it, Davie?"

"I brought you a couple of things." He threw over a bottle of reasonable malt. "I owed you that from the Waverley, remember?"

"Bit late. But not too late to open it."

It was mid-afternoon by the time we finished it.

"How about it then?" Davie mumbled.

"How about what?"

"The job, asshole. Are you coming back into the directorate or not?" He pulled himself upright with difficulty. "I have a personal interest. You'd need an assistant."

"True."

"Am I going to get an answer?"

"Not yet."

"I didn't let you down, did I?"

"No, Davie. What would I have done without you?"

"Up yours." He slumped down on the sofa again. "Pity about last night."

I nodded, thinking of Katharine and Amanda, still feeling an emptiness that the whisky hadn't done much about. I looked out over the line of rooftops. The sky was the lightest shade of pale blue. Through the window came the roar of the crowd at the Friday afternoon execution. I wondered what had happened to Patsy Cameron. And if my mother had finished reorganising the Council. Was resurrection on the cards for the body politic? If there was enough new blood, I might be tempted to take the job. On my own terms.

"Oh, I almost forgot," Davie said. "I got you this as well."

He tossed over a small plastic bag. It was an E-string for my guitar.

I had to laugh.

THE BONE YARD

The dung really started to fly on Hogmanay, 2021. The last day of the last month is supposed to be a time for celebrating the good things that happened in the old year and for anticipating the joys of the new one. In Edinburgh that means getting slaughtered. Not even the Council of City Guardians has managed to put a stop to that part of our heritage. But this time someone took getting slaughtered literally. It didn't come as a complete surprise. Ever since the new wave of ultra-keen young guardians took over in 2020, there's been an undercurrent of tension in the "perfect city". Everything's been tightened up so much under the new rulers. They call them the "iron boyscouts" in the ordinary citizens' bars when they reckon there's no informer around, or when they're too pissed to care about being sent down the mines for a month. There's too much supervision of everyone's activities, too many regulations, too much control. And as the city's schoolchildren find out in their sex education classes, if you bottle everything up, you're sure to become a pervert. Or a dissident. Or both.

I would never turn down a murder investigation. The problem was that this case didn't start off being one of those. Or rather, it did. But I just didn't realise.

Christ, I wish I had. Whatever way you look at it, I could never have guessed I'd end up in the Bone Yard. I'd trade my entire collection of blues tapes – W.C. Handy and Big Bill Broonzy included – to have missed that gig.

Chapter One

The weather set its trap with all the cunning and skill of a poacher who invites his extended family round for a New Year's banquet then realises his cupboard is bare. In the early afternoon the sky was bright, Mediterranean blue without a hint of a cloud. Citizens ventured out with only one sweater instead of the usual three and tourists imagined that unbuttoned raincoats would be adequate protection. There were even a few guardsmen and women around without their standard-issue maroon scarves. They all got a couple of hours of reasonable warmth, then the sun went west and the temperature swapped a minus for a plus reading faster than politicians pocketed envelopes stuffed with banknotes in the years before the UK fell apart. I was standing at my living room window when people in the street below started jerking about as if a mantrap's serrated jaws had suddenly closed around their legs. It wasn't exactly warm in my flat, but at least I had a glass of barracks malt to ward off the cold.

"What have you got on tonight, Davie?" I asked, glancing over my shoulder. "For God's sake, leave my guitar alone. The neighbours will start complaining."

The bulky figure on the sofa raised his middle finger, scratched his beard and continued strumming. "And a happy New Year to you too, Quint. If they put up with you playing the blues, I don't see why they should be bothered by this."

3

"Possibly because they like the blues, while what you're playing is just a wee bit passé."

"Nothing wrong with 'Flower of Scotland'."

"Nothing apart from the fact that Scotland ceased to exist seventeen years ago." I took another pull of whisky. "And the fact that your lords and masters outlawed the song."

Davie discarded the guitar and picked up his glass. "They also banned the blues, Quint."

"Which shows you what a bunch of tossers they are."

"That's enough abuse of the Council, citizen." Davie didn't look too bothered as he poured himself more malt. "Unfortunately I'm on duty tonight. I've got to supervise patrols in the tourist area."

"Which is why you're getting your drinking in now, is it?" I asked. Not that Davie's consumption of alcohol would affect his ability to do his job. The Council may have been struggling to provide Edinburgh's population with decent food, but he was still fit enough to take on anyone in an Olympic wrestling competition. Except there haven't been any Olympics Games for a long time – too many countries have been reduced to warring city-states.

I peered down into the street below. It was rapidly sinking into the gloom of twilight. Under the Energy Directorate's recent electricity rationing plan, the streetlights don't come on until as late as possible.

"So, no chance of a romantic Hogmanay with Fiona, then?" I said. Davie had been spending more time than his rank are meant to with a fellow auxiliary. I did a double-take. "Jesus, look at this. There's a lunatic coming along Gilmore Place."

"Not very likely, given the Council's policy on unproductive citizens. They're all banged up in homes for life."

"Not this one." I followed the guy along the street. First he pressed himself into a doorway on the other side. He waited, then slowly stuck his head out to take a look. And then he sprinted across to the near side in what could charitably be described as an ungainly fashion, narrowly avoiding being hit by a superannuated Supply Directorate van. "Look at him now."

Davie joined me at the window and we watched as the man in the street continued his antics. He was around six feet and thin, like all citizens, in his early twenties, as far as I could make out in the murk. He was wearing an orange woolly hat and the standard dark blue overcoat ordinary citizens obtain with clothing vouchers. From the doorway three down from mine, his head appeared slowly, looking towards the Tollcross end of the street.

"He seems to be checking if he's being followed," Davie said. Then he burst out laughing. "Bloody hell, what a jackass."

Our man belted across the road again, his legs kicking high like a pony that's just seen the vet get out his biggest syringe. Again, the head poked in and out nervously from a doorway opposite.

"Check out your lot and see if they're chasing him." I kept an eye on the strange guy while Davie flipped open his mobile and called the guard command centre in the castle. If it hadn't been for the cold and the location – my flat's on a street where tourists only come if they were born with a jellyfish's sense of direction – I'd have assumed he was a street performer in the year-round arts festival that's the mainstay of the city's income.

Davie signed off. "No. They didn't have a clue what I was on about."

"Don't worry. I think we're about to find out."

The young man had crossed the road, legs all over the place again. We watched as he disappeared from view directly beneath my window.

"You don't think he's on his way up here, do you?" Davie asked dubiously.

"He's a client all right," I replied. "Care for a small wager?"

"Bollocks to that. You know I don't bet with you any more,

Quint." Davie's barracks commander had lost patience with the number of bottles of whisky he used to take from the mess to cover his wagers with me. The one we were drinking now was my Hogmanay present.

I listened for footsteps on the stair. They weren't long in coming. The knock was quiet, just a couple of tentative taps.

"No, I'll get it," I said, waving Davie back to the sofa. "Your uniform isn't likely to turn him on."

I opened up and let in the guy from the street. At close range he looked much more normal. He pulled off the woollen cap – presumably a gift from a doting mother who could only find orange wool in the city's stores – and revealed thick brown hair shorter than the regulation one-inch length. His face was thin and his brown eyes seemed to be far too big for the rest of his features. He smiled hopefully.

"Citizen Dalrymple?" He glanced over my shoulder, but didn't look particularly concerned by the sight of Davie in his City Guard's grey tunic with the maroon heart. If anything his smile got broader.

"The same," I said. "Call me Quint. And that's Hume 253." I didn't give him Davie's name. That would have been too much of a shock for an ordinary citizen – auxiliaries are supposed to be faceless servants of the city and if you don't address them by barracks name and number, you're nailed for non-compliance.

"Em, right." The young man fiddled with his hat then stuffed it into his pocket. "The name's Aitken, Roddie Aitken." He gave another smile, as if what he was called was a private joke.

"Fancy a dram, Roddie?' I asked, holding up the bottle.

He stared at it like he'd never seen whisky before. He may well not have seen barracks whisky before. The look on his face suggested either that he had a massive hangover or that he was one of the few Edinburgh citizens who have an aversion to alcohol.

"Sit down," I said, pointing to the place on the sofa next to Davie. "Don't worry, he won't bite."

Davie wasn't too impressed by that kind of talk in front of a citizen.

"So, Roddie," I said, giving him what I thought was an encouraging smile. "Who's following you?"

The guy looked like I'd just accused him of being sympathetic to the aims of the democrats in Glasgow. He sat bolt upright and looked over towards the door, as if he were gauging whether he could beat us to it.

"Don't panic," I said. "I saw you in the street."

Roddie Aitken relaxed a bit and smiled weakly. "I must have looked like a right ..."

"Aye, you did," Davie said with a grin.

The young man laughed. He didn't seem to be intimidated by Davie's presence; some of my clients would rather forgo their sex sessions than talk in front of an auxiliary. "I heard you help people out," he said, turning to me. "Is that right, citizen Dalrymple?"

"Quint," I said. "Remember?"

He nodded apologetically.

"And I do help people out, as you put it."

"But you're not in the guard?"

"Not any more. I have contacts though." I nodded at Davie. "Why? Have you got a problem with the guard?"

Roddie Aitken shrugged. "No, not at all. It's just that I told them about my problem and they ... well, they haven't followed it up."

It wasn't the first time I'd heard that story. There aren't enough auxiliaries in the Public Order Directorate to deal with every citizen's request for help. One of the reasons I didn't rejoin the directorate when I was invited a couple of years back was that there's plenty to do cleaning up their omissions and lapses.

The fact that I'm regarded as Mephistopheles without a disguise by the new wave of headbangers in the Council is neither here nor there.

"What exactly is your problem, citizen?" Davie demanded with typical guardsman's subtlety.

"Yes, you'd better give us a clue, Roddie," I said, gesturing to Davie to lay off him. "Don't be shy. Hume 253 often works with me."

Aitken thought about it for a few moments, then got stuck into his story. It often happens like that. Clients spend the first few minutes with their noses twitching like dogs carrying out extensive research on an unfamiliar leg, then they suddenly start rubbing themselves up against it like the trousers are on heat.

"I told the guard about the hooded man yesterday morning. They said they'd get back to me today, but they haven't. The thing is, I'm not sure what it's all about. Jimmie reckons that the guy was trying to have a real go at me, but I didn't see the knife . . ."

Davie's eyes were rolling and mine probably weren't too stable either. "Hold on a second, you've lost us," I said. "We've got a hooded man, a knife, a Jimmie, the guard and you. Make some connections, will you?"

Roddie Aitken laughed and his face took on an even more boyish look. It was hard to tell how old he was. Maybe that's why he was dubious about the whisky. "I knew it would sound crazy," he said.

Davie got up and went over to the window.

Suddenly the young man's face looked older. His eyes were wide open, fixed on the figure in uniform. "Is he there?" he asked in a taut voice. "Can you see a big guy in a long coat with a hood?"

Davie stared down at the street, lit now by the dull glow of streetlamps on low power. Then he turned back to us, shaking his head slowly. "No hooded men, no one dressed up as Santa Claus who's got the date wrong, no one chasing people down the road with a knife. How many beers have you had today, laddie?"

Roddie looked offended. "None." His face reddened. "I don't like drinking that much."

"Let's start from the beginning," I said, giving Davie a look that he ignored. "Someone in a coat with a hood has been following you, right?"

He nodded, glancing at Davie with an injured expression. I felt a bit sorry for him.

"So how often have you seen him? When did all this start?"

Roddie sat up and pulled his orange hat out. "Look, I think I'm wasting your time. I didn't really want to come. It was Jimmie who—"

"Hang on," I said. "You can't just walk out. I've got my tongue hanging out like a kid whose girlfriend's decided she won't undo her blouse after all."

He grinned shyly, then sat back again. "Fair enough, citizen . . . I mean Quint."

"Right. Fill me in then."

"The first time I saw the guy was on Christmas Eve. I work in the Supply Directorate — the Deliveries Department. Food mainly, sometimes some booze, cigarettes for the nightclubs, that sort of thing."

I was interested. It's unusual for someone as young as Roddie Aitken to get a job as a delivery man. The older members of that department hog the driving duty because it gives them the chance to pilfer — if they have the nerve to risk a spell on the city farms or down the mines.

"It was in the Grassmarket, across the road from the Three Graces. I couldn't see a face or anything. It must have been about half seven in the evening and they hadn't turned all the lights on. Anyway, I was in a hurry — they'd suddenly realised they were short of whisky."

"How did you know he was interested in you?" Davie asked.

Roddie Aitken raised a finger to his lips and shook his head slowly. "I didn't really. It was just . . . he was staring at me, really hard. You know, giving me the eye."

"Nothing else happened?" I asked.

"No. I went into the club and made my delivery. When I came out, he wasn't there any more."

Davie leaned towards him. "You say 'he'. How do you know it was a man?"

Roddie's forehead wrinkled as he thought about that. It looked to me like he did more thinking than the average citizen. I wondered why he wasn't an auxiliary.

"Can't say for sure. He was big – not huge, but big enough to be a pretty unusual woman." He smiled at the idea. "The hood part of his coat had a kind of high neck as well; that's why I couldn't see much of his face."

"Not much to go on so far," Davie said.

"I know. Then I saw him again three days ago, last Saturday night about half nine. This time it was on Nicolson Street, near my flat. I looked round a couple of times and he was still there, about twenty yards behind me." He shrugged. "Then I turned into Drummond Street where I live and he didn't show."

I wasn't too excited so far. Christ, the guy himself didn't seem to be very bothered. But something about his expression, a tightening of the skin around his eyes, suggested the punchline was worth waiting for.

"Then he showed up again the night before last." Roddie turned to me, his eyes wider. "I'd been working late. One of my mates in the department was sick – pissed, I should think – so I was delivering vegetables to the shops. I got back to Drummond Street just before curfew at ten. The sky was dead clear and there was a frost. That must have been why the footsteps sounded so loud. This time I didn't see him till I was about fifty yards from my door." He stopped to catch his breath, looking at both of us. "Then he started running. I turned round and saw the figure in the long coat and hood. He had something in his hand.

I ... I couldn't see what he could possibly want with me so I didn't run, just walked a bit more quickly."

I began to get the distinct feeling that Roddie Aitken was too laid back for his own good. I reckon I'd have been down the road faster than the mob in London after the millennium when they spotted anyone who looked like a city trader or a lawyer.

"I didn't really see what happened next," he said. "Jimmie, my neighbour, opened the street door and pulled me in as the guy hurtled past. Jimmie swears blind he saw a big knife, but I don't know ..."

"What exactly was this Jimmie doing at the door?" I asked.

Roddie smiled. "He's a nosy old bugger. Always sits at his window. He said he saw the man in the hood and didn't like the look of him, so he came out."

Davie stood up again and headed for the window. "And you reported this to the guard?"

"Jimmie told me I should." Roddie Aitken shrugged. "I suppose he had a point – after all, he saw the knife. There are some crazies around, even in Edinburgh."

He was right there. But I couldn't figure out why even a crazy guy would follow a delivery man around. "Is there anyone who's got a grudge against you, Roddie? At work, for instance?"

He looked at me innocently, as if the idea were ridiculous. "No. I get on fine with everyone, Quint. I reckon it's just a piece of nonsense." He paused and glanced down at his hands. They had suddenly started to shake. "At least I did, until I saw him behind me as I came along Lauriston Place on my way here."

That explained why he'd been acting like a five-year-old on speed in the street. Davie was already on his way towards the door.

"What colour was the coat?" he asked.

Roddie shrugged. "I'm not sure exactly. Dark – maybe navy blue or black."

The door banged behind Davie.

"Have you got a complaint reference?" I asked.

"Aye." Roddie handed me a crumpled piece of official paper numbered 3474/301221. It told me that citizen Roderick Aitken, address 28f Drummond Street, age twenty-two years, next of kin Peter Aitken of 74m Ratcliffe Terrace (relation: father), had reported an attempted assault by a person unknown (probably male). The location and a description of the assailant were also given. I was pretty sure that the guard would have paid about as much attention to Roddie's report as they pay to the city's few remaining Christians when they complain that the Moslem tourists get more religious tolerance than they do. The thing is, the Christians are right. Maybe Roddie Aitken was too.

"Look, how do you feel about this, Roddie? Do you reckon the guy is really after you?" I fixed my eyes on his. "You'd better come clean with me. Are you in trouble?" I was thinking of his work — maybe he'd got in some heavy-duty black marketeer's way.

Roddie opened his arms to protest his innocence. "I haven't got a clue, Quint, honestly. I'm straight." He looked at me with his wide brown eyes. "All I ever wanted was to be an auxiliary, but I failed the exams two years ago because my maths is so crap. I'm having another go next month. I don't do what some of the others in the department do — pilfering, selling black and the like."

I opened my mouth to speak but he beat me to it.

"And I haven't been telling tales either. None of my workmates knows I'm doing the exams."

I believed him. He was a pretty wholesome citizen, the kind who should have been in the guard instead of arselickers who don't give a shit about the city. Like all of us, he could have done with a better diet and a shower more than once a week. But he gave the impression that he was proud to be an Edinburgh citizen. There aren't too many like that these days.

"All right," I said. "I'll see what I can do."

"Great. I can't pay you very much ..."

"Don't worry about that. The Public Order Directorate subsidises me. After a fashion." I looked at my watch. "There isn't much I can do tonight though."

Roddie stood up. "No problem. I'm going out with my friends."

"Right. Stick with them and ring my mobile if you see the guy again." I scribbled the number on a piece of paper. "I'll come round to your place tomorrow and talk to your neighbour."

He pulled his hideous orange hat down over his ears. "What time do you think you'll come?" He suddenly looked a bit awkward.

"Some time in the middle of the day." I wasn't going to let him off the hook. "What's the matter? You don't like drinking, so you won't have a post-Hogmanay hangover. Not planning an illicit sex session by any chance, are you?" Citizens are only supposed to have sex with officially approved partners.

His face was red, but he looked pleased with himself. "Well, I've got this girlfriend, Quint, and I'm hoping . . ."

"It's okay. I won't tell Hume 253."

A second later Davie came back shaking his head. "No sign of the mystery man."

I went to the door with Roddie and put my hand on his shoulder. "I'll see you tomorrow then. Don't worry about the idiot in the hood. Have a great Hogmanay."

"Thanks, Quint." Roddie headed down towards the street. "Same to you."

"Not much chance of that," I called after him. "I'm going to the guardians' annual cocktail party."

"Lucky you," he replied, without a trace of irony.

He'd have had a great future as an auxiliary.

Chapter Two

I pulled on the least crumpled of my black sweatshirts and a reasonably clean pair of strides, also black. I wouldn't wear anything smarter to a Council do on principle and anyway, my only suit is retro enough to be banned on the grounds that it might bring about a 1990s nostalgia cult. Then I checked myself out in the mirror. The usual suspect. One thing to be said for food rationing is that it keeps you trim. My jawbone looked like it was about to break through the parchment of my face and I didn't seem to be big enough for my clothes. My half-inch-long hair was continuing its deep and meaningful relationship with greyness, but at least my teeth hadn't fallen out. Yet.

Coming up to seven. They'd soon be kicking off at Parliament House, not that I intended to arrive on time. I took a last pull of whisky, decided against having a blast of B.B. King then hit the road. Davie had offered me a lift in his guard Land-Rover when he went off to the castle for his shift, but I prefer walking. You never know what you might come across on the perfect city's streets. Hooded men lurking in doorways perhaps.

As I headed past Tollcross towards West Port and the Grassmarket, I found myself trying to put the last year's chaos into some kind of order; 2021 wasn't likely to take up too much space in Edinburgh history, not even in the make-believe version the Information Directorate was no doubt working on at this very moment. Most of the old guardians had been eased out in 2020 — thanks mainly to my mother, as senior guardian, at last coming to her senses and resigning — and for the rest of that year the new guardians kept their eye on the ball reasonably well.

"How are you doing, Quint?" The old man who hands out the *Edinburgh Guardian* at the corner of Lothian Road and Fountainbridge interrupted my reverie. "On the piss tonight?"

"After a fashion. How about you, Andy?"

He opened his worn duffel coat. "Look. I managed to get hold of a bottle of stout to bring the New Year in."

I nodded, suddenly feeling guilty about the malt I'd been gulping. Christ, even last year the average citizen managed to find enough bevies to do the job. "Have a good one when it comes, Andy," I said.

"Aye, laddie, you too."

I walked on, seething. This is how Edinburgh is now. Things were buggered from the start of 2021. The city prides itself on being independent, but that doesn't mean it can survive in a vacuum. There was a disastrous flu epidemic in the Far East and that sent tourist numbers from China, Korea and Japan right round the U-bend. Then the Russian mafia thought it would be a neat idea to lob some former Soviet warheads into the Middle East to screw up oil production and, all of a sudden, a lot of Arabic-speaking tourists had better things to do than mess about in Edinburgh's shops and clubs. So revenues did a nose-dive and we only get meat once a week, a beer at the weekend if we're lucky and enough coal to keep ourselves as warm as penguins on an ice floe. It's a pretty good recipe for civil unrest. But the iron boyscouts — fifty per cent of the guardians are female but somehow "iron girlguides" doesn't have the same ring to it — instead of patting us on the back and sweet-talking us about how the good times are just round the corner, decided to apply the thumbscrews. Everything's by the book now, no leniency. Step out of line and you're in the shit. But as they say on the streets, at least the shit's warmer than your average citizen's flat.

The castle rose up before me. It was lit up like a flagship in pre-independence times on an evening when the admiral had his pals round for a pint or two of pink gin. That was the kind of thing the Enlightenment Party, the Council's forerunner, had vowed it would put a stop to. Everyone in the city would be equal, the same opportunities for all and so on. And here I was on my way to a reception where guardians and senior auxiliaries would be offering foreign dignitaries the best food and drink the city could provide, without an ordinary citizen in sight. If we could eat hypocrisy, there'd be no problems with malnutrition.

I came down into the Grassmarket and my nose filled with the delicate odour of cow dung. A couple of days a week, cattle are run in here by herdsmen dressed in seventeenth-century costumes as a spectacle for the tourists. The Agriculture Directorate swears the beasts are all BSE-free. I hope they're right — there are sometimes rumours about outbreaks in the city farms, followed by the secret culling of infected herds. I edged round the cowpats. A squad of labourers was clearing them up without much enthusiasm. Beyond the skeletal trees in the middle of the broad street is the Three Graces Club where Roddie Aitken had his first sighting of the hooded man. It's another example of the Council's double standards. Strictly tourists only are allowed to watch a floorshow that gives the imagination the evening off, especially when the Three Graces themselves are on. I suppose Canova's marble sculpture of the goddesses in the City Gallery might be a turn-on to a few perverts, but the performers in the club make sure everyone in the audience gets the point — using a lot of pointed accessories that the sculptor didn't find space for.

I looked across at the replica of the ensemble on the pavement outside the nightclub. Even at this early stage it was surrounded by potential customers who were running their hands over the Graces' rumps. When the original was first brought to Edinburgh for some ludicrous amount of money in the 1990s, I can remember people referring to it as the Six Buttocks. I can also remember my mother giving me a major earbashing when I did the same. She never was one for levity. Then again, when she was senior guardian she did plenty to establish the city's reputation as the Bangkok of the North. I never quite understood how she managed to reconcile that with the Council's ideals of sexual restraint and the inviolability of the body. Obviously filling the city's coffers took priority. Ah well, I couldn't hold it against her now. She died last January. I didn't see her much after her resignation and the lupus she'd been suffering from for years gave her a bad time near the end. But I sometimes feel an unexpected sense of loss. I reckon my old man does too, not that he'd ever admit it.

As I walked up the West Bow past souvenir shops bedecked with tartan scarves and plastic haggises, it occurred to me that perhaps I was being too hard on the present Council. After all, they were only continuing the policies of their predecessors, with a zeal my mother and her colleagues would have approved of. Then again, there's nothing worse than a young zealot. I should know. In a previous existence I was one. Before Caro died seven years back and my career in the Public Order Directorate became about as meaningful as a 1990s European Union directive on the configuration of bananas.

I stopped outside a shop and watched a Chinese family buying what looked like Edinburgh's entire stock of souvenir playing cards. Their faces were wreathed in smiles, from the aged grandmother with suspiciously black hair to the infant cradled in her father's arms. I shivered and stamped my feet as the cold bit hard. But it wasn't just the chill that was getting to me. In the rush to establish a just and equitable society, we forgot about friendship and affection, not to mention love. We get physical at weekly sex sessions, but there are no sessions for emotion. Then I thought of Davie and his Fiona. Even though auxiliaries aren't supposed to get emotionally involved, they seemed to manage all right. Maybe it was my own fault. I was still hung up on a woman I hadn't seen for nearly two years. Katharine Kirkwood. She came to me because her brother had gone missing and we ended up in a multiple murder case. Then Katharine left the city. God knows where she was. She'd probably erased all traces of me from her memory by now.

I walked up to the Royal Mile and glanced at the gallows where they give the tourists a thrill with mock hangings. I was going through one of my regular depressive phases. There's only one known cure – taunting guardians and senior auxiliaries. I headed to the reception with a spring in my step.

I resisted the temptation to spit on the Heart of Midlothian as I passed in front of St Giles. It used to be the tradition, but if you do that kind of thing nowadays you're asking for trouble. They don't mention it in the City Regulations (a document which I've come to know intimately in my line of work) and I don't imagine anyone would complain if a tourist who'd read Walter Scott gobbed on the brass plaque that marks the site of the old Tolbooth. But the maroon heart is the emblem of the city and the guard are pretty touchy about it being messed with by ordinary citizens. Christ, I'd almost talked myself into emptying out my throat.

But I was interrupted. A horse-drawn carriage with a group of Africans in colourful robes missed me by about an inch on its way to the neo-classical façade of what was once known as Parliament House. It's called the Halls of the Republic now – you can't get away from Plato in this city. The Council only uses it for over-the-top receptions like this one. They prefer the Gothic pile of the Assembly Hall for their daily meetings. They have a point in one respect. This building was where the Scottish law courts were based before the Enlightenment won the last election in 2003. Since the Council rapidly dispensed with the concept of an independent judiciary and gave the Public Order Directorate responsibility for the administration of justice, they'd have been pushing their luck in the irony stakes if they'd located their base here. Besides, the draughts in the Halls of the Republic are even worse than down the road.

The guardsmen and women on duty at the entrance took one look at my clothes and moved towards me *en masse*, hands on their truncheons. Then they recognised me and stepped back. Some of them nodded as I came up — they were the ones who'd heard that I'm good at what I do. The rest belonged to the persuasion who regard me as a boil on the body politic. The way they were glaring at me suggested they'd like to take me round the back and use their service knives to lance me.

Inside the building a red carpet leads to the main hall. Auxiliaries dressed in medieval costumes lined the corridors. Maybe they gave the foreign dignitaries a thrill, but they did nothing for me. The old hall was another story though. It was packed with people who'd already got well stuck into the magic, but I wasn't paying attention to them. It was the seventeenth-century roof that caught my eye: great oak hammerbeams arcing over the throng like the stained bones of some gigantic creature that had perished in the dawn of time. There were open log fires roaring in the ornately decorated fireplaces, their flickering light glinting on the varnish of the beams and catching the colours of the painted windows. One of them shows the charter of the newly independent city being handed over by a suspiciously well-fed citizen to the first senior guardian.

"Is that outfit the best you could do, Dalrymple?"

I gave up perusing the decor reluctantly and grabbed a crystal glass from a passing waitress who was dressed up as one of Robert the Bruce's camp followers, complete with disembowelling knife.

"Tell the truth, Lewis. You couldn't bear the disappointment if I turned up in a suit." I took a slug of the whisky. It was a dark, smooth malt that the Supply Directorate must have been keeping in reserve for this sort of occasion: there are no trading links with the Highlands any more and the whisky produced by the city's two distilleries is a sight worse than this.

The public order guardian shook his head in disgust and sipped mineral water. He used to be famous for his rum and cigarette consumption before independence, but guardians don't allow themselves any vices. In the case of coffin nails, they don't allow anyone else that vice either: they banned them, along with TV and private cars, not long after they came to power.

"So, have you been enjoying youself telling the foreigners how little crime there was in Edinburgh last year, Lewis?" I was pleased to see my use of his name in public was giving him the needle. Guardians are supposed to be addressed by title only.

"And what if I have, citizen?" he said combatively. "The directorate's kept things under a tight rein."

I laughed. "That's true enough. No murders, not many muggings—"

"None at all in the central tourist area," he interrupted.

"Only a few burglaries in the suburbs," I continued. "And officially, there's no drug consumption, no rape, male or female, no gunrunning" – I glanced up from my glass and saw that Lewis Hamilton was beginning to look pleased with himself – "no pornography – at least among ordinary citizens – no bribery, at least none reported." I gave him a smile before skewering him. "And a black market that runs as efficiently as any other department in the city."

He looked around, eyes bulging, and stepped closer. "Keep your voice down, man. You know perfectly well that a carefully regulated black market is necessary to maintain equilibrium."

Yet another example of Council hypocrisy. Citizens get nailed if they're caught skimming off goods from city stores or delivering short, but all the time auxiliaries are keeping tabs on the black economy. Actually, to be fair to Lewis Hamilton, it's something that's come about under the iron boyscouts and I reckon he's not too keen on it himself. But he's one of the few survivors from my mother's team, so he hasn't got much room for manoeuvre.

The guardian moved back and eyed me balefully. "I don't understand your attitude, Dalrymple. The directorate gives you your ration vouchers and allows you to work in your idiosyncratic fashion. Why do you have to be so bloody bolshy?"

I couldn't help laughing. Lewis sometimes sounds like a caricature of a mid-twentieth-century colonel. But he had a point. I could have gone back into the directorate on my own terms after the murder case in 2020, but I didn't fancy the boneheaded hierarchy. Better to stay outside, keep up my private investigations and help him chase dissidents when he gets desperate. I thought I might come across some trace of Katharine that way too, but I've never even had a sniff.

"Good evening, citizen."

I turned and was confronted by another reason I've kept my distance from the directorate: Hamilton's deputy, known in the trade as Machiavelli. A scheming, arse-licking piece of slime who'd stab his boss in the back if the lights went out. Fortunately for Lewis, the directorates have their own power supply and their electricity doesn't go down like it does in ordinary citizens' houses.

"How's life, Raeburn 03?" I said, pronouncing his barracks number like it was a virulent strain of groin infection.

He returned the favour by giving me a supercilious smile from beneath his feeble beard as he drew his superior away for a private chat. I watched them as they retreated to the area in front of the statue of Viscount Melville. The body language was revealing. Raeburn 03, wavy blond hair gleaming in the light, was doing a Uriah Heep, rubbing his hands like they were covered in best barracks lard and bending his skinny frame towards Hamilton, who was bending over backwards to keep his distance.

I grabbed a refill and caught sight of my father with another former guardian. The Council usually ignores ex-members but it invites them to the Hogmanay reception to keep them sweet. Hector didn't use to turn up, but since my mother died he's been more assertive. I went over.

"Hello, old man."

"Hello, failure." The skin around my father's eyes creased and he nodded to me slowly. "I wasn't sure you'd come, Quintilian." He loves to use my full name. He should do. It was his idea.

"I wouldn't miss a chance to network with the city's movers and shakers," I said ironically. "How are you, William?"

The shrivelled figure at my father's side quivered as if the force of my breath was almost enough to knock him over. He used to be science and energy guardian when my mother was in charge, but it didn't look like he had a lot of energy reserves left now.

"William," he repeated in a querulous voice. "I'd almost forgotten my name. They still call me 'guardian' in the retirement home. William Augustus McEwan," he said slowly. Then he seemed to revive. "I'm still going, Quintilian. Hector has been telling me about your exploits."

"Uh-huh. Don't believe everything the old man says."

"But I do, Quintilian, I do." William McEwan smiled sadly. "The city needs more like you." He looked around blearily at the mass of people. "The new guardians, they're going to throw everything we worked for away." He shook again and held on to my father's arm. In their faded tweed jackets and worn brogues, surrounded by loud-mouthed drinkers gabbling away to hard-faced young auxiliaries, the pair of them had the appearance of time travellers who'd got stuck in the wrong millennium.

I tried to inject a light-hearted note. "The Council has about as much desire for more citizens like me as it has for an outbreak of AIDS among the city's nightclub staff."

William McEwan shook his head weakly. "You're wrong,

my boy. They're going to need you, all right. They don't know what they're letting themselves in for."

I've rarely seen anyone look more solemn. Even Hector, never one to keep his feelings about the boyscouts to himself, looked dubious. "Have another whisky, you old misery guts," he said. "You don't get this quality of dram in the home."

But his companion was peering round the room again, apparently looking for someone. As he was doing that, I caught the medical guardian's eye and raised my glass. Despite her sober black dress and flat-heeled shoes she stood out, her short, silver-blonde hair and high cheekbones a striking combination even among a gaggle of ambassadors' wives in expensive outfits. She raised an eyebrow at me. If she hadn't been a guardian, and therefore sworn to celibacy, I might have tried to forget Katharine by having a go. As things are, there's no chance.

Hector started mumbling about some less than fascinating discovery he'd made about Juvenal's sexual peccadilloes. My father's spent years combing the pages of the old Roman misogynist, presumably because it keeps him close in spirit to his wife. A waiter in a pair of tartan trews came up with a silver tray full of canapés that ordinary citizens wouldn't have recognised as food. As a representative of that body, I did my duty and grabbed as many caviar, lobster and *foie gras* dainties as I could.

"Here, William," I said, turning to the ex-guardian. "Have some of . . ."

But he was off, piling across the hall like a man with a mission. I almost choked on my vol-au-vent when I saw who he'd approached. Then he started waving his arms about with surprising force.

"Oh, Christ," said my father.

"Oh, Christ is right." I handed him my evening meal and went to rescue William McEwan. The person he'd chosen to give a piece of his mind to was the senior guardian; and although the senior guardian is supposed to be a leader among equals, the present one's more like a deity than a servant of the city. He'd been groomed for the top since the day he started the auxiliary training programme. He had the kind of record that other auxiliaries would sacrifice their closest colleagues for – triple As in every exam he ever sat, four bravery commendations during border duty and numerous prizes for his knowledge of Plato. His calm authority seemed to inspire worryingly mindless levels of devotion in his supporters. The tall figure in an immaculate powder blue suit turned to William like he was an irritating insect, smiling apologetically at his guests. But as I approached, it seemed that the guardian's brow furrowed and it even looked like he was being shaken by what he was hearing. His eyes, pale blue between the black of his hair and wispy beard, held the old man in an unwavering stare. Which meant that young blue eyes didn't register my arrival.

"And what about the Bone Yard?" William McEwan demanded, all traces of querulousness vanished from his voice. "What about those poor—"

He broke off and gasped as the senior guardian gripped his wrist.

I put my hand on William's shoulder and pulled him gently away. That broke the senior guardian's flinty gaze and he swung his eyes on to me, briefly stopping to take in my missing right forefinger.

"Citizen Dalrymple." The deity favoured me with a thin-lipped and very brief smile. "I'm afraid the former guardian is not very well. I suggest you remove him before he makes a spectacle of himself." He turned back to the men in suits he'd been addressing and ushered them away from us.

"What was all that about, William?" I asked as I led him and Hector to the nearest corner. "What's the Bone Yard?" But he was shaking, all the energy he'd summoned up now spent like a battery's last surge, and I didn't get any answers to my questions. Not long afterwards I put Hector and him into a guard vehicle and sent them back to their retirement home. What a way to spend Hogmanay.

It didn't get much better. I hung around and consumed as many canapés and as much whisky as I could manage. And I chatted up a few foreign businessmen's wives, but never got beyond them telling me how much they liked shopping in Edinburgh because of the low prices. When midnight came, I joined hands and sang "Auld Lang Syne" like the rest of them. It was worth staying that long to see how awkward some of the guardians looked when they tried to be spontaneous. Machiavelli in particular had the horrified expression of a snake that's just slithered into a convention of secretary birds. That's when I decided I'd seen enough.

Outside by St Giles I took in a few deep breaths to clear my head. Bad idea. My lungs tensed up like they'd just been injected with ice water. For a moment I even thought I was going to pass out. It was the idea of landing on the frozen pavement that made me get a grip. I headed home, the distant singing of revellers in the suburbs echoing in my ears like it did when I was a kid and Scotland won the rugby Grand Slam. Tonight was the only night of the year when the curfew isn't enforced. I suddenly felt wide awake, the whisky only a faint throb in my temples, dead certain that I wasn't going to sleep for hours. I stopped at the corner of George IVth Bridge and Roddie Aitken flashed into my mind. I wondered if he was all right. I even considered walking down to Drummond Street and knocking him up. Then I remembered he had a girlfriend. I'd be really popular if I turned up at this time of night.

So I wandered back to my place and shivered through the wee small hours listening to the blues at low volume. When I eventually crashed out, Katharine Kirkwood and the medical guardian refused to keep me company, even in my dreams. That was a great start to 2022.

Chapter Three

It was still dark when I came to. Workmen seemed to have been round during the night and poured a ton of gravel down my throat. My feet had made an abortive break for freedom but hadn't got any further than six inches from the edge of the bedcover. They were so cold that I was forced to get up and knead the circulation back into them. After that I was wide awake and there was no point in going back to bed, despite the fact that New Year's Day is one of the few official holidays recognised by the Council.

I worked at what the Supply Directorate describes as my "desk, plywood, ordinary citizen issue" — more like a picnic table with rickety legs that I've had to shore up with volumes of ancient philosophy — and brought some of my missing persons reports up to date. Most of them were just people who'd been called up for extra duty in the mines or on the farms. The Labour Directorate is supposed to notify their next of kin but the paperwork is for ever going astray. And then there are the citizens who get sick of the Garden of Edin and cross the border without having the nerve to let their family know. I've lost count of the number of times I've had to tell tearful mothers and disbelieving partners that their loved ones have done a runner. I try to do it with a bit more delicacy than the City Guard.

I gave Roddie Aitken until eleven to do what he had to do with the girlfriend he was so bashful about, then headed off to his flat. There was no point in trying to call him since the only phones available to citizens are the public ones at the end of every third street. In the early days of the Enlightenment it was claimed that the telephone system was too expensive to maintain and that the mindless nattering it encouraged wasted time which could be put to more productive use. Everyone knows the Council just wanted to control the flow of information.

It was still cold enough to make deep breathing a hazardous occupation, the sky clear and deceitfully bright. I walked along Lauriston Place, the soot-stained granite of the City Infirmary on my right and what used to be George Heriot's School on my left. Its flag-topped turrets and octagonal dome now house a hotel dedicated to the wealthiest of post-communist China's businessmen and women. No prizes for guessing which building is better looked after. I walked on through what used to be university territory. The Medical School is an auxiliary training centre, while the McEwan Hall is now called the Edinburgh Enlightenment Lecture and Debating Hall – the dialogues of Plato which underpin the city's constitution are analysed on a daily basis here. The D-shaped building's former name reminded me of the ex-science and energy guardian and his performance at the reception last night. What the hell was he on about to the senior guardian? And what the hell was the Bone Yard? I didn't like the word much. It made me think of graveyards, cities of the dead, tombstones canting over as the corpses beneath decomposed and the earth subsided. Very cheerful on the first morning of the New Year.

Drummond Street is across the road from the university Old College, a great Adam building around a quadrangle topped by a dome high above ground level. They still light it up at night. Since the university was the spiritual home of the Enlightenment – a lot of its early leaders were professors like my parents – I suppose the current Council feels it's worth the electricity to commemorate the place, although most of the iron boyscouts fancy themselves more as hard-nosed enforcers than intellectuals. But they still aren't practical enough to sort out the city's bureaucracy, as my missing persons files show.

I wandered down Drummond Street towards number 28. There was no one about; even the kids seemed to have hangovers. I stopped and cocked an ear. Dead quiet for a few seconds, then in the distance the raucous cries of the gulls desperately hunting for scraps in this underfed city. It struck me that I had nothing in the flat to eat and the food shops were closed for the day. Maybe Roddie Aitken would have some bread. He seemed like the kind of guy who'd be organised enough to stock up on provisions.

I pushed open the shabby street door and let out the usual reek of disinfectant failing to mask sewer gas and citizens who only shower once a week. It was tempered with the acid stink of vomit, as you'd expect after Hogmanay. Flat f was on the second floor. Someone across the landing from Roddie had defied Housing Directorate regulations and put a pot on the floor containing a gigantic plant with wide leaves so shiny they looked plastic. The branches had almost reached the filthy skylight. I didn't blame them for trying to find a way out of the dingy staircase.

I went up to Roddie Aitken's door and knocked. Not too hard – I didn't want to sound like the City Guard – but hard enough and long enough to wake him even from a sex-induced slumber. No answer. I knocked again. While I waited, I looked at the faded blue door. Down by the keyhole there were some recent scratches, quite deep. He probably couldn't get the key in last night while pissed. I pressed my fingers on the panel. It swung open on hinges that badly needed oiling.

"Roddie?"

Still no answer.

"Roddie, where are you? It's Quint, Quint Dalrymple."

Like most flats, mine included, the door opened straight on to the living room. Chaos. I'm not the most tidy person, but even when I'm arseholed I don't wreck the joint like Roddie had done. The standard-issue armchair and sofa were upside down, their fabric torn and cushions shredded; the books citizens are encouraged to read (philosophy texts, classic novels, that sort of thing) had been scattered around the floor; the kitchen cupboard had been emptied, cereals and potatoes all over the place. Even if Roddie had invited the city rugby champions round, he wouldn't have had this much cleaning up to do.

Then I noticed his orange woollen hat. It was lying on the underside of the inverted table and it had been ripped to shreds. I began to get a seriously bad feeling about the scene.

I knocked on the bedroom door. Nothing. I opened it hesitantly, then drew breath in so sharply I almost choked.

Roddie was there all right. I saw immediately why he hadn't been answering.

His throat had been torn out.

I was bent over the kitchen sink, gasping and shaking. Trying to throw up, but aware very quickly that even though I hadn't seen a murder victim for nearly two years, I'd still seen too many in my life to be able to react like a normal human being. I wasn't sick in my stomach, but in what passes for my soul – sick that I'd abandoned Roddie to this, sick with responsibility and guilt. Jesus, I liked the guy and his naïve enthusiasm.

I splashed water on my face and stood up in front of the mirror. Shook my head and called myself a lot of names. And swore a solemn oath that I'd catch the evil bastard who slaughtered the boy who came to me for help. Then I went back to the door and looked at the horror on the bed.

I forced myself to be dispassionate. It's not difficult if you've been an auxiliary, even one who was demoted seven years ago like me. Auxiliaries pride themselves on being able to handle any crisis. One thing I definitely was not at that moment was proud. But I had to do my job. Roddie deserved the best I could give him even though it was far too late.

The first thing I did was call Davie. He was asleep after his night shift, but I heard the exhaustion vanish from his voice even over the mobile.

"Fuck." The word rang out like a pistol shot. I knew it was one aimed at himself. "Bloody hell, Quint, I thought the lad was just imagining things." He shot himself again with the same word. It sounded like we were both guilty about what had happened to Roddie Aitken. "I'm on my way."

I called Lewis Hamilton. He'd have to be directly involved as there hadn't been a violent death since the last murderer ran riot. I hoped to the god I don't believe in that we didn't have another one like that on the loose. I also called the medical guardian and asked her to handle the post-mortem herself.

Before the guard arrived and turned the staircase into even more of a war zone, I carried out a quick private inspection of the flat. I didn't go far into the bedroom because there was a lot of blood on the floor and the killer would have left prints and traces. But the living room was another story. There were no visible signs of blood here, suggesting that the murderer had worn protection over his feet in the bedroom then removed it. I was thinking about the hooded man Roddie had described. What could be his motive? Smuggling? Black-market goods? There was no need to kill for those – plenty of people would willingly provide whatever you wanted for a price. But the way the place had been trashed, it certainly looked like a search had been undertaken. I hunted around for any evidence of pilfered supplies. Roddie Aitken definitely hadn't struck me as that kind of delivery man, though he might have sold me a dummy. But I found nothing in the living room. Perhaps there would be something in the bedroom. Or perhaps the killer had found what he was after.

In the distance I heard the high-pitched wail of sirens. It wouldn't be long before I had to face Roddie close up.

Hamilton came in looking pale, a team of people in white

plastic overalls at his heels. "Good God Almighty, Dalrymple, what have you found?" He peered over my shoulder into the bedroom and flinched. The public order guardian never did like dead bodies.

I filled him in about Roddie's visit and request for help, though I kept quiet about the hooded man for the time being. Scene-of-crime personnel were already starting to take photos and sketch the room layouts; they seemed to have memorised the manual I wrote when I was in the directorate.

The medical guardian turned up, also in white plastic. "I'm impressed, citizen," she said with a tight-lipped smile. "You even work on city holidays."

"You don't mind handling this personally, do you?" I asked. "It's the first murder for—"

"I know my job," she said tersely, then handed me some overalls. "Who's in charge on the public order side?"

"I'm taking the case." I glanced at Hamilton, who looked a bit dubious. "I know I found the body, but that doesn't disqualify me." If Hamilton knew how fired up I was to catch Roddie's killer, he'd have been even more dubious about letting me run the investigation, but I wasn't planning on telling him about the oath I'd sworn.

Davie came in, a grim look on his face. I beckoned to him to come over. "I'll need Hume 253 to work on this with me, guardian."

"Very well, Dalrymple." In the old days Hamilton wouldn't have let me lay down the law — that was his party piece. Now he's too busy protecting himself from the iron boyscouts, who were well pissed off when he refused to resign with most of my mother's gang.

I got Davie to oversee the scene-of-crime squad and told him to look out for any sign of illicit goods. Then, when the photographers finished with the longer-range shots, the medical guardian led me into the bedroom. We had to step around some large patches of partially dried blood on the worn carpet. Standing by the bed, we looked down at the mangled upper torso; a heavily stained sheet lay over the lower part of Roddie's body. His chest and arms were bare, splashed with blood from the gaping wound in his throat. The medical guardian, known to citizens who were prepared to take a chance as the Ice Queen because of her silver-blonde hair, was making preliminary observations into a small tape-recorder. The trachea had been ruptured and over two square inches of skin and cartilage torn out.

The guardian was bent over the wound, a magnifying glass in her hand. "The tears in the tissue are uneven," she said, standing up slowly. "It looks like a bite."

That was the way it struck me too. "A human bite?" I asked, pretty sure what the answer would be.

The Ice Queen nodded. "I think so. I can't see any signs of the deep laceration you get with bites from dogs and other animals with long canines."

"Any teeth marks we can match up with dental records?"

She was bending over the body again. "It's a terrible mess, citizen. We might be lucky."

"Look." I pointed to the swollen skin on Roddie's wrists. "He was tied down." Whatever was used, the killer had taken it with him. The thick marking suggested rope.

"That would have helped the assailant to bite his victim, but you'd still expect him to have been writhing around. I wonder if he was knocked out." The guardian examined Roddie's head. "No sign of any blows here."

I had a sudden flash of the hooded man running down the street. The neighbour said he'd seen a knife. I looked at the bloody sheet over the lower half of the corpse. Christ. What were we about to find underneath it?

The Ice Queen glanced across at me. It seemed she was on the same wavelength. "Ready?" she said in a low voice, her fingers on the edge of the sheet.

"Go."

Carefully she lifted Roddie's shroud. I forced myself to take a deep breath, blinked my eyes once and focused on his lower abdomen.

"Oh, no." Even the medical guardian, highly qualified stomach cancer specialist and fully paid-up member of the ultra hard-hearted wing of the iron boyscouts, was having trouble with this vision of horror. "I can't believe someone could do this to one of his fellow human beings."

I parted company with her there. I'd come across several vicious bastards who happily sliced open their fellow human beings. But I saw her point. This was gross even by their standards. Where Roddie's genitals should have been there was nothing except a great hole stretching right up into the groin.

"The penis and scrotum are missing," the guardian said.

I had a look under the bed. Nothing.

"It seems the killer took them when he or she left."

The Ice Queen's glare lived up to her nickname. "Citizen, are you seriously suggesting that a woman carried out this atrocity?"

"We're hardly in a position to rule anything out so far." But I didn't want to fight with her. "Forget that for now."

She'd already done so. Her head was over the wound. "Citizen," she said, her voice registering surprise. "There's something inside here."

"What is it?"

"It looks like the edge of a clear plastic bag."

I bent down and caught a glimpse of it. "Get it out," I said. She hesitated. "Get it out," I repeated impatiently.

She shook her head. "No. I want to wait till we get him on the slab. Pulling it out now might compromise other traces."

She was right there. I looked up at Roddie's face, something I'd been avoiding doing much of so far. The eyes were bulging and his lips were drawn back from his teeth. There was blood on the teeth. I had a piercing flashback to Caro dying on the dirty floor in the barn on Soutra, her foot jerking spasmodically.

"Oh, Christ," I muttered under my breath. "How come nobody heard him screaming?" I looked over at her. "Guardian, we're going to have to prise his mouth open. I think his tongue's been taken too." ·

She nodded slowly. "That'll have to wait for the mortuary too. I estimate he's been dead for at least nine hours. Rigor mortis is well advanced."

I thought of how I'd almost gone to see Roddie when I left the reception, then spent the early hours listening to Robert Johnson and shivering under a blanket. Not for the first time I felt pitifully inadequate.

Davie shook his head slowly as the body was removed by Medical Directorate personnel.

"Jesus, Quint, who did that to him? Do you think the hooded—"

I raised a finger to my lips and motioned in the direction of Hamilton. "Keep him to yourself till we finish up in here."

He nodded. "Right you are." He looked round at the auxiliaries who were dusting for fingerprints and itemising what was on the floor. Some of them had moved into the bedroom now. "What do you reckon went on in here last night?"

The public order guardian came over to us, his face greyer than the guard tunic he often wore instead of his guardian-issue tweed jacket.

"Well," I said. "For what it's worth, we're not just dealing with a drunken argument that got out of control. I think the victim was tortured because the murderer wanted to know where something was – something that was valuable enough to kill for. There's no way of telling at this stage whether he found what he was looking for."

"Is there a sexual slant to it as well?" Hamilton asked.

"Could be, in a seriously perverted way." I shook my head slowly. "I'm not sure though. It's all a bit contrived. We'll have to wait and see what's been put inside the body."

Hamilton gave an involuntary shiver. "I've never heard of a plastic bag being secreted inside a murder victim before."

"Me neither."

"I gather you think the killer cut the tongue out as well," the guardian said, avoiding my eyes.

I nodded. "At first I thought it was to keep him quiet, but there would still have been some noise. We'll probably find out from the neighbours that there was music playing." One of the Supply Directorate's standard-issue cassette players was lying smashed on the floor.

"Do you think the victim knew the killer?" Hamilton asked.

I shrugged. "Your guess is as good as mine. What else have we got? The scratches round the lock suggest that whoever put the key in had a pretty unsteady hand."

"Drunk? Shaking?" Davie suggested.

"Maybe the latter. Maybe the victim was being threatened at the time."

There was some shouting outside the door. A guardsman stuck his head round.

"Neighbour, guardian," he said. These days auxiliaries often speak like words are rationed. Why not? Everything else in the city is.

I remembered the old man Roddie mentioned. "Let him in, guardsman."

A small figure almost ran in, slewing to a halt in front of us.

"It was Roddie, wasn't it?" he demanded desperately. "It was Roddie they carried out."

"You're Jimmie, aren't you?" I looked at the short, stocky man in front of me. He was bald on top, but he made up for that with the largest pair of eyebrows I'd ever seen. It was like Nietzsche's moustache had acquired a twin and migrated.

"Aye," he said, peering at Hamilton and Davie with the

mixture of fear and loathing affected by most ordinary citizens. "Jimmie Semple."

I put my hand on his arm and led him back towards the door. "Why don't we talk in your place?" I glanced over my shoulder in an futile attempt to pacify the guardian. "I'll be back soon." It was obvious to me that the old man would clam up like a 1990s government minister in front of a parliamentary committee unless I got him away from anyone in the guard. Hamilton still fondly imagined that citizens would do anything an auxiliary told them.

"Who are you, son?" Jimmie Semple said as he took me into his flat on the ground floor. "You don't exactly have the look of one of them bastards."

"Quint's the name. Quint Dalrymple."

The old man sat down in his armchair at the window. "Oh, aye, I remember you. You were the one who caught that killer a couple of years back." He shook his head. "Something like this has been waiting to happen ever since the fucking boyscouts turned the screw." Then he caught and held my gaze. "What's happened to Roddie, citizen?"

"Call me Quint." I didn't look away, though I'd have liked to. "You were right upstairs, Jimmie. It was him they took away."

"That bastard in the hood got him. I knew he would. I told Roddie to be careful, but he didnae listen."

"You're wrong," I said, sitting opposite him and leaning forward. "He did listen to you. He came to me for help."

"Did he tell you about the crazy guy with the knife?" the old man asked.

I nodded.

He swore under his breath, spittle landing on the carpet by the toe of my boot. "So congratulations on a job well done, ya shite."

I couldn't think of anything to say for a bit. "Look," I said eventually, "I liked the lad. He only came to me yesterday afternoon. It was when I came round today to follow up on his problem that I found him."

Jimmie Semple looked back at me, his expression softening. "So you didn't think he was just wasting your time?"

I shook my head.

"Aye, well, I'm sorry if I was a bit . . ."

"Forget it. Will you help me find the man in the hood?"

His eyes were wide, bloodshot, under the dense growth of his brows. "Aye, son, of course. But what can I do?"

"Tell me everything you saw and heard. Last night and the night Roddie was chased down the street."

He told me about the hooded man first, but there wasn't much to it. He hadn't seen a lot more than Roddie, confirming only that the attacker was tall and solidly built and that the face had been obscured by the hood. He wasn't sure about the colour of the coat either – another triumph for the Council's enlightened policy on streetlamp brightness. He didn't even have much to say about the knife. It might have been a hunting blade, or even a carving knife. Christ. A blood-freezing image of the Ear, Nose and Throat Man came up before me like a spirit from the underworld: he used long knives to butcher his victims as well as to take off the end of my right forefinger. But he was long dead and buried, of that I was certain.

"What about last night?" I asked. "Did you see Roddie?"

"Aye, he came by on his way out." The old man glanced over at the dusty clock on his mantelpiece. "Must have been about eight o'clock. He was on his way out to meet his pals for Hogmanay."

"How did he seem?"

"Och, he was fine. He wasnae bothered about that lunatic." Jimmie brought his hand down hard on his knee. "He should have been though."

"He mentioned a girlfriend."

"Aye. Good-looking lassie. I don't know her name. I only saw her from the window a couple of times."

"Jimmie, did you hear Roddie come back last night? Did you hear anything at all from his flat?"

He shook his head and looked at me with an expression of infinite sadness. "No, son, I didnae. I wish I had. I had a half-bottle of whisky I'd been saving all year, you see. I was dead to the world long before midnight." He gazed across at me, a sheen on his eyes. "How did Roddie die?"

I mumbled some bullshit about the case being subject to Public Order Directorate security regulations and left him to the view from his window.

He was better off not knowing what happened to his friend upstairs. Roddie would be on the mortuary table by now, the medical guardian waiting for me before she started the post-mortem. I wished I was on another planet. Preferably one on which I was the only human being.

Chapter Four

———◦◦◦———

I left Davie in Drummond Street taking statements from the rest of Roddie's neighbours. Hamilton dismissed the guardswoman who was behind the wheel of his maroon Land-Rover and drove towards the infirmary. It was mid-afternoon by now, the sun already low in the western sky and the shadows lengthening in the city. The air was even colder than it had been, making the breath of the people unfortunate enough to be out on foot plume around their heads like the ink squirted by a nervous octopus.

"What kind of monster would do that, Dalrymple?" The guardian glanced at me. "Don't tell me you think it's an auxiliary." Two years ago he'd never come to terms with my idea that the killer was one of the city's servants. I had the feeling he was less sure about the rank below his these days. Then again, he didn't think much of his fellow guardians now either.

"I haven't a clue, Lewis. It's too early to say," I said. "You haven't heard any reports of a hooded man in the city centre, have you?" I tried to make the question sound nonchalant.

He looked blank and shook his head.

I told him what Roddie and Jimmie Semple had seen.

"It isn't much to go on, is it?" he said morosely.

"It might be all we get." I looked out the side window as we passed the Potterrow Entertainment Club. It was once a famously shitty student union, but ten years ago the Tourism

Directorate converted it into an electronic games centre. No Edinburgh citizens are allowed in, of course. The building's concrete walls are heavily stained with the soot that has built up since coal was reintroduced as the main heating fuel; the nuclear power station at Torness was shut down soon after the Englightenment came to power. A gaggle of Filipinos stood around outside the entrance stamping their feet and waving their arms in the cold. The amount of tartan knitwear they had on should have kept them warm. Maybe the quality of wool isn't as high as the Marketing Department claims.

"I don't think I'll bother with the post-mortem, Dalrymple. I've got some paperwork to catch up with." Hamilton had always been squeamish during autopsies. He used to attend them just to keep an eye on me, but apparently he'd got beyond that stage. Progress indeed. Then he spoilt it all. "You can manage on your own, can't you?"

"What do you think?" I said sarcastically. That was always the problem with the first generation of guardians: they treated everyone like primary school kids.

"All right, all right," Hamilton said wearily. "Obviously you'll need to attend the Council meeting tonight."

"Obviously." I relented a bit. "I'll give you a call beforehand and let you know what we find."

He pulled up and let me off outside the infirmary's grey-black granite façade. It seemed like years since I'd walked past it at midday on my way to Roddie's. Sometimes I wish I'd found another line of work. But, like the Labour Directorate says, "Every citizen has a talent that the city needs." Every citizen except the bastard who did for Roddie Aitken.

I found the Ice Queen in the mortuary antechamber, fully kitted up and ready to go. She gave me a brief nod, then handed me a set of protective clothing. Even in layers of green medical gear she looked pretty amazing, her figure firm and her complexion smooth. I made sure she didn't see the way I was looking at her. You don't want to play that kind of game with guardians, especially not guardians who can handle a scalpel.

"All right, citizen," she said. "Let's see what we've got."

I usually try not to get too affected by what's laid out on the mortuary table. Otherwise I'd keep away like Hamilton. But this time was different. I'd seen Roddie Aitken alive less then twenty-four hours earlier. He'd been sitting on my sofa talking in his boyish voice without much concern about the strange person who was following him. Watching the medical guardian and her assistants going about the normal procedures – removing the plastic bags over feet and hands, scraping fingernails, plucking sample hairs – made me feel seriously uncomfortable. From the bottom of the table I could clearly see the corner of the plastic bag that had been pushed into the wound in the groin. But the guardian wasn't to be hurried. She was examining the torn skin on the neck.

"I'll cut this whole area away now," she said. "It looks like there's at least one reasonable impression of bite marks."

"Good," I said without much enthusiasm. "Now all we can hope is that the killer visited a dentist in the city." The problem was that state-funded dental practices more or less died out in the years before independence and there were plenty of people growing up then who couldn't afford treatment. Even though the Council set up free dental care for all Edinburgh citizens not long after it came to power, a lot of them steer clear of the surgeries. The fact that the Medical Directorate spends as little as it can on pain-relieving drugs may have something to do with that.

"What do you reckon was the cause of death?" I asked. No harm in hurrying the Ice Queen along.

Her head was over Roddie's chest. "Still too early to say. Possibly heart failure brought about by the shock of what was done to him." She pointed at the deep cuts in the flesh of the upper thighs as well as at the gaping hole.

The senior pathologist who was assisting her nodded vigorously in agreement. I got the feeling that he would rather have gone for a walk in the badlands beyond the city border than contradict his superior.

The door opened and a thin figure wearing a green gown over a guard tunic entered. One glance at the hands which almost immediately started rubbing together was enough for me to identify Hamilton's number two, Machiavelli. He bowed his head punctiliously at the medical guardian, who completely ignored him, then at the lower-ranked auxiliaries in the room. They had to acknowledge him as they couldn't risk showing what they really thought of him. Apparently I'd recently turned into the invisible man. No way was he getting away with that.

"What are you doing here, Raeburn 03?" I asked in a loud voice. "On work experience?"

His body stiffened. "I could ask you the same question, citizen," he said after he'd run his eyes over the body in front of him.

I didn't like the way he was looking at Roddie. "Presumably you haven't spoken to your boss recently," I said. Mentioning an auxiliary's senior officer is the best way to make him flinch. Machiavelli flinched. "I'm in charge of this case," I continued. He didn't look at all pleased at that piece of news. Maybe he'd thought this would be an opportunity to make a different kind of name for himself in the directorate – Sherlock Holmes or Inspector Bucket instead of the Renaissance schemer.

The medical guardian had moved down to the middle of the table. She extended the incision she'd already made in the upper part of Roddie's abdomen to the point where the wound began. I glanced at Machiavelli and was surprised to see that he looked a lot less queasy than his boss used to when the dissecting knife went in. His eyes were fixed firmly on the Ice Queen's rubber-sheathed fingers. She parted the skin, examined the area, took some samples and finally laid hold on what had been rammed in to the cavity.

"There you are, citizen." The guardian held up the plastic bag. It was about six inches square, covered in blood and dotted with bits of internal debris. Something I couldn't make out was weighing down one corner.

"What is that?" Raeburn 03 asked in a strangled voice. Maybe what he'd been watching was getting to him after all.

I let the photographer do her work, then took the bag from the guardian. On the scrubbed surround of a sink I ran a finger between the sealed opening – it was one of those bags that are used for frozen food and the like. Machiavelli was at my shoulder.

I turned the bag up and let its contents slide out.

"What on earth . . ." Hamilton's deputy stretched his hand out.

I grabbed his wrist and squeezed hard. "Excuse me, Raeburn 03. You're on my territory."

He gave me a glare that Medusa would have been proud of then stepped back a few inches.

I concentrated on the find. It was a cassette tape, made of clear plastic with the brown tape visible inside. There were no paper stickers on the outside and no writing to identify what had been recorded on it. I was, however, willing to bet my collection of Johnny Guitar Watson tapes that something had been recorded on the cassette. It looked to me like the killer was playing a very nasty game indeed.

"It's not a standard-issue cassette," Machiavelli put in. "There's no Supply Directorate serial number on it."

He was right. Citizens are only allowed to listen to music approved by the Heritage Directorate, which they can obtain free from the city libraries.

I looked at the cassette again. Near the top edge was a line of what looked like Chinese characters. Standard-issue cassettes are imported from Greece as part of the deal involving package holidays in Edinburgh for Greek nationals. So what we had here was technically a piece of contraband. More important, it suggested that the murderer had links with the world outside the city borders. Which raised the spectre of dissidents or gangs of psychos. Bloody hell. This was getting worse by the minute.

"Shouldn't we listen to find out if there's anything on the cassette, citizen?" Hamilton's number two had changed his tone. Now he was almost conciliatory. Bollocks to that.

"We're going to," I said, putting the cassette into a bag of my own. "At tonight's Council meeting." That dealt with him. Unless Hamilton was hit by a bus in the next couple of hours, Machiavelli wouldn't be deputising for him in the Council chamber and so he wouldn't hear a thing. At least until he wormed it out of one of the numerous iron boyscouts who liked his style. He must have been doing them a lot of favours.

"Citizen?" The medical guardian was back at the top end of the table. Her assistants had been wrestling with Roddie's jaws. "You were right. His tongue has been removed."

I got a lift in a guard vehicle back to Drummond Street. Davie had spoken to most of the neighbours. They'd all been well into the bevy from the early evening, but some of them said they heard music coming from Roddie's flat after midnight. The guy across the stairwell had knocked on his door to wish him happy New Year but got no reply and assumed he was pissed like the rest of them.

I told Davie about the cassette. "Let's borrow a machine and listen to it. I don't want to go into the Council meeting blind. Or deaf."

We borrowed Jimmie Semple's cassette player and set it up in Roddie's flat. The scene-of-crime people had finished, having found, so Davie told me, no fingerprints apart from Roddie's and no sign of illicit goods. They'd left the place as it was, so we had to step over books and cushions to get to the single power point. I pushed what was left of Roddie's orange hat under the sofa — it was giving me a lot of angst.

I stuck the cassette in and waited for what I was pretty sure was some kind of message from the killer.

What I got was a hell of a surprise.

"Is that what I think it is?" Davie asked after a minute.

"If what you think it is is Eric Clapton playing 'Tribute to Elmore', then yes, guardsman, it is."

We listened until the music stopped and left the tape running. There didn't seem to be anything else recorded.

Davie rubbed his beard. "Well, boss, you're the expert. What does it mean? What's this got to do with Roddie Aitken?"

"And why was it stuck inside him?" I looked into the darkness outside, then glanced both ways in the street below. No hooded man. "God knows."

"A non-standard-issue tape with banned music on it." Davie nudged my arm. "It must mean something, Quint."

I wasn't arguing with that. A series of unpleasant thoughts had struck me. The blues had been banned not long after the Enlightenment came to power because the drug gangs that used to terrorise the city took them as their trademark. The leader of each gang gave himself the name of a famous bluesman – Muddy Waters, Howlin' Wolf, John Lee Hooker – and the gang members followed suit. My love affair with the blues had started before that. When I was a kid in the nineties, contemporary music was so poor that my friends and I ended up turning to what we thought was the genuine tradition. But I couldn't say the blues were only a source of pleasure to me. The psycho who killed Caro and eleven others called himself Little Walter. And now we had a clown messing about with Clapton and Elmore James. This was bad news almost on a par with the Stop Press from Sarajevo in August 1914.

"It's an instrumental," Davie said, breaking into my thoughts.

"A chance for 'God' to show off his skills on the bottle-neck that Elmore was famous for. What's your point, Davie?"

He shrugged. "I was just thinking that if there had been a lyric, it might have told us something."

I headed for the door. It was half six and I needed to talk to Hamilton before the Council meeting at seven. "It might have," I said over my shoulder. "But then again, we might not speak this particular language. The message is presumably directed at someone who does."

Davie's boots clattered down the stair behind me. "I thought you knew all there is to know about the blues, Quint," he said.

I shook my head. "Not when they're being played by a lunatic, my friend."

Some of the most unpleasant experiences of my life have occurred in the Council chamber. As a result, I hate the place. The building used to be the Assembly Hall where the Church of Scotland had its annual knees-up. It was an attempt at steepling Gothic splendour, but its blackened façade strikes me more like the castle of a vampire with a taste for coal dust. Hamilton was doing an imitation of a sentry on autopilot outside. Behind him the central tourist area was lit up brighter than a Christmas tree in the days before trees became an endangered life form. In the suburbs beyond, where the ordinary citizens live, the lights were a lot dimmer.

"Are you aware of the fact that Raeburn 03 was at the autopsy?" I demanded, warming up for the fight I was about to have with the boyscouts.

The guardian looked surprised. "I was not. Did he get in your way?"

"He did, Lewis. Pull his chain, will you?"

Hamilton smiled grimly. "With pleasure." His face darkened. "We're in trouble, aren't we, citizen?"

"I reckon so. This killer's more than just a butcher. He's playing mind games too." I told him about the tape.

The guardian swore under his breath, an action which would have definitely convinced his colleagues that he was past it. Guardians pride themselves on being above coarse language. Me, I'm a big fan.

"Come on, guardian, we're going to be late." I let him go first through the doorway and up the wide staircase. Busts of Plato were all over the place, the philosopher's wrinkled brow and featureless eyes giving a greater impression of fallibility than the first Council intended. He was their master, *The Republic* and *The Laws* the cornerstones of the new constitution. Unfortunately he didn't specify how to deal with murderers who stick music cassettes inside their victims.

We were admitted into the chamber. When my mother was senior guardian, there had been a vast horseshoe table. The Council members sat round it and people like me who had to give reports sat between the horns and felt small. The iron boyscouts have changed things. In an attempt to show that they're even more devoted to Plato than their predecessors, they emptied the hall of all its furniture and remain on their feet throughout the daily meetings. As the meetings sometimes go on long into the night, they've taken to moving around the hall – the senior guardian playing at Socrates wandering the streets of ancient Athens with the rest of them as his interlocutors. I suppose it keeps them off the freezing streets of Edinburgh.

"Good evening, guardian. Citizen." The senior guardian nodded briefly at us and led us into the middle of the hall. The other thirteen guardians gathered around. They were all carrying clipboards. I saw the medical guardian. She had her notes under her arm and her hands stuffed into the pockets of her light brown tweed jacket.

"The meeting is in session," said the senior guardian, his head held high and his hands behind his back. He looked like a preacher about to address a congregation, the thin beard backing up his earnest expression. "I understand from the public order guardian that Citizen Dalrymple is to lead the investigation into the unwelcome discovery at Drummond Street." He glanced at Hamilton. For a moment I thought there was going to be trouble about control of such a serious matter being given to a non-auxiliary, but the senior guardian let it pass. He knew I could do a better job than anyone in the Public Order Directorate. "Perhaps you will favour us with your report, citizen," he said, turning his unwavering eyes on me.

"All right," I said. I've always got a kick out of trying to stamp my authority on the guardians. Shocking them out of their routine is a good ploy. "Let's start with a bit of music." I pushed through the ring of tweed jackets and put the cassette in the player that was kept in the chamber.

I couldn't really say that Clapton went to the top of the Council charts. Most of the boyscouts were too young to have much more than a vague idea of what kind of music they were hearing. Those who did know – like the heritage guardian, an expert on eighteenth-century Scottish art who had the look of a poorly preserved mummy but was actually five years younger than me – tried to appear scandalised that the blues should be heard in the Assembly Hall. As for the senior guardian, he kept his head held high. There was a faint smile on his lips but I couldn't make up my mind if he looked more like a tolerant saint suffering for his faith or a public-school headmaster about to use his cane in the old days. The music stopped and there was a long silence.

"Thank you for sharing that with us," the senior guardian said eventually. "I presume this was the cassette that was found inside the victim."

Obviously the grapevine was working well.

"It is, guardian," I replied.

"And what exactly is the significance of this particular . . . how shall I describe it . . . piece?" The guardian moved towards where I was standing by the cassette player, his colleagues close behind.

I shrugged. "Search me, guardian."

He gave me a thin smile. "But you know what it is and who performed it?"

"Oh, aye. It's Eric Clapton's 'Tribute to Elmore'. Elmore being Elmore James, leading proponent of the bottle-neck guitar."

Some of the guardians made a note but most didn't bother.

"Very interesting, citizen," said the heritage guardian, holding his pen vertically like a child trying to attract the teacher's attention. "But what did the murderer mean by putting it—"

"I think we're getting ahead of ourselves, guardians," interrupted Hamilton. I'd been wondering how long he'd keep quiet. "Clearly some information about this case has become available to you already." He looked around balefully. "I'd like to know how."

Nobody volunteered an answer. Gossip between the directorates is the lifeblood of the system, but none of the iron boyscouts could admit that openly – certainly not in front of an ordinary citizen like me. I let them stew for a few moments, then outlined what I'd found in Roddie Aitken's flat. This time all of them took notes.

"So, to summarise," the senior guardian said when I'd finished. "We are dealing with a murderer who took care to leave no fingerprints, who took advantage of the only night of the year when there is no curfew to effect his escape, who tortured his victim to discover the whereabouts of some object as yet unknown and who left this piece of music as some kind of message."

Not bad for a scientist. And the senior guardian isn't just any scientist. He was a senior researcher in the mechanical engineering faculty at the age of twenty-one and a key member of the Science and Energy Directorate a few years later. The word is that when he became senior guardian he never even considered assigning his original directorate to someone else. But no matter how much they fancy themselves, guardians aren't investigators and he hadn't mentioned everything.

"Correct – as far as it goes," I said. Then I gave them something else to chew on. "I'm assuming the murderer was the hooded figure seen by the victim four times before he was killed. What does that tell us, guardians?"

Rustling of papers and eyes definitely lowered. I felt like a professor leading a seminar for a group of students who were never given reading lists.

"What are you getting at, Dalrymple?" Hamilton asked suspiciously. He wasn't impressed that I was springing something we hadn't discussed on him.

"Simply this. The hooded man — not that I'm necessarily convinced it's a male at this stage — showed himself several times to Roddie Aitken. Why? Why didn't he just follow him back to his flat the first time and do what he did last night?"

The senior guardian was nodding, his lower lip caught between his teeth. "I see what you mean, citizen. He was trying to frighten his victim."

"Very good, guardian," I said. "The killer was trying to frighten him into handing over something."

"But what was that something?" Hamilton said, his brow still furrowed.

"I don't know," I said, shrugging my shoulders. "Either he found what he was looking for in the flat or—" I broke off. It had occurred to me that maybe Roddie never had what his killer wanted. He didn't seem to be the kind of guy who was into the black market. So why was the bastard after him? Could it be a case of mistaken identity or was it something more sinister? Possibilities started to bombard me.

"Wake up, citizen," said the medical guardian, her pale face looking unusually impatient. "Or what?"

"Or . . . I don't know," I said, smiling lamely.

The senior guardian gave me a dubious look then turned to the Ice Queen. "Very well. Let's have your report." He paused momentarily before addressing her. "Guardian."

One of the problems the guardians have constructed for themselves is how to address each other in front of ordinary citizens. I'm bloody certain they use their first names when they're on their own, but they can't do that in front of the likes of me.

The medical guardian ran through her preliminary report, putting the time of death around two a.m. and the cause of death shock-induced heart failure. She thought the knife the killer used had a large non-serrated blade — possibly a hunting knife. (Or possibly a standard-issue auxiliary knife, but I didn't feel like raising that point for the time being.)

"We are carrying out tests on matter removed from the

victim's fingernails," the guardian said. "No other traces of the killer have been found, apart from the bite mark on the throat. This is being analysed as I speak and I am cautiously optimistic that we will have sufficient data to carry out a search of dental records." She looked around her colleagues, ending at the senior guardian. "I hope to be able to provide further information at tomorrow's meeting."

"Thank you, guardian." The senior guardian turned to me. "Anything else you feel we should know, citizen?"

I could think of a lot of hints concerning the way they run the city, but I bit my tongue. "We'll be looking at all aspects of the victim's background and following up leads." I gave the information guardian the eye. She was a nervous-looking redhead who had survived from my mother's time. "Are you intending to publicise the killing?"

"That is a matter for the Council," the senior guardian said, his gaze hard. "I suggest you get back to your investigation, citizen."

I headed for the door, then decided to give them a farewell gift. "Guardians," I said over my shoulder, "we're not dealing with an average murderer here. This one walked away with Roddie Aitken's tongue and genitals as well as leaving us a cassette. A cassette that was not standard issue and suggests some connection with the world beyond the city border." I turned and faced them. In the air above the guardians' heads I could almost read the word "dissidents". It has the effect on senior auxiliaries that "Brussels" used to have on Conservative politicians in the 1990s.

I hadn't finished with the Council. I wasn't going to sleep easy tonight and I didn't see why they should. I moved to the door then turned back to face them.

"One of the few things I'm certain about in this case so far is that this isn't the end of the killer's activities. This is just the beginning. Pleasant dreams, guardians."

Chapter Five

"Where to?" Davie asked from the driver's seat of the guard Land-Rover he'd laid his hands on for the duration of the investigation.

I stood by the railing looking out over the racecourse in Princes Street Gardens towards the ravaged stump of the Scott Monument; the top twenty yards of the space-rocket-shaped steeple fell off a few years back, making a mess of a tourist group from Hong Kong. Frost glistened on the floodlit grass while voices from the tourist restaurants and bars on Princes Street echoed around the surfaces of the ground, the granite buildings and the castle rock. Everything was hard, like the guardians wanted to be and the killer definitely was.

"The hooded man's out there somewhere, Davie," I said, turning to him. "Somebody knows him."

"His friends and relatives maybe don't know that he likes biting people's throats out." Davie shook his head slowly. "Why Roddie, for fuck's sake? Why him, Quint?"

"Let's see if we can find out." I climbed into the rust-spattered Land-Rover. "To the City Archives, guardsman. At the double."

"Now you're talking." Davie gave a sardonic smile as he started the engine. "There's nothing I like better than an evening with the files."

"Sorry. You'd better call Fiona."

"I already have. She's not expecting to see much of me in the immediate future."

We crossed the Royal Mile on the way to the main library which houses citizen archives. I felt sorry for the disruption to Davie's love life, but not too sorry. At least he had a woman in the city. All I had were memories of one who was dead and one who had disappeared.

"Right, what have we got?" We'd been through Roddie Aitken's records and compiled lists of people to be interviewed – questioned, the guard would call it, but I prefer the subtle approach.

Davie leaned back in his chair and stretched his muscular arms, then picked up the checklist we'd made. "Parents: Peter and Morag, 74m Ratcliffe Terrace."

"I'll do them." That promised to be a lot of fun. The local bereavement advisor would have been round by now, but they're often unfeeling enough to make things worse for the families. I'd been coming across this more and more in the last few months. In the past, auxiliaries in the social care and welfare departments had been trained to cope with the needs of citizens. Now most of them were like miniature iron boyscouts, with all the social graces of the worst football fans in the years before the sport was banned by the European Union because of match-fixing and street warfare.

Davie made a note. "Friends: apparently three close male friends and two close females, one of them his cousin."

The Council keeps tabs on citizens by making them declare the friends they see more than once a month. God knows how many auxiliaries that occupies updating files and carrying out spot checks.

"Do you want to make a start on them tomorrow?" I said. "We'll need to try and track down this girlfriend he had. Maybe she's one of those two. If not, he might have met her at a sex session."

Davie nodded. "Then there are his workmates."

"We'll check them out in the archives first. The likelihood is some of them will have black-market offence notifications. We may need to put them under surveillance rather than blunder in."

"Right." Davie raised a finger. "I've just thought of something else. The report Roddie made to the guard about the hooded man."

I grinned. "Well done, guardsman."

Davie's finger was now simultaneously moving up and down and swivelling. "I suppose you had that on your personal list?"

"Of course I did. You're the expert on the City Guard. See if you can find out why no action was taken."

"I can tell you that now, Quint. You know how busy we are, especially over the Christmas and New Year period."

"You never know what you might come across." I stood up and looked around the high shelves packed solid with grey files. They ran for over fifty yards to the far end of the basement which was thirty yards wide – and these were only the archives for citizens like Roddie Aitken who live in the central areas because of their jobs. There are six other citizen archives, not to mention each of the twenty barracks archives where auxiliaries' files are kept, and the central guard archive in the castle. Christ, what had the Council done to the city? Turned it into a paper mausoleum, where people's souls are confined to the archives and their lives programmed more carefully than the computers the guardians keep to themselves. This wasn't why the Enlightenment won the last election. Or why, even until recently, Edinburgh citizens preferred Council rule to the chaos caused by the drugs gangs in the past.

I roused myself. "Come on, Davie. We'll be late for your chief." Hamilton had called an hour earlier and suggested we meet at my place to co-ordinate tomorrow's activities. Now I came to think about it, the guardian had never been in my flat before. He must have fancied a change from his rooms in the castle.

I felt a wave of exhaustion wash over me as we drove towards

Tollcross. It's always the same at the beginning of an investigation – there are so many angles to cover, so much you're unsure about. Sleep is the first casualty, but you can usually rely on the odd adrenalin rush to keep you awake. I got a very large one as we turned into Gilmore Place.

"Jesus, Davie. Pull in. Look down there." I pointed down the street towards the door of my staircase. The curfew had been in effect for a couple hours so there was no one about. Apart from a figure in a long coat with a hood.

"Bloody hell." Davie cut the engine and drew in to the kerb.

"Leave the lights on," I whispered. "We won't see a thing otherwise."

We both leaned forward and watched the hooded man. He was leaning against the wall by the doorway, head bowed. It was difficult to gauge his height and weight because of the voluminous coat and the limited light we were casting.

"He must have seen us," Davie said, his hand straying down to his service knife.

True enough. I knew what he was thinking. The bastard looked like he was waiting for me. I can recognise a challenge when I see one. He had some nerve showing himself on the streets, especially after curfew.

"Stay here. I'm going a bit closer."

"Are you out of your—" Davie shut up when I raised my finger to my mouth.

I opened the door carefully and set my feet on the icy pavement. Then walked slowly out into the middle of the street.

A movement came from the hooded figure, a twitch of the head to tell me I'd been spotted. But he stood his ground. I stepped forward, my heart doing a passable imitation of Willie Dixon producing a particularly thunderous riff on the bass guitar. I got to within ten yards and could see that the coat was dark grey.

Then everything moved into overdrive.

I heard the roar of a clapped-out diesel engine and more lights came round the corner behind me. Hamilton. I'd forgotten about the guardian and his sodding rendezvous. In the few seconds it took me to wave at Davie to get in his boss's way then run forward to my door, the hooded man was off like a greyhound.

I went after him, but he was always going away from me; he obviously kept himself in a lot better shape than I did. I knew where he was headed. Round the corner to the right, there's a yard where the Tourism Department store scaffolding for the tattoo they put on in the summer. If he got over the fence into it, he had a good chance of getting away altogether. My lungs were bursting as I came round the turn. The hooded figure was a good fifty yards ahead, his legs apparently unhindered by the coat. He would hit the fence any second now and it isn't high enough to put off someone as fit as him.

I ground to a halt, spitting something sticky and salty from my mouth, and pulled out my mobile phone.

"Davie," I gasped, "send vehicles round to the other side of the store in Gilmore Place Lane. Quick, he's over the fence."

Over the fence didn't do justice to the fugitive's leap – he sailed over like he was a champion vaulter with his pole concealed about his clothing. I waited for a minute then walked painfully back to Davie and Hamilton.

They were following the chase on their mobiles. I could tell from their expressions that the hooded man hadn't been sighted. We drove round and watched guardsmen and women comb the piles of scaffolding. There was nothing.

And nothing over the next few hours from all the guard units across the city, despite Hamilton's fierce instructions to spare no effort in the chase.

It was beginning to look like we were after one of the supernatural creatures that filled the world's TV screens before the millennium – our very own file stamped "X".

✳   ✳   ✳

In the morning Hamilton was apologetic. He had to be. I made it clear to him what I thought about the timing of his arrival in Gilmore Place. He muttered something about wanting to see how the other half lived. Jesus.

"Still no trace of your hooded man, Dalrymple," he added dolefully.

I was at the leaded window of his office in the castle, looking out over the ice realm that the city had become overnight. The suburbs were wreathed in smoke from the coal fires while the glass frontages of the shops across the gardens glinted in the sunlight. To the right, tourists slipped and slithered their way up the Mound. It was closed to buses in the early morning. In the old days there had been an electric blanket under the road, but the Council gave up using it a couple of years ago because of the electricity restrictions.

"You'd have thought there would have been some footprints around the depot he passed through," I said.

"Scuffmarks and the like. Nothing useful."

I had another bone to wrestle over with him. "So the Council decided not to publicise any details of the murder?"

He looked up briefly from his papers. "Majority decision, yes." Hamilton often fell into using the clipped sentences favoured by professional army officers and robots.

"And were you one of those who voted in favour?" I asked, sitting on the edge of his wide desk. That always got to him.

"No, I wasn't actually," he replied, glaring at me.

"What's happened?" I asked sarcastically. "Have you suddenly become a supporter of the free flow of information?" As far as I was aware the Council hadn't brought April Fools' Day forward.

"Certainly not." That was more like Hamilton. "I simply feel that in a murder as gruesome as this one we stand more chance of catching the perpetrator if we have the citizen body on our side."

"Very good, guardian." I got off his desk in surprise. "We've finally found something we agree on."

He looked at me and shook his head hopelessly.

My mobile rang.

"Good morning, citizen." The Ice Queen's business-like tones. "First the bad news. There were no traces of the murderer under the victim's fingernails. But the good news is that I have a profile of part of the killer's upper jaw. Do you want some of my people to help with the archive search?"

Two guardians trying to be helpful in one day. That was unusual. I handed her over to Hamilton to co-ordinate their directorates' efforts. And went to interview Roddie Aitken's parents.

Ratcliffe Terrace. When I was a student a year before the Enlightenment we used to go to a bloody good pub there which had an antique panelled bar and a moulded ceiling. The beer wasn't bad either. It got burned down by one of the drugs gangs not long after independence. Now it's a day care centre – all mothers are working mothers in the perfect city, and children are looked after by city staff from six months.

I slipped for about the tenth time that morning as I got out of the guard vehicle and headed for number 74. Davie'd just called to say that he'd spoken to two of Roddie's friends and was on his way to the third, one of the women. He hadn't found anything that looked significant so far.

The stairwell smelled the same as mine and every other in the city – boiled root vegetables, dodgy sewage and rancid citizens. I climbed up to the fourth floor, feeling the muscles tight in my legs from my ineffectual sprint last night. The place was dead quiet, everyone except the Aitkens at work. I'd asked them via the guard to stay at home.

The door was in surprisingly good nick – it had been repainted recently. I wondered where the paint had come from.

The Housing Directorate hasn't been doing much maintenance of citizens' houses in the last few years.

"I'm Dalrymple," I said to the tall, balding man who eventually opened the door. He was stooping slightly, an expression of childlike bewilderment on his slack face. "You can call me Quint."

"Quint?" he repeated blankly.

"Come away in," said a strong voice behind him. A woman who was nearly as tall as Peter Aitken appeared, nudging him gently out of the way. "I'm Morag, Roddie's mother," she said, offering her hand. "You'll be the investigator we were told to wait for."

I repeated my name.

"Quint? Is that short for Quintus, the fifth born?" Her eyes were dark brown like her son's and lively. Although her hair was pure white, the softness of her face suggested she was younger than her husband.

"No, it's short for Quintilian."

"The Roman orator and grammarian," Morag Aitken added. She'd probably taken advantage of the Education Directorate's continuing education programme. She led me and her husband, who was lagging behind, into the living room. It was a bit larger than mine and efforts had been made to decorate it distinctively. Someone had provided a series of pretty impressive watercolours depicting Edinburgh skylines.

"Mine," Roddie's mother said, following the direction of my eyes. Then the façade cracked momentarily. "Roddie always liked them." She took a deep breath then made an attempt at smiling. "Sit down, the pair of you."

"I met your son," I said, forcing myself to look at them. "I . . . I liked him a lot."

"Aye," his father said. "Everybody liked him." His voice broke towards the end of the sentence.

Morag Aitken was studying me. "How did you come to meet Roddie, Quintilian?"

"He visited me on Hogmanay." I was watching them carefully to see how they would react. "He had a problem he wanted my help with."

"What sort of problem?" Their voices came simultaneously. They glanced at each other in surprise.

It was obvious Roddie hadn't told them about the hooded man. Was he keeping it secret or did he just not want to scare his folks?

"Oh, just a minor hassle at work," I said, looking down at my notebook.

"What was it?" Morag Aitken asked insistently. "Roddie never had any problems in the department."

"That's right," her husband said. "All the other delivery men thought he was a great lad. His superior told me he had high hopes for him."

I would be checking that, but the impression I was getting from the parents tallied with my own. Roddie was a genuinely good lad. So why had he been tortured and killed?

"I'm sorry if this seems like an insulting question, but it may be important." I found it difficult to look these seemingly decent people in the eye now. "Did Roddie ever . . . em, bring anything home from work?"

Morag Aitken drew herself up like a lioness about to remove a jackal's head. "That *is* an insult, citizen. Roddie was brought up to be totally honest."

I glanced at Peter. He was nodding his head. I believed them. "If it's any comfort to you, that's what I expected to hear."

Roddie's mother gave me a long stare, then nodded sternly. "That is some comfort, Quintilian."

I was quiet for a few moments.

"He mentioned a girl. Do you know her?"

"A girl in the romantic sense?" Morag asked, giving me a sharp look.

"I think so. He wasn't too specific. We're talking to some of his friends . . ." I showed her the list of names.

"Those are his oldest friends from school," his mother said. "But he never said anything to me about a girlfriend."

I wasn't particularly taken aback by that. If Morag Aitken had been my mother, I don't think I'd have been too open about my sex life.

"In this city, girlfriends are hardly encouraged," she said. Neither are married couples like Roddie's parents, but the Council allows citizen weddings if people are insistent enough.

I stayed for another half-hour filling in Roddie's background and finding nothing at all to suggest that he'd ever been a bad boy. On the contrary, he would have been an ideal trainee auxiliary – apart from the fact that he wasn't the callous type favoured by the iron boyscouts.

They showed me to the door. Something about the way Peter Aitken was looking at me made me think he wanted a private word. I said my farewells to his wife, then engaged him in conversation about the paint he'd used on his front door. That got rid of her quickly enough. It turned out that he'd had it from a friend in the pub and not from his son.

"That girl you were asking about," he said in a low voice. "He did mention her to me once. He was very pleased with himself." He glanced back into the flat. "Morag's a bit . . . well, she never liked the idea of Roddie being with a woman."

"Do you know her name?"

He shook his head. "Sorry, son." Then he gave me a conspiratorial smile. "But I do know that he met her at a sex session."

"Cheerio, then, citizen," I said loudly, seeing Morag Aitken's white head looming in the hallway behind.

"Find the bastard who did that to my lad, son," Peter Aitken said in a feeble voice.

I hadn't forgotten what I'd sworn at Roddie's bedside. I might have known it would be this way. *Cherchez la femme.* The story of my life.

* * *

I met up with Davie at my flat. We found some stale baps and floppy slices of cheese and ate them for lunch. I glanced through the letters requesting help that people push under my door, while Davie told me about Roddie's friends. It was as his parents said. He'd known them all from primary school. None of them had the faintest idea why he'd been killed. What was interesting was that he'd kept his girlfriend secret from them all.

"Look at the state of this writing," I said, holding up a tattered standard-issue recycled brown envelope.

"What is it?" Davie said, his mouth full. "One of the Dead Sea Scrolls?"

The tiny, perfectly formed letters certainly looked like those of an ancient scribe. My namesake Quintilian must have got letters like this all the time. I opened the flap carefully and pulled out a single piece of the off-white writing paper citizens get from Supply Directorate stores. When I deciphered the address at the top, I discovered to my surprise that it was from my father's retirement home in Trinity. I looked down at the signature.

"It's from William McEwan."

"The former guardian who misbehaved himself at the reception the other night?"

"You heard about that, did you?"

Davie grinned before taking another bite. "The story goes that the senior guardian froze him out in a big way."

"'Quintilian,'" I read, "'I fear there is nothing even you can do about the great injustice of the Bone Yard.'" I looked over at Davie. "The Bone Yard. I heard him mention that at the party. Have you ever heard the name before?"

Davie sniffed suspiciously at a bottle of milk from my tiny citizen-issue fridge. "The Bone Yard? What is it? A new nightclub?"

I read on. "'I am breaking the Council's confidentiality oath by writing this letter, but I cannot keep silent any more. The next time you visit your father, come to my room. We are guilty of a great wrong and I must share it with you before it is too late.'"

Davie was making tea on my electric ring. "Bit melodramatic, don't you think?"

"You never know with the old ones." I remembered William at the reception. "He was wound up about it enough to go for the senior guardian's jugular."

"I'd have it black, unless you're keen on tea-flavoured yoghurt," Davie said, handing me a mug. "So what does it mean?"

"God knows," I said, shaking my head. "I'll check it out when I next see Hector." I looked at my notebook. "Right, then, back to the files. Let's check out Roddie's workmates."

We spent the afternoon in the archives. Some of the guys who worked with Roddie had been done for black-market activities, but none of it looked too serious. I turned my list over to the public order guardian — he'd enjoy terrorising them.

Meanwhile Davie and I went off to Roddie's local sex centre to hunt the mysterious girlfriend. The poor woman was probably looking forward to her next meeting with him, completely unaware of the murder. I hoped to hell I wasn't the one who would have to tell her.

Chapter Six

The tourists braving the cold on the Royal Mile had forced smiles on their bluish faces. The sky was overcast now and the temperature had gone up by a few degrees. I suppose that was as good a reason as any to feel cheerful. But tourists are only in the perfect city for a week or two. The rest of us have to live here permanently – no foreign holidays, no dancing in the streets (apart from Hogmanay) and no time off for good behaviour. All that most citizens have to look forward to is the weekly sex session. Even that's less exciting than it sounds, especially if, like me, you haven't ever really come to terms with having sex with complete strangers. Then again, you can get used to anything.

"Don't you think it's a bit strange that none of Roddie's friends knew anything about this girlfriend of his?" Davie said as he turned down St Mary's Street.

"Not necessarily. Maybe he was just keeping her to himself. He wouldn't be the first guy to do that."

I looked out at the grimy buildings on both sides. As soon as you leave the Royal Mile the atmosphere changes. No more souvenir shops, expensive tea rooms or restored medieval façades. You're into ordinary citizen land, although the Council has made a bit of an effort to tart up the Cowgate further down. It's here they run the cattle along to the Grassmarket and the tourists who watch sometimes venture into the pubs. They're still pretty shitty though. When I was a student we used to call the Cowgate the ninth circle of the inferno. The bars stayed open all night and the road was full of paralytic lost souls bewailing their fate and desperately searching for friends who'd long since buggered off home. The curfew's put paid to all of that.

Davie pulled up outside the Pleasance buildings. A sign on the wall described them as Citizens' Leisure Centre Number 13. In pre-Enlightenment times they were part of the university – there was a theatre, squash courts, bars and the like. Now it's a licensed knocking shop. Unusually for this city, tourists are not allowed in. They're catered for in the much more upmarket facilities run by the subtly named Prostitution Services Department. And they have to pay. At least citizens get laid for free. But we pay for that privilege in other ways.

"How do you want to play this?" Davie asked before we got out.

I knew what he meant. Guardsmen are about as welcome in sex centres as a tingling in the urethra. The places are run by low-ranking auxiliaries who do their best to convince clients that they have only citizens' interests at heart. Of course, copies of the records they keep are collected in the middle of every Sunday night by plain-clothed guard personnel. Where would the Council be if it didn't know exactly who was screwing who? Maybe that's how the celibate guardians get a thrill.

"Let's go in together," I said, grinning at him. "It's a bit chilly for you to stay out here." Davie's a useful guy to have around auxiliaries who think they're something special. Which means more or less all auxiliaries.

The middle-aged reception clerk looked me up and down with a practised eye but ignored Davie completely. Then she picked up the phone on her desk.

I cut the connection. "Hold on, citizen Macmillan," I said, reading the badge on her flat chest. "A few questions before you call your supervisor." I showed her the Council authorisation Hamilton had given me earlier in the day.

"I'm only on the door," the woman said in a dull voice. "I don't know anything." Her face was fleshless, the skin pocked with scabs. Another triumph for the medical guardian's Dietetics Department.

"You don't know anything about what?" I asked, giving her an encouraging smile. "I haven't even told you what I'm after yet."

"I don't know anything," she repeated sullenly. This is how citizens are nowadays. Hyper-suspicious of the Council and all its works.

I showed her the photograph from Roddie's file. "Recognise him?" I saw her eyes flicker.

The skin around her mouth loosened and she almost smiled. "Oh, aye, that's Roddie. Roddie Aitken. He's been coming here for a long time."

Five years, I calculated. Citizens attend weekly sex sessions from their eighteenth birthdays.

"Roddie's fine. We all like him here," she said, her face suddenly hardening again. "What's he done?"

"Don't worry, he hasn't done anything," I said. That was true enough. I sat on the end of her desk and gave her another smile. All that did was make her look down at her thin thighs, which were poking out from the short skirt sex centre staff are required to wear. "Who was he with in the last few weeks?"

Citizen Macmillan seemed to freeze for a few seconds before she answered, her eyes still lowered. "I can't remember. I'm only on the door. It's not my job to—"

"It's not your job to do what, citizen?" The man's voice was as smooth as the duvet cover in a tourist hotel bedroom. I almost believed he was unconcerned.

He didn't wait for the receptionist to answer. "And you are?"

"Dalrymple," I answered, flashing my authorisation again. "I need to see your files."

"Where's your barracks number badge, auxiliary?" Davie demanded. You can't take him anywhere.

The supervisor smiled urbanely. "I do apologise, guardsman. I must have left it on my desk. I'm Moray 37." His low barracks number indicated that he'd been a member of the Enlightenment before independence. He led us down a corridor, his long legs sheathed in an unusually tight pair of cream trousers. He didn't look like he would last a day on the border, but he'd have got in as an auxiliary before the boyscouts restricted the rank to heavy-duty headbangers.

"Well, here we are," he said, tossing carefully tended locks of black hair back from his forehead. "*Chez moi.*"

The room we were in was a file-spotter's paradise. Apart from the table and chair a couple of paces in from the door, the furniture consisted entirely of gunmetal filing cabinets. Judging by the neat array of pens, pencils, notepads and proformas on the tabletop, I reckoned Moray 37 was that file-spotter.

Davie picked up a barracks number badge and tossed it to the auxiliary, who gave him a brief smile.

"Well, gentlemen, tell me how I can be of service." The supervisor sat down in front of us and propped up his head on the extended fingers of one hand. He was probably tired after a hard morning with his pencil and rubber.

"A citizen by the name of Roddie Aitken," I said. "Do you know him?"

"I think not." Moray 37 almost pulled it off. If his eyelashes had quivered for a micro-second less, I'd have gone for it. "Should I?" he asked with a studied lack of interest.

"Citizen Macmillan at the door says he's very popular around here," I said, watching him carefully.

The auxiliary fluttered his lashes deliberately this time. "Citizen Macmillan doesn't know the meaning of the word popular." He leaned back and pulled open a drawer in the nearest cabinet. "Aitken, Roderick. Here he is." He pulled out a grey cardboard folder and opened it. "Aitken, Roderick." His features were blank. Too blank. "I can't say I remember him. It appears he's one of our people though. Next due in on Saturday."

No chance of that. I wondered whether Moray 37 had really heard nothing on the grapevine about the murder or whether he knew more about Roddie than he was letting on. Time for the third degree. I gave Davie the nod.

"Do you think I'm funny, auxiliary?" Davie asked mildly.

Moray 37 raised an eyebrow. "You're about as far from funny as I am from playing in the front row of the barracks rugby team."

Davie leaned over the table until his face was a few inches in front of the supervisor's. "So why are you laughing at me?" he demanded.

"I can assure you, guardsman . . ." There was no way that sentence was ever going to reach the finishing post.

"You're taking the piss. My boss and I come in here asking questions and what do you do?" His beard was close enough to tickle Moray 37's cheeks. Davie brought his fist down hard on the table. "You give us the runaround."

The supervisor's eyes sprang open wide, then his gaze dropped. "I . . . oh, very well . . . you can see the file for yourselves."

"Thank you." I took it and looked down the attendance sheet. Next to the dates of sex sessions is entered the name of the partner. Unmarried ordinary citizens must, as the city regulations put it, "enjoy sexual congress" once a week with a different member of either sex, depending on whether they have declared themselves hetero or homo. (Bisexuals aren't catered for – they made the original guardians feel insecure, don't ask me why.) This was supposed to be a way of widening people's sexual experiences and ensuring that everyone screwed everyone, whether they were handsome, ugly, fat (not many of them nowadays), thin, spotty, greasy-haired or whatever. Believe it or not, the Council actually reckons this improves social cohesion. I've had sessions with women who definitely did not have that effect. No doubt there are several female citizens who would say the same about me.

There wasn't anything special about Roddie's attendance

sheet. I made a note of the last six female names he had been with. Then I flicked through the other pages. One detailed his sexual preferences (oral sex was one – how unusual); another, the comments made by his partners to centre staff afterwards. They were mostly complimentary, although one woman didn't think much of his technique. The last page gave the results of his most recent medical check-up, which were clear.

"Satisfied, citizen?" Moray 37 asked. His voice sounded just a bit tense.

I smiled at him. "No. Show me the reception records."

The auxiliary went as grey as the white bread in the city's bakeries. This looked promising.

"I'll come with you," Davie said as Moray 37 got up and headed back to citizen Macmillan's desk in the entrance hall. He suddenly seemed to be carrying a great weight.

They were back in a minute, Davie holding another grey file. The auxiliary sat down slowly.

It only took me a few seconds to discover what he was worried about. "Well, well," I said. "The Council is going to be very upset. You haven't been balancing your records, have you?"

Moray 37 now looked like he was about to lose control of his lunch. He shook his head distractedly.

What I'd found were the check-in slips for Roddie's last three partners. And the juicy bit was that, while the attendance sheet showed three different names, the slips all had the same one. Moray 37 could be demoted for this. Regulations state that citizens are forbidden to enjoy sexual congress more than once with the same partner unless what's called a "long-term relationship permit" has been issued.

"Did you know about this, Moray 37?" I asked, showing him the slips.

"I . . . no . . . I . . ." His shoulders dropped. "Well, yes, I did have some idea . . ."

"Some idea?" Davie yelled. "What the fuck does that mean?"

The auxiliary shifted around on his chair as if a burrowing creature had just broken through the fabric of his trousers. "You know how it is, citizen," he said, looking at me hopefully.

I did but I wasn't going to tell him that.

He started shuffling paper. "Sometimes citizens form emotional attachments. They like to see the same partner every week."

"And what do you get for arranging these romantic trysts?" I asked.

"What do I get?" Moray 37 tried to look outraged. "I'm an auxiliary. My job is to serve citizens."

Davie sounded like he was about to choke. "Your job, in case you've forgotten, is to serve the city."

"Which isn't exactly the same thing," I said. "Don't tell me you did it in the cause of young love."

The supervisor squirmed again. "Obviously you have no understanding of the feelings experienced by young people."

He was wrong there, but I still wasn't buying it. Auxiliaries, even older ones, aren't known for acts of charity to citizens. Maybe someone was pulling his chain, but short of taking him up to the castle and setting Davie loose on him in a big way, it didn't look like I was going to get much more out of him.

I looked at the name on the last three check-in slips. It was an unusual one. "Get me Sheena Marinello's file, auxiliary."

Now Moray 37 had the look of a pre-independence banker whose company car had just been surrounded by a crowd of ex-customers objecting to the way their savings had gone walkabout to the Cayman Islands. He moved away.

"I'll be right behind you," said Davie with a death's-head grin.

They went to the filing cabinets, where Moray 37 put on a performance of failing to find the file that would have won an Oscar in the days when Hollywood producers made the occasional watchable movie, rather than the Christian fundamentalist garbage they come up with now.

"Apparently the file's been — how did you put it, auxiliary? — misplaced," Davie said from the far end of the room.

I can't say I was surprised. "Can you describe how she looks, Moray 37?"

He shrugged. "Medium height, dark brown hair, shoulder length, freckles on her cheeks — nothing particularly special."

"Don't discuss this conversation with anyone, auxiliary," I said as I left his office. "That way, if you're lucky, you might stay in your job."

He looked ridiculously grateful.

In the corridor I heard the usual noises from the cubicles where citizens get their weekly hour of congress: music, lowered voices, grunts, moans, even a soft, satisfied sigh. I can't remember the last time I emitted one of those. Well, I can. It was with Katharine, and it was in my flat rather than in public.

The late afternoon shift of clients had started and there was a queue in the entrance hall. The receptionist was checking in a middle-aged couple who were glancing at each other dubiously. I waited for them to head off down the corridor, clear space between their bodies. There's nothing worse than being allocated a partner you don't even vaguely fancy.

"Citizen Macmillan," I said. "One question."

Her mouth slackened and her eyes opened wide.

"Don't worry. I'm not investigating you."

She didn't look like she believed me.

"Sheena Marinello. I know you've seen her. Describe the way she looks, will you?"

"Describe the way she looks?" The thin citizen laughed once, with surprising bitterness. "She's a bloody stunner. The kind that men do anything for. Beautiful body, perfect face, legs up to her neck." She shook her head slowly. "Roddie couldn't believe his luck."

We walked out into the cold past more ordinary citizens: young lads with lust in their eyes and standard-issue condoms in their pockets, women who'd seen it all before standing wearily in line. Roddie Aitken had got more out of his sex sessions than most. But who exactly was Sheena Marinello, and why had the supervisor been so vague about her charms? Time for another trip to the archives.

Where I discovered something very interesting. There weren't many women called Marinello in the citizen body, and only one whose first name was Sheena.

"Look at this, Davie." I showed him the front cover of the file. A single word had been rubberstamped in black on it.

"Bloody hell," he said. "Was Roddie Aitken having sex with a ghost?"

"Marinello, Sheena Pauline, deceased 12.3.2021." I read the handwritten date from the middle of the stamp, then opened the file. "She was past the age for compulsory sex sessions anyway."

Davie looked at the photograph. "Over sixty by a mile. So what's been going on at Moray 37's sex centre?"

That made me laugh. "You're not on parade now, guardsman. I know what goes on in barracks."

"All right, all right," he said with a scowl. "One of my female colleagues fancied a bit of rough."

I nodded. Occasionally auxiliaries got bored with barracks sex sessions and got themselves into ordinary citizen centres. That explained why the supervisor had looked guilty and why Sheena Marinello's file had been misplaced. It wasn't the first time dead citizens' identities had been assumed.

"Are we going to pick Moray 37 up?" Davie said as we got back into the Land-Rover.

"Hang on a minute. Let's see if the dental records search has turned up anything." I rang the medical guardian on the vehicle's mobile phone. She sounded totally unexcited to hear my voice, but she did inform me that no match had been found for the bite mark in the records so far.

Great. I looked up George IVth Bridge to the corner of the Lawnmarket where the gallows stand and thought about taking

Moray 37 in. It would mean curtains for the supervisor's career if we did. I didn't reckon he deserved demotion and the rest of his life being shunned by citizens for being an ex-auxiliary just because he'd done a colleague a favour. On the other hand, this mystery woman might be the only lead we had to Roddie's killer. Before I could decide, my mobile rang.

"Dalrymple? Hamilton here."

I knew immediately that he had something shit-hot to tell me – he'd never use his name rather than his title on the phone unless he was seriously wound up.

"Another body's been found."

I signalled to Davie to start the engine.

"Where is it, Lewis?"

"Among the ruins of Holyroodhouse."

"The palace?" Not a million miles from Roddie's flat or from the sex centre. I pointed to Davie and we moved off at speed. "We're on our way."

"As am I. And Dalrymple?"

I had to hold the phone to my ear with my shoulder as both my hands were otherwise involved. Davie had taken the corner like a Formula One man in the days when spending millions of dollars driving round and round in circles was an acceptable part of popular culture. "What, Lewis?"

"It's a woman this time."

I felt my stomach somersault.

"Not an auxiliary by any chance?"

"How on earth did you know that?" Hamilton asked in surprise.

"Call it a hunch, Lewis. Out."

I could live without that kind of hunch.

Chapter Seven

We raced down the lower reaches of the Royal Mile past bright lights, flags and startled tourists – into the black hole straight ahead of us. In the last hour night had fallen on the city. The ruins of the palace were as dark as anywhere in Edinburgh. Holyroodhouse had been the epicentre of the catastrophic riots that followed the heir to the throne's second marriage to the daughter of a Colombian drugs baron before his coronation in 2002. It wasn't only his fault. We'd been strung along for years by political parties who'd set up devolution but kept their sticky unionist fingers very much on the controls. The crown prince's attempt to improve his family's cash reserves wasn't a brilliant public relations exercise though. His involvement with a drugs heiress went down like a lead zeppelin at a time when the UK was being torn apart by drugs-related crime. Just as well he wasn't staying at the palace. The masses would have had no problem blowing him up as well.

"Hope you've got a torch," Davie said.

"Hope the directorate manages to find a generator." The Council had left the ruins exactly as they were. It liked the idea of them as a reminder of the bad old days, but it didn't like the idea enough to put up any lights.

"We're okay," Davie said. "They're way ahead of us. A generator must have been authorised as soon as the body was found." He pointed at the glow that was faintly visible beyond the first line of stones.

"Course it was. There's no expense spared when it's an auxiliary who's been murdered."

"Thank you for that observation, citizen." Davie's imitation of Hamilton's solemn tones made me laugh.

Not for long. Guardsmen and women were moving around among the crush of official vehicles, their faces drawn and pallid in the headlights. The main thing they're taught during auxiliary training is how to put a lid on their emotions. It looked like the collective pressure cooker was about to blow. I got out and immediately felt my feet begin to freeze.

Another Land-Rover pulled up, sending a shower of gravel over my tingling legs. Hamilton and the medical guardian got out.

"Over there, guardian." A guard commander had arrived at Hamilton's side like a dog that was desperate to please. "Raeburn 03 arrived with the scene-of-crime squad."

That was all I needed. Machiavelli had been out of my hair for the last twenty-four hours. I might have known the louse would try to lay his eggs again.

Hamilton strode away angrily towards a fifteen-foot-high section of the ruins that had been part of the picture gallery wall. Light from the generator that had been set up shone round the shattered edges. It was a good sheltered place for a murder. Not many citizens or tourists bother to walk here, especially in winter.

I went round the back and found Hamilton laying into his subordinate.

". . . and I specifically told you to keep your nose out of the murder case, Raeburn 03. Dalrymple's in charge."

Machiavelli stood there rubbing his hands and bending forward in a way that combined acquiescence with a complete lack of respect — a good trick if you can pull it off.

"I heard the initial call for assistance, guardian. I judged it was a serious matter and——"

"You judged it was something your friends in the Council would like inside information on, auxiliary," Hamilton roared. "Well, that's my job. Get back to the castle and play with your files."

Machiavelli straightened himself up, shot me a vicious glance and moved off slowly, trying to salvage some credibility in front of directorate personnel. I don't think he pulled that trick off.

"Did Raeburn 03 touch anything at the scene?" I asked a heavily built guardsman with a grizzled beard.

He shook his head. "I arrived with the first squad. We were told to keep everyone back until the guardian arrived."

"Who found the body?"

The guardsman nodded at a tourist with a pair of binoculars round his neck who was leaning against the wall further down. His knees didn't look too steady.

I turned to the Ice Queen. "Shall we have a look then?"

She was already kitted out in plastic overalls. I pulled mine on and walked with her to the tarpaulin that lay in the centre of the lit-up area. The ground was rock hard, with no sign of any footprints.

The guardian nodded to the guardsmen at the tarpaulin corners. They lifted it and rolled it back, averting their eyes.

It was a bad one. I've seen a lot of victims' bodies, but this one was in a hell of a state. She was on her back, naked apart from the remains of a brassiere, the cups of which had been ripped apart with a sharp blade. I couldn't see initially if she fitted the description we had of Roddie Aitken's girlfriend because her head was tipped back, displaying a bloody hole in her neck. The blood was frozen. The icy sheen of the body made it look even more grotesque – like a frozen mummy rather than a woman who'd recently been alive.

"She's been here for at least twelve hours, probably more." The medical guardian was on her knees beside the upper body. "The throat appears to have been bitten in the same way as the previous victim."

"That's not the only similarity," I said, pointing to the groin. The corner of a plastic bag was protruding from the mutilated vaginal opening. There were several deep cuts in the flesh of the upper thighs too.

"The wrists were bound as well." The guardian indicated ice-flecked weals in the skin.

"How did she die?" I asked.

She went back up to the head.

"Difficult to tell. Could be shock again, especially in an ambient temperature like this." The guardian examined the ground beneath the neck. "Loss of blood perhaps."

"How about the mouth?" I bent over the victim's head. There were frozen traces of blood around the chin. As with Roddie, the jaws were locked together and the teeth bared in a ghastly rictus.

"You'll have to wait, citizen. It's certainly a possibility that the tongue was cut."

"He'd need to keep her quiet, even out here in the middle of the night." I shook my head. "Why can't the butcher use a gag like anyone else?"

The Ice Queen stood up and stretched her arms. "Excuse me for encroaching on your territory, citizen, but didn't you have some theory about the tape being a message?"

"So?"

"So the removal of the tongue isn't just a way of stifling screams – it's symbolic too. The music speaks, not the human voice."

It wasn't a bad idea, especially as the Clapton track was an instrumental. It made me shiver though. What kind of lunatic leaves symbolic messages in his victims? Serial killers aren't usually too hot on semiotics.

"How do we know she was an auxiliary?" I said, turning to Hamilton, who was keeping his distance and looking in the opposite direction.

"I know her," said the grizzled guardsman I'd already spoken to. "She's in my barracks. Moray 310 is her number."

Was her number, more like. So she was in the same barracks as the sex centre supervisor. Things were beginning to connect.

The face of the tourist who found the body appeared behind the guardsman. The guy was in his late fifties, grey-haired and shaking from the cold.

"I insist you take me indoors," he said in a caricature of what was once called the Queen's English. "I explained to the officer that I was perfectly willing to make a statement, but I am not enamoured by the prospect of freezing to death before you can be bothered to take it."

Davie asked for the man's passport. "US national," he said. "Oliver St John Stafford."

He was probably one of the numerous ex-British citizens who jumped ship when crime in the UK made life less than rosy. You don't get any tourists from England itself in the city these days – the Council regards England as a wasteland harbouring hundreds of drugs gangs in search of new markets. It's one of the few things the iron boyscouts have got right.

"We'll send you up to the castle in a minute, Mr Stafford," I said with a brief smile. I wasn't keen on the prospect of permanently losing touch with my feet either. "Just tell me how you found the body, please."

He touched his binoculars. "I was birdwatching in the park. I thought I caught a glimpse of one of the American thrushes which sometimes make it across the Atlantic and—"

"What time was this, Mr Stafford?" I asked with an even briefer smile.

"It was about four, I suppose. The gloaming was well advanced." He looked pleased with himself for having got a Scots word in, not that his vowels were very convincing.

"Did you see anyone else in the vicinity?"

"Good God, no. Far too cold for anyone except a dedicated twitcher like me."

"What did you see when you arrived here?"

The fatuous smile was wiped from his face. "What did I see? I . . . Well, I was after my thrush and I came round the corner over there and found . . . found the woman."

"What was the first thing you noticed?" I gripped his arm to focus his mind. It's surprising what sticks in people's memories.

"The first thing I noticed were her clothes and the things from her bag." He moved his head rapidly from side to side. "They were all over the place." Then he lowered his chin to his chest. "My first impression was of the mess a bird of prey makes when it catches a smaller bird — feathers torn out and left all around."

I hadn't noticed the woman's clothing because of the restricted range of the lighting. Looking around in the surrounding gloom, I made out the white overalls of scene-of-crime people collating objects. Clothes and possessions scattered about. I remembered the mess in Roddie's flat. The killer had been looking for something again.

I sent Davie off with the birdwatcher.

A guardsman came round with plastic cups of black tea — the Public Order Directorate often fails to get hold of enough milk.

"What did the killer do for light?" Hamilton asked, cursing under his breath as he scalded his tongue.

I took hold of his elbow and led him out of the ring of artificial light. "Look above Arthur's Seat."

The moon, a day past full, had just cleared the summit of the hill. It shone out with frozen radiance over the aptly named Enlightenment Park.

"Would that have been enough for his purposes?" Hamilton asked.

"He might have had some kind of portable light as well." I beckoned to the nearest scene-of-crime officer. "Any sign of the victim's torch?" Auxiliaries are issued with torches and the batteries to run them; ordinary citizens are denied access to both, in order to restrict movement after curfew.

The young guardsman shook his head.

"So the murderer took hers," the guardian said.

"That doesn't mean he didn't have one of his own too," I said, stamping my feet. Circulation was long gone below my knees.

Hamilton's nostrils flared. I knew they would. As far as he's concerned, my chief suspects are always auxiliaries.

"Can we wrap this up, citizen?" Even the medical guardian looked like the cold was getting to her.

I nodded. "What about the post-mortem?"

"Tomorrow morning. She needs to thaw out."

I could have insisted on having it done during the night, but I had plenty of other things to be getting on with. Like why the victim was wearing a bra that was a lot flashier than the standard-issue number.

I went over to the pile of clear bags that contained the rest of her clothing and held them up to the light one by one. Black track suit bottoms – fair enough. White T-shirt and maroon and white running shoes – ditto. But black fishnet stockings? And high-cut white silk knickers matching the bra?

"She was in the Prostitution Services Department, citizen." The guardsman with the grey beard was at my side.

"You amaze me."

"Worked in one of the clubs. She must have been on her way back to barracks when the piece of excrement caught up with her."

"Any idea which club?"

He looked at me and nodded slowly. "The Three Graces in the Grassmarket. She was one of them."

The Three Graces was where Roddie Aitken made deliveries and had his first sighting of the hooded man. Coincidence?

"I need a photograph of her," I said.

The guardsman set off towards one of the directorate personnel who'd been at work around the body.

"A photograph of her alive," I called after him.

"Oh, right. If you come back to Moray with me, I'll get you one from her file."

I called Davie and told him to meet me at the sex centre. Then I followed the guardsman to his vehicle. The moon was higher in the inky sky now and my feet were blocks of ice dug from the deepest glacier in Greenland. But they were nothing compared with the freeze-dried heart of the beast who was loose in this benighted city.

Citizen Macmillan recognised the photograph I'd been given at Moray Barracks immediately.

"Aye, that's Sheena Marinello all right." She shook her head and muttered something abusive. "So she was an auxiliary." The photo showed the dead woman wearing a guard tunic, her hair plaited in the requisite female auxiliary style. "I thought she was a stuck-up bitch."

"Is the supervisor on duty?"

"Is he fuck. He left about half an hour ago looking like his arse was on fire."

We left her to the queue of customers that had built up behind us.

"We've got two choices," I said as we got back into the Land-Rover.

"And neither of them involves eating, I'm sure," Davie complained.

"Oh, guardsman, I'm sorry, are you hungry? We'll just stop the investigation for an hour so you can refuel. After all, it's only a double murder."

"Up all your orifices, Quint," he replied. "So what are the two choices? Check if the supervisor's gone back to his barracks and . . . ?"

"Actually, you might get a chance to eat at the other one."

"Great. Let's go there." He turned the key and waited for the prehistoric starting motor to engage.

"Fair enough." I picked up my mobile and called Moray

Barracks. They hadn't seen the supervisor since midday. So I called Hamilton and asked for all barracks to be alerted about the missing auxiliary.

"Where are we going then?" Davie enquired when I finished.

"To the Three Graces in the Grassmarket. Or rather, the Two Graces as it now is."

"A sex club." Davie shook his head vigorously. "I couldn't possibly, citizen."

"Uh-huh."

We got there in under three minutes.

Although it was only eight o'clock, there was already a large crowd of tourists around the replica of the Three Graces outside the club. We were told to get to the back of the queue in at least ten languages as we pushed our way through. At least I think that's what was being said.

A couple of gorillas in dinner jackets three sizes too small blocked my passage. Then they saw, in rapid succession, my authorisation and Davie. They let us through. Next we were greeted by two girls in toga-like robes which showed more than they covered up. The things some people have to do for the Council – and auxiliaries can't say no to any duty they're assigned.

"Who's in charge?" I asked.

"Watt 94, citizen. You'll find her at the bar."

"Good. I could do with a drink."

The girls parted the curtain and we went down into the club proper. It was large but there still weren't enough tables. The air was full of smoke – tourists being the only people in the city allowed tobacco products – and I had to blink my eyes to see what was happening on stage. Then I had to blink them again to convince myself I hadn't fallen into wet dreamland. So did Davie and he's about as prone to shock as the journalists who covered what MPs got up to in the days before MPs became extinct like the dodo and the elephant.

On the raised stage there were three nymphs cavorting to the sounds of a seriously languid saxophone. Cavorting doesn't fully cover what the women were doing. They were all completely naked, their hair done up in ribbons like the originals in Canova's sculpture. They were also standing close together. There the similarities with the work of art ended. Each of them was holding a pair of very large, knobbly dildoes and applying them to any opening they could reach. One of the three, presumably the dead auxiliary's replacement, was definitely not having a good time – or at least wasn't covering that up very well. The crowd, which contained a lot more men than women, was yapping and cackling like a pack of exceptionally ravenous hyenas. The noise got even louder when one of the Graces lay down and spread her legs. Another got down between them and started lapping at her colleague's groin. Meanwhile the third, the unhappy one, simultaneously plunged a green dildo into her own fanny and a purple one into the crouching auxiliary's arse. Wonderful stuff.

"Duty calls, guardsman." I manhandled Davie away to the bar that ran down the left side of the room.

"You didn't exactly have your eyes lowered, Quint," he said with a grin.

"I'm following up an important line of enquiry."

"Oh, aye."

I leaned against the polished mahogany of the bar. The burly barman was looking a bit uncomfortable in his Doric chiton and sandals. I asked him for whisky and Watt 94.

"What can I do for you, citizen?"

I turned to see a tall, middle-aged woman in lace blouse and tartan evening skirt. She had short black hair, bright red lips and eyes of burnished steel. You can always spot a senior auxiliary, even when they're out of uniform.

I flashed her my authorisation and emptied the glass that had appeared in front of me. It was tourist-quality whisky – a sight better than even barracks malt.

She eyed my glass coldly and nodded. "I was expecting you."

"Were you now? How come?"

She glanced over her shoulder then sent the barman away. "You know how it is. Bad news travels fast. You're here about Moray 310, I take it." Her voice was so deep I had trouble picking it up over the drone of the saxophones in the band.

"I'm also looking for a male auxiliary from her barracks – Moray 37. Seen him in here?"

She shook her head. "My men on the door would have told me if one of our own people had tried to get in." Auxiliaries are supposed to get their kicks only in barracks sex sessions.

"So tell me about the dead woman."

She shrugged. "I was only posted here a couple of days ago. I can show you her file . . ."

"I'm a big boy, Watt 94. I can find files by myself."

Spots of colour appeared on her cheeks, then that reliable old auxiliary self-control kicked in. "Really. Well, instead of wasting my time, you should go behind stage and talk to the club co-ordinator. She knows everything there is to know about the Three Graces."

I pulled Davie away from a plate of deep-fried miniature haggises. The Dietetics Department would never let Edinburgh citizens overdose on suicide food like we used to before independence, but the tourists can eat as much of it as they like.

On stage the Graces had got bored with their sex aids and were fiddling around with a trio of rough-looking young men in leather shorts. The Three Disgraces, presumably. We passed through another curtain and entered a shabby backstage area manned by a stage crew who were paying no attention to the show. Two of them were hunched over a chessboard. That's the way your more old-fashioned auxiliary spends his leisure time.

"Where's the co-ordinator?" I asked.

One of the guys stuck a thumb out and jerked it in the direction of a dim corridor.

Davie was about to take issue with the guardsman's manners, but I shook my head.

At the end of the corridor was a row of mirrors and sinks. At the last sink was someone I hadn't seen for some time. "Patsy? What the hell are you doing out of your cell?"

"Well, well, the great Quintilian Dalrymple." The woman took a step back and appeared in all four of the mirrors between her and me. Suddenly I had four ex-brothel keepers in their mid-fifties to deal with. They all looked in pretty good nick, blonde hair perfectly coiffured and well-stacked figures squeezed into black velvet dresses. On the other hand, none of them looked particularly pleased to see me.

"What are you doing here, Patsy?" She'd once been in charge of the Prostitution Services Department.

"New career," she said, giving me an acid smile. "You can't be sure of anything in life."

"I didn't have you down as a philosopher."

She ignored that. "So what's happened to my star performer? All they told me was that she's had a accident."

"You're going to have to spend some time training up her replacement."

Patsy turned to me, her face suddenly slack. "What happened to her?"

"Someone bit out her throat and cut her apart," I said, watching her closely. Patsy used to know a lot of the city's hard men. "She wasn't the first, either. Any idea who might have done it?"

"I'm just an ordinary citizen now, Quint. I only know what I hear around the club." She looked up at me, her eyes wide apart. "Is there another lunatic out there like the last time?" Suddenly she looked like a frightened old woman despite the layers of make-up and the tough talking.

"Maybe. So what have you heard around here? What can you tell me about Moray 310?"

"Oh, for fuck's sake, Quint, she had a name."

"I know," I said in a conciliatory voice. It's usually me who gets pissed off when auxiliaries are referred to by barracks number. Maybe I was turning back into what I'd once been. Shit. "What can you tell me about Moira?" The guardsman who gave me the photo had told me the victim's first name.

Patsy rested her rump against the edge of the basin. "She was a complete natural. I couldn't teach her much. Men just had to look at her and she had them under her spell. It was the way she moved. Slow and seductive, like a snake. She made the guys feel it was them who were shafting her, not that piece of rubber." She laughed softly and looked over at me. "I've only seen two other women who had that kind of power."

I knew what she was about to say.

"Your friend Katharine was one of them." She held her eyes on me to see how I reacted.

"Thank you for that, Patsy," I said with a scowl. "Let's get back to Moira, shall we? Was she involved in anything else?"

"Anything the Council wouldn't approve of, you mean?" Patsy gave me a bitter smile. "Why would you believe what I tell you, Quint?"

She had a point. She'd been known to have trouble with the concept of truth. But we were friends once, in the far distant past when I was in the directorate and she was turning herself from the city's number one madam into a high-ranking auxiliary.

"I trust you, Patsy," I said, smiling back at her and glancing around at the decrepit washroom. "Why would you lie? Things don't get much worse than this."

"That's true enough," she said, nodding. "Moira was ... clever. Cunning. She was one of those auxiliaries who pretend they have the city's interests at heart but are really only looking after themselves."

"There are a few of those around," I said ironically.

"Aye, a few." She laughed. "Well, I can spot that type a mile off, so I always kept an eye on her."

This was getting interesting.

"But I never picked up on a thing."

No, it wasn't.

"She was smart, kept a tight grip on herself, even when the punters got her pissed."

"So this conversation's been a waste of time," I said, putting my notebook back in my pocket.

Patsy shrugged and turned back to the mirror. "If you say so, Quint."

I headed for the door.

"But there's one thing I can't work out . . ."

I hit the brakes.

"She was on the phone in the corridor a few days ago." All facilities like this have phones for the staff to keep in touch with their barracks control room. "And she was really scared. Shouting and screaming. Till she saw me at the other end of the passage."

"What was she saying?"

"She kept repeating the same thing. I couldn't make any sense of it."

I went up to her and took hold of her fleshy arms. "What was it, Patsy? What was she saying?"

"'The electric blues.'" She looked at me uncomprehendingly. "She kept asking, 'What about the electric blues?'"

I let go of her and stepped back, thinking of the tape we took out of Roddie Aitken. Eric Clapton playing electric blues. Then I thought of the auxiliary's semi-frozen body, the legs splayed wide apart.

I was bloody sure another tape had been left inside her. The question was, what had been recorded on it?

Chapter Eight

It was a long night. Davie and I waited for the surviving Two Graces plus the victim's replacement to take a break from delving into each other. They were no more ecstatic about our delving into their relationships with the dead Moira than the new girl had been on stage. It soon became obvious that they thought their ex-colleague was a supercilious cow who kept herself to herself outside business hours. None of them had any idea exactly what she got up to when she wasn't at the club, but the general idea seemed to be that she was doing a lot of freelance whoring among the wealthier tourist clientèle. Patsy had the same impression. So where had the dead woman stashed her loot?

"Moray Barracks?" Davie asked as we came out into the freezing night air of the Grassmarket.

I nodded. "She was asking for trouble if she kept currency or jewellery in her barracks, but we have to start somewhere."

Davie pulled away from the even larger crowd that had gathered outside the club. Performances go on until four in the morning – no wonder the performers have trouble looking enthusiastic. "Do you think it could be a tourist who killed her?" he asked, swerving to avoid a Japanese guy in a Black Watch kilt.

"Christ, Davie, don't let Hamilton hear you saying that. That would be even worse than an auxiliary. Think of the dilemma that would give the Council. As far as it's concerned, tourists' arses exist primarily for us to kiss, not for tourists to shit out of."

"It's not quite like that, Quint," he said testily. "Without the income from tourism, the city would be more or less insolvent."

I love it when Davie turns back into a model auxiliary and spouts the Council's standard line. I didn't find it very convincing. "So you approve of your fellow auxiliaries spreading their legs for the tourists, do you?"

He gave me the glare guardsmen use when citizens are massively out of line. "Of course I fucking don't, but how else are we going to attract the business? These days people from the successful countries don't just want package tours that take in a few museums and medieval banquets. They want cheap sex."

I nodded, looking out at the crowds of half-cut foreigners wandering around the Cowgate. They want cheap sex, horse-racing in Princes Street Gardens, casinoes on every street corner, whisky and tartan knitwear. What they don't want is to bite people's throats out and hide music cassettes inside them. I didn't have much idea of what was going on, but I was sure of one thing: Edinburgh's latest multiple murderer was a home-grown product, born and bred in the city like his victims. Which led me back to another thought. Where was the bastard hiding out? Someone must know him; someone probably saw the bloodstains on his clothing after the second killing. So where the hell was he? I called Hamilton and asked him to get his people to check all the barracks' patrol reports. We might be lucky. Perhaps some vigilant guardsman had spotted a suspicious character in the early hours but failed to pull him in. Perhaps some citizen on his or her way to the early works buses had reported a strange man in a long coat. And perhaps Edinburgh citizens go to bed every night reciting "Our Senior Guardian who art in heaven . . ."

We would have got a warmer reception at Moray Barracks if we'd walked in sporting bubonic plague sores. Eventually my Council authorisation prevailed. I looked up from signing the sentry's log and saw Hamilton's deputy Machiavelli exiting at speed. The guardsman at his side had a guard rucksack on his back.

"I hope you're not going to lower morale even further by asking awkward questions," said the barracks commander, a doleful guy with bald head and thick brown beard who'd been called down to meet us. He looked like Friar Tuck after a particularly heavy night, except that he could probably count the number of times he'd smiled in his life on the fingers of one hand.

I gave him a smile of my own to show him he was already out of his league. "Awkward questions, Moray 01? Of course not. The morale of your barracks is much more important than the threat posed to the city by a psychotic killer."

That had some effect. The commander stepped back like I'd propositioned him, then struggled to regain his composure. A vein pulsed prominently in the middle of his forehead.

"Show us her cubicle. In person, please."

Moray 01 glanced at me to check I was talking to him, swallowed when he realised I really did want him to act as barracks porter and headed slowly down the corridor.

Moray Barracks is a seventeenth-century mansion that used to be a teacher training college before the Enlightenment. The Council decided it would serve their purpose better as the barracks covering the lower end of the Royal Mile and the Cowgate, not least because teacher training is now part of the auxiliary training programme. Auxiliaries learn hand-to-hand combat, survival skills (useful when they do their tour of duty in the notoriously dangerous border posts) and what are called public order skills; then those of them who want to teach are deemed ready for action and chucked straight into schools. At least there aren't many discipline problems in the classroom. The downside is that Moray House has been wrecked, its decorated walls knocked through to make dormitories and its moulded ceilings left in partial ruin. Very enlightened.

*　　*　　*

The commander led us through a female dorm, then a male one. I was on official business of course, so I paid attention to the semi-naked bodies on display in the first room. The female auxiliaries glanced across briefly, then ignored me as effectively as prime ministers used to ignore cabinet members in the old days.

We left the second dormitory and went up a wide staircase that had once been elegant and ornate and was now high quality drab, the steps chipped from heavy auxiliary boots. Moray 01 stopped at the first door on the next floor and pointed.

"This is Moira ... I mean Moray 310's cubicle." The commander made to depart.

"I haven't finished with you yet," I said, pushing the door open. The room beyond was quite large, containing a sofa, armchair, table and desk as well as a single bed. I looked at Davie then at the Friar Tuck lookalike. "I definitely haven't finished with you yet."

The commander was suddenly finding the carpet, which was in unusually good condition for a barracks, a source of great fascination.

"What's going on here, Moray 01? Why did the dead guardswoman have a room of her own instead of a dorm cubicle?"

He mumbled something about her overnight shifts and heavy workload.

"Come on, commander, all auxiliaries have times when they have to do the night shift. Why did Moray 310 — sorry, Moira, as you called her — get special treatment?"

The vein on his forehead had turned dark blue. Eventually he raised his head and faced me. "I'm not able to say. It's a Council matter, citizen."

"And this is a Council authorisation."

He turned to go. "So address your questions to the Council."

I glanced at Davie, who looked like he fancied playing

basketball with the commander's head. "Wait a minute. Raeburn 03, the Public Order Directorate official I saw leaving when we arrived, has he been in here?"

Moray 01 stopped but didn't turn round. "I don't see why he should have been, citizen. Now, if you don't mind . . ."

"Thanks for your co-operation," I shouted after him.

Davie stepped up. "Cool it, Quint. You aren't among friends here."

I nodded and looked around the well-appointed room. "Get a scene-of-crime squad down here, Davie, including a fingerprint guy. We're going to have to tear this place apart."

We did so. And found nothing special. Prints that were soon matched to the victim and other barracks members; underwear that was definitely not standard issue, but that came from the Prostitution Services Department stores rather than smugglers; and a couple of books of Eastern erotica that were presumably source material for the nightclub act. So either the killer got what he was looking for or she'd hidden it elsewhere. We spoke to some of her colleagues, but none of them was very close to her. They claimed to know nothing about her trips to Roddie Aitken's sex centre and I believed them. Most auxiliaries are very bad at lying.

At one in the morning my mobile buzzed.

"Dalrymple?" came Hamilton's voice. "We've picked up the missing auxiliary Moray 37. He's being brought to the castle."

"We're on our way."

Adrenalin and black coffee are the main things that keep you going during investigations, but it helps if you get a little help from your leads. With the sex centre supervisor we got the big zero.

Sample question: "Moray 37, why did you allow Moray 310 to impersonate a dead citizen and have sex with Roddie Aitken?"

Sample answer: "I was doing her a favour. I knew her in barracks when she was a trainee auxiliary."

Sample question: "Why did you risk your own position to do a favour for an auxiliary who didn't exactly lack the means of obtaining all the sex she wanted at the club?"

Sample answer: "Because she asked me."

Sample question (one of Hamilton's – you can tell by the stilted Council diction): "Why did you absent yourself from the sex centre without authorisation?"

Sample answer: "Because I panicked when I heard about the murder."

And so on. I kept after him, the guardian kept after him, but his answers didn't change. Eventually I concluded that he really had been doing the dead woman a favour. Maybe she fluttered her eyelashes at him and he couldn't say no, despite his sexuality (his file confirmed what his demeanour suggested). He had solid alibis for both murders and a search of his cubicle revealed nothing incriminating. At five in the morning we let him go, putting one of Hamilton's best undercover operatives on his tail. I had the feeling he was a dead end.

Davie and I got a couple of hours' uncomfortable sleep on the sofas in the guardian's outer office. I had a hazy dream about a drugs gang boss called Elmore, but that didn't do me any good. There never had been such a character – or one called James, or Eric, or Clapton, or God. Sometimes you can't even trust your subconscious.

Hamilton woke us up with more big zeroes. Apparently none of Roddie Aitken's workmates was into contraband any juicier than Danish bestiality magazines. And none of the barracks patrols had seen any hooded men with tell-tale bloodstains on their coats.

Then it was time to set off for the infirmary. For the next post-mortem.

I walked into the grey granite building in the pitch darkness that passes for morning at this time of year in Edinburgh. I felt the cold biting at my hands with sharp, insistent teeth, making the stump of my right forefinger tingle like it had just been touched by the blade of the Ear, Nose and Throat Man's knife again. That sick bastard would have enjoyed all this. But not even he went to the extent of planting tapes in his victims.

"Mind if I come with you?" Davie asked, catching me up. "I've never seen a post-mortem."

I looked at him in surprise. "Haven't you?"

"How could I? There haven't been any murders since the last ones you solved."

"No, I suppose there haven't. And you spent most of that investigation on surveillance."

"Aye. So can I come?"

I led him through the entrance hall with its patient line of thin, coughing citizens. The place was busy even at this early hour. "Suit yourself," I said. "Personally I can think of better ways to start the day."

"And I can't?" Davie stared at me fiercely. "You're always telling me to educate myself in the ways of the criminal."

"All right, big man, I said you could come. But promise me one thing."

"What?"

We stopped outside the mortuary and showed ID.

"Don't let the side down by losing your grip on your breakfast."

Another ferocious glare. "I'm an auxiliary, citizen. We never lose our breakfast."

"Right."

We robed up.

"We've got another bite mark," the medical guardian said, bending over the victim's neck.

"Which will no doubt match the last one but, like it, won't match anything in the records." I joined her at the upper body.

The skin was no longer under a sheen of ice and lividity was visible towards the underside. The auxiliary's teeth were still clenched, with dried runnels of blood leading down to the ragged hole in the throat.

The Ice Queen moved down to the lower abdomen. "Severe lacerations to the thighs and vagina. Mutilation of the outer labia and . . ." She lowered her face. "And removal of the clitoris."

I heard a sharp intake of breath from Davie. His face was about the same shade of green as his gown. "Before or after death?" I asked.

"I'll need to run more tests. It's difficult to be sure of the time or cause of death yet." The medical guardian looked up at me. "But given that the victim's hands were bound, at least some of the knifework could have been carried out while she was alive."

"Her feet weren't tied though."

She nodded. "True enough. You'd imagine she'd have been thrashing around."

"Maybe he stunned her."

"There's no indication of any blow to the head." The guardian took a pair of forceps and applied them to the object in the dead woman's vagina. There was a noise like the sound of an oar entering the surface of the sea as she pulled. Davie's breathing was very loud. I nodded towards the door but he paid no attention.

"There you are, citizen." The Ice Queen held the blood-encrusted plastic bag up. It was caught for a second in the flash from the photographer's camera.

"What a surprise," I said, blinking my eyes. "Another cassette."

"Not much doubt it was the same killer," she said.

"Have you got a cassette player in the vicinity, guardian?"

She had moved back up to the top of the table. "In my office."

"Let's have a break from this, Davie." I led him towards the door. His legs weren't too steady.

The guardian's voice came as I put my hand on Davie's elbow. It was sharp, the pitch suddenly higher.

"For the love of God."

Guardians, like all auxiliaries, are sworn atheists. Normally I would have been entertained by one of them referring to the supposedly non-existent deity. But not this time. I looked round to see her leaning against the slab. Her assistant was bent over the corpse's jaws, having just wrenched them apart, his head turned away. The Ice Queen was holding a pink and black shrivelled object in her forceps.

"It's a penis, citizen," she said, the timbre of her voice now deep and throaty. "A penis severed at the root by a very sharp knife."

Davie blundered out of the door, but I went back slowly to the table. There was no escaping the thought that it was Roddie Aitken's member which had been placed in the dead woman's mouth.

The Council chamber, seven o'clock in the evening. I had several things to share with the iron boyscouts and another couple I was going to keep to myself. Davie and I'd had a busy day.

"I trust you are making every effort to trace this homicidal maniac, citizen," the senior guardian said as his colleagues gathered round me like a family of tweed and brogue-clad vultures.

I resisted the easy shot; of course, the fact that the latest victim was an auxiliary was having an obvious effect on how seriously the Council treated my investigation.

"I'm making all the efforts I can, guardian," I said. "Unfortunately, so's the killer." I glanced at the chief boyscout. "But I don't think he's a maniac. He's been smart enough to avoid all the patrols, he's got a plan and he's running rings round us."

The senior guardian looked at Hamilton. "Is citizen Dalrymple out of his depth, guardian?"

"I'd like to see anyone else do any better," he answered brusquely. That was about as close to a vote of confidence as I could expect from Hamilton.

The senior guardian nodded at me slowly. His wispy beard made him look like a forgiving Christ, but the tone of his voice was more Old Testament. "Very well. Your report, citizen."

"If you don't mind, guardian," interrupted the Ice Queen. She was looking particularly stern tonight, her white-blonde hair combed back close to her scalp. "I have some test results that citizen Dalrymple is unaware of." She gave me a perfunctory glance.

"Enlighten us," said the senior guardian. If that was a reference to his other role as science and energy chief, no one seemed prepared to acknowledge it. There's no chance it was anything as flippant as a pun on the Enlightenment Party.

"Moray 310 died from loss of blood. I put the time of death at between five and six a.m. on Thursday 2 January." She looked around at her colleagues with their clipboards and their bowed heads. "Tissue and blood tests have confirmed that the penis found in her mouth was that of the first victim, Roderick Aitken." The heads remained bowed. The medical guardian caught my eye briefly. "Moray 310's tongue was removed as well."

"Is there some significance in that, citizen?" the senior guardian asked.

I shrugged. "The medical guardian thinks it's a pointer to the other messages he's sending."

"You mean the tapes?"

"Before we get on to that, senior guardian," the Ice Queen interrupted again – she really was taking her life in her hands – "I found something unexpected in the victim's stomach."

Now I was paying close attention. "What was it?" I asked.

The medical guardian suddenly seemed a lot less sure of

herself. Her head was bowed now as she flipped over pages on her clipboard. Then she looked up. "It showed up in the toxicological analysis of the stomach contents."

"It?" I shouted and was instantly surrounded by a ring of startled faces. "What is 'it', guardian?"

The Ice Queen pursed her lips at me. "'It', citizen, is a trace of a stimulant."

"A drug?" said Hamilton, his eyes wide. The years he spent fighting the gangs that used to traffic in controlled substances had left him scarred for life. "What kind of drug?"

"I told you," replied the Ice Queen. "A stimulant."

"Not one of those that are sometimes prescribed for guard personnel on the border?" I asked.

The senior guardian looked down his nose at me. "Those are not controlled substances, as you well know, citizen."

I did, but it's always worth winding the guardians up. Very occasionally they even lose their tempers. "So what is it?"

"A compound of one of the known methamphetamines and another substance that the Toxicology Department hasn't been able to identify." The medical guardian glanced at Hamilton. "Where did she get it, guardian?"

"Don't ask me," he replied, his cheeks red above the white of his beard. "We haven't found banned substances in the city for years." He glared at her. "Maybe you should check that none of your people has been experimenting in the labs."

"That'll do, guardian." The chief boyscout wasn't impressed with inter-directorate scrapping, at least not in front of an outsider like me.

I had a thought while they were squabbling. "Maybe that's what the killer's been looking for. Maybe this is all about drugs."

"Bloody hell," said Hamilton, to be given a bowel-liquefying look by his superior. "You don't think the drugs gangs could be forming up again, do you, Dalrymple?"

"Who knows what's going on beyond the border? There have

been plenty of drugs in the democratic states like Glasgow since they decided legalising them was a good idea."

Hamilton wasn't giving up. "They also still have high levels of criminal activity."

It wasn't the time for a debate about public order policy. "We'll need to close the Three Graces down immediately and see if we can find any sign of this new drug," I said. "All the staff will have to be searched and questioned."

That was more to Hamilton's taste. He was so anxious to get started that for a moment I thought he'd forgotten his incontinence pants.

The tourism guardian was in a similar plight — until the senior guardian assured him that none of the customers would be hassled. I might have known.

All of which overshadowed what I had to say about the tape that was inside the dead auxiliary. This time it was Jimi Hendrix playing "Red House"; the original studio version from 1966 — slow, sexy, very electric blues. And at least this time there was a lyric. So what the hell did it mean? The guy in the song hasn't seen the girl in the red house for ninety-nine and one half days; his key doesn't fit the door and he ends up going back across the hill to chase her sister. The expression on the Council's collective face said "And?" I didn't have much to suggest, except that Holyroodhouse where the auxiliary was murdered was now a kind of red house. They didn't buy it. Christ, I didn't buy it myself.

"Anything else, citizen?" asked the senior guardian.

Time for some more fun and games.

"A couple of things," I said, giving the group around me a smile to soften them up. "Why did the dead auxiliary have a room of her own rather than a cubicle in a dormitory? Her barracks commander suggested I take it up with the Council."

Silence for a time, then the senior guardian let out a long sigh. "What is the point of your question, citizen? Do you think that a single room is proof of corruption in high places?"

If only. No, I was just rubbing their noses in the reality of their supposedly equitable system.

"The Tourism Directorate recognises that certain key personnel need privileged treatment," the chief scout continued. "For the good of the city."

I let that pass without comment. "One last point. Roddie Aitken reported that he'd suffered an attempted assault by a hooded man to the guard."

They were still in a ring around me, like a herd of cows congregated in the middle of a field. I went into biting fly mode.

"Someone's removed that report from the guard operations file."

"What?" Hamilton looked like he was about to do serious damage to his cardiovascular system. I hadn't had a chance to tell him about my discovery before the Council meeting started. "How can you be sure the report was logged?"

"They are filed in numerical order, are they not?" said the senior guardian. He seemed to be very well informed about guard practices.

I nodded, unable to protect Hamilton from the bucket of shit he'd just thrown over himself. "The docket was torn out in haste. I found a small piece of the edge in the binder."

The public order guardian was shaking his head slowly. "I'll find out who took it, you can be sure of that. Probably the idiot who forgot to follow the report up."

Maybe. Or maybe there was someone in Hamilton's directorate who didn't want Roddie's complaint to be followed up. I wasn't sure how many other people in the Council chamber had the same thought.

We closed the nightclub and spent the rest of the evening looking for illicit drugs. We didn't find any. Davie and I were mobbed by a crowd of irate tourists when we left. They wanted naked flesh — not ours — but all I wanted was my bed. And I still hadn't turned forty. Pathetic.

Chapter Nine

———❦———

"Stop!"

"What the . . . ?" Davie stood on the brakes and pulled up in the middle of the deserted junction at Tollcross.

I put my shoulder to the door and leaped out on to the tarmac. I managed two paces, then fell flat on my face. My old friend the ice was back in force.

Davie pulled me to my feet. "What are you playing at, Quint?"

I started running again. "He was over there, in the shopfront."

"Who?"

I reached the butcher's. Even though it was chained up, the sour reek of meat well past its prime was still about the place. Nothing human though.

"The hooded man," I said. "I caught a glimpse as we went past." I ran out into the middle of the road and looked around in every direction. It was dead quiet, all the local citizens housebound by the curfew a couple of hours back. Nothing moved except the city flags under every streetlamp gently flapping in the chill breeze.

"Are you sure?" Davie joined me and peered about doubtfully. "I didn't see anyone."

I rubbed my eyes and tried unsuccessfully to swallow a yawn.

"I'm not sure of anything much at the moment, guardsman," I said eventually and headed back to the Land-Rover. The idea of the hooded man hanging around the vicinity of my flat again suddenly struck me as farcical. It was probably just my imagination messing me about. So I got Davie to drop me off and fell into a sleep so subterranean that not even the killer in my worst recurring nightmare could locate me.

And then, over the next couple of days, everything in the investigation went quiet. You get that sometimes – a burst of headless poultry activity at the beginning, followed by a becalmed state like the one the Ancient Mariner enjoyed so much. So what was going on? Had the killer found what he was looking for? Maybe the dead auxiliary had somehow got her hands on a new stimulant. Or maybe Roddie Aitken had pulled the wool over everyone's eyes and managed to smuggle it in. You sit around with ideas swooping through your mind like swallows catching flies on a warm summer evening when you haven't got anything else to go on. But unfortunately this was the freezing heart of winter and the leads we were chasing up didn't give us much to bite on. At one stage I tried to convince myself that the killer had found the drugs and departed to seek his fortune in a more liberal city like Glasgow. But I wasn't that gullible, not even for a fraction of a nanosecond.

The Council's policy towards tourists didn't help much. I wanted to check out any who were regulars at the Three Graces. It would have been easy enough to do as customers have to fill in a card giving their name and hotel, but the tourism guardian accused me of wanting to harass the city's customers. I assured the Council I would apply all my well-honed diplomatic skills, but they weren't having it. So instead I had to stick to what used to feature in twentieth-century police procedural novels, i.e. chasing up every boring detail. Meaning that Hamilton and I had undercover surveillance teams tailing as many of the two victims' friends and contacts as we could manage, including the sex centre supervisor and Patsy Cameron; that we searched all their cubicles or flats while they were absent; that Davie compiled a list of everyone who had access to the guard complaint register; that the bite mark and DNA data from the second victim were checked against dental and medical records (no joy); and that, in my spare time, I tried to work out what the point of the blues tapes was. It was all as about as useful as an enema during an epidemic of dysentery.

Then, on Sunday afternoon when I was walking across the ice rink that the castle esplanade had become and trying hard not to use my buttocks as skates, I got inspired. Sex reared its purple rosebud head and I immediately stuck my hand in my pocket – to pull out my mobile and tell Davie to meet me at the centre where Roddie and Moira had achieved congress. I'd just remembered that citizens can be allocated lockers if they want to keep personal equipment secure.

"What's up?" Davie said when I got there, his backside against the rust-shot maroon door of his vehicle. "Getting desperate?"

"Very funny, guardsman. You know former auxiliaries like me aren't allowed to defile ordinary citizens." That's why I have to spend every Thursday night with weird demoted women. One thing to be said for the investigation was that I had a reason for calling off my last session. The last thing I needed just now were distractions of a carnal nature. Well, almost the last thing.

It was a Sunday so there was a long queue outside the sex centre. As usual, citizens were grumbling about the fact that they had to meet here for sex rather than in their flats. The official line is that this way health standards are maintained, but everyone knows it's so that a firm grip is kept. It's not a joke though – any citizens caught having it off in unapproved premises get to acquire an intimate and long-term knowledge of potato picking and turnip tending on the city farms.

I pushed through to the front. Citizen Macmillan gave me a reluctant nod from her desk.

"Back again, citizen? Did you forget something?"

"Now you come to mention it . . ."

"Well, don't take all day. People behind you have got things to do."

I glanced round at the sullen faces in the reception area. They looked like children who've got to the front of the school dinner queue only to see that the last tray of chips has just run out.

"I won't keep you long," I said. "Roddie Aitken and Sheena Marinello. Did they have lockers?"

The receptionist's eyes flashed open at the mention of Roddie's name. "Where is Roddie? Why do you keep asking questions about him?"

I knew she didn't expect any answers. In some ways I would have liked to tell her what had happened to him — she was obviously quite friendly with him. But she was better off not knowing.

She shook her head slowly, her gaze lowered. "Roddie didn't. He wasn't one for sex aids or any of that kind of stuff." Then she looked up at me again and her lips pursed. "But she was. The cow always had a bag with her. She took a locker the day she registered."

What had been a dull murmur from the citizens behind me was beginning to get louder. I heard Davie clear his throat and everything went quiet again. It was one of those times when a guard uniform is a handy thing to have around.

"Were you wanting to have a look at her locker, citizen?"

The tone of citizen Macmillan's voice made me suspicious. "Don't tell me it's been cleared out."

She smiled triumphantly, pleased with herself for having got one over an authority figure, even one as marginal as me. "No, no, not yet. The supervisor told me to go through the locker file yesterday, but I haven't had the time yet."

"Or the inclination?" I said, returning the smile that had momentarily transformed her face. These days there are a lot of citizens who don't smile much. It wasn't always like that. For years after the Enlightenment, people were almost pathetically grateful that the Council had managed to restore order after the nationwide chaos the drugs gangs had caused. The fact that everyone had work and a place to live was a major improvement. But things have got a lot harder recently.

"Can I have the key?"

She handed it over and got back to checking in clients.

Davie and I beat a rapid retreat down the corridor.

"You don't want to mess around with citizens' sex lives," he said. "They were getting pretty restless back there."

"For a lot of them it's all they've got to look forward to every week," I said. "They don't have the privileges your rank enjoys."

"Oh, aye?" he said belligerently. "Privileges like patrolling the back streets of Leith in the middle of the night? Privileges like burying your tongue in the arse of every drunken tourist who asks for directions to the nearest brothel? Privileges like . . ."

I smiled at him. "Only joking, guardsman."

"Fuck you, Quint," he said, shaking his head in disgust.

"Here we are. Number 238." I put the key in the lock. "Any chance of a result in here?"

"I'm not betting on it, if that's what you mean," he replied testily.

"Cheer up, Davie. There might be a gold-plated clue lying waiting for us in this locker."

"Aye, and you might stop taking the piss out of the likes of me."

"I take it you're not optimistic then?" I said, pulling the door open.

At first glance it looked like he was right. The auxiliary hadn't left much behind. There was a bright orange dildo with a ridged top that could have done service as a witch's nose in the days when kids were allowed to dress up on Hallowe'en. And there were some pieces of good-quality black underwear, including a bra with holes for the nipples to poke through. I don't know why, but I found it comforting that Roddie at least had the chance to experience imaginative sex with a professional. Exactly what she was doing impersonating an ordinary citizen in order to screw a raw young guy like him I still found puzzling. I pulled out an object covered in light brown foil.

"What's that?" Davie asked.

"It's a malt whisky-flavoured condom, guardsman. Don't they have those in your barracks?"

"Not the rubber, jackass." He pointed past my leg at a small dusty blue object in the bottom left corner of the locker. "That."

"Bloody hell." I dropped to my knees and whipped my magnifying glass out. Then pulled a plastic bag over my left hand, picked the thing up between thumb and forefinger and reversed the bag. "Well spotted, Davie."

"So what is it?" he asked, peering as I held the bag up to the light. "A tablet?"

"Yup. We'll need to get it to the toxicology lab sharpish. Look at the colour. I've got a feeling it's what the killer was after."

"What do you mean look at the colour?"

"Wakey, wakey, Davie. Remember the music on the tapes? Remember what the dead auxiliary was saying on the phone?"

His eyes opened wide.

"Exactly. I reckon what we've got here is a prime example of the Electric Blues."

That was what I reckoned, but scientists don't deal in snap judgements. The chief toxicologist took my mobile number and sent me about my business without showing the slightest concern at my demand for a high-priority analysis. I considered pulling the senior guardian's chain since it was his directorate I was dealing with, but decided against it. He would probably just spin me a line about how the complexities of science aren't subject to being rushed.

So Davie and I went back to the castle and sat in the Land-Rover on the sunlit but still ice-coated esplanade. We went through the list of guard personnel who had access to the complaint file. There were twenty-three people on it, including the public order guardian and his deputy. I wondered about Machiavelli. He seemed to have taken Hamilton's warning to stay out of the case seriously. I hadn't seen him for a few days. Then I remembered where I'd last caught sight of the shifty bastard: departing rapidly from the dead auxiliary's barracks with a guardsman carrying a rucksack. What had he been doing there?

"I suppose you know Machiavelli?" I said to Davie.

He nodded. "Unfortunately."

"His reputation in the guard's that bad, is it?"

Davie shifted in the well-worn driver's seat. It wasn't the Land-Rover's luxury upholstery that was making him uncomfortable. He always gets fidgety when I start questioning him about his superiors. Auxiliary training and discipline are hard to get over. Except in my case, of course.

"Raeburn 03's ... well, he's the kind of guy who gets up people's noses. He's devious, always gives you the impression that he's working to his own agenda. Or at least some agenda that the rest of us don't know about."

Those were more or less my thoughts too, but I'd have used plainer language. As far as I was concerned, Machiavelli was a shite on legs.

"He's got friends in high places though," Davie added. "He always makes sure everyone knows how close he is to the guardians."

"Apart from Hamilton."

Davie laughed. "Aye. The guardian really hates the contents of his abdominal cavity."

"For someone who failed to make it through his first post-mortem, I'd recommend cutting down on the anatomical imagery."

"Very funny."

I looked at the list again, then out on to the glinting tarmac. "I can't see why the docket should have been torn out of the file deliberately, Davie. Maybe it's just a coincidence."

"Could be. It's not exactly unknown for bits of documentation to go missing."

I nodded and looked out towards the northern suburbs. In the distance behind the equestrian statue of Field Marshal Haig — someone who got away with murder on a grand scale — flashes of icy light sparked from the dreadnought grey surface of the Firth of Forth. Cold sea, cold sky, and, somewhere out there, the latest butcher of the city's young.

I shivered. "Time to check some more files. That should warm us up."

It didn't, but the chief toxicologist's phone call did. We ran out of the guard archive in the castle and burned over to the labs. They're in what used to be the university science area at King's Buildings. The site was secured with razor-wire as soon as the Enlightenment came to power because of the interest the drugs gangs had shown in the equipment and chemicals stored there. The Council has never bothered to take the wire down, even though it could make better use of it on the border these days.

"What is the provenance of this tablet, citizen?" the scientist asked after we'd cleared the security checks and got into his lab.

"You mean where did I get it, Lister 25?"

The chief toxicologist's thick lips gave a brief and surprisingly delicate twitch, like an actor greeting a colleague across a crowded room in the days before that profession became superfluous to modern society's needs. Lister 25 must have been very overweight in pre-Enlightenment days, but twenty years of auxiliary eating had left him with great folds of skin hanging from his face like an elephant on a controlled diet.

"Sorry, that's classified," I said, avoiding any excessive lip movements in case I encouraged him.

"I see." He turned to the lab table and picked up a test-tube with a pale-coloured sediment in the bottom. "It's just that this is very interesting, citizen. In fact, as far as I am aware, it's unique. In several ways."

That certainly was very interesting. "And what ways are those? I presume it matches the trace that was found in the dead auxiliary's stomach?"

"Indeed. But that trace was so minute that, though I say so myself, I did very well just to identify it. I won't bore you with the intricacies of its chemical structure, but this drug's chief claim to uniqueness is its strength. The dosage contained in a tablet this size would be enough to cause massive increases in mental alertness and sexual potency in an average-sized person."

It seemed a fair bet that was why they were called "Electric" Blues.

"How else are they unique?" Davie asked.

Lister 25 carefully lodged the test-tube in a rack and turned back to us, then gave another twitch of his lips. "The compound is also exceedingly dangerous for anyone with a weak heart. The effect of a dose this size taken more than once in such cases would be severe nausea, stiffening of the muscles, convulsions, coma, respiratory collapse and then death."

"Fucking hell," I said under my breath. "But the post-mortem on the dead auxiliary didn't report those effects."

"As I said, citizen, in her case the dose was minuscule. She was doubtless a healthy specimen and it appears that she put a tablet against her tongue for a few seconds." The scientist looked at me seriously. "You understand now why I asked you about the provenance. If there are quantities of this drug in the city, I can promise you that you will be picking up bodies on a regular basis. I am certain that no clinical trials have been carried out on this little beauty."

"Wonderful," I said, with a scowl. "I'll take your report to the Council this evening. What about manufacturing the drug? What kind of facilities would be needed?"

Lister 25's expression lightened. "That's the good news, if there's any to be found in this sorry tale. The compound is so complex that only a top-level chemist could produce it, and a well-equipped lab would be essential." He opened his arms and looked around the room we were standing in. "The labs in this building would fit the bill. Come to think of it, the six chemists on my staff would too. There aren't many other installations in the city that could do it." He raised his hand to pre-empt me. "And before you ask, citizen, neither I nor any of my people have had anything to do with these tablets. Whoever produced them should be put up against a wall."

He was bound to say his people were clean. And I wasn't capable of understanding their technical capabilities. I only did chemistry for a term at school before begging to be allowed to change to something that had more to do with my experience of the world. As far as I was concerned moles were small blind creatures that used to be turned into trousers, not something to do with chemical structure.

We left him to his test-tubes and bunsen burner. Before independence chemists would have worked for years to come up with a face cream to deal with those pachydermic wrinkles. Now they've got better things to do — or have they?

That evening's Council meeting was an uncivilised affair. I was the barbarian at the gates, of course. The boyscouts didn't take kindly to my demand for searches to be carried out on all regular customers of the Three Graces. Eventually they went along with it; that's the power the spectre of drugs-inspired chaos still has. They were even less impressed when I told them I'd already started checking airport records to see if any tourists with the symptoms described by the toxicologist had been flown out of the city over the last few days.

The toxicologist was also the cause of a set-to I had with the senior guardian. I asked him, in his capacity as science and energy supremo, if what the guy had told me about his team of chemists was true. Maybe I should have put it a bit more tactfully, but I've always thought that tact is for people who don't want anyone to know what they're really thinking. I positively enjoy sharing my thought processes with auxiliaries, especially guardians. Apparently the enjoyment isn't mutual.

The senior guardian immediately leaped on to a horse so high you could have got the entire Greek army besieging Troy into it. "Citizen Dalrymple," he said, his boyish face with its unlikely beard set hard, "I can give you my personal assurance that no laboratory in this city has been used to produce this drug."

I shrugged, trying not to look impressed but actually quite surprised. It's unusual to get a credible personal assurance out of a guardian – they aren't that different from twentieth-century politicians. He hadn't finished either.

"I can also assure you that no scientist in Edinburgh would have anything to do with an illicit substance such as this one." He looked at me like a heron that's just speared a fish and then decided it's not worth eating after all.

I left shortly afterwards, my tail more down than up. It's a bad idea to go into battle with the Council when you're short of ammunition. So far this investigation had come up with about as many bullets as a conscientious objector playing Russian roulette.

Outside it was another polar evening, the cold piling into my lungs faster than a crowd of tourists stampeding into the Tourism Directorate's whorehouses at opening time. Sunday night. I had to make the weekly visit to my old man. Even though I saw him at the reception not long back, he'd give me hell if I didn't turn up as usual. Davie was off trying to convince his regular skirt he still fancied her, not that he ever seemed to have much trouble pulling that off. So I called a guard vehicle and directed the driver to the retirement home in Trinity.

On the way down I found myself thinking again about the cassettes the killer had left in his victims. Had he used Clapton and Hendrix just because they were masters of the electric blues? And if it was some kind of message, who was it directed at?

Then I thought of the person who was my best friend when I first listened to those guitarists as a spot-ridden, music-crazed teenager; the guy who played drums in my first, ear-shattering band at university; the guy who used to run all the city's most profitable deals until I caught up with him. William Ewart Geddes. Billy. This smelled like the sort of dead smart, high-profit, totally immoral deal he'd have got himself into right up to his shifty grey eyes.

But then I shook my head and made myself come back to the real world. Billy was so crippled that he could hardly even move around in the wheelchair they strapped him into every day. There had been talk of him being allowed to continue making the deals the Council depended on when my mother was still senior guardian. But the iron boyscouts took one look at his record and packed him off to a home for the disabled. Not exactly the place to run a drug trafficking operation from. No, I was dreaming. I was also guilty as hell that I hadn't been to visit him for over a year.

In the end there's only so much you can do for your friends when they go bad. With relatives it's different. They can tear you to shreds every time you see them, they can turn out to be completely cynical in the pursuit of whatever they lust after – power in my mother's case. But when they go, they still leave you with a hole inside bigger than the one in the ozone layer our predecessors bequeathed us.

The Land-Rover pulled up outside the house in Trinity. I was a bit shaken. For a moment I almost thought I was getting sentimental.

Chapter Ten

The house was set back from the road, its front lit by the bright lamp above the door and the much dimmer ones in the old men's rooms. I looked up to the third floor. My father had the only room up there, just below the lookout tower that the early Victorian sea captain who built the mansion had insisted on. Hector had dug around in the archives — like son, like father — and discovered, to his great amusement, that the first owner had been drummed out of the Royal Navy for sodomy before he turned to trade. He was probably one of the few who got caught.

I knocked on the door and was admitted by the usual sour-faced nurse. I couldn't blame her for looking less than enchanted with life. Who would volunteer to be in charge of a bunch of semi-incontinent old curmudgeons who spent most of their time working out scams for getting their hands on the contents of the alcohol cabinet? Like the buggers in the navy when such an institution existed, retired citizens are entitled to a shot of booze every day — unless they misbehave, in which case it ends up in the nurse.

There wasn't much misbehaving going on tonight though. I walked across the hallway, breathing in the familiar reek of boiled fish and the wind it inspires, and popped my head into the common room. There was still an hour till bedtime and normally they were gathered around Scrabble boards or chess tables chuntering and rabbiting on like a convention of geriatric trainspotters. There were a few of them playing, but no one was saying much. I didn't have to ask why.

I wasn't too worried. The nurse would have told me if it was Hector who'd died. Then I remembered the note I'd received. Jesus, surely not. I took the stairs in threes and miraculously reached the top without hamstring damage.

"Who was it?" I said, stumbling into Hector's room. "Don't tell me it was . . ."

My father looked up from the array of books spread across his desk. "Ah, there you are, failure." He shook his head irritably. "I wish you'd learn to formulate comprehensible sentences."

"Not now, for God's sake. Who's died?"

That seemed to be comprehensible enough for him. He dropped his gaze. A shiver convulsed his long, thin body and suddenly he looked even older than he was. "Poor William. He should never have been in a second-floor room. He had trouble with his eyes . . . couldn't judge distances properly . . ." His voice trailed away.

I leaned over him and swung his chair round so he was facing me. "I need to know exactly what happened to him, Hector."

His eyes flashed as they met mine again. He was never down for long. "Why? He's not the first former guardian to go. You're not normally this interested."

I suppose that was a reference to my mother, but he was being a bit hypocritical. For years my parents regarded each other with maximum suspicion and he didn't exactly collapse with grief when she died. Then again, neither did I – it hit me later. But he had a point. I wasn't too sure myself why the former science and energy guardian's death had given me a frisson.

"How did it happen?" I asked quietly. Raising your voice with my father is always a waste of time. His time as a guardian and, before the Enlightenment, as professor of rhetoric at the university made him more or less invincible in verbal combat.

"He fell down the stairs this morning. Broke his neck, the silly old sod." The words were harsh, but the tone wasn't. I knew my father had been close to William.

"Did you see him?"

"I heard him, lad." He gave me a weak smile. "I was sitting here reading some Quintilian, curiously enough."

"What time was it?"

"Before seven. You know how early I wake. I heard his door open down below, then there was a sliding noise like he'd lost his footing. Then a series of bumps that I didn't fathom immediately, followed by a godawful bang." He looked up at me, his face white as he relived what had happened. "I got up from my chair and looked down the stairwell. I could see him, legs crumpled and his head at an impossible angle. He must have hit the floor head first. You know how hard it is in the hall."

I nodded. "Was anyone else about?"

"I started shouting. The woman dragged herself out of her pit and called an ambulance, but there was no point."

"Did William usually wake early too?"

Hector glared at me. "I didn't sleep with him, you know." He fumbled with his pen and eventually managed to screw the cap back on. Then he looked at me curiously. "No, as a matter of fact he didn't. When he arrived here after your mother cleared out the Council – apart from the stubborn buggers like Hamilton – I remember him telling me how much he was looking forward to staying in bed in the morning. Apparently he never liked getting up at the crack of dawn."

I had the strong feeling that something peculiar had taken place in the retirement home.

"Did you see anyone unusual around here this morning?"

Hector threw up his hands. "The place was full of stormtroopers. There was so much noise I couldn't concentrate on my reading."

"No, I mean before William fell. Any vehicles outside?"

"This room might be in the lookout tower but I'm not a bloody sentry, Quintilian." More glaring, then a reluctant sigh.

"I did glance out when I got up. There was nothing in the street." His eyes began to open wide and I backed off. "What are you suggesting, laddie?"

"Nothing. Nothing at all." I headed for the door. "I'll be back in a minute."

William McEwan's room was easy to spot. It was the one with the wide-open door and the stripped bed. The nurse hadn't wasted any time getting the place ready for its next occupant. I bent down and examined the carpet on the landing. It looked like a herd of waterbuffalo had been stampeding over it for centuries. The same could be said for the rug in the old man's room. I stood there for a few minutes and asked myself exactly what I was playing at. I'd heard the ex-guardian having a go at the chief boyscout, giving him grief about something called the Bone Yard. Then he'd sent me a note mentioning it again. Now he was dead. So what? I'd seen two people on the mortuary table who definitely hadn't died accidentally. And what was I thinking anyway? That the senior guardian had been so pissed off by the old man's harangue that he'd had him done away with. Even someone as cynical as I am about the effects of power on the individuals who exercise it would laugh at that idea. Then I saw the mark on the wooden floor beyond the rug.

I suppose it could have been made by William himself. Except that it was recent, and surrounded by several indentations that looked distinctly like those made by the nails on the soles of guard-issue boots. There's no way a retired guardian would have a pair of those; if he was lucky, he might have managed to keep a hold of his guardian-issue brogues like Hector had done. If Davie had been there, I would have bet him that someone had dug a heel in while dragging a reasonably heavy weight off the bed. The odds would have been pretty short as well.

I went back up to my father's room and tried to look nonchalant. I've never been much good at that. He knew I was on edge and conversation became sketchy.

I got up to leave before the nurse came round to turn the light out at ten. "When's the funeral?"

"Tomorrow morning, nine o'clock. Full Council attendance." Hector gave me a dubious look. "Are you planning on coming?"

I nodded slowly, suddenly wondering why William's death hadn't been mentioned at this evening's Council meeting. Surely they weren't trying to keep me away? That idea got up my nose in a big way. "I'll be there all right."

I said goodnight and went back to the Land-Rover. I'd already decided I wasn't going to wait till morning to visit the crematorium.

If the driver thought it was weird to be directed there, he didn't show it. His rank is taught to treat surprise as if it's the bad boy at the back of the class — ignore it and it'll eventually give up and find someone else to annoy. Oddly enough, I used to have problems with that tactic when I was an auxiliary. Probably something to do with my highly strung temperament.

Which was actually about as taut as a Hendrix e-string as we drove through the darkened streets to the northern of the city's two crematoria. It wasn't only that I was going way beyond my authority. That was limited to investigating the murders but anything's fair game in a murder case as far as I'm concerned. No, it had just struck me that I hadn't been back there since my mother's funeral. It was suddenly very clear to me that I didn't want to go anywhere near that soulless brick and concrete dump. So why didn't I just redirect the driver and forget about William McEwan? I'd have been hard pressed to answer that question. Suspicion? Hunch? Curiosity about this Bone Yard that seemed to be eating away at him like a liver fluke? I wasn't sure, but there was no one in the Land-Rover actually expecting answers to those questions so I let them ride.

The steel gate at the entrance to the crematorium driveway was chained up. I got out and pressed the intercom button. Even through the crackle I made out the voice that responded. I'd been hoping the city's chief ghoul might have taken the night off. Or gone back to the underworld. He didn't exactly sound overjoyed to hear my voice either.

In a minute he appeared on the other side of the gate.

"Citizen Dalrymple," he said drily, the stiff parchment skin on his face even yellower than usual in the artificial light. "You're almost becoming a regular."

"I'm pleased to see you too, Haigh. Hurry up. Unlike you, I'm not a creature of the night."

He finally got the chain open and let me in. I signalled to the driver to wait where he was. The less he knew of what I was about to do, the better for his future career.

"I imagine you have an authorisation, citizen," Haigh said. He put out his hand for it like a vulture flexing its claw as we walked into the dingy low building. The guardians have a very pragmatic attitude towards death. All that matters to them is disposing of the body efficiently, so what funds they've spent on the crematorium have been to maintain the furnace, not to tart the buildings up. It's never occurred to them that the bereaved might like to see off their relatives and friends in slightly more salubrious surroundings. No doubt that was why they kept Haigh on as facility supervisor too. His bony bald head and elongated limbs made even atheists cross themselves.

"Now, let me see, when was the last time we met?" the old bastard asked, handing back my authorisation.

"You know very well it was at my mother's funeral, Haigh," I answered, giving him the eye. "Shall we get on?"

He smiled, lips drawn back over seriously far gone teeth. "I also know that any personnel arriving at this facility during the hours of curfew have to be checked with guard headquarters. I'll just go and make the call."

I grabbed his fleshless arm before he could move off. "I don't think so, citizen. What I'm going to do now will be our little secret."

His jaw dropped. "What do you mean, citizen?" he asked suspiciously.

I gave him a smile to encourage him. All that did was make him look like a vampire who's just noticed the garlic festooned about the chosen virgin's negligée.

"William McEwan. You have him here?"

Now the virgin had whipped her cross out. "The former guardian?" he said haltingly. "Yes, he's here. Why do you ask?"

"I want to have a look at his papers."

The old bureaucrat's expression brightened. "Only his papers?"

"Before I take a look at the body."

He was back to being the panic-stricken vampire, this time with the first rays of dawn appearing over the eastern Transylvanian uplands. "You ... you can't do that. It's against regulations. I'll have to call ..."

"You'll have to calm down, citizen," I said, leading him briskly into his office. Then I gave him the eye again. "You'll also have to comply with everything I request." I glanced around his impeccably neat room with its cabinets full of perfectly organised files. "Otherwise an unexpected wave of chaos might suddenly burst over your records."

As I thought, the threat of messing with his files did the trick — anally retentive bureaucrats are easy to intimidate. He unlocked the drawer of his desk and took out a maroon file. Deceased ordinary citizens and auxiliaries get grey, but guardians are honoured with maroon. So much for death the great equaliser.

I flicked through the pages. I was after the post-mortem report, but all I got was a big zero from the Medical Directorate.

"How come there was no post-mortem, Haigh? It wasn't exactly death by natural causes, was it?"

The crematorium supervisor looked away shiftily. "Yes, I did notice that. I rang the Medical Directorate and was told that a post-mortem was not required. They didn't give me a reason."

"And you were happy with that?"

Haigh gave the smirk of the bureaucrat who has covered his arse with fifteen-inch armour plating. "If that's what the Medical Directorate decides, it's good enough for me. I logged the call, of course."

"Of course you did." I handed the file back. "Got your screwdriver ready?"

His face slackened again. "Isn't this enough for you? What more do you need to know?"

I went over to the nearest cabinet and grabbed a handful of folders.

"No, put those back. I . . . oh, very well." Haigh put the file away, took out his screwdriver and locked the drawer again. He was nothing if not careful. I wondered how many other people he expected to be interested in the recently deceased former guardian.

The hall and corridors of the crematorium were bloody freezing. I followed the supervisor down to the room where coffins were stored for the brief period allowed by health regulations before their contents go up in smoke (the coffins themselves are reused, of course). The place had hardly any lights and I suddenly had the nasty feeling I was being led into a fairy-tale fiend's lair. As if to reinforce that, Haigh looked over his hunched shoulder and gave me a grin Beelzebub would have been proud of. For all his protestations, I was sure this was the part of his work he liked best – messing about with the bodies.

"Here we are, citizen," he said, turning into a windowless room and putting on the light. There were three coffins on stands, all of them showing signs of wear and tear. The one Haigh headed for was in the best condition of the three.

"Screwdriver," I said, holding out my hand.

He handed it over reluctantly.

"Now, off you go back to your files," I said. I was pleased to see he could barely contain his disappointment. He wasn't giving up though.

"Regulations clearly state that a member of crematorium staff must always be present when coffins are opened, citizen Dalrymple."

"Are you attached to this screwdriver?" I asked.

He didn't get my drift.

"Would you like to be even more attached to it?" I brandished it at him like they taught us in the auxiliary training programme. The door closed behind him rapidly and I set to work.

Actually, I could have done with his help to lift the lid off when I'd undone all the screws, but I didn't want him to see what I was looking for. That was the problem. I didn't know what I was looking for myself. I took a deep breath and manhandled the lid off. And looked upon the face of William McEwan.

But it wasn't much like Schliemann looking upon Agamemnon's features. No gold mask, not even much attempt to arrange the face in a condition of repose. The poor old guy's eyes were wide open, his lips and teeth parted, giving him the expression of someone who's just woken up from a disturbing dream. But there would be no more lie-ins followed by leisurely breakfasts for this sleeper – only the ultimate substantial slumber.

I loosened the maroon and black striped Council tie and the white shirt under the tweed jacket that they'd dressed him in. His neck had that clammy chill feeling we all acquire eventually. I felt for the fracture, lifting him up. The head lolled loosely to the side. His neck was broken all right, and there was no obvious bruising to suggest that hands had been laid on him. And there was a large contusion on his forehead consistent with a fall. So far everything was in order. What had I thought I would find? A label saying "Assassination carried out by Council order"?

I shook my head and stepped back from the open coffin. I had a decision to make. It didn't take long. There was no point in getting this far if I wasn't going to go through with it.

I stepped forward again and started to undo the buttons of his shirt. I didn't want to, but I was going to have to examine the whole body for marks showing if William had been manhandled to the top of the stairs. This was what should have been done in the post-mortem that someone had decided wouldn't take place.

I was unzipping the former guardian's trousers when Haigh tried to come in. I shouted at him so loud that I was lucky William McEwan didn't come round and ask me what I thought I was doing. I asked myself the same question after I'd struggled to get his trousers off and found nothing; the fact that the laces on his scuffed old brogues were double knotted didn't help. Then my eyes fell on the shoes. They were lying on their sides on the floor where I'd dropped them. Why the hell would anyone tie double knots on a dead man's shoes?

I went to the bottom of the coffin. Even before I pulled his socks off, I could see William McEwan's feet were badly swollen. The black bruising all over the top of both feet showed that he didn't just have bad circulation. Some piece of shit had trampled all over the old man's feet, which probably had nothing more than bedsocks on them at that time of the morning. No doubt it was the bastard who'd left the marks of his boots on the bedroom floor. There was no way William had fallen down the stairs accidentally. Christ, with these bruises he'd hardly even have been able to walk two paces.

I backed away again and squatted down on the concrete floor. This time the decision I had to make took a lot longer.

After I put the clothes back on William's wasted limbs and tried unsuccessfully to close his eyes, I was nearly consumed by rage. Haigh saw how I looked as I stormed down the corridor and veered out of my way. I tossed over his screwdriver without making any effort to miss him and told him to put the lid back on the coffin himself. At that moment I was dead set on driving straight to Moray Place and asking the senior guardian what the fuck was going on. Then I got outside and the Arctic air brought me to my senses. Suddenly suicide didn't seem like such an attractive option.

Back in my flat I gulped whisky and tried to work out a plan of action. Whoever killed the ex-guardian had friends in high places, as the lack of post-mortem showed. On the other hand, I had very few friends on the Council. Hamilton might class himself as one if he was feeling charitable, but his own position in the Council was isolated. No, the only sensible way was to keep what I knew to myself and nail whoever was responsible when I had the whole story.

So I put on my black suit and turned up uninvited to William's service. Hector beckoned to me to sit beside him but I preferred to stand at the side where I had a good view of all the guardians and senior auxiliaries on parade. I saw Haigh lurking in the background and wondered if he'd told anyone about my visit. If he had, no one seemed to be too bothered. Judging by the lack of eye contact I was receiving, I might as well have stayed at home. The medical guardian was the only one who even batted an eyelid in acknowledgement of my presence, but I wasn't getting my hopes up — she looked as beautiful and as glacial as ever. Machiavelli was standing next to Hamilton with his nose in the air and his head angled away from the guardian in another tell-tale piece of body language.

What I was hoping might be interesting was the senior guardian's address. I reckoned I'd be able to spot if he was harbouring any guilty feelings about the old man's death, but I'd forgotten what a skilful performer the chief boyscout had become during his time at the top. He ran through William's achievements at the Science and Energy Directorate, expressed the city and the Council's gratitude and held his head high as the coffin disappeared into the floor. A statue would have given more away.

Outside, no one was inclined to hang about. The temperature was doing its usual impression of Tromsø on a bad day and there was no wake afterwards; since the guardians don't permit themselves alcohol, there wouldn't have been much point. I had a few words with Hector then led him towards a guard vehicle.

"Aren't there better ways for you to spend your time, citizen?"

I turned to face the senior guardian. I'd been wondering if he'd have the nerve to approach me.

"It's important to mark the passing of the old guard," I said with a thin smile. "Even if the passing is a bit premature."

I was hoping to catch even a hint of regret but there was nothing.

"Citizen, it's someone who hasn't passed away yet who you should be after – the murderer. Kindly get back to work." He strode off without a glance at my father.

"What did he mean?" Hector asked. "Are you working for the Council again?"

I nodded slowly.

Over the crematorium a cloud of smoke rose from the chimney. It was the last breath of William McEwan, floating away into the chill blue sky above the "perfect" city he'd served.

Chapter Eleven

I was running down an ice-rimmed street under a bright moon, my legs flailing, trying to catch up with a figure in a long, hooded coat. Then the figure stopped and turned to face me. I slowed to walking pace, my breath rasping in my throat and a stitch fastening my liver to my lowest rib tighter than an industrial sewing machine could. As the figure's face came into view I felt myself falling into an abyss. It was Roddie Aitken, lips bared and blood trailing down his chin. Then everything went black, darker than the universe before the big bang went off, darker than the soul of the killer I was trying to find. But I could hear voices. Not Roddie's, not any man's. They were women's voices, the voices of the women I'd lost. My mother, Caro, Katharine Kirkwood. They seemed to be getting closer, asking questions plaintively, accusing me of failing them. But I'd also lost the power of speech. Like Roddie, like William McEwan.

I woke up in a sweat-soaked bed reeking of nettles and seaweed. It took me a couple of minutes to work out that the smell came from the cup of barracks tea on my bedside table.

"Nice dream?" Davie asked as I staggered through into the main room of my flat. "You looked like you were well into an imaginary sex session."

"Sod off, guardsman. It was a nightmare actually."

Davie grinned. "That's the problem with random selection of partners."

I shook my head. "No, it was a real nightmare. Christ, this bastard case. We're going nowhere with it. Just waiting for the butcher to kill again."

"You read my mind," Davie said. "When you'd woken up properly I was going to tell you that none of the tails we've got on the two victims' friends and contacts has come up with anything significant." He tossed over a sheaf of papers. "Their reports up to yesterday evening."

At least the City Guard's bureaucracy was still doing its job, though personally I'd have given the undercover people an extra hour's relaxation rather than make them write up the day's events before they sign off.

"No more pills found anywhere either," Davie added, flipping the pages of his notebook then closing it. "So what are we doing today?"

I knew what I was going to do, but it was something that I didn't want to risk involving him in. "Can you keep an eye on all the leads we're following, Davie? I want you to keep Hamilton off my back as well. I'm switching my mobile off today."

"Oh, aye?" he said, raising an eyebrow. "And where exactly are you headed, Quint?"

"You don't want to know, guardsman. You do not want to know."

I reckoned I had about an hour at the most. I still had an "ask no questions", one of the cards issued by the Public Order Directorate to undercover operatives, from the murder investigation in 2020. It would get me into the Science and Energy Directorate archive all right, and my disguise would buy me some time from the senior guardian. If he was advised that someone answering my description was in his directorate files, he'd be down faster than the Archangel Gabriel when Lucifer got uppity.

And so it came to pass. I used the blue overalls I had when I was in the Parks Department a few years back, supplementing them with a bag of tools to make me look like a plumber. Pipes are always blocking up or cracking in the Council's Edinburgh and plumbers bring out the best in even the most granite-jawed sentry. I was also wearing a bright blond wig I'd picked up in one of the ragshops that ordinary citizens rely on when their clothing vouchers run out.

I strode purposefully up the steps to what used to be the Royal College of Surgeons in Nicolson Street. Trust the Enlightenment to choose a Playfair neo-classical temple for the city's science and energy base. The original Council members had little time for science. It had been misused so much in the late twentieth century, what with cloning (until the American religious right put a stop to that), the development of new, even more addictive consumer drugs and the nuclear industry's increasingly unchecked expansion. Such scientific experiments as were allowed took place in the King's Buildings where the toxicologist worked and at a few other locations, but the headquarters were symbolically situated in a building Plato would have approved of.

I got into the archive room and diagnosed a supposedly explosive leak. That scared all the file shufflers off. Then I locked myself in and headed for the records covering the years when William McEwan was guardian. In the limited time I had I was unlikely to find some as yet unidentified needle in this particular stack of bureaucratic hay, but I owed it to the old man to have a try. If he'd been keeping any documents to show me at the retirement home, they were long gone by the time I searched his room. I took a deep breath and started pulling open cabinets and maroon-coloured "guardians' eyes only" files.

As it turned out, I got even less than the hour I'd estimated. By the time the banging started on the steel-plated security door, I'd found nothing. But as nothings go, it was a very interesting one. What I wanted to know was, why was there a full set of top-security files covering one particular hot subject except for four months of William McEwan's period of tenure? That particular subject was what used to be the city's main source of electricity until the Council shut it down – the advanced gas-cooled reactor power station at Torness.

Whoever was laying into the door was doing a fair imitation of a blues drummer who's taken too many pills from the bag marked Speed Kills.

"Who is it?" I shouted, trying to stall them.

"Davie."

I was impressed. "How did you find me?"

"Are you going to let me in, Quint?"

I finished putting the files back and opened the door.

"There's been a sighting of the bastard in the hood," he said hoarsely. "A sentry's been attacked – knocked senseless. He's regaining consciousness now."

"The attacker got away?"

"What do you think?"

We came out into the watery sunlight. Clouds had been gathering while I was inside and it didn't feel as cold as it had. No doubt the weather was laying another ambush.

"Where are we headed?"

Davie started the Land-Rover's engine. "Raeburn Barracks. Apparently the sentry was patrolling the waste land where that school used to be when he saw a guy in a long coat in the bushes. I don't know any more."

"I know the feeling," I muttered as we roared down the South Bridge. "So how did you find me?"

"I was in the ops room when the sentry here reported a plumber with an outrageous wig," he said, turning to grin at me. "Who else could it have been?"

I looked away, pissed off that he'd clocked my disguise from a mile off. On the bridge a small boy in the maroon sweater all the city's schoolchildren wear flicked us a well-practised V-sign as we passed. I liked his spirit but I didn't give much for his chances if he tried that with the auxiliaries in his school. The Council is keen on the three Rs, but it's an even bigger fan of the three Ds: Discipline, Direction and Drill. I should know. My mother was the first education guardian.

Raeburn 497 was six feet two and about fifteen stone. That's how he survived. As it was, he was definitely a candidate for the small number of plastic surgery operations the Medical Directorate carries out each year – the Council has been having a big downer on non-essential use of resources.

"Shouldn't he be in the infirmary?" I asked the barracks commander.

"My medical officer's had a good look at him. She says his skull's undamaged."

Which was more than I could say for the young auxiliary's face. It looked like someone had been tapdancing on it with steel-toed boots.

"Can you describe the man who laid into you?" I asked, bending over the swollen purple features.

A brief shake of the head. "Not really."

I had to lean closer to make out the words. He'd lost most of his front teeth.

"The collar of his coat was pulled up and the hood was hanging down low."

Sounded like our man all right.

"What colour was the coat?"

"Dark brown. It was long, almost down to his boots."

"What colour were they?"

"Black. High, up to his knee. Badly scuffed." He shook his head a couple of times. "Not like any I've ever seen before." He tried to laugh and only succeeded in coughing up blood. "Except in the Westerns they show in the Historical Film Society."

Cowboy boots? I hadn't seen a pair of those since the ones I saved up for when I was sixteen fell to bits years later. Another pointer to someone from outside the city. No doubt you can buy all sorts of exotic footwear in democratic Glasgow – if you can fight your way to the shop. It didn't look like our man would have any problem doing that. But something was bothering me. I didn't have any recollection of the hooded figure I'd chased from my flat wearing that kind of footwear. I was pretty sure I'd seen an ordinary pair of work boots.

The sentry's breathing was heavy and he was obviously in a lot of pain. I turned to his commander, a barrel-chested specimen in the standard iron boyscout mode. Before I could ask exactly where the sighting had occurred, the door to the barracks sick bay opened and Machiavelli walked in. His face immediately turned greyer than the contents of the pies ordinary citizens have to put up with. I couldn't tell whether that was because of the guardsman's injuries or my presence.

"What happened here?" he asked, his eyes opening even wider as he approached the bed. "It's Raeburn 497, isn't it? He's inter-barracks unarmed combat champion."

I left the commander to fill him in. So our killer had taken out the city's best fighter. That made my day.

"Where were you when you saw him?" I asked the sentry.

He suddenly looked a lot worse, his head lolling over in my direction. "Fettes . . . near the foundations of Carrington House. He was in the bushes by the gates . . . here, I've lost my knife . . ."

He passed out. Just as well. His commander would drag him over the coals in the barracks boiler room for mislaying his auxiliary-issue weapon. I was overjoyed to learn that the murderer's collection of sharp blades had grown by one.

"Commander," I said, interrupting the conversation he was having with Hamilton's deputy, "This man's in a very bad way. For Christ's sake get him to the infirmary."

For a sworn atheist, Raeburn 01 showed surprising alacrity in complying. Maybe he was just programmed to obey anything in the imperative mood.

*　　*　　*

Davie and I drove up to the place where the guardsman had been attacked. It was only about a hundred yards from Raeburn Barracks, which shows you the nerve of the guy. But what the hell was he doing here?

Before the Enlightenment what's now a lattice of foundation stones with untended grass growing over them had been one of Scotland's most expensive public schools. Which is one reason why the drugs gangs, who started out in the urban nightmare of Pilton up the road, decided to blow the place up. A lot of the stone had been carted off and used in other less exclusive building projects – though since most of them were tourist facilities, that isn't exactly accurate. Down by the remains of one of the boarding houses, the city's number one headbanger had been given a lesson in unarmed combat by the city's number one murderer.

We hunted around the area that was cordoned off by City Guard tape. Apart from a few scuffmarks on the bone-hard ground, there was nothing to see. I don't know what I expected. The killer had been careful enough so far not to leave anything he didn't want us to have. After a while I squatted down by the unkempt bushes and looked up through the trees at the dull red ball of the sun to the west.

"You know what I think?" Davie said.

"Surprise me, guardsman."

"He was waiting for someone."

"In the bushes, within spitting distance of a barracks? Doesn't seem too likely. What citizen would willingly come here? It'd be a real risk." Then I raised my eyes to his. "You're not suggesting he was meeting an auxiliary, are you?"

Davie was suddenly looking uncomfortable. "Well, it's a possibility, isn't it?"

I thought of how Machiavelli looked in the sick bay. Something had washed all the colour from his face and I didn't think it was just the smell of antiseptic. But that was hardly conclusive. After all, Raeburn was his barracks. He had every right to be there even though his current billet was in the castle.

I stood up and shook the stiffness from my legs. "I wonder. Maybe the hooded man didn't have a meet arranged." I turned to Davie. "Maybe he was doing the same thing as we are."

"What do you mean?"

"Maybe he was looking for someone."

"An auxiliary?"

"It wouldn't be the first one he's targeted."

"Great. That means we've got the five hundred members of this barracks to check out."

"Forget it, my friend. The Council would never allow it. Anyway, what would we be looking for? All Raeburn personnel with guilty looks on their faces?"

I headed back to the Land-Rover. As we were driving away, I remembered the last time I'd been in the public school's grounds. It was when I was investigating the murders two years ago. An ex-drug gang member called Leadbelly who was one of the few remaining prisoners in the city's prison had been clearing stones from the site. He gave me some information that turned out to be useful and I gave him some blues tapes in return. As we turned south and the long line of spires and gables leading along the Royal Mile to the castle swung into view, I wondered what had happened to my informant. Then my mobile rang and the thought exited my mind as quickly as a warm spell on an Edinburgh spring day.

"What exactly were you doing in the Science and Energy Directorate, citizen?" The senior guardian's voice didn't suggest that he was making anything other than a mundane enquiry, but I sensed he was a lot more interested than that.

"Checking on labs with personnel who could have produced the Electric Blues," I lied.

"In disguise?" There was a silence that the chief boyscout presumably thought was meaningful. "You are wasting your time, citizen Dalrymple. No auxiliary would have anything to do with the manufacture of such drugs without a specific order from my directorate. No such order has been given."

I was sure that if it had been given, there wouldn't be any reference to it in the archive. I considered passing that thought on to him but decided I was enjoying my freedom too much.

"Are you still there, citizen?" The senior guardian almost sounded impatient, an unusually human characteristic for him.

"I am."

"What are you doing?"

I've never been able to handle close supervision. "Sorry, guardian, you're breaking up. I'll see you at the Council meeting. Out."

Davie glanced across at me. "Are you messing the senior guardian about, Quint?"

"Why? Are you going to do me for insubordination, guardsman?"

He shook his head, but the expression on his face was grim. "He might look like a saint in a Renaissance painting, but he used to have a reputation in his barracks for breaking people he didn't like." He slowed at the checkpoint on Raeburn Place and raised his hand to acknowledge the guardswoman on duty. She gave him a smile that would get her a job in the Prostitution Services Department any day.

"Friend of yours?" I asked.

"Auxiliaries don't have friends," he replied with a grin.

"Sorry. Close colleague?" I said, using the official term.

"Close enough a few years back."

"You seem to have been close enough to every female auxiliary under thirty-five in the city, Davie."

"Jealousy's a fearful thing, citizen." The smile died on his lips. "Listen, I meant what I was saying about the senior guardian. Are you going into battle with him?"

I looked out at the citizens trudging up the hill towards the centre for the evening shift in the city's hotels and restaurants, casinos and strip joints. Their backs were bent, their faces drawn in the cold. Was this really the best the Council could offer them after nearly twenty years? The Enlightenment's ideals of education, work and housing for all were still intact, but only just. I didn't have much faith in the iron boyscouts and I wasn't the only one. The question was, could anyone else do any better?

"Well, are you?"

Davie's voice roused me from my thoughts. "Am I what?"

"Are you going into battle with the senior guardian?"

I looked ahead into the grey, lowering sky. "I don't know, Davie. I'm beginning to get the feeling that he's declared open season on me."

A snowflake hit the windscreen and stayed there on its own for a few seconds. Another joined it. Then they got our range and a flurry of the white stuff carpeted the glass. The frayed wipers immediately had trouble clearing it. The Land-Rover slowed as Davie took his foot off the accelerator and peered out through the glass.

"Shit," he said. "This is going to cause chaos. You know what the city's like when it snows."

Buses with worn, remoulded tyres slewing across the roads, citizens late for work, tourists complaining — it's the same every winter. But I had a nasty feeling that the murderer wasn't the kind of guy to be deflected from his plans by a change in the weather. Of course, it would have helped if I had the faintest idea of what those plans were.

The snow kept pelting down, some flakes even managing to slip through the holes in the Land-Rover's bodywork. I felt them on my hands for a moment before they melted away, leaving as little behind as the hooded man who was haunting the city. And me.

The Council meeting was a lot of fun. Hamilton told them how none of his operatives had turned up anything and I told them about the attack on the guardsman at Fettes. There was a brief burst of outrage at this second assault on one of the city's servants, but as it wasn't in the same league as the murder of the female auxiliary, they soon shut up.

"Citizen Dalrymple." The senior guardian paused for effect after addressing me. His lips twitched in a brief and unconvincing smile. "I have the strong impression that you are merely waiting for events to occur in this investigation. Surely there is more that you can do to pre-empt the murderer." The tone of his voice was suddenly sharp and I remembered what Davie said about the chief boyscout's reputation. He was trying to muscle in on my territory. Normally I give anyone who tries that the verbal equivalent of a knee in the bollocks, but that would just have ended up with me being booted off the case. No, I had to keep the senior guardian sweet: that was the only way I'd be able to find out if he or any of his colleagues had anything to do with the production of the Electric Blues.

So I grovelled like a trainee auxiliary who's failed all his assessments and has to beg for one last chance before being reassigned to ordinary citizen's duties like cleaning the bogs in the city's nightclubs.

"I'm sorry my investigation hasn't uncovered anything significant yet, guardian. I'd appreciate any help you can give." Out of the corner of my eye I caught a glimpse of Hamilton's face. He looked like he'd just seen a tourist voluntarily donate all his winnings from the racetrack in Princes Street Gardens to the Council's urban renewal fund.

As I suspected, the senior guardian didn't have any specific advice to offer. He'd just been laying down the law. It's interesting how many guardians in this supposedly equitable city get a kick out of doing that.

"I won't tell you again, citizen," he said, fixing me with a steely glare. "Concentrate on finding the killer and leave the Science and Energy Directorate to me."

As far as I was concerned, that was as good as him hiring a mason to engrave in stone the words: "I have a secret that I'm not at all keen on you finding out about."

*   *   *

Hamilton caught up with me on the stairs outside the Council chamber. "What on earth was going on in there, Dalrymple? I know the investigation's ground to a halt, but there was no need to make us look quite so cack-handed."

I wasn't really listening to him. What was much more intriguing was the sight of his deputy Machiavelli racing up the stairs towards the senior guardian. His face was still greyer than a corpse's. I turned and watched as the pair moved out of the throng of guardians to a secluded corner. Then Machiavelli started waving his arms about like a windmill in a hurricane.

I'd have given a lot to hear that conversation.

Back in my flat I sank into the faded, lumpy cushions of my citizen-issue sofa, took a pull of what remained in the whisky bottle and considered my options. When I was in the directorate, people used to accuse me of excessive cynicism. This manifested itself in a distrust of authority – meaning Lewis Hamilton – and a predilection for conspiracy theories. Nothing had changed. In this particular investigation I definitely distrusted the city's top dog and I was bloody sure there was a conspiracy around the Electric Blues. Whether the two were connected was anybody's guess. Then I remembered Roddie Aitken sitting on this very sofa and telling his story. I remembered the way he'd laughed off the hooded man as if he were a harmless crazy guy and went off into the dark to bring in the New Year. It looked more and more like he'd been set up. I hadn't forgotten the oath I swore. I was going to find the bastard who cut him open. I was also going to find the bastards who put the killer on to him. No matter who they were.

This time I was sprinting up a hillside in the moonlight after a shadowy figure, my breath rasping in my throat and my legs brushing through bracken. For all my efforts, I couldn't gain on the figure. I caught a glimpse of a long coat as it breasted the summit. Then I slipped on the wet vegetation and went my length, knocking the breath out of my lungs. That woke me up with a jerk.

There was a faint light in my bedroom. As my senses cleared from the dream, that began to puzzle me. I'd made sure the candles were extinguished before I crashed out at midnight. I sat up in bed and looked towards the door. The light was coming in through a slight gap between the door and the jamb. My heart skipped a few beats. The seal on the bedroom door is good and I always pull it to. It never opens itself during the night. I put my breathing on hold and listened carefully. Nothing, not a sound. But what was the source of the light? It couldn't be Davie. His arrivals were about as subtle as a herd of rhinos. An icy thought stabbed into my mind. The hooded man. He'd been in the vicinity at least twice. I felt my hands tremble then the rest of my body followed suit. The auxiliary knife that I should have handed in when I was demoted was in my bookcase, behind my copy of the collected works of Sir Arthur Conan Doyle. All I had in the bedroom were my clothes. I forced myself to take a series of deep breaths. As I completed the fifth, I heard the unmistakable sound of the strut creak in the middle of my sofa. Jesus, there was definitely somebody there. I felt around under my bed for my boot, the only offensive weapon I could think of, gripped it hard and tensed every muscle in my body. Then powered myself out of bed and through the door.

Although the light from the single candle on the coffee table wasn't bright, it was enough for me to make out a single figure sitting on the sofa. The figure was wearing a long, dark-coloured coat.

Chapter Twelve

A moment of gut-freezing shock as what the killer had done to the groins of his two victims flashed in front of me, then I was put out of my misery. The figure raised its head and the light cast by the candle fell on the face.

"Hello, Quint. Still in love with your bed, I see."

I tried to step forward then decided against it. My knees were suddenly weaker than those of a 1990s prime minister confronted by a backbench revolt. A series of shivers ran up my spine. I tried to make out the features, which were ringed by crewcut brown hair, but there was no need. I knew this person from the languid, hoarse voice.

"Katharine?" I managed to get the name out, but inducing an auxiliary to tell a joke about Plato would have been easier. "Is it you, Katharine?"

She stood up and let the coat drop from her shoulders. "At least you remember my name. Should I be pleased?"

It came to my attention that I was standing in an unheated room wearing nothing more than a pair of grubby citizen-issue underpants and brandishing a well-worn size eight boot. For some reason this irritated me.

"What the bloody hell are you doing sneaking around other people's flats in the middle of the fucking night?" I threw the boot to the floor, narrowly missing my bare and very cold feet.

"You'd better put some clothes on, dear. You'll catch your death." A smile flickered across Katharine's lips, making her face look less gaunt. The shortness of her hair had the effect of increasing the size of her green eyes. I felt them on me.

"Make yourself even more at home than you have already," I said, turning tail and heading back to the bedroom. "Nothing much has changed since you were last here."

I sat down on the bed and tried to get a grip. Katharine Kirkwood. I never expected to see her again. After the murder investigation a couple of years back, she jumped the border fence. Edinburgh hadn't been too kind to Katharine in the past so what was she doing back here? Surely she wasn't risking arrest for her unauthorised departure from the city just to say hello.

I fumbled with my flies and pulled on a heavy sweater. It's against regulations to burn coal after curfew and I didn't fancy risking another run-in with the senior guardian – he was energy supremo, after all.

Katharine had pulled her coat round herself. It was brown and had a high collar, as well as a hood. I sat on the sofa, forcing her to move over. As she did that, I noticed her footwear – worn work boots rather than the cowboy variety.

She turned to look at me, her face eventually loosening to a faint smile.

"You look all right, Quint," she said.

"Oh, thanks. What were you expecting after two years? All my teeth to have fallen out and my hair to be whiter than the stuff that's clogging up the streets?"

"Why are you angry with me?" she said, her eyes flashing. "I've taken a lot of chances to get to you."

I nodded. "Yes, you have, haven't you? I was impressed by that leap you made into the storeyard. Course, you've always been good at jumping."

"Haven't I just? Was that Davie with you in the Land-Rover?"

I ran my eyes over her. She was thinner but fitter-looking than before. Like all of us, she could have done with more to eat. Still, whatever she was involved in wasn't doing her too much harm.

"Didn't you want to hang around so you could lay into him like you used to?" I asked. Davie and Katharine had never got beyond the stage of intense mutual suspicion.

"I wasn't sure it was him. Then that other Land-Rover arrived. I don't want the guard to know I'm back."

"What about at Tollcross the other night? Was that you too?"

She looked at me uncomprehendingly and shook her head. So that had either been the killer or my imagination playing tricks.

I picked up the whisky bottle and held it up to the light. Enough for a slug each. I offered her it.

"No, thanks. Try this." She handed me a half-litre of Russian vodka.

"Jesus, where did you get real vodka?" I let the spirit wash down my throat. Warmth instantly spread through my abdomen.

"We can get anything from the traders — when we have something to trade." She took the bottle from my hand. For a moment I felt her fingers on mine. The flesh tingled as if she'd spilled acid. That was my body's way of reminding me that the first time we had sex was in this room. I didn't actually need that reminder.

Neither did Katharine. "Are you pleased to see me, Quint? Or have you been through too many sex sessions to remember what we did in that armchair?" Her eyelids were wide apart and the corners of her mouth twitched.

I leaned forward and kissed her. For a few seconds she was still, then she put her hand against my chest and gently pushed me back.

"You're not answering my questions," she said, her voice even hoarser than usual.

I shrugged. "All right. Yes, I'm pleased to see you. No, sex sessions haven't erased the memory of our love."

"Fuck you," she said with a laugh. "I don't remember anything about love."

I took the vodka back and drank. "Don't you? Why are you here then?"

"That's just typical of a man," she said, shaking her head. "Not everything revolves around your cock, Quint."

I gave her a weak smile. "Very little has been revolving around that recently. I'm on a case."

She looked interested. "Are you now?" She pulled the bottle from my fingers and drank. "Any chance of you telling me what it's about?"

It was time to be masterful. "No."

She laughed and I felt the hairs rise on the back of my neck. She had the most arousing laugh I'd ever heard. I reached out for her hand. The long, thin fingers were another part of her that used to fascinate me.

"Don't, Quint. This is serious."

"So's this."

She stuck both her hands inside her coat. "You want to know why I came? All right, I'll tell you, mister investigator. You're about to have a major drugs problem in this city."

I sat up as if a hatpin had just worked its way through the cushion.

"And that's not all," she said, turning towards me and fixing me in her gaze. "The gang boss who's setting it up is a complete psycho."

She wasn't telling me anything I hadn't begun to suspect but how did she know all this? "Anything else?" I asked, trying to conceal my surprise.

She nodded, her expression quizzical. "I don't really understand this bit. The guy who told us about the drugs had escaped from one of the local gangs. He was delirious most of the time and he kept saying the same words over and over again."

My mind was in turmoil. What was she going to hit me with now?

"It seems to be a place," she continued. "Or at least the code-name for a place."

"Tell me, Katharine."

She ran her fingertips down her cheek then twitched her nose like she'd just sniffed industrial-strength disinfectant.

"The Bone Yard," she said, shrugging her shoulders. Then she realised I was as jumpy as a male tourist near the stage in the Three Graces. "What is it, Quint? Have you heard of it?"

I nodded slowly and reached for the bottle again. It looked like it was going to be a very long night.

Katharine shivered and closed her eyes. After a couple of minutes I began to wonder if she'd fallen asleep. Then she gave a start and sat up straight again.

"Where have you been hiding out in the city?"

"We've got some contacts here." She frowned and looked at me suspiciously. "Are you working for the Council again, Quint?"

"Yes, but not full time. Don't worry, Katharine. I'm not going to hand you or your friends over to the guard."

"You'd better not try," she replied, her expression harder than a barracks rugby player's. Then she shivered again, this time uncontrollably.

I put my arm round her shoulders. "What is it, Katharine?"

She let out a sob then swallowed hard. "Food," she said with a gasp. "I haven't had anything for a couple of days."

"Glad to see your people have been looking after you," I said on the way to the kitchen that takes up one corner of my main room. "I haven't got much myself. I've not been in a lot recently."

"You don't have to tell me that," Katharine said weakly. "I've been looking for you all over the city."

I found a can of stew that had escaped Davie's notice and opened it. The electricity was off so the cooker was no good. "Have this," I said, handing it to her. "You're taking your life in your hands eating it cold. God knows what state the meat's in. There are rumours that the Supply Directorate's been having problems with diseased cattle."

She started wolfing it down. "You'd have been much better off coming with me out of the city, Quint," she said between mouthfuls. "At least we have clean herds on our land."

Some dissidents run collective farms, defending them against the lunatics and criminal gangs who maraud about the country.

Katharine had finished eating but she was still trembling. I touched her hand. It was freezing. There was only one solution.

"Come on," I said, pulling her to her feet. "You're the one who's going to catch her death. The bed's the only warm place in this flat."

She didn't resist, but as I pulled off her coat and bundled her under the covers she looked at me sternly. "I haven't forgotten what they taught us in auxiliary training about keeping each other warm on night exercises. But that's all that we're going to do, all right?"

I gave her my best salute and crawled up against her. After a while she stopped shivering and moved so that there was a gap between us.

"Right, Quint. Let's get down to business."

Her business in the past had been purveying sexual services to tourists in the city's biggest hotel, but I didn't think mentioning that would be a good idea. She seemed to have lost interest in carnal matters.

"Okay," I said, letting my head sink into the sack of straw that the Supply Directorate classifies as a pillow. "What do you want to tell me about first? The drugs, the psycho or the Bone Yard?"

She glanced down at me and twitched her head. "It doesn't matter. As far as I can see, they're all part of the same story."

I was afraid she'd say that.

"Our fields are in what used to be East Lothian, south of Dunbar," she said after a long silence. "There are about a hundred of us — enough to look after the animals, work the crops and guard the fences. I made sure we got a hold of rifles and ammunition not long after I arrived. Most of the gangs keep their distance." Katharine glanced at me dispassionately. "Any who don't, we shoot."

"Which is why firearms were banned in Edinburgh," I put in. "Mob rule's a dangerous thing."

She glared at me. "We're not a mob. Anyway, it's not as simple as that and you know it, Quint. This city's got plenty wrong with it from what I've been hearing."

I got my hands out from beneath the covers and tried to calm her down. "All right, cool it. I'm even less of a fan of the Council than I used to be."

She kept her gaze on me, then laughed. "And you never exactly gave the guardians your unconditional support in the old days." Her face became serious again. "Quint, I heard your mother died. I'm sorry. You must have had a hard time."

Those words affected me more than the official tributes at the funeral. Katharine had first-hand experience of the catastrophic mistakes my mother had made when she was senior guardian, but she was still sympathetic. I'd missed her openness.

"Anyway, our fence guards found the guy who deserted a couple of weeks back," she said, leaning over me to reach for the vodka. My nostrils were filled by the reek of unwashed clothing and sweat which didn't completely obscure the delicate smell I remembered from the few times we'd been naked together.

Katharine gulped then quivered as the spirit fired up inside her. "He was in a bad way physically and mentally. He took a couple of bullets in the abdomen when he slipped out of the gang's camp. And he was raving. At first we thought he'd messed himself up permanently on some brain-damaging drug."

Electric Blues, for instance? I took the bottle and swallowed from it. There wasn't much left. At least we were keeping ourselves warm.

"So what did he say that sent you back into the city you love so much?" I asked.

Katharine gave me the kind of look that guardswomen reserve for the barracks jackass when they draw him as sex session partner. "In one of his relatively lucid periods he told me about this formula for a hot new drug that his gang leader had got a hold of. Apparently it was pretty complicated and needed a good chemist in a well-equipped lab to produce it."

"And his gang boss had a contact in the city who could arrange that?"

She nodded then looked at me sternly. "Am I telling you something you already know, Quint? This isn't a one-way transaction."

"I'll tell you what I'm working on, Katharine." I squeezed her arm. "Honest."

She pulled her arm away. "You'll tell me after I tell you? Sounds like kids playing doctors and nurses."

"We can do that too if you like."

Her face went blank and her body jerked away from mine.

"What is it, Katharine? What's the matter?"

She was gazing straight ahead into the darkness, the candle on the bedside table casting its dim light on to her profile. Although she looked thinner, the lines of her features hadn't changed in the two years since I'd last seen her. But she'd been strong then, hardened by her experience of prison and the Prostitution Services Department. Now her toughness seemed more of an act.

"I . . . I had a bad time after I went over the wire. There are a lot of animals out there."

"Tell me, Katharine."

She kept her eyes off me. "No, Quint. I can't. It's over now."

I touched her hand with one finger. "No, it isn't. You're still in pain." I sat up and moved closer to her. "Remember when I told you about Caro? You persuaded me it would do me good to share the pain. I didn't believe you at first, but you were right." Her eyelashes quivered and for a moment I thought she was going to weep, but she kept control. "Let it go, Katharine. You can trust me."

She turned slowly towards the light and looked into my eyes. Then she shuddered briefly and dropped her gaze, like a deer that senses the stalker's gun but can't find it in herself to turn tail.

"There was a gang in the hills east of Lauder," she said slowly. "They lived off the sheep that have run wild there since the original farmers were massacred years ago." She lifted her eyes to mine and I saw the hatred in them. "They really were animals, Quint. They called themselves the Cavemen. The morons had burned down all the cottages in the area, so they had to dig themselves holes in the ground. Bastards." She spat out the last word and lapsed back into silence.

"They caught you?" I asked haltingly.

She gave a bitter laugh. "I thought I could look after myself. But not against those madmen. They even slashed each other with their skinning knives in their desperation to get at me." She looked at me, her gaze suddenly unsteady as she finally began to lose control. "I was tied to a tree for a month before I killed two of them and escaped."

"Jesus." I tried to put my arm round her.

"Don't!" Her shout must have woken most of the neighbours. "Don't, Quint," she repeated, her voice back to something approaching normal volume. "I . . . I haven't been with a man since then."

I moved away. "I understand, Katharine."

She looked at me in disbelief.

"Or at least I'm trying to understand." In fact I was way out of my depth and suffering from cramp in both legs.

"So now you know," she said, her face loosening into a faint smile. "After years spent satisfying tourists, I've turned into Katharine the Untouchable. Funny, isn't it?"

I wasn't laughing. Suddenly I had a great urge to change the subject. "The guy who told you about the drug formula. What did he say about the psycho who was running the deal?"

Katharine nodded, happy to stop talking about what she'd been through. "He was completely terrified of him. Remember, this was a man who was delirious most of the time, but even when he was raving he kept going on about the Screecher."

"The Screecher?"

She nodded. "That's what the leader of his gang was called. He was terrified the Screecher was going to track him down and cut him to pieces for deserting."

Cut him to pieces? That sounded familiar.

"What else did he say about him?"

Katharine shrugged. "Nothing very coherent. I had trouble making sense of it. About the drugs, his boss . . ."

"And what about the Bone Yard?" I asked, trying not to sound too interested.

"He kept repeating that and moaning — not just from the pain of his wounds, but as if it were something horrendous that he could barely live with."

Like William McEwan, I thought. But not like the senior guardian. I hadn't seen many signs of spiritual disturbance on his saintly face.

"He never explained what it was though." Katharine settled back on her pillow, her eyes flickering. She was about to pass out, but I needed more.

"So where is he, the wounded gang member? I need to see him for myself. It sounds like he could do with hospital treatment as well."

She shook her head weakly, her eyes firmly closed now. "He's long past that stage, Quint. He died a week ago."

"Shit." The first half-decent lead I'd got in the case and it vanished quicker than the beggars on Princes Street after the Enlightenment came to power.

Katharine turned over, her back towards me. "Look in my coat pocket. I've got his ID."

Santa Claus does exist after all. Even though he'd arrived a bit late this season.

*   *   *

I came to as the front door slammed.

Katharine sat up straight. A wicked-looking knife that I hadn't noticed before glinted in the faint glow from the streetlights. "Who's that?" she whispered.

"Davie. Get back under the covers."

I jumped out of bed and reached the door before he came in.

"You're up early, Quint," he said. "It's only seven o'clock. What happened? Guilty conscience keep you awake?"

"Something like that," I mumbled, suddenly aware that I was seriously short of shut-eye.

"Here." He tossed me a brown paper bag, which I failed to catch.

"Croissants? Jesus, Davie, where did you get them?"

He looked over from the kitchen where he was starting to make coffee, a grin spreading across his bearded face.

"Fell off the back of a Supply Directorate van, did they?"

"Are you suggesting that a guardsman is capable of dishonesty? That's a serious offence, citizen." His face didn't look very serious.

"Aye, and so's nicking tourist provisions." I headed back to the bedroom with my share of breakfast.

Katharine's head emerged from the covers.

"Take these," I said in a low voice.

"What about you?"

"I'll pick something up later. Now listen. Stay here all day. I'll get back as soon as I can. It's not safe for you on the streets." I pulled on my trousers and put the dead gang member's ID card in the pocket.

She raised her eyes to the ceiling. "I can look after myself."

"Please," I said, putting my hand on hers. "There are some serious crazies out there."

She pulled her hand away, not too fast, and looked at me accusingly. "You never told me about the case you're working on."

"I will." Then, before she could move, I leaned forward and kissed her once on the lips. "Later."

If her expression was anything to go by, I was lucky not to walk into the main room with the haft of her knife protruding from my chest.

Chapter Thirteen

———◦◦◦◦———

Davie and I went out into the cold. Darkness still prevailed in the sky overhead and the underpowered streetlights weren't making too much of an impression on it. They were helped a bit by the thick carpet of snow that was lying on all the surfaces. It reflected their feeble glow and muffled the sound of the buses on the main road. Citizens unlucky enough to be working in the mines were already heading for the collection points, scarves wrapped around their faces. Eyes were sunk as deep in their sockets as those of the prisoners on Death Row after the last, desperate UK government reintroduced capital punishment.

Davie had parked the Land-Rover away from the pavement as the snow had drifted near the buildings. Walking into the road, I caught sight of thin parallel tyre tracks about two feet apart. Probably some poor sod in a wheelchair going to the infirmary for an early morning appointment.

"Where to then?" asked Davie.

"The main archive on George IVth Bridge."

"Not again," he groaned as the starter motor whined and eventually fired. "This case is about as much fun as the paper chases we did during auxiliary training."

"Don't knock it, guardsman. It's the only lead we've got." He was about to ask me about it. I'd have to tell him eventually but I didn't want him to know about Katharine yet. I spoke before he could. "Did the guardsman who was attacked yesterday have anything more to say?"

Davie shook his head. "I checked with his barracks commander late last night. Apparently he was still pretty shaky."

"He took a hell of a pounding."

Davie swung carefully round the snow-covered junction at Tollcross, slowing to walking pace as we passed a City Guard emergency unit. A Mines Department bus had mounted the pavement and turned an *Edinburgh Guardian* kiosk into firewood. The passengers were standing around looking dazed and confused, but happy; whatever happened next, they'd missed at least part of their shift in the frozen earth.

"I wouldn't worry," Davie said as he accelerated up Lauriston Place. "I played rugby against that guardsman once. He used his head like it was the business end of a battering ram. He probably bangs it against a wall himself if he doesn't get his daily ration of hits."

At the archive I sent him off to see if Hamilton's people had reported anything overnight. That made him very happy. Then I told him to come back as soon as he'd finished, which didn't impress him so much.

Even at eight in the morning there were plenty of auxiliaries in the archive. Paper has come to dominate this city in the eighteen years since the Enlightenment came to power. Here were large numbers of highly educated people spending their lives chasing files. Winston Smith in *1984* would have felt very much at home, though his first name wouldn't have made him popular with the Council — too redolent of what's still seen as the bankrupt legacy of the British establishment. The Enlightenment regarded computers as socially divisive and educationally sterile, so they got rid of as many as they could. Those the guardians have kept are used to run the Council's classified records, but there aren't enough to go round for that. Just as well. That means I can still find a lot of sensitive information in the archives.

I found a quiet corner and took out the ID card Katharine had given me. Under the bright reading light it didn't take me long to discover something very interesting. The card proclaimed that Hamish Robin Campbell had been born on 27.11.1970, had the status of ordinary citizen, was five feet nine inches tall, weighed twelve stone six pounds, had light brown hair, a complete set of teeth and an appendix scar; he was in the Leisure Department of the Tourism Directorate, lived at 19b Elgin Street and his next of kin was his wife Muriel Campbell. The photograph that stared out dully from the laminated card was of a balding, sad-faced man who looked like he'd been working too hard for too many years. In that respect he was no different from most of his fellow citizens who'd invested their lives in the Enlightenment. Except they don't carry fake ID cards. If you've seen as many as I have, you can spot a ringer faster than the annual strawberry ration disappears from the city's foodstores.

I had a pretty good idea where this particular specimen came from too. The City Guard's Documentation Department is staffed by skilled forgers and graphic designers. The problem is, they're all auxiliaries and auxiliaries are by training and nature perfectionists. They make a really good job of every false ID they produce for undercover agents, with the result that those IDs often look more convincing than the real cards the Citizen Registration Department issues.

So what was going on here with Hamish Robin Campbell? Was he a former guard operative who'd deserted? Or could he be an active undercover man who'd penetrated the gang that was run by the crazy guy he called the Screecher? The obvious person to ask would be Hamilton, but that wouldn't prove much. I'd never heard of covert guard operations being run outside the city borders and, anyway, Campbell might have been handled by one of the iron boyscouts without the public order guardian's knowledge. I also wanted to keep this to myself till I found out more about the dead man and his links with the drug formula.

I had a plan about how to do that but it would need careful timing. In the meantime I checked the Deserters Register for

Campbell's name. It wasn't there. Either he'd managed to leave the city without being missed or his name had been deliberately kept out. Then I checked the Accommodation Index and discovered that there had once been a Muriel Campbell living at 19b Elgin Street, but she died in 2016. That was as much confirmation as I needed that the ID had been produced by auxiliaries. It's standard procedure to use an address that checks out superficially, but the forgers in the castle aren't required to update secondary details. Now I was sure the card was fake. But I wasn't looking forward to what I had to do next.

"Davie, I need to get Hamilton out of his office for a while."

If he was surprised, he didn't show it. "You're keeping something to yourself, aren't you, Quint?" He made a skilful adjustment to the Land-Rover's steering as we came on to the esplanade. Judging by the way other guard vehicles were slewed about the snow-covered expanse beneath the castle entrance, most drivers had decided that parking in the normal neat ranks was not essential today.

"Is it that obvious?"

"Aye." Davie laughed. "You get this faraway look in your eyes when you're on to something tasty. Like a kid opening the *Enlightenment Encyclopedia* at the page headed 'Human Sexuality' for the first time."

"Very funny, guardsman." I gave him a stern look. "What page number is that again?"

He pulled up by the sentries. "Volume three, page four hundred and thirty-seven." He undid his seatbelt and looked back at me thoughtfully. "I suppose I could get the guardian to come down to the operations room to go over the roster of personnel involved in the investigation. These days he almost licks your feet if you ask for his advice."

"Poor old sod. The iron boyscouts think he's a joke."

"Well, I don't," Davie said defensively, "and neither should you. He's been asking what you're up to."

"Has he now? Tell him I'm checking on the guardsman who got his brains rearranged yesterday."

Davie nodded. "Okay. Give me ten minutes before you go to his quarters."

I put my hand on his arm. "There's the small matter of the clerk in his outer office."

Davie grinned. "Oh, don't worry about Amy. I'll tell her you're on official business."

"I can do that myself."

"Aye, citizen. But will she keep quiet about your visit afterwards?"

He headed off through the gate, acknowledging the guards. I sometimes wonder if there are any female auxiliaries in the city who he hasn't provided with an unforgettable sex session.

Hamilton's clerk was middle-aged and faded, her hair as grey as the auxiliary-issue suit she was wearing. But there was a red glow about her cheeks. Whatever Davie said to her seemed to have done the trick. As soon as I went in to the outer office she looked down at her papers. As I went in to the guardian's office, I heard the outer door close behind her. I was on my own. The question was, for how long?

The last time I used Hamilton's computer was during the search for the murderer two years ago. I was banking on the chance that he hadn't changed his password since then. I sat down, logged on and entered the word "colonel". Then I hit the return key and waited, feeling my heart pounding in my chest. The screen flashed and the Council Archive main menu came up. I highlighted the City Guard line, then the Confidential Operatives line in the subsidiary menu that followed. I was asked again for a password. As in all systems, users are instructed not to use the same one that they use for initial access. But Lewis Hamilton was a leading proponent of the Enlightenment's anti-information technology position and he used his terminal about as often as I agree with current Council policies. The chances were that he used the same password. I entered it and waited for alarm bells to ring. They didn't. The menu of the file containing details of all the guard's undercover operatives appeared. I was in.

I glanced at my watch. Nine thirty-three. I hoped to hell Hamilton was buying Davie's strategy. Tea is brought round at quarter to ten in the castle. That would give Davie an extra chance to stall the guardian.

I went into the Operatives' Aliases option and entered the name on the ID card. There was a brief pause and then the file came up. Hamish Robin Campbell: alias approved 12.8.2018. That was interesting. It showed that the guy had been undercover for three and a half years. I noted down the barracks number of the auxiliary who had assumed the alias, which was Watt 103. Things were looking promising. Then I requested the reports Campbell had filed on his activities and my luck ran out as comprehensively as the guy's at the end of the queue when the whisky runs out on a Saturday night.

The screen told me that Campbell's reports were "Not Available". That's jargon for "So Secret That Even Guardians Don't Have Access". There was only one person who could call up "Not Available" files and that was the chief boyscout. Who knows what his passwords were? "Baden" and "Powell"?

I went back into the main menu and tried to bring up Watt 103's service record. All auxiliaries' data are held in the Council Archive, but I was pretty sure this particular servant of the city had officially died a long time before Katharine came across him. And so it turned out. Watt 103 didn't feature as a serving auxiliary, but there was a reference to him in the "Auxiliaries – Deceased" archive. According to that, he had died of a heart attack in the infirmary on 4 December 2019. Unless he'd come back to life like a cataleptic character in an Edgar Allan Poe story, someone had been messing around with the records. And whoever that was had fallen foul of the cross-referencing system, suggesting he or she didn't have a complete grasp of the archives but also hadn't wanted to involve a professional clerk.

I heard the outer office door bang. After a delay that made my heart shake, rattle and roll there was a knock on the door of the inner office. Then another knock. I waited, frozen to the seat in front of the terminal, ready to claim I was a technician updating Hamilton's software and fully aware that wouldn't do anything more than buy me a little more time. Then I heard footsteps moving away and the outer office door close again. The guardian's notorious temper seemed to have put the visitor off entering without permission. That was the first time I'd ever felt grateful that Hamilton was such an irascible old bugger.

It was obviously time to get out but I still wanted to know more about Watt 103. I scrolled down his personal details and came to a piece of information that made all the tangled nerves I'd suffered in the last twenty minutes worth while. The auxiliary who staggered to Katharine's collective farm south of Dunbar had been trained as a physicist before the Enlightenment. Not just any kind of physicist either, but a nuclear physicist. After the Council was established, he'd been involved in the decommissioning of Torness nuclear power station. I sat back in the chair after I logged off and looked out through the leaded windows towards the gull-grey water of the Firth of Forth. Torness nuclear power station went out of service in 2007. So what was one of the few remaining nuclear physicists in a city where coal has been the main fuel for fifteen years doing over the border? And what was he doing in a gang that operated close to the city's former main source of energy?

I smelled a very large mutant rat glowing brightly in Edinburgh's Enlightenment gloom.

I met Davie and the guardian in the corridor outside the operations room.

"Ah, there you are, Dalrymple." Hamilton was looking twitchy, which isn't usually a good sign. He started running his hand back and forward through his beard as if the Council had just decreed that auxiliaries must be clean-shaven but that razors aren't allowed. "There seems to be a bit of a problem."

It was unlike him to be vague, even when he ran into trouble.

"What is it?" I asked, glancing at Davie. He didn't look particularly bothered.

"It's my bloody deputy," the guardian replied.

"Raeburn 03? He hasn't fallen under a bus, has he?"

Hamilton glared at me. "That isn't funny, Dalrymple. I don't think much of him as an individual but he's an excellent administrator."

Most of that was for Davie's benefit. I wondered if the guardian knew that his number two was known as Machiavelli by everyone else in the guard.

"So what's the problem with your excellent administrator?" I asked.

"We don't know where he is," Davie put in. "No one's seen him since yesterday evening."

That sounded interesting. "When you say no one, you mean no one you've asked so far," I said.

Davie looked at his notebook. "All personnel on duty in the castle, all personnel in Raeburn Barracks . . ."

"How about the senior guardian?" I looked at Hamilton.

"He's been informed. He hasn't seen him since the end of the Council meeting last night."

I nodded, remembering Machiavelli's urgent conversation with the chief boyscout outside the Council chamber. "I think we'd better run a check on your deputy, guardian. Is your computer operational?"

Hamilton strode away down the passage. "It was the last time I looked. Useless piece of junk. I don't know what you expect to find there."

"It's amazing what you come across in the database some-times," I replied, grinning at Davie.

We set off after him, our boots ringing like drumbeats on

the flagstones. I wondered where Machiavelli's auxiliary-issue footwear was at this moment; and if he'd gone there willingly.

Hamilton was overjoyed when I offered to handle the computer. I was pleased too. That way he wouldn't notice the tell-tale line informing him that he'd logged off ten minutes ago. I remembered to ask him for his password. He went all coy and wrote it down rather than say it in front of Davie.

I got into the senior auxiliary section of the Serving Auxiliaries archive and typed in Raeburn 03's barracks number. It was then that the guardian began to have second thoughts.

"Em, Dalrymple," he said, leaning over my chair. "What exactly do you expect to find out about my number two? You know how many checks personnel have to go through to reach his level in the hierarchy."

I looked up at him. "He's a missing person, isn't he? Guard regulations state that anyone absent from their post for more than three hours is required to attend a review board."

Hamilton looked at me like a medieval abbot who'd suddenly detected signs of demonic possession in one of his monks. "Since when did you care so passionately about guard procedure?"

I shrugged. "I did write most of the regulations when I was in the directorate."

"That was a long time ago, citizen. You surely can't suspect Raeburn 03 of any involvement in the murders."

Even I wouldn't have gone that far, at least not yet. "Look, guardian. He's been very interested in the case since the beginning. He turned up at the first post-mortem, he was in the second victim's barracks not long after her body was discovered, he's been—" I broke off. Telling Hamilton that I was suspicious about Machiavelli's friend the senior guardian was probably not a very good idea.

"Well?" demanded Hamilton. "He's been what?"

I gave him a smile to pacify him. "He's been someone the Council has had its eye on for promotion."

My smile had the wrong effect. "You mean when it manages to get rid of me?" the guardian said, his cheeks scarlet. "Well, I'm not going anywhere. This is my directorate and I'm staying till I drop."

Behind him Davie had his eyes raised to the inlaid ceiling. "I know that, guardian," I said, scrolling down Machiavelli's service record. I realised that I knew as little about him as I knew about his superiors in the Council. They'd all appeared out of the woodwork when my mother's regime began to crack.

"Auxiliary training 2010 to '12, then a year on the border, a couple of years in Raeburn Barracks administration, three years in the guard, a year in the Tourism Directorate ... that's interesting, guardian. Your deputy was in the Prostitution Services Department."

"Get on with it, Dalrymple."

I could see from Hamilton's expression how impressed he was by that aspect of his deputy's career. "Then he was in the Science and Energy Directorate for a year. As assistant to the present senior guardian no less."

"That's probably why he follows him around like a lost sheep," the guardian growled.

"Uh-huh." I kept on scrolling, then stopped abruptly. "And his last posting before this one was in the Finance Directorate, from 2019 to '20." I paused. There was no way Hamilton was going to let that pass without comment.

"Yes. As one of your friend Heriot 07's assistants." The guardian sounded like he'd just inhaled deeply in a pigsty. "I wonder what he learned from him."

"My ex-friend Heriot 07," I said, trying to stall him. Heriot 07 was the barracks number of Billy Geddes, who used to run all the city's money-making scams. I was beginning to wish I'd kept a much closer eye on him since he'd been confined to a wheelchair. Jesus. There were wheelchair tracks in the street outside my flat this morning.

The door burst open.

"What is Citizen Dalrymple doing at your terminal, guardian?" The senior guardian's voice wasn't exactly sharp. He still sounded like he could sweet-talk the Lord God Almighty into passing on to him the secret of eternal life, but there was an edge to his voice that would have put the wind up Satan. "Kindly leave us, guardsman." Davie didn't hang around.

Hamilton hit the shutdown function. "I was supervising the citizen, senior guardian."

"Never mind that." The chief boyscout moved into the centre of the room and looked around like a pre-Enlightenment estate agent working out his percentage. "About Raeburn 03. I am handling the search for him personally." He gave me a stare that he no doubt hoped would send my body temperature through the floor.

"I think there may be some connection with the murders," I said, looking straight back at him. You could almost hear the clang of invisible sabres crossing.

"I will be the judge of that, citizen. If any such connection exists, you'll be the first to know." The senior guardian turned his attention back to Lewis Hamilton. "In the meantime, guardian, you will not pass any information from the Council Archive to citizen Dalrymple. Understood?"

The guy was about thirty years younger than Hamilton, but he was treating him like an auxiliary trainee on his first day in uniform. Lewis had his face set hard, but there was nothing he could do.

"I wish to speak with my colleague, citizen." That was guardian-speak for "Close the door on your way out, scum."

I left them to it.

And spent the rest of the day trying to work out how to dig up more information on Machiavelli, Billy Geddes and the dead physicist Hamish Robin Campbell. By the time I went back to the flat, I was beginning to make progress on two of those fronts.

Chapter Fourteen

There was a tap on the door just after eight o'clock that evening.

"Where the fuck have you been?" I yelled. "I told you to stay indoors."

Katharine stood in the doorway of my flat, shaking off melting snow like a dog that's been in a river.

"You told me?" she said, eyeing me blackly. "And who exactly are you to tell me what to do?"

I got up and went over to the kitchen area, not wanting to show her any more of how I felt. "You must be freezing. I'll make coffee."

She spread her coat over a chair and sank down into the sofa. "Coffee," she said wistfully. "I haven't had that for a long time."

"Not many people in the city have – at least, not decent stuff. You can still find it if you know the right people."

"How corrupt."

I turned and saw that she was smiling ironically. "How realistic, more like. Since you object so strongly on moral grounds, can I have your share?"

She didn't reply but the smile remained on her lips.

"So where have you been?" I asked, handing her the least chipped mug I possessed.

She laughed. "Now he wants to know where I've spent my day."

"For Christ's sake, Katharine, there's a double murderer out there." I gave her what I hoped was an unconcerned shrug. "Anyway, it's better for me if you don't hang around here. I don't fancy being done for harbouring a deserter."

She was about as far from buying that line as the city was from purchasing a fleet of Chinese limousines to ferry citizens to the mines.

"If you must know," she said with a nervous flick of her head, "I was trying to score some drugs in the Cowgate."

"You were what?" My voice went soprano.

"Don't worry. I was pretty subtle about it."

Somehow I managed to get a grip on myself. "Let me just get this straight, Katharine. You went down to the street in the city that's most infested with undercover operatives and tried to find out if a new drug has appeared. You do know that Edinburgh has what *Time* magazine described as the most ferocious anti-narcotics programme in the western world, don't you?"

She gave me a monarch-of-all-she-surveys look that would have impressed the long dead Margaret Thatcher. "Of course I know about the Council's drugs policy. I also know that there are ways and means for tourists to get hold of stuff."

I slumped back on the sofa beside her. "Don't tell me. You pretended you were a tourist."

She shrugged. "Obviously it worked," she said in a remarkably convincing sing-song Scandinavian accent. "The guard haven't turned up on my tail."

"Not yet they haven't," I said, resigning myself to the idea that my staircase might at any moment become a physical training location for most of the auxiliaries stationed in the castle. "Did you get a sniff of anything?"

Katharine shook her head. "Bugger all, apart from some hash that even schoolkids in the old days would have laughed at."

"So for some reason it's not being distributed yet. That confirms what I know from guard sources."

"Well, I'm glad I've been of some service," she said acidly.

"It wasn't worth the risk, Katharine."

"I can look after myself, Quint. You know that."

Except when there's a gang of Cavemen around, I thought. I didn't share that with her.

"What about you?" she asked. "Found out anything interesting?"

I had to make a decision. I looked across at her, wondering if it was a good idea to involve her in the case. I'd get shat on from the stratosphere if the Council discovered I was sharing classified information with a deserter. On the other hand, I needed all the help I could get if it turned out that senior auxiliaries like Machiavelli had been bad boys. She turned towards me when she felt my eyes on her and fixed me with her bottomless green gaze. It was no contest. But I needed to check something out first.

"Did the guy who died ever say anything about the old nuclear power station at Torness?"

Her eyes were still on me. There was a long pause before she spoke. "No, he didn't. At least not that I understood. He was raving most of the time. Like I told you, he just kept going on about the Screecher and the Bone Yard."

I'd begun to wonder if there might be some connection between Torness and the Bone Yard. But even if there were, what could that have to do with the Electric Blues and the killings in the city?

"That was truly disgusting," Katharine said, pushing her empty plate away.

"Sorry. It's not like it was when supermarket chains still existed. These days, if something's out of season, you don't get it, end of story."

"So in winter the only vegetables are potatoes, turnips and

kale. They don't have to be half rotten though. And as for the tinned soup . . ."

"I suppose you're spoilt on your farm."

"You obviously haven't tried growing root crops without the benefit of machinery." She sat upright. "Anyway, you still haven't told me what you found out today."

I nodded. "I'm going to. But, Katharine . . ." I waited for her to look at me. "It won't be like it was the last time we worked together two years back. You won't be an official member of the team. Davie and the others can't know about you."

"Suits me," she replied. "What makes you think I wanted to be in the team?"

"Nothing. But you risked your freedom by coming to tell me about the drug formula, so you must still have some feeling for the city."

She laughed harshly. "I don't give a shit about the city, Quint. The Council has always done exactly what it wants with it." She broke off and looked down. "But you're right in a way. I was an auxiliary once and I swore an oath to serve the bloody place. As far as I'm concerned that means the people. And the people are being fucked by the system."

"You'd get on well with the democrats in Glasgow."

"I'd have gone there long ago if there weren't so many gangs of lunatics between us and them." She looked up and her eyes flared in the dim light. "Are you going to tell me what you know or not?"

"Okay. I'll just put some music on." If my place had been bugged, Katharine and I were already up the Crap River without a punt-pole. But at least the bastards wouldn't find out the latest news. Muddy Waters seemed appropriate.

"You remember Billy Geddes?" I asked as the master belted into "The Hoochie Coochie Man".

"Your schoolfriend? How could I forget him? I thought he was crippled."

"He is. And even though the Council under my mother would

probably have kept him on as a deal-maker, the iron boyscouts cut him loose without a second thought. Or so the archive shows. He was demoted and packed off to a disabled persons' home in Merchiston a year and a half ago."

Katharine opened her hands. "And?"

"And I found when I went there this afternoon that he hasn't been seen since 18 November last year."

"Maybe he died."

I shook my head. "There's no record of that. And no record of a transfer to another home. Christ, the guy's in a wheelchair. He can't go far on his own."

"So what are you saying, Quint?"

I sat back, shaking my head. "I don't know exactly. But it's too much of a coincidence that Billy the arch-fixer disappears at the same time a new drug is developed." I took a deep breath and filled her in about the Electric Blue we found in the dead auxiliary's locker. She was unimpressed that I hadn't told her last night, but I made up for that by mentioning Machiavelli's disappearance.

"I remember that bastard from the guard," Katharine said, screwing her nose up. "I might have known he'd lick his way to the top."

I nodded. "The problem is, both he and Billy are dead-ends until we can track them down. I've got Davie doing a check on all the city's disabled facilities, but I don't reckon he'll turn anything up."

Katherine looked at me, her forehead lined in frustration. "What are we going to do then?"

I raised the stump of my right forefinger. "Never fear, Quintilian's got a plan."

She looked seriously unconvinced. "What is it then, smartarse?"

I tried to make it sound impressive, even though it was a last resort. I could only think of one senior scientist to consult. "I've been feeling a bit under the weather recently. I'm going to see the chemist."

I'd got Davie to find out where the chief toxicologist lived. It turned out he was one of those typical first-generation auxiliaries who was totally dedicated to the job. Either that or his manner put off even other scientists, because he avoided his barracks and spent his off-duty hours in a room above his laboratory. I deliberately didn't give him any advance warning of what I thought would be *my* visit.

Katharine saw it as *our* visit. "I'm coming with you, Quint."

"No, you're not. Word about you will get back to the Council."

She smiled at me sweetly. "We'll just have to make sure he keeps quiet about us, won't we? Don't worry, I'll think of a way to do that."

"What about the driver?" I demanded. "Oh, forget it." I called the castle and asked them to send me a vehicle. The auxiliary who brought it down would have to call for another Land-Rover to pick him or her up, but that was someone else's problem. My problem, and Katharine's, was whether I could remember how to drive after two years on my bicycle.

"I'd rather have ridden a mad cow," Katharine said, jumping down outside the labs as soon as I skidded to a halt in the snow. Mixing concrete with a straw would have been easier than finding gear in the clapped-out vehicle.

"Was I that bad?"

"No wonder cars were banned by the Council. You'd have reduced the population to double figures on your own by now."

"Thanks very much. I take it you'll be walking back." I led her to the gate. The guardswoman on duty waved us past when she saw my authorisation and the "ask no questions" which I'd passed to Katharine. I got directions to the chemist's room.

"Let me do the talking, all right?" I said as we walked into the building.

"Oh, you know what you're going to say, do you?"

It was a fair comment. I reckoned the city's chief toxicologist would answer my questions because something about him had given me the impression that he wasn't the iron boyscouts' number one fan. That didn't mean I had a very clear idea of how I was going to get him started.

We climbed to the fourth floor, our footsteps ringing down empty corridors which smelled of noxious substances and the sweat of scientists who, like everyone else in the city, don't see the communal baths often enough. At the far end of a long passage we came to a door. A scrap of paper with the words "Chief Toxicologist" had been stuck to it with a drawing pin. The city has better things to spend its money on than laminated signs, even for senior auxiliaries.

I put my ear to the faded black surface and heard the faint sound of music. I couldn't make out individual notes but the rhythm was familiar.

"He'll keep quiet about our visit," I whispered to Katharine with a smile.

"Why?" Her face was blank.

"Watch." I raised one hand, knocked twice quickly and turned the handle. The chemist hadn't locked it. He was probably too caught up in the music. "Good evening, Lister 25."

"What?" The chief toxicologist's pachydermic features appeared from behind a lateral shelving cabinet filled with files, beakers, test-tube racks and pot plants. "What do you think you're doing, citizen?" He moved across to the cassette player.

"Leave the music," I said. "Robert Johnson was a genius in my book."

Lister 25 stood still, his ungainly form bent over the low table. "You like Robert Johnson?" he asked in amazement. "You know who Robert Johnson was?"

I shrugged. "Like I said, a genius. This is one of my favourites." I glanced at Katharine. "'Kind Hearted Woman

Blues.'" She ignored me. "I don't think you're a genius though, Lister 25. Playing banned music in a Council building isn't going to do your career much good."

The chemist turned the volume down and twitched his lips at me. "My prospects are severely limited as it is, citizen. Who's your friend?"

"You don't want to know," I said.

Lister 25 nodded slowly. "I see. But you do want to know something."

I smiled. "Correct."

"And if I help you, my illicit addiction to the music of black America will remain unknown to my superiors?"

"Correct again. You can trust me. I'm a blues freak too."

"Sit down," said the chemist, waving expansively at a pair of unsound-looking plastic chairs. "I will endeavour to comply with your every demand. Is it about the matter we discussed on your last visit?" He looked doubtfully at Katharine.

"The Electric Blues?" I said with a laugh. "What do you think of the name?"

The toxicologist gave me a supercilious glance. "Electric blues were a travesty of the original Delta sound, citizen."

"You reckon? Well, whatever. I'm not here about them."

He rubbed his jowls pensively. "Really. I'm intrigued."

"Did you ever know a physicist by the barracks number of Watt 103?"

He went pale faster than a tourist who's put the last of his holiday money on a donkey masquerading as a horse at the Princes Street Gardens racetrack.

"Are you all right?" Katharine said, moving quickly to the sink and running him a glass of water.

Lister 25 was trying to take deep breaths. "Why are you . . . why are you interested in Watt 103, for God's sake?"

He must have been about the same age as the dead man. "How long have you known him?" I asked.

"Since the first year of university," Lister 25 gasped, finally bringing his breathing under control. "Alasdair was a brilliant physicist."

"A nuclear physicist," I said, watching his reaction.

The toxicologist nodded, then looked down. He'd started to knead the loose skin on the back of his left hand.

"When did you last see him?"

He shook his head weakly. "I don't remember exactly. Two or three years ago."

"What was he doing then?"

Lister 25's breathing again began to sound like that of a diver who's had his oxygen line slashed. "I . . . I . . . don't . . . don't . . . know. Class . . . classified work."

"You're going to do him an injury, Quint," Katharine said, settling the chemist gently in his chair. "Stop this. Stop it now."

I nodded reluctantly. "Just one more thing," I said. "The Bone Yard. Have you ever heard of it?"

Between more gasps and choking, the toxicologist managed to nod that he had. But he seemed not to know anything about what the word referred to.

"Ask . . . ask the senior . . . the senior guardian," he said as we were leaving. "He . . . he has . . . he has all the files."

I knew that already. And the chief boyscout was the one person I couldn't ask about the Bone Yard. He'd warned me off already and I had a nasty feeling that if I asked again I'd end up in a box like his predecessor as science and energy guardian. And anyway, what did all this have to do with the murders? I couldn't see what the link was. But I was getting more and more convinced that there was one.

Katharine decided against walking back through the snow-carpeted streets of southern Edinburgh. It wasn't a good decision. I still couldn't make much sense of the Land-Rover's gear-box.

"You take the bed." I put the candle I'd lit on the table.

Katharine shook her head. "I'm all right on the sofa. I haven't had much to do with beds recently. We sleep on sacks of straw on the farm."

"All the more reason to renew your acquaintance with a mattress now. What do you think Supply Directorate beds are?" I sat down and pulled out my notebook. "Anyway, I've got work to do."

She came over. "I can help."

"I wish you could. This investigation's going nowhere faster than the old parties at the last election."

"That bad?" She smiled then looked at me seriously. "What does the Bone Yard mean, Quint?"

"If I had any clue about that I wouldn't be sitting here chewing the end of my pencil."

She shook her head impatiently. "No, I'm not talking about your investigation. What do the words 'bone yard' refer to?"

I shrugged. "Cemetery, according to the dictionary."

"So have you checked out the city's cemeteries and grave-yards?"

"Checked them out for what? There are dozens of them. And since the Council brought in mandatory cremation back in 2006, nothing much has gone into them."

She smiled grimly. "Which means they'd be good places for illicit activities like drug trafficking, doesn't it?"

I sat back and heard the flimsy chair creak beneath my weight. "But there hasn't been any trafficking, Katharine. We'd have found bodies by now. The Electric Blues are fatal for people with weak hearts."

She nodded slowly. "Okay. What other angles have we got?"

I grinned at her. "You should have taken up my mother's offer to join the Public Order Directorate."

She was quiet for a minute. "I suppose if I'd stayed in the city, the Cavemen wouldn't have got me," she said eventually in a low voice.

"Christ, I didn't mean that, Katharine."

"It's all right, Quint. It was a long time ago." She got up from the table and moved towards the bedroom. "I'll see you."

"Yeah. Goodnight." I watched her svelte figure move into the darkness, then heard the door close tight. She might think it was a long time since she'd been abused by those neanderthals but she wasn't anywhere near getting over it. Then I thought of Caro. It was nearly seven years since the Ear, Nose and Throat Man had killed her and I still had vivid dreams of her. Not often, but enough to make sure I felt guilty at every sex session. That's what the Council's managed to do in its relentless search for the utopian state. It imagined it could appeal to people's desire for knowledge and self-advancement, but all it's ended up doing is pandering to their animal appetites. All anyone thinks about apart from screwing is getting enough to eat.

Which brought me back to the Bone Yard. It suddenly came to me that the city is indeed full of bone yards. But unlike the cemeteries, these ones operate to full capacity. Every day of the year Edinburgh has to feed thousands of tourists as well as its own citizens. So the perfect city is extremely well endowed with slaughterhouses.

Chapter Fifteen

I woke up to a thud from the direction of the front door and looked at my watch blearily. Six thirty-two. The postman had beaten Davie. I staggered over from the sofa and picked up a brown A4 envelope. Then all traces of sleep were blown away as quickly as the smoke from the city's myriad coal fires when the east wind kicks in.

I'd recognised the small, ultra-neat handwriting. I received something from the same correspondent only a few days ago. It was William McEwan. I looked at the postmark. It was dated 4 January 2022, the day before the old man went head first down the stairs. The post in Enlightenment Edinburgh doesn't run to standards Mussolini would have approved of, but it gets there in the end. And the envelope was unopened. It had escaped the random checks the Public Order Directorate makes on citizens' mail.

I ran my left forefinger under the flap and pulled out a sheaf of stapled pages. On the front was a brief handwritten note, which read:

Quintilian,
    In case your regular visit to the home is delayed, I am sending you this classified minute. I have other documents which I copied illicitly before I left the directorate, but

they are too sensitive to trust to the post. I hope this will
bring you down to Trinity soon.

W.M.

Not soon enough, unfortunately. I stood in the centre of my
freezing living room flicking through the pages. Then sat down
on the sofa and took a deep breath. No wonder the Science and
Energy Directorate archive was missing a lot of files.

The minute was of a meeting between McEwan and the senior
guardian dated 14 October 2019. Of course, the chief boyscout
wasn't senior guardian at that time. My mother was. At the
meeting they agreed to follow the recommendations made in
the Science and Energy Directorate's feasibility study, which
was written by none other than Watt 103, a.k.a. Hamish Robin
Campbell, the man who had died at Katharine's farm. And what
did he write a feasibility study about? Whether the two advanced
gas-cooled reactors at Torness nuclear power station could be
reactivated.

I sat back and tried to work out what the hell was going
on. The minute was marked "Senior Guardian/S.& E. Guardian
Eyes Only", which was interesting. It suggested that the rest of the
Council – which, in an unusual link with the pre-Enlightenment
UK cabinet, is defined in the city's constitution as a body bearing
collective responsibility – hadn't been briefed about what was a
major policy change. After the horrendous disaster at the Thorp
plant at Sellafield in 2003, nuclear power became about as popular
as a doctor with syphilis. So the Enlightenment had come to
power with a promise to shut down Torness at all costs. What
were my mother and William McEwan doing planning to start
it up again?

I went over to the sink and splashed water on to my face.
Maybe they hadn't actually gone ahead with the plan outlined
in the minute. Surely some news of a big operation like that
would have filtered out. On the other hand, why had the files
gone from the archive? And why had William McEwan been so

agitated about the Bone Yard? It looked like my idea about the city's abattoirs was off target after all.

Katharine came out of the bedroom in a pair of my faded citizen-issue pyjamas. I was so engrossed in my thoughts that I didn't give her anything more than a mumbled greeting. And completely forgot that Davie was both late and in possession of a key.

He chose that moment to make an entry.

"Hello, Davie," Katharine said without any sign of surprise.

He took in her short hair and gaunt features, then what she was wearing. "Oh, aye?" he said, turning to me. "Got your fancy woman back, have you?"

I was never one for pig in the middle. "I'll just sit down and let you two get on with it." When they worked together in the last murder case, Davie and Katharine had what could best be described as a relationship based on mutual loathing. He didn't like her dissident record and work in the Prostitution Services Department, and she thought he was a typical boneheaded guardsman.

"I am not anybody's fancy woman," Katharine said haughtily.

Davie ran his eye over her again. "I see what you mean. Times been hard on the other side of the border?"

"Not as hard as the ones the females in your barracks must go through waiting for the sex session roster to be posted."

"Children." I waved the minute at them. "I've just got a big break in the case. Can you postpone the verbal boxing contest?"

"Not really, Quint," Davie said, his cheeks red above the thick curls of his beard. "She's a deserter. I should take her in."

"Just try it, guardsman," Katharine said, leaning forward on the balls of her feet like a lioness about to pounce.

"Oh, for God's sake, what's your average age?" I demanded, glaring at them. "Above eight, by any chance? Look, this investigation's just gone critical in more than one way. For the next few days we need to keep our canines out of each other's throats."

Davie and Katharine exchanged glances that were still hostile enough to petrify a Leith hard man in the days before they all joined the guard, but at least they both kept quiet.

"That's better," I said. "Davie, I hadn't intended to tell you about Katharine, but since you've got into the habit of coming in without knocking . . ."

"You said I could," he protested with a pained expression.

"Go and make some coffee, will you? We need to have a serious look at what we're going to do next."

Outside, the noise of the early morning traffic suddenly seemed a lot quieter. I drew the curtain and saw a cloudful of large snowflakes so thick that I could hardly make out the flats across the street. As visual metaphors for how much Edinburgh citizens know about the activities of their guardians go, it wasn't bad.

I filled them both in about the Torness minute and tried to make it clear how dangerous it might be if they were to tell anyone else. Then I mentioned a pretty dodgy strategy I'd worked out for getting into the senior guardian's personal archive. It involved a lot of dressing up and judicious use of the "ask no questions". Neither Davie nor Katharine looked impressed, but since they weren't liable to end up down the mines for impersonating a rodent control technician, they couldn't complain too much. As things panned out, I didn't need to open my make-up bag after all.

My mobile buzzed and Davie answered it. "It's the guardian," he said, handing it over. "Sounds hot."

It was nothing like the inside of an advanced gas-cooled reactor, but it was still enough to get my circulation going.

"Dalrymple? We've found Raeburn 03."

"Dead or alive?"

"The former." Hamilton's voice took on the usual diluted quality it acquired when he had to talk about violence. "Cut up like the others."

"You haven't touched anything, have you?"

"I haven't," he said defensively. "The guardswoman who

found the body brushed off the snow to find his barracks badge."

"What's the location?"

"The summit of Blackford Hill."

"We're on our way." I grabbed my jacket. "Come on, Davie."

Katharine was standing by the table. "What do you want me to do, Quint?"

"Stay here and don't answer the door."

Davie turned from the front door. "You could always do a bit of early spring cleaning."

She raised her middle finger.

If Katharine stayed inside my pit all day I'd perform oral sex on the senior guardian. I didn't tell her that though. She was always one for a challenge.

"What was Machiavelli doing up here?" Davie asked as he steered the Land-Rover up the steep slope of the snow-covered road past the observatory. Scene-of-crime people were already taking photos of tyre tracks and cordoning off the area.

"Good question. We'll have to see if he was killed here or somewhere else." My mind was already racing ahead. What if he'd been in the surrounding area before the murderer got to him? I could think of one place he might have been visiting – the laboratories at King's Buildings. Maybe he'd recently acquired an interest in chemistry.

There was only a faint line of light in the sky to the east. A generator was being set up ahead of us by the directorate's technical squad. The guardian loomed out of the darkness.

"Jesus Christ, Dalrymple," he said, shaking his head slowly. "I don't know how much more of this I can take."

"What's the problem?" I asked lamely.

There was a shout from ahead of us, then the floodlights came on in a sudden blaze. I blinked and tried to focus.

"See for yourself," the guardian said, tramping off to his vehicle.

I moved towards the light.

Davie was on my right. "Bloody hell," he said with a rapid intake of breath. "I see what he means."

The body was lying just below the trig point at the summit. There was a carpet of fresh snow on it. Machiavelli was in a rough crucifix position with his legs about six inches apart, feet towards us as we laboured up the hill. But the position wasn't what caught the eye. Despite the snow, a great crimson gout was visible. It was about six feet long and a couple of feet across and stretched out from the neck to the concrete pillar. From the neck. The body in the grey guard tunic had been decapitated on the spot. And I could see no sign at all of the head.

You'd think the snow that had fallen on Edinburgh overnight would be a useful source of traces – footprints, spots of liquid and so on. The problem is it also covers things up.

"What have we got then?" I said to Davie after we'd spent more than enough time crawling around in the snow beside the body.

"Not a lot," he replied, blowing on his fingers and then trying to flip over the pages of his notebook. "Except terminal bloody frostbite."

A guardsman came up with plastic cups of tea that was as grey as a citizen-issue block of writing paper. I gasped as my lips soldered themselves to the rim of the cup.

Hamilton came up to where we were standing about five yards from the body. His face was looking a lot redder than it had done earlier. Maybe he'd supplemented his tea with barracks whisky.

"I don't suppose there's any doubt that it's my deputy."

I shook my head. "We checked that. Obviously another body could have been dressed in his uniform, though God knows why anyone would bother impersonating him."

"Have some respect, Dalrymple," the guardian said, giving me a ferocious glare. "The man's been butchered."

"Sorry," I said. It is a bit out of order to talk ill of the dead, even those who've been behaving suspiciously. "He had a distinguishing mark. A scar on his pelvis from a bone-marrow graft. It's Raeburn 03 all right."

The medical guardian came over, peeling off surgical gloves and dropping them into a bag held out by one of her assistants. Her ice-blonde hair almost merged into the snowy backdrop – apart from the wide red stripe that extended from where Machiavelli's head should have been. "Clearly the victim was alive when he was decapitated because of the spurting," she said. "But he may well have been unconscious. He'd been badly tortured like the others."

I nodded. We'd logged knife wounds on the thighs and abdomen, but no organs had been cut out to make a cavity and no tape had been secreted.

"The deep rope burns on his wrists suggest he was kept tied up for some time," added the Ice Queen. "I'll know more about the state he was in prior to death once I've run tests on the stomach contents and so on. The same goes for the time of death. I'd tentatively put it at around four a.m." She turned to go.

"I'll see you in the mortuary when I've finished here," I said.

"I'll be waiting for you, citizen."

Davie and I watched her move off across the trampled snow, her shape still eye-catching in the protective white overalls that made the rest of us look like semi-inflated rubber dolls.

"To get back to business, gentlemen," Hamilton said irritably. "Did the killer leave any traces?"

"We're still looking," I replied. "The snow's an effective shroud."

"There are Land-Rover tracks leading down the road," Davie said. "They may well come from the guard vehicle used by Mach ... by Raeburn 03."

Hamilton looked like he was about to ask Davie about the dead man's nickname so I intervened. "And the guardswoman who found the body at ..." I checked my notes. "At six twenty-one a.m. saw no sign of anyone."

"What brought her up here?" Davie said.

"She told me she saw wheel tracks leading up from the main road and followed them," I replied. "She did well considering the amount of snow that had already come down on top of the tracks."

"Amazing, Dalrymple," Hamilton said with a snort. "A good word for the guard from you of all people."

I smiled at him. "I've got no problem with individual guard personnel. After all, I have a very good assistant." Davie looked about as comfortable as politicians in the old days used to when someone mentioned poverty in the Palace of Westminster. "Of course, that may have something to do with the training manuals your directorate uses, guardian."

Hamilton decided this was a good time to depart, his boots crunching into the snow as he headed for his Land-Rover.

"Thanks a lot," Davie said. "My career in the directorate just took a major nosedive."

"Because you're identified with a demoted auxiliary like me?" I laughed. "Tell the truth, guardsman. You love it when I have a go at the guardian."

"No, I don't." He started stamping his feet up and down and clapping his hands together. "Anyway, guard procedures work well enough, no matter which tosser wrote them. And what have you found out here that the rest of us haven't?"

He had a point there. Even if we had found plenty of traces, they wouldn't necessarily have got us any closer to discovering the killer's identity. Or motive. I watched as Machiavelli's headless corpse was wrapped up by Medical Directorate personnel. Beyond them the city's skyline stretched out in the light of morning which had been gradually increasing while we were on the scene. I ran my eyes along from the castle's turretted bulk and down the Royal Mile's line of spires and rooftops. In the east Arthur's Seat crouched like a somnolent lion, its flanks albino white apart from the vertical black scars of the crags. The Ice Queen's staff carried the shrouded body to a battered pre-Enlightenment ambulance that the mechanics in the Transport Directorate had miraculously managed to keep together. The city was going to pieces in all sorts of ways, and someone was taking individuals to pieces. But why had the murderer removed a senior auxiliary's head from this frozen hilltop in the middle of the long Edinburgh night?

I spent the day at the autopsy and checking out Raeburn 03's rooms in his barracks and in the castle. There were no traces of Electric Blues in his stomach and no bags full of the drug in his wardrobe. That would have been too easy. Machiavelli and his accommodation were as clean as a model would-be auxiliary's locker in the tented training camp in the Meadows. I did find copies of his namesake's works on his bedside table, but they're required reading for his ranks so I didn't even smile.

In the evening I attended the Council meeting. I thought there was a chance that the senior boyscout would be shaken up by Machiavelli's gruesome death but if he was, he wasn't showing it. What did get me going was his reluctance to accept that the latest murder was connected to the earlier two. Fair enough, there was no tape. But the other similarities convinced me that it was the same killer. Not for the first time I had the impression that I would make plenty of progress with the case if I tied the senior guardian to a chair and gave him the third degree. There was about as much chance of that happening as there used to be of insurance companies responding quickly to claims in pre-independence times. I considered trying to get Hamilton to give me access to his computer again so I could check out his deputy further, but that would have been a waste of time. What the senior guardian says goes. Unless you're an insubordinate schemer like I am. I went back to my flat to scheme.

"What do we do now?" Davie asked.

We were sitting in the Land-Rover in Gilmore Place under the light of the streetlamps. It was glowing dully on the grey sludge that the morning's snow had become.

"Good question," I said. "We haven't exactly got much to go on." There had been no reported sightings of Machiavelli's Land-Rover during the time he was missing, so we had no idea where he'd been before the killer caught up with him. The vehicle had been found in a back street near the King's Buildings with only Machiavelli's and other guard personnel prints on it. The sentry's log at the chemistry labs had no record of Hamilton's deputy being there. And there were no witnesses around Blackford Hill — everyone had been asleep in their uncomfortable beds.

"What did the medical guardian have to say in the Council meeting?"

I shrugged. "She just confirmed that the time of death was around four in the morning and that the cause of death was severing of the carotid arteries. The wounds on the thighs and abdomen and the rope marks on the wrists were similar to those of the previous victims."

Davie looked up from his notes. "And the weapon?"

"A sharp knife with a large blade, would you believe?"

"Great." He closed his notebook. "Like I said, what next?"

I opened the Land-Rover's door. "Ask me that tomorrow morning, guardsman."

"Don't do anything I wouldn't with that deserter woman, Quint," he said, leaning out of the window.

I looked back at him sternly. "As a loyal auxiliary, I know you wouldn't do anything at all with a deserter, my friend."

"That's exactly what I mean," he replied, slipping the vehicle into gear and pulling away.

What I called him was drowned out by the racket from an

exhaust pipe shot through with more holes than a 1990s election manifesto.

In the stairwell's feeble light I made out a hooded figure sitting on the floor across the landing from my front door. My heart seized up for a couple of seconds, then I remembered who else wore a long coat.

"Katharine?" I moved towards her. "What are you doing out here?"

She raised her head slowly. Her face was pale, the rings around her eyes so dark that for a moment I thought she'd gone three rounds with the city's female boxing champion. She opened her mouth, whispered a few words I didn't catch and pointed with an unsteady hand at my door.

I followed the direction of her arm. And froze as solid as the ground around the concrete post at the top of Blackford Hill that morning.

"Tell me it's not what I think it is," Katharine said faintly.

I pulled out my mobile. "Davie?" I shouted. "Get back here. Now!"

"Tell me, Quint," Katharine repeated insistently, her breath catching in her throat. "Tell me."

I stepped carefully over the flagstones and knelt down in front of the discoloured bag that had been hung from my doorknob. I could make out the stamp of the Supply Directorate. It looked like a flour sack but I knew very well it didn't contain that substance. More like a single, heavy object the shape and size of a football. On the floor beneath the sack were spatters of coagulated and partially frozen blood.

"Fucking hell," I said under my breath, then jerked backwards as the street door below slammed. The sound of nailed boots sprinting up the stairs filled my ears.

"What is it?" Davie yelled as he careered on to the landing, narrowly avoiding Katharine's legs.

I pointed at the sack. "What do you think's in there?"

His eyes widened. "Oh, no."

"Oh, yes." I pulled on rubber gloves then lifted the weighty bag off the handle and set it down gingerly. "Knife."

Davie handed me his service weapon. I took a deep breath and cut through the string round the top of the sack. Parted the flaps of material. And looked down on the severed head of Raeburn 03.

I heard Katharine move and waved to her to keep back.

Davie leaned forward, his lips drawn back in a rictus of disgust. "Bloody hell," he hissed. Then he clutched my arm. "What's that in his mouth, Quint?"

"Give me your torch."

I tilted the head over and shone the light at the senior auxiliary's swollen lips. The teeth were apart and a flat object covered in transparent plastic was protruding about two inches from them. I looked closer. There was no way I'd be able to open those hardened jaw muscles without an expanding clamp. That was a job for the medical guardian. But I already knew what was in there. The killer had provided another piece of music. And it had been personally delivered to me.

Chapter Sixteen

———◆◆◆◆———

As I knelt down beside Katharine, the staircase lights flashed three times.

"Come on, that's the curfew," I said. "Let's get you inside." I looked over my shoulder at Davie. "Call the medical guardian, will you? And don't let anyone inside the flat."

He nodded, glancing down at the sack and what had been inside it. "This should keep everyone occupied out here."

I pushed Katharine in gently as the lights went out and lit a couple of candles. She slumped down on the sofa, her chin resting on her breastbone. Her breathing was uneven. She looked like an explorer who'd given everything and was now resigned to the end.

"Hey," I said, sitting beside her and touching her hand. It was ice cold. "How long were you out there?"

She shivered but no words came.

I squeezed her chilled skin. "Tell me, Katharine. I need to have an idea of when the . . . the sack was put on my door."

She shivered again, this time more violently then laid into me. "You only care about your fucking investigation, don't you, Quint? It was the same the last time. I should have known better than to come back. I don't mean anything to you, do I?"

I left the question unanswered, feeling the sting of her words turn into a warm sensation deep inside. So it wasn't just concern about the drug formula that had brought her back to the city. Apparently she had some interest in me after all.

"I've only been back for about half an hour," she said, looking away from me. Then she let out a great sob.

I took a chance and put my arm round her shoulders. She resisted for a few seconds, then moved towards me.

"I . . . I couldn't touch it," she said, her voice quivering like a frightened child's. "I couldn't get to the door handle."

"It's all right, Katharine. I didn't exactly have a great time touching the sack myself."

She raised her head and looked at me in the candlelight. "No, there's more to it than that." Her eyes burned into mine. "You see, I knew what it was."

I stiffened involuntarily, suddenly gripped by the horrific thought that she had some involvement in the killing. "How, Katharine?" I asked, my voice unsteady.

"I've seen a man's head in a sack before," she said, her eyes still fixed on mine. Whatever else I read in them, it wasn't guilt. She'd been in bed with me all last night.

Outside on the stair there was the pounding of many feet. Davie knocked and stuck his head round the door. "They're here."

"I'll be out in a minute," I said, then turned back to Katharine. "When did you see a head before?" I got her to her feet and steered her towards the bedroom.

She sat down on the bed and wrapped her arms round herself. "The time I told you about with the . . . the Cavemen . . . the leader was a madman and he used to lay into his own men all the time." She glanced up at me, then looked down again. "Two of them started fighting over me . . . Christ, I don't know why . . . they all had plenty of time to do whatever they wanted . . . and the leader, he just waded in and grabbed one of the guys by the hair . . . he had this long bayonet and he . . . he hacked the head off . . . then he put it in a sack and made the other Caveman wear it round his neck . . ."

"Jesus, Katharine."

She looked up again and shrugged. "I was happy at the time, though I made sure I didn't show it. One animal less." Her voice broke. "But you don't forget things like that."

I sat down beside her. "No, you don't. You wouldn't be a normal human being if you could."

Katharine laughed bitterly. "No way am I a normal human being, Quint."

"You think anyone else in this room is?" I stood up. "Look, I'm going to have to get out there. Stay here. I'll be back."

She fell back on the bed like she'd been poleaxed. "I spend my life waiting for you, Quintilian Dalrymple."

As I pulled the covers over her, it struck me that there were plenty of less encouraging things she could have said.

"What do you think, guardian?"

The Ice Queen looked up from the mortuary table on which Machiavelli's head had been placed. Behind her the body had been laid out on another table. In the bright lights it looked like a scene from one of the television pathologist series that were so popular in pre-Enlightenment times. Except that hospital finances in the 1990s wouldn't have stretched to two tables for the parts of a single body.

"What do I think?" the medical guardian asked irritably. "I think there are better ways to spend an evening."

I was surprised. I'd always assumed that the Ice Queen was in the habit of shutting herself up in the morgue's refrigerated storeroom overnight.

"On the other hand," she continued, "I know that this head belongs to that body and I know that this is our killer's third victim."

That was more like it – competent analysis a robot would be proud of. "What about the tape?"

"Quite so." The guardian straightened up and beckoned to her assistant to remove the contents of the dead auxiliary's mouth.

I followed her over to the sink. "Any thoughts on the victim?"

The Ice Queen gave me a sidelong glance. "You surely don't expect me to speculate on matters outside my field, citizen."

I grinned. "They aren't exactly outside your field. Mach ... Raeburn 03 was very well connected in the Council. If he was a target, who's next among your colleagues?"

She shook the water from her hands and made a passable attempt at indifference. "I really don't see what you're getting at. The other victims had no such connections."

I handed her a paper towel. "Maybe the killer's working his way up the hierarchy. Ordinary citizen, auxiliary, senior auxiliary — next, a guardian?"

She dropped the towel in a bin, managing to imply that my line of thought should go with it. "I'd keep that idea to yourself, citizen," she said, looking across to the table. "Your tape's been ejected."

I almost fell over. Verbal humour from the Ice Queen was about as likely as spontaneous cheering during a debate on *The Republic*. I took the tape from her sidekick and headed for the machine.

Before I got there the guardian's mobile rang. She spoke briefly and signed off.

"An emergency Council meeting has been called, citizen. Your presence is required."

I started walking again. "What, now?"

"Now."

I slotted the cassette into the cassette player, desperate to hear what was on it. I wasn't disappointed.

Great music, but not exactly consistent with the other pieces. Then I got the message. And experienced meltdown.

The Council chamber. If the senior guardian was shocked by the discovery of Machiavelli's head, he wasn't showing it. That wasn't the case with his colleagues. They were standing around him with their mouths open like a group of statues in the middle of a fountain. Fortunately the water supply had been turned off.

"What is on the tape, citizen?" the chief boyscout asked after the medical guardian had confirmed that the head went with the body.

I went over to the machine and hit the play button. The exquisite sounds of Paul Kossoff's guitar washed over the guardians. I was pleased to see that at least one of them looked to be getting into the rhythm surreptitiously.

"And that was . . . ?" the senior guardian asked when the music finished.

"'Fire and Water' by Free," I replied. "There are those who say that Paul Rodgers had the finest voice of all British rock singers."

"Really?" said the senior guardian in a voice that sounded interested but I was bloody sure wasn't. Then his expression livened up a bit. "Did you say rock singers? The other pieces of music were blues, were they not?"

I shrugged. "Free were influenced by American rhythm and blues like a lot of bands in the late 1960s. Paul Rodgers sang plenty of blues standards in his time."

The senior guardian's eyes locked on to mine. "So why exactly was this song chosen, citizen?"

I was pretty sure he was squaring up to me, daring me to come out into the open. In fact, that was probably why he'd called this emergency meeting – to make sure I came up against him in front of the other guardians rather than in private. He knew I'd been digging in the Science and Energy Directorate archive and he knew I'd heard William McEwan mention the Bone Yard. But he didn't want to give me the chance to ask him any awkward questions. Like whether the song had anything to do with his directorate. I reckoned it did. "Fire and Water" sounded to me like a pretty unsubtle hint at nuclear reactors. The ones at Torness used to produce the equivalent of millions of fires and needed plenty of water in their cooling systems. But I needed something more solid before I could lay into him.

"The song's a typical lover's complaint," I said innocently. "The guy's having a hard time with a woman who blows hot and cold." I gave the Ice Queen a quick glance and was rewarded with her normal glacial gaze.

Lewis Hamilton was shaking his head in annoyance. "What's the point? Isn't there any connection with drugs?"

"Not one that's hit me so far," I replied. "I'll need to think about it."

The chief boyscout finally decided that staring me out was a waste of time. "I trust you'll let us know when your thought processes bear fruit. Another point, citizen. Why was the head left on your door?"

Good question. I'd been wondering about that myself. The hooded man had followed Roddie Aitken to my flat, so he probably knew about my involvement from the beginning. The fact that he'd risked being spotted with his unsavoury bundle suggested either that he had something against me or that he wanted to get me in even more deeply than I already was. Which might explain the choice of "Fire and Water" as the latest musical offering.

"Well, citizen?" the senior guardian asked, his saintly features beginning to tighten impatiently.

"Well what?" I replied with a lot more impatience. "There are plenty of people who know I'm running the case. The murderer may be one of them."

"Plenty of people?" Hamilton's forehead furrowed like it always did when he came to a conclusion that offends him. "The murders haven't been publicised, Dalrymple. The only people who know about them are auxiliaries."

I let a wide smile blossom across my face. He'd just buried his foot in the shit. I didn't have to add another word, so I turned on my heel and left the boyscouts to it.

*　　*　　*

I let myself into the flat as quietly as I could and lit a candle. Then I sat down at the kitchen table, feeling its flimsy legs bend as I leaned on it, and tried to do some serious thinking.

The main problem was that this wasn't simply a multiple murder investigation, which would have been bad enough. There were too many things going on at the margins – like William McEwan's death, the new drug formula, the nuclear physicist who ended up at Katharine's farm, the Bone Yard. How the hell did they all come together? Could it be that they were all part of an agenda that did not include a future for the Council? Then there was the music. I had the definite impression that someone was pulling my chain, someone who knew how much I was into the blues. The first two pieces obviously referred to the uppers they'd called Electric Blues, but now there was "Fire and Water", which I reckoned was a reference to the nuclear part of the puzzle. But why? What was I being told? That there was some connection between the decommissioned power station at Torness and the new drug?

The bedroom door opened and Katharine stepped into the dim light of the candle. She rubbed her eyes, but I wasn't paying much attention to them. The only garment on the lower half of her body was a pair of knickers. Her long legs looked in good condition – that's what you get if you work on a farm where there's no machinery. I had a look at them then went back to the black material covering her crotch. Presumably an itinerant salesman had called at her place since the Supply Directorate in Edinburgh provides only off-white underwear.

"What are you doing?" she asked. "It's the middle of the night."

"I am a creature of the night, my dear," I said in an attempt at a Lon Chaney accent.

"Creatures of the night who've got any sense spend it in bed." She headed back into the other room.

I pursued her after a diplomatic gap of a second or two. By

the time I got there she was already back under the covers. I threw my outer layer of clothing off and slid under the thin blankets, shivering. Katharine was facing the other way but she pushed her rump towards me. I moved into the warmth that her body was making. Her legs burned against me. I couldn't tell if she'd gone back to sleep or not, but she was very still. Then I remembered the Cavemen and what she'd been through. Suddenly I didn't feel like making any further moves. So I absorbed her heat and fell into a surprisingly dream-free sleep.

Which lasted until about six in the morning, when I woke up to the realisation that I was going to have to take some life-threatening decisions. I felt even worse when I saw that the other side of the bed was empty.

"Morning." Katharine appeared at the door with a mug of coffee. "I thought I heard sounds of the kraken waking."

"You're up early," I mumbled, trying to clear a way for words. My mouth was gummed up better than a glue-sniffer's nasal tubes in the days when you didn't need a guard permit for adhesive substances.

"The life of the soil," she said, sitting on the bed and drinking from her own mug. "You've almost run out of this stuff. You're going to have to get Davie to pilfer some more."

"Do you mind? I earned that from a client who works in one of the tourist restaurants." I gulped the coffee down. "Anyway, I've got other plans for him today."

"Have you now?" Katharine looked at me severely. "And what about me? If you think I'm going to stay in this shithole . . ."

"Before you insult my home any further, one of those plans involves you."

"I hope you don't expect me to dress up as a guardswoman and spend the day with him."

"Not exactly. I'm going to tell him to get you an 'ask no questions'."

"Can't I use yours?"

"I might need it. Until you get it, do you think you'll be able to bear staying in my shithole?"

She shrugged, then nodded non-committally. I wasn't convinced she'd stay but I had more worrying things on my mind. Like disturbing the senior guardian's breakfast.

"So you'll sort out Katharine's 'ask no questions' and take it to her at my place, Davie?"

He was staring out at the New Town's Georgian houses in the early morning gloom and looking pretty unimpressed. "What are you playing at, Quint? She a bloody deserter. If the public order guardian finds out . . ."

"Well, you'd better make sure he doesn't." I slapped him on the thigh. "Lighten up, pal. She's given me some pretty useful information."

"Oh, aye? And where's it got you? I haven't noticed any murderers sitting in the castle dungeons."

I nodded slowly, feeling the wet greyness of the walls in Forres Street seeping into me like a dose of pneumonia. "Someone's playing games with us, Davie, and I'm not having fun. Especially since I don't know the rules."

"The great Quintilian Dalrymple doesn't know the rules?" he asked ironically.

I wasn't in the mood, so I did what I normally do when he takes the piss – assaulted him verbally using numerous words banned by the Council. He enjoyed it almost as much as I did. Eventually we got back to business.

"Something else, Davie. Do you know anyone in the Fisheries Guard?" The sum total of the Council's navy is half a dozen converted trawlers that protect the city's fishing boats from the modern version of pirates – that is, headbangers from Fife armed with ex-British Army automatic rifles.

"Those lunatics? Aye, I went through auxiliary training with some of them." He looked at me seriously. "What's going on?

You don't want to mess with those guys. They're a bunch of total psychos."

"Who don't pay that much attention to what the guard command centre tells them to do?"

Davie shrugged. "They don't need to. The captains have their own patch to patrol. They have carte blanche to deal with raiders however they want. All they need the castle for is to approve their ammunition supplies."

That was what I wanted to hear.

Davie was peering at me suspiciously. "What are you up to, Quint?"

"Me? I'm going to have a chat with the senior guardian."

"Is he expecting you?" Davie asked as I got out of the Land-Rover.

"Put it this way — I don't think he'll exactly be surprised to see me." I stopped and turned back to him. "Keep your mobile on. If you don't hear from me in an hour, come knocking on his door."

"What?" The idea of making an unauthorised call on the chief boyscout looked about as palatable to him as a plate of citizen-issue black pudding.

I walked down the slippery road towards the checkpoint that restricts access to Moray Place. All the guardians have their residences in the circular street that surrounds a small park. The original members of the Enlightenment had thought it appropriate that Council members live together, despite the fact that they'd cut themselves off from their families. Then again, living together didn't have any dubious connotation as far as they were concerned. My parents were both guardians in the first Council and they'd given up living with each other in any significant way years before the last election.

I flashed my authorisation at the guardswoman by the heavy gate. She was young and hard, her fair hair drawn back tight in the regulation ponytail.

"Which guardian are you visiting, citizen?" she demanded, her hand on the telephone in the sentry box.

I didn't want to give the senior guardian any advance warning. "Your boss, the public order guardian," I said with a winning smile.

She was very far from returning that. "The guardian is at the castle, citizen."

"I don't think so. He told me to be here at seven thirty on the dot." I was pretty sure the guardswoman wouldn't risk annoying Hamilton by checking on his whereabouts.

His temper was to my advantage again. She took her hand away from the phone and raised the barrier. "It's number seven," she said.

"It's not the first time I've been here," I said as I walked past her. "Unfortunately."

Around the corner she couldn't see that I carried on past the residence that Hamilton rarely used and headed for the senior guardian's. In the gloom before sunrise the streetlights, which are kept on overnight here for security reasons, cast sparkling circles of pale orange on the icy paving stones. I was thinking about the infrequent visits I made to my mother here. The last was after the end of the murder case in 2020. I was usually torn to shreds by her and I had a nasty feeling her successor was about to keep up the tradition.

I knocked on the black door. It opened before I could blink. The male auxiliary on the other side must have been as close to it as the Three Graces' chiffon wraps are to their buttocks.

He ran an eye down me and made to close the door again.

"I'm Dalrymple," I said, sticking my authorisation in his face. "The senior guardian's expecting me." Well, that was a bit of a liberty, but there was some truth in it.

"I have no record of any appointment," the auxiliary said, stuttering slightly. He must have been in his late twenties but he suddenly looked like he needed a nappy. You often get that with members of his rank when the bureaucracy fouls up.

"Look," I said, pushing past him. "It's bloody freezing outside. I told you, the senior guardian will—"

"The senior guardian will do what, citizen Dalrymple?"

I looked up to see the man himself standing halfway down the ornate staircase, a file under his arm. Apparently I was too late to interrupt his breakfast. Then again, deities don't need to bother with food and drink.

"I need to talk to you," I said. At my side I felt the auxiliary flinch as I deliberately omitted his superior's title.

There was a pause as the chief boyscout considered my fate.

"Very well. I was just going into the library. Will you join me?"

I wasn't sure whether the excessive politeness was for the benefit of the auxiliary or whether he always behaved like this out of Council meetings. It knocked me off the course I'd decided on. But only for a few moments.

"You often came here when my predecessor was in office, I imagine," he said, sitting down in a leather armchair beside the open fire. The walls were lined with books as high as the ceiling. They seemed mainly to be scientific tomes. Over by the barred window was a row of gunmetal cabinets. I wondered if they contained the files that had been removed from the Science and Energy Directorate archive.

"Citizen?" the guardian said less politely.

"What? Oh, no, not often. I only ever came here on official business."

The guardian nodded, his ascetic face beneath the wispy beard expressing approval. "My predecessor took the regulations very seriously."

"Much more seriously than she took her family," I said, looking into the fire's dull flames. I could feel his eyes on me still.

"I'm sure she knew what she was doing." The guardian drummed his fingers lightly on the grey file on his knees. "What is it that you want, citizen?"

This was it. Crisis point. I'd tried unsuccessfully to work out a way to do this diplomatically. I had to go for broke. I linked eyes with him.

"What exactly is the Bone Yard, guardian?"

I was hoping I could provoke a reaction from him like William McEwan had done at the Hogmanay party. But there was nothing – no giveaway intake of breath, no sweat on the forehead, no trembling fingers. He looked at me with his saint's eyes, strong but strangely compassionate, then shook his head slowly.

"No."

I didn't understand and it must have been obvious because he said it again.

"No, citizen." Now his eyes were less compassionate, but they were still strong, as determined as the craziest guardsmen's, the ones who volunteer for permanent border duty.

That seemed to be it. He said nothing more.

"What do you mean 'no'?" I asked eventually.

"I mean no, you are not to pursue any line of enquiry about this subject." His thin body was taut now, coiled in the chair like a snake about to dart forward. "I mean no, the Bone Yard has nothing to do with the murders you are investigating. I mean no, you are not to discuss the subject with anyone else. Including any of my colleagues on the Council."

"But there are indications that the Electric Blues and this Bone Yard place are connected." I returned his stare but I couldn't do much to deflect it. Time for the killer blow. "And there are indications that your directorate is or has been involved."

Again, nothing. He was about as impervious to attack as a pre-Enlightenment prime minister with a massive majority.

"Indications are not evidence, citizen," he said imperiously. "And even the Council's justice system needs evidence."

For a split second I thought he was being ironical about the regime he ran, but the set of his mouth told me that was a vain hope.

"Let me put my cards on the table," I said, resorting to dishonesty – I had no intention of telling him about William McEwan's minute and what I'd found out about the nuclear physicist. "The song 'Fire and Water' that we found on, or rather in Raeburn 03 made me think of the old nuclear power station at Torness." I kept my eyes on him, but he was as solid as the Bass Rock. "I was wondering if it might be the Bone Yard I heard the former guardian talking to you about."

There was only the slightest relaxation in the chief boyscout's body, but it was enough to tell me that he thought he was off the hook.

"Really, citizen. William McEwan's mind had obviously begun to wander. I can assure you that the Bone Yard is in no way connected with Torness. You have my word on that." His eyes hardened again. "On the other hand, the murders do seem to have some connection with the drug." He stood up rapidly. "If you wish to remain in charge of the investigation, I suggest you make some progress with it quickly. And forget the Bone Yard."

"But what is it? What is the Bone Yard?" I asked desperately.

"Believe me, it is no concern of yours, citizen," he said firmly then pressed the bell for his secretary.

That was it. I was out of the house like a guardsman on a charge being marched to the latrines with a mop and bucket. But though I didn't show it to the auxiliaries and guard personnel who were assembling for the morning shift in Moray Place, I felt pretty pleased with myself. For one thing, I'd got out of the lion's den alive. For another, I was certain that the senior guardian's word was as worthless as a time-expired clothing voucher. It's never a good idea to tell an investigator that something isn't his concern.

Now I needed Davie's contacts in the Fisheries Guard more than ever.

Chapter Seventeen

———◇◇◇———

I got back to my place to find Davie and Katharine facing up to each other over the kitchen table. An "ask no questions" was lying between them on the surface. It looked like she'd given him a few choice suggestions as to where he could put it.

"Christ, am I glad to see you, Quint," Davie said, glowering at Katharine like a wee boy who's had his football nicked by a nimbler and much faster girl. "You can forget any chance of me working with this deserter."

"No, I can't." I looked at them as appealingly as I could. "I need all the help I can get."

"That's why I came back, Quint," Katharine said.

"Oh, aye?" Davie sneered. "You haven't done much so far."

I gave up and went over to my cassette player. After half a minute of Albert Collins playing "How Blue Can You Get" at full volume, they let go of each other's throats. I risked another few bars then shut the noise down.

"Got that out of your systems, children? Because I'm in deep shit in this investigation. And if my clothing's impregnated with the brown stuff, then so's yours." They seemed to be getting the message. Davie even looked mildly ashamed. Not Katharine – that would have been a major surprise. But at least she wasn't disagreeing.

"Would you mind telling me what's going on, Quint?" she asked, slipping the "ask no questions" into her pocket.

That seemed like a good idea. So I filled them in about where William McEwan's memo and the latest song were leading me. And about my meeting with the chief boyscout.

"I don't see what all this has got to do with the murders," Davie said, his face contorting as he tried to keep up.

"Neither do I. Call it a hunch, call it my genius for detective work . . ."

Katharine laughed. "Maybe we should go for the former so your head doesn't contract elephantiasis."

"Thank you." I smiled sourly at her.

Davie was still fighting it. "You just said the senior guardian told you to forget the Bone Yard and everything to do with his directorate. You're surely not planning on going up against him?"

I gestured to Katharine to keep quiet. I knew she'd have no problem working against the senior guardian. She probably kept herself awake at night longing for a chance like that. But Davie was different. He was a serving auxiliary, sworn to uphold the orders of the Council and its leader. And I needed his connections in the guard if I was to pull off what I had in mind.

"Look, Davie, I'm not saying the senior guardian's involved. But I don't believe his directorate has always been in the clear."

He rubbed his beard and looked at me dubiously. "What are you going to do then?"

"It doesn't work that way, guardsman. Either you're in or you're not. We haven't got time for committee meetings every half-hour."

He stared at me, glanced at Katharine then nodded slowly. "I suppose you'll need someone reliable to watch your back."

"That's a 'yes', is it?" I asked.

"Aye." He grinned and I grinned back. That's what I like about Davie. Once he's made a decision, he forgets all about the mental wrangling that led up to it.

"You're welcome to his back," said Katharine, unimpressed by this display of male bonding. "As far as I can remember, his front is much more interesting."

I didn't know whether to be encouraged by that or depressed by her uncertainty. It seemed best to move on.

"You asked what we're going to do." I looked at them both before I hit them with the big one. "We're going to take a trip to the old nuclear power station at Torness."

If the Supply Directorate hadn't rationed pins, you'd have heard several drop.

When we'd worked out as many angles as we could, Davie went off to talk to his friends in the Fisheries Guard. Katharine headed for the Central Library to pull a plan of the power station; I didn't want to risk going back to the Science and Energy Directorate archive. And I spent the rest of the day with Hamilton following up the few leads Machiavelli had left. Those didn't amount to much. There were several unauthorised absences from compulsory barracks philosophy debates, but he wasn't the first senior auxiliary to keep away from those. And we didn't find any traces of Electric Blues in the quarters of the few auxiliaries he was close to.

So the day passed, to be concluded by an uneventful Council meeting. I was keeping my head down in advance of the approaching night's programme of recreation and the senior guardian was so impressed by my reticence that he expressed only minor criticisms of my report. Not that I'd told him anything significant. The real fun was just about to begin.

We stopped at the retirement home on the way to Leith. I left the other two in the Land-Rover and ran up the stairs. The nurse made a half-hearted attempt to get in the way, but gave up when she saw it was me.

"Hello, old man," I said, gasping for breath as I went into

the room on the top floor. The only light was a pool of yellow on the desk.

My father looked up from his books. "Hello, failure. It's a bit late for social calls, isn't it?"

"Yes, well, it's not exactly a normal visit."

"I thought as much from the way you're twitching around," he said with a surprisingly lewd laugh. "Like a boy about to get his hands up a lassie's skirt for the first time." As he's got older, Hector has become increasingly scabrous. That's what you get from reading Juvenal all day.

"It's a bit more serious than that."

Hector stood up slowly from his chair and raised himself painfully to his full height. For all the aches and pains the old man suffers, he still has a commanding presence. "What exactly have you got yourself involved in, Quintilian?"

"Em, it's a bit sensitive."

My father's eyes flashed. "Are you going to tell me or not?" he demanded.

I smiled. "No, I'm not." I handed him a brown envelope.

"What's this? Pocket money like those arsehole MPs used to take in the old days?"

"What would you do with pocket money? You've got all the dirty books in Latin you need." I heard a single blast from the Land-Rover's horn. It was time to stop messing around. "Look, Hector, we're doing something a bit risky. It's all written down in there. Don't open it unless . . . well, unless I don't show up again."

His expression was grave now. "That bad?"

I nodded. "And make sure you keep it somewhere secure. If it comes to the worst, your guess is as good as mine as to what you do with it."

"I'll think of something." He looked at me with a mixture of tenderness and annoyance. "You'll never learn, will you?"

I laughed. "On the contrary. I made sure I learned everything you taught me."

He shook his head. "I never taught you to be so headstrong, laddie."

I turned to go. "Oh, yes, you did."

"Quintilian?"

I glanced back at the tall figure. The lower part was out of the circle of light and he looked like a ghost whose nether parts had been removed. In his case, probably by my mother.

"This has to do with what Willie McEwan was saying, hasn't it?" he said slowly.

"Aye, it does."

"Good for you, lad." His voice was suddenly faint.

I left before the scene got too heavy.

"They'll be waiting for us in the docks," Davie said as I got back into the Land-Rover.

"Sorry."

Katharine looked at me in the dull light from the dashboard. "Are you all right, Quint?"

"Of course. Nothing I like better than breaking every regulation in the book as well as several that have never even occurred to the Council."

"Boasting again," muttered Davie.

We were lucky with the weather. Well, as lucky as you can expect to be in the perfect city in January. At least the sky had clouded over and the night was murky enough to give us the illusion that our activities were going ahead in private. The reality is that there are informers all over the place, though the Fisheries Guard base in the docks is probably as secure as anywhere. The fact that it was cold enough to emasculate a king penguin was in our favour too, but you'd have had a job convincing me of that as I jumped out of the Land-Rover and kissed goodbye to the circulation in my feet.

Leith began to get trendy around the time I was born in the 1980s, its old warehouses and merchants' offices metamorphosing into duplex apartments and wine bars for bankers and the like. There are none of them left now, just good citizens working in the Labour Directorate's facilities. I've always hated the place. Our family dentist lived and practised down here. He spent most of my childhood practising on me and never seemed to get any better. The dank streets outside the port area were quiet, the lights off as it was past curfew time. Leith is about as far as you can get from the tourist area and its inhabitants were all supposed to be tucked up in bed with a cup of what the Supply Directorate, with its vivid imagination, calls cocoa. A foghorn droned lazily as we waited for the gate to be opened, its melancholy sound sending a slow shiver up my spine.

"What's the matter?" Katharine asked. "Having second thoughts?"

"Two hundred and second more like."

Then there was movement ahead of us. The gate swung back and a beaten-up guard vehicle which bore a vague resemblance to a Transit van backed towards us at speed.

A burly guardsman, wearing – I'm not kidding – an eyepatch, stuck his head out. "Follow me!" he yelled, then set off like there was a time bomb in his cargo space. The fact that the head I glimpsed was completely bald and had a deep dent on the crown did nothing to settle my nerves.

"Do you know him?" I asked Davie, who was struggling to keep the Transit's single tail light in view.

"Aye, that's Harry – Jamieson 369. He's a complete nutter."

"What a surprise."

"You know what happened to his head?" Davie looked away from the narrow road across a swingbridge and grinned.

"Eyes front, guardsman," I said, holding on to the bottom of my seat. Katharine couldn't have looked less bothered if she'd tried.

"A couple of headbangers on a raiding ship had a go with crowbars."

"I suppose he didn't even notice."

Davie laughed. "How did you guess?"

We finally caught up with the other guard vehicle. Near the mouth of the old Imperial Dock – now called the Enlightenment Dock, of course – I made out a hulk alongside which must have been raised from the seabed very recently. Then I realised that guard personnel were carrying stores on board down a narrow gangway.

"Jesus, we're not going out in that, are we?" I asked, pointing my open mouth in Davie's direction.

"What did you expect?" he answered, putting his shoulder to the driver's door. "This is the Fisheries Guard, not the High Seas Fleet."

Katharine and I followed him out.

"Evening, Davie." The bald guardsman called Harry was standing on the damp dockside. He was wearing filthy oil-stained overalls. "These'll be your pals. No." He raised a hefty, blackened hand. "I don't want to see any ID." He grinned broadly. "That way, when you fall overboard, I'm in the clear."

"Very funny," I said. "Where's the captain?"

This time he laughed out loud. A bull with a hard-on would have bellowed more decorously. "Captain? Our magnificent vessels haven't got room for wankers standing on the bridge telling the crew what to do." He leaned towards me and I made the disturbing discovery that the stoved-in area on the top of his skull was pulsing like it had its own heart.

"But if you're looking for the guy in charge, that's me."

I commented on that under my breath, making sure my lips didn't move. Davie and Katharine were already walking the plank down to the rotting ex-trawler's deck.

"After you," said the skipper.

I set off, feeling my boots slip on the gangway and trying to remember when I'd last been on a boat.

"Down into the bowels," dirty Harry yelled, pushing me towards a door beneath the wheelhouse. Apart from a faded maroon heart painted on the superstructure, the ship would have had no problem masquerading as a raider.

"Right," the guardsman said, pulling out a bottle of barracks whisky and gulping from it before offering it round. "It just so happens that this vessel's going on routine patrol in eastern waters tonight." He looked at our faces one by one, holding his gaze on mine. "Eastern waters between Dunbar and Cove. Any good?"

I nodded. That covered the area of the power station.

"But you'll need to understand one thing," the bald man said, his face cracking into a grin again. "My business is beating a thousand kinds of shite out of fish thieves. That takes priority over your wee outing. They aren't very nice people, pirates, so if you're not into violence, you'd better keep your heads down."

"What makes you think I'm not into violence?" Katharine asked, taking hold of a fish knife from a rack on the wall.

Harry laughed like a kid who's come across the key to his father's booze cabinet. "My kind of woman," he boomed.

Maybe it was just me, but I had a bad feeling about the way the cruise was starting off.

We had moved out into the firth, six deck crew members taking positions at the vessel's bow and stern. They were all carrying light machine-guns. Fisheries Guard personnel are among the few who get their hands on the Council's small store of high-quality firearms. Officially guns were banned after the last of the drugs gangs were dealt with seven years back, but truncheons and auxiliary knives aren't much good against pirate ships. Until you board them, at least. I reckoned Harry and his crew had done that often enough over the years.

After we cleared the dock, Katharine and Davie had crashed out. I went up to the cramped wheelhouse and watched the bald man at work. He swung the wheel with the natural seaman's easy mastery, his mouth set in a solid smile suggesting he lived in hope that raiders would appear as soon as possible. He acknowledged my presence with an unconcerned nod but didn't waste his breath on talking. Eventually I decided to give it a go.

"Your people don't seem to give a shit about us or what we're doing on board, guardsman."

"What makes you think I do?" He grinned humourlessly. "Citizen." He managed to imbue that word with all the guardsman's loathing of ordinary citizens who get themselves involved in auxiliary business. I hadn't put him down as a bigot. A psychopath, yes.

"I was one of you lot once," I said, trying to impress him. "My barracks number was—"

"I know who you were." He leered at me in the feeble light from the navigation instruments, no trace of even a hard man's smile on his face now. "You were the fuckhead who got a lot of my mates killed in the drugs wars."

That was one way of looking at it. I decided to move the conversation back towards its original direction.

"Your people, they will keep quiet about this, won't they?"

Nice one, Quint. Judging by the way the skin on his scalp had gone all tense, I'd managed to insult him and his beloved crew.

"My people always keep quiet," he replied after a long pause. "Citizen."

I'd completely screwed up on the diplomacy front so I reckoned I had nothing to lose. "Like they've kept quiet about what happened at Torness a couple of years back?"

Now things got very subdued in the wheelhouse. The trawler's engine ploughed away beneath us and the waves belted into the bow, fortunately not too heavily. I looked ahead and saw nothing, not a single light. Or anything else. I hoped my companion knew where he was going.

"So that's what this is all about," the guardsman said eventually. "I thought as much." Then he clammed up again. This was like having a conversation with Rip van Winkle – as soon as it got interesting, decades of nothing.

"Were you out in eastern waters that night?" I asked,

trying very hard to pretend I knew what had happened at the power station.

"Out in eastern waters," he repeated. "That would be a good title for a book, eh? 'Out in eastern waters.' I like it."

"Great, why don't you use it for your memoirs?" I said, choking on my impatience. "So were you? Out in eastern waters?"

"Sure we were," he said, suddenly looking at me seriously. "I suppose you'll be wanting to hear the story."

Do the bears in what remains of Edinburgh zoo shit in the shrubberies?

So the bald man with the eyepatch and the dented head told me what he'd seen. End of wisecracks for a bit.

"I don't know why I'm letting you in on this. Still, Davie told me you're okay and I owe him one. That lunatic saved my life on the border when I was on my first tour. It'll be hours before we get there even if the pirates don't distract us and, now I think of it, I could do with telling someone the story. We were warned that we'd have a lifetime of shovelling coal if we ever opened our mouths and we haven't. But it isn't right. It festers inside you like something a surgeon should have dealings with."

"December 2019," I said.

"Aye. The fifth." Harry shook his head then spat out of the open side window. "It's not a date I can see myself ever forgetting. It was a night like this. Heavy cloud and no chance of making out the campfires on the hills over in Fife. I was pissed off. I wanted to practise my celestial navigation." He paused and reached for the bottle of barracks malt he had near the wheel. "That's why so few people had any idea about the explosions."

"Explosions?" I said, my gut going leaden.

"That's right, citizen. The fuckers had been messing about with the reactors, from what I could gather on the emergency channel. We were about five miles offshore when it started. Christ, the flashes were bright for all the cloud. The power station buildings suddenly looked like they were ten feet away."

"What did you do?"

"What do you think we fucking did?" He turned on me and I could see the rhythmic pulsing in his damaged skull. "I may look like a headcase, but I'm still an auxiliary. We went in to pick up the injured."

"What about . . . weren't you worried about the fallout?"

"I never even gave it a thought, pal." He glared at me again. "You did say you used to be an auxiliary, didn't you? We look after our own, remember?"

An image of Caro lying on the floor in the barn during the attack I planned came up in front of me, then disappeared into the murk that was all round the boat.

"What's the matter, citizen? Don't you want to know what we found?" the bald man asked, a dead smile plastered across his face. "Well, I'm telling you what we found even if you've lost the stomach for it." He gulped whisky again. "Fuck all is what we found. As soon as I radioed in my position I was ordered to return to base. Just like that. No discussion, no argument. Goodnight, Torness." He laughed bitterly. "Course, it didn't end there. A squad of special guards was waiting for us in Leith. We were confined to the ship until senior auxiliaries from the Science and Energy Directorate arrived and told us to zip our lips together about the firework show or else."

"One of those auxiliaries is now the senior guardian, isn't he?"

"I think I'll give that question the body swerve." He laughed, this time with a trace of humour. "In fact, I think I've told you all I'm going to, citizen."

I nodded slowly. He'd already said enough to make this freezing cruise worth while. "Thanks, Harry," I said, taking the bottle from his thick-fingered hand. "I wish you'd call me Quint."

The bald man glanced at me with his single eye. "And I wish I had the nerve to sail this bloody boat right across the North Sea. To hell with the fucking Council." He grabbed the bottle back and grinned malevolently. "And to hell with you, citizen Quint."

At least he'd managed to say my name.

After I swallowed some more whisky to help me get over the shock of hearing a serving auxiliary badmouth his lords and masters, I went down to the cramped cabin over the engine compartment and passed out with my head next to Davie's on the table. I woke to the smell of good-quality coffee. No doubt it had been looted from a raiding ship.

"It's dawn," Katharine said, handing me a metal mug so battered it could have come from Schliemann's excavations at Troy. "We're lying a couple of miles off the power station. The big man wants to know what we're doing next." She smiled faintly. "And so do I."

"Ah." I ran my hand through my hair and considered what Harry had told me about Torness. "My plans are in the process of being changed."

She moved away haughtily. "I'm sure you'll let me know when you've got them straight."

"No, I mean . . . oh, for Christ's sake, sit down, Katharine." I nudged Davie and was greeted with his version of a grizzly on the morning hibernation ends. "Time for a wee chat." I took a gulp of coffee and filled the pair of them in. By the time I finished, neither of them looked very happy.

"Are you sure about this?" Davie asked dubiously. "I never heard any rumours about explosions. If they were that big, wouldn't people in the city have seen or heard something?"

"It's a long way, Davie, and there was cloud cover. Anyway, if you don't believe me, ask your mate with the Grand Canyon in his skull." I turned to Katharine, wondering how many fearful thoughts had just passed through her mind. "Your farm's not many miles inland from Torness, is it?" I said softly.

She nodded, her face registering confusion rather than panic. "I wasn't there then, of course. But none of the others ever mentioned it."

I was trying to work out a way to broach the next difficult topic but Davie steamed in ahead of me.

"Any sheep with two heads?"

Katharine was obviously even further ahead than that. "No," she replied calmly. "And no unexplained illnesses or deaths either. Human or animal."

Feet pounded down the steps.

"Oh, you've finally woken up, have you?" Harry shook his head disapprovingly at Davie.

"You, being a member of the superior race, don't need to sleep, I suppose?" I said.

"That'll be right." Harry let out one of his roaring laughs. "So, have you changed your mind about going ashore for a picnic by the sarcophagus, citizen Quint?"

I felt Katharine and Davie's eyes on me.

"Doesn't sound like a particularly good idea after all," I said.

The bald man laughed again. "You got that right, pal. I wouldn't have let you go anyway. What I can do is take us in to about half a mile range so you can look at the place through binoculars. You're in luck. The cloud's lifting and the pirates must all be stoned. The sea's as empty as a foreigner's wallet after the Tourism Directorate has finished with it."

He thundered back up to the wheelhouse, leaving us to our thoughts. Mine would have done serious damage to a Geiger counter.

Grey, freezing morning that stung my eyes and laid waste to my circulation a couple of minutes after I went up on deck. Straight ahead of us stood the great rectangular block of the power station, stark and incongruous against the snow-covered fields behind. I looked through the binoculars Harry had handed me. The concrete end walls were heavily discoloured but between them bright yellow sheeting covered the entire extent of the central façade.

"Not much sign of damage," Davie muttered.

"Obviously they had to cover it up," Katharine said. "People in the tourist planes would soon have noticed if the place had blown up."

I nodded. "They must have rerouted them inland until they fixed the sheeting. But still . . ." I lowered the bins and rubbed my chin. "If there had been any serious radiation leak, monitors abroad would have picked it up. Not every country in Europe's as chaotic as this island."

Katharine moved nearer, running her lower arms along the rusty deckrail. "What are you getting at, Quint?"

I shrugged. "Maybe it was very localised. Maybe the reactor core wasn't affected."

Davie stood up straight and breathed in deeply, then thought better of it. "Christ, is the air safe around here?"

"I've been in this area dozens of times since the fireworks," Harry shouted from above, then bellowed out a laugh. "Do I look any the worse for it?"

Katharine and I exchanged glances.

"I'm not going any closer though," the big man continued. "So make the most of it."

We did. I scanned the high wire fencing. Yellow signs with the nuclear symbol had been hung every few yards. The fencing extended all the way along the pier which had given the only access to the power station. The Edinburgh land border is miles away and the technicians had to come by boat in the early years of the Enlightenment.

"Quint, what's that?" Katharine had grabbed my arm hard. "Over there by the gate."

I looked through the bins again. Surely not. The words I'd first heard William McEwan use to the senior guardian leaped up like one of the traps laid by the Viet Cong to skewer foot-soldiers in the jungle. It looked like Torness really was the Bone Yard. The unmistakable components of a human skeleton, completely bare of all remnants of flesh and clothing and splayed out in the shape of a St Andrew's cross, were clinging to the densely strung wire.

On the way back to Leith, Harry told us he reckoned the skeleton had been put there to scare dissidents or any other interested parties away from the power station. Maybe they were meant to think the fence was electrified, though there hadn't been much juice coming out of that edifice recently. The Science and Energy Directorate had apparently deserted the place completely. Left it and whatever nuclear nastiness was in it to the east wind and the fauna of what used to be East Lothian.

It was nearly dark by the time Harry navigated his pride and joy back into the Enlightenment Dock. I decided against reminding him to keep quiet about our trip.

"Good luck to you, Davie," he said as we started slithering up the frozen gangplank. "And to you, hard woman. Pity we didn't get the chance to see you fight." He let out a restrained roar. "I'm not wishing you luck, citizen Quint. You're way, way beyond the realms of luck."

I raised a finger to the daft bugger. He was right though. Even if I'd found the Bone Yard, I hadn't got anything to use against the senior guardian. Let alone the madman who'd been practising his butchery skills in the city.

"What are we going to do now?" Katharine asked as we got into the Land-Rover.

"Aye, what next, Quint?" said Davie.

"Stop ganging up on me, will you?" I yelled, burying my hands in my pockets and sinking my chin down on to the jacket that had done such a bad job of keeping the sea air out. I'd suddenly found myself thinking of Roddie Aitken. That was making me feel as blue as Mississippi Fred McDowall when he sang "Standing at the Burial Ground".

Chapter Eighteen

We headed down Ferry Road towards Trinity. I wanted to call in at the retirement home to let my old man know I was all right. On the way I turned my mobile back on. Less than a minute passed before Hamilton was on my case.

"Dalrymple? Where the hell have you been?" His voice was tense.

"What's happened?" My heart missed a beat as the idea that the killer had struck again hit me.

"Nothing's happened, man." That couldn't be right. He sounded like a ferret had crawled into his auxiliary-issue long johns. "I've been ringing your number every half-hour and getting unobtainable."

"Oh." I tried to play it cool. "I've been checking out various archives. I forgot I'd turned it off."

"And where's Hume 253? I haven't been able to raise him either. What have you been doing with that 'ask no questions' I issued? I suppose you think I was born yesterday." With his heavy beard, he'd have been a big draw in the infirmary's neo-natal ward. "Anyway, what have you got to report at tonight's Council meeting?"

That was a good question. I turned the question back on him while I scrabbled around for something to fob his colleagues off with. Unfortunately he had even less than I did. It was going to be a fun evening.

* * *

We were in luck. The senior guardian was preoccupied – I'd like to have known what with – and let Hamilton and me off the hook.

I went back to the flat and found Katharine asleep on the sofa. Her face wasn't tense like it was when she was awake and she looked much younger. I put my hand out and, without touching her, moved it slowly downwards above her short hair and the contours of her cheek and jaw. I had a sudden flash of her as she straddled me in my armchair a couple of years ago, her neck taut as she simultaneously forced herself down on me and bent her upper body back. The fact that I hadn't attended a sex session for nearly a fortnight suddenly became very apparent.

Then I heard someone begin to pound up the stair in archetypal guard fashion. So did Katharine. She was instantly awake, sitting up and at the ready. Her face was lined again, the moment of repose gone.

Davie shouldered open the door, carrying a large movable feast in both hands. "Guess what I've got here," he said, looking pleased with himself.

"Rations stolen from ordinary citizens?" Katharine asked with a sour smile.

"Shut up, will you?" I hissed, stuffing a tape of Council-approved folk music into my machine. I didn't want anyone to hear what we were about to discuss, let alone notice that I'd acquired a non-paying lodger who featured on the Deserters Register.

"You don't have to have any of it if your heavy-duty moral scruples get in the way," Davie said to Katharine.

That was it. I'd had it with them. "You're a pair of tossers," I shouted. "We've got our noses in all sorts of forbidden places and all you two can do is take the piss out of each other." I gave them the sulphuric acid glare I inherited from my mother. I've practised it a lot less than she did but it seemed to get through to them. "I'm not joking. Either give me some decent back-up or fuck off out the door."

They both looked pretty sheepish.

"So what have you got there, Davie?" I asked after a strained silence.

"Em, right, there's a pot of barracks stew, with decent meat in it "—he poked around in the dark brown contents of a cast-iron pan—" well, semi-decent meat."

Katharine's nose twitched dubiously.

"And wholemeal bread," Davie continued, "barracks beer, apple crumble and — wait for it — real cream."

"Real cream?" Katharine leaned forward, an interested expression on her face. "Where did you get that?"

"What's it to you?" Davie looked affronted. "You reckon I took this—"

"You remember where the door is, don't you, guardsman?" I said, burning him with the acid look again.

He glanced over his shoulder then sat down at the table. "It came from the guard kitchens," he muttered. "If it's any business of—"

"I'm not joking, Davie," I yelled.

We settled down to eat to the strains of bagpipes and fiddles. It could have been worse. At least there weren't any accordions.

"Right, team, we have to talk." I pushed my plate away and emptied my glass of barracks heavy.

Katharine took the armchair, leaving Davie to join me on the sofa. "It's about time we sorted things out, Quint," she said. "I haven't got a clue what we're doing and I don't think you have either."

"Thank you for that constructive opening."

"I'd have to go along with her there, Quint," Davie said, keeping his eyes off me.

"You as well? Now I really know who my friends are." I pulled out my notepad and started flicking through the pages. That didn't get me much further. "Okay. Review of where we stand. The cruise on your pal Harry's floating shipwreck wasn't a complete waste of time."

"That is reassuring," Katharine said.

It was her turn for the vitriolic look. "We've got confirmation that something disastrous happened at the power station near the end of 2019."

"Aye, but what's that got to do with these murders?" Davie said, opening his arms wide like a drunken tourist who's forgotten where his hotel is.

"That's the difficult bit." I drew a square on my pad, wrote "Torness" in it then sketched in the coastline. "How far's your farm from the power station again, Katharine?"

"About ten miles, I suppose. We never go that way because of the—"

"Because of the gangs," I interrupted. "In particular, because of the gang led by the headcase known as the Screecher?"

She nodded. "So?"

"So maybe the Screecher got nosy and took a trip over the fence."

"In which case, either they were his bones on the wire," said Davie, "or he glows in the dark."

"He might have sent one of his minions in," I said.

Katharine leaned forward and nodded her head. "He had a nuclear physicist in his gang, remember? Maybe the Screecher found him at the power station."

"Maybe," I said. "And maybe the Screecher used what he learned from him to put the squeeze on someone in the Council. By threatening to spread the word about the explosions."

Davie's hand came down hard on my knee. "Don't piss about, Quint. We all know the senior guardian's the most likely person to have had the squeeze put on him – Science and Energy is his directorate. Are you sure about this?"

"No," I said with a hollow laugh. "Except there are those files missing from the directorate archive. The ones you know who's probably got in his private library."

Katharine sat back, shaking her head. "Even if you sneaked a look at them, they wouldn't necessarily show any link to what's been going on in the last couple of months."

"True enough." I flicked through the pages again. This time I felt a couple of twinges. The first had to do with the toxicologist, but I let that one go for the moment. The second was much more pressing. Roddie Aitken had just made another appearance in my thoughts.

"What have you come up with?" Davie asked.

"Is it that obvious?"

"You're smirking like a kid who's got off border duty by playing with himself during his assessment."

Katharine yawned. "I'd have thought that would get him a permanent transfer into the City Guard."

"Children," I said, glaring them into submission. "Answer me this. As outlined in the manual I wrote for the directorate, what's the basic rule of investigating practice?"

Davie scratched his beard. "Always triangulate data?" he suggested without much confidence.

"Wrong, guardsman," Katharine said with a superior smile. "Always compare initial evidence and statements with subsequent data." It was a long time since she'd done her auxiliary training, but what I wrote in the *Public Order in Practice* manual seemed to have stuck.

"Very good. Unfortunately I haven't been following my own instructions."

"Meaning what?" Davie demanded, pissed off that a demoted auxiliary who was also a deserter had shown him up.

"Meaning that, in all this chaos, we've forgotten about the first victim."

Now Katharine was looking puzzled. "The young man? I assumed he had something to do with the Electric Blues."

I shook my head. "We never found any evidence of that. And he definitely didn't strike me as a drug trafficker."

Davie got up and went back to the table. What was left of the apple crumble did a disappearing act. "Me neither," he mumbled with his mouth full.

"What are you saying, Quint?" Katharine asked.

"I'm saying that tomorrow morning we hit the Delivery Department files and find out his movements over the last few weeks."

"But I've been through those files," Davie said.

"Yes, but we weren't particularly interested in where he'd been delivering, were we? Maybe he went somewhere that's linked with the drugs. Like, for instance, where they're produced."

He nodded, not looking too convinced. Soon afterwards he went back to his billet. Katharine went to bed and didn't move when I lay down on the other side. I left a space between us which she didn't move into. I didn't feel confident enough to stake a claim. As I drifted off, thankful at least that the bed wasn't moving up and down like dirty Harry's ship of fools, I remembered the oath I'd sworn. I'd been ignoring Roddie, but I was back on track now. I didn't care about the other two victims much, though even corrupt auxiliaries don't deserve to die the way they did. But I cared about Roddie and his killer was going to find that out. I slept surprisingly well that night.

The next morning was warmer and the snow was gone from the streets. It had turned into huge amounts of water that the works buses were spraying over citizens on the pavements. Their faces were even more sullen than they usually are first thing.

Davie steered the Land-Rover down to the Supply Directorate depot off the Canongate. In pre-Enlightenment times it had been part of Waverley station, but the Council blocked the railway lines leading in and out of the city soon after independence. That was part of their policy of securing the borders and getting a grip on the drugs gangs. The fact that it enabled them to control everything that went on in the city was purely incidental, of course.

The depot is gigantic, nearly half a mile long. The sentry at the gate took one look at the guard vehicle and waved us through without checking our IDs, which meant that Katharine didn't have to show her "ask no questions". I'd wondered about bringing her along – if we ran into Hamilton and he recognised her, we'd be in serious shit – but on balance it seemed safer to keep an eye on her. God knows what she'd have got up to on her own.

We drove into the great covered area. Rows of packing cases and piles of stores stretched away into the distance. In the early days the Council decided to concentrate all the city's supplies in one heavily guarded location to discourage thieving. That had the additional advantage of providing huge numbers of jobs for citizens involved in recording, packing and delivering the stuff. In fact, that may have been the only advantage because there's probably more pilfering and black-market-controlled stealing now than there ever was before.

Davie drove down the central passage towards the office section. We passed great heaps of potatoes and turnips, the bitter-sweet stink from the latter invading the Land-Rover; then boxes full of cheap clothes run up in the Council's sweatshops, not that the guardians refer to them as such; and finally, shelves full of the tattered books that are bought in on the cheap from other cities' ransacked libraries. Personnel from the Information Directorate's Censorship Department were sorting through them, tossing the rejects into crates marked "For Burning". The Council gets more heat from books than it does from the nuclear power station at Torness. There must be some sort of moral in that.

Katharine was shaking her head. "There's enough food in here to keep the city going for years."

Davie nodded. "Aye, and this depot doesn't handle the meat. You should see how much of that they've got in the cold stores at Slateford."

That reminded me of the Bone Yard. Not long ago I thought it might have something to do with the slaughterhouses in that part of the city. Something about that idea still nagged at me.

"So why are Edinburgh citizens all so thin and hungry-looking?" Katharine was saying. "Why doesn't the Council increase the entitlement to food vouchers?"

Davie shrugged, looking away as he pulled into a parking space beside a Supply Directorate delivery van that was held together with wire.

"Don't forget the tourists," I said as I opened the door. "They get first bite at the cherry. And at the sirloin steak."

Davie slammed the door on his side. "Sirloin steak?" he asked. "What's that, then?"

The deliveries supervisor, a middle-aged woman with grey hair and the wan look of someone who's seen it all and isn't convinced it was worth the bother, greeted us without enthusiasm. But at least she was efficient.

"All the delivery documentation pertaining to Roderick Aitken was removed from the main archive after his death. I will have it sent up to the meeting room for you to inspect." She gave Davie a sceptical glance from behind the stacks of files on her desk. "I hope you get more out it than you did the last time you were here, Hume 253."

We went up grimy stairs to a room furnished with a table and chairs that wouldn't have found space in a junk shop in the old days. No one could accuse Supply Directorate staff of creaming off quality goods to brighten up their place of work. I looked out of dirty windows at the scene that stretched across the depot's endless concrete floor. Forklifts raced around like crazed dung beetles, loading and discharging, endlessly moving things from one location to another. Armies of staff paraded around with clipboards, checking deliveries off and distributing bits of paper. The system seemed to work but it didn't exactly make you rejoice in the regime. A single computer would have saved an awful lot of hassle. But then there'd be citizens hanging around with nothing to do and the Council couldn't have that.

A couple of porters arrived with our very own collection of delivery sheets, waybills, receipts and rosters. We settled down to the kind of job that archivists dream about. I had some fun but the others struggled. After an hour we compared notes.

"There doesn't seem to be any pattern to the goods he delivered over the last three months," Katharine said, pushing away the files she'd been working on. "New carpets to tourist hotels, fruit, vegetables and other supplies to food stores, beer to the citizens' bars. About the only thing he hasn't delivered is sex aids to the recreation centres."

"The old hands keep that job for themselves," Davie said with a grin.

"What about you?" I asked.

He pulled a face that suggested he'd been wasting his time too. "No pattern with the vehicles he's been driving either." I'd put him on to that in case there were any Roddie had been assigned frequently; we could then have looked for a secret compartment where drugs might have been stashed. "Transits, Renaults, some Polish contraptions I can't pronounce the name of. They even had him on a bicycle distributing styluses for the record players in the tourist clubs." He raised his shoulders. "Nothing regular."

"Which leaves me," I said, giving them a triumphant smile. "And I've got several goodies."

"Oh, aye?" Davie came round the table.

"What is it, Quint?" Katharine kept to her chair, but her voice betrayed her interest.

"What I've got is three places where he made more than six visits in the last month of his life, i.e. December. I haven't gone any further back yet. I reckon any lead will be recent rather than months in the past."

"I wish you'd told me that," Davie complained.

"Why do you think the frequency of visits is important?"

Katharine said, ignoring him. "Surely he could have gone only once or twice to the place we're after?"

"You're right, he could have. But let's hope he didn't. Otherwise we're going to be driving around the city for the rest of our lives."

She nodded. "Fair enough. So where are these three places?"

"Number one, the zoo."

"Animal feed," Katharine said, checking her notes.

"Yup. Number two, a sawmill near a village called Temple about ten miles south of the city."

"Pine slats, two by fours and dormitory partitions."

"Right again. And number three, Slaughterhouse Four at Slateford."

"Don't tell me," said Davie. "Sirloin steak."

Katharine actually laughed at that. "Among other things. So where do we go first?"

I knew where I wanted to go first. It was finally time to check out the city's meat production facilities.

"How are we going to manage this on our own?" Katharine asked as we came out of the depot.

"We aren't," I replied. "If we're going to have any chance of finding the laboratory that's been producing the Electric Blues, we're going to need expert help."

She thought for a moment then turned to me with a satisfied smile. "The toxicologist."

"Correct. Head for the King's Buildings, Davie."

He turned down St Mary's Street, glancing at me as he span the wheel. "Won't we need some back-up, Quint?"

"You mean, shouldn't we inform Hamilton?" I asked with a laugh.

He wasn't impressed and gave both of us the benefit of his guardsman's assault glare. "That as well. I seem to remember a lot of references in your handbook to keeping senior officers fully informed."

"True enough," I said. "But that handbook was written for serving auxiliaries, not demoted ones like me."

"And me," put in Katharine.

"Also, telling Hamilton and calling in more guard personnel to help with the operation will mean that what we're doing gets leaked within half an hour. I don't want that. Don't worry, Davie, I've got to report to the Council tonight. I just don't want to give any advance warning of this line of enquiry."

I braced myself as he slammed his foot on the brakes at the junction with the Cowgate. Five or six cattle galloped nervously towards the Grassmarket, the herdsmen in medieval costume being applauded by a small group of tourists who presumably had nothing better to do with their time. At least those cows had escaped the city's slaughterhouses – for the time being.

I left Katharine and Davie in the Land-Rover outside the labs and went to find the chief toxicologist. This time he wasn't listening to Robert Johnson in his private quarters, but was supervising a team of white-coated, masked, rubber-gloved chemists who were siphoning off a clear liquid with extreme caution.

The toxicologist saw me through the glass panel. I gathered from his energetic semaphore that he didn't want me to come any closer.

"Citizen Dalrymple," he said as he eventually emerged, pulling down his mask. "You caught me at a very delicate procedural juncture."

Classic senior auxiliary gibberish. "What is it you've got in there?" I asked.

He looked around to see that we were alone. "It's a new variant of the e. coli virus. We found it in some salami that a Danish tourist imported illegally."

"Jesus. Has anyone been infected by it?"

He shook his head. "The man himself was repatriated the day he arrived and no other samples of the meat have been found."

"Thank Christ for that."

The chemist laughed, the folds of flesh on his face wobbling alarmingly. "Don't worry. It happens all the time."

"Right," I said, not particularly reassured. "If things are under control here, can you spare me some time?" I told him about the search for the Electric Blues lab.

He looked intrigued, then his face fell. "Wait a minute, citizen. Does the Council know about this?"

I pulled out my authorisation. "As you can see, you're required to give me all the assistance I want."

"You aren't answering my question," he said, his jowls quivering.

"Look, the Council will be briefed about this tonight." I could see he was wavering. I considered putting him on the spot for his addiction to banned music, then I thought of a better way. "Have you lost any senior staff in the last six months or so, Lister 25?"

He looked at me in surprise. "It's funny you should mention that, citizen. I was going to call you after your last visit but it slipped my mind. Lister 436. She was an excellent toxicologist – I'd been grooming her to take over from my present deputy. Then she was suddenly transferred to the senior guardian's private office last ... let me see ... last November, it must have been. Yes, late last November. I haven't heard from her since." Then he looked at me again, his wrinkled skin turning an even sicklier yellow shade than normal. "Surely you don't think she's been involved in the production of that drug?"

I didn't think it was necessary to answer that question. "Are you coming to see if we can find the lab?"

The chemist already had his white coat off. "If I find that a student of mine's been producing a substance like that, there'll be serious trouble."

He may have looked like an elephant that's been on a crash diet, but I wasn't planning on getting in his way.

Slaughterhouse Four is one of the many parts of Edinburgh that the tourists don't see. At first glance it doesn't seem like a place of death, unless the wind happens to be blowing towards you from it. The main block is a large Edwardian building with high windows and saucer domes at the corners. In the field and yards in front of it doomed sheep and cattle give a rustic touch to the rundown urban surroundings of soot-blackened housing and potholed roads.

"Right, we're going to have to be quick," I said as Davie pulled up outside the checkpoint. "If there is something illicit going on here, whoever's involved will clear out as soon as they hear we're about the place." I looked at the toxicologist on the front seat beside me. "I'm not going to spell out to the facility supervisors what we're after. When they see you, they'll probably assume it's something to do with hygiene or infection control."

"Are we going to split up?" Katharine asked from behind.

I nodded. "You go with Davie. If you see anything that looks like a lab, call me. Lister 25 and I will check out the resident science officer first."

As we cleared the sentry post, a heavy drizzle started to fall, weighing down our clothes with an evil-smelling spray in the few seconds it took us to get inside the abbatoir. Instantly the mild bleating and lowing from the animals ouside was replaced by the rattle of the machinery on the killing line and a high-pitched shrieking that made my stomach flip.

As I heard the heavy steel door clang behind me, I suddenly wondered where the butcher of humans had been since he decapitated Machiavelli. He'd been quiet for too long. I was sure of one thing, though. He'd feel very much at home in Slaughterhouse Four.

Chapter Nineteen

I've been through a lot of post-mortems but they don't compare with Slaughterhouse Four. The most diligent serial killer would have to work weeks of overtime to get into the league of mayhem that's staged there every day. I'd consider turning vegetarian if the Supply Directorate could come up with alternative sources of protein, but soya and pulses don't exactly flourish in the city's farms.

The toxicologist and I put on protective overalls and walked up the killing line. The animals can't be stunned electrically because of the power shortages, so big men in blood-spattered clothing club them with round-ended iron bars. The petrified squealing is enough to make you lose yesterday's breakfast as well as today's. Then chains are lashed around rear ankles and the jerking carcasses are winched up. Slaughtermen with long-bladed knives wait for them down the line, yelling and joking to each other. You'd think they'd be disgusted by their work but people get used to anything. A spray of warm red liquid lashed across my chest, making me jerk backwards.

Lister 45 grabbed my sleeve and pointed to the right. There was a double door that had been secured with a heavy chain.

I indicated it to the auxiliary who'd been assigned to us. "What's in there?"

He put his mouth up to my ear and shouted above the din

from the conveyor belt. "The Halal line. For the Moslem tourists, you know? We're not allowed to go in from this side."

That sounded interesting. Even though the numbers of Moslem tourists has fallen recently because of the unrest in the Middle East, there are still a good few around. And the region does have a historical involvement in the drugs trade. Could there be a connection with the Electric Blues?

"Open it up," I said, beating the auxiliary's doubtful look down without having to pull out my authorisation.

He eventually managed to turn the key in the padlock and the door swung slowly open. The Halal line is in a poorly constructed extension to the main building, angled so it faces Mecca. There's no conveyor belt so the slaughtermen get very close to their victims. Pairs of bearded guys in bloody aprons were wrestling sheep to the floor and cutting their throats. In the background a Moslem clergyman was reciting from a book. All of them looked up and stared at us with undisguised hostility as we came in.

I walked past the holy man, who had rushed up and started to gesticulate wildly. There was a small room to the rear and I could see a couple of men in white coats through the glass door. They turned to me too, but they weren't aggressive, they were just proud of their work. They held their hands out to me as I shoved open the door. Each contained the glassy jelly of a sheep's eye.

"Thanks, but no thanks," I said, swallowing what had just arrived in my mouth.

The toxicologist came in, ran a practised eye around the place and shook his head. "We're wasting our time, citizen," he said. "Let's leave before these people get really annoyed."

We left the Moslems to it and rejoined the Enlightenment's atheist killing line. There isn't much to choose between them really. But as far as I'm concerned death isn't a religious matter – it's much more serious than that.

"Nothing," said Davie, pulling off his protective overalls. "We've been through the admin block, the packaging area and the coldstores. He shivered. "And they're bloody cold, I can tell you. There was no sign of anything like a lab."

Katharine nodded in agreement, gulping tea from one of the mugs that the supervisor had sent in to us. We were in what passes for a meeting room in Slaughterhouse Four. It must be one of the few rooms in the facility that doesn't have blood on the walls.

"Same here, I'm afraid," I said. "We did the sheep lines — ordinary and Halal — and the cattle." I'd discovered from the supervisor that pigs, poultry (including pigeons trapped at night in the city centre) and what are called "other sources of meat" (horses, donkeys and clapped-out camels and the like from the zoo) are processed in Slaughterhouses One to Three. But Roddie Aitken hadn't made many pick-ups or deliveries to those.

"Are you sure this is sensible, citizen?" Lister 25 asked, his wrinkled face partially hidden behind a mug. "I mean, if I were setting up a lab to produce illicit drugs, I wouldn't do so in a slaughterhouse."

I shrugged. "Maybe this was just a transit point. The Electric Blues might be made elsewhere then brought here for onward distribution." I looked round their pale faces and wondered how many of us would be stuffing our faces with meat that night. "And maybe I'm just following a lead up my own backside."

Davie turned up his nose. "In that case, I want a transfer back to the castle before you make me go the same way."

"Not yet, my friend." I headed for the door. "There are still two other locations to check, remember? Meanwhile, I've got to go and spin a yarn to the Council."

Outside it was pitch dark beyond the narrow ring of light by the slaughterhouse entrance. From the pens there came the sighing and coughing of invisible animals. They wouldn't be there for long. Like all the city's killing lines, Slaughterhouse Four works non-stop shifts. But the main beneficiaries aren't ordinary Edinburgh citizens. Our meat is rationed, while the tourists pay Third World prices for prime beef. That's the perfect city's version of equality.

Hamilton was waiting for me on the ground floor of the Assembly Hall. I'd deliberately timed my arrival to minimise his chances of picking my brains before the meeting.

"What the bloody hell have you been up to, Dalrymple?" he growled. "I heard a report that you've been poking around one of the slaughterhouses."

As I expected, it hadn't taken long for news of our activities to get back to him. "Don't worry," I said. "You'll hear all about it at the meeting."

"Did you find anything?" the guardian asked as we went up the stairs towards the Council chamber.

"Not a sausage," I said with a tight smile.

"What?" He followed me in, looking bewildered.

There was already a gaggle of guardians around the chief boyscout. He looked over their heads as I approached and watched me with a serene expression which didn't convince me for a moment.

"Well, citizen Dalrymple, have you anything to report?" he asked, an almost undetectable edge to his voice. "Anything at all?"

So that was the way he wanted it. "Yes, I have," I replied, smiling as he blinked involuntarily. I was sure he knew where I'd been, but it would be interesting to see how he reacted. I wasn't planning on telling him my line of thinking though. "We picked up a lead that linked Roddie Aitken with Slaughterhouse Four in Slateford."

"What was the nature of that lead, citizen?" The senior guardian was watching me as closely as I was watching him. The other guardians had stepped back a couple of paces to follow the duel.

"Supply Directorate records show that there were three locations that Roddie visited frequently. One was Slaughterhouse Four." No visible changes on the chief boyscout's face.

"Unfortunately, there was no sign of a lab capable of producing the Electric Blues."

"And what are the other two locations?" the senior guardian asked quietly. Too quietly, even by his standards. I reckoned there were knitting-needle teeth like a Moray eel's behind those saintly lips and I wasn't going to take any chances.

"The Three Graces club was one," I lied. "We've already taken that to pieces."

The chief boyscout kept after me. "And the other?" The tone of his voice rose a touch higher than the question required. I was sure he was desperate to know whether I was on to the lab.

I felt Hamilton's eyes on me. There was no option, but I felt a stab of guilt as I condemned him and a lot of his personnel to a wasted night. "The other?" I said, squeezing the moments for all they were worth. "The other is the City Distillery in Fountainbridge."

The skin on the senior guardian's face slackened just enough for me to know that he'd bought my dummy. So had Hamilton.

"The distillery?" he said incredulously. "It'll take us days to search that rabbit-warren, man."

It wouldn't, but he'd certainly be tied up long enough to give me the chance to check out the other places. I wasn't happy about messing him around, but I had to make sure the senior guardian knew nothing about where I was really heading until I had enough evidence to confront him.

"We'll get going as soon as the meeting's finished," I said, trying not to look too enthusiastic.

"The meeting has finished for you, citizen," said the chief boyscout, moving down the chamber with his flock of acolytes. "You are excused the rest of the proceedings as well, guardian."

Lewis Hamilton should have been embarrassed at being treated in that offhand way by someone so much younger, but as we walked out he was beaming more than a poor man who'd won the lottery in the days before the last British government rigged the draw in favour of cabinet members.

Obviously he hated meetings with the iron boyscouts as much as I did.

The next few hours needed careful planning. Before Hamilton and I went to the distillery with a couple of squads of guards, I called Davie and asked him to start checking out the zoo with the chief toxicologist. I also told Katharine to wait for me at my flat.

And then I pretended to be totally committed to the farce that I'd set up in the distillery. On the face of it, there was a reasonable chance that one of the city's two whisky-producing facilities concealed a drugs lab, given the presence of chemists and suitably equipped premises. In fact, it had occurred to me in the Council meeting that if the chief boyscout didn't have other things on his mind, he might have asked me why I'd visited the slaughterhouse before the potentially more suspicious distillery.

Hamilton and his white-overalled staff had great fun stomping around the ramshackle distillery. Thirty years ago it was a state-of-the-art plant, but during the Enlightenment it's been allowed to run down because of lack of funds. There's never been any question of cutting back whisky supplies to citizens and auxiliaries though, despite the guardians' own abstinence. Whisky and beer are the legalised opiates in their utopia.

After a couple of hours, I decided to leave Lewis to it. "There are some things here I want to check in the archives," I said, waving a sheaf of papers I'd abstracted from the facility supervisor's files.

"You can't go now, Dalrymple," the guardian said, looking round from a steel cabinet in the one of the labs. The distillery chemist was sitting in the corner with his head in his hands as one of Lister 25's staff painstakingly disassembled a maze of glass tubes, balloons and beakers. "We're making excellent progress."

Except you're going to find even less of a sausage than we did at Slaughterhouse Four, I thought.

"I won't be long." I walked away quickly and he didn't follow.

Outside, my planning hit a rough patch – transport. Davie had the Land-Rover at the zoo. I didn't fancy having a guard driver with me where I was going so I commandeered the nearest vehicle, a pick-up truck with more rust than is on what's left of the Forth Rail Bridge, and had another go at remembering how to drive. The last time Katharine almost bailed out. My technique didn't seem to have got much better. I swerved out on to the main road and missed one of the city's garbage trucks by the length of my forefinger – the one that's short a couple of joints.

I called Davie and asked how he was getting on.

"Nothing so far," he replied. "We've done the clinic, the foodstores and the admin block."

"Watch out for the peccaries," I said.

"What?"

"Nothing. I'm on my way to pick up Katharine."

"What are you driving?" he asked suspiciously. "More to the point, how are you driving?"

"Very safely indeed."

"Oh, aye."

I signed off. The jokes were over. Now I had to drive ten miles out of the city in pitch darkness through numerous guard checkpoints. I hoped it was going to be worth it.

The curfew was well under way and I had enough trouble even navigating to my own flat.

"About time," Katharine said as she climbed in. "I've been bored stiff up there."

I headed for the junction. "Jesus!" Katharine put her hands out in time to stop her head hitting the windscreen.

"Sorry. Bloody guard. They drive like lunatics."

"They're not the only ones. Didn't you see them, Quint?"

I was leaning forward like a myopic pensioner. "The lights on this thing are about as much use as a guardian in a drinking competition."

Somehow we made it past the checkpoints that the guard have erected at every mile-post without any more near misses. Katharine called ahead on the mobile before we reached each one and we only had to flash our "ask no questions". Apart from guard patrols, the roads were empty and completely unlit. It was like driving through a desert, although the temperature was a bit lower than the Gobi even on a bad night. Then we came out of a dip in the road about five miles out and were blinded by the lights of one of the city's coal mines. They work round the clock like the slaughterhouses. I spent some time down one after I was demoted. Cutting sheep's throats is probably only slightly more unpleasant, especially if being two thousand feet underground in a dripping, gas-ridden tunnel gets to you.

We turned off and were enveloped by the night again. Now there were tall trees on both sides of us, bending over the road ahead like great predators about to pounce. The pick-up's engine suddenly coughed, making both of us jump. You can be sure that the limited quantity of diesel the Council imports is the scrapings from the bottom of the oil companies' tanks; they don't give a shit about a city that has banned private cars.

We came to a crossroads that was unmarked. Since citizens' movements are carefully controlled and the drivers in the Transportation and Supply Directorates know where they're going, the guardians have dispensed with signposts. It takes you back to Britain during the Second World War, except that people knew who the enemy was then. These days that isn't so clear.

Eventually we reached the last checkpoint before our destination.

"Blue Sector Sawmill?" I asked the guardswoman on duty.

"Straight ahead, about three-quarters of a mile. What are you doing out here at this time of night?" She flashed her torch at us, holding it on my face.

I leaned out and pushed the beam down. The last thing I needed now was an eager auxiliary calling in to the guard command centre and reporting my presence out here. I held out our "ask no questions" and hoped that the guardswoman wasn't old enough to have known me when I was in the Public Order Directorate. There wasn't any sign of recognition. Usually young auxiliaries on their first tours of duty are the ones who get stuck on their own in the middle of nowhere. It's supposed to be good for their characters.

I accelerated away, following the road as it ran along the edge of a steep valley. I had a vague recollection of being driven out here to visit some friends of my parents when I was a kid. My old man told me that the village of Temple on the other side of the river had historical associations with the Knights Templar. I had a sudden vision of men in chain mail and white tunics emblazoned with red crosses, men who used a higher purpose like religion to justify slaughter. For some reason that made me think of the senior guardian.

"I can see a light ahead," said Katharine, bending forward to squint through the cracked windscreen.

It was the single maroon lamp displayed by facilities manned by City Guard personnel. We traversed a couple of humpbacks in the road, but that wasn't why I was feeling queasy. Davie hadn't called in with anything from the zoo, so this was it. If we didn't find something here, it would be back to letting the killer call the shots. And to being used as a urinal by the chief boyscout. Apparently even saints have to empty their bladders somewhere.

The auxiliary who appeared at the sawmill gate was built like a lumberjack, though the Supply Directorate hadn't managed to come up with an appropriate checked shirt. He rubbed his eyes and screwed them up when he saw the "ask no questions".

"What is it you're after?" he asked suspiciously, admitting us into a Victorian farm courtyard stacked with piles of wood. "We don't work a night shift here, you know."

"I need to see all the rooms in the facility," I said, putting on the standard do-what-I-say-or-it's-the-mines-for-you voice that undercover operatives affect when they're checking up on their colleagues.

The auxiliary wasn't impressed – he was old enough to have been through this kind of idiocy dozens of times – but he went into what was obviously the office and threw some switches. The steading was flooded in light, the ornate gables and casements looking as incongruous as a sober tourist in the Grassmarket after midnight. In the nineteenth century it wasn't a crime to embellish places of work. The Council prefers breezeblocks and concrete.

We followed the lumberjack, who turned out to be the sawmill supervisor, into the various storehouses, cutting yards, machine rooms and accommodation areas. The auxiliary dormitory was well-behaved, shiny-faced guardsmen blinking in the unshaded overhead light; but the citizen workers were rebellious, at first grumbling about being woken up then running their eyes hungrily over Katharine. They get drafted for month-long tours of duty and there are no sex sessions during that time, so I couldn't really blame them. Katharine returned their stares blankly and one by one they lowered their eyes.

All of which would have been fascinating for a social psychologist studying the effect of enforced labour, but it got us nowhere. The nearest thing to a sophisticated chemical lab was the wood treatment room and the nearest thing to dangerous chemicals were the drums of creosote lining the walls.

The auxiliary led us back to his office and offered us tea. "I don't suppose you want to tell me what that was all about?" he asked over his shoulder as he tinkered with a guard-issue spirit stove.

He seemed like a pretty reasonable guy. He was past middle age, probably one of the original breed of auxiliaries who used to believe in the Council's aims and now aren't so sure. I decided to satisfy his curiosity. You never know what you might pick up if you treat people like human beings.

"We're on the trail of some illicit material," I said. "There's a chance it moved between here and the main depot."

The lumberjack turned round and faced me. I suddenly noticed that the whites of his eyes were cloudy and wondered how much he could see. That was maybe why he'd been posted out here, where all the damage he could do was to his own fingers on the circular saw.

"What kind of material would that be then?"

"I don't think you want to know that, my friend."

"That bad?" He handed a mug to Katharine. "There you are, lady." He was running the risk of getting his head in his hands to play with using that form of address with her, but she didn't seem to regard him as a threat. Or a patronising arsehole. "Well, was there a particular driver involved?"

There didn't seem to be much harm in telling him that.

"Roddie Aitken?" he said, his face breaking into a grin beneath the shag pile of his beard. "Good lad, Roddie. What's he been up to?" Obviously the guard jungle drums hadn't been beating this far out of Edinburgh.

I looked down at the mug he was holding out to me. "He . . . he had an accident." I didn't have the stomach to be more precise.

"Nothing serious, I hope." The auxiliary gulped from his own mug. "Must be a couple of weeks since I last saw him."

I nodded. "The manifests say he was picking up different kinds of wood."

"Aye, that's right." The lumberjack nodded, then his eyes shifted slowly away from mine.

It was one of those moments when you suddenly realise you're on the brink of something big. You don't get much warning, only a couple of seconds when the hairs on the back of your neck rise as if a barn dance has just started on your grave.

"Course, he wasn't only collecting from us," the auxiliary said, rubbing his afflicted eyes again then giving a strangely melancholic smile. "There were some packages that came down from the other place too. Only they never say anything about it in the documentation."

I was suddenly finding breathing difficult. "The other place?" I asked hoarsely. "What other place? I didn't see any lights except the one above your gate." I glanced at Katharine.

"Me neither," she said, her gaze locked on the auxiliary.

He shook his head. "Oh, there's no light over there at night. Most of the poor sods behind the walls prefer the darkness. Not that they have much choice."

I slammed my mug down on his desk, splashing hot liquid on the back of my hand. "For God's sake, what is this other place?" I shouted.

He gazed back at us then sighed like an aged wise man finally giving in to his disciples' demands for enlightenment.

"The other place?" he repeated in a low, unwavering voice. "You won't have heard of it. Most of the guardians don't even know it exists."

"What?" Katharine said incredulously. Even she was losing her cool.

The sawmill supervisor blinked his lustreless eyes. "They call it the Bone Yard."

Chapter Twenty

"So you have heard of it," the lumberjack said. He could obviously see more than I thought. He was smiling faintly at the expression of shock on my face. It must have rivalled Agamemnon's when his wife produced an axe in the bathroom at Mycenae. Then the auxiliary's voice hardened. "That means you must be working for the fuckers in the Science and Energy Directorate."

Still struggling to get my head round what was going on, I waved my hands at him ineffectually. "Public Order Directorate," I gasped. "Special investigator."

He sat down again, looking marginally less ferocious. "Well, there's plenty to investigate up there, I'll tell you that for nothing."

"Come on, Katharine," I said. "Let's get going."

Throughout this exchange she'd been motionless, an inscrutable look on her face.

The lumberjack let out a long, deep laugh that wouldn't have been out of place in a cemetery at midnight. "Your Council authorisation won't get you anywhere up there, citizen special investigator. The guards will be on to the Science and Energy Directorate before you can blink." He leaned forward and looked at both of us. "I get the impression you'd like what you're doing to stay a secret for as long as possible. Am I right?"

I nodded at him and smiled. There used to be a fair number of auxiliaries like him in the early years of the Enlightenment – people who hadn't forgotten what it was like to be a normal human being rather than a Council slave.

"There's a ten-foot stone wall with barbed wire on the top all the way round the place," the lumberjack said. "The only gate's in front of the old house. The wankers up there reckon their security's tighter than the prison on Cramond Island's."

"What exactly goes on up there?" Katharine asked.

The auxiliary examined his hands with their swollen fingers for a few moments. "What they say they do – not that they ever say much since they're a squad of specially chosen lunatics who never go back to the city and have as little to do with us as they can – what they say they do is dispose of cattle with new strains of BSE. That's why the place is guarded so closely. Supply deliveries and pick-ups are made here, supposedly to avoid any chance of contamination. We do see cattle trucks going up the road occasionally." He opened his clouded eyes at me knowingly. "Very occasionally."

I leaned forward into the ring of light round his desk. "But there's more to it than that, isn't there?"

"Aye, there is," the auxiliary said, nodding slowly. But I don't know what. You'll have to find that out for yourself." Suddenly he gave me a conspiratorial wink. "Bell 03."

His use of my former barracks number showed he knew who I used to be. I wondered if he'd recognised me the minute we arrived. Perhaps he'd served with me in the directorate. There wasn't time to ask.

"Can you get us inside?" I said.

He shook his head. "Forget it. I'm quite attached to this posting and I don't want to lose it. Not even for you." He smiled at me apologetically as he tugged his beard with his fingertips. At least he wasn't one of those guardsmen like Harry who held it against me that their friends had been killed in the drug wars. "But I will tell you the best place to get a look over the walls. After that you're on your own."

I glanced at Katharine. She shrugged, apparently unconcerned by the prospect of trying to penetrate a high-security facility. She was used to being on her own. So was I, but this was carrying things to extremes.

The lumberjack was unrolling a detailed City Guard map. Katharine and I gathered round like carrion crows alighting on a carcass. Except I had the feeling that this particular carcass still had a fair amount of life in it.

We went back the way we came for a mile then took the pick-up down a narrow lane that ran past a pine wood, driving slowly with only the sidelights on. The auxiliary reckoned the best way to approach the compound was from the rear, where the sentries were only placed every hundred yards. But we had to get there while it was still dark. We left the vehicle in a copse and headed off across the fields, following the compass bearing I'd worked out at the sawmill.

"Quint, why don't you call in Hamilton and have him pull the place apart?" Katharine asked in a low voice as we stumbled over the rough ground in the faint light of early dawn.

"I wish I could." Just after we started walking I'd tripped and landed in a ditch full of half-frozen water. Now my hands and arms were shaking uncontrollably. "But I'm certain that the senior guardian would put a stop to that before we got five yards beyond the gate."

"So the great Quintilian Dalrymple's going to act the hero." A smile played across her lips.

"No one's forcing you to be here," I hissed, peering at the solid mass that was beginning to rear up on the ridge in front of us. The truth was, I wasn't sure what I was going to do, even if we did manage to get inside. I'd spent so much time and effort searching for the mysterious Bone Yard and I was bloody sure it was the key to everything else that was wrong in the city. But

I was also in the process of committing the investigator's worst strategic error: getting close to the solution and then hoping that everything will work out for the best. Sometimes it's the only option you have.

The house inside the walls was built by a Victorian mines magnate who had political aspirations. According to the lumberjack, Gladstone had been a frequent visitor. Since the old Liberal's favourite hobby apart from rescuing fallen women was chopping up timber, it was surprising that the forest behind the wall was so thick. I wasn't complaining. The profusion of branches hanging down over the walls made life difficult for the sentries. From behind the ruined chapel outside the compound – no sharing a pew with the peasants in the village kirk for the original owner – Katharine and I took in the lie of the land. The sun was rising but there was a mist so we weren't as obvious as we might have been.

"What next, Quint? If we sling over that rope your friend gave us, we should be able to get on to the wall in that sheltered place."

I took a quick look at the sentry posts. They were built up on the inside with only a couple of feet of planking cut with slit-holes showing from where we were. I had a feeling that the senior guardian would not be canonising whoever was in charge. Like a lot of top-security facilities in the city its impregnability was a matter of rumour rather than fact.

"Okay, go for it," I said, squeezing her arm. "I'll be right behind you."

"You'd better be," Katharine replied, looking over her shoulder. "After all, you're the one who knows what he's doing here." She was away towards the wall before I could respond to that crack. Then the rope with the steel hook the lumberjack had given us flew over the wire on the top. It seemed to get a good purchase on something on the other side. I hoped it wasn't a passing guardsman's throat.

Katharine hauled herself up, the long skirts of her coat stuffed into her belt, then signalled to me to follow.

I stepped out and froze. There was a movement in the sentry box to my right. A period that felt like several decades, but in reality couldn't have been more than five seconds, ground by. I couldn't move back into the cover of the chapel wall in case that convinced the sentry that he or she had seen something. Swivelling my eyes, I satisfied myself that the maroon beret had drawn back from the slits in the planking. And ran for the wall like a frightened rabbit. It was only as I was halfway up the rope that the idiocy of the situation struck me. Taking refuge inside the walls of a top-security facility was carrying even my advanced appreciation of the bizarre a bit too far.

"Come on, for God's sake," Katharine said, holding out her hand as I began to struggle.

I took it without a second thought. I've never been much good at climbing ropes and I'm not proud either. There was a nasty moment when the barbed wire acquainted itself with my thighs, then I was over, pulling the rope up with me. We shinned down the other side and dived into the undergrowth. It was drenched in an icy dew.

"What next?" Katharine asked. "We can't see a thing from here."

"How do you fancy crawling through this?"

She pulled her coat skirts out. "No problem. I'm properly equipped." She glanced at my donkey jacket and soaked trousers contemptuously. "Unlike you."

So we crawled through the bracken and ferns till we reached the inner edge of the wood. In the distance at the far end of the enclosed land stood the main house, a large two-storey edifice in sandstone with enough windows to suggest that the man who built it either had an army of offspring or a lot of fawning friends who came to stay every weekend. Between us and the house was a fenced field where a couple of very sane-looking cows were chewing the cud. Away to the left was a much newer building, a long, low line of breezeblock huts with shuttered windows. Late period Council style without a doubt. And at the far end, a taller building without a single window from which a brick-built chimney rose high above the tops of even the oldest trees. That was where we were headed. Except we got distracted on the way.

The first thing we came across was a clearing in the wood. The surface of the ground seemed to be flat, then I noticed that it was covered by separate slabs of dull grey metal.

"What are those?" Katharine asked, looking around the open space. "There must be over thirty of them."

We went closer. And I saw a yellow-bordered symbol on each slab that immediately brought Torness to mind.

"Jesus."

"What is it, Quint?" Katharine asked again.

I went closer. There was no doubt about it. The international warning for radiation danger was on every slab. What's more, you didn't have to be a metallurgist to get the idea that the metal was lead, or an undertaker to recognise the slabs as grave markers.

"Jesus," I repeated. "This is it. This is the Bone Yard. Literally."

Katharine stared at me, then glanced away towards a narrow gap in the trees on the other side of the clearing. "Someone's coming," she said quietly.

I looked across the clearing and saw two figures approaching. The normal reaction would have been to melt back into the undergrowth and I almost did that. Then I realised that the figures weren't looking at us. They were dressed in citizen-issue grey coats that were several sizes too big for them and their heads were covered by the flat caps that absolve the Supply Directorate from providing the population with umbrellas. They were also concentrating so hard on the path in front of them that I began to wonder if there were mantraps under the worn grass. Then the leading one stumbled and the other person put out a hand

and supported his or her companion – it was impossible to tell which sex they were from our position. From their slow, unsteady progress, I got the impression they were very old.

Katharine nudged my elbow. "What do you think?" she whispered. "They don't exactly look dangerous."

We stood still as the figures reached the grave that was nearest to their side of the clearing. The lead slab was surrounded by a rim of fresh earth. The two of them stood staring down at the grave, arms round each other's back. It was then I realised that stooping seemed to be their usual stance. After a while one of them knelt down slowly and placed a small sprig of holly on the surface of the metal. There was a long silence, then a solitary crow cawed from behind us. The two figures raised their heads instinctively and looked straight at us.

I wanted to run across the clearing and reassure them we meant no harm, but that would have meant stepping over the graves and I didn't think that would endear me to them. Then it became obvious that they weren't disturbed by our presence. In fact, the one who was kneeling started carefully repositioning the holly on the slab. Perhaps they hadn't seen us after all.

"Come on," I said to Katharine under my breath. "They're the best chance we've got of finding out what the hell's been going on around here."

We circled the clearing and walked towards the figures slowly but without stealth. As we approached they finally seemed to register our presence, but they didn't speak – just turned and lifted their faces when they heard our footsteps.

I heard Katharine draw breath in rapidly. I could see why. The kneeling one was a woman. I knew that from the softness of her skin and the delicate line of her jaw and neck, even though her face was blotched with dark red lesions and her eyebrows had disappeared. Her male companion's face was also heavily marked and his limbs were shaking with rapid movements. But their eyes were what was hardest to look at. If the lumberjack's were clouded, theirs were almost completely opaque, like watered-down milk. That was why they hadn't noticed us for so long.

"What harm are we doing?" the woman asked querulously. "Alec's at peace now. You can't get anything else from him."

Katharine and I exchanged helpless glances.

"You're not doing any harm," I said. "We're not on the staff here."

An expression of what looked like joy flashed across both their faces, to be replaced almost immediately by a terrible sadness. It was as if they'd been waiting for this moment for years, only to realise as soon as it arrived that salvation from what they were going through was an impossible dream.

"Not on the staff?" the man repeated, his ruined features contorting as he struggled to work out who we were.

The woman rose to her feet with difficulty, holding on to her companion's arm tightly. "Surely you haven't come over the wall?" she said, her voice fraught with fear. "You'll never get out again, you know."

"We'll see about that," I said, trying to sound more in command of myself than I was. "In the meantime we need your help. Will you be missed for a few more minutes?"

The man laughed. It wasn't a pretty sound, but it raised my spirits. Whatever he'd suffered, at least he could still laugh. I saw that Katharine was smiling.

"They won't miss us. Now that we can't work in the labs or with the cattle, they're just waiting for us to join the others here." His head started to shake like his arms and legs. The woman drew him gently away from the grave.

"Come on," she said. "We'd better get into the cover of the bushes."

Katharine took her arm but she shook it off firmly. We let them move slowly ahead.

In the undergrowth they lowered themselves carefully on to the trunk of a fallen tree and sat hand in hand like a couple of kids who'd strayed away from a school picnic.

"If you're not on the staff, who are you?" the man asked suspiciously. "No one's ever volunteered to enter this place before."

"I'm Dalrymple," I said, preparing to launch into a sanitised account of what we were up to. I didn't get the chance.

"Quintilian Dalrymple?" they said in unison. I wasn't aware that my name had become part of a Gregorian chant. "The investigator?"

"Yes," I replied. "How do you know?"

"We haven't been here all our lives," the woman said. "Though it often feels like it. We knew about you when we were in the Science and Energy Directorate." She shook her head slowly. "Your mother was responsible for all this, you know."

I'd been wondering when my mother, the former senior guardian, would come back to haunt me. The lesions on the couple's faces were a silent reminder of the lupus that had ravaged her. But I suspected that what they were afflicted by was even worse than that.

"Don't worry," the man said. "We won't hold it against you." He sighed deeply like a torture victim who's tracked down his abusers but can't find the strength to avenge himself on them. "We're long past that."

"Tell us," Katharine said simply, squatting down on the damp bracken in front of them. "Tell us what they did to you."

"Very well," the man said. "This is our story. I hope you both find it informative." His voice broke towards the end of the sentence but I couldn't tell if that was the effect of emotion or his physical condition.

I settled back against the gnarled trunk of an ancient oak and shut out the harsh call of the crow that was still haunting the wood. Maybe it had found a rabbit – or something larger. Then I leaned forward and listened to the old man's soft, uneven tones.

"We're ... we were mechanical engineers. Specialising in

steam turbines. Before the Enlightenment we worked at Torness. Of course, after the plant was decommissioned, we had to retrain."

The woman laughed bitterly. "Coal. I hate the bloody stuff. We spent most of our time patching up what passes for a coal-fired power station in this benighted city."

Her companion nodded. "Until we were called into the Science and Energy Directorate in 2019 and told we were to be part of a top-secret team. They gave us false identities as ordinary citizens."

"To work on starting up the nuclear plant at Torness," I said.

They were seriously shocked. "You knew?" the woman exclaimed. "How? No one outside this hell-hole is supposed to have heard about the project we took part in."

I looked at their devastated faces. "Not quite no one. There were a few others. My mother and the science and energy guardian, for instance."

"Guardians," the man said. "Why would they talk?"

I considered defending William McEwan, but time was running out. The longer we were in the compound, the greater the chance we'd be caught.

"We heard your mother died, Quintilian," the woman said, giving me a surprisingly sympathetic look.

"She did. Last year." I paused for a moment, amazed that the woman could feel anything for the guardian who was at least partially responsible for what had happened to her.

"It would never have worked," the man continued. "All our colleagues were agreed on that. But there was great pressure on us to come up with a positive recommendation. The deputy guardian . . ."

That's what I wanted to hear. Some dirt on the one-time deputy science guardian who was now senior guardian.

"He was like a man with a mission. For him Edinburgh's very survival depended on the gas-cooled reactor." The man lowered his head. His hands were shaking even more than they had been. "He forced us to break into the sarcophagus round the fuel elements. You see, the Council had been in such a hurry to close down the plant that it took the easy way out. Instead of spending money to make the reactor safe, it did the minimum. Then encased it in concrete."

Katharine had gone very white. "You mean it's still live?"

The woman shook her head slowly. "The original Council wasn't that irresponsible. Basic safety procedures were followed. It just wasn't a very good idea to break into the core." She was suddenly looking even frailer.

"There were explosions," I said softly.

The man nodded. "It could have been a lot worse. The radiation leak was minimised and the city was lucky. There was a south-westerly wind and the cloud was carried over the North Sea. There have been so many leaks from old reactors in Russia and the Ukraine that it probably hardly showed up on the monitors abroad."

"So the only people who suffered were us," the woman said, her voice shrill. "The forty of us who were in the immediate vicinity. We had no chance. Seven died on the spot."

Katharine put her hand on the woman's. This time it wasn't shaken off. "They brought you here?"

"They could hardly let us back into the city, could they?" said the man. "The tourists would have disappeared overnight." He looked at me with his milky eyes. "Besides, we've been useful to them. All the city's viruses and contamination have ended up here."

"BSE," I said, glancing away in the direction of the cattle.

"And worse," the man said, shaking his head.

There was something else I wanted to check. "Did you know the auxiliary Watt 103?"

"Oh, aye," the woman said brightly, then shook her head. "Poor Alasdair. He was even worse off than us. They made him stay at Torness. There were four of five of them. They had to monitor the reactor after the sarcophagus was closed up again." Now she was looking at me. "Do you know what happened to him?"

Katharine squeezed the woman's knee gently. "I was with him when he died not long ago. He got out of Torness."

"I'm glad," the woman said. "He was a good man and he deserved better from the Council."

"So did you all," Katharine said, bending her head and resting it on the woman's thigh.

I was thinking about what the lumberjack said about the cattle trucks. "If they're monitoring BSE there must be a laboratory here."

"There are several labs," the woman said. "They had us working there before we got too shaky. Not that we know much about chemical procedures. We were nothing more than lab assistants." She laughed weakly. "Probably the most overqualified assistants in the world."

The man smiled at her, his mottled skin seeming almost to crack. For all the agonies and indignities they'd suffered, they were both undefeated. The iron boyscouts should have been shot for taking advantage of them.

"So chemists had to be drafted in?" I said.

The woman nodded. "There are three of them. The woman in charge is a toxicologist by specialisation. She's not been here long."

I was prepared to bet my entire collection of crime fiction that she was the one the chief toxicologist had been grooming to succeed him. I tried for a royal flush.

"When you were working in the labs, did you ever see any blue pills being produced?"

There was total silence for a few moments. Even the ravenous crow had decided to give it a rest. Then they both nodded.

"She called them Electric Blues," the man said. "I overheard her on her mobile once. She wasn't too pleased when she saw me, but who did she think I was going to tell?"

That was it. Time to call in the cavalry. I had my mobile halfway to my lips when Katharine sprang to her feet and cupped her ear in the direction of the clearing.

"Guards," she said, motioning to us to hit the ground.

I hadn't heard anything, but her experience of field operations was a lot more recent than mine. Then heavy boots came crashing through the bracken, getting nearer and nearer.

Until they stopped a couple of tree-trunks away.

"I'm fucking freezing out here," said a male voice. "Have you got that bastard whisky?"

"Aye."

A screwcap was undone, then gulping could be heard.

"Christ, that's better. Here you are, Jim."

Not exactly standard guard language, but the headbangers posted out here probably didn't give a shit about regulations.

"Where the hell are those stupid old fucks?" the first voice said. "Do you think they've croaked?"

I watched the faces of the ex-engineers. They were motionless, their lips slack.

"If they haven't yet, it won't be long. Their lead boxes are ready for them." A guttural, soulless laugh. "Come on. The commander'll be looking for us if we don't report back soon."

The sound of their legs brushing through the undergrowth faded.

Katharine helped the others to their feet. "I'm sorry you had to hear that," she said. "Those guardsmen are scum." She settled them on the fallen tree. "Won't you tell us your names?" she asked, looking at each of them in turn.

"Our names?" the woman said slowly. "Our names? The Council took those away from us years ago when we became auxiliaries."

"Yes, but surely you remember them."

The man turned towards her and smiled. "This is the Bone Yard. You saw the blank slabs. No one needs names here."

I swallowed hard then punched out Hamilton's number on

the mobile. For a horrible moment I thought I wasn't going to get a connection. At this range nothing was certain. Then I heard the buzz and breathed out.

"Dalrymple," I said when I heard the guardian's voice. I told him where we were, then lowered my voice. I was so wound up that I'd been shouting. "I've found the lab where the Electric Blues are being produced."

"You have? Well done, man. I'm on my way."

"Bring as many squads as you can," I said. "And don't take any shit from the sentries on the gate — this is a top-security facility."

"Are you sure? I've never heard of it."

"That's the wonder of top security, Lewis. Two more things."

"Go ahead."

"Bring a camera. In fact, bring several cameras. This place needs to be recorded for posterity."

"Right. And the other thing?"

"Whatever you do, Lewis, don't tell the senior guardian where you're going. It's a matter of life or death."

Chapter Twenty-One

Davie always did fancy himself as a racing driver. He caught up with Hamilton by the suburbs and called me again when the convoy of guard vehicles was approaching the gate.

"The guardian's demanding entry now, Quint. They don't look too happy on the other side. Hang on ... bloody hell, that was neat. The guardian just grabbed the sentry's mobile and smashed it against the gatepost."

It looked like Lewis was taking my point about the need for secrecy seriously. I just hoped there weren't many more mobiles inside the compound.

"Right, we're on our way in," Davie went on. "Where are you?"

"We're breaking cover now. Meet us at the labs behind the big house. Out."

I nodded to the others. "They're here."

Katharine was helping the man and woman to their feet. "It's over," she said, smiling at them. "You'll soon be free of this place."

They both shook their heads. "Where else is there for us? Our friends are all over there," the man said. The two of them looked over towards the clearing with its lead slabs as if their eyes were drawn by an ineluctable force. "That's where we want it to end. With them."

I couldn't argue with him. But I was going to use them first. I felt bad about it but I had to convince Lewis Hamilton that the senior guardian was even more off the rails than the last train that tried to cross the Forth Rail Bridge after independence.

"Can you take us to the labs?" I asked.

They nodded and we set off through the bracken. As we cleared the woodland, a shot rang out to our right. I made out a guardsman on the wall with a rifle and, further along, a sentry slumping back in his box. The guardian really was taking my warning seriously. Firearms are only issued in extreme cases. Then I saw the sentry's arm move upwards. There was another shot and he was still.

My mobile buzzed.

"Dalrymple? Are you all right?"

"Yes, Lewis. What's going on?"

"My people spotted one of the sentries with his mobile to his mouth. I hope he didn't get through to whoever he was calling. We think we've secured all the other mobiles."

"If you haven't we might be fighting a civil war." I signed off and led the others out into the open. In the enclosure ahead the cattle gazed at us without interest as they ruminated. They were in luck. Their date with the furnace and the tall chimney had been indefinitely postponed.

Guard personnel were swarming all over the place. Outside the labs a small group of white-coated figures had been assembled, their hands cuffed behind their backs. Hamilton was strolling around like an officer on parade. He'd been waiting for an operation like this for years. He was about to learn something about the chief boyscout that would make him even more pleased.

Davie came towards us.

"You okay, Quint?" he called, his eyes widening as he took in our companions. It looked like he'd made the connection between the state they were in and what had happened at Torness.

"Don't worry, lad," the man said, smiling faintly at him. "We're not as radioactive as that."

Davie realised his mouth was hanging open like a whale's in plankton-gathering mode. He closed it, stepped forward and took the man's arm, giving Katharine a grim smile. If it was safe enough for her, he wasn't going to hang back.

"What is this place, Dalrymple?" Hamilton shouted as I came into range.

"This is the Bone Yard, Lewis. Did you bring a camera?"

"Three, plus directorate photographers."

"Good. There's plenty for them to work on. One of them can start with these people here." I indicated the shuffling couple beside me. "You can send another over in the direction we've just come from. There's a clearing marked out with lead slabs that you'll be interested in."

"And the third?"

"There's a lab in there that should have a large number of small blue objects in it."

There was a sudden movement to my right. I turned and watched as the chief toxicologist's loose frame covered twenty yards at amazing speed.

"Is it you, Eileen?" I heard him say, his voice cracking. "And you, Murdo? I was told you'd both died a couple of years back."

"We're still going, Ramsay," the woman replied, clutching at his arm. "Not for long though."

The toxicologist's face was wet. "So this is what they called the Bone Yard," he said, shaking his head. "I heard the name a couple of times but I was told never to repeat it."

You didn't have to be Einstein to work out which of the city's scientists had given him that instruction. I left them to their shared pasts and went over to a tall young woman in a white coat. She had her head bowed as if the scene with her former lab assistants was causing her pain. There was more on the way.

"You're in a quicksand full of shit, Lister 436," I said to

her. "Your only chance of avoiding a long and unhappy life on Cramond Island is to come clean about the Electric Blues right now."

Her eyes jerked around for a few seconds, their dark brown colour in striking contrast to the ashen white of her skin. She was obviously wondering if selling out the senior guardian was a sensible option. A quick glance at Hamilton's miniature army helped her make up her mind. She led us in and showed us her chemistry set.

We had a council of war in the long conservatory that had been the staff's messroom. Old copies of the *Edinburgh Guardian* were scattered around the wooden floor, which was buckled all over as if moles had been trying to effect entry. Except no self-respecting mole would have wanted anything to do with the lowlife that made up the guard personnel here.

"Right, we've collected documents and taken photographs of everything," Hamilton said. "And all the Electric Blues we could find are in my Land-Rover."

"Make sure they don't fall out on the way back," Katharine said, making it sound like she had no faith in the guardian's competence.

I glared at her. I'd already spent more time than I should have persuading Lewis not to arrest her. Now he was doing his impersonation of Krakatoa seconds before eruption.

"It's one forty-three," I said, trying to move things along. "We can only hope that no word got out about our presence here. So the question is, what next?"

"We call an emergency Council meeting and divest the senior guardian of his powers forthwith," Hamilton said. He'd been overjoyed when we found papers in the lab linking the top level of the Science and Energy Directorate – i.e. the chief boyscout – to the drug production. But he was letting himself get a bit carried away.

"That might not be too clever," I said. "If we give the senior guardian the chance to defend himself, he might manage to turn this against us. The rest of the guardians think he walks on air as well as water. He did give most of them their jobs, remember."

"But we've got all this evidence," Davie said.

"We have now," I said. "But how long for? We're going to need as many copies of the photos as we can get."

"I'll see to that," the guardian said.

"And I've got to be sure I can make the bastard see reason," I said.

Hamilton looked at me quizzically. "Meaning?"

"Meaning that if he starts using staff loyal to him to locate our evidence, we have to stop him in his tracks." I had a thought. "Davie, give your mate Harry a call. Tell him we need his crews for a bit of shore-based headbanging."

Hamilton looked like he was lost at sea. I just hoped we weren't all going to end up as food for the fishes like the fat man in that gangster movie half a century ago.

"Lewis, I need you to find out where the senior guardian is." Katharine and I were with Hamilton in his Land-Rover on the way back to the city.

"Simple. He's required by Council regulations to advise the guard command centre of his whereabouts at all times." The guardian made the call. "He's been in meetings with a Chinese trade delegation all day and he's expected back in his private accommodation at four o'clock."

That was good news. If he'd been busy negotiating, he wouldn't have had much chance to wonder about what we were up to.

"Right, I'll land on him unannounced there. Somehow I think he'll find the time to see me."

"Dalrymple, surely you don't think the senior guardian's the killer," Hamilton said haltingly. "I mean, he's over-zealous and autocratic but he does have the city's best interests at heart. Even I have always been convinced of that."

I couldn't suppress a laugh. Over-zealous was a major understatement. The chief boyscout was so zealous he could have walked into a senior position with the Spanish Inquisition when he was at primary school. But Lewis had a point.

"No, I'm pretty sure he's not the murderer," I said. "At least not the one who killed Roddie Aitken and the female auxiliary. But considering he was responsible for everything that's been going on in the Bone Yard, I'm taking every precaution I can."

The sun was already low in the sky to the west. All around us sodden brown fields dotted with patches of half-frozen water stretched away into the distance, lined by bare trees with scarecrow branches. I shivered in the blast of cold air that was coming in the holes in the Land-Rover's bodywork. I found myself wishing I could put my arm round Katharine and feel the warmth of her. But she was sitting bolt upright in her long coat, her eyes fixed on the rutted road ahead. The Enlightenment wanted to get rid of the cult of the individual which had supposedly destroyed the United Kingdom's social fabric in the years around the millennium. All it achieved was to make us into even more self-reliant, emotionally illiterate citizens – and I speak from a position of considerable authority on emotional illiteracy.

"Right, Davie." We were round the corner from the checkpoint in front of the guardians' accommodation in Moray Place. I was leaning in the window of the pick-up which he'd driven in from the track where Katharine and I left it. "Have you got everything clear?"

"Do you mind?" he asked sardonically. "I'm a trained auxiliary."

"That's very reassuring, guardsman. Are Harry and his guys in the picture?"

"Aye. They're up at the castle waiting to be given copies of the photos and documents. Katharine and the guardian are handling that." He grinned. "Should be interesting to see if she ends up in the dungeons."

I gave him a frosty glare.

"Then Harry's people will take up positions near the six embassies you specified."

"And you've told them that if they don't hear anything by six p.m. they're to make the deliveries?"

"I have, Quint. Calm down, will you?"

"Calm down? That's easy for you to say. You're not the one who's got to squeeze the senior guardian's nuts."

He laughed. "You're having more fun than a guardsman in the barracks bar who's just come off border duty."

"Is that right? Make sure you come and join me if I'm not back in half an hour." I started to walk away.

"Quint? You don't want to forget this."

I turned back and took the object he was holding out. True enough, I needed to be properly equipped before I could contemplate facing the city's top dog.

Security around the guardians' quarters has never been exactly minimalist, but now Moray Place resembled the Red Square on May Day in the time before Moscow turned into an eastern version of Tombstone. It took me a lot of shoving to get through the serried ranks of guard personnel to the senior guardian's residence. It looked like someone was seriously worried about his personal safety.

The young female auxiliary at the door took an instant dislike to me. I managed to get my authorisation out before she could practise her unarmed combat skills on me.

"Where is he?" I asked, pushing past her.

"In his study." The auxiliary was already on the internal phone.

I headed up the ornate staircase, thinking of the times I'd come here to see my mother as I pulled on Katharine's coat. This meeting promised to be even more life-threatening than those ones. I slowed down outside the high door, took a deep breath, pulled up the hood and walked in with my head bent forward.

There was a sudden intake of breath then a long silence.

"Why are you wearing that coat, citizen?" The senior guardian's voice possessed almost its normal level of control, but there was enough wavering at the edges to make me sure my choice of apparel was having an effect.

"I thought it might set the mood for our meeting," I said, taking the coat off and moving towards the large mahogany desk. On my way I noticed the painting that the chief boyscout had hung above the Adam fireplace. Each guardian is entitled to borrow one work from the city's galleries and – surprise, surprise – his was the exquisite, sombre-toned El Greco entitled *The Saviour of the World*. Some world. Some saviour.

"Am I to understand that you have at last made progress in your investigation, citizen?" The guardian remained seated at the desk, his head resting on the high back of his chair like a king receiving a tedious courtier.

I spread my hands on the desktop and leaned towards him. "I spent the morning at the Bone Yard." I leaned closer, my eyes locked on to his. "It's time for the truth, you lying bastard." Spots of my saliva landed on his beard. I didn't offer an apology.

The chief boyscout was pale but still in command, at least of himself. "The truth? That's a notoriously slippery concept, citizen."

I slipped my hand round his beard and pulled his head across the desk. "The truth, you callous fucker, or you won't have to wait for the real hooded man to catch up with you."

His body had gone slack but his eyes were still hard. "Very well, citizen. If you would let me go . . ."

I pulled my hand away and watched as he rearranged himself in his chair.

"The truth," he said, his voice a lot less composed than he'd have liked. "If you've been to the special facility––"

"The Bone Yard," I shouted.

"The Bone Yard." He pronounced the words with a curious movement of his lips as if they were ones he should never have been forced to utter. "If you've been there, surely you know the truth, citizen."

"What I know is that you imprisoned the people who were exposed to radiation at Torness and directed all the city's muck, like BSE-infected cattle, at them." I felt my shoulders shaking. "And what I also know is that you set up production of the Electric Blues there. You realise that the drug's potentially lethal for people with weak hearts, don't you?"

The guardian shrugged then looked at me imperiously. "I see that my actions have failed to win your approval, citizen."

"Failed to win my approval? Jesus, don't you people ever speak plain English? What you did was criminal. Don't you get it? You forced those people to break through the sarcophagus, then you locked them up and used them as slave labour. Without bothering to mention any of that to the Council."

His eyes flashed. "The original decision to return to Torness was taken by my predecessors, Dalrymple. One of whom was your mother."

"Don't think I won't be carrying that with me for the rest of my life." A vision of the couple in the Bone Yard, their ravaged faces and crippled frames, had jumped up before me. "But that doesn't get you off the hook."

The guardian gave me a tight, totally humourless smile. "You're missing the point. As a demoted auxiliary, you obviously can't be relied upon to maintain your familiarity with the works of Plato so—"

"What is this bollocks?" I yelled, slamming my hand down on the desktop. This was exactly the kind of line my mother used to take when she had to explain herself and it pissed me off even more than queuing for food vouchers on a Friday afternoon. "Don't tell me the Enlightenment's favourite philosopher wrote something that justifies the bullshit you've been coming out with for the last two years."

He twitched his head at me impatiently. "Indeed he did. Don't you remember the noble lie, citizen?"

"Sounds like a major contradiction in terms," I replied, but something was stirring in the depths of my memory.

The chief boyscout rose to his feet like a preacher about to address his congregation, which made the prospect of listening even worse.

"There was a myth that human beings were formed from earth. Those destined to rule had gold mixed in with them, while warriors had silver, and farmers and artisans iron."

It came back to me, despite the fact that I always tried to steer the discussion in philosophy debates towards more mundane matters like how to eradicate the drugs gangs. "One of the many myths that indoctrinate people into believing their roles in life are predetermined, so they buckle down to their daily toil," I said. "I can see why it would appeal to the Council."

The guardian ignored my irony. "The Enlightenment has always given citizens the chance to better themselves."

"Oh, aye? Apart from selling their souls and becoming auxiliaries, what opportunities are there in the city now?" I suddenly found myself thinking of Roddie Aitken. All the Council's precious system gave him was an early cremation. "Anyway, what's the myth got to do with your noble lie?"

He smiled harshly at me again. Never mind gold or silver, he had enough iron in his soul to rebuild the Forth Bridge. "During the discussion it is suggested that rulers are entitled to lie in order to protect the interests of the state. Would you like the page reference to *The Republic?*"

"No, I fucking wouldn't." I leaned across the desk and grabbed his beard again. "You've got absolutely no chance of convincing me that the lies you've been telling are noble, pal." I pulled his face right up to mine. "In my book you're personally responsible for four murders. I don't give a shit about the two auxiliaries, but I care more about Roddie Aitken and William McEwan than you can even begin to imagine."

The chief boyscout didn't try to protest his innocence or deny that William had been murdered on his orders. For the first time he was looking frightened. Not an attractive emotion in a golden ruler but an emotion all the same. Maybe I was beginning to get to him.

"Listen to me," I said, loosening my grip. "When this is over there'll be nowhere for you to hide in Edinburgh, I promise you that. But there's still a lunatic out there and catching him is a fuck sight more important than what used to be your career." There was a flash of what I took to be resistance in his eyes. "And don't even think about arranging any accidents for me. I've got people ready to turn over photos of the Bone Yard and papers about the Electric Blues written in your own fair hand to a selection of embassies."

He nodded his head slowly in acquiescence and I let go of his beard.

"Right, I want to finish this investigation and I want to finish it fast. You've got some Electric Blues here, haven't you?"

He nodded, keeping his eyes away from mine.

"They're the ones the killer's been looking for all over the city, which is why three people have been cut apart and why you've turned Moray Place into Fort Knox. The killer was blackmailing you about Torness, threatening to tell the rest of the world what you've been covering up. He passed you the drugs formula and told you to set up production. Then what happened?"

"Whatever you may think, I am not a common criminal," the guardian said indignantly. "I had no intention of allowing that character to traffic drugs in the city. I enlisted the help of Raeburn 03 in the Public Order Directorate."

"And he thought it would be a bright idea to double-cross the hooded man? He got that wrong, didn't he? The killer reckoned Machiavelli had the Electric Blues. When he found he didn't, it was off with his head."

He didn't make any comment about the auxiliary's nickname. Perhaps he'd known about it all along. "That was unfortunate. The hooded man, as you've been calling him, wanted a woman when the deal was agreed. We gave him one of the Three Graces; she passed him a small sample of the drug as well as keeping an eye on him. The foolish woman also kept some of the pills for herself. We decided to lead him astray by making out that the delivery man Aitken was stealing the drugs on behalf of a rival dealer. The female auxiliary kept Aitken under surveillance too."

"By screwing him? You bastard," I said, raising my fist and watching as he jerked back into his seat. "You set Roddie Aitken up. When this is over, you'll be very sorry you did that." I managed to bring my breathing under control. "And you let me stay on the investigation in case I made things easy for you by catching the hooded man."

He nodded.

"I know more than you think," I said. "I know about the nuclear physicist Watt 103. He ended up in a gang run by a lunatic called the Screecher."

The senior guardian smiled humourlessly. "You have been busy. Apparently the Screecher got into Torness last year and killed the other scientists. He kept Watt 103 alive for his technical knowledge. I think he was planning to reopen the sarcophagus to strengthen his hand.

"Jesus. So who is the crazy bastard under the hood?"

He sat dead still for a few seconds then his face took on a supremely malicious expression. He looked like a bodysnatcher who's just come across a prime specimen dangling from a tree in a deserted wood.

"You know him, citizen," he said in a whisper.

I grabbed his beard again, feeling several strands come away in my fingers. "What do you mean I know him? Who is he, you fucker?"

Despite the damage I was doing to his facial hair, the chief boyscout seemed to be enjoying himself. Now the smile on his lips was so mocking that I badly wanted to lay into him. It's a hell of a long time since I've been violent. I applied long-forgotten auxiliary training to rein myself in.

"Let me describe him, citizen," he croaked, sprawling on the desk as I tugged harder. "Big man, over six feet two, at least sixteen stone . . ."

"Knows how to handle a knife and likes inflicting pain," I continued, unimpressed at being strung along. "Smart, judging by the way he chose the songs on the tapes, probably a devotee of the blues—" I broke off. Jesus, a devotee of the blues who was also getting himself involved in drugs trafficking. Maybe the bastard wasn't coming into it cold. Maybe he had plenty of experience in the business. I let the guardian go and rocked back on my heels.

"As I said, citizen. You know him." He was still smiling viciously, like a public executioner fingering the blade of his axe. Then he struck. "He stood watching while your woman friend was strangled by the Ear, Nose and Throat Man. He was that psychopath's leader."

I was back in the barn on Soutra seven years ago during the attack on the city's last remaining drugs gang; men turning to run and leaving a slim, shuddering form on the floor. Caro. She died a few seconds after I got to her.

"The Wolf," I said incredulously. Then I made the connection with the gang leader's name. The Screecher. No doubt he thought that was a really neat pseudonym for a blues singer.

I focused on the guardian again. "You're even sicker than I thought you were. You've been dealing with Howlin' Wolf? You set the Wolf on Roddie Aitken? You let the Wolf play games with me while he was cutting your own auxiliaries to pieces?"

I couldn't hold myself back any longer. It only took a split second. The head-butt spread his nose over his face like a ripe plum. That was the first instalment of his payment for the lives of Roddie Aitken and William McEwan.

Then I sank back into a chair and sat there quaking. The Wolf. Jesus. We really were up against Edinburgh's public enemy number one.

Chapter Twenty-Two

I called Davie in and got him to handcuff the chief boyscout to the arm of his chair. Now that I had him where I wanted him there was no need to use Harry's guys as postmen, so we called them off and got them to assemble at the castle. Hamilton and Katharine soon joined us in the senior guardian's study.

"What happened to him?" Lewis asked, bending over to examine the comatose figure on the desk.

"Remember those operations women used to get done before the Enlightenment to make themselves more appealing?" I asked. "He was in urgent need of one."

"Not only women had nose jobs," Katharine said sharply.

Lewis Hamilton seemed to be impressed by what I'd done to his boss. "I take it he was responsible for everything," he said, shaking his head in disgust. "What did he tell you?"

"Not as much as he might have. I got carried away before he finished." I filled them in on what I'd learned.

Hamilton looked even more disgusted when he found out that we were up against the Wolf. "Good God, man, I assumed that bloodthirsty lunatic left Edinburgh years ago and went to prey on the youth of some less stable city."

"Well, he's back home," I said. "The question now is how do we track him down?"

"Use the drugs?" Davie suggested. "They're what he wants, aren't they?"

Hamilton wasn't keen. "What are you proposing, guardsman? That we tie them to a tree in Princes Street Gardens and wait for him to pick them up?"

Davie shrugged. "It was only an idea."

"Bait," I said, nodding. "It's reasonable enough." I pointed at the figure that was still slumped over the desk. "We could use him instead of the drugs."

"I don't think I'll be able to sell either of those options to the Council," Hamilton said. "It's going to be hard enough to get them to accept that their hero's been concealing all these horrors."

"So how are we going to find the killer?" asked Katharine.

I went over to the window and looked out through the trees into the circle of grass in the middle of Moray Place. It was there that the hunt for the last killer ended. Something about that case was beginning to resurface in my mind, but it was like a deep-sea diver avoiding the bends: coming up extremely slowly. Whereas I was certain we needed to nail the Wolf quickly before he used his knife, let alone his teeth, again. Why had he been quiet for so long?

It was coming up to the time of the Council meeting. We were going to confront the guardians with the photos and papers that proved the senior guardian's guilt. Hamilton drafted in squads of guards to seal off the area around the Assembly Hall, just in case any of the chief boyscout's supporters were inclined to resist. Davie called Harry and told him to bring his people down to Moray Place. We needed an escort we could rely on for the guy with the flattened nose and they had the right qualifications.

In the Land-Rover surrounded by burly figures in oil-and-salt-impregnated uniforms, the senior guardian was doing his best to look like an early Christian martyr. His long hair and wispy beard, the latter now matted with blood, added to the effect. He sat with his hands manacled to guards, his chin up and his eyes set in a glassy stare.

"What's the plan then?" Davie asked as we drove through Charlotte Square. It was so cold that the breath of the tourists around the gambling tents stood up from their mouths like periscopes above the surface of a dark ocean.

"Council meeting first," I said, glancing round at the senior guardian. "The last one for you." He made no sign of having heard me. "Then a detailed interrogation in the castle," I continued, turning back to Davie. "He knows things that'll lead us to the Wolf, I'm sure of it."

Katharine was crushed up against me in the front seat. I felt her arm and leg move. "How are you sure, Quint? Another one of your hunches?"

I didn't reply, just looked out as we passed the shops and restaurants on Princes Street. Their garish lights and banners were giving tourists the come-on like an aged tart in serious need of cosmetic surgery. Or even a total body transplant.

I turned to the senior guardian. "There's something I don't get about the Bone Yard. Why did you bury the bodies of the auxiliaries who'd been exposed to radiation? You could have burned them in the furnace there."

He gave me a brief, superior glance. "Scientists don't destroy material that might prove useful in the future, citizen."

I looked away in revulsion.

We skidded on the Mound's icy surfaces then pulled round the corner. Guard personnel waved us into Mound Place and Davie stopped by the railing separating the road from the steep slope of the gardens. An evening race meeting was in progress despite the weather. They use guard sprinters when it's too cold for the horses.

I ran my eye around the steps leading up to the Assembly Hall. A couple of guardians, one of them the Ice Queen, were looking at us dubiously, puzzled by the extra security. I don't know if they recognised the figure in the back of the vehicle.

"Right, get him out," I said to Harry and his men.

Doors creaked and the Land-Rover began to empty. I followed Katharine out of the passenger door and stopped to stretch my legs. During that process I made the mistake of blinking. I was aware of a sudden flurry of movement to the rear. That flurry came as the senior guardian wrenched the two guardsmen who were attached to him towards the railing. They stuck their free hands out to stop themselves, but he whiplashed forward like he'd been jabbed with a cattle prod. The point of the black-painted railing upright came out of the back of his neck, forming a small pyramid trimmed by strands of bloody hair. As cosmetic surgery goes, it was pretty radical. The irony of the city's chief official committing the heinous crime of suicide in front of the Assembly Hall wasn't bad either.

In the background to the right, the broken spire of the Enlightenment Monument rose up into the darkness, like a vandalised roadsign pointing to a utopia that no one believes in any more.

The Council meeting was pretty fraught. After the medical guardian had supervised the removal of the senior guardian from the railing and confirmed that he was dead, Hamilton hit his colleagues with the Bone Yard evidence. They were white-faced and quiet, like schoolchildren whose chemistry teacher had just drunk battery acid in front of them. It wasn't difficult for Lewis to get himself elected temporary senior guardian. Considering that had been his ambition for at least fifteen years, he was very cool about it. I wasn't surprised to hear them vote for a total news blackout about the Bone Yard and the chief boyscout's suicide as well. A report of the latter might have resulted in Edinburgh citizens dancing in the streets.

Afterwards we went up to the castle. No mutilated bodies had been discovered, there were no reports of violence. Christ, there weren't even any reports of "suspicious behaviour", the guard's blanket charge for citizens who get up their noses. So where was the Howlin' Wolf and what was he doing?

"Maybe he's crossed back over the border," Davie said. We were sitting at Hamilton's conference table tossing ideas around.

"Maybe he has," I said. I was looking out at the bright lights of the city centre.

"You don't believe that, do you, Quint?" Katharine said, leaning back in her chair. She had her coat buttoned up. Hamilton's idea of heating would have gone down well in ancient Sparta.

I shook my head then glanced across at the guardian's computer terminal. When in doubt, hit the archives. Except that in this particular case I knew I'd be wasting my time. I spent years trying to trace the Wolf and his gang members in the records when I was in the directorate, but he'd made sure they all kept out of the Council's bureaucracy from the second the Enlightenment came to power. I still got up and went over to the machine, unable to resist the temptation. Maybe there was something in the previously restricted files on the deceased senior guardian that referred to the deal with the Wolf.

But there wasn't. As I'd already discovered, the chief boyscout knew all about what to include in the archives and what to keep to himself. The filing cabinets in his study contained pharmacological reports and production schedules of the Electric Blues, but nothing about distribution or the Wolf. I did find out from the chief boyscout's personal file that his first sexual encounter was with a man who'd been a senior figure in the Church before independence, but he was hardly the only teenager who'd been down that path.

At midnight we called things off. Davie drove Katharine and me back to my place. As we swung round the bend at Tollcross and entered the blacked-out zone outside the tourist centre, I found myself dredging my memory for the thought that had eluded me earlier. It was something about the last murder case that being in Moray Place had provoked. The deep-sea diver was still controlling his buoyancy as carefully as a Supply Directorate clerk distributes ration books, but I was close, I almost had it.

We arrived outside my flat. I got out stiffly, forgetting how cold it was. The icy road surface did for me again and I landed hard on my arse, which put all thoughts of how to catch the Wolf temporarily out of my mind. The fact that Katharine was laughing at me didn't help the process of ratiocination either.

"Jesus Christ, what a day," I groaned, dropping on to the sofa.

"Don't forget last night," Katharine said. "And yesterday. It seems you need to make an application to get a night's sleep these days."

I reached out for the bottle of whisky on the table. "Two fingers for you and two fingers for me," I said, holding it up to the candle flame.

She raised an eyebrow but didn't refuse her share. "What happens next, Quint?" she asked, pushing my legs away and sitting down next to me.

The whisky had an instant effect. The faces of the people I'd been involved with over the last twenty-four hours flickered before me like the frames of an old film: the lumberjack who'd recognised me; the fragile inmates of the Bone Yard with their clouded eyes, their blotched complexions and their soft, sad voices; the toxicologist dashing to greet them, tears coursing down his wrinkled face; and the senior guardian, his face splashed with blood from his shattered nose and, at the last, his body hanging like a hooked fish from the railing spike.

"What happens next?" I repeated wearily. "We try to find the Wolf before he gets bored with selecting his victims and goes back to indiscriminate mayhem. He used to be an expert at that."

Katharine nudged me with her elbow. "That wasn't what I meant." She put the fingers of one hand on my chin and turned my face towards her. "What happens to us?"

My mouth experienced a sudden attack of paralysis. I could look at her, take in the way her eyes were wide apart and fixed on mine — but speak? No chance.

"You've been so distant, Quint. It's like I don't exist," she said, nudging me in the ribs again with enough force to make me wince. "I suppose you think I only came back to the city to tell you about the drugs formula."

The function of movement returned to my mouth but I was having difficulty forming a sentence with the words in the right order. Eventually I made the grade.

"Wait a minute, Katharine. You've not exactly been sending out too many signals yourself. What did you expect me to do? Listen to your story about the Cavemen then drag you to bed?"

Her face slackened and she gave me another smile. I'd seen more of those in the last five minutes than I had since she came back. "I'm sorry. You were so good about all the shit that happened to me." Her gaze dropped and her voice became less assured. "I suppose I just thought you'd be glad to see me again. Treat me like a long-lost lover rather than a psychiatric case."

I slid my hand over hers. She didn't move it away. "I thought you'd given up on men," I said. "You did kind of give that impression, Katharine."

She laughed. "I kind of gave that impression because I had given up on men, Quint. But you were never just one of them to me. I saved your life, remember." She moved her face close to mine.

I wasn't too sure where this debate was headed. "So because of that you have some kind of hold over me?" I asked, leaning my forehead against hers.

She nodded then put her lips against mine. At first she didn't make any attempt to kiss me and I didn't respond. Then we seemed to get used to each other and there was a lot of tongue contact.

Eventually she pulled away. "Come on, let's get under the

covers. Otherwise they'll find us like Captain Scott and his friends in the morning."

We stumbled into the bedroom, arms round each other. Her coat proved to be as big a source of trouble as it had been since I first laid eyes on it. We finally got our outer layers off and took refuge in my bed. It was dark under the covers but we didn't seem to have forgotten the general layout of each other's bodies.

"God, I haven't been near a shower for days," I said as my shirt came over my head.

"And you think I have?" Katharine replied from the region of my lower abdomen.

Once I was sensitive about what got up my nose, but years of weekly visits to the communal baths have put paid to that.

"Katharine," I gasped, suddenly feeling her mouth on my cock, "a condom, I've got one in the ..."

A few seconds later her face came up to mine. "Too late," she said, her voice deep and alluring. "How long do you need to get hard again?"

"Twenty minutes?" The hard points of her breasts were rubbing against my chest and her groin was crushed against mine. I was forced to recalculate. "Quarter of an hour?"

"I'll settle for ten minutes," she said, breathing into my ear. "That's my best offer."

I closed my eyes and moved my hands down her back. "Done," I murmured, wondering exactly what kind of deal I'd just signed off on.

It turned out that I was party to an agreement similar to that entered into by Cleopatra and Mark Antony – something along the lines of "Forget the major crises taking place in the outside world, let's spend the rest of our lives screwing". Except that the rest of our lives in this case meant the next four hours. That was a long way beyond what I thought would be the limit of my energy reserves, as well as a strain on my stash of condoms.

I must have fallen into an abyss of dreamless sleep because the next thing I knew was the flailing sensation of coming up for air after a long dive. It wasn't just me waking up though. What also resurfaced was the thought that had been bothering me last night. Who says sex isn't good for the mind?

I sat up in bed, only vaguely aware that my shoulders were in the process of becoming a heat-free zone. My mind had just gone into overdrive. The murder case two years ago. Remembering that in Moray Place had set off the chain of ideas that I couldn't get hold of at the time. But now I had it. I'd made the connection I needed to identify that murderer by using information I'd got from a former member of Howlin' Wolf's gang who was a prisoner in the city's sole prison – the gang member known as Leadbelly. He might be able to help me again. But was he still alive? The last time I saw him he looked like he was a living skeleton and that was nearly two years ago.

I toppled out of bed and scrabbled around in my clothes for my mobile.

"What's going on, Quint?" Katharine asked, sitting up and rubbing her eyes.

"Lewis?" I said, waving at her to be quiet. "Are you in the castle? Good. I want you to log on to your computer."

"What are you talking about, man?" the guardian said in confusion. "It's not even six o'clock." You have to wake up very early in the morning to beat Lewis Hamilton.

"Don't argue, just get over to the terminal. Ready? Okay, do exactly what I tell you. Call up the main directorate menu. Got that?"

There was a long pause. "All right, it's on screen."

"Highlight the Corrections Department option."

"The Corrections . . . ?"

"Just do it!" I shouted.

"I have," Hamilton replied tersely.

"Highlight Cramond Island."

"Done."

"Highlight Prisoner Register."

"Done."

"Right. Are there any prisoners who entered the facility in 2015?" I couldn't remember Leadbelly's prisoner number but the year he was captured was burned on my memory permanently because of Caro's death.

"There's only one," the guardian said at last.

"Highlight his number."

"Done."

"Okay," I said breathlessly. "Scroll down the file and see if there's any reference to his drug gang name of Leadbelly."

There was an extended silence. I could feel my heart pounding like a bass drum played by a Sumo wrestler.

"Here it is," the guardian shouted, almost making me drop the mobile. "Code-name Leadbelly. Entered facility 23.5.2015."

It was him. Since he was on the register, the chances were he was still alive – unless the Corrections Department had failed to update its archives.

Hamilton was continuing to read. "Known confederate of Howlin' ..."

I signed off, called Davie and told him to pick us up. It was a long shot but I reckoned it was worth it. Leadbelly had delivered the goods in the past and he was our best chance of finding the Wolf now. He was probably our only chance.

The tide was out so we were able to cross the causeway to the island. There was thick, freezing fog and I could think of numerous places I'd rather be. Starting with the Bahamas.

"How are your thighs?" Katharine asked from behind me.

"In need of a serious massage." At one stage last night she'd been on top, pounding up and down on them.

"I'll remember that next time."

I smiled to myself. "You reckon there'll be a next time, do you?"

"I do."

I looked over my shoulder and saw the grin on Katharine's face. Behind her Davie was trudging along with his head bowed.

"What's the matter with you, guardsman?" I called.

He raised his head. "Oh, nothing," he said morosely. "Being forced to watch a performance of *Romeo and Juliet* first thing in the morning is quite uplifting, really."

"Asshole," I said, realising as the word left my lips that Katharine had come out with it at exactly the same time. That was a bit worrying.

The guards at the gate knew we were coming. They admitted us to the prison yard. The place was like the set of a low-budget movie based on an Edgar Allan Poe story. *The Fall of the House of Usher*, perhaps. I almost expected the high walls to cant over at any moment and plunge us without a sound into the icy waters of the estuary.

Katharine stood on the flagstones, running her eyes round the cell windows. She'd spent three years on the island for dissident activities. It didn't look like she was overjoyed to be back.

One of the guards led us into the accommodation block and down damp steps to an interrogation room. The door slammed to behind us and in the single bulb's dim light I became aware that there was a hunched figure covered with a threadbare blanket on the floor in the far corner. No movement came from it.

"Leadbelly?" I said in a low voice.

Nothing.

Davie stepped up, ready to haul him to his feet. I shook my head.

"Leadbelly? It's me, Dalrymple. The guy who sent you the Huddie Ledbetter tapes." That had been the deal when he gave me information before. He'd been amazed that I kept my part of it. But that was nearly two years ago. God knows what life in the tomb of the island had done to his memory since then. The original Council tried to rehabilitate prisoners, but the iron boyscouts never gave a shit about the few remaining lifers.

Thin fingers appeared at the edge of the blanket, pulling it down to reveal a skull that Poe would have swooned over – hairless, unwashed, skin shrunken over uneven bone. An eye sunk deep in its socket glinted out at us.

"Huddie?" came a croak. "Huddie's dead and buried." There was a vacant laugh. "Lucky bastard."

I went over to him and knelt down, gagging at the stink that rose up to greet me.

"You remember me, don't you, Leadbelly?"

"Aye, I remember you. What the fuck do you want this time?" The words were harsh but the tone had a touch of the bitter humour that flourishes in hell-holes like this – until the inmates succumb to disease and malnutrition.

"Howlin' Wolf." I let the name sink in.

Leadbelly moved his head. Now both his eyes were on me. "What about him?"

"He's back."

I became aware of a grating noise that was gradually getting louder. When I saw the prisoner's shoulders shaking, I realised that this was his version of laughter.

"And he's been killing people."

Leadbelly didn't stop laughing immediately, but the noise and movement slowly came to a halt.

"What the fuck do you expect? He wasn't called the Wolf just because he liked the old guy's music." He began to crank the laughter up. "The Wolf does the business and suddenly Leadbelly's popular again. That's a real fucking joke."

I leaned forward into the pollution cloud that hung over him. "If you give me what I need, I'll get you out of here."

That shut him up. After a minute I began to wonder if I'd given him heart failure.

"I said, I'll get you out of here."

He jerked into life again. "I heard you." He let loose a manic cackle. "I was just trying to work out if I can trust you."

"I got you the tapes, remember?"

"Aye, you did." He thought about it again. "All right, what is it you want to know, man?"

"The Wolf, he had a lot of safe houses in the city, didn't he?"

Leadbelly nodded. As his head came down, I saw evidence of insect life on his scalp. "Let me guess. You want the addresses. You're fucking crazy, man. There were dozens of places over the years."

"Yes, but not in the last few months before we hit you at Soutra. We busted most of them and forced you out of the city, remember?"

The prisoner looked at me blankly, then nodded. "Aye, you're right. Seems like a century ago."

"Safe houses, Leadbelly. Or contacts – were there any friends or family?"

He cackled again. "We were a bunch of psychos, for fuck's sake. We didnae go back to our mothers for high tea on Sunday afternoons."

"I'll get you out," I repeated. Talking the Council into that would be the thirteenth labour of Hercules – the one the big man would have given the bodyswerve – but I'd think about that later.

"I reckon you might too." Leadbelly pulled himself to his feet. He was way beyond ordinary malnutrition. It looked like his bones had been on a diet. "Okay, here's the stuff. Two places you fuckers never found. A top-floor flat in the New Town. St Stephen's Street. I can't remember the number, but there was a tourist shop two doors further down selling Independent Edinburgh Rock and shite like that." He paused to draw breath. "And a house down beyond Jock's Lodge. What was it? Oh, aye. Mountcastle Street. It was number 35. I remember that because it's my prisoner number." He opened the blanket and showed the label stitched on his filthy striped tunic. "He used to take women there and give it to them." He looked over my shoulder and bared the rotten stumps of his teeth at Katharine.

"Let's go," I said, turning to the others.

"Here, what about me?" Leadbelly called.

"I'll be in touch. I said you could trust me."

A deranged baying followed us down the dank passage. Maybe it was just ironic laughter. Or maybe it was a salute from Leadbelly to the former leader of his pack.

Chapter Twenty-Three

⊷∘◇∘⊶

The tide was lapping at the sides of the causeway and we had to move quickly.

"All the flats in St Stephen's Street were turned into hostels for cheapskate tourists three or four years back, weren't they, Davie?" I said over my shoulder.

"Aye. There's no way he'd go there."

"Mountcastle Street's our only chance then. It's not so far from Roddie Aitken's flat and the palace ruins where he did for the female auxiliary." I was gasping for breath, the frozen cottonwool of the fog massing in my lungs. "He could have cut across the park."

Davie was suddenly right behind me. "Doesn't that street back on to the old railway sidings at Craigentinny?" he asked.

"Bloody hell, you're right. It's the perfect place to lie low."

Not long after independence when the Council was busy sealing off the city, a wagon carrying a tank of some highly toxic chemical had come off the rails at the sidings. The fumes killed a lot of the local residents, making the guardians even more determined to cut road and rail links with the outside world. The surrounding area was evacuated and the houses left deserted. As the citizen body was gradually reduced by desertion and illness, it never became necessary to repopulate the area. So the guard patrols it less regularly than most places.

"It's still a bit of a longshot, isn't it, Quint?" Katharine said.

I turned and looked at her. Our rapid pace across the causeway didn't seem to be affecting her at all. Her cheeks were red but her breathing was almost normal, whereas my legs were about to give way.

"Longshots are my speciality, remember?" I said, as we hit the mainland and headed for the Land-Rover.

She didn't look very convinced.

Davie turned off the Portobello Road and drove into the wasteland. None of the houses had windows or doors, none of them even had window or door frames. Since the Supply Directorate provides only the most basic fixtures and fittings, the houses have been easy targets over the years for citizens still hankering after the do-it-yourself superstores that used to enhance every suburb. The gaping holes in the buildings made them look like open-mouthed skulls whose eyes had long since gone to the carrion birds.

We coasted to a halt before the corner of Mountcastle Street.

"Are you sure you don't want back-up?" Davie asked, his hand on his mobile. "I've only got my truncheon and my service knife."

"I've got a blade too," Katharine said, lifting her sweatshirt.

"Whatever happens, you're staying here," I said to her with as much authority as I could manage.

"Who are you to give me orders, Quint?" she asked, her green eyes flashing. There was no sign at all of the night before's tenderness. "I saved your skin the last time we did something like this."

It was hard to argue with that. I turned to Davie to see if there was any hope of help from him, but he was deeply immersed in the view from his side window.

I weighed up the options. "All right. Call Hamilton, Davie. Tell him where we are and what we're doing. That way, if we blow it, he'll be here to pick up the pieces. You could let Harry know as well. Even the Wolf would think twice about mixing it with his guys."

I turned to Katharine as he hit the buttons. "I'm not giving you orders, for God's sake. But you're better off out of it. The Wolf and his gang killed women for fun." A vision of Caro lying on the barn floor with her leg twitching came up before me.

Katharine moved her face close to mine. "We're in this together, Quint. Come on, let's finish it."

The intensity in her voice surprised me. For someone who reckoned this was a longshot, all of a sudden she was very committed.

"Okay," Davie said, "they're all on their way." He gave me a serious look. "Why don't we wait for them, Quint?"

Katharine dug her elbow into my side. "No, let's check the place out now."

I wavered between them, then sat on the fence. "We'll do a recce. That way, if it's clear, we won't be wasting too many people's time."

Now it was Davie who was looking unconvinced. I shrugged at him and followed Katharine out of the Land-Rover.

We were crouched down behind the crumbling garden wall of number 33. The fog had risen a bit and we could see the open gap where number 35's front door had been. There was no sign of anybody, no sound because of the fog's muffling effect. Nothing but cracked paving stones, overgrown gardens and litter carried by the wind from the inhabited regions. The houses in the street were semi-detached and quite large. They must have had at least three bedrooms.

"Right, here's how we'll do it," I said. "Katharine, you go round the back and look into all the ground-floor windows there." I stared at her sternly. "Without going inside."

She nodded reluctantly.

"Davie, you and I'll go in the front. You take the upstairs and I'll take the downstairs."

"Quint," he said desperately, "they'll be here in a few minutes. Let's just hang on."

Katharine glared at him, then moved away quickly before we could stop her.

"Oh, for fuck's sake," Davie grunted, heading after her on all fours.

By the time we reached the front entrance, Katharine had already disappeared round the side. I stuck my head over the edge of what had once been a bay window. And swallowed back a surge of vomit. The carcass of a sheep lay spreadeagled on the floor in a pool of coagulated blood. All but one of the legs were missing and the belly had been split open and ransacked like a stolen handbag. The animal had probably been taken from one of the pens near the palace in the Enlightenment Park.

I tapped Davie's shoulder. "I think it's him. Get Katharine back to the Land-Rover."

He nodded and moved away to the side of the house. I took a deep breath and went in the front entrance. The floor was uneven and damp. I almost slipped as I looked cautiously into the right-hand front room. There were piles of sodden cardboard all over the place, but no other sign of habitation.

Then I heard it. The beginning of a shriek that was cut off. It came from the back of the house. I instantly thought of Katharine and ran down the corridor. To the left was what had been and apparently still was the kitchen. In the far corner were the remains of a fire and sheep bones gnawed clean of meat were strewn across the floor. But no people.

"In here, cocksucker." The voice from the other rear room was deep but strangely unsteady. "I've found myself an old friend." There was a harsh laugh. "Haven't I, darling?"

I felt a pain in my chest like I'd just been clubbed by an iron bar. I moved towards the doorway.

"Well, well. And now I've got another old friend." Howlin' Wolf was standing against the hole where a fireplace had been. I'd only ever caught a glimpse of him once, when he and the Ear, Nose and Throat Man turned away from Caro's body. He was big, almost as big as the animal who strangled her, his face and upper chest covered with a heavy beard. But it was the eyes I remembered – tiny, screwed-up sparks of malevolence. He had his arm round Katharine's neck. She was on her tiptoes, her cheeks blazing red as she fought for breath.

"The great fucking Quintilian Dalrymple," the Wolf said, grinning at me. "The shithead who chased me and my boys out of the city. Looks like it's time for some bills to be paid." Again his voice wavered. It was out of synch with his hulking frame.

I leaned forward on to the balls of my feet and tried to make things out in the unlit room. Katharine's head was twitching, her eyes fixed on me. She seemed to be telling me to stay back. But it was the Wolf's face that I was trying to see. The small patches of skin between the top of his beard and his piggy eyes were blotched with crimson, as was his forehead. I'd seen lesions like that very recently.

"You've found an old friend?" I said, playing for time and wondering where the hell Davie had got to.

Katharine struggled in his grip, her eyes protruding unnaturally.

The Wolf laughed again, like a demon looking forward to an eternity of pain. "The bitch here. I know her very fucking well." He pulled her round to face him. "Isn't that right?"

Katharine's feet were completely off the ground now and a harsh choking sound was coming from her. I stepped forward.

"Stand still, you," the Wolf shouted. "I've already seen one of your women die."

Bastard. I froze. Gradually he lowered Katharine's feet to the floor.

"I reamed this one's ass many a time, fucker." He coughed

and spat out a discoloured lump. "Maybe I'll ream it again in a minute. After I've cut her."

"You're the one who's reamed, Wolf," I said, trying not to look at the top of Davie's head which had appeared at the far end of the window. "You've got radiation sickness, haven't you? It's got much worse in the last few days. That's why you've been lying low." I gave him a bitter smile. "Don't worry, there are plenty of lead coffins available in the Bone Yard."

"The Bone Yard?" he said, coughing again. "You know where it is, fucker?"

"I found it, thanks to your cassettes. And I've got the Electric Blues. And the guard's top squad of headbangers is on its way." I wasn't planning on sparing him anything. "And I found you because Leadbelly told me about this place."

His head jacked upwards. "Leadbelly spilled his guts? Did he fuck, liar!"

I raised my shoulders with as much nonchalance as I could find. "How else could I have tracked you down? You had some kind of stash here, didn't you? What was it? Drugs? Weapons?"

He spat on the floor again. "Both. You chased us out of the city before I could clean the place out. There was a sack of ancient Es in the loft." He gave me a murderous glare. "And a set of butcher's knives that I'm going to use on the bitch and you."

Katharine's eyes bulged as the Wolf tightened his arm again.

"So you were the leader of the Cavemen," I said, trying to stall him. "And later you moved east and set yourself up as the Screecher."

He laughed again. "I like my people to live in fear. They know to keep away when I sing my blues."

I heard the noise of engines in the distance. Glancing over at the Wolf, I saw that he had his ear cocked.

"Running out of time, fucker," he said, pulling a long-bladed knife out of his belt. "Say goodbye to the woman." He didn't wait for me to speak, just raised the knife and brought it down with slow deliberation towards Katharine's abdomen.

The moment seemed to last for ever. Then there was a blurred movement from my left. Katharine immediately dropped to the floor like a stone. The Wolf stayed upright, his small eyes suddenly open very wide. For a couple of seconds it seemed he'd lost the plot. Davie was at the window, staring at the haft of his service knife. The blade was embedded in the wall an inch from the Wolf's head. Then the Wolf shook his head and looked down at Katharine. There was only one thing for it. I charged him, feeling the crunch as his own knife penetrated his chest and went right through into the plasterboard behind. I watched as his eyes slowly stopped twitching, then stepped back. The Wolf fell forward like a statue on to the cracked concrete, his head turned to one side with the hood of his coat lying partially over it. There was a long rattle in his throat then I heard the words "The Killing Floor", followed by a fading gasp. Trust the animal to die with the title of one of his namesake's songs on his lips. I stood up, giving him one last look. His eyelids were still wide apart but nothing else was open for business.

There was a stampede of auxiliary boots in the hallway.

"What happened?" Hamilton asked, taking in the scene.

Katharine got up slowly. Her breathing was still laboured and her whole body quivering. She raised her head. "Yes," she said quietly, "what happened?"

"The Wolf's dead," I said, moving my eyes away from her and feeling empty inside. "And we're even."

I shouldered my way through the guard personnel into the front room that didn't contain the sheep's remains. I suddenly had an intense desire to be alone.

Dirty Harry and his guys moved out, looking disappointed that they hadn't had a chance to deal with the Wolf themselves.

Hamilton came in after a few minutes. There was a mixture

of shock and delight on his face which made him look like a child in pre-Enlightenment times who'd discovered how easy it was to get away with shoplifting. "I can hardly believe it, Dalrymple," he said.

"What can you hardly believe, Lewis?" I said, trying not to lose my train of thought.

"After all this time, we finally got the scum."

I nodded. I obviously looked distracted enough to get his attention.

"What's the matter, man?" he asked impatiently. "This is a triumph. It's exactly what we need to get the Council back on an even keel."

Something gave way inside me. "Bugger off, will you, Lewis!" I shouted. "I don't give a fuck about the Council. If it hadn't been for the Council and its bastard leader, none of this would have happened."

The guardian retreated, muttering something about how the strain of the investigation had obviously got to me.

I turned away, dimly aware that the last of the guard personnel were leaving the house. My words to Hamilton took me back to what I'd been thinking about before. Was it right that the senior guardian was responsible for everything? He'd tried to keep what happened at Torness and what was done with the survivors secret, leaving himself open to blackmail by Howlin' Wolf. He'd set up production of the Electric Blues, even though he later tried to double-cross the Wolf. And he'd used people like Roddie Aitken without caring what happened to them. All that was clear enough. So it came down to the Wolf. He was clever; all the years he kept ahead of us when I was in the directorate proved that. And he knew about the blues, so he could have worked out the idea of the tapes in order to put me on the trail of the guardian and the Electric Blues. Obviously the idea was that I track down the drugs and the lab that produced them so that he could muscle in later on. But that didn't quite ring true. The Wolf was sharp, but he was also a psychopath. As the murders showed, he was at home with mayhem. I had the feeling that someone else was involved.

Katharine came in. Her neck was ringed with livid bruises. "Quint . . . I . . ." She wasn't looking at me. "I know what you're thinking. I'm not denying it . . ."

I went over to the hole where the window had been and stared out over the potholed road. There were criss-crossed tracks from guard vehicles all over it. "You're not denying that the reason you came back to the city was to track down the guy who abused you? You're not denying that you found out from the deserter who died at your farm that the Screecher used to be in charge of the Cavemen? You're not denying that you played me for a jackass just so that you could get a chance to pay the bastard back?" I glanced at her, trying to look indifferent. "I told you, Katharine. We're even. What more do you want?"

"Stop it!" she shouted, her face screwed up and her fists clenched. At first I thought she was going to hit me, then I saw the wetness around her eyes. "I'm not denying I wanted to kill him. He made me hate myself more than I ever thought I could." She gulped for breath. "But I didn't only come back for that. There was the drugs formula. It could have hurt a lot of people." She came closer. "And there was you, Quint. I came back for you as well. Even if you don't believe me, I did."

I was listening to her, but as she'd been speaking something else had struck me. The Wolf taunted me about Caro, made a crack about how he'd already seen one of my women die. How the hell did he know Caro was my woman? Because of auxiliary regulations we kept our tie as secret as we could. Only people who were very close to us knew about it. That made me sure about who else was involved in it all.

I took a step towards the door, then froze. There were a few seconds of silence then I heard the faint noise again. And again. Creaks on the ceiling and another sound I couldn't place immediately. A kind of muffled rolling. I raised my hand, caught sight of the stump of my right forefinger, looked back at Katharine then felt my mouth open even wider. There was someone else in the house.

I ran into the hallway, skidding and crashing my elbow into the wall. Then took the stairs three at a time.

Chapter Twenty-Four

I raced into the upstairs front room like a greyhound after a hare and choked on what I inhaled. Despite the open holes in the walls, the room stank like a cesspit. Looking at the heaps of excrement on what was left of the floorboards, I realised that it actually was a cesspit. One inhabited by a misshapen dwarf on wheels.

"You forgot about me, Quint." The voice from the shrunken, chair-bound figure in the far corner was scratchy, like an astronaut's coming across the airwaves from a distant planet.

"I did, Billy." I watched as William Ewart Geddes, former deputy finance guardian and my oldest childhood friend, pushed his wheelchair forward a couple of feet. That was as far as the missing floorboards allowed him to go.

"But I never forgot you." The voice had hardened. Calculating eyes glinted at me from a filth-encrusted face. Billy's clothes were in tatters, his trousers open and streaked with shit.

"What's been happening to you?" I said, stepping closer. "What did the Wolf do to you, Billy?"

He laughed harshly. "The Wolf? The Wolf did nothing to me. He's been the best friend I ever had, Quint. The best, you hear?" His eyes were locked on me.

"But you need nursing, Billy. In your condition . . ."

"In my condition?" he screamed, spittle flying from his disfigured lips. "And who was responsible for my condition, Quint?" He'd obviously spent the time since I'd last seen him building up a major grudge against me.

"The blackmail and the drugs were your doing, weren't they, Billy?"

He nodded. "Oh aye. I was the best deal maker this city's ever had. The fuckers in the Council could have used me, but they turned their noses up at me and shunted me off to the home. I was going to get them for that. The Wolf was in this to make a heap of money but I wanted to wreck the regime."

"The Electric Blues would have killed plenty of innocent people."

"Who gives a fuck about innocent people? Nobody's innocent in this stinking city." He pushed himself backwards with surprising strength and banged into the wall.

"Not even Roddie Aitken, the first victim?"

Billy made an attempt at shrugging with his damaged shoulders. "That saintly hypocrite in the Council told us the boy was working for another gang. That made him expendable."

"Expendable?" I shouted. "He was set up, Billy. He knew nothing about the drugs or anything else. Jesus Christ, you didn't use to be like this."

He laughed again. "Exactly, Quint. You're finally getting the picture. I didn't use to be like this." He nodded down at the wheelchair, strands of filthy hair dropping over his forehead. "That's why I brought you into the game." He looked to one side of me. "Tell your friends to leave us alone. This is between you and me."

I motioned to Katharine and Davie to move back from the doorway. "You set all this up so that you could have a go at me as well, didn't you, Billy?"

"Don't flatter yourself," he said dismissively. "I had dealings with the Wolf years ago. He provided the city with essential products from time to time."

"Drugs, you mean."

He nodded. "Drugs and chemicals, mainly for medical purposes. He had contacts with other cities that we couldn't deal with officially."

"So he managed to get you out of the nursing home when he was looking for a lab to produce the Electric Blues."

Billy stared at me like a spider weighing up a fly. "Correct. And because I made a point of gathering information all the time I was in the Finance Directorate, I knew about the blast at Torness. I heard rumours about the Bone Yard. I ended up in this chair before I could find out exactly what it was."

"I found it, Billy. It was the chief boyscout's version of a concentration camp for the people affected by radiation."

He showed no emotion. "Was it there the drugs were produced?"

I nodded.

"So you worked it all out, you fucking smartass." Now there was a manic glint in his eyes. "Even where we were holed up. How?"

I told him about Leadbelly. "But I haven't found out everything, Billy," I said, trying to placate him so I could get closer without him snarling at me. "The songs were your idea, I suppose?"

"Of course. I knew you wouldn't be able to resist them."

"And 'Fire and Water' was to put me on to Torness and the senior guardian?"

"You made the connection?" He cackled triumphantly. "I knew you would."

I took a step closer. "But why did you do it so abstrusely, for Christ's sake? You could just have got the Wolf to scratch out a message in Roddie Aitken's blood."

"To turn the screw on the senior guardian. He had the Electric Blues and we wanted to make sure he didn't do anything hasty with them." He looked at me as if I were a moron. "Anyway, do you think telling the Wolf what to do was easy? The only way I could sell him the idea of the tapes was by appealing to his extremely well-developed sense of the macabre. The guy wasn't good at taking orders." He stared at me blankly. "You killed him, I suppose."

The way he held his gaze on me made it clear that he meant "you" singular rather than plural. I nodded. "I'm not going to play a lament for him, Billy. When I got involved in the case, the Wolf started following me around, didn't he?" I was thinking of the time I'd seen the hooded man in Tollcross and the wheelchair tracks outside my flat.

"Sometimes he was totally out of control. The radiation did something to his brain. The stupid bugger got through the fence at Torness and started messing around with the damaged sarcophagus."

"I know."

"Of course you do." Billy laughed bitterly. "Shades of what happened at Sellafield years ago, eh? You'd better send some conscripts out to clean things up."

"Fancy taking charge of that operation?" I demanded.

"It would beat going back to the home I was in." Billy's eyes locked on to mine again. "The one you gave up visiting."

I inched towards him. "So why did the Wolf take you to my street?"

"I made the mistake of telling him who you used to be. He had it in for you in a big way since you'd dealt with most of his gang and driven him out of the city. I only just talked him out of confronting you that morning." Billy's lips drew back from discoloured teeth. "It was his idea to hang the auxiliary's head on your door." He spat out a malevolent laugh. "Not that I had any objection."

I moved closer, breathing in his stench. "You told him about Caro too, Billy," I said accusingly.

He didn't look away. "Everyone has their weak point. The Wolf wanted to know yours."

"You were her friend as well as mine, for fuck's sake."

He pounded his shrivelled arms on the wheelchair. "Exactly, Quint. I *was* her friend. You *were* my friend. But nothing lasts for ever."

"You twisted little bastard," I shouted, stepping over the gaps in the floorboards. "I'm taking you in front of the Council. This time it'll be Cramond Island for you, not a nursing home."

He looked at me placidly, a mocking smile on his lips. As I bent over him to get a hold of the wheelchair, I saw his eyes narrow. Then I remembered the set of butcher's knives the Wolf said he'd stashed in the house.

"Sit still, citizen." The medical guardian's voice was unusually sharp. I suppose I should have been grateful that she was stitching my neck herself.

"How many's it going to be?"

"Thirteen, I think. Lucky for some. If your assailant hadn't been in such a weakened condition, the meat cleaver would have severed your head. That would have been a pity." The Ice Queen looked even less compassionate than she sounded.

"The Torness survivors," I said. "Are they being looked after?"

She nodded. "They're in an isolation ward here." She shook her head slowly. "They won't need it for long though."

"So you're not even letting them die where they want to, near their friends?" I asked, wincing as I turned to look at her. "Does that make you proud to be a Council member?"

Her perfect features beneath the white-blonde hair were lifeless, as robotic as ever. I didn't expect an answer and I wasn't disappointed.

"Done," she said, snipping the thread.

I got up and headed for the door.

"Citizen," she called. "Nothing like Torness and the Bone Yard will be allowed to happen again, you can be sure of that."

I glanced back as I reached the door. "No, I can't, guardian," I said. "And neither can you."

I found it difficult to get too excited about the Council meeting that evening. Hamilton had the boyscouts well under control and it was pretty obvious that most of them would be back in auxiliary uniform soon. The Science and Energy Directorate was already organising an expedition to check the reactor casings at Torness. I let Davie report on the final stages of the investigation. It wouldn't do his career any harm and I was finding it difficult to care any more.

"Anything further?" Hamilton asked, giving me the eye when Davie finished.

"Billy Geddes – Heriot 03 as was," I said. "I want to recommend that he isn't sent to Cramond Island. He isn't up to it physically." I needed to clear my account with Billy. I was still guilty that I hadn't visited him often. Maybe the violence that Howlin' Wolf let loose on Roddie and the others could have been avoided if Billy hadn't wanted to get back at me so much.

Hamilton looked at me curiously and made a note. "It's not exactly your jurisdiction, Dalrymple, but we'll take your view into account. Anything else?"

"The prisoner known as Leadbelly," I said.

"Number 35 in Cramond Island," Davie put in, going for broke in the efficiency stakes.

"I offered him an amnesty."

Lewis Hamilton looked like he was about to explode, but eventually he made another note. Two down, one to go.

"And finally, there's Katharine Kirkwood."

"Don't tell me," the guardian said. "You want her desertion charge removed from the guard register."

I nodded, running my eye round the so-called iron boyscouts. Their faces were slack and pale, but whatever happened to them, they had a future, unlike the radiation victims from the Bone Yard. Katharine had done a hell of a sight less harm than the guardians and I'd have pointed that out if any of them had objected. They kept their mouths shut.

"Very well," Hamilton said, nodding and closing his note-book. "It only remains for me to offer you the thanks of the Council and the entire city for your good work, citizen Dalrymple. Should you desire to return to a senior post in the Public Order Directorate . . ."

I raised an eyebrow at him and turned away. Then they started to applaud, which got me to the door even faster.

Outside the Assembly Hall I leaned against the railings and looked out across the city. The lights of the centre blazed as much as ever, burning up the city's precious coal reserves. The idea of bringing Torness back into service wasn't a bad one but anyone can have good ideas. It's how you put them into action that's difficult. I glanced to my right. A few yards in that direction the senior guardian had skewered himself. Thinking of Roddie Aitken and William McEwan, I didn't have it in me to feel regret for his suicide.

I heard voices from round the corner. A squad of cleaners appeared. Most of the citizens were laughing and joking despite having drawn the much hated night shift. All of them looked thin and drawn, clothes loose on their undernourished limbs. I thought of the Bone Yard. It wasn't just the place where the city's untouchables had been confined. The Bone Yard was Edinburgh itself. The citizen body was skin and bone, struggling to survive. But people still seemed able to make something of their over-regulated lives. They deserved better than they'd been getting from the guardians. But would the next Council improve anything? And did I have a part to play in the "perfect" city any more?

There was a rustle of clothing at my side.

"What are you doing out here, Quint?" Katharine's voice was hoarse, still affected by the bruising to her throat.

"I walked out on the tossers," I said without looking round. "Don't worry. You're in the clear."

I felt her eyes on me.

"I don't care about that." She laughed softly. "Anyway, I've still got my 'ask no questions'."

"You're all right then."

"Don't be like this, Quint," she said desperately. "I told you the truth. Okay, I didn't only come back for you." She moved up against me. "But the case is finished, isn't it? And I'm still here."

I turned to look at her. "Yes, I suppose you are."

She leaned forward and kissed me once on the lips.

"It's not you, Katharine," I said. "It's Edinburgh. Deep down inside I love this city. But it's the kind of love that makes you suffer and I don't know if I can take it any more."

"So come back to the farm with me," she said, touching the back of my hand with her fingertips. "There are none of the city's problems there. Just hard work and home-grown food."

"It's an idea," I said, nodding. Then I looked back out over the lights of Princes Street. But no matter how hard I tried, I couldn't conjure up fields of potatoes and kale. I kept thinking about the chief boyscout and the noble lie he'd quoted from Plato; that people's natures are predetermined and that their rulers have the right to lie in the interests of the state. It's a myth but like all myths there's some truth in it. In which case the next Council would be just as dangerous as the last one. There was one difference though. I wasn't going to get fooled again.

"Why are you smiling?" Katharine asked.

"I may just have rediscovered my vocation," I replied, turning to face the blackened Gothic façade behind us.

She looked at me, a smile gradually fading from her own

lips like the winter sun's last glow over an icy lake. Fire and water, I thought.

Davie ran down the steps and came towards us, his arm raised.

Katharine squeezed my hand once then walked slowly away, her long coat flapping in the wind. At the corner of the lane she stopped and looked back at me for a second before pulling up her hood and disappearing into the night.

WATER OF DEATH

Edinburgh, 2025 – an independent, almost crime-free oasis surrounded by anarchic city-states. Except global warming has turned the summer into the Big Heat and water, like everything else, is strictly rationed.

The ruling Council of City Guardians has been forced to become more user-friendly. Citizens now live only for the weekly lottery draw while serving the tourists in the year-round festival. So when a recent lottery winner goes missing, subversive investigator Quintilian Dalrymple is called in to deal with a minor case of the summer-time blues.

Then a body is discovered face down in the Water of Leith – the only clue to the death, a bottle of contraband whisky. Quint thinks he sees the first traces of a ruthless conspiracy to destabilise the city.

The Council, increasingly fearful of losing its grip on power, expects Quint to stop the tormentors dead in the water. But he is having serious difficulty distinguishing friend from foe during the Big Heat. Meanwhile the body count, like the temperature, keeps on rising ...

Don't miss Paul Johnston's new novel WATER OF DEATH available from Hodder & Stoughton in hardcover from June 1999.

Turn over to dip your toe in the water ...

WATER OF DEATH

Edinburgh, July 2025. Sweat City.

When I was a kid before independence, summer was a joke that got about as many laughs as a hospital waiting list. There was the occasional sunny day, but you spent most of the time running from showers of acid rain and the lash of rabid winds. To make things worse, for three weeks the place was overrun by armies of culture victims chasing the hot festival ticket. Now the festival is a year-round event – though a lot of the tourists are only interested in the officially sanctioned marijuana clubs – and "hot" doesn't even begin to describe the state of the weather. Over the last couple of years temperatures have risen by three to four degrees, causing tropical diseases to migrate northwards and bacteria to embark on a major expansion programme. Scientists in the late twentieth century would have got closer to the full horror of the phenomenon if they'd called it "global stewing" – except we haven't got enough fresh water to stew anything properly.

What we do have is a cracker of a name for the season between spring and autumn. To everyone's surprise the new-look, user-friendly Council of City Guardians didn't saddle us with an updated designation for the period (think French Revolution, think Thermidor). Our masters were probably too busy discussing initiatives to relieve the tourists of even more cash. As the blazing days and stifling nights dragged by, ordinary citizens gave up distinguishing between the months of June, July and August. And even though the classic *noir* movie hasn't been seen in Edinburgh since the cinemas were closed and television banned by the original Council, people have taken to calling this season the Big Heat. That kills me.

Still, in Sweat City we're really civilised. Unlike most states, we've done away with capital punishment and the nuclear switch has been flicked off permanently – the reactors at Torness were recently buried in enough concrete to give a 1990s town planner the ultimate hard on. On the other hand, the Council set up a compulsory lottery last year, turning greed into a virtue and most citizens into deluded fortune hunters. Deluded, very thirsty fortune hunters given the water restrictions.

Then some grade A headbangers came along and raised the temperature even higher than it had been during Big Heat 2025. Giving me a pretty near terminal case of the Summertime Blues.

Chapter One

———○◇○———

I was lying in the Meadows with a book and heat-induced headache, making the most of the shade provided by one of the few trees with any leaves left on it. It was five in the afternoon but the sun still had plenty of fire in its belly. The rays glinted off a big hoarding in the middle of the park. It was advertising the lottery. Some poor sod who'd won it was dressed up like John Knox, a bottle of malt whisky poking out of his false beard. "Play Edlott, the Ultimate Lottery, and Anything Goes", the legend said. If you ask me, what goes, what's already gone, is the last of the Council's credibility. There's an elaborate system of prizes ranging from half-decent clothes, to bottles of better than average whisky like the one Johnnie the Fox had secreted, to labour waivers and pensions for life — but only for a few lucky sods. Edinburgh citizens were so starved of material possessions in the first twenty years of the Council that they now reckon Edlott is the knees of a very large Queen Bee. They even willingly accept the value of a ticket being docked from their wage vouchers every week. I think the whole thing sucks but maybe I'm biased. I've never won so much as a tube of extra-strength sun protection cream.

All round me Edinburgh citizens were lying motionless, their cheeks resting against parched soil that hadn't produced much grass since the Big Heat arrived. I was one of the lucky ones. At least I was wearing a pair of Supply Directorate shades that hadn't fallen to pieces. Yet.

I rolled over and peered at Arthur's Seat through the haze. People say the hill looks like a lion at rest. These days it's certainly the right shade of sandy brown though the desiccated vegetation on its flanks gives the impression of an erstwhile king of the beasts who's been mauled by a pride of rabid republicans. As it happens, that isn't a bad description of the Enlightenment Party which led Edinburgh into independence in 2004. But things have changed a hell of a lot since then. For a start, like the nerve gas used by demented dictators in the Balkans twenty-plus years ago, you can smell Edinburgh people coming long before you can see or hear them. Water's almost as precious as the revenue from tourists here.

I glanced round at my fellow citizens. If Arthur's Seat is a lion, we must be the pack of ragged hyenas that hangs around it. Everyone's in standard issue maroon shorts (standard issue meaning too wide, too long and not anything like cool enough) and off-white T-shirts. Those whose sunglasses have self-destructed wear faded sunhats with a Heart of Midlothian badge on the front. Up until the time of the "iron boyscouts" – the hardline lunatics who ran the Council of City Guardians between 2020 and 2022 – only the rank of auxiliaries was entitled to wear the heart insignia, which has nothing to do with the pre-Enlightenment football team. The present Council's doing its best to make citizens feel they have the same rights as the uniformed class who carry out the guardians' orders. Except the auxiliaries don't have to wear clowns' outfits.

The hard ground was making my arms stiff. I stretched and made the mistake of breathing in through my nose. It wasn't just that the herd of humanity needed more than the single shower lasting exactly sixty seconds which it gets each week. (One of the lottery prizes is a five minute shower every week for a month.) The still air over the expanse of flat parkland was infused with the reek from the public shithouses that have been set up at the end of every residential street. Since the onset of the Big Heat, citizens have had no running water in their flats. People get by one way or another and the black-marketeers do good business in bottles, jars, chamberpots – anything that will hold liquid. But the City Guard has to patrol the queues outside the communal bogs first thing in the morning. It doesn't take long for dozens of desperate citizens to lose their grip and turn on each other.

It was too hot to read. I lay back and let an old blues number run through my mind. No surprises what it was – "Dry Spell Blues". Before I could work out if Son House or Spider Carter was singing, the vocal was blown away by a sudden mechanical roar.

"Turn that rustbucket off, ya shite!" A red-haired kid of about seventeen jumped to his feet and started waving his arms at the driver of a tractor towing a battered water trailer. They come daily to refill the drinking water tanks at every street corner. It stopped about fifty yards away from us.

"Aye, give us a break or I'll give you one," shouted another young guy who obviously fancied himself as a hard man. The pair of them had done everything they could to make their clothes distinctive. They had their T-shirt sleeves folded double and their shorts stained with bleach, pieces of thick rope holding them up. Sweat City chic.

The driver had switched off his engine. Now that he could hear what was being broadcast to him, he didn't look happy. He was pretty musclebound for someone on the diet we get and the set of his unshaven face suggested he didn't think much of the Council's recent easy-going policies and their effect on the young.

"You wee bastards," he yelled, waddling towards the kids as quickly as his heavy thighs allowed. "Your heads are going down the pan."

There was a collective intake of breath as the citizens around me sat up and paid attention, grateful for anything that took their minds off the stifling heat. I watched as a woman sitting with a small child near the loudmouthed guys started gathering up her towels and waterbottles nervously.

Our heroes took one look at the big man coming their way, glanced at each other and turned to run. Then the tough guy spotted the woman's handbag. She'd left it lying open on the ground as she leant over her child.

"Tae fuck wi' the lot o' ye," the kid shouted in the local dialect

which the Council outlawed years ago. He bent down to scoop up
the bag and sprinted after his pal towards the streets on the far side
of the park. "Southside Strollers rule!" he yelled over his shoulder.

The woman shrieked. Her kid joined in. The citizens nearest to
them crowded round to help but nobody else moved a muscle. Even
the tractor driver had turned to marble. It wouldn't have been the
first time they'd seen a bag snatched by the city's new generation of
arseholes. It wasn't the first time I'd seen it either. Maybe because
I'd once been in the Public Order Directorate, maybe because I was
theoretically still a member of the Enlightenment, maybe just because
I fancied a run – whatever, I got to my feet and gave what in the City
Guard we used to call "chase".

Bad idea.

After fifty yards they were still going away from me, dust rising
from their feet and hanging in the air to coat my tongue and
eyes. But after a hundred yards, when my lungs were clogging
and my legs had decided enough was enough, the little sods
had slowed to not much more than a stride. Evidence of loading up on illicit ale and black market grass, I reckoned. Then
I cut my speed even more. People who get into those com-
modities at an early age usually learn how to look after themselves.

They turned to face me and started to laugh in between gasping
for breath.

"Hey, look, Tommy, it's the Good fucking Samaritan," the red
head said. Obviously he'd learned something in school, though the
Education Directorate would have preferred something more in line
with the Council's atheist principles to have stuck.

Tommy was rifling through the woman's bag, tossing paper
hankies and the Supply Directorate's version of cosmetics away
and stuffing food and clothing vouchers into his pocket. When
he'd finished, he looked up at me and smiled threateningly. The
teeth he revealed were uneven and discoloured.

"Get away, ya wanker," he hissed, raising his left fist. It had the
letters D-E-A-D tattooed amateurishly on the lower finger joints. I

was betting the right one had the word 'YOU'RE' on it, spelt wrong. "Come on, Col. We're gone."

He'd got that right. I took my mobile phone from the back pocket of my shorts and called the guard command centre in the castle. As soon as I started to speak, the two of them turned back towards me, their eyes empty and their fists drawn right back.

Like I said – bad idea.

"Are you all right, Quint?"

"What does it look like, Davie?" I took a break from flexing my right wrist and stood up to face the heavily-built guardsman who'd just arrived in a Land-Rover and a dust storm.

"Bloody hell, what did you do to those guys?"

I walked over to the bagsnatchers. The carrot head was leaning forward on both hands, carrying out a detailed examination of what had been his lunch. Tommy the hard man was still on his arse. Unfortunately he'd turned out to have a jaw that really was hard. I had a handkerchief wrapped round my seeping knuckles.

"Where did you learn to fight like that, ya bastard?" he demanded, trying to get to his feet. Then he ran his eye over Davie's uniform. "I might have fuckin' known. You're an Alsatian like him." The city's low life refer to the guard as dogs when they're feeling brave.

Davie grabbed the kid's arm and pulled him upright. "What was that, sonny?"

Tommy decided bravery was surplus to requirements. "Nothing," he muttered.

"Nothing what?" Davie shouted into his ear.

"Nothing, Hume 253." Tommy pronounced Davie's barracks number with exaggerated respect, his eyes to the ground.

"That's better, wee man. And for your information, this citizen is not a member of the City Guard."

"He fuckin' puts himself about like one," Tommy said under his breath.

Davie grinned at me. "And there was me thinking you'd forgotten your auxiliary training, Quint."

"Quint?" the boy said with a groan. "Aw, no. You're no' that investigator guy, are you? The one wi' the stupid name?"

Davie found all this highly amusing. "Quintilian Dalrymple?" he asked.

"Aye, the one who's in the paper every time you bitches cannae do your job."

Too much adulation isn't good for you. "So what are you going to do with this pair of scumbags, Hume 253?" I asked.

Colin the carrot finally managed to get to his feet.

"Cramond Island, I reckon," Davie replied. "The old prison'll be a great place to give them a hiding."

The carrot hit the dust again.

"You cannae do that," Tommy whined. "We've got rights. The Council's set up special centres for kids like us."

He was right. In their desperation to be seen as having citizens' best interests at heart, the latest guardians, or at least a majority of them, haven't only given citizens more personal freedom – apart from anything involving the use of water – and a lottery. They've organised a social welfare system that treats anyone who steps out of line as an honoured guest. To no one in the guard's surprise, petty crime has risen even faster than the temperature.

"Who are the Southside Strollers?" I asked.

"What's it to you?" Tommy said, giving me the eye.

Davie grabbed his arm and stuck his face up close to the boy's. "Answer the man, sonny."

"Awright, awright." Tommy had gone floppy again. "It's our gang. We all come from the south side of the city."

"And you spend your time strolling around nicking whatever you can?" I said.

Tommy shrugged nonchalantly, his eyes lowered.

A couple of auxiliaries from the Youth Development Department looking desperately eager to please turned up to collect the boys. Colin the carrot was busy holding on to his gut, but Tommy flashed a triumphant look at us.

"Just a minute, you," I said, moving over to him. I stuck my hand into his pocket and relieved him of the vouchers he'd taken, leaving a streak of blood from my knuckles on his shorts as a souvenir. "Oh aye, what's this then?"

The pair of them suddenly started examining the ground.

"What do you think, Davie?" I said, opening the scrap of crumpled paper and sniffing the small quantity of dried and shredded leaves.

Davie shook his head. "If it was up to me . . ."

"But it isn't," the female auxiliary from the Welfare Directorate said, stepping forward and looking at the twist of grass. "Underage citizens are our responsibility, not the City Guard's. We'll see they're rehabilitated."

Davie looked at her disbelievingly. Like most of his colleagues, he had serious difficulty accepting the Council's recent caring policies. Not that he had any choice.

Tommy smirked then bared his teeth at me again. "You're dead, pal."

"Oh aye, Tommy?" I said. "And what does that make you?"

I handed the grass to Davie. We watched the miscreants get into the Youth Development Department van than I turned back to get my gear.

"The future of the city," Davie said morosely as he caught up with me. "Giving these headbangers special treatment is only going to make them harder to control later. Anyone caught with black market drugs should be nailed to the floor like in the old days."

"Hand that stuff over for analysis, will you?" We both knew that wouldn't make any difference. The guard's no longer permitted to give underage citizens the third degree so they probably wouldn't find out where the grass came from. I shrugged. "Stupid bastards. I told them to keep their distance but they had to have a go."

Davie laughed. "They weren't the only ones. You sorted them out pretty effectively, Quint."

"I'll probably end up on a charge. Unwarranted force."

"I don't think so. I'll be writing the report, remember."

The citizens under the trees were pretending they'd gone back to sleep. Davie's presence was making them shy. Even in the recently approved informal shirtsleeve order, the grey City Guard uniform isn't the most popular apparel in Edinburgh. The woman came to reclaim her vouchers, flashing me a brief smile of thanks. She probably thought I was an undercover guard operative.

"I'll give you a lift home," Davie said as we headed for his vehicle. "What were you doing here, anyway?"

"Trying unsuccessfully to find somewhere cool in this sweat pit to read my book."

"What have you got?" Davie took the volume from under my arm and laughed. "*Black and Blue*? Just like the state of your knuckles tomorrow morning."

"Very funny, guardsman."

"Isn't that book on the proscribed list?" he asked dubiously.

"The Council lifted the ban on pre-Enlightenment Scottish crime fiction at the end of last year. Don't you remember?"

"I just put a stop to crime," he said pointedly. "I don't read stories about it."

"That'll be right. You said something about taking me to my place?"

Davie wrenched open the passenger door of one of the guard's few surviving Land-Rovers. "At your service, sir," he said with fake deference. "Number 13 Gilmore Place it is, sir."

But as things turned out, we didn't make it.

Tollcross is as busy a junction as you get in Edinburgh. A guard vehicle on watch, a couple of Supply Directorate delivery vans, the ubiquitous Water Department tractor and a flurry of citizens on bicycles constitute traffic congestion these days. There was even a Japanese tourist scratching his head in one of the hire cars provided by an American multinational that the Council did a deal with. The lack of other private cars in the streets was obviously worrying the guy.

"Why were you frying yourself in the Meadows, Quint?" Davie asked. "There are bits of grass around the castle that actually get watered. It's quieter there too."

I looked at the burly figure next to me. He was still wearing the beard that used to be required of male auxiliaries, even though the current Council's made it optional. God knows what the temperature was beneath the matted growth.

"Quiet if you don't mind being stared at by sentries," I replied. "Since they moved the auxiliary training camp away from the Meadows, it's become a much more relaxing place."

"Asshole." Davie was shaking his head. "Anyone would think you hadn't spent ten years as one of us." He laughed. "Till they saw how handy you are with your fists."

My mobile rang before I could tell him how proud I was to have been demoted from the rank of auxiliary.

"Is that you, Dalrymple?"

I let out a groan. I might have known the public order guardian would get his claws into me late on a Friday afternoon. Not that his rank take week-ends off.

"Lewis Hamilton," I said. "What a surprise."

"Where are you, man?" he demanded. "And don't address me by name." Lewis was one of the old school, a guardian for twenty years. He didn't go along with the new Council's decision allowing citizens to use guardians' names instead of their official titles.

"I'm at Tollcross with Hume 253."

"Distracting my watch commander from his duties again?" Davie had been promoted a few months ago though that didn't stop him helping me out whenever something interesting came up.

"And the reason for your call is . . . ?" I asked.

"The reason for my call is that the people who run the lottery need your services."

I pointed to Davie to pull in to the kerbside. "Don't tell me. They've lost one of their winners again."

"I know, I know, he'll probably turn up drunk in a gutter after a couple of days . . ."

"With his prizes missing and his new clothes covered in other people's vomit. Jesus, Lewis, can't you find someone else to look for the moron? Like, for instance, a guardsman who started his first tour of duty this morning?"

Hamilton gave what passes for a laugh in his book. "No, Dalrymple. As you know very well, this is a high priority job. One for the city's freelance chief investigator. After tourists my fellow guardians' favourite human beings are lottery winners." I knew he had other ideas about that himself. As far as he was concerned, Edlott was yet another disaster perpetrated by the reforming guardians who made up the majority of the current Council. He particularly despised the culture guardian, whose directorate runs the lottery, for what he called his "lack of Platonic principles", whatever that means. I don't think Hamilton was too keen on his colleague's eye for a quick buck either. The underlying idea of Edlott was to reduce every citizen's voucher entitlement for the price of a few relatively cheap prizes. Still, the public order guardian's aversion to the lottery was nothing compared with the contempt he reserved for the Council members who forced through the measure permitting the supply of marijuana and other soft drugs to tourists. As I'd seen in the park, foreign visitors weren't the only grass consumers in the city.

"Any chance of you telling Edlott I'm tied up on some major investigation, Lewis. I mean, it's Friday night and the bars are ..."

There was a monotonous buzzing in my ear.

"Bollocks!" I shouted into the mouthpiece.

Davie looked at me quizzically. "Bit early to hit a sex show, isn't it?"

I got the missing man's name and address from a new generation auxiliary in the Culture Directorate who oozed bonhomie like a private pension salesman in pre-Enlightenment times.

"Guess what, Davie. We're off to Morningside."

"What?" Davie turned on me with his brow furrowed. "You're off to Morningside, you mean."

"Your boss just told me this is a high priority job. The least you can do is ferry me out."

Davie looked at his watch and gave me a reluctant nod. "Okay, but I'm on duty tonight and I want to eat before that."

"You pamper that belly of yours, Davie."

He gave me a friendly scowl.

We came down to what was called Holy Corner before the Enlightenment. The four churches were turned into auxiliary accommodation blocks soon afterwards. They form part of Napier Barracks, the guard base controlling the city's central southern zone. The checkpoint barrier was quickly raised for us.

"Where to then?" Davie asked.

I looked at the note I'd scribbled. "Millar Crescent. Number 14."

He headed down the main road, the Land-Rover's bodywork juddering as he accelerated. Ahead of us, a thick layer of haze and dust obscured the Pentland Hills and the ravaged areas between us and them. What were once pretty respectable suburbs became the home of streetfighting man in the time leading up to independence. It had only been used again in the last couple of years and the parts beyond the heavily fortified city line a few hundred yards further south were still an urban wasteland. It was haunted by blackmarketeers and the dissidents who've been trying and failing to overturn the Council since it came to power. On this side of the line, the Housing Directorate has settled a lot of the city's problem families into flats that used to be occupied by Edinburgh's blue rinse and pearl necklace brigade. The Southside Strollers were the tip of a very large iceberg.

"Ten minutes, Quint," Davie said, as he manoeuvred round the water tank and the citizens' bicycle shed at the end of Millar Crescent. "That's all I'm giving you." Then his jaw dropped.

I followed the direction of his gaze. A young woman was on her way into the street entrance of number 14. She was wearing a citizen issue T-shirt and work trousers that were unusually well-pressed despite the spatters of paint on them. She also had a mauve chiffon scarf round her neck that had never seen the inside of a Supply Directorate store. She had light brown hair bound up in a tight plait and a self-contained look on her face. Oh, and she was built like the Venus de Milo with a full complement of limbs.

Davie already had his door open. "Well," he said, "make it half an hour."

We climbed the unlit, airless stairs to the third floor. The name Kennedy had been carved very skilfully in three inch high letters on the surface of a blue door on the right side of the landing. The incisions in the wood looked quite recent.

"This is the place," I said, raising my hand to knock.

"Where did she get to?" Davie asked, looking up and down the stairwell.

"Will you get a grip?" I thumped on the door. "Exert some auxiliary self-control."

"Ah, but we're supposed to come over like human beings these days," he said with a grin.

"Exactly. Like human beings, guardsman. Not like dogs after a . . ."

Then the door opened very quickly. The woman we'd seen stood looking at us with her eyes wide open and a faint smile on her lips.

"Dogs after a . . . ?" she asked in a deep voice, her dark brown eyes darting between us. A lot of citizens would have made the most of that canine reference in the presence of a guardsman but there didn't seem to be any irony in her tone.

There was a silence which Davie and I found a lot more awkward than she did.

"Em . . . I'm looking for citizen Kennedy," I said, pulling out my notebook and trying to make out my scribble in the dim light. "Citizen Fordyce Kennedy."

"My father," she said simply.

"And you are . . . ?"

She looked at me blankly for a couple of seconds then smiled, this time with a hint of mockery. "I'm his daughter." She hesitated then shrugged. "Agnes is my name."

"Right," I said. "So is he in?"

"Of course he isn't in," she said, her voice hardening. "That's why we called *you*."